SKIRMISH

SKIRMISH

A House War Novel

MICHELLE WEST

DAW BOOKS, INC.

DONALD A. WOLLHEIM, FOUNDER

375 Hudson Street, New York, NY 10014

ELIZABETH R. WOLLHEIM

SHEILA E. GILBERT

PUBLISHERS

www.dawbooks.com

First Printing, January 2012
1 2 3 4 5 6 7 8 9

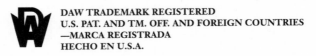

DAW TRADEMARK REGISTERED
U.S. PAT. AND TM. OFF. AND FOREIGN COUNTRIES
—MARCA REGISTRADA
HECHO EN U.S.A.

PRINTED IN THE U.S.A.

This is for the readers who've waited so patiently for the events that follow *The Sun Sword*.

Acknowledgments

Every book is a challenge, and every book is a joy. This has been especially true of *Skirmish*. I started chapter one more times than I have for any other book (although *Hidden City* came close). During that process of constant false starts, I was a bear to live with. During revisions, I was just possibly worse.

Luckily, my home team has developed a sense of humor about my writing process (which is probably why they're still sane). So, in no particular order, credit is due my sons, Daniel and Ross, my exceptionally patient husband, Thomas, my Australian alpha reader, Terry (and Skype for when we discussed revisions and which elements could be changed, tossed, or enshrined); my mother and father, who manned the fort, and made sure my entire household was not falling down on top of me; my Monday and Friday night extended family.

My away team is also, at this point, family—and just as tolerant. Sheila Gilbert, my long-suffering editor (and publisher), Debra Euler, my managing editor (well, okay, she's DAW's managing editor, but I'm sure on the wrong days if you asked her, she'd say I personally need one of my own), and Joshua Starr who answers phones, emails, and tweets; Marsha Jones, who now gets all the difficult picky questions about who-does-what when it comes to rights and things like e-books. And of course Betsy Wollheim who did not even blink on the very last time I will ever drink wine at a DAW dinner. (I fell asleep. It was survivably embarrassing. I think. I'll let you know the next time I see her.)

No book is an island. No author is an island. If it's true that we learn to write in isolation, if it's true that the words are ineluctably our own, it's *also* true that those words on the page don't magically become a book on their own.

And when they do become a book, there are the readers. I have the best readers in the world.

Author's Note

When I started *Hunter's Death*, Jewel Markess ambushed me; I had intended her to be a minor character through which the events in the poorest of the city's streets could be viewed. I knew there were demons, and worse, beneath the city streets; I knew that they were preying on the people who, in theory, no one would miss. I hadn't counted on Jewel Markess, of course, and by the time I had finished Jewel's *first scene*, the shape of the novel shifted.

I finished *Hunter's Death*. By the end of *Hunter's Death*, I knew how many of the character arcs would close; I knew what the end of the entire long sequence would be; I knew that Jewel ATerafin had taken the first steps on a path that must lead to a House War for the heart of Terafin. I also knew about the characters that hadn't appeared yet.

I began to write the arc that would introduce those characters. Jewel was part of the six-book series, *The Sun Sword*. Sixteen years had elapsed between the end of *Hunter's Death* and *The Broken Crown*, and Allasakar had had the time to recover, to summon the *Kialli* in force, and to plan. And he'd had time to bring a god-born child into the world—while he was on the plane. Jewel's role in *The Sun Sword* led her to the brink of a House War—but that wasn't resolved in *The Sun Sword*.

I finished writing *The Sun Sword*. I started *The House War*, with the intent of writing a braided narrative—one that could move between the early past of the den and its formation, and the fracturing of the House Council in the quest to determine its next ruler. In fact, I started the first book six times. The only beginning that worked was the one for the book that became *Hidden City*. But I'd intended to write a braided narrative between the past and the present—and there was no way to make that work, given Rath.

Readers of *The Sun Sword* were then left in the present while I followed the beginnings of Jewel and her den.

The book you hold in your hands is the first book that takes place in the present time line—but it takes place *after* the events of *The Sun Sword*. In fact, it starts the day after the last appearance of Jewel Markess ATerafin in that series.

To understand the events in *Skirmish*, the best thing to do is to read *The Sun Sword* before you start this book. I realize, however, that not everyone will want to do this, because the series doesn't just follow Jewel.

Between now and the publication of *Skirmish*, I will work on a "story so far" which will encapsulate the key events that occur in *The Sun Sword*, with regard to Jewel and her den. I'll put this up on my web site (http://msaga-rawest.wordpress .com). It will, of necessity, be very spoiler heavy, but for readers who have only been following *The House War* series it will be essential; many things will make little sense otherwise.

Prologue

27th of Corvil, 427 A.A.
The Common, Averalaan Aramarelas

HANNERLE LOVED WINDOWS. She loved, especially, the long, low bay or bow windows that were so expensive to have built. She didn't like full panes of flat glass; those, she had said, with decided lines etched a moment in both corners of her lips, reminded her too much of the storefront. It wasn't that she disliked the store; the store had been built, and its custom grown, by the dint of her organization and will. If Haval was, in his own modest opinion, the genius who created the dresses by which they earned a comfortable living, Hannerle was the foundation that allowed that genius to flourish. The store had been her idea. But the windows that girded either side of the doors were meant to display and to sell; to offer a pleasing and enticing view to the men and women on the outside.

So it was in their bedroom that the most glorious of the windows above the shop resided. The bed, which sat, headboard to the wall, in the center of the room, couldn't be seen from the street; nor could someone sitting or lying in that bed see those streets. They could see the sun; they could see the tops of buildings that sat opposite them; they could see the azure of sky on a clear day.

Hannerle was not a woman who understood what the word "relaxation" meant. She was up at dawn, in the kitchen or the store tidying, cleaning, cooking—and, if Haval were being honest, complaining; complaints were, in the opinion of his wife, the luxury one earned by doing the work. Although she professed to love windows and light, she seldom took the time to look at either.

Her husband entered the bedroom and walked directly to the windows. He paused to examine the curtains; they were older now, their color faded. They would have to be replaced. He opened them with fastidious care, anchored them by the tassels that hung concealed by their fall for just this purpose, and let the light in. The sky was an astonishing shade of blue, which wasn't unusual at this time of year. The air was cool, but the glass shut it out. Unlike his wife, who disliked the view of the streets, Haval looked down; the streets at this time of day were full. People in various shades of color and in differing cuts of cloth walked past the window heading toward their destinations, heads often bent slightly into the wind. They carried baskets or bags, most of which had yet to be filled judging by the easy way they moved.

He expected no custom today. A sign now hung in both windows and across the closed—and locked—doors of the store apologizing for his unexpected and unannounced absence. He bowed his head a moment. He had no need to school his expression; his reflection made clear that he had none. His face was a mask. His posture was neither slumped nor upright as he turned, at last, toward the room's other occupant: Hannerle.

She lay beneath sheet, blanket, and comforter; the counterpane had been neatly folded and lay across only her feet above the footboard. She slept.

She had done nothing but sleep for three days now. He had tried, several times, to rouse her; nothing worked: No sound, no movement, no amount of shaking or pleading. She could, with effort, be moved into an upright position, and she swallowed liquid if it was dribbled slowly and evenly into her mouth. But she did not wake.

Doctors—for Haval had money—had come and gone in slowly dwindling succession. Healers, however, had not; the healer-born were beseiged at the moment and the Houses of Healing closed to all who did not come bearing a writ from *Avantari*, the Kings' Palace. It mattered little; the doctors had been clear. His beloved, curmudgeonly wife was suffering from the sleeping sickness. They had no official name for it, yet, not that the naming of things much concerned Haval; some in the streets called it the dreaming plague.

"Is it contagious?" Haval had asked, in a very subdued voice appropriate to a man of his age.

"Clearly," the oldest of the doctors had said. "But we aren't certain how. Proximity to the affected doesn't seem to matter."

"And I am, therefore, unlikely to catch it from her?"

"You're as likely to catch it from someone in the Port Authority," was the crisp reply. "But it's best, if you've sons or daughters, to have them check in on you every day, or at least every other day. You're caring for your wife; if you fall prey to the illness . . ."

"Understood." Haval had no sons or daughters. "When will she wake?" he had asked, although he knew the answer.

The doctor hesitated for just a moment, and then said, "I'm sorry. I don't know if she will."

"Have any of the others?" He knew the answer to this question as well. He wasn't even certain why he'd asked.

"I'm sorry," the doctor repeated.

Haval thanked him for his time. And paid him.

He took a seat beside the bed in silence, his wife's right hand caught between both of his. Hers was limp, but warm; she slept. What he now knew about the disease was fragmented but reliably accurate. It had started perhaps three weeks ago, near the beginning of Corvil; it had gone undetected for the first week because its spread was not concentrated in one area, and because it was only in the second week that older children and otherwise healthy adults in their prime had been affected by it. The victims were spread across the economic spectrum; they were also spread across gender. There were *no* reliable symptoms to indicate that one had caught the disease. There was no accompanying fever, no rash, no coughing—nothing. Prior physical exhaustion wasn't a requirement either.

No, people simply went to sleep . . . and failed to wake.

Just as Hannerle had failed to wake.

"Hannerle," he said quietly, bending his head toward not her ears, but that hand, "I've heard word." He wasn't particular proud of this fact, because the information he imparted had required no finesse, no investigation, none of the subtle contacts which were his quiet pride. No, this word was impossible for any but the sleeping or the dead to miss; it had spread through the Common and the High Market like fire in the dry season.

"The Terafin is dead."

It was not the first time Hannerle had been ill, of course. It *was* the first time she had been both ill and utterly silent. Like any man whose wife's chief luxury was the volume of her complaints, he would have sworn that silent was the preferred state. But over the years, sharp and clever humor had worked its roots deep into the heart of her complaints; they amused him; the silence was bitter and cold.

He fed her water slowly and with painstaking care; he checked the fire burning in her grate; he changed her clothing. Although it was Hannerle's job to fill the silence with her frequent chatter, he spoke. He couldn't be certain that she wasn't listening, that some part of her wasn't somehow awake and trapped inside a body that couldn't respond. He kept her company, and although he could have done so while he worked, she had once made him promise to leave his work behind when he crossed the threshold of what was nominally "their" bedroom. He left his work behind.

But in the late afternoon he rose, because some idiot had taken to ringing the bell on what was clearly the wrong side of locked doors which prominently told all visitors that he was *not here*. He was not, therefore, in the best of moods when he made his way down the stairs and into the storefront, where his cloth, his threads, and his various beads lay strewn across the counter. On the other hand, he was perfectly capable of feigning almost obsequious delight on the very slim chance that such delight be, by the social status of the idiot, required. The fact that said idiot clearly failed to heed what was written did not, in fact, imply that they couldn't read; Haval often found the opposite to be true. But there was nothing that Haval was incapable of feigning, except perhaps youth.

He understood better why his signs had been ignored when he saw who waited at the door: a young man—young enough that the use of the word man dignified his age—who wore the livery of the Merchant Authority. He carried a letter with the air of the determined and faintly terrified, and it was clear—by his persistent worrying of the bell pull—that he was tasked with making *certain* that this official document was delivered to its intended victim. Only tax collectors and the very earnest were capable of this level of persistence.

He therefore opened the locked door.

The young man bowed. He didn't introduce himself, but to be fair, Haval didn't ask; messengers served a function that required different manners.

"You are the proprietor of the store?" the visitor asked, his voice high enough that Haval privately downgraded "young man" to simply "young."

"I am," Haval replied, holding out one hand.

"This is for you," the young man said, although it was already obvious.

Haval glanced at the back of the envelope and frowned. "I'm not expecting any correspondence," he began. The slight rounding of the young man's eyes made him reconsider. "Are you to wait for a response?"

"No, sir. But I am to obtain a signature of receipt."

"I . . . see. Very well, come in. May I ask who sent the letter?"

The boy nodded vigorously. His answer explained his anxiety. "Lucille ATerafin."

In spite of the solemn silence of the preceding three days, the two words, huddled side by side and spoken in such a fashion, piqued Haval's curiosity. He signed a statement acknowledging receipt of the letter and let the boy hurry—at a brisk jog—away from his store before he returned to Hannerle's room. He only broke the seal once he was ensconced in the chair closest to the bedside.

At one time in his life, such a letter would have constituted the work he had faithfully promised to keep out of the bedroom, but it had been decades since that had been the case. He slid a letter opener into the top upper corner of the closed envelope and cut it cleanly. Then he removed the single piece of paper that had been folded and deposited within. He read it three times before he refolded it and placed it on the bedside table. His wife would have recognized the way he then sat, for fifteen minutes, in silence. She wouldn't have approved.

"Hannerle," he finally said. "I appear to have been granted an appointment with Jarven ATerafin."

Hannerle was, of course, silent. This silence, however, was not glacial.

"No, no, it's not like that. I realize I *am* getting on in years, but I honestly cannot recall *requesting* such an appointment. Even had I, I assure you I would have politely rescinded that request in the wake of the current Terafin tragedy."

He paused. Memory, and a deep understanding of his wife's temper, allowed him to silently fill in her part of the conversation.

"The handwriting is definitely Lucille's. I'd recognize it anywhere." He would, on the other hand, recognize hundreds of handwriting samples with ease. "I would hazard a guess that this is entirely Lucille's doing, and while it is safe enough—for a value of safe which I'm aware isn't yours—to annoy Jarven, annoying Lucille is trickier." He rose and headed toward the closets that girded the walls.

"The appointment, however, is for less than an hour from now."

Haval disliked tardiness. He also disliked being rushed. Curiosity, however, had reared its head, and he fed it because it *could* be fed. He welcomed the distraction. He had chosen to dress as a merchant of middling means; a merchant of humble means was not appropriate for the Terafin offices within the Merchant Authority, and today he had no wish to stand out.

Two guards stood on either side of the double doors that led to the offices; they wore Terafin livery, which was to be expected. He handed them the letter that Lucille had penned, and they examined it in silence before nodding curtly and allowing him to pass.

Lucille waited on the other side of the doors, sitting behind her bastion of a desk. Paperwork was placed in deplorable piles across its visible surface, but she lifted her head the minute he stepped across the threshold and the doors closed at his back.

"Can I help you?" she asked, in exactly the tone of voice one would use if one wished to imply the opposite.

Haval was instantly on his guard. "Yes," he replied, the single word clipped and cool. "I have an appointment to speak with Jarven ATerafin."

She raised one brow. It was astonishingly similar to the movement of Hannerle's brow, and were he another man, he would have lost heart. But he understood that she meant him to play a role here, and if Lucille was temperamental and extraordinarily territorial, she did little without cause.

"Haval Arwood." He had lifted his chin, lowering his shoulders as he did; he stood at his full height and looked down at her.

She pulled a book that had, until that moment, been standing on end on her desk. She even read it with care, and took a pen to mark something beside what was presumably his name. "Please take a seat," she said, rising. "I'll inform Jarven that you've arrived."

Curious, Haval thought, as he took one of a handful of chairs positioned in front of the desk—and therefore in front of the watchful eyes of the resident dragon. Curious, indeed.

She took five minutes to return, during which time Haval sat. He observed the office itself; it was not, as one would expect, quiet. Paperwork flowed from one desk to another, often accompanied by curt instructions; there were at least eight men and women visible, all of whom looked harried. He recognized four—two women and two men; the others were new to him, although it was true that he seldom attempted to visit the Terafin Merchant Authority offices.

He merited no more than a glance or two from the office workers, which was troubling, as he had adopted a posture that should have been worthy of none. Clearly, Lucille expected his presence to be noticed; she also expected it to be marked. For that reason, she was chilly upon her return, and her instructions, as she led him to the closed door of Jarven's office, were loud and clear: Jarven was a busy man, and he didn't have time to waste. Lucille was not, strictly speaking, incapable of being friendly, but it was not the trait for which she was known; she was known, instead, as a veritable dragon, and the Merchant Authority was her hoard. Her clipped, curt orders made of Haval Arwood a man among the multitudes of grasping—and useless—would-be entrepreneurs.

She was, in her way, a consummate actress—a fact that Haval had never fully appreciated before today; she even closed the door a little bit too loudly at his back. She didn't *slam* it; that would have been unprofessional. But no one in the exterior office could fail to mark it for the dismissal it was.

He set that thought aside as he turned toward the room's single desk. It was wider and longer than the desk Lucille occupied, and it looked as if it were a display piece; not a single paper was out of order. There was an inkstand, a quill, and a small stack of untouched paper in a tray; there were a few books that had been neatly organized and wedged between two large, marbled bookends.

Haval glanced from the desk to the man who occupied the chair behind it. The years, until this moment, had been kind to Jarven ATerafin. Jarven watched his visitor in silence. After a moment, he gestured to the two chairs that faced the desk, and Haval nodded. He slid into the rightmost one; it was the farthest, by only a foot or two, from the desk itself.

"ATerafin," Haval said, lifting his chin.

"Haval." Jarven rose. The movement wasn't graceful; the weight of age had descended at last. The man who theoretically ruled the Terafin offices in the Merchant Authority sought the refuge of the window, and the street-side view it offered, just as Haval might have done. "You've no doubt heard word?"

"I am neither dead nor sleeping. Yes, I've heard."

"And what, exactly, have you heard? I admit that I haven't the stomach for rumormongering, at the moment. Or rather, I haven't the stomach to listen."

"I have heard only that The Terafin is dead," was Haval's cautious reply.

"Truly?"

"I speak of credible rumors."

"And those that lack credibility?"

"I feel they are beneath notice, Jarven, and it pains me to repeat them."

"I will trouble you to take those pains." He pushed the curtains aside and held them open while he watched the streets below the window.

"Some have said she was assassinated."

Jarven said nothing.

"Some have said she was executed by the Kings themselves."

More nothing. Since Haval was the master of silence, he bore up under it well, although it chaffed him. Jarven had always had that effect. "Some have said she was murdered by demons."

At that, Jarven lifted a hand, and Haval was suddenly grateful for the chair.

"Have you heard any other rumors?"

"There *are* no other rumors at the moment, Jarven."

The older man winced. "To be expected, I suppose." He let the curtains drop, and turned to face his visitor. "You are perhaps wondering why I called you here."

"I am, indeed, although I believe it was Lucille who instigated this meeting."

Jarven smiled, and if it was a faint smile, it was genuine. "And how much do you truly think my dragon instigates?"

"Rumor," Haval replied gravely, "implies that she owns the entirety of the Terafin Merchant arm that is not connected with the Royal Trade Commission."

"She has her hands full, at the moment."

"I noticed; the training of new employees is always trying; it is why I have none."

"Would you care for tea?" Jarven asked quietly.

"Tea?"

"Indeed."

"Perhaps. It's been chilly these past few days. I wouldn't find something stronger unacceptable."

"Ah. I might."

"Shall I fetch Lucille?"

"No. I believe that I would like to walk, Haval. I'm in want only of company."

"If you consider a humble—"

"Humble? You?"

"—A *humble* dressmaker worthy company, I would be honored. I think Lucille's approval will be withheld, however."

"Oh, probably. But it will give her something to fuss about."

Haval was politic enough not to point out that Lucille seldom lacked something to fuss about.

Jarven's version of a walk lasted until a carriage could be called. His simple tea didn't take place in the Common; nor did it take place in any of the establishments located nearby. It required crossing the bridge to the Isle. Haval was surprised enough to allow Jarven to absorb the tax incurred by the bridge crossing. The carriage stopped outside of the Placid Sea.

It was not an establishment with which Haval was intimately familiar, although it wouldn't be the first time he'd crossed its threshold; it would, however, be the first time he had done so as a merchant.

"My apologies," Jarven said, when they were seated. "But the bustle of the Authority and the Common at the moment is something I wish to avoid."

"I can understand that," Haval replied, "but I cannot stay for long." He hesitated, and then said, "Hannerle has fallen to the sleeping sickness."

Jarven said nothing, although his expression softened. Haval wanted no sympathy, and where it was unwanted, it was impossible to offer. In its place, Jarven did something vaguely more disturbing; he set a small stone down on the center of the table, to one side of the bread basket. He tapped it three times.

"Jarven, I want no difficulty," Haval said, his voice softening, his expression hardening. "At this time, at my age, I cannot afford it. Do you understand?"

"Is there a man anywhere who desires difficulty?"

Haval said nothing. Wine arrived, handled by a silent man who immediately withdrew.

"In the perfect world," Jarven continued, as the waiter receded, "we would sit in our diminished, familiar domains; we would drink our tea and conduct our business—trade deals or dresses, it matters little—and we would think, and hope, for safety. We are neither of us young men."

"And in our imperfect world?"

"We might—or perhaps you might—do the same."

"And you?"

"The Terafin is dead," Jarven replied, as if that were an answer.

For Jarven, ATerafin for the majority of his life, it was. With obvious reluctance, Haval said, "Did she announce no heir?"

"Not after the death of Alea, no. Even had she known that her life was in danger, it is unlikely in my opinion that she would make an open declaration."

Haval didn't ask why. He had some suspicion, and he desired no confirmation.

"Alowan is also dead."

"I . . . had heard rumors." Almost against his will, and certainly against his better judgment, Haval added "You think there will be a struggle for the seat."

"You think otherwise?"

Haval grimaced. "ATerafin, have I mentioned this is not a discussion I wish to have?"

"Yes. But misery enjoys company." Jarven lifted his glass by its stem and looked at Haval through the red transparency of wine.

"Very well. I will keep you company in your misery, but not for much longer; I must return to Hannerle." He hesitated, and then lifted his own glass, as if it were a shield.

"There is one other piece of news that might not have reached your ears, given the remarkable din of current information."

Haval was now weary of the game—of all games; mention of Hannerle's name had robbed them of their glitter. It was his wont to control the flow of conversation; to guide it, as if he were stone and words were a small stream he could part. With Jarven, however, it was always a contest, because Jarven desired to exert the same control. There was no such thing as small talk between the two men. Even if one of the two made the attempt, it would never be trusted; every word, every nuance, and every silence would be weighed, examined, tested. It was the nature of the game.

"The presence of the Twin Kings at the manse on the purported day of The Terafin's assassination?"

"Ah, no. You do have decent sources; I will grant you that point. It is true."

"The current near-war between the Houses of Healing and *Avantari?*"

"Between Healer Levec and *Avantari.* No, but again, I will grant you the point."

"The presence of demons in Terafin? I grant you that the last point is given very little credence in more intellectual circles—which is possibly why it's been spread at all."

Jarven was silent again.

"What news?" Haval finally asked, as if the words had been dragged out of him.

Jarven reached out and tapped the stone again; he did not remove it from the table. His expression as he met Haval's gaze was as smooth and neutral as Jarven's many lines and wrinkles allowed. "Jewel ATerafin has returned from the South."

There were sounds in the room, but they were the sounds that any room contained: breath, stifled movements, breeze through curtains. For a moment, two men for whom words were both weapon and art were in want of words. But when one discussed matters of import, words had to be handled with care.

"When?" Haval finally asked. He expected Jarven to hesitate.

"On the day The Terafin was murdered." Each word was blunt and guileless. Jarven was capable of honesty, as was Haval; capable did not, however, imply probable.

"Some word would have reached—"

"Word will," Jarven continued. "But she did not arrive by road or vessel."

"How, then?"

"Magic," was Jarven's soft reply.

Haval knew enough about magic to know that such arrival—if indeed the claim was true—would be costly in many, many ways. "And how certain are you of your sources?"

"Haval, that is almost beneath you."

"It is, I admit, lacking in subtlety."

"I am entirely certain of my source in this case; it was an eyewitness to the events." He did not warn Haval that this must not travel farther than this room; the stone which he'd placed upon the table had already made that clear. Nor did the dressmaker ask who the eyewitness was. For one, Jarven wouldn't answer and might actually be offended, and more important, Haval now knew.

Haval weighed words, weighed questions, and watched his only audience. "You know who the contenders for the title are."

Jarven nodded; they did not exchange names.

"Tell me, Jarven, is Jewel among them?"

"If she were?"

"Pardon?"

Jarven winced. "Sloppy. That was sloppy, but you are under some stress at the moment, and I will allow myself to forget it."

Haval drank the wine. He seldom drank. It was a passable vintage. "What are you asking of me? In the event that she could be considered a contender—and given her background, that claim would be both tenuous and more readily contested—I would remain a dressmaker. What, exactly, do you feel my relevance would be?"

"A question you must, at this moment, be asking yourself. Come, Haval, it would not be the first time you have offered advice to Jewel ATerafin."

"The advice offered her was advice about *clothing*, Jarven."

"Ah."

"Clothing and appearance."

"I see."

Haval snorted. In the endless minutes since Jarven had made his announcement, facts had begun to mesh and combine; he could no more stop this process than he could resist falling should he happen to jump off a cliff. Names, unspoken, came to him in a list: Rymark. Haerrad. Elonne. Marrick. Of the four, Rymark had one singular advantage: he was the son of Gabriel ATerafin, the former Terafin's right-kin, and therefore the most trusted man on the House Council. Haerrad had strong merchant concerns, and access to the most obvious money. Elonne was a quiet, elegant woman; she had poise and a ready wit, and she, too, had her own base of power within the House. Marrick, Haval knew less well; Marrick was genial, slightly underdressed, and charismatic in a very avuncular way. Nothing about Marrick implied either power or danger.

And a man who held a great deal of power without implying either was a threat.

He thought back to Lucille's abrupt and chilly greeting, and to her four unknown new employees. The fact that those four were already in place, and in such short order, made clear that the House Council had not expected The Terafin to survive for long. They were prepared for a struggle for the seat; they'd had the time to prepare.

If they were clever, if they were ruthless, and above all, if they could move with speed, it would be short.

"Gabriel serves as regent?" he asked softly.

"Gabriel, at the moment, is the titular head of the House Council, yes."

"Will he serve as regent until the succession is decided?"

"If he survives," was Jarven's soft—and surprising—reply.

Haval glanced at the stone in the table's center, and he drank again, the silence harsh. "How bitter will this struggle be? How far will it go?"

"In truth, I cannot answer. If the situation were different, I would say it would be decided swiftly—if messily. But the Kings are now involved, and it is not clear that they have a mind to step back. Nor is it clear to the House Council how they came to be present almost at the moment of The Terafin's death; there is some rumor that she herself summoned them. She certainly summoned," he added, "Sigurne Mellifas."

"And demons came, in the presence of the magi?"

"And demons came."

So many variables, so many combinations, now played like invisible notes between these two momentarily silent men. They had survived demons before, but they had no wish to repeat the experience; the shadows history cast were long.

"Let me answer your previous question with a different question," Jarven finally said.

"And that?"

"Tell me, Haval, in *your* opinion, is Jewel among those who will vie for the House Seat?"

28th of Corvil, 427 A.A.
Order of Knowledge, Averalaan Aramarelas

Sigurne Mellifas lit a candle.

Its soft, flickering glow cast more shadow than light in the darkened interior of her office. The moon cast more, but she had curtained the windows.

One candle, she thought. *One candle's length.*

Beyond—and beneath—the Tower heights, the magi were gathering in ones and twos. They would move with either purpose, reluctance, or great curiosity, toward the grand chambers in which the First Circle magi convened in times of emergency, pulled toward it the way rivers are pulled down mountains. Matteos would be fretting, because she had sent him ahead, divesting herself of the protection he was certain she required.

But there were some conversations she could not have within his hearing, and some conversations that perhaps would be best not had at all. She watched as the wax beneath the wick began to melt. The Tower was silent. She watched her wards with the gathered patience of decades, waiting. They were nascent. No one—no man, no demon—approached as the wax continued to melt.

The Terafin was dead. The creature that had killed the most powerful woman in the Empire was ash. Ash answered no questions. And questions? They abounded in this confined space. The Kings' questions. The questions of the House Council. The questions of the magi themselves, although those at least would be dealt with before the night—the long, long night—had passed.

Meralonne, she thought, *where are you?*

The runes continued to sleep. The candle flickered as she at last gave in to her unease; she rose, pulling her robes more tightly about her. She could feign age; could feign forgetfulness, could even feign frailty. No scruple prevented it. But she could no longer feign youth; it had passed, and with it, so much of her hopes. Had she not seen the demon with her own eyes, hope would be easier to grasp, and it would be far less painful. But summoned, she had.

Meralonne.

The stairs remained empty; the door remained untouched. The candle, however, continued to burn.

Meralonne APhaniel was not, had never been, docile. His temper was uneven, and he disliked—intensely—the papers by which so much information among members was shared. He was not fond of explanations—either given or received—and his pipe irritated at least half the members of the Order, regardless of their standing. He could be cajoled, when it suited him. He could be nudged; his ego could be pricked. All of these, Sigurne had done in her time.

But he could also be commanded, and that, she did so rarely it might never be noticed. Complaints about her tolerance of his habits, his temper, and his flagrant use of technically illegal magic littered her desk. Demands about the same did likewise. She had learned how to deflect most of them over the years. Even Matteos enjoined her to rein Meralonne in from time to time.

She had never explained to Matteos why she did not. One day he would know, and she dreaded the coming of that day. Her silence was not something that Meralonne himself demanded; if she had never offered explanation to Matteos, it was in part because the subtle negotiations that existed between Member APhaniel and the Guildmaster of the Order went unspoken. Meralonne had never threatened, and Sigurne had, likewise, refrained. They walked a knife's edge, balancing between the careful fabrication of ignorance and uncertain knowledge.

Always, always.

Something tugged at her wards; she saw their brief, dull glow—orange, all—but it was subtle and slight; it was wrong. Perhaps a child walking those stairs might have made that faint an impression; a child or one who used magic to approach with stealth. She suspected neither, but tested her wards, touching them without even a gesture to catch a glimpse of what lay beyond her closed door.

Darkness and magelights, nothing more.

But the wards continued their faint glow, tightening like a web, and she froze for just a moment, breath forgotten until the ache in her chest reminded her that it was a necessity. She turned from the wards and the door toward the closed curtains that blocked moonlight and starlight both. Placing one hand on the surface of her ancient desk—for comfort, not for support—she gestured. The curtains flew to the left and the right of the window, exposing the glass of the Tower's height. From where she stood she couldn't see the street.

Nor had she need. A foot beyond the glass, maybe more, stood the most difficult of her mages.

*   *   *

At the very height of the Tower, one might walk the roof undisturbed. Sigurne now closed the curtains and repaired to that roof, although the night was cold and the winds ungentle. Meralonne did not join her immediately; he stood, suspended in air, a weapon—a sword—in one hand. His eyes were the color of polished silver and his hair curled and billowed in the wind's folds, almost touching his ankles. He wore no other cape.

"It is not yet time," she told him, speaking softly.

His frown was slight and sharp, his brow momentarily furrowed as if her words were spoken in a language he didn't understand. As there wasn't, to her knowledge, such a language, she waited for a minute before she repeated the words. He closed his eyes, and even in the darkness she could see the pale sweep of platinum as lashes brushed flawless cheek.

Only then did he leave the whispering voice of the air to step, once again, upon something more substantial. "Can you not feel it, Sigurne?" he asked. She thought that he had not abandoned the wild wind; he had merely swallowed it.

"No," she whispered. "I cannot. I cannot feel it, I cannot see it."

"Surely that is your choice?"

She smiled and shook her head. "How many years have passed since we first met, Member APhaniel?"

He frowned.

She had not expected an answer. "Many," she told him. His sword still graced his hand, the edge a bright, crisp blue—a glimpse of azure, as if the blade had cracked the facade of night and allowed a sliver of day to leak through before its time. "What do you feel, Meralonne? What do you see?"

"Do you remember the snow, Sigurne?" He lifted his sword. "Do you remember the sky?"

"You already know the answer." She lifted a hand as if to touch him. Here, now, she couldn't. Not without calling upon reserves of a power best used in other ways.

"Do I?"

Ah, his eyes when he turned; they were wild, fey. Gray gave way to silver, the lie to the truth. He was never so dangerous as when he was like this; nor was he ever as beautiful. She wondered if it was always this way: those who had touched the edges of true, abiding power must define beauty ever after as inseparable from deadliness.

"No," was his soft reply. Had she asked the question aloud? "Had you,

Sigurne, you would have lived your life in a tower in the ice and the azure of the far North. I know who trained you, and I know who taught you; they were not the same.

"There are, of course, those who kill to gain power—or to hold it. You, Sigurne, are not among that number; you have taken power here, and you hold it the way a Matriarch might. But the death of the Northern Mage availed you nothing. You were too weak to take what he had built and make it your own, and you did not have that desire." He lowered his sword, although its edge still gleamed. "There are those who kill simply to gain their own freedom. Had you been that, you would have fled long before I arrived."

"I was that," she said, voice rough. "I wanted my freedom."

"Freedom? From life? You were not yet old enough to consider life a burden."

She didn't argue, although mere decades past, she would have.

"You watched. You waited. You bore witness. You were willing to pay for that privilege with your life."

"Until I saw it with my own eyes, I could not be certain he would die." She forced the brief, rough edges from her voice. "You saved my life, then. Why?"

"Because you did watch, Sigurne. And I knew, the moment I saw you, that you had both seen *and* understood. I was not certain how long you would live, and yet, here you are: the Guildmaster of the Order of Knowledge. Conversant with the customs and the powers of the *Kialli*, but respected and trusted by the Kings and their divine parents regardless.

"You have seen my hand in the training of the warrior-magi, Sigurne, and you have seen their power take an . . . unexpected turn. This sword?" he lifted it once again. "You have now seen its like in the hands of your own. Not all are capable of forming such a weapon with will and power alone, but half, now. Half of my students."

"Meralonne—"

He lifted a hand. "Give me but a few moments more, Sigurne. A few. Can you not feel it?"

"I have already said—"

"Yes. You have. Let me ask you a different question, one closer to your own heart. You have misgivings about my work with your mages. You have always had those misgivings."

She stiffened.

"When you saw the weapons—and I admit the bow surprised me; I think it unique, in all of mortal history—you were afraid."

She did not trouble herself to deny it. With Meralonne, there was no point. He understood her well enough to know how fear drove her; it was not a weakness he—or any man—could exploit.

"Why, then, did you not withdraw those mages from my service? Why did you allow me to expand their number?"

It was Sigurne who looked away. She had no candle to mark time, although she had the moons, and she watched them, their distant silver faces so much like his eyes.

"What did he tell of you the ancient days?"

"Only that men had fallen far from the height of their power."

He did not believe her, which was fair; she was lying. But she could. "The Terafin is dead."

His gaze sharpened.

"You had not heard?"

"I am in service to the Kings' armies in the South, as you well know."

"Yet you are here."

"Your summons was urgent. How did she die?"

"*Kialli.*"

"*Kialli* here, as well?"

It was the answer that she had dreaded, although it was also the one she'd expected. "How large are their forces in the Dominion?"

"They have already moved openly within the Terrean of Mancorvo; they have shed the pretense of humanity at least there."

"They own those lands?"

"Ah, no. But it was closely run. The kin failed there, and I believe that we will see the whole of their forces gathered, at last, in Averda. There are events that are troubling, even to me. I would not have said that they could coordinate an attack within Averalaan while they concentrated upon the Southern War."

"And what does it mean? What do you fear?"

"The Shining Court," he said softly.

She raised a hand, and he fell silent. "What of her new companions, APhaniel?"

"You speak of Jewel ATerafin?"

She nodded.

What he said next surprised her. "She has now walked roads that you will never walk; she has seen things that have not been seen since the gods themselves ruled the world. Three at least of her companions have seen what she has seen; you must draw your own conclusions from that. You could speak with her," he added.

"You know why I cannot. At best, I could speak with Gabriel ATerafin; should I request an audience with Jewel, it would merely accentuate her power in a House divided. She will no doubt already be in danger; she will no doubt be heavily observed. She is seer-born; she has value. Are her companions a danger to us?"

"Only inasmuch as Jewel is. While she lives, I think they will not be of concern to you—but I cannot guarantee it."

"And you are now so well acquainted with Jewel Markess ATerafin that she has taken to confiding in you?"

At that, he chuckled, and she exhaled slowly in relief. "Ah, no. But you can feel the winds of Winter when she speaks; you can almost touch the turning of the seasons when she glances at you. You can see shadows of the Winter Court in its glory when she walks, Sigurne."

"Faded glory, then. She seems mortal, to my eye."

"She is, and you are now being deliberately provocative. I have traveled all this way at some personal expenditure of power."

"And you weather it . . . well, APhaniel."

"You did not answer my question."

"No, nor you, mine."

He bowed. "Then let me show kindness, in my own fashion. The end of days is coming, Sigurne, inexorable as dawn, dusk, or nightfall. The winds change, the Cities of Man rise. Soon, you will see the ancient waken from its slumber; I do not know what form it will take."

She caught his elbow in one hand; he had settled enough that it was almost safe to do so. "How long?" she whispered. "Decades? Years? Months?"

He reached out and gently lifted her chin with the tips of his fingers; her eyes widened. He had not touched her in this fashion for many, many years. "Perhaps a decade, Sigurne. But I feel it will be less—much less."

"You do not fear it."

"No. Never." He smiled, but the smile was no longer sharp and cold. It was worse; it was tinged with pity. "I would hurry it, if I could, Sigurne; you have few years left, and if you die, you will never see what unfolds."

"I would never see it at all, if it were within my power."

"Yes. That is the strange and confounding truth about you; you comprehend beauty; you understand those things that are truly terrible; you have even raised hand against them. But you deny your own desire."

She shook her head and lifted her chin further, breaking the contact. "I have many, many desires, Meralonne. I do not deny that power is compelling; I never have. But it is simply one desire, one reaction." She made her way to the edge of the Tower and looked down, to the web of light that the streets below were gradually becoming. "There is beauty in birth, and beauty in life, even mortal life, which passes so quickly. Perhaps especially in mortal life; one has to stop, to witness, or the moment is gone; it cannot be captured or lengthened for eternity.

"There is beauty in peace, Meralonne, and you will never know it. But I know it."

"That beauty, if I grant you its existence, is exceptionally fragile."

"Yes. But the desire to protect the fragile is strong."

"I admit that I have never fully understood why you would work so hard, and so thanklessly, to give to others what you yourself will never have."

She nodded. "I desire power, Meralonne, because it gives me the illusion that I have the ability to protect others."

"It is not entirely illusion."

"No, perhaps not. But it is not absolute; even were I a god, I would face failure, at least from time to time."

"And yet you continue."

She lifted her chin and gazed for a moment at the moons. It was easier, sometimes, to speak to him when she could not see his face. "Yes. I am not what I was. Nor am I *Kialli*. My memory is not perfect. My rage is not eternal. Even pain that I swore I would never forget has dimmed with time. One failure is not enough—although I admit it comes close when the days are dark—to become all that I see or know.

"It is what the young forget: one failure does not render all past success—or future success—meaningless. It is only if we surrender to despair that we fail in perpetuity, because we cease to try at all."

"And is all of your life to be that struggle?"

"Has not all of yours been?"

He was utterly silent for a full minute; she could not even hear the sound of his breath. The wind was gone.

She waited, as she had waited a handful of times before, and was re-warded by the sound of a brief, dry chuckle. Her own expression did not change as she turned to face him.

There he stood: his familiar robes dusty with travel, his hair once again a straight fall down his back, his sword absent. "Sigurne, you are a marvel. It is a growing wonder to me that men can look at you and see only your age."

"And not a young girl's heart, APhaniel? Not my inner beauty?" She winced.

"You have never had a young girl's heart; it is the lack that makes you so luminescent." He bowed. "I will tell you this, for I must return to the generals and the army; they will harry me if I am absent for too long, and I am less inclined to be either patient or subservient these days. Guard Jewel Markess. Guard her well. She has a role to play in this that I cannot clearly see, and if the situation in the South were not so dire, I would take leave of the Order to watch over her myself."

"You will not stay for the Council meeting?"

He grimaced. "I see little point. Among other things, I seem to have left my pipe in the encampment in the distant South, and I could not endure such a trivial meeting without it."

She let him go. She wanted him at her side, but knew what the possible cost of that decision would be. "Meralonne."

He nodded.

"Win this war. I do not, at this distance, care what decisions you undertake to guarantee that victory."

"Do not labor under the illusion that this battle is the whole of the war."

"If we lose, I fear it will be."

Chapter One

26th of Corvil, 427 A.A.
Terafin Manse, Averalaan Aramarelas

WHEN THE KINGS RETREATED from the Council Hall, noise and movement returned to the men and woman granted the rings of governance. Arann, injured, leaned against the closest wall; Finch clutched Teller's arms, her face as white as her knuckles. Celleriant sheathed his sword; the demon dissolved, the menace and size of his form sinking into a soft, gray ash that could not maintain a shape. Rymark clutched the document he had declared the legal will and intent of The Terafin; Haerrad, bleeding in the doorway, had barely moved when the Kings left the room, so intent was he on Rymark.

Gabriel was the color of demon ash; the silence was profound.

No. The silence of the woman who had ruled and guided this house for years was profound. The color of her blood. The vacant, unblinking stare of eyes that sought ceiling only because of the way she had collapsed.

Gabriel spoke. The Chosen moved. Everything was strained, everything was wrong.

This is what Jewel remembered as she strode down the gallery—and against the tide of people running without purpose, although they didn't know that yet—toward home: the West Wing. She had longed for home for months—at times she had been certain she wouldn't survive to return to its comfort—and now that she was here, she could barely see it at all, although it surrounded her as she moved.

* * *

Jewel did not immediately head to the kitchen, although she had called the meeting there. Instead, she went to the room in which Morretz now lay. His eyes were closed, his face ashen; his chest neither rose, nor fell. His body was stiff with death.

Ellerson entered the room in silence. He tendered Jewel a perfect, silent bow; as she now knelt by the side of Morretz, she had nothing but silence to offer in return. There were questions, of course. There would always be questions. The den had answered most of the urgent ones. They had answered them, and then they had let her go without answering any of theirs in return—because Morretz was here, Morretz was dead.

Gabriel had the Chosen to guard and tend the body of The Terafin. Alowan had not been called; Jewel thought it an understandable oversight, given demons, Kings, and mages. She had therefore walked in haste to the wall upon which lay the simple magic that would alert the healerie—and Alowan—of the need for his presence.

Finch had stopped her. Finch had caught her hand. Finch had told her that Alowan was no longer in the healerie.

And why? Gods.

Alowan was also dead. Dead days ago. The flowers that lined the halls, the small portraits, the keepsakes and mementos offered as a sign of affection, respect, and loss were still in evidence in every corner of the galleries and the courtyard; they lined the walls of the great hall, and no servant had sought to remove them. They had tidied the more egregious of the wilted petals; that was all.

But they would be removed now. They would be replaced. Alowan had been loved, yes. But The Terafin had been the heart of the House; word of her death had spread. Word, weeping, the silence that comes when no words can convey horror, loss, shock. Jewel knew; she had been there to witness the death of Amarais Handernesse Terafin, and she had experienced all of them.

"ATerafin." Ellerson walked past Jewel, to the head of the bed in which Morretz now lay in his false repose.

She looked up at him in bitter silence.

"Allow me to tend to Morretz."

"He's dead," was her flat reply.

"Yes. And he has no family within Averalaan. Nor does he have any living relatives that we are aware of in the Empire. His contract has been carried out with honor; his Lord is dead." When she failed to reply, he gentled the stiff perfection from his voice. "He is a domicis of the guild-hall, and it is to us he returns. We will see to his funeral and his burial."

She still stared. At Morretz. At his silent face, at his hair, now gray and lank. She had heard him speak only a handful of times in all of the years she had known him. But in silence, he had been Amarais Handernesse Terafin's living shadow. He had become as necessary to The Terafin's life as it was possible for any other person to be. He had lived to serve her.

He had died to serve her.

"ATerafin," Ellerson said quietly. "He cannot be buried with her."

"Why not?" The words escaped her before she could catch them and bind them. They were too raw, too choked, and even speaking them, her eyes teared.

"You know well why. She is—she was—The Terafin, and in the eyes of the patriciate, Morretz was a servant. He was not even a servant granted the House Name."

"He couldn't *take* it. He was—"

"Yes. Domicis, and proud to be so. To take the name she offered—and if it eases you at all, she did offer it—he would have had to compromise the principles of the guildhall. To be ATerafin is to have an interest in affairs of the House."

"She was his life, and the House was hers—of course he had an interest in the House!"

"There is a subtle difference. He devoted his life to her life. He was not beholden in any way to anyone but The Terafin. Being ATerafin, however, implies a connection, a responsibility, to the House."

She shook her head. "She was the House, Ellerson. *She* was the House."

"No, Jewel—although it might anger you to hear it, she was not. House Terafin still stands. Its merchant concerns, its responsibilities to the Crowns, still exist, as does its seat in the Hall of The Ten. She shaped, guided, and ruled the House—but the House, like a kingdom, continues beyond her. That has always been the case, and she knew it well.

"There is only one hope for continuity," he added quietly. "And Morretz gave his life to achieve it."

She was silent. Numb. But she would not move from Morretz' side.

Ellerson did not leave. When he spoke, it was not to reiterate his request, not immediately.

"ATerafin, do you know how I came to serve in this manse sixteen years ago?"

She shook her head. She knew—very, very well—how he had come to *leave* that service. Was surprised at how it still stung, given how much she had lost today.

"Morretz came to me in the guildhall. I had taken leave of active service and intended to spend the rest of my productive years teaching. I taught Morretz," he added. "Before he came to serve The Terafin, he was my student. It was I who judged him capable of that service. When Morretz first arrived at the guildhall, he was angry, confused, and in search of a cause to which he could devote his life. If the cause were a worthy one, he could then forget that he had ever had a life of his own.

"I will not trouble you with all of the reasons this is a poorly conceived desire; it is a common desire, and it leads many to our doors. Almost all of those who do arrive to petition the guildhall for entrance for this reason do not, in fact, remain."

In spite of herself, Jewel looked up. "Why?"

"Because they are looking for some form of service that will allow them to avoid making any decisions of their own. They are looking for service as justification for their existence. They come to us empty, and they ask us to fill that emptiness."

She nodded.

"You have seen the Chosen. You are held in esteem by the captains, and I believe you hold them in high esteem in return. Is this not the case?"

"It is."

"They have devoted their lives to the life of The Terafin."

She nodded again.

"Could they have done so if they were unformed and desperate young men? The willingness to lay down a life is not enough if they themselves consider that life to be almost without value. The Chosen are tasked with making choices and decisions in the absence of their Lord. She trusts them implicitly and explicitly. She trusted her domicis in the same fashion."

No, Jewel thought, glancing at Morretz's lifeless face. She had trusted him more.

"He offered advice and counsel. That advice and counsel did not come from an empty place. I was proud of him. As a student, he was one of my most challenging—and one of my most successful." Ellerson smiled; it was a bitter smile. "I have no children. Perhaps, in the end, this was not a wise decision on my part, but to have a family, I would have had to leave the service entirely. Morretz, inasmuch as a man can be whose life was devoted to another, was as close to kin as my chosen vocation permitted.

"I watched him grow. I watched him flourish. I watched him gain the knowledge required to serve a lord of power. I watched him slowly surrender his despair and his pain until it no longer defined him. Did it shape him? Of course it did. But it did not define him, in the end.

"Give him back to me, and I will take him home."

Jewel rose then. "He's yours," she said, voice too thick, too heavy, for more words. She turned and left the room.

The kitchen had never seemed so far away as she trudged toward it, head down.

The sounds in the wing were wrong. The ceiling was thick and flat; there was no tenting, no wagon cover; there was no sand and no sound of leaves in night wind. There were no stars. There was no sun. The voices she heard—at a distance—spoke Weston, not Torra.

This was home, yes.

But The Terafin was dead. Morretz, dead. Alowan—gentle, wise healer—dead as well. She had always considered home to be the place the den lived—but tonight, it felt empty, it felt hollow. She walked the halls and before she reached the dining room that led to the kitchen, she passed Celleriant. He stepped in behind her and began to follow.

Not now, she thought. She'd grown accustomed to his presence. Accustomed to armor that the Chosen would never wear; accustomed to the sword that no longer occupied his hand. The sight of his platinum hair seemed almost natural. When had that happened? How?

She had seen the way Finch and Teller watched him. She had answered their brief, signed questions.

This was home. It would never be the same as the home she had left. Had she stayed—had she stayed, it *might* have been. Had she been here—but no. No. She swallowed, squared her shoulders, continued to walk.

Celleriant had not chosen to serve her. He had failed his Queen, and Jewel was his punishment. She could probably order him to leave—but she wouldn't, and they both knew it. Nor would she now abandon the Winter King, although he had vanished somehow, as he often did.

"These people are my kin," she told Celleriant as she faced familiar swinging doors. "I would die before I see them come to any harm." She didn't wait for his reaction; instead, she pushed the doors open and walked into the kitchen.

*　　*　　*

There was no joy to be had at this homecoming. Not for Jewel. Not for her den. The enormity of two deaths—three—lay between them, around them. The woman who had given them the names that defined all but one of their number was gone.

Jewel's den was silent as she walked to her chair; silent as it scraped in its familiar way along the floor. She sat heavily, folding her arms across the table in front of her. By dint of will she didn't allow her head to sink into them. But her throat felt swollen and thick and she sat there in silence for far too long. Her hands were sun-dark; she knew her sojourn in the South had reddened her hair. She felt as if she had stepped out of the wrong season—the wrong world—and the passage had taken the hope of homecoming from her.

She glanced at Arann. They had all taken wounds today, but most of those were figurative. Arann's, as part of the House Guard, were more. *No,* she thought, numb now. He was not just a House Guard. She recognized the subtle change in insignia; he was Chosen. Somehow, in her absence, he had made his personal vow to The Terafin. What would happen to him now? What would happen to *any* of the Chosen? They had failed in the only charge they valued; she was dead.

Arann's wounds had been tightly bandaged, but blood had seeped through those bandages; in the dim light of the kitchen it seemed a much darker red.

Celleriant did not take a seat at the table; nor had she expected it. He walked to the wall behind her chair, and stood there in perfect, forbidding silence. She was more aware of his presence in the kitchen than she had been for weeks. She swallowed. She could see brief hand and finger gestures, and realized with a pang that they weren't meant for her.

And she was not the only one who had brought newcomers, although newcomers had always come to the den through her. Quietly seated, his shoulders curling toward the ground in almost exquisite embarrassment, was a boy she—to her shock—recognized. Adam. Adam of the Arkosa Voyani. He glanced at her, but when her eyes met his, he looked away instantly, paling. That stung.

"Adam," she said, falling into the Torra that now came so effortlessly.

He looked up instantly. She smiled at him, hoping her smile had no edges; it was a genuine smile. He was alive. He was alive, he seemed healthy, and he was—against all odds and hope—with her den. She wanted to ask him how, or why, but he seemed so nervous she was afraid it would sound as if it were an interrogation.

"He was at the Houses of Healing," Finch said quietly—in Weston.

"Levec had him there. It was Adam who told us you were still alive. Levec cares about him," she added, "but Adam wasn't comfortable there." She swallowed and then continued. "He's staying with us at the moment. It's been a bit awkward."

"Awkward? Why? Is Levec causing trouble?"

Finch shook her head. "In the last couple of weeks, there's been a new plague that's spread through the city."

"It's the wrong season for the Summer sickness."

Finch nodded. "It's not—I don't think the healers believe it's entirely natural."

"I don't follow."

"Adam is healer-born. Levec said—" She shook her head. "Adam's healer-born."

"And he let him stay *here?*"

Finch smiled ruefully, her face relaxing into the familiar expression at the octave change in Jewel's voice. "I don't think he was happy with the decision—and it's been difficult. Adam is new to the city. He's new to the Empire. His Weston is only barely passable."

"How barely?"

"He can buy a few rudimentary things and ask very simple directions. His Torra's not street Torra, either—but he understands most of it. Levec's lost younger healers before. He *hates* to let them out of his sight." Jewel didn't blame him. "It's not that Levec wanted him here—but Levec let him choose."

"And Levec's been checking up on him ever since?"

Finch shook her head.

"Tell me."

"This sickness—they call it the sleeping sickness, the dreaming sickness. People fall asleep and they just don't wake up."

"At all?"

She nodded; Jewel caught the hesitation in the gesture. She waited. Finch finally said, "Adam can wake them. They don't stay awake," she added in a rush. "But . . . Adam can wake them for a while. He's the only one who's been able to even do that much. So he's necessary, in the eyes of the Kings and the Houses of Healing."

"I'm surprised Levec doesn't have a room here as well."

Finch and Teller exchanged a glance. It was Teller who said, "He has a guest room."

". . . So what you're saying is I might accidentally wander across Levec—not the world's friendliest man on the best of days if you didn't happen to be born a healer—at any time?"

"He doesn't use it often."

Jewel almost laughed. It would have been wild and raw—but better by far than tears. Adam was alive. So many people weren't—but Adam was, and he was here, and that was an unlooked for gift. She looked across the table at where he was trying to look smaller.

"Adam."

He looked up instantly. Glancing around the table, he then said, "Matriarch."

It took Jewel a few seconds to realize he was applying that title to *her*. "Adam, I'm not—"

"I didn't know," he continued, in uneasy Torra. "I didn't know what you were when we met. I apologize if I gave any offense."

"Adam, I'm *not* a Matriarch."

"These people are your kin," he replied gravely. There was the tail end of a question in the words.

"Yes. But not in a way that your sister, Margret, would understand. We weren't born to the same parents. We weren't born to related parents, either."

"But you are all ATerafin."

She glanced at Angel, who couldn't understand what they were saying. "Almost all, yes."

He digested this in silence. After a long pause, he said, "My sister?"

"She is well. Adam—the Arkosa Voyani have left the Voyanne. They now dwell in the City of Arkosa, in the Sea of Sorrows. She's alive."

"My cousin?"

"Alive as well." More than that, she did not offer.

"And the Serra Diora?"

Jewel couldn't help but smile at that. He was fourteen years of age, and the Serra Diora was possibly the most beautiful woman Jewel had ever seen. The most beautiful mortal woman. "I left her in the camp of the Kai Leonne. She is alive, she is well."

The door swung open; Avandar entered the kitchen. After a moment, so did Ellerson. They stood on either side of the doors, watching; neither domicis had ever joined them at the table. Jewel looked at Ellerson and then looked away.

"Avandar, how is Ariel?"

"She is sleeping."

"Naturally?"

He raised a brow. "She was both frightened and exhausted. Ellerson has seen to a room for the child; I am not certain that she is best left on her own."

Jewel nodded. She almost rose to go see the girl herself. But she couldn't decide if leaving to check would be an act of concern and affection or an act of rank cowardice, and she suspected it was the latter. She stayed in her chair.

Everyone was watching her now. She was acutely aware that the first person she had spoken to was Adam. But it was hard to face her den, because The Terafin was dead. She was dead and Jewel's return had not saved her.

Teller said quietly, "Jay."

She swiveled to look at him.

"She knew. She knew you had to leave. I think she understood why."

Jewel nodded.

"You don't believe you had to be—wherever it was you went." It wasn't a question. Teller knew her so well. "But *she* did."

"Teller—I was there. I was there, and I'm not even certain if I was necessary. The war in the South isn't over. We need to *win* it."

"How bad will it be if we don't?"

"Henden bad. Dark Days bad. But if we lose and the Dark Days come again, there won't be a Veral. There will never be a spring." Her hands became fists on the table. "And I'm not *there* for that. The army's almost in place, but I won't see the battle; I won't be able to help there. And the Commanders are going to be furious. With me. With the House.

"I'll miss the battle. I arrived too late for The Terafin." She pushed herself out of her chair.

"Jay," Finch said, also rising, but with less force. She glanced toward the door, at Ellerson. Jewel's gaze was dragged there as well.

"Why is he here?" She spoke softly, as if there was any hope that Ellerson would fail to hear the words.

"We needed him," Finch replied.

"*I* needed him sixteen years ago, but he still left." Gods, the words. The words just fell out of her mouth. She wanted to grab them and swallow them whole. And she wanted to scream or shout or rage—not at Ellerson, although he was part of it. At the world. At death. At the demons and the Lord of Night and The Terafin, whose order had killed Morretz for *no reason*. He had come South, using a magic that he did not have—and had never had—the power to survive.

For what purpose?

Rymark had, in front of the *Twin Kings*, claimed legitimate right to the Terafin Seat in the Hall of The Ten. He had implicated Gabriel, his father, in his lie; he had produced a forgery of a document that he claimed was signed by The Terafin *and* the right-kin. Gabriel had not spoken a word. Jewel wasn't even certain what he would have said—he was rescued by Haerrad. Haerrad, clearly injured, had survived what was an obvious attempt on his life to contest Rymark's claim.

Jewel could no more declare herself the legitimate heir—the only one—than she could bring the dead back to life, not unless she wanted to join them. At this very moment, that didn't seem like such a bad idea.

The *only* reason she had been summoned back was to fulfill her promise to the woman she had served for all her adult life—and she couldn't do it. Not yet. Maybe not ever.

It was Angel who rose next. The movement was slow and deliberate; he abandoned his chair and then took the time to tuck it neatly under the table, a signal that for him, Kitchen council was over.

"Jay," he said quietly as he approached her, his hair in its familiar spire, his expression oddly gentle. "We don't have to do this tonight." He lifted his hands in clear den-sign, asking for a vote. One by one, her den nodded. Jester, utterly subdued and silent, Carver, grim and pale, Teller and Finch in silent concern. Only Arann hesitated; Arann, injured in the battle in the Council Hall. Daine's consent was given quickly, perfunctorily; he rose—they all did—and headed *straight* for Arann, who was trying very, very hard to put him off without drawing Jewel's attention.

She didn't speak—not aloud—but she gestured a short, curt command. Arann's shoulders slumped as Daine took both of his hands and held them tightly. "Come to the healerie," he said.

"The healerie?" Jewel said sharply.

Daine glanced at her. "I was in training with Alowan," he said. "And I'm all there is for a successor."

She blanched. "Alowan—"

"I'm not Alowan, Jay. Most of the House isn't aware of what I can—and cannot—do. But the healerie was important to Alowan Rowanson. It's the only thing he left behind. I want to keep it running. I want to keep it going. The House needs a healerie. And it's the only thing I can do for him, now."

"Levec will have my head."

"Probably. He wasn't happy when I told him."

"Daine—"

But Daine smiled almost bitterly and shook his head. "It's my risk to take."

She opened her mouth again, but this time no words came out.

Daine didn't have that problem. "Do you understand why Alowan served The Terafin?"

She swallowed. Nodded.

"I serve you in the same way, for the same reason. You can't forbid it, if you're smart. You need me here." Pursing his lips in a way that was at odds with his age, he frowned at the much larger Arann. "So do the rest of you. You're not dying, Arann. It won't hurt." He led Arann away, and Arann followed.

Angel approached Jewel while the doors were still swinging behind their vanishing backs. "We can do this in the morning," he told her.

"But there's so much—"

"It'll still be here in the morning." He smiled; it was a brief, pained grin. "And gods help you, Jay, *you'd* better be here as well."

She heard what lay behind both the words and the smile, and flinched. "Angel, I didn't mean to leave that way. I didn't mean to—"

"It doesn't matter. It's done. But, Jay—never do it again. Don't go where I can't follow."

"Can I promise to try my best?"

"No."

Avandar was already gathering the lamps. Around her, in silence, the den drifted through the doors, allowing Angel to speak for them. It was Angel who led her to her room, Angel who opened the door, and Angel who threatened to sleep on the floor in case she suddenly vanished again. It was Angel who drew the curtains, Angel who approached the magelight that sat cradled in its burnished stand. No lamps now. He whispered the stone to a warm glow; it made his hair look gold. Like a very odd crown, she thought.

"They'll call a Council meeting in the morning," she told him, as if this had only just occurred to her.

He shook his head. "Let them. At the moment, there's no one in charge."

"They'll have to call Council meeting, Angel. The Kings *were there*. They wouldn't interfere if The Terafin had been poisoned or stabbed or shot—but she was killed by a very large, very deadly demon. House Terafin can't claim this as an entirely internal affair anymore. Not after that Henden. We'll need to come up with a plan to deflect Imperial control, or the House will be crippled."

"Not more than it already has been."

She couldn't find words to answer him.

Avandar waited by the door in silence. Only when Angel left did he move. His robes were familiar Terafin robes, and he lifted a familiar chair, dragging it across the thick, dark carpets until it rested within plain sight of the illuminated bed.

"No," she told him softly. "You're exhausted. You need sleep more than I do."

He sat. That was all. It was his most effective way of disobeying an order that she only barely wanted to give.

27th of Corvil, 427 A. A.
Terafin Manse, Averalaan Aramarelas

The night, not unexpectedly, was bad. Jewel woke several times, jerking upright and staring, in wild-eyed silence, into the pale glow of her room. Avandar did not sleep. His hands tensed around the armrests of a chair that couldn't be comfortable for long hours at a stretch, no matter how careful its craftsman had been.

"Jewel?"

She rose. He remained in the chair, although she was aware of his gaze as she gathered up the very few things she had brought with her from the South.

"What are you doing with those?"

She didn't answer. Instead, she dressed. The clothing she had worn for most of her sojourn in the South had been Voyani in make and style; practical, loose, comfortable. She therefore faced the contents of her closet as if they were a sentence for a particularly odious crime. She set her dusty boots aside in favor of shoes that were far cleaner and far more polished; she found a dress, drew it out of the closet, and paused. It was blue, yes— but today, blue was not the right color.

Heading farther back, she found the dress that she had worn at Alea's funeral. It was serviceable, and even if it wasn't, it was the only official mourning dress she had.

"I think that is not required for breakfast," Avandar rose now. "Dress simply. You will not be allowed to hide in your wing for most of this day; take what freedom and ease you can."

Setting her jaw, she shook her head. "This is what I want."

Once dressed, with Avandar's help—her hair did need work, but if she was allowed a little ease, this is where she chose to take it—she left her room. She hesitated to one side of the door—the wrong side. "Avandar, where is Ariel?"

He led her further down the hall, pausing at the door that was next-to-last.

Jewel knocked at it once. Then, shaking her head, she entered the room. The curtains were open. Moonlight silvered the window.

Ariel was sleeping on the floor beside the bed. She had a pillow; she'd removed the counterpane. She was a slender child; she was almost lost in the folds of cloth and the darkness. But she sat up a little too quickly when Jewel entered the room. Jewel, in her strange Northern dress, approached with care, holding both of her hands palm out, to make clear they were empty.

"I'm sorry," she said, in soft, soft Torra. "This room must be confusing." She knelt at Ariel's side.

Ariel said nothing. Her eyes were wide; in the darkness, Jewel couldn't distinguish pupil from iris.

"This is my home. The people here are my family. It's colder in the North than it was in the South, so we wear different clothing. I'm sorry," she said again. "You're safe here. I—I'll be busy, so you might not see as much of me, but I'll come to see you when I can."

Ariel still said nothing, and after a long pause, Jewel rose and left the room. She shouldn't have brought the child here, and knew it—but leaving her in the middle of an army hadn't seemed like the better option. She stood outside of the closed door, head bowed against it for a full minute.

The den habitually used the breakfast nook—and nook was a misused word for a room that size, in Jewel's opinion—in part because their schedules differed so much, and they seldom ate together. The dining room seemed cavernous and empty when its long table was occupied by only two.

On this morning, however, they drifted into the dining room by some sort of silent consensus. They didn't go to the kitchen; neither Jewel nor Teller had called it.

The Terafin offices in the Merchant Authority had understandably been closed; Finch was therefore at home. The office of the right-kin, however, was being besieged; Teller should have been absent. But Teller, dressed for work, and at odds with the more casual morning clothing of Carver, Jester, and Angel, came to the table anyway. Daine came to breakfast in the pale robes of the healerie, as well. Adam, however, did not. Nor did Celleriant. Arann was not yet on duty; he was seated at the foot of the table, as far from Daine as it was possible to sit, and still be in the same room.

Jewel sat at the head of the table, watching as the den gathered. They noticed what she was wearing—how could they not? White, mourning white, edged in black and gold. She hated it now as much as she'd hated it the first time she'd worn it. It was a *dress*. A dress might indicate some small part of the loss she felt—but it offered none of the rage. She struggled to set it aside. If there was one small corner of the world that didn't deserve it, it was this one.

Instead, in silence, she pushed aside the breakfast dishes that had been laid in front of her. She wasn't hungry. She knew she needed food—but apparently that information would not impart itself to her stomach. Ellerson attended and directed the servants who had come bearing their multiple trays in somber silence. Jewel tried very hard not to meet his gaze, or draw it.

When she had cleared enough space, she set four things on the table in front of her hands: three leaves, and three strands of hair twined in a bracelet. The hair was fine enough that it should have been almost invisible; it wasn't. It was Winter white against the gleaming wood grain.

It was the leaves that drew all eyes first: one was silver, one was gold, and one was diamond.

They stared for a moment. It was, predictably, Finch who spoke first, but she spoke with her hands, asking permission to take—to touch—what Jewel had placed on the table. Jewel answered the same way. Finch rose and lifted the leaf of gold—the warm color, not the cool ones—and raised it to the light.

Heavy, Finch gestured.

Yes. "It's gold."

"The others are silver and diamond?"

"Yes."

The leaves now drifted down the table, as if hands were wind; they settled for a moment and then passed on. No one, however, touched the hair that curled there in a very slender bracelet.

When the leaves returned to her, she bracketed them with the palms she placed flat on the table. "I don't know where to start. But those will give you some idea of just how strange the journey was."

"Did you save the Princess?" Carver asked.

Jewel did not pretend to misunderstand. It was a vision of a lone woman that had driven her to the South—but she had expected, however reluctantly, to travel with the armies under the three Commanders. "I don't know. The Princess—and that is not what she's called in the Dominion—is with the army. One of the armies. Given what those armies now face, I think salvation is going to be in short supply."

They were silent for a long moment, waiting.

"I didn't mean to leave Averalaan the way I did."

"No kidding," Jester said. His arms were folded across his chest, and he balanced his chair on its hind legs. She half expected him to extend his own legs and cross them on the table—but he glanced at Ellerson before he did, and kept them where they were. The dining room was *not* the kitchen. "Is it always going to come down to demons?"

"No. There are gods and other people in the mix as well." Her smile was a brief, bitter twist of lips. "It probably won't make much difference to people like us, though. The mages will argue about their classifications, if any of them survive."

"Other people?"

"My long-haired friend." She hesitated again. "He was in the kitchen last night. His name's Celleriant, although his own people call him Lord Celleriant."

"He's not here."

". . . No."

"Is he den, or isn't he?"

That was, of course, the question, wasn't it? "He serves me."

Jester gestured, den-sign.

"No. And he won't learn to speak it, either. I'm surprised he conde-scends to speak Weston."

"Do you trust him?"

". . . No." She grimaced. "And yes. I don't *like* him. But . . . he's one of mine."

Teller said, "He killed the demon that killed The Terafin."

Finch, at the same time, said, "He reminds me of Meralonne APhaniel."

"Meralonne?"

"On the night the demons came to Terafin. The night the stranger died in the foyer."

Jewel stared at Finch for a long, thoughtful moment. "Sigurne trusts Meralonne," she finally said.

It was Angel who said, "We trust *you*. If you want him, that's all that needs to be said. You've never been wrong before."

Against her will, Jewel said, "I didn't choose Celleriant."

"Then how—"

"When we escaped from the demons in the Common, we ended up on a hidden, ancient road." She swallowed. "And we met the Wild Hunt there."

She could not bring herself to speak of everything she had seen while walking that road, but she spoke of the forest of trees, from which she'd taken the leaves. She spoke of the Winter King in his castle of glass and ice, and she spoke of the Winter Queen at the head of her host, riding the endless and hidden roads, searching for her King, that she might depose him at last. She spoke of the Winter King—her Winter King—the great, white stag who could find his footing in any terrain, even the air itself.

"He was a man, once."

"When?"

"When the gods walked, I think. Long before the founding of the Empire. And before the Blood Barons. The Winter Queen gave him to me. She was riding him," Jewel added, her voice falling. "She ordered Celleriant to serve me as well. It was punishment for his failure." She stopped the sentence, but not in time.

"His failure to do what?" Angel asked sharply.

Avandar raised a brow; his lips settled into a sardonic half smile.

"His failure to kill me."

The silence deepened Avandar's amusement. It predictably did nothing to endear Celleriant to the rest of the den. "He won't try it again," she said, when no one dared to put the question into words. "He was ordered—by the Winter Queen—to serve me. He'll serve. He doesn't *have* to like it."

"Do the rest of us?" Angel demanded.

"Not more than he does."

She spoke of the Festival of the Moon in the Tor Leonne, of the Voyani Matriarchs, and of the masks. This was harder because if the story itself retained the same dreamlike quality of description, the events had occurred in what was theoretically the real world—if that had the same meaning, now. But she hesitated on the edge of the Sea of Sorrows. After the silence had grown awkward—beyond awkward, really—she took a deep breath and continued.

She spoke of the desert crossing; she spoke of the wagons that had taken flight, like small ships in the air. She spoke, at length, about the storm in the desert, about its end, explaining more fully how Adam had almost died, where almost meant could not be saved without a healer who could call him back from the bridge to the beyond, where Mandaros waited to offer judgment. Although the circumstances of that near death had not been entirely clear to the den when they had first met Adam, the reason he still lived was.

The den, in turn, explained in more detail Adam's role in The Terafin's continued—and tenuous—survival. It was a very muted breakfast, with more words than food passing lips.

When Jewel spoke of the rise of the City in the desert, she was once again in a land of dreams; the den couldn't grasp it. It wasn't that they didn't believe her—they did, and would; it was that they couldn't conceive of it. No more would Jewel have been able to do the same if she hadn't witnessed it herself.

But when she again fell silent, Teller nudged her—with den-sign, almost flailing to get her attention—and she continued with the trek out of the desert, at the side of the Serra Diora. She couldn't help but describe the Serra; she was a woman whose beauty could leave poets tongue-tied and at the same time desperately in search of words, as if by words they might capture and hold, in eternity, the flowering of a beauty that could not otherwise defy time.

She had found Ariel there, missing fingers, silent and terrified. After a long hesitation, she mentioned the demon who had brought—and abandoned her—to Jewel's care. "She's not a demon," she added quietly, into the various textures of den silence. "She's a child whose family died. I think it happened during the Festival of the Moon. She's not—she's not den, not exactly. She's too young to make that choice. But I couldn't just leave her there."

They accepted it without argument. Celleriant, no. Avandar had taken time. But Ariel was a child, and at that, an orphan—and that meant something here. Jewel was grateful

She spoke of Yollana of the Havalla Voyani and the passage into the Terrean of Mancorvo, and there she once again stalled. She did not speak of Avandar; nor did she speak of the ghosts who lingered in anger in the forests of the Terrean; nor did she speak, in the end, of the dead who waited, silent and accusing, for Avandar Gallais. But she found words to describe the Torrean of Clemente, its Tor'agar, Alessandro. She found words for the battle that occurred in one of the villages, when the waters rose and the demons revealed themselves among the ranks of the Southern clansmen. Yet even here, she faltered.

They knew, and they allowed it. There was just too much, there. Too much. Kallandras and Celleriant. Mareo kai di'Lamberto. The wild water. But no. It was more than that: it was Avandar. Warlord.

She turned to glance at the man she could not, for a moment, think of as domicis; his eyes were dark, his expression remote. Teller followed her gaze, and she shifted it, glancing at her arm, her sleeve, the brand hidden.

"We survived. We escorted the Serra Diora—with her sword—to the side of Valedan kai di'Leonne, the man she chose as her husband. And then—Morretz came." She flinched, fought for words and found them; they were rough. "Morretz found us, and we came home. We came home late."

She closed her eyes and opened them again, quickly. The expression on Amarais' dying face was carved into the darkness beneath her closed lids, a waking nightmare, an endless accusation. She swallowed. "The Terafin called me home. And I'm here. Haerrad is injured—it wouldn't break my heart if he died. Rymark has claimed—in front of the Twin Kings—the legitimacy of rule."

"They can't believe—"

"It doesn't matter. It's never mattered. Legitimacy of rule, in the absence of The Terafin, is defined entirely by the ability to take, and hold, the House Council. She could have anointed him in public with her own blood and it wouldn't matter. Haerrad won't accept him. Neither will Elonne or Marrick.

"There was a demon in the manse," she added soflty.

"There were at least two; one killed Alowan. It was hiding in his cat."

Jewel closed her eyes and opened them again, for the same reason. The den watched her, silent now. Avandar and Ellerson stood by the doors against the walls, their faces absent any expression. She barely glanced at Ellerson, and hated herself for it. He had been here for her den when she hadn't. He didn't deserve her anger or her pain, and she couldn't quite stop it. But she could stop herself from *acting* on it, and that would have to do.

She was ready when the knock at the outer doors interrupted her silence; she'd expected it. Ellerson left immediately, and in his absence, she glanced around the well-lit table, its perfect, polished surface nothing at all like the kitchen's. People's feet were not on the tabletop either; years of habit and some well-drilled lessons had made that almost unthinkable.

She knew what they wanted. She knew.

But The Terafin was dead. It had been less than a day.

She knew, Avandar said, as she clenched her teeth against the intrusion of his silent voice. It was another thing she did not want, and he was well aware of it. *She called you home because she knew. She held her post, Jewel; she held it for as long as she was capable of doing so—with the aid of your den. But she held it for a reason.*

Ellerson returned. He bowed, briefly, toward the table. "Jewel, Finch, Teller. Your presence has been requested by Gabriel ATerafin. The House Council is meeting within the half hour."

The Council Hall was packed. Jester and Angel accompanied them, as adjutants; it was allowed, but today, they were likely to be consigned to the galleries above. Avandar, as domicis, was allowed to stand behind Jewel's chair, and today, she felt his dour presence as a solid comfort; he was normal. Nothing else was.

Sigurne Mellifas stood by the door, her face unusually pale, her eyes ringed in dark circles. She looked older than she had the last time Jewel had seen her, although perhaps that was a kindness of memory. Older, she looked harsher. The almost grandmotherly frailty with which she usually cloaked her power had been discarded; she reminded Jewel of no one so much as Yollana, Matriarch of the Havalla Voyani. It was a strangely comforting thought.

Every member of the House Council who entered those doors was required to stand a moment in front of Sigurne. Only Jewel could see the light that the mage wove in the air between them. Every member of the House Council was also required to accept a very plain, gold band from the hands of the mage. Jewel had seen their like only once before; she knew what purpose they served. They exposed the demonic, if it was hidden safely within human flesh.

Jewel took hers without comment and slid it over her finger. When it failed to melt, she said, "Member Mellifas. Guildmaster."

"ATerafin." The reply was cautious and remote.

"The ring is not necessary. I can see."

"The rings were made fifteen—perhaps sixteen—years ago. They serve a purpose."

"Yes. But it is not a purpose that this meeting requires. I am here." When Sigurne failed to move, Jewel said, in a much lower tone of voice, "Ours cannot be the only House thus infiltrated; the rings might serve a better purpose offered to any other House Council." She liked this woman; she always had. But as she stepped over the threshold into the Council Hall, she accepted that her affection changed nothing. She lifted her voice. The acoustics in the hall were very fine. "The House Council meeting is a matter of both urgency and privacy. There is much to be discussed here that is not the business of those who are not Terafin and not appointed to the House Council.

"We appreciate your concern," she added, her voice loud enough to fill a hall that was becoming silent as people left off their smaller conversations to listen. "And we value it highly. It is seldom that the Guildmaster of the Order oversees such tasks. But I have returned from the armies in the South, and I can serve the same function as your spells and your rings. I am ATerafin," she added. "This is my home."

Sigurne studied Jewel's face for a long, long moment, and then she nodded. She gathered the rings that Jewel had so pointedly—and publicly—dismissed. "ATerafin."

"Guildmaster."

Sigurne left. Jewel hoped that she retreated to a quiet, warm room that had both tea and a bed. Given Sigurne, and given Sigurne's almost legendary hatred of demons, she highly doubted that was in the guildmaster's immediate future.

* * *

There was no blood on the floor. Jewel crossed it, looked at the marble beneath her feet; there was no sign at all that the woman who had ruled this House for decades had died here less than a day ago. The table had been repaired—in haste, and probably with magic—and the sundered chairs had been replaced; were it not for the chair that sat empty at the table's head, this might have been a normal day, a normal meeting.

But the chair did sit empty. Jewel glanced at it, hoping against hope that The Terafin would stride through those doors to occupy it once again. She was probably the only member of the House Council who watched the empty chair with that desire. It drew all eyes. Haerrad, injured, was nonetheless seated, and if there was one blessing today, it was the fact that the whole of his ire was focused on Rymark ATerafin. Elonne watched Rymark as well; hells, they all did. Rymark had produced a document—signed by The Terafin, and witnessed by the right-kin—that proclaimed Rymark ATerafin heir. They expected him to produce it again, at this meeting.

But for a man who held such a document in his keeping, he looked as grim and angry as Haerrad. Jewel frowned.

When the House Council had taken their seats, and the adjutants—the full complement—had been, as Jewel suspected they would, removed to the galleries, Gabriel ATerafin rose. He was not, technically, right-kin, because there was no Terafin—but no one sought to silence him as he opened the meeting.

"We are here, today, to discuss two issues." Save for only his voice, the room was silent. "The first, the matter of The Terafin's funeral."

Cautious words returned. He let them. Jewel was silent, but Finch and Teller were not, although half of their muted conversation was in densign. She watched. They were not—quite—at home in this hall. Had The Terafin been at the head of the table, Jewel would have been. She had spent half her life as a member of this Council, and if the first four years had been rough—and they had—she had grown accustomed to the smooth, polite talk that served as barbed argument across this large table.

She had no words to offer. The single, public act of defiance that had marked her return to the Hall had momentarily robbed her of voice. She wanted to go to the Terafin shrine now, with The Terafin's corpse; she wanted to lay it upon the altar and wait. She wanted to pay her final respects in the privacy of that remote shrine—and she was certain it would never happen.

"Three days," Haerrad said. "If the funeral begins on the second of Henden—"

"It is not enough time," Elonne countered, voice cool. "She was The Terafin, not the head of a lesser House. The Kings will, no doubt, be in attendance, and with them, the *Astari*. We may inform them that the funeral is three days hence, but we will be invited to reconsider that date."

"The Kings are not Terafin," Haerrad snapped.

"No. But if we hold the funeral in three days, they will not be here to pay their respects—and every other member of note in any of The Ten will mark their absence."

Jewel almost found herself agreeing with Haerrad, and that was never a good sign; she chose silence. Teller, however, did not. He concurred with Elonne. And so it went, until Gabriel raised a hand.

"The Terafin deserves the respect of the Kings." His voice was quiet. It was also resonant.

Haerrad opened his mouth, thought better of words, and closed it again.

The fourth day of Henden was set as the first day of the funeral rites.

The first *day*. As a concept, this was new to Jewel. Glancing at Teller and Finch, she saw signs of a similar lack of comprehension, but they, like she, kept their ignorance to themselves, alleviating it by inference as they listened. The funeral rites of monarchs and Exalted were, apparently, extended to the ruling head of each of The Ten, from the greatest to the least, and one day did not suffice to allow the correct respect—and presumed grief—of the populace to be shown.

Therefore the first day was given to grief and respect, and it was the first day rites that would almost certainly draw every man, woman, and child of power or notable rank in the City through the Terafin gates. The House Council agreed on a staggering sum of money to be devoted to the grounds and the manse itself in preparation for those three days; had they the luxury of time, the sum would, of course, be less.

Jewel, who hated the extravagance of excessive pomp and display, could find no voice to raise objection. This was for The Terafin, and it would be *seen*. It wouldn't be seen by Amarais, but it didn't matter. She wanted the world to know just how valued, how important, how beloved The Terafin had been, and if the world operated on money, she would live with that.

Of course, it wasn't about Amarais for much of the House Council.

They were jackals, carrion creatures; they wanted the House. It was about the House itself. Respect paid to The Terafin accrued to the House they wanted to rule in the very near future. She *hated* the conflation of respect and grief with bolstering their own future identities—it made her want to scream in fury.

She didn't. She swallowed the rage, instead—because she knew that half of it was directed at herself. She came home *too late*. She *had known* what The Terafin faced—and she left her to face it alone. There had been demons and death in the South; things ancient and terrifying. But nothing she had seen in the South seemed to justify her absence from the House—and the death of The Terafin only confirmed its pointlessness.

"The second order of business." Gabriel's crisp, clear voice broke her train of thought—and she wanted it broken. She dragged her gaze from the surface of the Council Hall table and fastened it onto the man who had been right-kin. But she glanced at Rymark on the way; he was silent, his expression angrier than it had been. He did not rise; he did not raise hand or voice; he did not call upon the House Council to once again witness his presentation of claim.

"In the absence of an acclaimed House Ruler, House Terafin will require a regent. I assume there *is* an absence of such acclaim."

Silence.

Haerrad, grinning, said, "Clearly."

"The House Council will now entertain the claims of those who feel they are worthy to rule House Terafin."

Elonne rose first. She rose slowly, gracefully, deliberately. She gave the entire Council table one steady measured glance. "I am Elonne Derranoste ATerafin. I have been responsible for the merchant routes along the Southern Annagarian coast, and to the Western Kingdoms, and if the Council deems it wise, I will lead Terafin."

Gabriel did not call for a vote. Gerridon ATerafin rose. He was a junior Council member, although he was no longer *the* Junior Council member; that was reserved for Finch. Or Teller. "I offer support to Elonne's claim."

"Thank you, Councillor," Gabriel said. Gerridon sat.

Haerrad rose next, but he waited until Elonne had fully resumed her seat to do so. "I am Haerrad Jorgan ATerafin. The more difficult land-locked routes in the Dominion have been mine; they have prospered, even during the war. In my hands, Terafin will likewise prosper, regardless of events that occur outside our domain."

Sabienne ATerafin rose from across the table. "I will support Haerrad's claim," she said quietly. "Given the manner of both Alowan and The Terafin's deaths, a Lord who retains his power during martial difficulties is necessary."

"Thank you, Councillor."

Haerrad took longer to sit than Elonne had.

Marrick rose third. He was the only man to smile at the Council table, but it was a restrained smile, for Marrick. "I am Marrick Bennett ATerafin," he said, bowing slightly. "I am not, it is true, martial—but during my tenure as Councillor, I have made gains within the Queens' Court, on behalf of the House, and within the Makers' Guild; Guildmaster ADelios has thrice in the past year accepted invitations to the House—when they have come from me. Such are the alliances I have built, and will continue to build, to strengthen Terafin when I rule."

To Jewel's slight surprise, Iain ATerafin rose. Of those who had taken a stand, he was the oldest. His hair was white. His clothing was neat, tidy, and entirely unremarkable; it was neither too fine nor too coarse. He was, according to Teller, very good at his job—which involved the internal financial workings of the manse itself. He rarely raised his voice, but no one doubted that he had a spine; the Master of the Household Staff reported to him when more staff was required, in her opinion. She did not always get that staff, and Iain was demonstrably still alive.

"I support Marrick in his claim," Iain said quietly. Of the support offered, Iain's was the most significant, and judging by the expression on Haerrad's face, Jewel was not the only person to be surprised.

"Thank you, Councillor," Gabriel said. He gazed across the table.

Rymark, his son, rose. "I am Rymark Garriston ATerafin. I claim the right of rule by designation."

"By designation," Haerrad said, pushing himself up from the table in obvious anger. "Now that the Kings do not crowd our shoulders, let us see your document."

"It is in the keeping of Gabriel ATerafin."

All eyes turned to Gabriel. Gabriel met his son's angry gaze, and it seemed to Jewel that it was Gabriel who blinked first. But if he did, he did not then produce the offensive document Haerrad had demanded. He said, instead, "Who stands as Rymark Garriston ATerafin's second?"

Verdian ATerafin stood. She was very much a younger version of Elonne, although her hair was paler, and her eyes gray; she was, and had always been, striking. She served as liaison with the Port Authority. "I support Rymark ATerafin's claim."

"Very well. It must now be asked: will three of you cede your claim to any other?"

Silence.

Gabriel nodded; the answer—or lack—was not a surprise to anyone who crowded this room. "Put forth your nominations for regent."

Teller rose. "I nominate Gabriel Garriston ATerafin as regent. He has served as right-kin for decades, and he knows the political affiliates of the House, and its internal structure, well. If the office of right-kin becomes the office of Regent, there will be very little disruption in House Business, as seen from the outside."

Haerrad drew breath, which usually served as a warning. But Haerrad's supporter, Sabienne, rose. "I will second that nomination. Gabriel ATerafin has chosen to support no claim to the House Seat; he has made no claim himself. Both of these facts are necessary in any Regent the Council now chooses—and only those who are otherwise very Junior could claim to do neither. The strongest members of this Council cannot take the Regency cleanly—if at all. Gabriel has the experience necessary to guide the House while the Council considers all claimants, and their worth."

She sat.

Haerrad did not speak further, although Jewel imagined there would be many words said after the meeting was at last over.

Gabriel said, "I will accept the nomination with a clear understanding that when The Terafin is chosen, I will retire."

"And if you do not serve as Regent?" Teller asked.

"I will retire now. A man cannot be right-kin to more than one Lord in his life."

It was Teller who now turned to the table, in much the same way. "Gabriel ATerafin as regent," he said clearly and in a voice Jewel hardly recognized. "Vote."

Chapter Two

28th of Corvil, 427 A.A.
The Common, Averalaan

THE SIGN ON THE SHOP'S closed door didn't look promising: *Closed for business due to family emergency.* Jewel hesitated, and glanced briefly at the length of the shadows that now pooled at their feet. Four sets of feet: Avandar's, hers, Finch's, and Teller's. To say she'd had a sleepless night wouldn't have been entirely accurate, but it was close, and at the moment, she wanted nothing so much as to crawl back into the carriage, out of the carriage, and into her room in the West Wing of the Terafin manse. It was cool in the city, even in the sun, although early morning sun was seldom warm in any season but summer.

Teller and Finch exchanged a glance; Jewel caught it because she was watching them. They'd clearly learned to rely on each other a lot in her absence; she wondered if either of them was aware of how much.

"What should we do?" Finch finally asked—this time of Jewel.

Jewel winced. The idea that the shop would be closed on the sixth day of the week hadn't even occurred to her.

"There are other shops," Teller offered. It was tentative. "We could choose one of them."

Not choosing one was not an option. As House Council members, no matter how junior—and although Jewel was young, she was not so junior as all that—they had no choice but to dress "appropriately" for singular and important occasions. Jewel often minded the fuss and the expense, which she considered a colossal waste, given how *many* starving people that money could be used to feed, but not this time.

This time, she needed funereal clothing for The Terafin, and it was the *last* such display of respect she could give the woman who had saved, and changed, all of their lives.

For years now, Haval had made—had insisted on making—all of the significant clothing in Jewel's life. He traded gossip as it pleased him for the custom of House Terafin, as he liked to call it, and she traded the same, probably more recklessly. Haval was slippery, canny, and shrewd. He also disliked emergency work, and as all three of them needed suitable attire before the fourth day of Henden, this was an emergency. It was a costly one, or would be, by the time he was done.

If he accepted the commission at all.

Jewel stared at the sign for a long moment, and then she reached up for the bell pull and began to yank at it as if it were a lifeline and she were drowning. She pulled for five minutes and the store failed to come to life.

"Jay," Teller began. He stopped. Through the window with its precisely lettered sign, he saw movement from the back of the store. The shadow resolved itself into a familiar figure, his face completely free of any expression at all.

Jewel stepped away from the door as he approached it. She glanced once at the sign, and once at her nerveless hand, still wrapped around the bell pull. The hand, she removed. Haval opened the door.

In the morning light, she thought he looked pale, his skin stretched and delicate with wrinkles. Certainly his eyes were ringed with dark circles. But he was Haval; the momentary expression of age or fragility cracked and shattered as he smiled. He even bowed, standing in the doorway. "Jewel," he said.

It was bad. She knew it was bad. He usually remembered to call her Jay except when he was offering subtle—or not so subtle—advice. But Haval was one of nature's natural liars. After five minutes in his presence—even if he was circumspect and near-silent—anyone would believe anything he chose. Anything at all.

She'd never learned enough about Haval to know, clearly, when he was lying; the only time she could catch him was when her own gift, her own "natural" talent, emerged. Avandar was better at reading the inscrutable dressmaker. But Avandar was silent and near-invisible, as he always was in Haval's presence.

"Are you—are you really closed for business?" Jewel managed to ask, when Haval rose from his deep and embarrassingly perfect bow.

"I am, at the moment, very busy—but I am not entirely adverse to commissions from valuable customers." He stepped away from the door. "Please, come in." He didn't remove the sign, however. "I would like to speak in the back room. If we are seen in the front, people will question the veracity of my carefully scribed sign."

"You . . . heard that I was back," Jewel said, following where he led.

"Yes. If knowledge of your return concerns you, take comfort in the fact that it is buried beneath much larger news." He paused, turned, and said, "Ah, forgive my lack of tact, ATerafin. I've slept very little these past two days, and I am not at my best."

She nodded, and took the opening he'd offered. "Actually, we're here because of the larger news."

"We?" He glanced at Teller and Finch. His gaze—as always—slid past Avandar.

"Finch, Teller, and I. The funeral begins on the fourth, and we need clothing appropriate to our station within the House—for however long we actually manage to *keep* said station." She could now feel Avandar's chilly glare boring a hole through the back of her head, and ignored it.

She expected some sign of outrage, because while Haval was perfectly willing to work on tight deadlines, he detested them, and made it known—usually by charging vastly more than he otherwise would. He said nothing; instead he turned and continued his slower than usual march into the back room.

Jewel stopped in the doorframe. Teller walked into her back. The room was almost spotless. There were a total of five chairs, two tables, and a solid, respectable desk. Bolts of cloth rested against the wall opposite the door, admittedly in several high piles; boxes and jars held beads of various colors. There were even small tables of the type that were easily moved, and upon which tea was usually set in a pinch.

"Ah, you've noticed," Haval said, as she snapped her jaw shut.

Of all the things she'd heard or witnessed since her return, this—small, trivial, politically unimportant—shocked her the most. In all of her years of coming to Haval's shop, she had never, ever seen the back room so tidy. It was almost as if . . . Haval didn't live here anymore.

But Haval was standing there, breathing and speaking, his hands by his sides. She raised her eyes to meet his gaze, and her own hands tightened into fists. "Haval," she said quietly, "where's Hannerle?"

"She is currently indisposed. Please, take a seat."

"No."

"ATerafin?"

"No. Where is she? How is she indisposed?"

"That is more personal than I wish to be at the moment, and frankly, if I accept your commission, we will have no time for trivial details." He walked to his desk, opened a drawer, and fished out a measure.

"How long has she been indisposed?"

"Jewel," Avandar said, before Haval could sidestep the question for a second time. "The question is inappropriate; Master Haval has given the whole of the reply he wishes to give at the present time."

Jewel nodded and took a seat. Avandar, however, wasn't fooled. He came to stand by her side, and he placed one hand on her shoulder. Haval gestured Teller into the center of the room, and Teller, in a silence tinged with compassion, lifted his arms and turned obligingly in whichever direction Haval indicated. Finch did likewise, first shedding one layer of clothing at Haval's request.

But when it was Jewel's turn, although she stood as requested, she failed to keep silent. "Is she sleeping, Haval?"

He heard the question, she'd said it so close to his ear. But there was no change at all in his breathing, no shift of muscles to alter his expression. He took the measurements, writing each down with fastidious care. He didn't even fail to meet her eyes—he did, several times. But there was nothing to acknowledge the question, no indication that she'd either hit or missed.

His hand was steady as he wrote down the numbers that reduced her to a size with which he could work.

"Haval."

"I have what I need at the moment; if you wish to choose appropriate cloth, please do."

"We'll leave it up to you. You're still better at it." She turned toward the door as he set aside all of his measurements. "Haval—"

He lifted a hand. "I think it advisable to refuse your commission, but against my better judgment, I will accept it. Do not make me regret my generosity."

"How much will your generosity cost?"

A shadow of a smile touched his lips. "Not more than three times what the work would have cost had you the time to plan ahead. I will have to visit House Terafin when I have something to actually fit."

"We can come here," she began.

"I think, in this case, it would be less difficult for me to attend you there."

"There'll be more people listening there."

"Yes. But I will say nothing that will not bore the listeners, and you will be forced to do the same."

"But I need—"

He raised a hand. "Jewel. Jay. I am not what I was. We each have our responsibilities in our respective homes for at least a little while longer."

She knew that had never stopped him before. She even opened her mouth to say as much, but it was pointless; Haval could be impenetrable when it suited him. She glanced once at her silent, stiff domicis, and once at Teller and Finch, both of whom had let her do what little talking there was.

"If we could wake Hannerle, what would it be worth to you?"

His silence was profound because it encompassed everything about him for just a few seconds: all motion, all breath, all expression. He didn't answer.

Because he didn't, she continued. "We can't *keep* her awake. Whatever this sickness is, we don't have that in us."

"How can you wake her at all?"

"Answer the first question first." Her voice was colder and harder than it should have been; that much, she'd learned from Avandar in her time.

"There is very little in my possession with which I would not part. If I thought it would satisfy, I would offer the robes in exchange. I will not insult you by doing so," he added. "But I will not, in turn, be insulted; I will not take on faith that you have the power to do so."

"Fair enough. Pretend that we can, for the moment."

"If you cannot keep her awake, there is less value in the waking."

Jewel nodded. Avandar drew breath, and she raised her hand in curt den-sign before he could use it. "I believe that we can continue to wake her, if she falls asleep and can't wake on her own. It's not a cure. It's as close as anyone can come, at the moment."

"And you would continue to wake her?"

"It depends on you."

"What do you want, ATerafn?"

"I want your ears. I want your eyes. I want your gossip and your ability to penetrate other people's gossip."

"And that is all?"

". . . no."

His smile was chilly; it contained no hint of surprise. "It's been decades, ATerafin, since I have worked in any official capacity."

"I don't give a rat's ass about official."

"You should," he told her softly, his voice as cool as his smile had been before it deserted his face. "You intend to take the House Seat, do you not?"

Silence.

I told you this was unwise, Jewel. Avandar spoke in the distinctly uncomfortable internal voice. Jewel, still silent, did the same. *Haval is not a fool.* Almost as if he grudged it, the domicis added, *he is, and has always been, dangerously perceptive. He is, and has always been, dangerously deceptive. He must be handled with care.*

I think we need him. Her reply was not much different than a spoken reply would have been. It wasn't, in fact, different than the spoken reply had been on the carriage ride to Haval's shop.

I did not press this point, Avandar replied. *But I will press it now. What do you mean "I think?"*

I need him.

You have come this far without anything but the clothing he crafts. I wish you to be clear on your reasons for this unwise approach.

Not a single member of her den would have continued to argue with her after she'd made such a definitive statement.

No, they would not. But I am not your den; I am not looking to you for either leadership or guidance.

The worst thing about this type of speech—a gift from the mark he had left on her arm—was these arguments. Avandar of old—Avandar before the sojourn in the South—would have stifled all urge to argue when in the presence of witnesses; now that the witnesses couldn't *hear* him, he didn't stop.

You know as well as I that this is different. I'm at a disadvantage from the beginning—

A disadvantage that you wouldn't have if you had accepted The Terafin's desire early enough to plan.

She didn't argue that point because she couldn't. Instead she said, *I need him. I need him at my side until this is over.*

I do not materially disagree with this statement; I wish you to understand what the cost of his indenture may be. Do you think he will survive in your service?

I . . . don't know.

Jewel, your friends are your weakness. The fewer you involve, the less difficult this will be in the end.

My friends are my weakness?

Yes. You fear to lose them.

It was true. But the other truth was as undeniable: Her friends were also her strength. She'd missed that, in the South.

She looked directly up at Haval. "Yes," she said quietly. "I intend to take the House Seat."

"May I ask why?"

"I promised The Terafin."

"There are some promises it is unwise to make."

"I wasn't her first choice. But all of her other choices died before she did. I'm what's left, Haval. I'm all that's left."

"And your claim?"

"I have the writ designating me heir."

"Which isn't worth the paper it was written on."

Jewel winced, but nodded; it was true.

"I think you fail to understand what—and who—you are up against. This will not be a minor scuffle; in my opinion, fully half of those who are standing now will be buried before this is over. The casualties will not be limited to the House, although it is the House that will suffer the brunt of them."

"If they kill outside of the House—"

"Who will go crying to the Kings? If you think the laws of exception governing The Ten will keep outsiders—such as myself—safe, you are hopelessly naive."

"Is that your answer?"

Haval turned to Finch. "You were made House Council members because she intended you to support Jewel's claim?"

Finch glanced at Jewel, but nodded.

"And she made this explicit?"

"She threatened to revoke the House Name if we didn't accept the promotion."

"I see." He turned back to Jewel, but Finch hadn't finished.

"We have the sword," she said quietly.

"Pardon?"

"We have The Terafin Sword. She gave it to—to one of us. As proof of Jay's claim."

"Who else is aware of this?"

"No one."

"And you can swear that?"

Finch nodded.

"Then let me ask you a different question, Finch. Teller, you may also answer if you desire. You understand that your chances, as House Council members, of surviving this war are less than fifty percent in my opinion?"

Finch paled.

Teller, however, said, "If they're that high, I'll be surprised."

"And you are willing to take that risk?"

"We have no choice. It's not about the promise Jay made. That promise was the only thing that kept The Terafin going at the end, but she's dead; she won't care now. And we're not dead yet; we don't want to die."

"There is no guarantee whatsoever that Jewel can save you—"

"It *doesn't matter*. She can save the House. She can save what the House is, and what it means. If Marrick or Elonne succeed, the House will be different, and I think we could live with it. But if Haerrad or Rymark succeed—" Teller shook his head. "We can't just stand back and allow it."

"Why not throw your support behind either Marrick or Elonne, in that case? Either of the two have resources that are greater than yours."

Jewel cleared her throat. "We're not convinced that Marrick and Elonne will survive."

Haval was still watching Finch and Teller. "And you are convinced that Jewel will?"

Finch said, "Jay will survive." There was no doubt at all in her words. Before Haval could speak again, she said, "We know that it's likely most of us won't. But even if they kill us all, Jay will survive. She's hard to kill. They destroyed half of the Common, and they couldn't kill her." She bit her lip; she was pale. Jewel saw that, and it hurt. "You don't understand, Haval."

"I understand Jewel ATerafin."

"Yes. But you don't understand *us*. The Terafin took all of us, not just Jay. For years now, we've survived—and prospered—because of her. We were afraid, when we came to the House, that there'd never be a place for us; we were all orphans, we came from the poor holdings, we had no acceptable clothing, and very poor manners. We knew that Jay was important, that Jay was valuable. We knew that we were suffered because of that.

"But she saw something in *us* as well. She gave us positions in the House. We learned. She taught us. We love the House in our own way. Maybe it's not the same way Jay does—maybe we can't do that because we're not Jay. It doesn't matter. We love what the House was, under her command. We don't want to see it turn into something else. Yes, she's dead. Yes, betraying the dead isn't a crime—not on the streets, not where we grew up. But it's *not* the dead we'll betray if we just give up and do nothing.

"It's the living. It's everyone *else* in the House. It's Lucille and Jarven and the servants and the cooks and the gardeners and the merchants. We're not children anymore. But some of them are. We don't plan to walk to our deaths; we don't plan to sit still in the dark, cowering. But we have a choice that some of them don't have.

"And we want—we need—your help."

"A heartfelt speech, ATerafin," Haval said, in cool, exact tones. "Heartfelt speeches, however, are best visited upon the young and inexperienced or the old and sentimental. In the event that your exposure to Jarven has led you to the mistaken assumption that I am part of the latter category, I must offer correction. I am not.

"You have been a valued and valuable customer of my establishment for well over a decade. Jewel, I am aware that your . . . offer . . . was meant to display some stiffening of spine on your part, and some tendency toward tougher negotiation than has been your wont."

"I'm not—"

"You pay a premium to come here, and you always have. The only exceptions to that general rule have been on those occasions when you are not personally negotiating. You have a sentimental attachment to my establishment, and to me personally, that weakens any negotiation you undertake. I am a fair man, and I attempt not to take advantage of this fact." Haval sat, gracefully and silently, on the chair closest to the center of his desk. He slid a drawer open, retrieved a blotter and paper, and slid it shut again. The room was silent. It was overly crowded as well; he greatly desired to send them all on their way. Measurements lay on the desktop as well, and if he intended to make suitable funereal attire, he needed all of the time remaining.

But he did not take it, not yet.

"Because I have not agreed to your terms, I am *still* endeavoring to be a fair man. Jewel, your opening gambit in this case does, I admit, make it less of an issue. Since I am aware that you are frequently less observant than you should be—a failing shared by a majority of this city's inhabitants—I am attempting not to respond in anger."

He knew what she would look like, which is why he didn't bother to turn; she could see the stiff but perfect lines of his back and shoulders as he folded his hands for a moment in front of him.

"Hannerle," he said, after a long pause, "would, if offered the same . . . deal . . . that you have offered me, refuse it with prejudice. She only barely tolerates the gathering of harmless gossip; she guards against anything more active on my part as if her life depends on it. And," he said, choosing this moment to shift his chair so that he might face her, "she is not wrong."

He waited. There was a reason for it; he was not angry, although he had implied the opposite; he was annoyed, but his annoyance was procedural, not emotional. He was also curious. But he believed that Jewel did indeed possess some method of waking his wife; that the waking would not be permanent.

"Do you understand what the base weakness of your opening offer was?" He now steepled his hands in front of his chest.

The girl who had once walked into his shop had been eclipsed by the woman, but they were connected by some of the same essential qualities, although this woman was infinitely better dressed. He saw the familiar tightening of jaw, the slight furling of hands—but they went no farther. Her hands did, however, move up to the hair in front of her eyes. She would no doubt push hair from her eyes at least a dozen times before this conversation was over.

She swallowed and nodded.

"Please," he said, loosing his hands to gesture briefly with open palms. "Elucidate for me so that *I* may be certain."

"Hannerle isn't half the devious bastard you are," was the slowly worded reply. "She doesn't lie. She doesn't pander. She cooks, she cleans, and she keeps this whole place running just so you can make dresses."

"I will point out that I frequently went to the wells; I am not entirely—"

"Did you want the explanation?"

"I wanted something less personal and more concise; I should perhaps make allowances for personal style. My apologies."

"I've known her just as long as I've known you. She makes me help in the kitchen. She complains about you while we're working. She even loves you."

"And the significance of these?"

"I care about her. I consider her a friend. I can't threaten to withhold something that'll help her."

"Ah, no, you *can*."

"I can't do it in a way that makes it believable."

"I believe that you believed you could, because you are under a great deal of pressure, and the demands of those you have chosen—as Finch made clear—to protect cannot be tossed away for the sake of one person. However, in my own arsenal, Jewel, I have Hannerle herself. Come." He rose. "Why don't you say hello to my wife?"

Haval wasn't certain how she would respond. Oh, he knew that she would follow him into the most light-filled room in their dwelling, but he didn't know whether she would do it bowed by the weight of a guilty conscience. It was troubling, that she still possessed that. He himself felt no twinge of it at all. But she moved to the door almost before he reached it, as if she were eager to enter, eager to see the sleeper who wouldn't wake. As if, in spite of her intentions, this one old, round woman with a querulous temper and a tendency to turn breath into nagging, was momentarily more important than a House.

He hadn't lied—implying anger which he was *entitled* to feel, even if he didn't, could hardly be counted as a lie; Hannerle would choose death before she saw him pressed into the type of service that he had once performed. He glanced once at the domicis, a man who had weathered the passage of years very, very well. He was certain that a few delicately worded sentences would make clear to the man the scope of Haval's previous profession.

But he was himself uncertain if Jewel actually knew what she was asking of him.

He entered the room where his wife lay abed. The sun was not yet high, and light came through open curtains in spokes; the room was perhaps dustier than was ideal. He did not approach the bed; he might have, but

Jewel was there before he could and Finch and Teller shadowed her. Only the domicis kept his distance.

Jewel, therefore, took the single seat by the bedside, and Jewel, not Haval, picked up the limp, cool hand of his wife. Jewel spoke to her, voice low, words even. She wasn't a patient girl; she was up before five minutes had passed—but she didn't seek escape. Instead, she touched Hannerle's forehead with the back of her hand, and gently brushed strands of hair to one side or the other.

"Does she drink?"

"I have given her water already."

"I could—"

"No." He waited, counting seconds until Jewel hugged her.

"ATerafin," he said stiffly. "Jewel."

She ignored him. "Avandar."

The domicis did not look pleased. "I think it unwise."

"We don't have another way of doing this. We can't take her by carriage—she's not small enough that we can manage to sneak her into the House. Not now. Probably not even a decade ago, when there wasn't a hint of a succession war."

"And then she will be in the House. It would be better if—"

"We can't. We can't ask him to come here. He's already going to attract attention because he's traveling with Levec almost every damn day to *Avantari*. His destination affords him some protection; it's also going to raise eyebrows. I don't want him to become the next Alowan. What he does for her, no one else can know. No one can attribute it to him."

"Perhaps I might be included in this logistical discussion?" Haval suggested.

They both turned to look at him.

It was Jewel who looked away first. "You win," she said. "I blink. I fold. Whatever it is that people do when they try to play a game with a bum hand."

"And you are suggesting—" His brows actually rose. He could have stopped them had he desired, but saw no advantage to hiding a shock that any person in the Empire might have shown. "You're not suggesting that he take her to the Terafin manse by *magic*?"

"I'm open to any other suggestion," was her flat reply. "But without a good reason, we can't have the healer in question come here. If Hannerle's awake, you can figure out a way to sneak her out of the House. Hells, if she's unconscious and you can think of a reasonable way to sneak her *in*, that would be our first choice. The rest of us would go by carriage, you included. For the next few days you have every reason to be in the House—tailors will be coming and going all over the manse. But not unconscious ones."

"May I ask a question while I consider these options?"

Jewel nodded.

"What did you intend to offer me? Or were you aware of Hannerle's condition?" Jewel's silence, so loud with facial tics, was answer enough. "I believe I will have words with Jarven ATerafin. He told you, Finch?"

Finch was also silent. Her silence was meeker and smoother. "Jay wasn't certain she believed him."

"Very wise of her. Unusually wise. What else did he tell you?"

"Not very much," was her diplomatic response. She even smiled apologetically as she said it. As lies went, it wasn't—but her smile was smooth as sword steel.

"And did he happen to mention his reasons for being so generous with other people's information?"

Finch's brow folded. "Pardon?"

"Did he suggest you use this to your advantage?"

"No. But he knows that Jay's fond of Hannerle. He thought, given everything, word might not reach Jay in time."

In time.

Had she said it to be cruel? No. No, not Finch. But he thought her angry, at the moment, and words could be said in anger that might never be thought of otherwise.

Haval lifted a hand to his eyes. When he lowered it, he looked tired and overwhelmed. Her expression softened, as he'd intended.

"I remember," Jewel said, as they stood in silence, "that you once told me a good lie worked because it used things that were true as foundation."

"That is not *entirely* what I said; I assure you I would have been somewhat more exact." He exhaled, straightening as he did. "There are other things you must learn. It is possible to threaten someone when you have no intention of carrying out that threat. We call that a bluff. It is not possible, however, for *you* to use this particular bluff on me. I am too aware of your foibles, and also aware of your current circumstances.

"I am not a foolish man. Sometime in the very near future the bluff could become truth, even in your hands. Your context will shift, Jewel. It will change. You feel you are desperate now—but you are far from it. You will understand the difference. I do not wish that on you," he added, softening his voice. "But if you intend to take the House—and I understand that is your decision and you will not be moved from it—you will be forced to do things that you have never considered before."

Jewel lifted a hand; it was trembling. "Enough, Haval. Enough. I'm sorry. I shouldn't have—"

"Attempted to use a weapon against me that wounds you almost as deeply when you wield it? No. Never do it again."

The domicis actually chuckled, and this time, Haval turned to look at him. "I wish you luck, Haval," Avandar said, his lips still etched with the lines of a particularly dry smile. He was, in Haval's opinion, a handsome man, and a distinguished one. "I have attempted to teach Jewel ATerafin similar lessons on occasion. She can be forced to listen; she cannot be forced to obey."

"Ah. Perhaps that is your difficulty. I have no need to be obeyed. I tell her what she should have already observed, no more, no less. She—like so many—observes what she pleases, and she evaluates it in a similar fashion. Because she is canny, she is often partially correct. If I sound either irritated or displeased, it is because, if she cannot learn from her errors with regards to other people, she should *at least* know better than to make such rudimentary errors while *I* am her opponent."

"And are you?" The domicis said, the sly smile still gracing his face.

"You, on the other hand," Haval replied, "are canny, perhaps in exactly the same way I am; I cannot help but think that you were offered your contract in the domicis hall for *exactly* this fight, in the end. The Terafin was an admirable woman in almost all ways; she saw far, and she planned for many, many contingencies. I do not believe that you—that any of you—have yet seen the full range of the plans she set in motion before her death."

Finch took a step toward Haval; Teller caught her hand and shook his head. It was a single, economical movement. She halted, waiting.

Waiting, Haval thought, for Jewel to speak.

"Avandar," Jewel said crisply.

Avandar's silence was chilly, but he nodded. "I will meet you in the West Wing. I would appreciate it if you survived until then."

Jewel snorted, which made Haval wince. It was *not* a sound that should have come from the mouth of a member of the Terafin House Council; it was certainly not a sound that would be allowed The Terafin. He studied

her clothing; she wore it the way she always had: gracelessly, but ener-
getically. Her bearing was not—would doubtless never be—regal. She
exuded neither confidence nor power.

"ATerafin," Haval began.

"You haven't come up with any suggestions as to how we sneak Hannerle into the manse," was her practical reply. "Which means you don't
have any."

"Not at the moment, no."

"Then we'll do without."

"I have not agreed to any terms."

"No. I told you, I surrender. I'm going to do this regardless, and I'd
appreciate it if you just shut up and accept it. If you want, you can run
out into the streets after the magisterial guards; we'll be long gone by
then, with any luck."

"I think they would frown on kidnapping."

"They'd probably do a hell of a lot more than just frown. You want her
to wake up, don't you?"

"I do."

"Then leave it, for now. Work, do whatever it is you need to."

"I think Hannerle will be confused and possibly annoyed—"

"Enraged?"

He winced. "Or, indeed, somewhat angry, if she wakes in a strange
room and in a strange place. If I am there, I can calm her."

"Fine. You can come back with us. You'll need to bring her home, regardless."

"Then give me a few moments to gather a few things. Finch, if I may
borrow your help?" he added, as he headed out of the room.

Haval's definition of a "few things" was like Jay's definition of a "little
trouble." It was also, sadly, in line with his definition of a "few moments,"
and involved a lot of carrying. He moved tall bolts of white cloth and tall
bolts of black cloth, none of which were light. They were easier to handle
than the small jars of pins and beads, and the heavy box full of needles and
thread.

"You realize," she said, while she was carrying the third bolt, "that
we're going in a carriage, not a wagon?"

"Ah, yes." He picked up the measurements he had made and slid them
into a pocket. "If we had more room or more time, I would take more."

She nodded, although she couldn't imagine how much *more* he could take with him.

"The Merchant Authority is closed tomorrow," he said, as he picked up a few small items and also deposited them in pockets. "Which is good. I find this type of tight deadline taxing."

Finch nodded. "I'll be home, but Teller will spend most of the day in Gabriel's office."

"And the House Council?"

"There's a meeting later this afternoon, but it should be brief. The only items of import so far have been discussions about the funeral and the guests invited to attend the burial itself. The great hall's been opened up, and the servants have been working like a small army; as far as I know, we have three Senniel bards who will either sing or play during the procession and the burial. The Kings and the Queens will also be present, so the House Guard's been busy as well. The gardeners have been weeping in frustration," she added, with a pang of sympathy. This was *not* the time of year for the gardens, and absolutely not the time of year for a burial.

But death didn't particularly care about the weather or the season; it came when it came.

They had reached the door with the last of Haval's "few" items, and Finch waited while he adjusted the sign proclaiming his absence, and locked the door firmly. The carriage was already waiting, and given the day, it received its share of baleful glares. They were *carefully* baleful, on the other hand, given the prominence of the Terafin crest and the size of the horses.

Haval was not required to carry his cloth and his tools; the footmen who met the carriage did that. Nor was he required to use the tradesman's entrance, because he had arrived in the same carriage as no less than three members of the House Council. He took care to look smaller and more nervous than he might otherwise have looked, and he walked several steps behind Finch. Jewel led, but she led in the unconscious way she always had. Her stride was wide and unfaltering, even given the skirts she wore; her step was heavy and certain. It wasn't elegant and it certainly wasn't graceful; Hannerle might have approached a kitchen counter in just the same way that Jewel ATerafin now approached the wing of the manse she called home.

She would have frowned—and not silently—had she heard the comparison, but there it was: something in Jewel reminded him of his wife. They were not the same woman, not even close to the same woman. Jewel was cursed with an earnest heart and a hope for the future that never wavered enough to break, something that Hannerle had never had. His wife believed in the present, and held onto it with a ferocity and a focus that defined her.

But they were both practical women, and they both had a temper that on occasion caused crockery to break. They were both fiercely protective of their homes, their families. Hannerle's home and family had always been small. Jewel's had grown.

It had grown, Haval thought, beyond her capacity to protect. She hadn't realized it. Not even The Terafin's death had yet made that clear. But she would understand it in time. Had he been a man who found prayer useful, he might have prayed now: let it be a long, long time in the future.

He was not a man for prayer, and not, in any case, pointless prayer. He trailed behind the three House Council members, deflecting the brief glances of passing servants and House Guards.

Marrick. Elonne. Haerrad. Rymark. Each had their strengths and weaknesses; each had, over the course of a decade, built a base of power on which they might both stand and maneuver. If rumor was to be believed, Rymark had gone as far as claiming a writ of inheritance from The Terafin herself. Rymark was canny, if cruel; he was clever. He was also the blood son of Gabriel ATerafin, the man who now held the House Council together until a successor emerged. That successor, if it was not his son, would emerge from the shadows his son's corpse cast.

Jewel had gained little height in the past fifteen years; she was small, her shoulders slender. She walked like a boy in the streets of the hundred holdings. He was uncertain whether or not she had ever actually killed a man. He was certain she had *seen* death, but seeing it and causing it were in no way the same. Death was not her gift, but he could see no clear path to the future she wanted if it could not become her tool.

All this he thought dispassionately, even coldly, as the famous galleries of the Terafin manse passed by him. He had an eye for geography that was almost as sharp as his eye for human detail; he knew the statues, the arms, the paintings, and the windows, and knew as well when the next turn would lead into the west hall in which Jewel's home was situated. He knew the tabards of the House Guard well; the tabards of the Terafin Chosen were similar. He saw both on display, and wondered, briefly, what would become of the Chosen; they had not, to his knowledge, been disbanded yet, although the Lord to whom they swore their life was now gone.

Frowning, he accepted his sparse knowledge of the minutiae of the guard structure within the House. He would have to ask Jarven who the Captain of the House Guard now was. He disliked even the thought of having to all but beg Jarven for information; it pricked at his dignity.

But . . . it gave him something to think about. Walking as he was, he couldn't retreat to smooth seams and stitching; nor could he soothe thought with the numbing task of perfect beading. The only other option was Hannerle, and that was not a place he wished to revisit, he had spent so much time by her side thinking of little else.

The doors to the wing opened as Jewel approached them, and he realized that wish or no, he would now do exactly that. An old man stood in the opened doors, bowing in greeting as the three members of the den approached. "Jewel. Finch. Teller."

It was Finch who spoke. "We have a guest," she told him, turning toward Haval. "And we require a room in which he can work in relative peace."

The man nodded briskly, and waited until they had all entered, even Haval; he sent the overburdened footmen on their way while he disappeared to prepare tea and something that smelled very like hot cider with a touch too much cinnamon. Only when the footmen had left and the doors to the wing had closed at their back did he speak again.

"He is not the only guest on the premises."

"Ummm, we know," Finch replied. "We had no real way to send word."

One white brow rose. It was as much criticism as the older man seemed prepared to offer, at least in the presence of guests. "I have taken the liberty of assuming the guest's stay will be for an unspecified length of time, and I've opened a room for her use." He turned to Jewel. "Avandar is taking a brief rest; he will join you shortly."

Shortly.

Haval glanced at Jewel, who seemed both unsurprised and unfazed by the comment. Jewel's domicis had always radiated an unseemly confidence—even arrogance—for a man in his chosen profession, but Haval was honestly surprised. A short rest for the magic he'd used implied a depth of power that no domicis in Haval's experience should have. It was novel.

Jewel rose, tea in hand. So far, her hand was the only thing that had touched it, but the room was chilly, even with wood burning in the grate. "Take us to her," she told the man. Her tone was rough and cool. Finch cast her gaze at the carpets. Even when she chose not to speak, she was expressive, which was unfortunate. Haval noted that Teller was not.

The man bowed and led them past the sitting room into a hall that was girded by modest doors on either side. He paused at the third door on the right and opened it. Haval, following at the same distance as he had in the external halls, was last to enter the room. Hannerle was already in bed, her head propped up by pillows. She was not, however, alone.

One young man and one boy stood beside her, on the side of the bed farthest from the door; they were both looking up at Jewel as Haval approached.

Jewel lifted a hand, signaling with a brief sweep of three fingers; the older of the two nodded. The younger, however, seemed to take no information from the gestures. Interesting.

"Daine, why are you here?"

Daine had now transferred his gaze from Jewel to Haval. She coughed and said, "This is Haval. The woman in the bed is his wife, Hannerle. Neither of which answers the question I just asked. Why aren't you in the healerie?"

"Jester called me. He said Avandar had brought a guest."

". . . Jester told you to come. To our wing, in the middle of the day, without any visible reason."

Daine said nothing. Given the shift in her tone, this was probably wise, at least for another few minutes. It became less wise with the passage of time, however.

Haval cleared his throat loudly. "Adam and Daine are both healers." It wasn't a question.

Jewel nodded; she knew there was no point in lying, not to Haval; she had brought Hannerle here for one purpose.

"And it is Adam who can achieve your minor miracle."

She nodded again.

"Adam is not from the Empire."

"Adam is new to the Empire, yes. Before you ask, no, I didn't bring him here."

"You knew he was healer-born."

"Haval—it's long, complicated, and entirely irrelevant, but *yes*, I knew he was healer-born. He was given into Levec's keeping, and Levec doesn't let go of much. Believe that here was not where I expected to find him. He's so young—"

"He is not much younger than you were, when you first became involved with Terafin."

"He looks younger than I felt at the time."

"They always do. I cannot tell you how young you all look to me, and I know what I was doing at your age. Will he start soon?"

"Yes. Just as soon as Daine answers my question."

Daine now squared his shoulders and gained two inches of height. "I'm here," he told his den leader, "because I want to see what Adam is doing. I know he's different. I know I can't do what he does—if Levec can't do it, I'm surprised anyone can. But we have no idea how far this will spread, and I want to be familiar with what it does. And with what he does."

Jewel offered no further argument. The damage was already done, and it was Haval's guess that Daine also lived in this wing, which made travel between the wing and the healerie vastly less suspicious than it might otherwise have been. "Adam."

Adam nodded and silently took one of Hannerle's hands in his; Daine took the other. They both closed their eyes almost simultaneously. Haval had seldom seen the healer-born at work; he had certainly seen his share of doctors, but doctors didn't have the peculiar ability to draw memory and knowledge from the minds of those to whom they were ministering.

He watched. "You understand that Hannerle is not likely to evince gratitude when she wakes in a strange bed?"

"Yes. But that's not my problem."

"It may well be, if you insist on having your dress made on time."

She chuckled at that. It wasn't forced. She even walked closer to the bed, and after a moment, Haval joined her. "How angry would she be?" she asked in soft Weston.

Haval did not choose to mistake her meaning. "It would break her heart," he replied.

"And will you?"

"Break her heart?"

Jewel nodded.

Haval didn't answer. He watched the rise and fall of his wife's chest; watched the play of magelight over her pale hair. Her skin was sallow and her wrinkles more pronounced, she'd lost so much weight. She wasn't fond of strange rooms, but she would wake in this one, if she woke at all.

Haval knew Jewel well. He knew that her inexplicable absence from her den, her House, and the Empire, had made changes in her; he was not certain how deep those changes were, or how dangerous. As always, he was curious; curiosity was the one weakness, the one appetite, that he struggled to deny. He could control it, but he could never entirely banish it; it troubled him, moved him, angered him; it brought him to life. It defined half of who he was. But Hannerle defined the other half, and he had managed, over decades, to hold those two halves in such perfect balance they looked whole.

That balance had faltered.

He wasn't certain when, but knew why: Hannerle did not wake. She had—hopefully through no choice of her own—withdrawn from his daily life; she had left him in the silence of his own thoughts and the routines of his unmoored habits. He had cleaned, in her absence. He had cleaned like a compulsive, returned to her side to dribble water into her mouth before he once again moved away. She was the center of his orbit, but the orbit grew.

Wake, Hannerle, he thought, watching her still face. *Wake.*

They had built their life together. They had built the store and its varied clientele with care; they had built their connections to the merchants who traveled from the South and the West. They had started in a modest, rented space and had graduated into their own building. Children had not come, and that had been the one blight in Hannerle's existence; it had not overly troubled Haval. He understood all the ways in which children were a burden; they colored the world, and they made it vastly more dangerous simply by breathing. They were a weakness that he did not want, but he would have accepted that weakness for the sake of his wife.

She had been so young when he had first seen her; so young, so blunt, so assertive—and yet, so strikingly naive. It was a peculiar naïveté, however. He could—and frequently did—lie to her, but the lies she accepted as truth were often small. She didn't demand truth; she simply demanded silence, once with the open palm of her hand. He could coax her; he could charm her; with care, he could manipulate her.

She had, therefore, never known the full scope of his activities. But she had nonetheless understood what they encompassed. She did not ask him who he served, or how; she asked him, instead, to stop. To choose.

He so chose. But her absence, and the certainty that the absence would never abate, had unraveled at least one lie—one observational infelicity that galled, because it was not an *intentional* lie; it was one that he had told himself, and even believed. It was their life, but he had built it, in its entirety, from his desire for, and comfort in, *her*. She had played no games, when she offered him the choice. What had she said?

Ah.

It's not that I don't trust you, Haval. I do. And I even know it's foolish, you lie almost as often as you draw breath. But your lies aren't cruel, they're not petty; they're even meant to comfort. It's why I've always accepted them from you, when I'd've gutted any other man or woman who tried.

But love, for me—it's practical. It's a practical thing. It's not just passion or romance. Her hair had been dark, and her eyes dark as well; the whole of her expression seemed hollowed by shadows. He'd lifted his hands to touch her face and she'd flinched.

I know there are no certainties. You could fall to disease. You could be carried from me in an accident. I accept those. When I promise you forever, it's a promise of intent; I can't control the moment of my own death. But I'd live with those fears. Do you understand? I'd live with them.

The fears that I have now—I can't live with. Accident, yes. Disease, yes. But not poison, not dagger, not sword, not unexplained disappearance. I can't build a future with that much fear. I trust you; I don't trust your enemies, whoever they might be.

Hannerle . . .

And I understand that it's part of who you are, and if I had any intelligence, I'd've never fallen for a man like you at all. But you lied, when I wanted to believe you, and I chose to believe. I can't choose that, anymore. I'm selfish, I'm greedy, and it's not enough. If you can make a life with me now, make one. But make it a life that has no more fear in it than it must. *I'll leave my family. I'll work, and work hard. I'm not an empty-headed girl; I know how to work.*

But I want to face a future with you, not alone. If that's not what you want—if that's not what you need—I'll cry, and I'll keep walking.

Hannerle. Haval bowed his head. He had chosen the life she'd offered. He loved that life. But that life, without her, was *not* his. He accepted it, standing in the Terafin manse, surrounded by Jewel's den. Had he not met Hannerle, had he not inexplicably fallen in love with her, he would no doubt have been dead these past fifteen years, and not peacefully.

Hannerle could not live with fear.

Haval could. Until Hannerle, all of life had been a game of fear and chance, but it had satisfied his curiosity and his intellect.

She stirred. He was uncertain how much time had passed. Her eyelids began to flicker, as they sometimes did when she slept or dreamed. Her mouth moved, her lips moved. He understood, then, that she would wake.

He glanced at Jewel and found, to his surprise, that she was watching him, not his wife.

Hannerle's eyes flickered open. Her lips changed shape, falling into the frown that habitually started mornings in which she'd slept unexpectedly late. She lifted her arms, or would have; they were both attached to hands that were held by two different men. Adam and Daine opened their eyes as she tugged her hands free and pushed herself up on the bed. It didn't last long.

"Haval?" she croaked, as her gaze fell upon the one person she expected to see when she woke. "Where am I?"

He cleared his throat. "You are in a room in the Terafin manse, Hannerle. Can you not see young Jewel? She's returned from the South."

Hannerle looked at Jewel, which did nothing to ease her confusion. "I can see her, but why am *I* here?"

The two healers stepped away from the bed; everyone did but Haval. He approached it, smiling at and for his wife. Knowing, as he took her shaking hands that he could calm her, that he could explain—because she was practical. But he knew, as well, that this was a respite. She would sleep again; it couldn't be prevented. This was not a cure.

Hannerle could not live with fear, but Haval had now accepted that he could not live with empty hope. Oh, he could endure it. But it wasn't *enough*.

"ATerafin," he said, although there were three in the room.

Jewel knew who he meant.

"I accept your offer."

Chapter Three

1st of Henden, 427 A. A.
Terafin manse, Averalaan Aramarelas

TELLER ENTERED THE OFFICE of the right-kin half an hour before anyone but the House Guard or the men and women employed by Gabriel would. There were Chosen at the doors of Gabriel's personal office, and Chosen at the doors to the outer office. Before The Terafin's death, the numbers had increased from two to four; those numbers did not decrease in the aftermath.

Barston, of course, helmed his great desk, as he had always done. Teller wondered if he would leave the office when Gabriel did, or if he would agree to serve whoever succeeded Gabriel. The Terafin chose his or her right-kin. Teller was no longer the new and nervous assistant, but in spite of his years in this office or its adjuncts, he always deferred to Barston in any circumstance that allowed it. Barston was still a stiff, formal man with a severe and unamused expression permanently fixed to his face. It had taken Teller a few years to understand the dryness of Barston's humor; it had taken him more to learn the boundaries of what appeared his boundless support and devotion to the etiquette and rules that governed the patriciate in general, and Terafin in particular.

He therefore bowed to Barston as he entered. Barston, of course, knew who it was. He looked up from his ledger of appointments. In the pale light that was not quite dawn and not quite night, he looked exhausted. "ATerafin," he said briskly.

"Barston," Teller replied. Barston could seldom be moved to use Teller's actual name. He had done so on some occasions in the past, but there was a comfort that had gone out of the House with The Terafin's death, and it wouldn't return until a new Lord took both sword and seat, if then.

"There have been several requests for appointments, ATerafin."

Teller frowned. He now had an office—a small one—of his own within Gabriel's domain; it had two doors, with some detailed carving at the height, and a window which was habitually open to let light enter. The glass could even be raised, to let breeze through. It was not raised at this time of year. His office was not so fine as Gabriel's, and it was not nearly as important, but Teller had, over the past five years, been ceded some small part of Gabriel's duties. He met with outsiders and visitors, often visitors of note, and he conveyed the gist of his many conversations to Gabriel. On occasion, when Gabriel deemed it necessary, Teller had reported to The Terafin directly.

"Am I a fool to hope that those requests come from people outside of the House?"

Barston raised one iron brow.

"I'm sorry. If I weren't on the House Council, Barston, I wouldn't have absented myself from the office yesterday. But neither Finch nor I have any clothing appropriate for a funeral of this import."

"You have failed to ask who made those requests," was Barston's response.

Because the office contained only Barston and Teller, Teller said, "How long can I continue to fail?"

"In safety?" Barston replied, surrendering. "Until the day after the funeral services. You will not, however, want to avoid all of the requests." He lifted a few papers—they looked, on brief inspection, like letters—and handed them to Teller. "Gabriel wishes to speak with you as well."

"He's here?"

"No." This was said in a distinctly chilly way. "But he should be here very soon."

Teller nodded. He turned toward his office, and then turned back. "Barston, a question. If it is too bold or too naive, tell me."

"I am not the right-kin," Barston replied. "My opinion, and I judge it likely that you wish me to give one, carries very little weight or significance. Remember that."

Teller nodded as if he believed any of it. He didn't. But Barston did.

He was not, in the parlance of the young in this House, an ambitious man. The whole of his ambition was this office and its running. He was very like a domicis that way.

"Gabriel has said nothing about his hopes for the occupant of the House Seat."

"He cannot, as regent."

"Who would you favor, of the four likely contenders? Who would you advise us to offer our support to?"

Barston was silent for a long moment. Too long; Teller was certain he wasn't going to answer. He did not, however, remain silent. "Have you asked Jewel ATerafin who she intends to support?"

"Yes." Technically, this was true.

"And her answer?"

"She doesn't have a good one."

"And she has been part of the House Council for well over a decade. If she does not have a suitable answer, then you cannot expect one from me."

Teller nodded.

Barston surprised him. "Who do you intend to support?"

"I don't know. If Gabriel would declare himself, we'd throw our support behind him in a second." This was also true. It pained Teller to lie to Barston.

"Gabriel will not."

"Why?"

"I believe," Gabriel ATerafin said, "that I made my reasons clear on the floor of the Council Hall."

Teller hadn't even heard the door open. He had the grace to redden; Barston didn't even blink. "ATerafin," he said, transferring his attention to the man who commanded the office, "there are a number of issues we must deal with."

"I notice you've lost an assistant," Gabriel replied, without pausing.

"He was not a suitable candidate given the current situation within the House," was Barston's rather severe reply. "And I feel that this is a very poor time to replace him."

"I can help," Teller said, before Gabriel could answer.

They both looked at him. Barston's glare held very strong disapproval.

"The opening of mail is *not* an appropriate duty for a member of the House Council, unless that mail is entirely personal."

Gabriel grimaced. "He is correct, of course. He is *always* correct. Come,

Teller; we've a few minutes before the office is open, and I'm unlikely to find any other time in which to converse."

Teller rarely entertained Gabriel in his small office; if there was a matter of import Gabriel wished to discuss, he discussed it behind his own desk. But Teller had long since given up being nervous in the presence of the right-kin. Barston could make him more nervous. Teller had two chairs in front of his much smaller desk; he offered one to Gabriel, and Gabriel sank into it as if standing were truly painful. Teller took the other chair.

"You have appointments with other members of the House Council," Gabriel said, when Teller was seated. It wasn't a question.

Teller grimaced. "I don't."

The regent of Terafin raised one brow.

"Barston hasn't made any appointments, given the funeral."

"Those were your instructions?"

Teller's brows rose, and Gabriel offered a tired chuckle in response. "I suppose that was an unfair question. Asking Barston for advice, however, is likely to be unproductive."

Teller had the grace to redden. And the strength to say, "Can I ask you for the advice that Barston considers inappropriate to offer?"

Gabriel looked down at his hands, which Teller took as a no. He was therefore surprised when Gabriel spoke. "Has it not occurred to you—collectively and individually—that you are in just as good a position to offer that advice as to receive it?"

"I'm so new to the House Council I don't—"

Gabriel lifted a hand. It wasn't den-sign, but it might as well have been. "You've worked in this office in one capacity or another since you came to the manse. You're not the youngest member of the House to be appointed to the Council."

No. That was Jay.

"Finch has likewise been heavily involved in the economic concerns of the House since that time. She's worked under both Jarven and Lucille, and while I wouldn't wish Lucille on anyone, Lucille is sharp, canny, and observant. Finch occupied Jewel's role in merchant operations during Jewel's absence, and did so both quietly and competently. It is not as if you come to the Council with no knowledge. You both understand elements of the patriciate and elements of the political entanglements that come with either ambition or monetary concerns.

"I have told you why I will not throw support behind any of the Council members who desire the seat, but I will repeat myself now. I am old enough to have no desire to take the helm, and I am trusted—inasmuch as any member of the Council can be trusted by any other member of the Council. I served Amarais Handernesse ATerafin. When she declared herself as a contender upon the death of the previous Terafin, I declared myself as her supporter." This was not what Gabriel had said in the Council Hall.

"She is dead. And I? I am tired, Teller. If I had one hope, one wish, even a week ago, it was that I not outlive her. Thus, the hopes of men who have power.

"I want the House to continue. There is no other man or woman who could have been acclaimed regent in my stead, or I would have declined. Alliances, such as they are, are forming even as we speak. They are also breaking in the same fashion. The merchants are now jockeying for position; I believe some handful have hopes of replacing Jarven; he is older than I."

"He's not notably more weary," Teller told Gabriel quietly.

"No. I do not discount either Jarven or the influence of his support. As regent, I do not have a right-kin, but the duties I previously performed cannot be neglected. All of the time I have is now devoted to both of the roles I have undertaken. Were I to support any one of the contenders, what do you think would happen?"

Teller said nothing.

Gabriel was not content with silence. "Teller?"

"You wouldn't survive."

Gabriel nodded. "If I die, what do you think will happen?"

He hadn't thought about Gabriel's death at all. He didn't want to start now, but he saw clearly that silence was not an option. He compromised. "Your regency buys us time."

"An interesting way to word it. Yes. It buys time. If I am very lucky, I will survive to pass the House to the man—or woman—who emerges as The Terafin. How do you think that will happen?"

Teller looked down at his own hands. When he looked up, he met Gabriel's steady gaze. "I think at least two of the current obvious contenders will be dead first, and their supporters will be forced to choose among the survivors."

"And?"

Teller looked away. Then he rose and began to pace, a habit that would have deepened every unhappy line in Barston's face. "If one of the surviving contenders has an obvious advantage, the House will fall in behind them. The other survivors will remain on the House Council, possibly enriched in one way or the other simply because they've survived." He hesitated, and then said, "If everyone is reasonable."

Gabriel nodded, watching him. "Do you think that everyone will be?"

". . . no."

"How so?"

He hesitated again, and this time, he wasn't certain he *could* speak. Gabriel waited. Teller had never been so aware of the passage of time. "Gabriel—"

"I ask for a truthful opinion, Teller. No more. But certainly no less. What you say will not leave this office."

Teller closed his eyes, drew breath. "Marrick has made a lot of connections outside of the House. He's . . . friendly. He seems harmless. He listens well. He has a sense of humor. The merchants—at least the seafaring ones—like him; he can drink most of them under the table."

"Not exactly a quality one would laud in a ruler."

"No. But he can do more than that. He owns lands within the hundred holdings, and he owns one ship, that I know of, which flies under its own flag, not Terafin's. He can speak both fluent Torra and some Rendish. But he's canny. I don't think he'll flinch from violence; he's not afraid. But he knows when to cut his losses. If he stands at the end of all this, and he hasn't accumulated enough support, he'll fold more or less gracefully."

Gabriel nodded.

"If Elonne is alive, so will she. She also owns properties across the holdings; I'm not as certain how many. She owns the lease for at least two of the actual stores in the Common. She doesn't own a ship, and she doesn't have Marrick's connection with the Port Authority because of that; she does own some land outside of the city, and I think she owns one mine. She isn't Marrick, but neither was The Terafin; she's more severe and less approachable.

"She also numbers the Queen Marieyan among her personal friends, and through the Queen, she maintains some access to the ears of the Kings."

Gabriel raised a brow.

"Of the four, she also has the closest personal ties to the priests of Cormaris and the Mother. Some significant part of her personal wealth is donated to both churches every year. She is very like The Terafin in outward appearance."

"Do you think she is very like the former Terafin in other ways?"

"I don't know. She has the grace and the elegance."

"The ruthlessness?"

"She'll do what she has to do, but if she feels she doesn't have the resources necessary to take the House without destroying large parts of it in the process, I believe she'll concede victory to those who do."

Gabriel nodded.

Teller continued, ill at ease. If he'd had any idea that this conversation would happen, he'd've talked to Jay before he left the wing. "Haerrad has the closest ties with both the Kings' armies and the House Guard. He's almost the opposite of Marrick in every social respect; he's neither friendly nor comfortable. He served in the armies in his youth, and everything about his bearing is military. If he were to take the seat, he would almost certainly have the support of The Berrilya."

"Which would guarantee he'd have no support at all from The Kalakar."

Teller nodded.

"Haerrad's power within the House, because of his connections with the House Guard in general, is probably the most dangerous for any of the contenders. He's not well-loved by the merchants, but he *is* respected. In the previous two trade wars, he was the first to condone use of lethal force in defense of the caravans on the trade routes, and he made certain that any of the caravans on any routes he was responsible for were heavily guarded."

"This did not endear him to the Kings."

"No. It didn't. But Haerrad is aware that he gains nothing from their approval. The House knows that he will pause one half step short of open defiance of the Kings in defense of House Law or territory. Like Elonne and Marrick, he has a number of properties within the holdings; like Elonne, it's not clear what those properties are." Jay had some suspicions, and those suspicions enraged her; Teller thought it good that their ability to investigate hadn't revealed anything solid. "But Haerrad would have to be dead—and probably in pieces—before he'd concede anything. I don't think he'd care if he destroys large parts of the House in the process; those parts would not be loyal to him, and they therefore wouldn't be of value.

I'm pretty sure he'd feel confident that he could rebuild anything he destroyed—and he'd be happier because he could rebuild it in a way that suited him.

"If he's one of the members left standing, he'll be The Terafin."

"And you think the chances are good?"

"Someone tried to kill him the same day The Terafin died."

Gabriel nodded. "He's accused no one."

"Publicly, no."

The new regent raised a brow in genuine surprise. "What have you heard?"

"Rumors, no more. We believe they originated with Haerrad."

"The rumors?"

"That Duvari—present at the time—ordered the assassination attempt."

"It would not be entirely beyond credibility," Gabriel replied after a long pause. "Haerrad would not be a Lord to Duvari's liking."

"No."

"You don't lend credence to the rumor."

"I'm undecided," Teller replied. It was safest. "The rumors won't harm Haerrad. Any laws he's broken in the past have always been internal affairs. The House believes—especially at this time—that someone who can stand against the Kings' demands is necessary."

"You've heard, then."

Teller met Gabriel's gaze and held it. The room was dense with uncomfortable silence; it was Teller who chose to break it first. "Yes. But some Royal Intervention was expected, surely? The Terafin didn't die by normal means. Even if the House wished to claim her death a simple assassination, it's impossible. The Kings themselves were present. They arrived too late—but they saw the demon that killed her. Sigurne Mellifas came, and she declared it no simple act of magery, no illusion. We will be under the eyes of the Kings—and the Order of Knowledge—for some little while yet.

"This buys the regent time."

"And if the regent doesn't desire that time?"

"He'll serve it, anyway."

"You speak with such confidence, Teller."

"Barston would kill me if I dissembled."

Gabriel laughed. He had barely smiled at all in the past few weeks;

Teller heard the warmth and affection in the older man's voice and was surprised at how deeply it pained him.

"Barston would, indeed. If the gaining of stature within the House has not yet changed you, it is because Barston has not yet had enough time. He has always taken these things quite seriously. But where Barston would not allow you to dissemble, Teller, I can do no less. You've spoken of three contenders. Tell me, now, of the fourth."

The desire to point out the passing of time came and went as Teller met the eyes of the man who had been, in all ways, his benefactor for over fifteen years. There were very few men—or women—that Teller held in such high esteem, and he knew that laughter would not be the result of anything he chose to say about Rymark ATerafin. Rymark was Gabriel's blood son.

Teller inhaled. How much did he trust Gabriel? With his life? With Jay's? Gabriel had steadfastly refused to support any contender; he held himself above suspicion. But Rymark was his *son*.

"Teller."

"I can't tell you anything that you don't already know," Teller replied.

"Tell me what I know, then. Let me take your measure."

"Why?"

Gabriel offered no answer but silence. His silences were always textured; they were like the emotions that lay beneath words, unspoken, unvented. This one was no different.

The quietest and most scholarly of Jay's den now chose to speak two words, watching Gabriel's expression with a care that would have delighted Haval. "Rymark lied."

The silence deepened, and it chilled. Teller waited for questions or denials, but Gabriel offered neither. Teller had chosen risk; he had chosen honesty. He hadn't dressed it in formal words or speech; he hadn't veiled it. Perhaps he should have. Perhaps, in the future of this office, he would come to regret it.

He drew breath and began again. "Rymark ATerafin is one of the senior members of the House Council. He is less economically independent than the other three; he owns no lands directly, although he does control some of the lesser leaseholds in the hundred. He has some merchant interests, but again, they're minor, and much of his efforts have gone into the import and export of exotica. He has some contacts within the Merchant

Authority, and a very strong base of support within the Order of Knowledge; that support does not fully extend to the Council of the Magi. He is a Second Circle mage, and the only mage-born man to sit upon the House Council.

"He has, however, cultivated many of the merchant houses, and he has connections—strong political connections—among them which he has already begun to bring to bear. None of the other contenders have his breadth of knowledge. There isn't a language with which he's not familiar; nor are there many laws, in any country. He has support among the House Guard; it doesn't rival Haerrad's, but no one else does, either. He has friends in *Avantari*, and more than a passing acquaintance with the Princes. If his personal finances are the weakest of the four, he nonetheless has access to funding that can put him on level ground." Teller stopped. He had faint hope that that would be enough; Gabriel dashed it quickly. In truth, they had little time.

"And in the event that one of the other four seemed most likely to take the seat?"

Teller exhaled. "I'm sorry, Gabriel," he said, lowering his head a moment. "If Rymark is standing, he will never acknowledge superior force. Like Haerrad, he will fight until there are no others." He looked up. Gabriel's dark eyes, unblinking, caught his gaze and held it.

He rose. "Thank you, ATerafin."

Teller caught his arm. "I've answered your questions, Gabriel. Can you answer at least one of mine?"

"I can try. Let us hope for both our sakes it is a brief question and a brief answer; Barston is soon to be fending off requests on our behalf, and they are likely to be increasingly uncivil requests."

"You won't break your word. You won't support any of the four. You don't think that all four will be left standing. What do you think will happen, now?"

"In truth? I do not know. The presence of the Kings' agents will cripple the early fighting; it will make the struggle more subtle. This may save lives; it may not. If I were one of the four, I would consider Elonne and Marrick to be the lesser threats. Even were I Elonne or Marrick, I would be maneuvering around the other two, in the hope that they both perish. A long succession struggle will harm the House; there is no question. Perhaps the Kings are aware of it, and they seek to hamper Terafin, long the first among equals." He inclined his head. "We have work to do."

He made it to the door, touched the handle, and stopped, his back toward his younger colleague. "Yes," he said, voice soft enough it wouldn't have carried over any other sound. "He lied. And there is only one way you could say that with certainty."

"Haerrad accused him of lying."

"Haerrad would accuse The Terafin herself of lying, had she appointed an heir before her death," was the grim reply. "Elonne and Marrick have been more circumspect in their response."

"They weren't bleeding."

"As you say." He still didn't turn from the door. "You are not Haerrad, Teller. You will never be Haerrad. Or Elonne, or Marrick, for that matter. When you speak of Rymark ATerafin's lie with such conviction, the source of that conviction is not ambition. You have spoken briefly—but well—about the situation that I, as regent, now face. But you have failed, perhaps, to mention the possibility of a fifth contender."

Teller froze.

Gabriel didn't see it. He didn't wait for a response; instead, he opened the door and left Teller alone in his small office. Teller made his way to the chair he normally occupied, and he sat, elbows against the desk's surface, hands against his face. What he hadn't said—what he hadn't the courage to say—was what he himself had seen when the demon had appeared in its deadly, terrifying glory: Rymark's expression. Rymark, of the four, had shown no surprise and no horror.

He wondered if Gabriel had seen his son's expression. Wondered, but was afraid to ask. He had no desire to hurt Gabriel. But the question *needed* to be asked. The person who posed the question needed to be able to survive asking it. Because if Rymark's expression meant exactly what it appeared to mean, this wasn't just another succession war. It was larger, darker; its outcome threatened to shadow an Empire, not just its most powerful House.

1st of Henden, 427 A.A.
Merchant Authority, Averalaan

Finch had discovered, with the passage of time, that death didn't stop the wheels of commerce. It might stop some of the cogs in those wheels, but that was a matter of misfortune for the cogs.

"That is not entirely true," Jarven told her, sitting back in his chair and surveying the steam of his most excellent tea as it swirled in the air above the cup. "If the Kings die, commerce stops almost entirely. It is one of the reasons The Ten—and the Merchants' Guild—pray for Royal Safety."

"I'm seldom privy to the prayers of the powerful," was Finch's pert reply.

Jarven raised a brow. He almost raised two.

"I'm sorry. It's—it's been a long week, and it's not going to get any easier for a while."

"Ah. No, Finch, it is not." He lifted the cup. His hands in this light looked delicate and aged. "How are the new additions to the office coming along?"

"I think you should ask Lucille."

"Lucille is *quite* busy, Finch."

And I'm not? Finch had graduated from her position as undersecretary to the busy and vociferous Lucille ATerafin; she now worked in her own small office, overseeing the more standard trade deals—most notably the renewal of grants. Anything difficult or flashy was passed, as a matter of course, to Jarven's office. Finch—and Lucille, of course—still *saw* most of the particulars of those contracts and proposals; Jarven insisted. She lifted her own cup of tea. Over the years, she'd become used to Jarven and his tea. It wasn't exactly ceremonial, but it contained the elements of familiar ritual, and he insisted on it.

Lucille insisted on showing Jarven the respect that she felt was his due, which was probably the real reason it was tolerated in an otherwise frenetically busy environment.

"They seem friendly enough," was her cautious reply.

"Do they indeed? How friendly?"

Finch smiled. "Not too friendly, but not too ingratiating."

"Ah." The old man sounded disappointed. "Do you recognize them?"

She did. They were all ATerafin, and most of them were her age; Paule was perhaps two years younger, although it was hard to tell.

"And can you tell me, young Finch, to whom each owes their current situation?"

"No. Lucille has to accept a new employee, and they're all here."

"Lucille has final refusal," Jarven said, in the tone of voice that implied correction. "She can exercise this refusal as often as she considers wise. While The Terafin lived, wisdom was not at issue; The Terafin didn't question her decisions."

No one with half a thought would, in Finch's opinion. She'd seen grown men reduced to tears of rage by Lucille. Several times. But she understood what Jarven was implying. "If any of the four were people she was likely to refuse, she's shown no sign."

"Ah. And Lucille is not capable of subtlety?"

"It's not exactly her middle name."

Jarven chuckled and sipped tea. Loudly. "Has Lucille come to any decisions about the rulership of the House?"

Finch almost dropped her tea, which would have been nothing short of disaster, as she liked her skin where it was. "P-pardon?"

Jarven raised a brow. "Finch, please. Gaping like that is beneath you. I merely asked a question that anyone of note in the House is now asking themselves."

"Themselves, Jarven. Not me."

"Not you? I'm surprised."

Finch carefully set the tea back down on the tray. "No one has asked me directly," she finally said.

"Which has the benefit of being the truth; I must admit that I'm in awe of your ability to dance out of reach of that question. You will not, however, be able to continue such a dance. You are a member of the House Council." He didn't bother to set his tea down; he drank it. "Have you opened any discussions with Lucille?" His gaze was sharp and clear. She both loved and hated it.

"We haven't even had the funeral yet," was her steady and quiet reply.

"Very well. How is young Jewel?" Jarven asked, eyeing the tea biscuits that Lucille had also laid out. The presence of biscuits or other edible food signaled the high probability of both long tea and tricky discussion; Finch had literally flinched when Lucille had peremptorily handed her the tray.

"She's now returned to the helm of the mountain mineral concessions," Finch replied. This was neutral enough; it was information that anyone with half an ear in the office would have.

"And that is all? I have heard the most astonishing rumors about her return."

Finch was tired of games. Jarven would tire of them only after he tired of breathing. "She's exhausted, Jarven."

He nodded. "The rumors?"

"Which ones? I admit that some of the servants' rumors have our hair standing on end; Carver's putting them out, one at a time, but it's taking real work."

"She rode a stag into the House Council Hall?"

"Oh."

"That was not rumor."

"No, sadly. That was true."

"She numbers, among her personal guard—and not her House Guard, which has at least doubled—someone who might not be human."

"That one's true as well."

"The Chosen have offered her their support."

"That's false."

"Ah. A pity."

"Not for Jay."

"Have the Chosen simply failed to petition her directly?"

Damn it. "She's not accepting visitors at the moment, no. She loved The Terafin, Jarven. Whatever else you hear, that much is true. She took the death very hard; she didn't even arrive in time to see her alive."

"Of her den, she is the most senior of the House Council. Rumor has it," he added, and Finch had *never* loathed rumor so viscerally, "that that is not the only reason she is of extreme value to the House, and to whomever rules it. You should try the almond biscuits, Finch. They're very good. What does Jewel intend?"

"Jarven—"

"You know that any discussion held in *this* office cannot be heard. There is no magestone; it is not required. All of the offers and negotiations are considered delicate enough the protections are built into the walls."

"Yes, but you'll know."

He chuckled. "Indeed."

Finch had had enough. "Who," she said, picking up her cup again, as if it were a shield and not a hazard, "will you support?"

He smiled. It was an unusual smile; it was almost predatory. She had seen Jarven for over a decade. She had been sent to his office with tea on a daily basis: rain, shine, or crisis notwithstanding. On receiving each of her three promotions, it had been made clear by Lucille that this giving of tea was still one of her primary duties, regardless of the increase in her workload.

During all of those days, months, and years, Jarven had rarely shown her the smile he offered now.

"I will," he said quietly, "offer support to none of the current contenders. I have made my impartiality in that regard quite clear. It is why there are now four new employees under my watchful eye."

"It's a small wonder Lucille hasn't strangled you. Or," she added balefully, glancing at the teapot, "poisoned you, at any rate."

He chuckled again. "It's a large wonder, in my opinion. They will watch the office now. They'll listen. They're probably cursing," he added, with a genial smile that was almost smug, "at the length of our little discussion."

"Which won't do me any favors."

"Not entirely, no. Not at the moment. You understand that most of the House is not yet divided? The Terafin's death was unexpected; the manner of her death was horrifying. Members of the House Council have not yet made their decision; members of the merchant fleet, while pressured, are doing their own investigations."

"Is that a delicate way of saying entertaining offers?"

"Finch, you wound me. Of course it is. At the moment, the four new employees are passing on those offers as quickly as their little mouths can move. They are also, as they can, expediting the paperwork of the merchants whose association would be deemed the most advantageous. Are you doing anything similar?" After a moment of silence, he shook his head. "That will not do, Finch. You've been with me for almost two decades—"

"Fifteen years."

"Sixteen, which is closer to twenty than ten. Don't be a pedant. As I was saying, you've been with me for almost two decades. You have a much better understanding of the minutiae of this office; you certainly understand which of the various merchants and merchant houses will prove most valuable. Not all of the assumptions are gained by a mere week's work; not even careful perusal of the filed paperwork can grant that kind of knowledge in so short a span of time.

"The four new employees will also be watching each other with more care. They've spoken with Lucille, inasmuch as they deem it wise; they've no doubt approached you as well."

"They haven't."

"Ah. That shows more wisdom than haste generally allows. Tell me, Finch, why do you think they have been more or less silent around you?"

"Lucille would kill them?"

He laughed. "Well, there is that. It's not the acceptable answer, and I'll trouble you to give me one before you leave."

Finch sighed. "I'm a member of the House Council. Even if I'm newly appointed. No one can withdraw that from me—and I don't think Gabriel would try—without diminishing the value of the Council within the House. Any offers made to me will be made by the leaders of their factions."

"And those?"

"The other House Council members."

"Good. I will let you leave now; I believe I have some dreary appointments of my own. The office will, of course, be closed for the three days of the funeral."

As she rose and placed everything on the tray, he said, "I hear you've employed Haval as your dressmaker?"

Her arms stiffened. "We have. Jay always employs Haval, when she's given any choice in the matter."

"Always?"

"Always."

1st of Henden, 427 A.A.
Terafin Manse, Averalaan Aramarelas

Haval's return to the Terafin manse was through the trade entrance, as befit his station. The trade entrance, in the manse, was quite congested; the House Guards were out in force, and the presence of clothing in various states of repair did nothing to stem their obvious suspicion of any outsider. He would have accepted this without irritation had their questions and observations not been so *rote*. He could have cheerfully and carefully carried poison in every pocket of his smock and they wouldn't have blinked.

But he understood why they were being so officious a few meters past the door itself; there, he saw the tabards of the Kings' Swords in prominent display. The gray complemented the varying blues of the Terafin colors, but its presence clashed with them in other ways. Neither set of guards were comfortable.

His understanding deepened when he saw the severe and unadorned robes of the Order of Knowledge in the open halls nearest the manse's great kitchen. He didn't recognize the members of the Order; most of them were younger than Haval. Nor was he ultimately troubled; the worst of the magi, excepting only the exceptional and formidable Sigurne Mellifas, were in the Dominion of Annagar, waging war alongside the Kings' armies. Now was not the time that the Empire wished to see any demonic activity, if there was ever such a time.

But such wishes counted for little in the face of reality. Demonic activity had been detected, and the most powerful House in the Empire was now without a leader at that very moment.

Haval no longer, to his lasting regret, required great effort to feign the effects of age; he required rather more to hide them. Today, it was not required. He fretted only because time, until the funeral itself, was so short, and he had been forced to give up even the hope of a good night's sleep. It deepened the circles beneath his eyes.

It took almost an hour to run the full gauntlet of guard, guard, and mage. Given the funeral services—and it was a full funeral of no less than three days—Haval was not the only clothier to grace the endless line. Nor was he, by any stretch, the only merchant; he was one of the more forbearing. The Terafin galleries, however, were almost empty in comparison, and he traversed these quickly, with the aid of a servant whose sole occupation seemed to consist of escorting visitors. Against his better judgment, he allowed the servant to help him carry his wares.

But he noticed, as he walked, that there were flowers strewn across the gallery floors, nestled mostly in the corner made of walls and floor. Among the flowers there were letters and other small mementos—paintings, drawings, unlit candles. Some—not all—of the hanging paintings had been covered in black and white; some of the draping cloth was edged in gold. The House mourned, in its fashion.

"She was greatly loved," Haval said to his guide.

The man nodded gravely; it was a gravity at odds with his age. He didn't speak, which left Haval no opening to continue, and perhaps that was best. The doors to the West Wing—guarded by four men in House colors—came into view.

"If you require assistance when you're ready to leave, please let the guard know; someone will return for you."

Haval thanked the servant. He also turned and answered the same set of questions posed by the very first guards he'd laid eyes on. The questions were, however, perfunctory; he was expected.

Haval entered the sitting room. Ellerson was waiting for him. Haval didn't pretend to understand why there were two domicis in such a small space; he understood that Jewel was not entirely comfortable with the older one, and understood, as well, that the discomfort was personal. He would have asked this domicis to lead him to the rooms in which the fittings would take place, but was interrupted in this perfectly reasonable request by the sound of raised voices.

He recognized one of them quite well.

Both men turned in the direction of the shouting, and when they turned back, they exchanged a brief and almost rueful half smile.

"I must extend my apologies," Ellerson said, offering a perfect bow. "Jewel ATerafin was expecting you, but I believe her . . . meeting . . . has gone on longer than she intended."

Haval nodded. "From the sounds of it, it will be some time; might I trouble you for tea?"

"Of course. I will inform her that you have arrived."

Haval took a seat. The chairs were large and comfortable, and a fire was burning in the expansive fireplace not far from the chairs. There was a small, dark table to one side of the chair, and it was to this table that Ellerson brought the requested tea. The shouting, in this room, was muted.

"Jewel wishes me to inform you that she will join you as soon as she is able," the domicis said.

"Are they all in this meeting?"

The domicis hesitated; it was a brief silence, one a less observant man might have missed. "They are. Finch and Teller are with Jewel now, and their fittings must be seen to first, as they are expected in their respective offices with minimal delay. I have therefore taken the liberty of placing your clothing and your tools in one of the guest rooms."

"Thank you. I took much longer to gain entrance than I anticipated, and I am unexpectedly weary. I did not think to be questioned by the Kings' own Swords; I certainly did not expect to be inspected by the magi."

Ellerson's head bobbed in something too formal to be a nod. "You will encounter both again on any visit in the near future."

"I see." Haval knew better than to ask the domicis why. He also knew that the domicis could answer. It was always slightly frustrating to have so much information so close at hand without being able to touch it. But slight frustrations had never deterred Haval. Information that was easily available was almost without value.

Teller joined Haval within the half hour. Haval had always approved of Teller; today was no exception. He was calm, even diffident; his confidence was quiet, not loud. He could stand in a room without attracting attention, but if he required attention, he could carefully grab it. But his expression was never neutral; it was never forced.

"I'm sorry," the younger man said, as if to reinforce this point. "Jay'll be with you soon, but I'm in a bit of hurry." He waited for Haval to rise and then led him—quickly—to his rooms. There he shed the outer clothing he'd been wearing, and donned what Haval had brought with him instead. Haval took his measurements, frowning and pinning as he worked. Teller, like Jewel, didn't care for pins or needles; unlike Jewel, he didn't flinch or hold his breath when they were being added.

"How is Hannerle?"

Haval glanced up from his work. He reminded himself that he liked Teller and that it was an entirely reasonable question, and therefore refrained from accidentally jabbing him with the wrong end of a pin. "She is," he said, pins held in his mouth somewhat blunting the edge of his voice, if not the words, "in a very, *very* unfortunate mood."

"That's bad?"

"It was bad enough that I considered it unwise to bring her with me— and I could have used her help." Given the levels of unexpected interrogation, it had been more than wise to leave her at the store, proof that Kalliaris did smile, on occasion. He finished his pinning. "You are not to gain much weight in the next day, is that understood?"

"Given work and sleep, I should ask how much I'm allowed to lose instead."

Haval managed to dredge some sympathy out of somewhere; he didn't inspect the source too carefully. "Believe that I have seldom dreaded the respectability of a funeral so intensely."

Teller slid—carefully—out of the jacket, and Haval equally carefully laid it flat between two thinning sheets, which were currently draped across the bed; Teller's rooms were very sparsely furnished, and the table—the single table—was already in use.

"Will Finch and Jewel be much longer?"

"Gods know. There's something going on in the Authority," Teller added. Haval noticed only the slightest of pauses between the first phrase and the minimal information of the second one. If hearing could be sharpened, Haval would have been holding a whetstone.

"Does that something happen to involve Jarven ATerafin?"

"Sooner or later, it has to."

"Oh?"

"Anything interesting in the Merchant Authority almost always seems to involve Jarven; if it doesn't, he sulks. According to Finch," Teller added with wry haste. "Lucille only gets involved in important, practical matters and again, according to Finch, she doesn't *start* trouble."

"And Finch now feels that Jarven is starting trouble?"

"Not in so many words, no, but she's feeling less than fully confident." The door opened. Teller's mouth closed.

"Ah, Finch. Just the person I wanted." Haval, pins more or less in hand, gestured her toward the small footstep on which Teller had been standing. "I'm informed speed is of the essence," he added.

Teller, in the background, was already changing into the attire he wore when in the office.

"Yes," she said. "I'm sorry. We had a message from Haerrad. It couldn't be easily refused as it was personally delivered, although Ellerson *did* try. How's Hannerle?"

"She is in fine fettle."

"That's bad?"

He chuckled; it was genuine. "Indeed. A less intelligent man might think she was trying to make him regret the lack of sleep and silence." At the small round "O" of shock she made, he relented. "She is confused and she is frightened. Finch, please—stand *still*. And straighten your shoulders. Thank you."

Jewel made her entrance as Finch attempted to follow his instructions. Haval took a brief break to do something about Finch's hair, which had not yet been bound in any way and now threatened the careful placement of his pins. It was long and fine, although its color was almost entirely nondescript.

"Good morning, Jewel. Before you ask, Hannerle is still awake."

Jewel grinned; it was a very tired expression. But where Finch and Teller were willing to listen more or less politely, Jewel was not. "Has she said anything?"

"Rather a lot."

This earned a chuckle. "Anything repeatable?"

"In this wing, yes; outside of it, no. Since I feel that a certain type of language devalues truly cutting wit, I will not repeat most of it."

"We probably said worse in the kitchen."

"No doubt. I did hear some of it—from the sitting room."

The den leader winced. "Sorry. We had a couple of minor emergencies, and talking people out of dealing with them in the wrong way took time. Speaking of which," she added, "I'd like to introduce you to someone."

The door opened again.

A familiar young man—Angel, not ATerafin—stood to one side of an entirely unfamiliar stranger. The second man was the one who arrested Haval's attention, and he did it so thoroughly the dressmaker forgot, for a moment, that he was pinning sleeves.

"This is Celleriant. Celleriant, this is Haval."

It was hard to say which of the stranger's features was the most arresting, but Haval settled on his eyes; they were a gray that was both cold and luminescent. It was either his eyes or his hair; his hair was a platinum spill that extended in a straight fall down his back, as if it were a cape. His features were striking: high cheekbones, tapered chin, pale, perfect skin, long neck. He was tall, slender, and his clothing—which Haval always noticed—was simple at first glance. But Haval spared more than a single glance for the cloth that draped from neck to mid-thigh because he wasn't entirely certain what the cloth was. It wasn't silk; it hadn't the sheen or the nubbled textures one would expect of silk. Nor was it anything as common as linen or wool.

It moved as he did, clearing the frame of the open door. Angel followed. Angel looked about as exhausted as his three den-mates, and in the light of the stranger's eyes, he seemed shadowy, insignificant.

"Would I be remiss in assuming that the source of this morning's possible difficulty was Celleriant?"

Celleriant's eyes narrowed. In the narrowing, he reminded Haval of someone, although no ready face or name immediately presented itself. This annoyed Haval greatly.

Jewel, however, heaved something too heavy to be a sigh. "No. For some reason, Celleriant thought that separating Haerrad's head from his shoulders was the acceptable response to an unwanted message. You won't notice the bruises Angel is sporting, but if you see Carver or Jester, they ran into Celleriant's shoulders or elbows."

Haval raised a brow. "Please tell me that he did not pull a sword."

"I would, but you always lecture me about lying."

"I lecture you about the very, very poor quality of the lies you attempt to tell. There is a difference; I have nothing against a competent lie."

Celleriant, silent until this point, glanced at Jewel. It was, however, to Haval that he chose to speak, and his voice was, like his face or his clothing, glorious and cold. "Haerrad, as he styles himself, is a danger. A threat."

Haval nodded. "My apologies, ATerafin. If you will just lift your arms—delicately, delicately!—I will be done. Unless the shoes you are wearing for the funeral services differ greatly in height?"

Finch shook her head.

"Good. This will not be my most outstandingly intricate work; I apologize. Hannerle has chosen to help, and the beading and lace will be done at the store; I will return either in the morning or in the late evening with something close to the finished work. Please, step down." As Finch left the stool, Haval motioned Jewel forward.

Jewel glanced at Celleriant and Angel.

"Haerrad is a danger, yes."

"And you feel that his death is unwarranted?" Celleriant asked.

Jewel's glance drilled into the side of Haval's face; Haval was busy once again laying out pins and rethreading needles; he had no need to look to know what she was thinking, her thoughts were so lamentably loud.

"I feel his death is necessary," Haval replied.

Angel coughed. Loudly. No one else made any sound.

"But his death is not the only necessary death. Lord Celleriant, why are you here?"

Celleriant looked to Jewel. Interesting. Jewel nodded, and then shoved random curls out of her eyes.

"I serve Jewel ATerafin," Celleriant replied, the words cool and proud.

"And that is your only concern?"

"What other concern would I have in such a diminished place?"

"I frankly haven't the slightest clue. But for the moment, let me take you at your word."

"You speak as if such courtesy is rare."

"It is, as you surmise, rare."

A Winter smile crossed the features of Celleriant, and Haval felt old. But he also, conversely, felt young—young enough to believe in Dragons and Gryphons and all manner of beautiful, fanciful death. "You are counted wise, among your kin?"

"Ah, no. I prefer not to be counted at all. Jewel, please. I realize you are not under the time constraints of either of your two companions, but *I* am. I am honestly thinking of adding a factor to the price I am generously charging for my work and my lack of sleep." Jewel removed her outerwear hesitantly. "Where is your domicis?"

"Not here."

Ah. "Very well. Yes, Celleriant, Haerrad is an issue. But the political situation in the House at the moment is somewhat delicate. If you have served Jewel ATerafin for *any* significant length of time, you will understand some of her shortcomings and some of her reservations. If you do not, or you will not acknowledge them, I will make them bluntly clear: She is squeamish. She does not like to kill."

"She is not capable of killing Haerrad," was the cool reply. "Nor was it my suggestion that she do so."

Jewel, standing exposed on the stool in a way that neither Finch nor Teller had been, now ground her teeth in annoyance. "If you serve me, and you kill him, it's the same damn thing; it doesn't matter whether or not it's *my* hand that wields the sword. What's so hard to understand about that?"

"You agree that he needs to die."

". . . yes."

"I could have easily killed him."

"He had House Guards with him."

"He had four. They were not significant."

"They don't deserve to die because I'm playing hide and seek with their boss!"

Teller cringed and took this opportunity to escape. Finch, after thanking Haval, did likewise; judging from their harried expressions this was more or less a rising replay of the argument that Haval had heard in the distance when he had first arrived. Angel, however, moved to the wall nearest the door and leaned against it, watching Celleriant moodily.

"If you believe that he will die alone, you are gravely mistaken."

"What she believes," Haval interjected as he helped Jewel into the skeletal outline of what would be the finest of the three pieces, "is that someone *else* will kill him. I do not think, at this point, she particularly cares who—although she should. He is not significant enough that the desire to kill him should drive all thoughts of caution to the winds."

Celleriant's very fine features did not shift at all, but his voice grew sharper. Clearly a repeat of the morning's argument did not deter him the way it did the less militant Finch or Teller. "You have already stated—clearly—as did your aides, that you do not believe you will achieve your goals with no deaths. While I do not understand the subtleties of mortal politics as well as you claim to, it is clear to me—and I believe clear to Teller at least—that the four who have openly claimed to seek the throne—"

"We don't call it a throne."

He waved a hand at the inconsequential correction, and Haval winced. It was, of course, a deliberate wince, meant entirely for Jewel's sake. "That the four who have claimed the *seat*, if you prefer, are also aware of this. They will not achieve their goals without killing."

"Killing and death are not the same."

"In this case?" Celleriant surprised Haval. He turned to the dressmaker. "What are the four now discussing?"

Haval frowned. He could dissemble, and considered it. "I am not a Lord," he finally said. "Nor am I considered a man of power; I have been a dressmaker for decades now, and I am content. It is not of me that you must ask that question; how would I know enough to answer it?"

Celleriant's frown was thin and edged, and his eyes narrow. "I fail to understand why your first statement would make you incapable of a cogent answer to the question."

"Pardon?"

"In the Court of my birth, only a very, very few are given the privilege of clothing the Queen; a *very* few. Most survive it; some do not. The fact that they are capable of emphasizing her glory does not turn them in one act into witless fools; it heightens the esteem in which they are held."

Haval was genuinely surprised. He was also, which was worse, suddenly curious. But he did not leap like a naive fool into that curiosity; he marked it instead. "You will find, in these lands, that dressmakers are not held to such high standards. The question of a dressmaker's survival is never an issue, for one."

"It is given to few," Celleriant replied, "to create beauty, or to enhance it."

"And it is instead given, in your distant lands, to the many to create death?"

"We do not create death; we merely cause it," was the cool reply.

Ah, he had stopped his pinning. He began immediately, given Jewel's known impatience for standing partially clothed in any company. She had, lamentably, already begun her ritual of pushing hair out of her eyes, and the partial sleeves were swinging, unpinned, in a most haphazard fashion.

"It is my belief that your aesthetics and ours are completely different," he told the stranger.

"Perhaps. Living in this place feels akin to burrowing with the rabbits in their small, dirt hovels."

Angel stiffened.

Jewel snorted. "Enough, Celleriant."

"But even here, I am not unobservant. You are called Haval?"

"I am."

"And you profess to no skill but the making of clothing?"

"I do."

"Then it must be common for dressmakers in this mortal Empire to also kill."

Chapter Four

HAVAL DIDN'T CEASE HIS PINNING. His expression did change; his eyes widened slightly and his brows packed more tightly together; it was brief. Jewel, however, understood that Haval was capable of perfect control of expression; he was capable of guarding his words, voice, and posture. Nothing that he wanted to hide escaped him, and what did escape was what he chose to reveal.

But the most revealing thing to Jewel was the fact that he did not stop. So she held out her arms, but she watched his face, trying to understand why he'd chosen to enact surprise while she could see it. Waiting, her breath short, for his denial.

Wanting it.

He met her gaze; he held it. And then, to her surprise, he offered her a slight and chagrined smile. "My dear Jewel," he said, gently folding her arms to test the pull across the back of her shoulders, "Did your Oma never tell you to be careful of the company you keep?"

"No one's likely to judge me by Celleriant; if he's in the room, no one's likely to see *me*."

He chuckled. He gave her that much. But he didn't give her more.

"Haval, how's Hannerle?"

He adjusted the pins in the shoulders of the dress with care. "She is, as you now surmise, concerned."

"I didn't—"

"No. She understands you, Jewel. I would say, in different circumstances, she might even be brought to approve. But that would take time, and we have little time."

"Haval—"

"You are now uncertain, ATerafin? Your man has made a single statement, and it has so unsettled you?"

Jewel, never good at hiding anything, bowed her head. But she lifted it again, and this time, she looked at Celleriant. She was angry, but she'd been angry since Haerrad's name had been carried into the kitchen by a diffident and cautious Ellerson. She was afraid. That fear had also come with Haerrad's name, because whenever his name was mentioned, she remembered Teller's injury. She remembered, as well, that the injury was a warning that implied—strongly—that it could have been so much worse.

Leave it alone, she told herself. *Leave it the hell alone.* But her mouth opened anyway. "Celleriant, why did you say that?"

He frowned. "I observed, Lady. Only that."

"He's an old man, and he *makes dresses.*"

"Yes."

"He doesn't—"

"Jewel," Haval said, catching her wrist almost gently. "What do you hope to gain? You already know what Lord Celleriant will say."

"We don't call him Lord here."

"Ah. But he is that."

"Not here."

Haval bent. "These are the shoes you will wear?"

She nodded.

"Good." He began to adjust the unpinned hem. "Answer my question while I work. What do you hope to gain?"

"I—I want him to understand that we're different. From him. From what he's known."

"And what have I told you about your lies?"

"They're bad."

"They are appalling. They are beyond simply bad, Jewel. Do you think that Celleriant has never killed?"

She shrugged. Her silence was stubborn, and it wouldn't last, not against Haval. "I know he's killed. He's probably done worse."

"Do you think he will never kill again?"

"... no."

"Yet you accept his presence."

"I have no choice in that."

"You have every choice in it. I believe your domicis—yours, not the older gentleman—is capable of removing Lord Celleriant should you but command his removal."

Celleriant wasn't particularly happy about this, but he didn't argue; he merely watched.

"You have chosen to accept his presence for reasons of your own; it is my surmise that nothing short of his death will remove him. He does not serve you in the way your den does; I am uncertain about the source of his allegiance, but I will trust your opinion in this particular case.

"Do you think that Avandar has never taken a life?"

Jewel almost laughed; it stuck in her throat and the sound that came out as a result sounded a little like she was being strangled. Angel crossed the room before she could stop him, but he said nothing, did nothing; he took up a position at her back and he held it, as if this was all he could do—and he knew it.

"Avandar has done more damage than small armies."

"I will not lecture you on the wisdom of saying that so openly; it is my guess that the only person in this small room who might be surprised at all is your Angel, and even there, I have my doubts. But you understand that it is unwise to make such a claim where outsiders might hear it?"

She nodded.

"You understand as well that these rooms are not generally magically protected in a way that makes them impervious to magical eavesdroppers?"

She was silent.

"Jewel. Jay," he added. "What I see in Celleriant, what I see in Avandar, what I see and have seen in many of my acquaintances, past and present— even in Ararath—is not different from what they see in me. I understand that ignorance is oft a comfort, and I am far more guarded than you will ever be; I will not say more."

"This is why Hannerle has always hated your work."

"My previous work."

"I don't want to hurt her," she replied, her hands in fists she couldn't unfurl.

"No. No more do I. Not every man or woman who has power indulges in games of death; nor do all who jockey *for* power assume that death is the collateral by which they will achieve it. But some, yes; they embark on dangerous games. It is in these games, in which the stakes are high and the danger equivalently high, that such men as we three have been involved, in the past."

"But that's in the past, Haval, and I—"

"The past is part, always, of the present. We cannot leave it behind in its entirety because it is the foundation of who and what we now are. It is true of you and your den as well; the difference is only in how the game is played and the reward sought.

"Did you truly not understand what you were asking of me, Jewel?"

She wanted to say no. No, she hadn't understood. She couldn't. She met his gaze, saw the lines etched around perfectly clear and lucid eyes, and looked away. "I didn't," she finally managed, "understand what I was asking of Hannerle."

"I will allow that as truth. But now that you do understand, Jewel, what will you do? I have committed myself, in all but deed; if you release me, I will withdraw. If, however, you do not, there is the small matter of compensation which will have to be discussed, and the compensation itself must of necessity be discreet. I will not be insulted if you withdraw your offer of employ."

"And if I don't?"

"I will only be insulted if you obviously undervalue the services I will provide—but inasmuch as you are unfamiliar with those services, I will attempt to be patient." He paused and then added, "If you are uncertain of suitable fees, there are, among your House members, people you might go to for guidance. They will understand the need for discretion, although at least one of them will be surprised at the need for that guidance."

She lowered her shoulders. "Are you done with me?"

Haval knew she was stalling for time. He raised one brow, no more, but nodded; she all but leaped off the stool. She was, however, careful in her dismount because long experience with Haval had taught her that messing up his careful pinning meant much *longer* stays on the stool as a result. Removing what was not quite a dress, but much more than cut cloth, she laid it carefully on the bed, adjusting undergarments she despised as she once again girded herself for daily House business. She envied Finch more than she could possibly say because Finch was required, by duty, to leave the manse; Jewel, now watched with excessive interest, was not.

Thus attired, she asked Haval to wait a moment, and went in search of Avandar; Angel followed. Celleriant, however, did not.

"Jay?"

She shook her head. "I need to find Avandar."

Angel said nothing else, but it wasn't required; Avandar met her in the waiting rooms. "ATerafin," he said, which meant he was still annoyed at the morning discussion. "Are the fittings done?"

"Yes, and Haval's packing his things. He'll probably be back later tonight, if we're lucky."

"I see. Is there some difficulty with his work?"

"No. Not the dresses."

"Ah."

There were whole days when she wanted any other domicis. "Avandar," she said, through slightly clenched teeth. "Do we really need Haval?"

"I believe I have answered this question before. If you wish to pursue the most aggressive course of action, the answer, to my mind, is a clear no."

"And if we wish to pursue something sane and humane instead?"

"I have, in my years of service, come to know much about the House, its politics, and its more powerful members and factions. I have taken some care to study similar forces outside of the House, but I am seldom far from your side, and those forces have offered neither opportunity nor threat to you."

She waited, her hands falling almost unconsciously to her hips, as if she were a much younger version of her Oma.

"Very well. Yes, you feel you need him."

"Why? Why does it have to be him?"

Avandar's smile was thin. "He is canny, Jewel, in a way that you will never be. He is observant in a way that I myself have never been. His instincts, on the very few occasions I have been privileged to observe him, are more than sound. There are very few men in the Empire that are like Haval. But that is not the answer you desire. He has no particular ambition on his own behalf; in a man with his talents, this is unusual. For reasons that are not entirely clear to me, he has a sentimental attachment to you. If you allow it, he will serve your interests more clearly and more devotedly than you yourself can.

"But the limits of that service will be found in your response to his advice and counsel. If you cannot take his advice or learn from his lead, he will, in the end, be wasted."

Jewel exhaled. It was a brittle sound in the otherwise silent hall.

"You are having reservations." Avandar didn't look particularly surprised; he looked slightly weary.

"I am."

"Become accustomed to them, Jewel. They will never stop. Win or lose, you will never be unaware of the cost. What you take from Haval, you take. There is a very good chance that he will not survive this struggle."

"It's not Haval I'm worried about."

Avandar's eyes narrowed into slits. *It is his wife, of course.* He was annoyed.

She didn't answer; not in thought and not in words. Instead, she turned back to her room, trailing two shadows, not one. She entered; Haval was almost finished his careful packing, and he looked up. Celleriant was standing by the nearest wall; he was watching Haval with open curiosity, which was much more than he usually showed.

"Who do you advise me to speak with about fair compensation?"

Haval smiled. "Two men. You will, in my opinion, benefit from approaching either, and for this reason, I counsel you to approach them both. Tact is necessary, as is discretion, but I believe your approach to at least one will be expected."

"Will anyone observing be happy about it?"

"No."

She had *so* hoped that the funeral would be behind her before the knives actually came out. She *hated* the politicking when The Terafin hadn't even been properly laid to rest. She hated every single member of the House Council who had sent her letters or invitations; she hated the merchants who had implied that they were willing to receive hers; she hated even the Kings, whose search for evidence of the demonic within the House was interfering with the necessary work of the funeral preparations. The only person she couldn't bring herself to hate was Sigurne Mellifas, who was also frequently seen traversing both grounds and galleries.

And she knew it was a waste of time. She knew that to say this at all would make her seem ten years younger, and not in a good way. She held her peace. It was hard.

Then again, she'd already lost her temper in the kitchen, and Avandar would make her pay for that one way or the other.

"Who?" she asked again.

"I encourage you to consider the options, ATerafin."

"Haval—I've no time for tests, today."

"Your entire life is about to become nothing but a continuous test, in which failure is likely to be marked by death—even if that death is not yours. I believe you had an Oma of whom you were fond? I offer you the advice she would have offered." In perfect Torra, Haval then said, "Begin as you mean to continue." He turned to Angel. "If you will help me carry my things, I would be grateful."

Angel nodded but didn't move; he wouldn't, until Jewel gave him the signal. She was pretty certain that Haval expected this.

Silence enfolded her as she stood, considering Haval's words. After a long pause she looked up at him; he hadn't moved. "I can only think of one," she admitted.

"And that one?"

"Devon ATerafin."

"Of the Imperial Trade Commission, senior aide to Patris Larkasir, also of the Imperial Trade Commission. Very good."

"The second?"

"I forgive your ignorance in this regard, but urge you to do more thorough research in the future. I will give you the name as a show of my good will, although I will point out that you are familiar with the person. He lives in the manse. His name is Jarven ATerafin."

"Jarven? Finch's Jarven?"

Haval chuckled drily. "The very one. I would have this conversation with Jarven directly, and not through Finch, although Finch has the easier and less suspicious access. And now, if you don't mind, I would like to borrow your Angel."

Jewel lifted her hand in curt den-sign; Angel nodded and began to carry the greater part of Haval's load.

Only after they had both departed did Jewel look to Avandar. "Well?"

"His advice is sound, but I understand why you have not, prior to receiving it, chosen to approach Devon."

"I don't even know if he'll have time to see me. Can it wait until after the funeral?"

Avandar raised a single brow, which was all the answer she needed. It wasn't the answer she wanted, however.

Devon ATerafin had rooms within the Terafin manse. They were not so fine as the rooms the den had occupied since their arrival, but to be fair, there were far fewer of Devon than of the den itself. His rooms, like most of the rooms senior members of the House occupied did not sport House Guards; nor, at this point, did they have private ones.

Devon, however, did not spend all of his time in his living quarters in the manse itself. They had been supplied for his use as a gesture that made clear his worth to the House—but it was a gesture meant to assuage the doubts of outsiders. Jewel was therefore uncertain that she would find him at home, should she even attempt to contact him.

It was an excuse.

Carver made it a very short-lived one. "He's been using his rooms," he said quietly, as they hunkered around the kitchen table looking as bleary-eyed as Jewel felt. The night's sleep had been anything but good. Avandar had spent the evening in her room supplying the light that stopped night-mares from echoing when she woke screaming their tune.

"You're certain?" Jewel demanded, although she knew he was.

He nodded. "Vivienne mentioned it to Merry."

Carver's connection with the servants in the manse had strengthened over time. He was even tolerated—barely—by the formidable Master of the Household Staff because he understood the rules that governed the servants. He only sidestepped them when he was certain that charm could prevent damage. In the case of the stiff, silver-haired dictator from whom servants regularly fled in tears, that was almost—but not quite—never.

"Is he taking meals in his room or in the dining hall?"

"In his room, for the most part." Carver hesitated, which was unusual.

"Spit it out."

"Duvari has visited Devon at least three times that we know of. The investigation into the presence of demons isn't going to go away any time soon."

"Teller said Gabriel had submitted a request for an audience with the Twin Kings."

"Did he get it?"

"Yes, but it won't occur until after the funeral services are over. The Kings will be here for those; so will the Queens and the Princess Royale."

"For all three days?"

"For at least the first day; I believe they are also committed for the third. We'll see the Exalted on the first day; the Triumvirate will perform the ceremonies."

Carver nodded.

Jester, however, said, "The point Carver forgot he was trying to make is this: Devon's going to be housebound as much as possible while the Astari are crawling around the grounds. It's easier for him now; he has leave from Patris Larkasir because of The Terafin's death. It'll be harder later—but if you need to speak with him, now's the right time."

"While Duvari could pop in at any second."

They all fell silent, considering that. Or all of them who were around the table. Celleriant was by the wall; Avandar and Ellerson were by the door. Jester, Angel, and Carver were here, but Arann, Finch, and Teller were gone, as they would be most days from here on in. Arann's rise in the House Guard, his entry into the Chosen, had changed his shifts for the better, for the most part—but the "better" hours were longer.

Ellerson cleared his throat. It had been a long time since he'd been her domicis, but that sound was as familiar—as painfully familiar—as breathing. "It is my opinion, ATerafin," he said, speaking to Jewel, "that you are considered a moderate threat."

"By who?"

"By all of the contenders. You have not put yourself forward as a possible candidate. You are nevertheless of value to *any* future leader of the House. You might also be of extreme value to any putative leader. It is clear to me that The Terafin's death occurred in your absence for a reason; whoever planned and executed it could not be certain that in your presence his plans would not go awry. Your vision is unreliable and it is not easily commanded, if at all—but where it exists, it is accurate and undeniable."

"Meaning?"

"Devon ATerafin's disposition is not entirely well known, but his standing within the Imperial Trade Commission makes his support valuable. He is likely to be at least partially observed. As are you."

"You counsel subtlety in my approach."

"Given the nature of your possible request, yes. But given the nature of the events within the House, it is also likely that a meeting with Devon would not be overly suspicious as long as it did not occur with any frequency."

"Avandar, could you mask my presence?"

Avandar glanced at Ellerson, but nodded. "There is a risk, however."

"And that?"

"I would use magic; if we approach the door and someone is exceptionally cautious, I will be noted."

Use of magic would probably ring clarion bells throughout the upper echelons of the House.

Jewel pushed hair out of her eyes before she let her chin sink into her hands. "Fine. Angel, Avandar, with me. Celleriant, you draw more attention than gold coins tossed in the streets of the twenty-fifth would. Stay here. Or, if you want, you can *discreetly* check the grounds for *Kialli*."

"I feel that was not entirely wise," Avandar told Jewel as they exited the West Wing.

"It probably wasn't. But I'm certain that demons exist on the grounds, and I want them gone. If I could kill them myself, I would. I'm tempted to try, regardless. Celleriant, on the other hand, *can* take them."

"So can I. And Lord Celleriant is unlikely to be subtle."

"If you want to join him, feel free. I've got Angel."

Avandar said nothing. Loudly. Jewel exhaled. "I'm sorry. That was uncalled for."

Angel's fingers moved in a mute *it's good*, but he didn't break the domicis' icy silence.

That silence carried Jewel like a wave to Devon's closed door. The halls weren't empty; they were crowded with various merchants and their attendants. One of those merchants almost bowled Jewel over, but he could be forgiven—he was carrying a flower arrangement that was taller than she was, and it made her hard to spot.

No one stopped her; no one called to her. She passed House Guards on duty and House Guards escorting visitors of import; she passed the very occasional servant who was being used as a guide. Once she'd cleared the main gallery and the halls, she expected the traffic to taper off. It did, but not entirely. She was not the only House member in desperate need of new attire on very short notice.

But eventually she came to Devon's rooms.

She hesitated in front of his door, and as she did, Avandar lifted the delicate brass knocker and rapped it loudly. After a few minutes, the door opened.

Devon, in burgundy bathrobes, stood in the frame. His hair was dark and wet, and his brows lifted as he saw who his visitors were.

Jewel reddened. "I'm sorry," she mumbled. "We've come at a bad time. We'll come back later." She turned quickly from both Devon and his door.

"Jewel." Two voices. Devon's and Avandar's. Jewel froze, forced her expression into something she hoped was businesslike, and turned again. Devon glanced at Avandar; Avandar merely waited.

"Please. There will be no good time before the end of the funeral services, and if you are not discomfited, I will not be." He pushed the door open and stepped back, leaving a small trail of water in his wake. "Give me but a moment, and I will change into something more appropriate for entertaining guests."

He disappeared, leaving said guests stranded in a sitting room that was much more modest in both size and furnishing than the den's sitting room. Jewel took a seat. Angel and Avandar didn't. It made her feel distinctly uncomfortable, so she rose; she couldn't manage to stand as still as either of her companions, however. There was a fireplace here; there were two paintings on either side of the mantel, and nothing above its center. One painting was of the Twin Kings, and the other, of The Terafin. It was the painting of The Terafin that Jewel approached.

It was a good likeness, but it was almost a decade old—or older. Time unraveled slowly as she traced the static and familiar lines of Amarais' jaw, her slight smile, her grave eyes. She wore blues; the dress itself was dark, the sleeves lined in lighter colors; she wore, as well, the Terafin Sword, although it was sheathed. Her hair was bound in a net that sparkled only where it caught light, transfixing it. Her gaze traveled to the left of Jewel's, fixed on some point that only the painter would fully understand.

She hadn't expected to see this here, and she was immobile, for a moment, at the unexpected bite of memory. Amarais was dead. She was gone. She would never frown or stare or nod or smile again. She would never invite Jewel into the privacy of her smallest rooms, to share wine, to share memories, to ask advice, to demand—everything. Jewel had never once told this woman of the depth of her endless respect for her; she'd never once spoken of the complicated love that grows out of near-worship, dipping and rising with the passage of years and the gaining of experience.

Is this what you wanted? she all but demanded. *Is this what you saw, for me? For your House? Did you know that it was demons that would kill you?*

But it had to be demons, Jewel thought, lowering her chin. It had to be. It was demons, after all, that had driven her den to House Terafin so many years past. Wasn't it fitting, in the end, that those very demons find a way to destroy the unexpected safety that she'd found here?

No.

No. That was too personal, and Jewel had rarely benefitted from making disaster a personal affair. Her nails were scoring her flesh; her hands had become fists, her knuckles whitened by their tightness, when she hadn't been paying attention.

"Jewel."

And of course Devon would pick this exact minute to return to this room. What Angel saw didn't hurt her; what Avandar saw, he would see no matter what pains she took to hide it. But Devon was not one of hers, and it pained her to be exposed to him, even momentarily. She forced her hands to open, forced her face to stiffen, before she turned away from the painting.

Caught beneath it, the lower edge of its frame disappearing behind her shoulders, the woman who had been The Terafin and the woman who intended to fulfill her promise to become the next one faced Devon ATerafin squarely.

Devon, in a dark shirt, dark pants, his hair combed back from his face, looked at them both, words deserting him for a moment. Jewel's expression was stiff, but her hands were shaking and her eyes—her eyes were not entirely dry. *Amarais*, he thought. He nodded to her; he did not bow. He was aware of both Angel and the domicis; only one of them could fade successfully into the background. He was aware, as well, that neither of them would interrupt or interfere; they were here for Jewel.

"ATerafin."

Jewel nodded.

"In truth, I had expected to hear from you before today; you are late." His lips curved in a brief, hard smile.

"Your legs are broken?" she asked, her words as hard as his smile, but infinitely less refined.

"Pardon?"

"You know where I live, and I'm pretty much always there."

"Ah." His smile softened around the edges. "The South has not changed you much, has it?" He was surprised when her glance slid away from his.

"Yes," she said, the single word almost inaudible. "I wasn't here."

If he felt any anger or any bitterness at her absence—and he had—he almost repented. Almost. "No." He turned, crossed the room, opened a cabinet, its glass doors reflecting diffuse magelight. As he opened it, he retrieved a small, square glass bottle. He also touched a small stone and spoke a single, low word.

Her eyes were as good as they'd always been. "Silence?" she asked.

"Yes. It is possible, even probable, that someone will attempt to listen in on our conversation; they will know that we—or that I—am cautious. It is not a sophisticated stone." He lifted the bottle; she shook her head. Neither of them drank when working unless the work itself demanded it.

"Duvari?"

"Oh, almost certainly Duvari, but I am entirely accustomed to that." He indicated a chair; she took it, and he took the chair directly opposite. "The House Council convenes on the seventh of Henden."

Jewel nodded.

"Will you announce your intentions there?"

She glanced at her domicis; Devon waited. When she looked back to him, she said, "Actually, that's not why I'm here." Which wasn't an answer.

"You will have to answer that question soon."

"I won't have to answer it definitively until the seventh, if then," was her curt reply.

"Now I *am* curious. Why are you here?"

"For advice."

"I am not perhaps the man of whom advice should be asked; my advice is likely to be somewhat compromised."

"Maybe."

"What do you wish to know?"

She looked at Avandar again, which was both expected and unacceptable. "Jewel," Devon said sharply. "The advice you receive from your domicis cannot be requested in so public a fashion; people will assume it is the domicis, and not the master, who controls the situation."

She stiffened and then, to his surprise, she smiled. It was both rueful and vastly more relaxed. "That's advice I've also received—from my domicis. I'm sorry. I don't quite know how to ask the question, now that I'm here."

"Ask. If your delivery is unwise or lacking, I will inform you."

"No doubt. I want to hire someone." Before Devon could ask who, or for what, she continued. "I'm not entirely certain how he'll do what he does—not in the specifics. To be honest, Devon, I'm not entirely certain exactly what he does."

Devon raised a brow; he couldn't prevent it.

"But he suggested I speak to you about—about appropriate compensation for his services."

"I fail to see why. He's a merchant?"

"No."

Devon nodded slowly. "What, exactly, do you think he'll do for you?"

"Ferret out information, mostly. Give me advice when I need it."

"That's all?"

She hesitated and then nodded.

He grimaced. "Jewel."

"It's not information that just anyone has, or can easily obtain. He's spent a small lifetime listening to gossip, and he knows which gossip is reliably true, and which is not. I don't know who he talks to. I don't know who'd talk to him—but people do."

"May I ask who your prospective employee is?"

"No."

"Very well. You wish him to spy for you?"

She looked surprised. He found it mildly annoying. But she didn't disagree. After too long a pause, she said, "Maybe. I've never asked him how he knows what he knows."

"In general, when one buys information, one pays for the information one receives."

"How am I supposed to put a value on that?"

"You aren't; the person who has the information generally defines its worth."

She took a deeper breath and then said, "What do the *Astari* pay you?"

Avandar's audible breath made perfectly clear that it was entirely the wrong question to ask, but it came a little late. If it hadn't, the quality of Devon's resulting silence had the same effect; it was as cold as winter steel, and it lasted for what seemed a very long while.

She waited, feeling her shoulders begin a slow gather toward her spine. Devon had long had that effect on her when his anger was cold and silent. "Why," he finally said, in a voice that matched his changed demeanor, "do you think that question is relevant?"

She wanted to leave, but compromised and squirmed her way out of the chair instead.

"Do you even understand what the *Astari* do?"

"They protect the Kings."

"Yes. But not in the way the Kings' Swords do. In discreet terms, the Astari are proactive, not reactive. Not every decision made by the Lord of the Compact is granted the Kings' dispensation. There is a balance maintained between the Kings and the Lord of the Compact; were there not, the *Astari* would be functionally illegal."

"You're implying that anyone who wants something similar to the *Astari* for their own use would be illegal, period, given they're unlikely to seek the Kings' dispensation."

"I would say, rather, that you're inferring that. Jewel, would you please sit down. Watching you pace like a caged beast is not conducive to complex discussion, at least not on my part."

She sat heavily.

"What," he said, the minute the chair had finished creaking, "do you think the *Astari* actually do?"

Instead of glancing at Avandar, she looked at the backs of her hands, which were now in her lap.

"Do you perhaps believe that they are an elevated variety of assassin?"

Since it *was* one of the activities the *Astari* were commonly understood to engage in, she was silent.

"I see. And you now feel that such services are necessary?"

"Devon—"

"Answer my question."

She looked up. "Yes. If not for me, then for someone. You know the four contenders. There is no way that either Haerrad or Rymark will concede victory to anyone else—anyone—if they're still alive."

"And you intend to assassinate them."

". . . no." Breathing hurt. "But one or both of them will be dead by the end of this. Both, if one of them is not The Terafin at that time. Tell me you think I'm wrong. Tell me, and I'll leave. I'll leave gratefully, Devon. I'll be *happy*."

He was silent, but still; the ice of his anger had thawed.

"But if you can't tell me that, understand me. If I sit back and wait for *someone else* to kill them, *knowing* that it'll happen, and praying for it like a vulture, how am I any better? Yes, I'm not the murderer, but I'm not innocent either. I'm just waiting on the sidelines and praying that someone else will do the dirty work so that I don't have to."

"That is an exaggeration, Jewel."

"And I'm aware that sending someone who *can* kill is pretty much the same as going myself, except that I'm not confident of my ability to be successful."

"So you are saying that you intend to utilize assassination as a tool?"

She rose. She couldn't stop herself. This was the discussion that she desperately did not wish to have with Devon. Or with anyone.

Devon didn't press her, which was a small mercy; it was also brief. "Let me return to your hypothesis. Your reasons for naming Haerrad and Rymark so openly seem sound on the surface, and in the political context of a House War, there *will* be deaths. I am unconvinced, however, that your acceptance of the necessity in these two cases is not personal.

"If I remember correctly, Teller was injured by Haerrad; it was meant to serve as a warning."

She said nothing at all.

"But Rymark has caused your den much less . . . distress. Why Rymark, Jewel? Answer carefully, and do not attempt to lie; I will merely find it insulting, rather than convincing."

The fear left her. Anger was all that remained, and it wasn't any weaker than Devon's. "Rymark," she said, in a cool, even voice, "killed The Terafin. If I do *nothing else* in this miserable war, I'll see him dead. I don't care how. I don't care when."

She watched his expression freeze in place. "What did you just say?"

"You heard me."

"I was not present at the moment of The Terafin's death, but from any intelligence gathered, neither were you."

Of all the things he had said so far in this small and suffocating room, this was the worst. But she couldn't flinch from truth just because it hurt her; she had to be stronger than that. "I didn't see the blow that killed her. I was there when she died."

"And yet you make your statement with complete conviction."

"I do."

Devon rose; he was inches away from her before she thought to move. The thought, she crushed. If she stepped back, she'd damn well do it by choice, not reflex. "I know what happened during the Dark Days, Jewel. If you seek to play games, no matter how costly, you *will not* play games with demons."

"I'm not the one playing them."

"If you have information of this kind, and you withhold it, you *are*. Why do you say that Rymark was responsible for The Terafin's death?"

"Because he was."

Jewel, Avandar said. *Have a care.*

I am. Don't interfere.

"Finch and Teller were there."

"And?"

"They saw Rymark. They saw the rest of the Council, but they were watching Rymark."

"Why Rymark?"

"Haerrad wasn't present."

He opened his mouth to speak, snapped it shut, and nodded. It was a fair answer, and even in anger, he was willing to acknowledge it.

"Rymark didn't appear to be surprised. And unlike anyone else in the Council Hall, he wasn't afraid of the demon at all. Finch thought he knew it would come."

"That is not proof," Devon said, his voice still sharp and cold, his words much less intense.

"If we play games of assassination, proof isn't required."

"I don't suggest you play those games."

"I wasn't aware that I needed your approval."

Devon took a step back and then returned to his chair, motioning stiffly for Jewel to do likewise; she demurred.

"After her death, after the death of the demon, Rymark announced that he had in his possession the legal writ declaring him as heir to the Terafin Seat."

"Again, that is not proof."

"No. But he lied, and we both know it. He would have had to have the time to prepare a well-forged writ. Alowan was assassinated prior to the attempt—by days—in order that The Terafin be without her healer."

Devon nodded.

"And an attempt on Haerrad's life was made at the same time as the attempt on The Terafin's." Jewel's voice made clear which attempt she wished had succeeded. "If you're accusing me of being emotional, I am. I'm even being irrational. But in this case, irrationality and rationality coincide.

"I think the demon was the last resort. Had the Twin Kings not been present, I don't think most of the House Council would have survived. Had Celleriant not arrived, the Kings themselves might have died."

"That would be your . . . newest servant?"

She nodded. "Someone in the House had to be responsible for her death."

"Why do you say that?"

Irritated, she said, "You know it yourself."

He said nothing, waiting. Devon, she knew, could wait for hours without any sign of flagging.

"No one else would benefit from Haerrad's death. Assassinating The Terafin could be a potent weapon if one wanted the Empire to be in turmoil—but assassinating the Kings or even the Princes would have a much more powerful effect. The Terafin's death would require a successor. If someone allied in some way with the demons could be that successor, her death would be useful and even necessary. Killing Haerrad would remove one of the most difficult impediments in the struggle for the seat."

"There are others."

Jewel nodded. "I don't care what you think, Devon. I'm not wrong." She looked with longing toward his closed door. "You don't have to answer the question I came to ask. I'll ask someone else."

"Who?"

"Does it matter?"

He ran his hands over his eyes and through his hair. "Jewel. Sit."

As if compelled, she obeyed, making a great deal more sound than he had.

"You understand that my loyalties have always been divided."

Had they? Jewel glanced over her shoulder at the painting of the Kings. "No," she finally said, although the word was soft. "I never thought they were divided. You served The Terafin when her interests didn't diverge from the Kings'."

"I respected—and admired—The Terafin."

"Yes. She was worthy of both. I wasn't around for the House War that made her what she was—but you were. If I had to guess—if anyone ever asked—I'd say that The Terafin was considered the best of the contenders by the Kings, or by Duvari. I don't know if you supported her bid—"

"I did."

"—But if you did, you did it with permission."

"You've grown less kind."

Jewel shrugged. "She accepted it. She accepted you. I understand why."

"And would you?"

"Accept you? It depends. What would you be offering that would require my acceptance?"

"You are still angry."

There wasn't any point in denying it. "Yes. You could have interfered, Devon. Not in The Terafin's death—there's no way you would have let her die. It wouldn't have served the Kings' interests, not when the army is fighting its distant war. But you could have saved Teller from Haerrad, that time. I'm certain of it. You didn't."

He didn't disagree. She almost wanted him to because he was right—there were some angers that slept without dying. When she touched them, they woke, and they burned as if they were still new.

"You understand why."

"Yes. I understand why. It doesn't mean it doesn't enrage me." She wanted to pace the room, but she managed to remain in her seat. Avandar had moved toward the back of her chair and stood there like shadow. "Why are you keeping me here?"

The line of his shoulders relaxed. "This is not the conversation I thought to have when you first appeared at the door, ATerafin. If you will not drink, allow me the opportunity."

"You don't drink when you're working."

"Ah. Perhaps. Perhaps not. I will, however, drink now."

Avandar was at the bar before Devon could stand. He poured something rich and golden into a short, squat goblet; this he carried to Devon and placed on the table in front of him. Devon stared at the glass for a long moment before he lifted it in the palm of his hand. Jewel watched, almost fascinated, as he began to drink.

"Before you left—and in such a dramatic fashion—you offered Amarais the only comfort you could offer her. I do not know what occurred in the South, although rumor has it that Commander Allen was . . . less than pleased at your disappearance."

"How would you know?"

"The magi have ways of communicating over long distances, and the Commander had already received permission to second your services for his war. I believe he communicated with Sigurne through one of the magi that now accompany the army."

Jewel had the grace to cringe, no more—the army was in the South, in a different country. But she? She was no less at war.

"She called you home," he added, staring at the liquid as if it were a mirror. "And you are home, now. Four of the House Council members are on the move; in truth, they have been on the move for months, possibly years. Yet you, Jewel, are not."

"Am I not to be allowed to bury her?" was the bitter reply. "I've never been able to bury my dead," she added, her voice low.

"You are not personally responsible for the burial, and you are not a child; you understand that she is dead. What happens to her corpse is a grace note, but it will not bring her back; nor will it alter the situation in which you find yourself. You hesitate, Jewel. You stall for time. You know that you cannot afford this. Were it not for the manner of her death and the unexpected presence of the Twin Kings, the leadership of the House might already be decided."

He drank again, slowly and steadily. "You were not the only person to offer her comfort before her untimely death."

This surprised her.

"Do you think she had no understanding of either who or what you will face? Demons, certainly, she did not expect—not initially. But she was canny, and she knew how to fight.

"She trusted you. In the end, I do not think you will betray her trust. But you have never seen what must unfold now. Yes, you've seen the politicking that occurs between merchants, both aligned and unaligned with the House; you've seen some hint of the violence that might occur. You've seen the assassination of Alayra; you've seen the deaths of Alea and Courtne, and were it not for those deaths, you might not now be in the position you *are* in. But those? Those were trivial games in comparison. Those deaths hurt Amarais immeasurably, but they did not deprive her of the House." He set the empty glass on the table, and Avandar, like a cold shadow, retrieved it.

Jewel hated—had always hated—the taste of liquor. But she liked the color, and wondered, watching Devon's stiff expression, if it might not one day come in useful. He took the glass that Avandar had refilled in silence.

"Devon."

One dark brow rose. "I had wondered if you had lost your voice."

"What did you promise The Terafin before she died?"

The other brow also rose. "I should have expected that," he replied, with a slight, but pained, smile. "You've always been perceptive. Not always, sadly, predictably so.

"What did she demand of me? Very little, Jewel. Very little that she didn't expect would naturally occur. One of the few fortunate things about imminent death is the lack of debt incurred. She was, of course, aware that some interest would be taken in the struggle for the House Seat. She was also aware that some preference might be given, discreetly, toward some of the claimants. She was *certainly* aware that one or two would find no favor at all."

"With Duvari?"

Devon didn't answer.

"Sorry. I shouldn't have asked."

"No, you shouldn't have. But you are new to this. If you were not, Jewel, you would ask for my support. Not all of the candidates know that I serve the *Astari*; it is possible that none of them do. I expect to speak with all four before the week is out. They will offer concessions in return for my visible support."

"You're not a House Council member."

"No. But the House Council is small, and it is not the whole of the House. I occupy a visible role within *Avantari*, and the merchants know me."

"What would they offer you for your support?"

"A better question. I am not entirely certain. I believe it's possible they will offer me the Merchant Authority office."

"But that's already occupied by Jarven."

"Indeed; they will also curry favor with Jarven."

"What would they offer him?"

"At his age? A settlement, in all likelihood—and at that, a valuable one. He is close to an age where retirement would be expected, and indeed such retirements often occur during the changing of the guard."

"I can't offer you that."

He raised one brow. "No?"

She snorted. Pushed hair out of her eyes. "You don't know Jarven."

"Ah. As it happens, I *do* know Jarven. It was Jarven who introduced me to Amarais, and it was Jarven who sponsored my first application into the House. I do not believe you've had much interaction with Jarven, however."

"I haven't."

"Ah. Finch?"

It was Jewel's turn to be silent. She knew he already knew the answer, and sometimes these silences seemed like stupid, pointless games. But people played them for a reason.

"Very well. You cannot offer me that, and between us, it is not a position I could accept. I am unlikely to make that clear to any of the other four. You will know."

She nodded. "I've nothing to offer you," she told him softly, "except this: I'll keep you. I'll keep your secret. I won't give you orders that you can't obey. I won't expect your service to the Kings to come second to your service to me."

"And will you resent it less, this time around?"

She looked at a point just past his shoulder, refusing to drop her eyes, but unable to meet his. After a long pause, she said, "Yes. Yes, because it's to *me*."

"And you value yourself less highly than you value your den?"

"Is there any point to that question? Short of starting a dissection of my character I've no intention of participating in, what do you hope to gain?"

He drank. "Nothing. My apologies, Jewel. I want more, however, than just that concession."

"I've nothing else to offer."

"Not yet. But if you become Terafin, the vast resources of the House will be yours."

"No, they won't. They'll be the House's. I can't promise you anything until I know what they actually are."

"Ah. How, then, do you intend to pay your prospective employee?"

"What?" She shook her head; he had brought the awkward conversation around again, leaving her struggling to keep up. After a long pause, she said, "I have some money; I have nowhere near as much as the rest of the House Council." Enough. "Devon—you probably know to the copper what I can access; you almost certainly know better than I do. What do you want, and what do you intend to do?"

"If you intend to rule the House, ATerafin, you will never make such an open admission of ignorance again."

"I'm not Amarais."

"No. No, you are not. Very well, Jewel. I want you to announce your candidacy."

"I'd have to do that anyway."

"Yes. But you will put it off, and it will be a disadvantage. There are people who are now waiting for you, and their neutrality puts them at risk; there is some pressure on them."

"And on you?"

He smiled. "Indeed. If you forsake your promise to the previous Terafin, I must choose another behind which to stand. It is not a simple matter to be both highly placed in the House and a member of the *Astari*, and it will require some time and some finesse to arrange, if that is even possible."

"Who would you choose?"

"Elonne, I think. Possibly Marrick. Haerrad is so antagonistic to both Duvari and the Kings, any approach on my part would lead to my death."

"Not Rymark."

"Not now. Not given what you have said. I will speak with Gregori; I believe he was present during the assassination."

"Gregor?"

"Ah. Never mind; he is another member of the House, a junior one." Devon leaned back in the chair and let his neck hug the hardwood at its height for a moment. Avandar refilled his glass and set it on the table. Devon closed his eyes, his face aimed toward the ceiling. "When I offer you my support, Jewel, understand what it means.

"Most of the work I have done for the House involves *Avantari* and the various Royal trade routes. Some of it involves less bureaucratic matters."

"I know." It was with Devon that she had been sent to the Merchant Authority so many years ago; it was with Devon that she had crawled through the dark basements beneath that Authority, where every shadow and every sound they made might be their death.

"It is in the less official functions that I would most be of use to you. It may obviate your need for any secondary employee to, as you put it, spy for you."

"And will you kill for me?"

"For you, Jewel? No. But there will be death in the manse—and beyond it—before this is done, and I cannot say for certain that I will not kill on command. I will advise you, as I can; I will provide what information I now have about the other four. It will not be complete; they are cautious, and I am forced to be cautious as well." He opened his eyes and added, "You have your domicis, and he is meant for a struggle of this nature. But you will have me, as well, and where I am not present, one or two others. We are not yours, but inasmuch as you serve our purpose, we will protect your life as if it were the very Kings'."

"Is it safe to offer me this?"

"It is safe to offer *you* this, yes."

"And would it be safe for me to refuse it?"

"Although you might doubt me, Jewel, yes. It would be safe. Duvari has no interest in your death at this moment. That may change—that will almost certainly change—in time. You will never speak directly to Duvari about the House or its war. If any word is passed to Duvari, it will go through me."

This time, when Jewel looked at Avandar, Devon let it be.

Avandar now turned to Devon. "She does not require another guard," he said in a cool voice. "She has me, and one other."

"You counsel her to reject my offer?"

"On the contrary. I would counsel her to accept the offer, but I wish to alter the provisions. I understand that Jewel is of value to you. She is of value to me, but my loyalty is completely undivided. You could not kill her while I was in the room, ATerafin, and you are skilled.

"But she has oft disregarded her own safety in favor of those that she cares for."

"That is a weakness she cannot afford."

"It is. But it is a weakness, nonetheless. Demanding that she become something entirely other than the woman she is is as much a fool's dream as her own dream of taking the House without death."

Devon nodded slowly. Jewel watched his expression shift and harden; it was subtle. Devon, she realized, didn't like Avandar. She wondered if he had always disliked him this much, or if this was new.

"Protect her den, in her stead. If you give her your word that you will do everything within your means to achieve their safety, she will believe you, and she will forgive any unforeseen circumstances that lead to your failure."

"Avandar, no—"

Avandar lifted one hand. "His duty when he arguably failed Teller was neither to you nor your den; it was to The Kings and The Terafin. He made no promise, Jewel, and no oath, to you. This would be different."

"I don't—"

"Trust him? No? And yet you feel comfortable enough to speak frankly in his presence; you willingly—and needlessly—expose your ignorance time and again. You cannot trust him to love what you love, no. I will accept that as fact because you cannot trust me to do likewise. You cannot trust him to obey your commands when his own imperatives and morals dictate otherwise—but Jewel, you trusted both The Terafin and Alowan, and that was true, as well, of them.

"I do not understand the hostility you feel toward Devon, but it is time to choose which of two things is greater: that hostility or your own needs in the matter of the succession."

Devon raised a brow. He also raised an empty glass, and after a moment, Avandar removed it and once again walked over to the cabinet. During all of this, Angel had been silently observing—and listening. He lifted a hand in den-sign, asking permission to speak. She nodded.

"Trust him."

Jewel stared at Angel as if an unexpected gulf had opened between them, swallowing the floor, the chairs, and anything else in the room in the process.

"Jay, he can't be what you are. No one can. If it was that simple, we wouldn't have followed you."

"But—"

"He'll do what you tell him to do here. He's not stupid enough to do otherwise. He'll do more, yes, and you can't prevent that—but he won't work against you. He's got knowledge and experience that none of the rest of us can offer. Let him in."

She was silent. Devon, drink once again replenished, watched her; he never once turned to look at Angel. But Angel hadn't finished.

"We know what we're up against. No, I'll take that back—we don't know. But we know that the chances we'll all survive are next to none. We know what The Terafin wanted—but Jay, we follow *you*. Always have."

"No," she finally replied. "The rest of us are all ATerafin."

"They wanted the name because you wanted them to have it. I didn't care what you wanted; I cared about what I wanted. I cared about my own pride. I wasn't willing to swear an oath to anyone else while you lived."

At this, Devon's brows rose—slightly—and this time he did turn in his chair to look toward the wall at his back. Angel's spire of hair bobbed as he met Devon's gaze with a nod.

"They want more from the House—"

Angel exhaled. "Yes. They do. But what they want from the House is a grown-up version of what they—what *we*—wanted from you when we lived packed in two rooms in the holdings. You're the only avenue to that future. We're not going to walk to our deaths; we'll make them expensive. But we're not going to avoid the fight, either. We can't.

"Devon ATerafin is an intimate part of that fight. If we didn't need him, The Terafin wouldn't have made him promise to support us."

Devon turned back to Jewel and set his glass on the table. He added nothing to Angel's words, and Avandar had once again achieved invisibility on the Devon scale of attention. Jewel, unfortunately, had not.

"Jewel," he began.

What he might have said was lost as his expression suddenly stiffened. A second later, so did Avandar's, and they both looked toward the closed door that separated these rooms from the rest of the manse.

Avandar headed toward that door first.

"ATerafin," Devon said sharply, "tell your domicis to be cautious. I believe magic is now being used in significant quantities not far from here."

Jewel felt the blood leave her face in a rush.

Celleriant.

Chapter Five

THE WINTER QUEEN had commanded Lord Celleriant to serve Jewel ATerafin.

It was therefore the Winter Queen's command that had brought him here, to the Terafin manse. This manse, with its small people and its equally confining concerns seemed to leech color and vitality out of all who inhabited it; absent was the wild fury of the elements and the subtle beauty of the hidden ways.

Celleriant had casually suggested that he and Viandaran could achieve, in minutes—or perhaps hours—what Jewel herself felt must be achieved: dominance over the House. She spoke of four possible rivals to the seat she would claim as her own; they were all, without exception, human; only one was talent-born, and his power, according to Viandaran, was insignificant.

Let us leave these rooms, Celleriant had said to Viandaran. *The four are closeted here, like rabbits in these crowded warrens. Let us kill them now.* He had offered Jewel his sword and his service, albeit reluctantly, for that very end, and what had he received in return?

Her anger and contempt. It was to be expected, and for that reason, it did not gall him—but Viandaran *did*. Here, he played servant to her master.

It is inadvisable.

Inadvisable? Of all of the men and women gathered beneath these many roofs, only Viandaran was worthy of note; only Viandaran was worthy of fear. Even in the Court of the Winter Queen, Viandaran's was a name that was considered apt for song or verse.

Yet he, too, chose to huddle, damping his light. Given the way the others treated him, he had also hidden the vast depths of his power. And to what end?

To play these pathetic, mortal games?

The world was shorn of glory. Once, it had been driven by, possessed by, and almost destroyed by a wild, savage beauty. Such beauty might be found around any corner, through any pass. Had there been death? Oh, yes. But it hardly mattered; death made life so vibrant, so immediate.

And the only thing that remained of it lingered on hidden paths, hidden roads. The Winter Queen.

He felt her presence, as all sworn to her service must, no matter where they might wander; he heard the attenuated music of distant bells, distant flutes, distant horns. It disturbed him; the Wild Hunt had been called in the lands of the distant South, but the Winter had not yet given way to the Summer. It was the Summer he yearned for; warm beauty instead of cold. The Summer, the Queen, and Mordanant, his brother.

Yet a different face, a different voice, troubled him as he walked these halls; not immortal, not perfect, not firstborn. A different song, both mortal and yet as beautiful, as haunting, as any voice raised in the Court of the Winter Queen save only her own.

Kallandras.

The Senniel bard faced war in the South; war, *Kialli,* and death. In the North? Celleriant faced squabbling mortals, too timid to lift sword. They might bare their fangs at each other, but only at a safe distance. It galled him. Even had they lifted swords, their weapons were like dining utensils in comparison to true weapons.

And yet, the assassin that had killed Jewel ATerafin's beloved ruler had been no mortal. That thought brought him his only comfort, even if scant—it had taken no great effort to kill the creature, after all. If the demon had managed to escape detection up until that moment, it meant two things: that someone within the House was conversant with the kin, and that the kin themselves were extending the humiliating effort to pass undetected among the rabble of humanity.

*   *   *

An hour passed, and the halls grew no less tedious, but they eventually led to doors that were all of glass, and faced the outside world. Celleriant had yet to see any significant portion of the city or the Isle, and he paused a moment before these doors. Beyond them lay grass and carefully constructed flower beds. He opened them and stepped out into the cool air.

This was a mortal garden. Yards away, trees—carefully pruned and cultivated—stood. They girded slender paths, which were marked by small statues and standing lamps. Along these narrow walkways, flowers had been carefully but hastily planted; he judged the weather cold for them, but understood that this was some necessary part of the funereal ceremony for those who lived huddled behind the walls he had momentarily escaped.

But here, he thought in disgust, mortality had leached all wilderness from the plants themselves, and all struggle; no weeds choked the flower beds, exerting their more primal power, and all that grew on the trees above were small buds; there were no leaves. Even had there been, they would be small and green; the wonder and the majesty of the ancient forest had never touched them. He could walk among them—and he now did—speaking and cajoling as he pleased, and they would never wake, never answer.

They lived, domesticated and fettered.

Is this the world you wanted? There was no answer. His question was meant for the gods, and the gods could no longer hear him; when they had been able to do so, they would never have deigned to reply. *Is this the only world in which the mortals could survive?*

It wasn't even a world worth destroying.

And yet, if he but closed his eyes, he could see the worn visage of Kallandras of Senniel; he could see the mark on his ear, invisible to mortal eyes, that spoke of oaths that death itself could not destroy. He could almost hear his voice; could see the elegant and graceful way he navigated the currents of the wild air, weapons in either hand that might have been made when Man was near the apex of its power.

Not for Celleriant, the love of mortals; not for Celleriant, the unhealthy obsession with their brief lives. But this one man had been born in this diminished age, and this one man had called him, in the end, by his name.

Where are you, Kallandras? What do you face?

He expected no answer, and received none; he wandered the grounds, restless, searching for anything that might bring a passing color, no matter how faint, to this dreary world. As he walked, his desire was answered; he found the one tree in the Terafin gardens that was not untouched by immortal hands. It was not alive; that, not even the Arianni could grant, but it was enchanted, and the magics were dark and cold.

"So," he said, speaking the ancient tongue. "I am not entirely alone in this place." He did not draw sword, not yet; instead he approached the tree's trunk. It was not a young tree; it was perhaps the oldest in this garden. Its leaves had not yet begun to flower, and its branches were thick and high.

He became aware, as he approached this single tree, that the mortals showed some respect for the age it had achieved; it was the centerpiece of a network of paths, and it was ringed by slender flower beds that, when in full bloom, would keep distance between any passing visitor and the trunk of the tree itself. Those beds had been turned, but whatever might be laid in them had not yet been brought.

In sight of this tree was a pavilion, and it was tented in colors that were somber: white, black, and trailing golden ribbons. It was large, and two smaller, sister tents—one entirely black and one entirely white—stood just beyond it. Celleriant smiled. The tents were empty, now, but they were clearly meant for use.

Ah. This, he thought, would be one of the areas in which the funeral services were meant to be held. He glanced at the tree's height again, and this time, he whispered a small benediction to the slight breeze that moved through the grounds, and it gathered beneath him. He cajoled it with more care than he had ever chosen to display when speaking with mortals, and it lifted him toward the lowest of the tree's branches. There, he drew even with the furled buds, and as he did, his eyes narrowed.

No mortal magic touched this tree; very little mortal magic was capable of this subtle infestation and influence over the form of living things. The magic that was there was deeply rooted, and it would express itself in the leaves, if only that. Reaching out, he grabbed a slender branch and snapped it off the tree.

Or he tried; the branch did not break. It stiffened, instead. The bark hardened, and the branch lengthened in an instant; Celleriant swiveled to the side before it pierced his chest; it nonetheless sheared through his tunic's left arm. Releasing the branch, he pushed himself back; the branch twisted as if it were an arm, as it followed, lashing out, supple where it bent. Once again, he dodged, but this time he felt the edge of the branch break skin.

It annoyed him. He coaxed the elemental air, and began to move as quickly as the anchored branch did; he was not yet ready to draw weapon against something as lowly as *a tree*. But the tree was not likewise constrained; the branches that faced Celleriant now shed all appearance of bark. This time, however, the buds burst into blossom, revealing leaves; they were a harsh, metallic red, livid and glowing even in the bright, cool sunlight.

The subtle aura of magic fled like clouds in a windstorm; in its place, the heart of the storm itself stood revealed. Celleriant's hair rose in fine strands as if electrified—and he was: this magic was ancient, wild. He understood what he faced mere seconds before the whole of the tree shifted its hundred arms and they converged on the spot where he stood suspended in midair.

The world was red; red and black. Buds burst, blossomed; leaves drew blood and grew from that sustenance. His blood, and he shed it because that was the price of carelessness. But he laughed, and his voice was like thunder in a sky so full of twisting limbs it was no longer clear or blue.

"Jewel, where are you going?" Devon's voice was at her back; she was sprinting. The halls weren't empty, but she'd never lost the ability to navigate crowds in an emergency; she could break her stride to pivot in order to avoid collision, and pick it up again smoothly. Angel could keep pace with her by moving in a similar fashion although he was larger. Avandar and Devon brought up the rear and she *knew* Avandar was less than happy about that position.

She took stairs two and three at a time, heading down, her palm skirting the surface of brass rails for balance. The manse's first floor was more crowded than the upper hall had been, and the gallery was worse still. People cursed her as they jumped to one side or another to avoid collision; she apologized without looking back.

Angel didn't ask where she was going; he followed. She was certain Devon and Avandar did the same. It didn't matter. By the time she could answer Devon's question, she was almost at the door that led to the Terafin grounds. She wasn't the only one. A handful of House Guards clanked their way toward the same doors from the opposite end of the hall. Armor had the advantage of weight and sound; people moved out of the way of the House Guards, and they didn't curse them in passage.

But she lifted her hand, palm out, and the guards slowed as they recognized the House Council crest she now wore. "Go," she said, pausing only for breath. "Summon Sigurne Mellifas. She's in the manse. Have her meet us in the gardens."

"Where, ATerafin?"

"She'll know," was the grim reply.

Jewel threw the doors open and ran out toward the grounds. She didn't have to look very hard to see where Celleriant was; he had cleared both ground and the height of the trees, wielding a sword that looked like barely contained lightning. Were it not for the sword, she might have missed sight of him, because what he now faced was infinitely worse: A black tree with leaves of scarlet and crimson, whose branches twisted in air as if they were limbs or tentacles.

"Avandar!"

He was there; the doors had slammed behind her, although the sound was distant and almost unremarkable. It wasn't the domicis who grabbed her shoulder, and it certainly wasn't Angel, who knew better; it was Devon.

"Jewel, what is that?"

The imperative to run deserted her; her legs were shaking. "It's a—it's a demon," she whispered, certain that she was wrong, but not certain why. It occurred to her, after the words had left her mouth, that he might have been referring to Celleriant, because Celleriant stood revealed in the heights. His hair was a white spill of something that seemed to gather and reflect light; his sword was pulsing like a pale, blue heart. He wore armor now, and he bore a shield; the black limbs that might once have been branches clattered audibly against it.

But even at this distance, Jewel could see his smile. It shouldn't have been possible, but she didn't doubt her vision; he was exultant in the way that only immortals could be, wild and unfettered.

Gardeners were running *toward* the manse, their tools carried in clenched fists as if they were weapons; their eyes were wide with both fear and purpose. They passed Jewel and her companions, heading straight for the glass doors; they paused only when they reached the House Guards, who had begun to spill onto the stone terrace. She heard their frantic babble, the syllables crashing and colliding in such a way that whole sentences were hard to distinguish.

But she saw Celleriant, and the rising black shadow. Drawing breath, she made her way down the stairs and onto the path that would lead her to them.

*   *   *

Stubbed toes and snarled hair made it clear that she needed to watch where she was going, but it was hard. She saw branches riven by sword and heard the clatter they made as they fell; she saw leaves—what might have been leaves—stiffen like tines, and she thought they broke skin, scraped armor. Walking while watching the heights, she ran into a slender lamppost, cursed in very liberal Torra, and looked back at the path again.

This time, she saw natural shadow in a shape that the grounds didn't usually contain, and she recognized the silhouette—in sunlight—of the Winter King. It moved and as it did, it gained solidity and form; she heard Devon's sharp intake of breath at her back.

Jewel.

Can you carry two?

He bowed his great antlered head; he was, to her surprise, amused.

"Angel," she said curtly, as the Winter King knelt on his forelegs, "get on."

Angel was more hers than anyone's; he looked dubious, but he didn't hesitate. He clambered—awkwardly—onto the sloping back of the great stag. Jewel climbed up behind him.

"He won't drop you," she shouted, as the Winter King rose and turned. "If he's willing to carry you at all, there's no way you can fall off."

"Jewel!" Devon cried. The second syllable was noticeably quieter than the first. The stag leaped forward on a path that should have been too narrow, and they were borne aloft.

Turning, cupping hands around her mouth, she shouted "Go back, Devon! Go back for the daggers—we'll hold it while we can!" She had no idea whether or not her words had carried, but she wasn't certain he'd need to hear them. Devon was pragmatic, practical. Practical enough, certainly, to trust the lives of companions to fate if necessary.

Jewel!

Join us, she told her domicis grimly, *as quickly as you can. I have no idea what he's facing, but it's—*

You said it was a demon.

It's not. And it is. It's— She shook her head; her hair flew at right angles.

Why, Avandar asked, *are you running toward it? Stay back, you fool.*

But back was gone as they approached what had once been a tree. The Winter King stopped before they reached its trunk; his hooves came to rest well away from the gnarled and exposed roots that lay between the artful construction of flower beds.

Above their heads, black branches swayed against the breeze, leaves now glittering like flat rubies. They reminded her of other leaves she had seen and taken, but these she would never have dared to touch.

"Let us down," she told the stag.

No. It is not yet safe.

"Then why in the hells did you bring us here?"

Look, Jewel. Look well. What, exactly, do you see?

She wanted to argue; she didn't. Short of throwing herself off his back, she couldn't. Instead, she did as bid: she looked at the tree.

This close, she could see the bark that had once enclosed it; she could see the ebony that underlay it, growing thicker as the minutes passed. The roots were darkest as they lay against the ground.

Winter King, she said grimly, *move. We're too close to the—*

She lost thought and the rest of the warning as the stones that lined—and made—pathways cracked; the Winter King leaped clear of the roots that broke free of their binding of earth and stone. They reared back like serpents readying to strike, and the Winter King lowered his head, his antlers both weapon and shield.

"Jay—"

"Hang on. Just—hang on."

She saw root and antler clash as the Winter King snapped his head up and away; the roots were attempting to snarl themselves around his tines. He lashed out with his hooves and she heard the crack of something far too solid. The landscape passed in a blur of black and green and gray; she tried to focus on the roots that were even now shaking themselves free in greater number.

It was the roots, she thought. The roots, not the branches; something was buried beneath the tree, and it had been absorbed.

Yes, the Winter King said, as she cupped hands around her mouth and shouted a single name. "Celleriant!"

Shearing the branches off seemed to cause no harm; they fell, and where they struck earth, they burrowed. Celleriant was wounded; he was angry. But the anger was not wild rage; it was akin to humiliation. He could not challenge this creature, this corruption of a tree that was barely full grown; it had no name, no voice, no status. It was an affront that it could injure him at all, but it had, and he felt the wounds—slight scratches, simple insignificant cuts, begin to burn.

But he heard the voice of Jewel Markess ATerafin beneath his feet.

"Not the branches! The roots, Celleriant!"

Fire cut across the height of the Winter King's antlers as Jewel shouted the words. Focused fire, it struck the tangled black roots. If proof were needed that these roots weren't entirely wood, the fire gave it; it bounced. Avandar rarely did anything as undignified as cursing; he was silent. She felt, rather than saw, his passing shadow as he approached the tree, skirting the ground by several feet. His flight wasn't Celleriant's flight, but it didn't matter.

"Avandar—the earth—"

"Not here," was his terse reply. "These lands are not a desert and you do not wish them to become one." Fire flew from his hands. Contained in the privacy of the Terafin grounds, it was technically legal; no writ would be required for the use of this much magic unless the House Council deemed it necessary. Jewel shook her head to clear it, amazed that she could even be thinking of bureaucracy at a time like this.

The tree cast little shadow, as if it was unwilling to part with even that much darkness. Avandar's second round of flame was slower, but no less focused, and it spread where it hit root; this time, it singed. The Winter King dodged; his hooves splintered roots when they were close to the ground. But they fell like shards or slivers and they were absorbed.

Above, Celleriant fought.

He heard Jewel's command. He understood what she desired, but it irked him. She couldn't imagine that this was beyond his understanding; she couldn't imagine that she, in her handful of mortal years, had seen more than he in his millennia. But the branches that fell lost form and shape, hitting the ground like a black rain that was quickly absorbed.

"The roots!" she shouted again.

Yes, if this were an ancient tree, it would be the correct form of attack, but that was impossible. Not here. He *knew* the ancient. He was of it. She was not. He wanted to tell her as much; he didn't. The Winter Queen had commanded him to protect—and follow—the mortal seer. Beneath him, secure on the back of the Winter King—one of only a handful to have survived, even in this lessened form—she still lived.

His shield drove him back as he blocked; the tree's branches had lost even the patina of what they had once been; they moved like snakes, coiling to strike, attempting to grasp and crush. He cut them down, shearing leaf from branch and branch from trunk. Beneath his feet fire rose in gouts; Viandaran had come, but he had not yet chosen to unleash the full force of his power.

It shouldn't have been required here, where mortals huddled like rabbits and cast a gray pall over everything they touched. But . . . *this* tree . . .

Sigurne Mellifas came last to the grounds, and she froze before the doors to the terrace were fully opened. Matteos was with her. He had become more stoic in his silences, but no less protective, as the years had passed, and his scars whitened as he saw what she saw. "Sigurne, wait," he said, but without much hope.

She gestured; the doors flew open with enough force to rattle glass. She offered no other response to his comment.

"Is that Meralonne?" Matteos demanded, squinting as he gazed into the sky over the Terafin grounds.

"No. He is still in the South."

"Then who?"

"At this distance, I cannot be certain; my eyes are not what they once were. Come, Matteos; follow." This was easier said than done; the lowest of the stairs that descended from the terrace were adorned with armored House Guards. They had unsheathed their weapons, but they had not advanced. Sigurne approved of this obvious caution; young men so seldom set aside their pride of position in favor of common sense.

She removed the heavy and easily recognized medallion that marked her as a member of the Order of Knowledge, and at that, mage-born. In her hands, it signified more: it made clear that she was the guildmaster. The House Guards did not, in theory, follow orders from any save the House Council or the regent, but theory often faltered in the face of the unknown and the obviously dangerous.

"Guildmaster Mellifas," one such guard said, bowing.

"I was summoned here at the command of Jewel ATerafin," she replied, giving him an authority upon which to pin obedience should an authority beyond her own be required.

"She's not here," he replied.

"No. She is, I fear, much closer to the danger." Lifting her hands, she passed them—obviously—over her eyes. "If you insist, Sentrus, I will take two guards, but no more. From here it is clear that swords are not our most effective weapon."

"You can see swords?"

"Just one," was her soft reply. "But if that sword is all but ineffective, nothing we wield will make any difference."

"Not nothing, Member Mellifas," a formal and familiar voice said. She turned. On the terrace, slightly—very slightly—out of breath, stood Devon ATerafin.

"Ah. You've brought weapons."

"I had one," was his grave reply, "at the behest of the Exalted. One, however, seemed insufficient."

"Keep your weapons, then," she replied, "and accompany us now."

He nodded.

Celleriant called the wild air and it woke enraged; like all wild things, it could be coaxed and cajoled, but it resisted a cage. He required a cage, now; he required its force as a weapon he could wield, not just as a landscape upon which he might stand and hold ground. The branches that attacked him did not increase in number; that much, at least, Viandaran's fire granted him. He whispered the only benediction that mattered: the name of the Winter Queen.

Then, gathering air, he shifted the position in which he held his shield, and unleashed the heart of the wind's fury. It could not strike him—although it desperately desired to do so—and chose instead to vent its rage on branches that twisted and moved; it flattened leaves, tore them from their slender, ebon moorings, and as it did, Celleriant dove forward, slicing a narrow path directly in front of himself. The shield was driven back into his chest as the tree attempted to do what the wind could not.

But nearer the trunk, the lashing branches were not so numerous; they were thicker, wider, and they moved less quickly. The leaves were the danger here; what the trunk lacked in flexibility, the leaves gained; they were launched like daggers, and embedded themselves across the length of his shield. He might have ignored them, otherwise, but to his consternation, they were not easily dislodged, and from their tips, red light began to spread across the shield's surface.

It wasn't—it shouldn't have been—possible. He raised his sword and swung it with a cry that even the howling wind couldn't dampen.

*   *   *

The Winter King's unexpected leap carried them much farther away from the base of the tree. But the distance didn't seem to faze the roots; they broke earth in a straight line between tree and the stag. Stones, dirt, and bulbs erupted above them. Reaching out, Jewel grabbed the tines of the stag's antlers; she cut her hand and cursed. Cursing, it seemed, was something that only the den did, when injured; Avandar, Celleriant, Kallandras, and Devon became utterly silent. But she needed that grip; she pulled herself over and around Angel, and balanced, like some street performer, at the base of the King's neck. There, feet as flat as she could make them, she looked at the tree. Not at Avandar, not at his fire, not at Celleriant or the sudden ferocious storm that whipped more dirt and debris up into the sky, but at the tree itself.

As if the ground was momentarily transparent, she could see its roots. They were spreading as she watched—twisting, breaking and re-forming as they sought to gain ground beneath them. She shook her head. Not those, she thought, but the deep roots, the roots that never saw sun or felt wind. How far down did those travel? What did they now draw sustenance from?

She could almost see the answer, but it was insubstantial, like shadow in fog; it had a shape that she couldn't discern, but must.

Something was wrong. Something worse than a tree that was no longer a tree breaking earth and sky in an attempt to kill. She had called it demonic, but no. Its power was red and black, yes—but it was like a tidal wave or earthquake; it belonged here.

Impossible, two voices said, as one: Avandar and the Winter King.

She staggered as something struck the Winter King in the side; he leaped, spilling blood. The blood wasn't absorbed as easily by the ground as the fallen black limbs that might once have been branches

Avandar—

Her words were lost as she tumbled. Angel joined her; the Winter King was yards away. Yards away and safe. Around Angel and Jewel, roots rose like a thicket, exposing not leaves, but thorns.

"Sigurne, if you please?" Devon said, voice low.

Sigurne understood both what he asked and why: she could see Jewel ATerafin, alongside a single member of her den, as the ground shifted to expose ebony vines with jagged thorns. She gestured in silence; Devon flew. He was not the master of his own flight, and in truth, he was ill accustomed to cooperation with the magi; his landing was rough, and it was off by a few inches. He took the brunt of his weight with bent knees, one dagger in each hand.

"Angel!" He held one dagger out, and Angel, no fool, took it almost before Jewel had turned. He retained the second; if the daggers did their work here, he'd have time to give one to Jewel.

Jewel shouted a warning; Devon's body obeyed. He threw himself to the right, landing to one side of a large, moving vine; into this, he thrust the dagger he held. The runes along the flat of the blade blazed with sudden, golden light, and the light grew so bright it seemed white. Something in the distance screamed in mingled rage and pain; the vine scorched and blackened. Devon released the blade and unsheathed another, while Angel struck a different vine.

Jewel stood between them, watching the ground.

"ATerafin," Devon said, more sharply than he intended. He caught her shoulder with his free hand as she knelt. Before he could pull her to her feet, Angel caught his wrist. They exchanged a single, silent glance—a brief one—before Devon released her. She hadn't even looked up.

"It's been a while since you've worked with her," Angel said softly. "If you intend to do it again, remember: Don't touch her, and don't interfere if she's not in obvious danger."

Devon looked pointedly at the smoking ruins of blackened vines that encircled them; Angel's grimace granted Devon the point. Angel turned; enough time had been spent on advice. He watched the broken ground as Sigurne Mellifas at last approached.

"I think it safe, for the moment," she told Devon. "At least on the ground."

Jewel bent further and laid both of her palms against the exposed earth.

Celleriant could not dislodge the slender spikes that had attached themselves to his shield; had he time, had he a moment's respite, it would have been a simple task. But this, this slow decay, was something he had not seen since—

He roared, his voice like thunder.

The tree shuddered. He flew up and away, gaining speed above the wild air's bitter protests; the branches that now sought to follow tore his cape, no more. As he gained speed, he gained height, divesting himself of gravity. Only at the height of the tree did he swerve and retrieve all of gravity in a second. He fell.

Falling, he sundered branches with sword, cracked them with shield; he accepted the stinging cuts of slender, ruby leaves. They followed him as he plummeted, but they curved in on themselves in a rush, twining and tangling, one over the other, until there was no way back.

But he had no intention of escape now. He struck the very trunk of the tree with the edge of his sword, and he held nothing back; he had no hope of surviving what followed if he showed any hesitance at all.

Jewel.

The tree's roots froze in place. Only the vines that had encircled Jewel were dead. Jewel lifted her face and blinked rapidly as Devon and Angel swam into view. She rose on unsteady feet.

Avandar, where is Celleriant? What has he done?

I can no longer see him, the domicis replied. *What has happened to the roots?*

I don't know. Whatever force animated them, it's withdrawn.

Gone?

No. She began to walk toward the tree. Angel cleared his throat.

"It's safe," she told him, without looking back.

"ATerafin."

Jewel stopped at the sound of a new voice.

"Sigurne?"

Sigurne Mellifas nodded. She was accompanied by Matteos Corvel, who looked much, much grimmer than she.

"It's Winter magic," Jewel told the Guildmaster of the Order of Knowledge.

"Yes." Sigurne lifted one guttered dagger.

"I thought Winter magic was demonic magic."

Sigurne was silent. It was the wrong type of silence. "Sigurne?"

"Why do you think this is not demonic in nature, ATerafin?"

Jewel looked up to the tree's height; it wasn't a question she could answer immediately—if at all. "Tell me about Winter magic, Sigurne. If it's not forbidden."

"It is not forbidden, but I have very little to say. It is not a mortal magic, and it is not a branch of magic that we can either develop or teach with any reliability. Those among my magi who are interested in Winter—and Summer—magics are also those who study lore and legend.

"There is a reason that the daggers in Devon ATerafin's possession are consecrated by the Exalted."

"Winter and Summer magics were the forms used by gods?"

"So we believe."

"Meralonne can use Summer magic."

Sigurne's silence shifted and changed. After a long, long pause she said, "So, I believe, can the young man who is now fighting in the air above us."

"Avandar, can you—" Jewel stopped. Took a deep breath. "Never mind. I see the Winter King."

He came across what might have been a fairy-tale clearing to reach her, and he knelt at once on both slender forelegs, bowing his crown of tines. He was wounded in several places, something she had never seen.

They will heal, he told her, in a tone of voice that forbade both concern and questions. *Climb, Jewel.*

How long had it been since he had experienced Summer?

Celleriant cleaved bark that was no longer bark, the edge of his sword sparking as it struck. Around him, leaves flew, cutting skin, hair, scraping armor. But the branches could no longer reach him; he stood within the heart of the trunk, in a gap made by the weight, and the force, of his sudden downward plunge.

How long had he lived in the lee of Winter, with its bitter, bitter ice and its beautiful, deadly cold? He knew Winter. But he remembered Summer, and the memory of the Arianni had no equal.

The edge of his sword began to shimmer as blue light made way for slow and certain gold; he spoke words that existed for one season alone, and he spoke them now in the secrecy of darkness and the imminence of death. Cold answered. Cold, a reminder that Winter reigned; Summer's time had passed and might never come again.

His laughter was wild and angry.

"Is that the best you can do? Think you that a simple passing regret has the power to destroy a Prince of the Arianni?" The hilt of his sword was warm and sticky with his blood; the leaves were now attempting to sever his arm at the wrist. They understood the nature of the danger, but not the nature of the sword itself, and he drove it down, plunging it into the growing shadow, cracking ice as he did. Black ice.

Once, he had plunged sword into white ice, burying it to the hilt, as he stood before the Winter face of Ariane. The ice had cracked only an inch from the buried blade, no more, as if making a statement. She could swallow the whole of his self with but a moment's hesitation, a moment's discomfort. She could contain him.

She was the only being that could. She had walked the world when the gods were young, and it had not destroyed her. But she could own it, break it, build it; she could destroy and she could create. On her own ground, there was no force that was her equal. Child and kin to those gods, she had been born, breathing, into the world; she could not forsake it.

But she had not been the only such child born.

Ice cracked like a brittle facade. Liquid, dark and thick, some mix of sap and unnatural blood, spilled from that fleshless wound. He began to sink into it as the leaves buzzed like insects near his open eyes.

Jewel stiffened. "Avandar."

"ATerafin."

"I need to go to Celleriant."

He gave her a familiar, questioning look. Sadly, what it questioned was her sanity. "That is not, at this moment, possible. Not for you."

"Can you go?"

"I could, yes. Not without injury."

"Could you command him?"

That look again. He didn't bother to reply.

"We have ten minutes, Avandar. Ten at the outside."

"And if we fail? If we choose not to take that risk?"

"We'll lose him." Her voice was flat and hard.

His was nonexistent.

Avandar.

You underestimate Lord Celleriant.

No, I don't.

"My duties as your domicis are focused on your well-being and your safety, ATerafin. Perhaps Member Mellifas might aid you. I, however, cannot."

Jewel bit back an angry stream of Torra, the den's cursing language of choice. She turned to Sigurne, a woman who now made her Oma look young. But before she could ask—if she even could—the Winter King said, again, *Jewel, climb.*

This time, she did as he asked. Angel started toward her; she shook her head. He turned to Devon, said something low. Devon nodded and something passed between their hands. Then her den-kin joined her, and not until he was firmly seated on the Winter King's back for a second time did the great stag rise.

I serve you, he told Jewel, as the muscles beneath her tensed. *But I am not your slave; you are not master of my will.*

Was she?

Of course. She was—and is—absolute; it is her nature. It is not, and will never be, yours; you are subject to the flaws and imperfections of both change and age. But in those flaws, ATerafin, there is power and a brilliance of a type that cannot be found in the eternal.

As he spoke, he ran, the cadence of his measured words a counterpoint to the urgency of his stride. The tree was not far from where they had stood in silent witness to the events unfolding above them, but Celleriant was; he was somewhere at the height of the tree, and they were too close to its base.

That changed. *You must hold on, now, ATerafin. Tell your leige. He must hold, as well.*

You can't carry us?

Here? I can. But only if you are willing.

His words made no sense at all; she was on his back, wasn't she? He was taking her exactly where she wanted—and needed—to go. What, in that, implied that she wasn't willing? She was becoming accustomed to a total lack of sense in the world. Sense was something small, hard, practical; it was human. It was mortal. Sense was her Oma.

Yes, he said, as he rose up on his hind legs at the base of the trunk. *Sense is practical. How many times, ATerafin, have you walked up the side of a wall?*

It wasn't, as Jewel quickly discovered, a rhetorical question. She grabbed the Winter King's tines, and felt Angel's arms surround her on either side as he scrabbled to do the same. He was silent; she was shouting. Wind tore the words away, made them nothing but a sensation in her throat and on her lips. She tightened her legs around the Winter King's girth and felt her inner thighs slide inches as he continued to run.

To run up the trunk, while the wind dropped leaves. Those leaves were deadly; she closed her eyes as they scratched the sides of her cheeks, drawing beads of blood. Behind her, Angel finally let loose with a curse, but he clung to the tines of the King, just as she did. *Kalliaris,* she thought absurdly.

It is not in her hands, ATerafin, but yours.

Her hands were slipping. But, eyes closed, she could feel the Winter King's muscles beneath her legs. She could feel—and hear—the wind's howl. She could imagine that she was riding in the middle of a flash flood in the desert, while above, the storm took the form and shape of a great dragon. The Winter King was willing to carry her now; he'd carried her then, as well—and for a similar reason.

But that ride had been effortless compared to this one.

Yes. But if you look, Jewel, if you look, seer, you will discern the path I follow, even in this. I cannot run pathless, nor can the Wild Hunt.

You go where she leads.

Yes. But she is a pathfinder, Jewel. If there exists a way, the Winter Queen will find it, no matter how narrow or dangerous the journey. This is a gift given to those who call the Hunt.

Celleriant—

He rides. It is not the same.

But the Winter Queen—

Oh, Jewel. Ariane has run those roads, just as I have run them.

Without thought, Jewel replied, *Celleriant will kill you if he ever hears you say that.*

Yes. But he and I do not speak. Why do you think she gathers the fallen and transforms them?

. . . I don't know.

She cannot be weak, was his soft reply. *But she is what she is, in its totality. What her mounts see, we see as mutes. What we hear, we cannot betray to her enemies.*

You can talk to me.

Yes, and that is the wonder, Jewel; how often do you think she has ceded her personal mount to one who is merely mortal?

Jewel had no answer. Although she was mortal—or perhaps because she was mortal—the presence of the Winter Queen was death—but a death so beautiful, a death so all encompassing it made life seem pointless and insignificant in comparison. Jewel had seen gods in the flesh in the Between, but it was Ariane whose face was rooted so deeply within her that she had only to close her eyes to recall the Winter Queen in all her deadly glory.

She opened her eyes to escape that memory, and regretted it; the air was red and black. But Ariane's gift was twined around Jewel's wrist, and as

Jewel's sleeves flew in the wind, she saw it: it glowed. Strands of hair that should have been all but invisible to the eye glittered as if they were fine spun crystal; one was blue, one was gold, and one was white. They flashed like miniature lightning, and when she could see again, the world had become . . . white.

The Winter King ran across a white desert, his breath leaving clouds in a trail.

The ice is thin.

Celleriant looked up into a sky of dead branches, dead leaves. Beyond them, he could see the lingering ghosts of the ancient forests that had once given voice to a world. He had—in a youth so long past him only memory retained its fragments—loved those forests. He had loved them as he had loved nothing else, although he would learn how shallow that love had been, in time.

Beneath the bowers of singing trees, their voices attenuated and slow to build, he had traced the networks of streams, brooks, and rivers, learning to walk on the surface of the rippling water without actually getting wet. Had he fallen? Yes. Many times. As a child, it had little troubled him.

Had he stumbled? Fallen? He was wet, now. Wet, in the warmth of Summer, was a benison. But the air was chill and cold—how else could there be ice? He tried to lift himself out of the water and realized that there was no riverbank in this place; no rocks on which to balance his weight. There was no grass.

Those were fragments of youth; he yearned for them as one can only yearn for lost things. What had silenced the forest's voice? Ah. Winter. Where had he been?

Ice cracked as he moved. It was thin. It slowed him. His breath rose in a wreath, like steam or fog. He saw his name swirl in the eddies before the wind carried it away.

The ice was thin, yes—but it hardened as he walked. It deepened beneath his feet. He slowed, then stilled, listening for familiar voices. Hearing none. Or hearing ghosts. What had happened to the forests?

At the height of the tree, the sun shone without warmth—but it was Henden; Jewel told herself it was because it was Henden. Her arms were red with cold, her hands shaking as they clung. Angel's hands, resting now almost on top of hers, were the only source of heat; the Winter King himself might have been a ghost. A solid ghost. She felt his fur as barding, his musculature as iron. She was momentarily afraid, but reminded herself, with what heat she could muster, that she had demanded to come here.

Yes, he said. Just that.

The landscape was strange. She knew she was riding up the trunk of the tree, but she saw the tree as horizontal. She saw it, bark covered in ice and snow, the height of its branches frozen and glittering in Winter sun. Its leaves were now encased; their color couldn't be discerned. As the Winter King continued to run, the snow thickened and widened until it formed a vast plain, glittering and cold, out of which only icy branches grew. Gravity reasserted itself in the normal direction.

You were not wrong, the Winter King said.

About what?

The trouble began in the roots. But as with any tree, what the roots touch travels to the branches if the tree is not to perish. We will find something buried there, in the end.

Given the gardeners, Jewel thought this statement more prophetic than historical. Especially considering the funeral and the dignitaries who'd been invited to attend.

But the imperative of the funeral—of the respect that was Amarais Handernesse ATerafin's due—had receded for a moment. Jewel held onto the Winter King and stared straight ahead as he ran. The tree seemed to go on forever. To the left and right, branches encased in ice formed patchy walls. Ahead, those branches were all that remained, as trunk gave way, at last, to the tree's crown.

At the heart of those many branches stood Celleriant; he, like the leaves, seemed encased in ice. He was frozen, but she could see the bright, burning blue of his sword.

He remembered now.

Celleriant, Celleriant. Long days spent forming the syllables lent them strength and a majesty that he did not, perhaps, deserve. He turned, or tried. His hands were encumbered and heavy; perhaps this was why he could not climb.

The Winter comes, Celleriant, and with it sleep.

You will sleep, Ancient?

All things which know life know sleep.

Am I not alive?

The rustle of laughter touched his upturned face. The leaves were falling. *You are alive.*

But I do not sleep.

Do you not?

No.

We pity you, Celleriant. There is peace in sleep. There is a promise of rest. It is earned. We grow into it, year by year. How is it that you do not sleep?

I don't know. There's too much to see, Ancient. Too much to learn. If I sleep your sleep, things will age and die before I wake again.

But new things will be born beneath our bowers. We are content. Tell us, Celleriant, if you do not sleep, how do you dream?

He had been young, then. Youth was its own country, its own terrain; the geography of folly could still be beautiful. *I dream*, he had told them, so defensively.

Of what?

Of life. I dream of the wind. I dream of flight. I dream of the earth and its mountainous heights. I dream of my kin, no matter how distant they are. One day, Ancient, I will find a calling and a duty.

So soon?

I have my sword, he'd said with pride. *I have my shield. I have called them myself, and they are of me.*

But they have no place in the forest.

He said nothing.

And the things of which you speak are not dreams, Celleriant. They are your bright and quick imaginings. They are figments of your desire and your will. They are the crown of the waking hours. But they are not dreams.

Then I want none of your dreams, Ancient.

No, indeed, although in time you may come to them anyway. We must part for now, for you will not hear our voices, and we will be unable to hear yours. We will wake again, Celleriant. In the turn of seasons, we will wake, we will be renewed. We will look for you in the height of the Summer; that is our promise.

The promised Summer had come, but Celleriant dwelled no longer in those ancient forests, for with Winter had come war, and with war, the Winter Queen.

* * *

It was Winter now. The coming of Winter presaged so many things: endings. Beginnings. He saw the ghosts of ancient forests and heard their tremulous voice and he felt an ache and a desire that became, for one moment, the whole of his desire for Summer. Winter without end was silent, still, cold. There was glory in it, there was majesty, and there was death. Not all things that Wintered survived to see Summer's return.

The water was just beneath his shoulders now; the cold had slowed the river's force, but not enough. He was heavy. He could not recall ever feeling so heavy. He tried to swim, but his hands were still full and they stung. He looked down; beneath the water, warped and wavering in his vision, were two things: a sword, a shield.

They have no place in the forest.

He struggled with their weight.

Chapter Six

THE BLUE LIGHT of Celleriant's sword began to flicker as the Winter King slowed.

"Can you take the branches down?" Jewel asked.

It would not help him.

"I don't care. It would help me." She started to dismount and Angel tightened both of his arms, trapping her between them.

"What in the Hells are you doing?" he all but shouted in her ear.

She shook her head as if to clear it. She felt the Winter King's presence; he was waiting. Watching. "I need to get down," she finally said.

If you do, you must leave your companion with me.

"If you get off his back, you're going to fall a lot farther than you think!" Angel's hands were white; his words were almost a hiss. "Jay!"

She pulled one hand off the Winter King's antlers, signing. Angel, however, didn't sign back; he held tight. "What do you see, Angel?"

"What do you mean, what do I see?"

"Exactly what I said. Tell me." Her voice was low. It must have transmitted the urgency she felt, because he drew a longer, more measured breath.

"I see what used to be the tree. It's black, and it doesn't look much like a tree anymore; its branches look like vines. The leaves are blood red. Down is a long way away," he added. "Don't look." He knew how she felt about heights.

"You don't see snow?"

Silence. After it had grown uncomfortable, Angel said, "I see Lord Celleriant. He's—he's trapped."

"Trapped how? Angel—I can't see what you see."

"Have you tried?" He was always perceptive—often at exactly the wrong time.

"No. No, I haven't tried—if I do, I'm sure I'll stop seeing what I *do* see. And I need it. I need it to do what I have to do. Tell me—what do you see?"

"He's impaled. He's impaled, Jay. His upper arms, his left thigh, the right rib cage. His eyes are open—but he's not looking at anything."

"His sword?"

"It's there. There are vines around it, but they're not touching the blade—only his wrist."

"Shield?"

"Same, I think. I can't see his wrist on that side."

Jewel lifted the hand with which she'd signed; it was the hand on which the twined hair of the Winter Queen was knotted. "What—what do you see here?"

His breath cut. "I can't—I can't take it off you."

"No. You'll fall. That's not what I asked, anyway. Angel—what do you see?"

"It's glowing. It's glowing—but Jay, I'd swear it was alive—it's . . . crawling. Squirming."

Jewel nodded and exhaled. "Let me go," she told him.

"I can't—"

"That wasn't a request. Celleriant is trapped, Angel—we'll lose him."

"You're certain that's a bad thing?"

"No. No, I'm not. But while he's here, I can't just surrender him. You need to hold on."

He was den. He hated to let go of her, but he knew and understood the tone of her voice; he trusted her, and the trust was stronger than his fear. "I will. Don't take too long," he added.

She laughed. It was the wrong laugh. But she let go of the Winter King's antlers completely, and after a tense minute, she unlocked almost numb legs.

Will you take him back down? she asked.

I will not let him fall unless he desires it.

She swung herself clumsily off his back. Her stomach lurched; she stumbled. For just a minute she felt the air rush toward her back, but it was only wind. It threw her hair into her eyes, where pieces of bark and ice joined it. Against the snow, she saw the Winter King's shadow; she stood in it a moment as if it were an anchor. His hooves didn't break the snow's crust. Her feet did. The relative difference in their weight didn't matter.

Maybe gravitas did.

The Winter King chuckled and nudged her shoulder with his flecked muzzle. *Not gravitas, Jewel, or you would already be lost. Not as I am,* he added. *That will never be your fate. In my youth, Jewel ATerafin, I would have said you wouldn't last a day.*

Yet you are here. Go. I will keep your Angel as safe as he allows.

She began to walk toward Celleriant. Beneath her feet, beneath the snow, the ground was solid. Her knees were no longer visible, and her skin stung with cold. A feral, small smile touched her lips and the corners of her eyes; her den would have recognized it. They'd wintered in the holdings. They knew cold could kill; it was a fact of life.

Stripped of wealth and the privilege of wealth, anyone could die in the Winter.

Celleriant.

Ice covered branching vines, things twisted so far out of shape they might never have been part of a tree at all. But they weren't a wall. There were gaps, and for thorns, red leaves, as covered in ice as everything else. Jewel caught a branch in shaking hands, ready to leap forward—or back—if it lunged. It was frozen in place, in shape. The moving mass of thorns below might have been a bad dream.

And this? she thought, snorting. Was this a *good* dream?

No, ATerafin, the Winter King said. *It is simply a dream. It is not even your dream. But it is strong. It is old. If you will it, I will carry you back to your kin. Pass beyond those branches, and I cannot guarantee that I will be able to save you.*

"I can't even guarantee that I'll be able to get past them," she said, uncertain of how far the spoken word would carry. Here, in this grim, vertical winterscape, the Winter King's voice was disturbing; she wasn't sure why. If he knew, he didn't tell her, and she concentrated on two things: the winding, cutting maze of branches and the man—if he was that—who stood suspended at its heart. His sword was dying slowly, like a candle that had reached not only the end of wick, but the end of wax as well. Candle stubs, on the other hand, had never been so cold or perfect in their final, sputtering moments. Arianni Lord, he was beautiful, the red of his blood like the delicate stroke of a Maker's brush—larger, more perfect, than life.

Jewel began to crawl over and under the looping curves of branches as if each were a miniature arch or groove. Leaves' edges, blunted by ice, scraped against her exposed skin. Reaching out, she pushed them away. Some snapped off in her hand, the stems were so brittle. She brushed them off and kept moving, wishing she had chosen to wear different clothing. Her shoes weren't meant for this weather, and she'd followed the imperative of instinct out the doors without bothering to grab a coat. Cursing in Torra, she ran into a snarl of branches, and began to work her way through them. They didn't grab her. They didn't cut her. But they only barely moved, and she was straining.

Avandar.

Silence.

She was used to his silences; she could've written screeds about them. But this silence had none of Avandar in it.

He cannot hear you, Jewel, the Winter King said.

Why not? You can.

Yes. I am here. He is not. I believe your Angel can hear the Warlord; the Warlord is not pleased.

Later, she'd ask him where he was. Or where she was. Now, she forced her way through the last of the branches and discovered that they grew at the lip of a small outcropping. She almost fell and reached in a panic for the curved limbs she'd been cursing so loudly. Breathing quickly enough to make her throat raw, she looked down. It was only ten feet. No, probably a little less, given how she felt about height. But it was a straight drop, a sudden plunge, and it reminded her that it wasn't height she hated—it was falling.

She looked across at Celleriant. He stood both above the ice and almost encased in it; he wasn't moving. She wasn't certain he needed to breathe, but if he did, he was in trouble, because he didn't appear to be breathing either.

His sword flickered. The intervals between light and its lack grew as she watched, her eyes unblinking. When they started to sting, she blinked; tears ran down her cheeks, but these tears didn't bother her.

"Celleriant!"

She hadn't expected an answer, because she was almost certain he couldn't hear a word she was saying. But she tried again, and a third time. There wasn't a fourth, not immediately. Instead, sliding down the edge of one vine, she took a deep breath and let go.

*　　*　　*

The ice was hard. It was hard, it was flat, it was cold, but ice was like that. She found her footing, wobbling on one knee. She'd tensed too much before the drop and had bruised or pulled something—but as long as she could stand and walk, it didn't matter. She stumbled, righted herself, and found momentum. It carried her to where Celleriant stood.

His feet were mired in ice; she couldn't distinguish them from the frozen water itself. She didn't try. She shouted his name a fourth time, in the faint hope sheer volume could crack the thin ice around his shoulders and his neck. No luck.

Celleriant, where are you?

No answer, but she didn't expect one. She looked up at his face. The difference in their heights was less pronounced because she was standing on the ice and he was partially beneath its surface; she looked at his eyes.

It was her turn to freeze. She had never liked Celleriant. He was everything that she'd always assumed—as an orphan in one of the poorest holdings in the city—nobility would be: cold, arrogant, completely devoid of humanity.

His first act, his first interaction with her, had been to attempt to drive her from where she stood in the open road. But it was an ancient road, a wild one; she had known what she fought for, and the road had responded. Celleriant couldn't force her to move, no matter what he rode or what he wielded; he had been unable to touch her at all, which no one, Jewel included, could have predicted. He had failed the command of the Winter Queen.

And the price for his failure?

To serve Jewel ATerafin. She hadn't wanted him. She didn't want him now. His suggestion that he casually slaughter—with Avandar's help—every living person in the manse had enraged her; she hadn't been in a mood that black for as long as she could remember. She knew he'd meant it. That was never going to change, because he wasn't mortal.

But he'd obeyed her furious denial. Jewel had learned the hard, harsh way that obedience was better than nothing. She'd had Duster, after all. But Duster had wanted the den. She'd been afraid of what she wanted, but she'd wanted it *anyway*. Celleriant?

No. Never.

Why had she taken Duster? Why had she worked so hard to keep her?

Because she'd needed Duster. In the end, she'd needed her. Maybe need and love had been so entwined Jewel hadn't been able to tell them apart.

She'd been younger then, and no question, she'd loved Duster as family. As kin. She could never love Celleriant. But she could need him. She knew she did need him. She'd accepted that sometime between their first meeting and this one.

What she hadn't considered then was that this icy, arrogant, inhuman immortal might need anything of his own; he'd always seemed above need, beyond it. But his eyes were wide with pain and longing, his lips thin with them. She'd never expected to see vulnerability from this Lord, and seeing it, wished she hadn't. Like everything else about him, it was larger than life; brighter, harsher, deeper.

He would sink into despair and loss and be extinguished, and at this moment—only this moment—the thought of that hurt her.

Be wary, Jewel, the Winter King said.

Of what? He's frozen, he's trapped—this is the only time he's ever been harmless.

He will not thank you for what you witness, was the Winter King's reply.

I'm not likely to rub his face in it.

You are not capable of dissembling in a reasonable or intelligent fashion. Do you think he will not know? Tread carefully, ATerafin.

She snorted a cloud of hanging white mist in response.

You understand what he cannot be. Do not forget this. Do not tell yourself a different story and believe somehow that it will become the truth; there is—for you—as much danger in that as there is in the demon kin.

But people *did* change. Not everything, and not all at once, and not as much as either you or they hoped they could—but they did.

Be wary.

This time she didn't answer. Instead, she reached out with both palms and touched Celleriant's face. Her hands were warm—and cooling quickly—and ice became water at her touch. His expression was still frozen, but there was none of the chill she usually associated with him in it.

Celleriant.

His arms moved. His hands fell—shield hand, sword hand. How, given the ice, she didn't know, couldn't say. But it sent a shock through her, a sharp pain that felt and tasted like fear. Fear was anathema.

She knew he was going to drop his sword and shield. She knew, as strongly, that he mustn't; that they mustn't break ice. They'd sink without a trace. He might remain standing, encased, but in any way that mattered, he'd be dead. She let her hands drop away from his shining face, and watched as water once again began to freeze.

Jewel—

She caught the sword as his fingers finally loosened their grip. The shield was entangled somehow around his forearm; he'd probably have to work a little to get it free, and work seemed beyond him at the moment. It was certainly beyond Jewel, because the hilt grew thorns—burning thorns. She cried out, but the cry had syllables to shape it; they were all Torra. The sword didn't want to be handled.

Certainly not by her.

It figured. Even frozen in despair, Celleriant was a snob; she was merely mortal; she was unworthy. And if he wanted to tell her that, she was fine with it—but he had to move his own lips. He had to move his butt out of its frozen, standing throne, and take the sword back on his own. She stumbled across ice, her knee still throbbing, the blade wobbling against surface and scratching a very loping trail in her wake. The sword was *heavy*.

Celleriant.

He looked up. It was a slow, steady movement. He was shaking, and strove to hide it. "Lady."

She wore Winter armor, but her visor was raised, and her hair trailed across her shoulders, regardless; she wore a cape of midnight blue, edged in silver. She bore a sword and a shield, and they shone with a white, white light, like the harshest of snows.

"You have come to offer me your service." Her voice, like her sword, was snow; her eyes were silver. Around her, armored men moved on their restive mounts; he was aware that they spoke. But the only voice he could hear was hers.

"Of what value is your service," she continued coldly, "when you are without even the humblest of weapons?"

Here, in the heart of the Green Deepings, the Winter was strong. Celleriant did not—could not—rise. "I have a sword, Lady. And a shield. I will be your weapon and your wall."

"I see neither. Have you misplaced them?" She glanced above his head then, her eyes rising to the silent bower of branches high above her face.

This was his forest. This was his home. It was dark and shrouded now, but surely Summer waited? He glanced at his empty hands. He heard the words of the ancient trees. There was no place in the forest for those weapons.

But he had summoned them. He had fashioned them. He had called them, and in the end, they had come. They were hers, even if they were absent; they had *always* been hers; he understood that the moment he had first laid eyes on her, although he had always been aware of her presence.

He called them now, in defiance.

He called them in fear.

But his hands remained empty.

She had no mercy in her; she was Winter, and she was absolute. Turning to her host, she motioned them forward; they spared him a single glance, no more. The hooves of their mounts left marks in the perfect surface of snow.

Ariane. Ariane. Ariane.

"What is your name?"

He stared at her. He opened his mouth. He could not remember being young, but he knew he was young here, now; he was callow, inexperienced. He could not bear even the weight of her momentary inspection, her icy disapproval. Yet he had yearned for it. He had yearned for it, even in Summer, when the voice of the forest had been at its strongest and warmest, and the air was filled with sound.

What is your name? Where is your name?

He could not rise. He could not move. He could not speak. In horror, in the depth of a humiliation he had never conceived of, he watched as the Winter Queen's expression froze.

Her eyes widened, and silver spilled like blood into the air. She said—she spoke—a single word of denial as she stiffened—and shattered.

Silent, he watched as shards flew to the right and left of Jewel ATerafin.

In her hand, burning like blue light, he saw his sword. He stumbled to his feet in sudden panic. The feeling was so visceral he might have been young again—a reminder that reminiscences elided the truth of youth.

"Wake up," she said sharply, her voice rough and unpleasant. "You'll die of—of exposure." Her words made no sense, and her grip on the sword would have pained him even if the sword had been a cold, dead slab of tempered metal. "Your shield is on your arm, if you can still see your arm. Celleriant, damn you, *look at where you are*. Look. *See it.* Your sword is going to bleed me to death while you stand there." She jabbed at air with his sword for emphasis, as if she could make punctuation purely physical.

He stared at her for a long, cold moment, and then he straightened, looking past her, looking past the blue edge of his sword. "ATerafin."

"Yes." She walked toward him as if drawn—or dragged. He held out a hand. "Give me your word that you'll hold onto it this time, or I'm not giving it back."

"You will find that very, very costly."

She snorted. It was a graceless, foolish sound. "Does it matter?"

"Pardon?"

"Does it matter how costly it'll be? You dropped it. I caught it before it hit ice."

"You do not understand the nature of that sword."

"No. But I understand what would have happened to you if I hadn't. Do you?"

He looked around at the bitter, broken landscape. After a pause, he said, "Yes. I . . . did not understand the nature of the danger."

And she had.

For just a moment he saw her as the scion—the diminished and undignified scion—of the ancient seers of the long dead Cities of Man. It was seldom that he chose to remember either their significance or their power; he did so now. She had been called seer-born by Viandaran, but this was the first time Celleriant had ever been convinced that she was—that she could be—a power in her own right.

In her bumbling way, she had been honest; her hand was bleeding. Her blood trailed down her wrist and across her sleeves; it also trailed down the hilt of the sword to the blade itself, where it evaporated.

She could hold his sword. She could not wield it, of course, but Celleriant doubted that she was capable of wielding any sword that was not wrought for imbeciles. Yet mortal men had died for daring to simply touch the hilt of his blade in the past. His own kin could not approach the blade as she had—although perhaps they were unwilling to pay its price.

"Yes, ATerafin. I give you my word that I will hold on to the sword. I will not let it drop here. I will never," he added softly, "be parted from it again."

She exhaled, losing color, but also losing the exaggerated posture of human anger. She pried her fingers from the sword's hilt; he saw that her knuckles had whitened and her skin was almost blue. He took the sword with care and frowned as he examined only its edge; in the gleaming light of this false Winter, its color had shifted almost imperceptibly. No one but Celleriant would notice; no one save perhaps Ariane herself.

"That is not the way," he told her coldly, "to blood this blade."

"You're welcome." She started to say more—she never seemed to be short of the babble that mortals so prized—but stopped herself. "So . . . do you know where we are?"

"I have some idea, yes."

"Good. Can you get us out of here?"

He stared at her as if she'd just asked him to cut off his own arm—or worse. It was an expression with which she was regrettably familiar, but not on his face. She laughed; she couldn't help herself. Her laughter didn't noticeably improve his mood.

"Do you mean to imply that you came here without *any* knowledge of where we now are?"

"Imply? No. If you want, I'll say it outright: I have no idea where we are."

"How did you arrive here?"

"On the back of the Winter King, if you must know. If it makes you feel any better, Ariane didn't specifically tell you to keep me alive."

"I cannot discharge the duties I was charged with if you are dead," he replied.

"Or if you are?"

He raised a pale brow. "My death would be considered an acceptable reason for failure."

She snorted. "Do none of your people have any sense of humor?"

His smile was slender and very cold. "We do."

"You win. Tell me where we are?"

"In a dream."

"A nightmare?"

"If you prefer."

"Do we have any control over the shape the dream takes?"

"Dreams are not my specialty, ATerafin. Do you normally exert that control over your own?"

"No. But mine can't kill me." She glanced down at her injured hand. "And I'm betting when we get out of this one, I'm still going to be bleeding."

He nodded as if the blood was inconsequential. "Come. Follow. Follow closely."

"Why?"

"The heart of the dream is waking."

Jewel looked at the mostly frozen water; from there, she looked up to where the growth of vines overhung what was apparently a small basin. "I came that way," she finally said, pointing.

He frowned. "Through the vines?"

"There wasn't any other way to reach you. *I* can't fly."

"No more can I, now." He began to walk, and his steps were apparently heavy enough to fracture the ice's surface. "Mortal dreams, like most mortal power, are echoes of the truth. Mortals can conceive of greatness, but seldom achieve it. Your dreams are different. You touch what is there—but not, if Viandaran's comments are true—deliberately. You stumble; you are mostly, but not entirely, blind."

"Nonetheless, you could travel here."

Jewel hesitated, and then lifted her wrist. Around it, the strands of Ariane's hair had thickened into a distinctive bracelet. Artisans might have crafted it.

Celleriant glanced at its twining strands. He even lifted a hand to touch them, but stopped short and pulled back. "I see. I will not even say that you do not understand the magnitude of her gift, ATerafin—but rather, that you are beginning to understand it." He shook his head and a smile—one that was neither cold nor cruel—touched the corners of his mouth and his perfect, gray eyes. "It is because of her gift that you walk here now, but it is not because of her gift that you are capable, in the end, of doing so."

"If this is a dream, can we wake up?"

He laughed then. The sound made the hair on the back of her neck stand on end; it was like lightning strike, and it was so close. "Perhaps you have always been sleeping; perhaps it is now that you truly begin to wake." He lifted an arm, and his hair began to move in the sudden breeze. "Witness, Jewel. The children of the gods are waking, and you have touched the edge of a single such child's power. It has touched you.

"The gods have always been transformative." He held out a hand and she stared at it until he said, "Yes, I mean for you to take it."

And, oh, it was cold when she did. It was like ice.

"Yes," he said, divining her thoughts. "It is like the ice here. The ice is mine. Emblem of Winter and the cost of Winter. Come, ATerafin. I begin to understand."

"Good. Explain it to me."

"We regret Winter when it is long past its season, and only then. There has been no Summer for centuries. It should be Summer now, for the Hunt was called and the Winter Queen rode. Yet we are still trapped in Winter, still frozen in time."

She waited to hear more, or tried; his grip on her hand didn't allow her to stand still. He began to drag her in the direction she'd pointed out, and the desire to preserve some dignity meant that she ran to keep up.

Celleriant had no difficulty climbing the side of the basin. Jewel might have, but he had her clamber up onto his armor-plated back and cling, arms twined around his neck. It should have been awkward, and maybe for her it was; he didn't appear to notice her weight. Nor did he have difficulty with the ice- and snow-covered vines. He drew his sword. Not for Lord Celleriant the indignity of crawling over, under, and around anything that stood in his way. But this time, the vines withered, defenseless; this time they sprouted no leaves, and drew no blood.

"They're not—not attacking you."

"No."

"Why? Why is it different this time?"

He glanced over his shoulder. "Winter reigns here."

"But—"

"Even dreams have their own rationale. It was to drive me—to drive us—here that the tree so distorted itself; it succeeded. But that tree and these vines are no longer one. Come."

She glanced through the passage he'd cut, at the exposed and sharp edges his sword had left. He built a bower of sorts as they walked, and Jewel frowned.

"I don't think it took me this long to reach you," she finally said.

"How would you know? Time passes differently here, if it can be said to pass at all."

"Then where are we going?"

"To the Winter King. If he carried you here, Jewel, he can carry you out. I do not guarantee that it will be entirely safe—but safety could not have been your first concern if you commanded him to bring you here at all."

"And you?"

One silver brow rose. "ATerafin, you surprise me."

"Maybe more mortals would if you paid attention."

"Perhaps. But in the Winter Court one pays attention to the things that can kill one."

"That's not true of everyone."

"No, ATerafin. It is not. But it has always been true of me." He cut through the last of the twisting vines. A pathway now opened up across snow imprinted by a single set of footprints; they were hers. "Go."

"Come with me."

"I will not ride the Winter King while I still breathe."

". . . why?"

"He will not carry me." He turned to glance at the fractured vines. "The dream is broken, ATerafin. I will emerge on my own. But I have some work left to do."

"Wait."

"One would think that it is you who are the immortal, given the time you waste. For what would you have me wait?"

"You're injured. In our world."

"Ah."

"You've taken wounds to your upper arms, and to at least your left thigh; I think there's also a wound in your chest."

He lifted a mailed hand and flattened his palm across that chest. Then he nodded. "You are correct."

"Celleriant—"

"They are not insignificant, but they are no longer my master. I have work to do here, and it will not wait, unless you desire the dreamscape to enfold The Terafin's funeral."

Still she hesitated, torn.

"This is not the first time you have left your kin in order to further your own goals." Celleriant had swallowed Winter. The fact of ice, the fact of cold that killed, adorned his voice and his words. She saw herself in them, hated what she heard. Truth was like that, some days.

"No. It's not." Turning, she began to sprint down the path her footsteps traced. The snow impeded her flight, but not by much, because she hadn't been struggling for all that long before the Winter King appeared. He knelt on his forelegs. Angel still sat astride his back, his arms shaking even at this distance, his hands around the King's tines.

Jewel.

"I got him. But he won't follow."

No.

"How do you know?"

It is still Winter here. We must away before the Winter ends; the path will go with it, and I am not winged.

She clambered up his back, between Angel and his neck; he rose. She tried to grip his horns and felt nothing at all in her palms except the bitter, biting cold. Her teeth began to chatter.

"Angel."

"I'm here."

"Aren't you freezing?"

She felt his shrug against her shoulder blade; she couldn't turn to look. "I'm cold," he said. "But I've got Rendish blood and I can't disgrace it by complaining about a little snow that I can't see."

She laughed; it was wobbly. "I've got Torran blood. I can complain when the water isn't even frozen. Avandar?"

"He's here. Almost here. There's a bunch of ash where there used to be wood, but he avoided torching the height of the tree."

"Is he pissed off?"

"What do you think?"

"I think I'm going to ask the Winter King to take us somewhere safe. Like the Winter Court."

Angel laughed. It was shaky. "Thanks for coming back in one piece."

"More or less one piece?"

"That, too."

The Winter King ran above snow that was painfully bright. His hooves disturbed none of it, but the wind did—and the wind was a blistering howl. Ice stung Jewel's cheeks. She was certain it would have done the same to her hands, but she couldn't feel her hands anymore.

I need to talk to Sigurne, she told the great stag.

She is waiting. She is as unhappy in her way as the Warlord is, but she is markedly more patient. A moment's silence, and then he added, *She is powerful, Jewel. Were she not old, she would be a danger in the future.*

She'll never be a danger to me.

How can you be so certain?

We want the same things for the people around us. For the City, she amended. *For the Kings. For the House. We probably want different things for ourselves. I trust her.*

Unwise.

Yes. But if I were wise, I wouldn't be riding you now, and Celleriant would be riding in the host of the Arianni. We are what we are.

In silence, the Winter King continued to run, and Jewel marked the moment when the snow gave way to the side of a tree, and the ground approached as quickly as if she were actually falling. She closed her eyes. She also held her breath, but that was less voluntary.

But the ground failed to hit her, and the Winter King failed to drop her, besides which, Angel's arms were on the outside of her body, hemming her in. The wind died and in the stillness that seemed like sudden—deafening—silence, she heard the quiet voice of the Guildmaster of the Order of Knowledge.

"ATerafin?"

She opened her eyes. "Angel," she said, under her breath, "Help me down. I don't want to fall on my face in front of the guildmaster."

He had his own trouble. The Winter King knelt obligingly. Angel's legs were shaking as he dismounted. So were his arms. But they would never be shaky enough to deny Jewel the help she'd asked for in such a hurried whisper.

"Thank you," she whispered. And then, because it was Angel, "I needed to know what you saw, Angel; I couldn't see it myself."

He nodded, no more, because Sigurne was approaching.

Jewel managed something like a crude bow.

"This is not the time to stand on ceremony, ATerafin."

"Good. I don't think I can, for much longer. Stand, that is." Jewel's legs collapsed beneath her. "But as long as we're avoiding formality, can you please call me Jay? Or Jewel?" She hated the latter, but Sigurne was old enough that she was allowed a little formality.

"Jewel, then," Sigurne said. "You are injured."

It wasn't a question; Jewel lifted her hands and opened them. Her palms were bleeding.

"How?"

"I—I picked up a sword."

"By its blade?" Matteos Corvel asked sharply. He was Sigurne's personal version of Angel. He was never far from her side—when she allowed it.

"Hush, Matteos. These are not the wounds one receives from mishandling a blade." Sigurne caught Jewel's hands in her own and examined them with care. She then frowned. "What is that on your lap, Jewel?"

Jewel looked down. Snared in the panels of her loose skirt was a single, red leaf. It glittered. "Don't touch it," Jewel told the mage. "It's a leaf."

"Is it now a danger?"

"I don't know. It's not attached to the tree anymore." Jewel took the leaf and shoved it hastily into her pocket.

"The tree," Sigurne said, looking up. Her eyes widened slightly, and her mouth opened, but not to offer words.

"What's happening?" Jewel's question was sharper than she'd intended.

"I believe your Celleriant is now ending the danger—to us."

"What's he doing?"

"Matteos, I believe it best that we retreat some little distance. Help me, please. Angel?"

Angel nodded, and pulled Jewel to her feet. She allowed this in part because it meant she could trust him to take care of things like direction and walking; she looked up. She looked up and her mouth opened on the same silence as Sigurne's had, but it stayed that way for longer.

Celleriant's sword was lightning; his shield must be thunder—he was the storm's heart. His expression couldn't be seen, but Jewel could feel it, even at this distance: rage, fury, and exaltation. Was he injured? He must be. But injured or no, he was as primal, as elemental, as unleashed fire, as desert storm. She had always thought him beautiful in a cold, sculpted way; that sculpture now moved, breathed, and fought.

The tree screamed.

It screamed in a rage not less than Celleriant's own; it looked at nothing but Celleriant. Neither did Jewel. She was aware of Angel's arms; aware of when she almost tripped over an exposed root; aware of when she stopped walking at all—but she couldn't take her eyes off Celleriant. He rose as if winged, and he plunged the same way birds of prey might, his sword before him.

Straight down without hesitation he flew, and only then did he disappear. But she watched; light exploded from the height of the tree in a single, brief flash.

"Jewel."

Celleriant did not emerge.

"It is over, for now."

Shaking her head, she turned to meet Sigurne Mellifas' gaze.

"Celleriant—"

"He will return. Do you not know this?"

"No."

"Ah. Let me see your hands."

Jewel lifted them automatically.

"Was it Celleriant's sword that you lifted?"

"Yes." Jewel frowned. "How did you know?"

"I did not, or I wouldn't have asked—but yes, I guessed."

"How?"

"I am a master of Lore, Jewel. It is—or perhaps was—the most relaxing part of my profession. His sword is old, and it is not meant for the hands of mortals."

Jewel frowned. "But Meralonne APhaniel uses a sword very like it."

"Yes."

Her frown deepened. "And mortals can't make them?"

". . . they can. You are perceptive, as expected; you see what I hoped not to say. But our weapons and his weapons will never be the same."

"Because we die."

"Because we are mortal and death is inevitable—the immortals can die, although not merely by existing for long enough."

Jewel shook her head and looked around the ruins of what had been immaculate landscape minutes or hours before. Someone, she thought, cringing, was going to pay for this.

Avandar appeared some ten yards away. He was noticeably less crisp and clean than he had been while speaking with Devon. Devon was, in fact, by his side, carrying two large daggers that looked as if they'd make good, decorative letter openers in the back offices of the Exalted's cathedrals on the Isle. Seeing them, Jewel frowned; it was a day for frowning.

"Sigurne, the consecrated daggers—they hurt the tree."

"They are effective against what was once known as Winter magic. Winter magic was used to great effect by the Lord of the Hells and his followers, but he was not the only one to use it, at least not according to ancient tales. It is thought that summoned demons have a form made of Winter magic and the demands of existence upon this plane; it is the reason the daggers have been of use against them."

"And if they arrived here without being summoned first?"

"It has never happened. But they are not creatures of this world; there is always a cost for arrival, and a price to be paid to remain."

"Why was it called Winter magic?" Celleriant's dream was of Winter, endless and soul-destroying. He served the Winter Queen.

"Jewel, I don't know. I know that the ancients could, in theory, use either branch—Winter or Summer—as appropriate. The demons, however, cannot use the latter now, and the Summer injures them greatly. The daggers are imbued as part of a ceremony that has long been handed down by the gods to their god-born children."

"Did any mortals ever use Winter magic?"

"Not to my knowledge—but to call it knowledge is a disservice; what we have are fragmented tales and ancient lays, no more. We sift them and attempt to understand the truth that underlies them, if any truth does. But our truth is not, perhaps, the truth that the gods faced when they walked this world in the flesh." She looked up once again to what remained of the tree's height. "There is one you could ask. Do not, however, be greatly surprised or annoyed if he fails to give you answers you find immediately relevant or useful."

Jewel shook her head. "I see you've met Celleriant before."

"Lord Celleriant? No. But I have had some passing acquaintance with things ancient in my time. This," she added, surveying the wreckage of the path, "is going to be distinctly unpleasant."

The vines had not shrunk; the stones that lined the path had not magically fallen back into place. Whole chunks of cold, hardened dirt added unwelcome texture to the flower beds.

Avandar reached Jewel's side, reached for her arm, and stopped short of actually grabbing it. The mark on her inner wrist, however, stung. "ATerafin," he said, using his most correct annunciation.

She stopped herself from cringing and turned to Devon. "ATerafin."

He looked grim, and spared her a glance, no more. "Sigurne."

"Yes."

"This is a disaster."

"It is," was her measured reply. "But how much more of a disaster would it have been had we discovered the nature of the tree's enchantment at the funeral itself? We must consider ourselves lucky." She glanced at his blades. "I will petition the Exalted without delay; they were to be present for the interment, and with luck, they might be persuaded to arrive early. I will withdraw for the moment, but I will not be far from the manse."

"You will remain in residence until the funeral is over?"

"I am hardly in residence now, ATerafin." She raised a silver brow. "I will not remain on the grounds indefinitely. But I believe, given my advanced age, I might accept an appropriate invitation to remain as a guest for at least the three days of the funeral rites. It would spare me the unnecessary rigors of travel."

"I will speak with the regent immediately."

"That will not be necessary," was the firm reply. To Jewel's surprise, Sigurne pinned her with a look that fell just short of demand. It was entirely familiar, but not on Sigurne Mellifas' face; the ghost of Jewel's Oma seemed to have taken possession of the otherwise kindly older woman.

"We have room," she heard herself say. "In our wing. I could ask Avandar—or Ellerson—to prepare one of the rooms we don't use. Will Matteos be staying with you?"

"That will hardly be necessary," Sigurne began.

Matteos, however, said, "Yes, absolutely."

"Umm, you have to understand," Jewel continued, forcing more words out now that the unexpected ones had landed her with an extremely significant guest, "that we don't have many guests, ever. Our wing—it's not exactly *formal*. We have a cook who comes in during the day, but we mostly—"

Sigurne lifted a hand. "I was not raised in the very formal confines of the Empire. I am sure the change will do me some good."

Matteos looked highly dubious.

"Does your Lord Celleriant also room with the den?"

"Yes and no. He doesn't require much sleep, and he doesn't really like socializing. Oh, and there's also a little girl in residence. She doesn't speak Weston, and she's very, *very* shy. I'm sure Gabriel would be ecstatic to arrange more appropriate—and more private—circumstances for your stay, Member Mellifas, and I—"

"Is anyone else in your wing?"

"Yes," was Jewel's defeated reply. "You'll meet them." She glanced at the sun's position. "You might also meet our dressmaker. I'll apologize for his mood in advance. Is there anything you need to fetch from the Order?"

"Yes. I will head there immediately, speak with the Exalted, and return. Thank you."

True to her word, she left them, Matteos by her side.

Devon glanced at Jewel after sheathing the daggers that they both knew were now as useless as they looked. "That was unwise," he said curtly.

Skirmish ✦ 163

"Did I have much choice?"

"There is always choice, ATerafin. Have you considered how other members of the House Council will view your choice of guests at *this* time?"

"That wasn't my first concern."

"No, and that is entirely understandable. But it *is* a concern nonetheless. You have entertained no guests of significance for any notable period of time; Sigurne's presence will change that. It may well change the way you are viewed, and not in a fashion you desire."

"What should I have said?"

"Nothing. She would have accepted Gabriel's offer of housing, and Gabriel's offer would be both necessary and entirely neutral."

"She meant to stay with me."

"Yes," he said, gazing thoughtfully at the ruins of the grounds. "Did you not consider that odd?"

"Not odder than a tree that turns into a Winter landscape and attempts to destroy one of my—" she stopped. "No, not at the time."

"And now?"

"Yes, of course. I assumed she wanted to speak with Celleriant at her leisure."

"Jewel—she will be our ally. She may well be yours. But she is not your liege, not a member of your den. You will have her in your personal space for at least five days, and during that time, you will be observed much more closely."

"I don't doubt it. I'm sorry. I have a weakness for autocratic old women. I was mostly raised by one, and I still have a couple of the scars. I knew we needed her," she added.

Devon relented as gracefully as she suspected he could, given his mood. "The Kings need her here, yes."

"The House needs—"

He ignored her attempted correction. "But your future in the House is not the future of the Empire. They are related; the Empire, however, will survive without you." He took a step away, and then looked back. "I intended to give you time to consider my offer."

"And now?"

"Now, ATerafin, unless you wish to engage in a public and entirely unbecoming argument, you will graciously accept it. I will play no further games; I will not seek to force you to come up with an offer that is not insulting simply to make you aware of the concessions you must otherwise consider. But you will accept my support, Jewel."

She swallowed. This Devon, she hadn't seen for a very long time. This one, she trusted, even though she knew he was a small part of the Devon ATerafin she had come to know over the years. She nodded.

"Very well." Her agreement didn't seem to please him. He surveyed the grounds again with disgust. "Duvari will not be pleased by the turn of the day's events."

"No one will be pleased, Devon."

His smile was grim, but not devoid of humor. "I wish you as much joy of the House Council—and the regent—as I will have of Duvari."

Teller took one look at Jay when she entered his office—via a somewhat agitated Barston—and forgot what he'd been working on. He rose, almost knocked his chair over in a rush to escape the wrong side of his desk, and ran to where she stood in the open door. She grinned. It was a very lop-sided grin. "Can we come in?"

Barston had her back, and not in the traditional sense of the word; behind Barston stood a nervous Angel and a grim Avandar. Angel didn't exist in Barston's hierarchy of importance, as he wasn't even ATerafin; Jewel, however, was a member of the House Council proper. Teller nodded frenetically at the older man. But Barston's lips were a pinched, whitening line.

"Master Teller," he said, reverting to a form of address that had been appropriate when Teller had first been his assistant what felt liked decades ago. Teller cringed inwardly. Outward cringing met with Barston's severe disapproval. "There is some concern at the moment among the House Guard, and word is traveling to the Chosen even as we speak."

"Understood. Jay, does your . . . appearance . . . have anything to do with the House Guard?"

"Not directly," she replied, in a tone of voice that held out very little hope for Teller. "We need to speak with Gabriel, though."

"You need to go to Daine in the healerie. Your hands are—"

"They're scratches. I'll get them looked at *after* we've had a chance to give Gabriel a heads up."

Barston cleared his throat. Loudly. Teller acquiesced. He wanted a moment in private to ask Jay what in the hells had happened—because it wasn't just her hands that were a mess; her clothing was rent and torn in places and her skin looked almost frostbitten—but he wasn't going to do that now. Maybe they'd have time after work—if work ever ended today; new emergencies tended to be added to the pile of merely stale ones.

Barston ushered them instantly toward Gabriel's office.

"Doesn't he have appointments?" Jay asked.

"I have cleared them," was the curt reply. "But I would appreciate it if you would be brief. If your appearance is any indication, there will be a small army of House members who will demand immediate action." He pinched the bridge of his nose and admitted that there had already been half a dozen.

"They don't even know what happened," she pointed out.

"They don't need to know anything to make demands. I'm surprised Teller has not made this clearer to you."

She didn't have a chance to reply because Gabriel looked up as the doors opened.

Avandar slid into the room and took up his customary position by the wall, hands at his sides; Angel stood by the wall on the opposite side of the door. That was unusual.

"Jewel?" Gabriel said, rising. He was much more graceful in his show of concern; for one, he didn't have to catch a falling chair when he left it.

Jay headed toward the desk as if unaware that she'd left both of her shadows behind. She probably was. "Yes. I'm sorry."

He didn't need to be den-kin to know that the news was bad. "Why are you injured?"

"We had a little problem on the grounds."

"The grounds."

She nodded. "I think the pavilion is more or less standing, but the tenting has been ripped beyond repair."

"The . . . tenting. Please tell me that you are not referring to the area in which the reception is to take place three days hence?" He also pinched the bridge of his nose. Gabriel was subject to headaches when things were enormously stressful; Teller thought he'd been suffering from one for a week now. Or more.

"I can't."

"Very well. What happened?"

"We're not entirely sure. No, sorry, we're sure about what happened—but we're not sure how or why. Sigurne—"

"Member Mellifas was present?"

"Yes. There was a very obvious magical disturbance. You know the old tree that overlooks the pavilion?"

"Yes."

"It's mostly dead, now. But before that, it was mostly not a tree anymore. The House Guards were called by the gardeners; the gardeners were in a panic."

"How exactly does this involve you?"

"One of my retainers discovered the inimical nature of the tree," she replied, with a perfectly straight face. Jay wasn't much of a liar, but if she could find a truth somewhere to hide behind, she put up a good fight. "Sigurne and Matteos arrived; the House Guard summoned them at my request."

"Your injuries?"

"They're minor. My retainer was more heavily injured in the fight."

Gabriel's eyes widened before they narrowed. "This retainer of whom you speak—would he happen to be the man who killed the demon responsible for The Terafin's death?"

"The same."

"He was not injured in that fight."

"No. He didn't consider the death of the demon to be much of a fight at all. This was different. Are you going to convene the House Council?"

Gabriel looked as if he would rather cut off his own hands. He grimaced. "We cannot rearrange the timing of the funeral rites," was the grim reply. "Let me accompany you back to the site to see the extent of the damage. We have *no* time, Jewel."

"Yes. I'm sorry," she added again. "But the tree was enchanted, and it must have been enchanted with the funeral in mind. Everyone's going to be there—it would have been a disaster in the best possible case."

"In the worst?"

"A slaughter."

"Then perhaps I must thank you. Believe," he added severely, "that I am nonetheless finding it difficult." He opened the door. "Barston!"

Barston was seated at his desk in front of Gabriel's pressing appointment schedule—and another, larger, set of papers that Teller recognized as a guest list. "Regent." He rose.

"Send for the Captains of the Chosen. Now."

"At once, Regent."

*   *   *

Barston had cheated; the Captains of the Chosen were already on their way, and it took less than four minutes before Gabriel's door was subject to the sharp rap of Barston at his most officious. He allowed Torvan ATerafin and Arrendas ATerafin into the office and closed the door at their backs. He didn't close the door quickly enough; Teller could see that there were now half a dozen people in the office, and he recognized at least one of them: Rymark ATerafin.

Gabriel did not look out the opened doors; he seemed marginally surprised at the speed with which his curt command had been obeyed, no more. But he sat heavily behind his desk, and he touched one of the paperweights that adorned it. Jewel's expression sharpened as he spoke a single word.

"Captains," he said quietly. "There has been a disturbance on the grounds."

Torvan and Arrendas exchanged a glance. There was history in it; a history built on friendship that had been thoroughly tested and hadn't—yet—broken. They waited.

"I would like you to serve as escort while we visit the site of the disturbance."

They saluted in perfect unison.

Gabriel rose. "I have a few words to speak with Barston before we leave. Please, wait for me here."

Jewel was confused. Gabriel had clearly invoked a magestone for the purpose of protecting the privacy of any conversation that occurred in this room—and then he'd gone and left it. She turned to glance at her domicis, but her domicis cleared his throat and looked—pointedly—at the Captains of the Chosen.

Torvan ATerafin looked down at her with some concern. "Jewel, your hands."

She wanted to pull her hair out in frustration; instead, she shoved it out of her eyes. "They're just scratched."

"Let me see them." It was not a very captainly thing to insist on, not when dealing with a member of the House Council. "Hands, Jewel."

Arrendas surprised her. He chuckled and shook his head. "Just show him your hands, Jewel, or we'll be here all day."

"We won't. Gabriel will come back."

They were both, in theory, working—and the work today was deadly serious. It would be at least as serious tomorrow and the next day, and for the three days that followed, because every member of the patriciate of any note whatsoever would be in attendance for The Terafin's funeral. The Kings would be here. The Queens. The Princes, but they would attend only one day, and that day didn't overlap with the Kings. In any case, there'd never been a bigger security nightmare in the House—because the last Terafin ruler that had died hadn't died at the hands of demons, and in particular, no evidence existed that implied enchanted bloody trees lurked on his grounds, waiting to destroy his visitors.

Jewel relented and shoved her exposed palms under Torvan's nose. He caught her wrists and lowered them so he could actually see them. His expression shifted instantly. "Where did you get these?"

"Thorns," she said promptly.

"Someone threw you into a burning bush?"

"They're *fine*, Torvan."

"Good. I'll accept your word, for now. But before you tell us why Gabriel needs an escort to visit the site of the disturbance, we would like to speak with you."

Chapter Seven

JEWEL GLANCED AT THE CLOSED DOOR. From there, her eyes went to the silence stone that Gabriel had so deliberately invoked.

"Jewel," Torvan said quietly, and with just a hint of humor, "You'll have to look at us sometime."

Squaring her shoulders, she did. "I'm sorry," she replied. "It's not that I've been avoiding you—you've been up to your ears in security details, and I've been trying to get a dress made." She grimaced as she said it. Haval would no doubt be short on sleep when he did show up. "I've just been thinking as far ahead as the funeral. I want it—and me—to be perfect for her. Even if she can't see it." Thinking of what had just happened to the grounds surrounding the pavilion, she cringed. So much for that.

"You have yet to declare your intentions to the House and the House Council," Arrendas said.

"I know. But the House Council won't meet again until after the last day of the funeral rites. I thought I had time."

"And that's why you've hesitated?" It was Torvan, this time.

She nodded. The truth was simpler than that. If she declared herself as a contender for the House, it put everyone in jeopardy, and it meant in an absolute way that Amarais was dead. Oh, she knew it. But some part of her held on—why, she didn't know.

"The other four have no such compunctions."

"No. But they've made it clear for years that they intended to succeed her." She looked at the closed door as if the very finely accoutred room was a cell. "I wish Gabriel had chosen to put himself forward."

"He won't."

"I know."

"Do you fully understand why?"

Jewel glanced at Teller; Teller didn't so much as lift a hand to help—and in Teller's case, a lifted hand would have been as good as words, given den-sign.

". . . no. I assume it's partly to do with the fact that his blood son is in the running."

Torvan's silence was chillier. Arrendas said, "The Chosen were not asked to stand down."

"Well, no."

"Jewel—the Chosen were The Terafin's. They *are* The Terafin's. The Terafin selects them, and they serve her. Not the House. Her, directly. They're counted as part of the House Guard in any other way. It's common practice to ask them to stand down and return to the House Guard when The Terafin to whom they swore their oath dies. We are, however, still the Chosen of House Terafin." He stopped speaking.

"Did she ask Gabriel to do this?"

"I haven't asked him." Arrendas glanced at Torvan and passed off the conversation.

"What do you think, Jewel?"

"I think she must have."

He nodded. "She meant for you to succeed her."

"I know."

"Jewel, do you *want* the House?"

"Pardon?"

"Do you want it? Do you want to rule House Terafin? Do you want to occupy the Terafin Seat in the Hall of The Ten?"

Jewel was silent. It was the first time she'd been asked that question, and instead of the automatic yes it should have engendered, she had nothing. She found words slowly. "For myself? No, Torvan."

He grimaced.

"But I can't think of anyone else I want to serve. Will that do, for now?"

"I don't know. Amarais wanted the House. From the moment she joined it, she wanted to rule it."

"I'm not Amarais."

"No, Jewel, you are not. Nor will you become her. She saw things in you that reminded her of her own sense of duty and responsibility, and she approved—but she never expected that you, coming from the holdings, would become a woman who was born to the patriciate."

Jewel glanced at the carpet. "I'm sorry," she said again. "I'm not ready for this conversation, not today."

"Be ready for it," was his reply. "The House is in danger. We have been prepared to serve you, as we served The Terafin before you, since you returned. We've been waiting for your call to arms. We've been under some pressure, as you must expect; we are not inexperienced, and we can deal with that pressure for some small time yet. But it must be a small time, Jewel. The Chosen cannot exist as a headless body for much longer; it will be absorbed, one way or another, in the conflict."

"Torvan—"

"Find the desire to rule Terafin. Find it somehow."

"It's so big." She was surprised she'd spoken, although her voice was so quiet and small she hardly recognized it as her own. She knew they were words she should never have said aloud. Avandar was silent—but forceful—in his agreement of this assessment.

Torvan, however, nodded. "It was never a small responsibility for The Terafin. You knew her; do you honestly think she was without doubt? Her choices in the long Henden of the Dark Days were, in her later estimation, the wrong ones; we survived. We survived. But the demons have returned; The Terafin is dead. We will bury her, and we will work to install a new Terafin in her stead."

"And you think that I'm the right person for the job? Or will you do this," she added, her voice sharpening, "because Amarais thought I was? Do you have no opinion of your own?"

Arrendas raised a dark brow. Torvan raised a lighter one.

"We trusted our Lord," Arrendas finally said. "As did you. Do you doubt her choice?"

"Every day."

"And do you not walk this path—even with hesitance—because of her choice?"

"Yes. And because of mine. I gave her my word; it was the *only* thing I could give her, in the end. It was the only thing she wanted from me; the only thing that would bring her *any* comfort." She looked at Torvan, waiting.

To her surprise, he smiled. "Yes, I have an opinion, Jewel Markess ATerafin. Would you hear it?"

"I asked, didn't I?"

"From the moment you first appeared at the front gates of the manse, I saw a leader in you. Those who followed you were not significant in status or number, but they were unwavering. You were willing to threaten The Terafin in order to preserve their lives—not your own.

"I watched as you worked at her behest. I know why you worked. I know who you worked with, during the darker days. I know what you faced. I know what it cost. And I know that you paid that price, and that you will continue to pay it. I understood what The Terafin wanted for you, and from you, long before you did, and I approved.

"I approve now, Jewel. If The Terafin had chosen Rymark as her successor, as he claims, I would have retired. She chose you. For you, I'm willing to wage the war that must be fought.

"You are not Amarais. She was a woman of steel; a living sword. What she carried in her heart, she exposed to very, very few—but one of those few was you. I do not expect that you will present yourself—to us—as that sword; it is not how you lead. But, Jewel, you do lead. And where you lead, people will follow, even though they risk death. Is this not the case?" He looked across the room at Angel, pinning him there with his steady gaze.

Angel proved—again—that he was no House Guard, no member of Torvan's Chosen; he offered Torvan a lopsided grin.

"Those who follow are not without fear. Teller, do you understand what you risk?"

"I risk no more—and no less—than Jay does," was his quiet reply. "But yes, Torvan, we know what we'll face."

He turned once again to their den leader. "You don't lead soldiers. You don't command armies. But neither did The Terafin. Absent soldiery, absent armies, there is still war, still death. But you inspire loyalty in those who have little ambition; you inspire ambition in them, as well. You will never wield sword in your own defense; that isn't your job. It's *ours*. Our job—for which we expect to be paid," he added, with a sudden grin, "and our privilege. Do you understand?"

She did. But she turned, half-blind, toward the door, and this time, she saw a pair of familiar hands signing. Angel's. *Agreed.*

You couldn't have philosophical discussions in den-sign, but Jewel understood the whole of what simple hand gestures couldn't convey.

Straightening her shoulders, she turned back to the two captains that Amarais had chosen—she understood that now—for her.

"I want—I need—to turn the whole House into my den. Minus the signing. I mean to do that. I would die before I give up my House to Haerrad or Rymark."

"But not Elonne or Marrick?"

"I don't understand them as well."

"Meaning you've yet to clash with them."

She smiled. "Pretty much exactly that, yes. I would trust Gabriel with the House; in that, I'm different from her. She believed—and because she did, we did—that she was the only person for the House Seat. Good intentions or ill didn't matter. I'm not that person; I don't have that certainty of vision." She grimaced, knowing it was an unfortunate choice of word.

"Gabriel is not willing to take it. If it puts you at ease at all, his reason is simple: he is not willing to kill his son."

"I don't think his son would suffer the same reservations."

"No. But that is not a matter to ever discuss with his father."

Jewel nodded.

"Gabriel cannot support you now," Torvan continued.

But Jewel understood what he didn't say. "He summoned you both to this room—with cause—because I was in it. He understands that I don't want attention or hostilities yet, but he gave us the opportunity to speak. He can't support me; he can help."

Torvan nodded gravely. "If I am not mistaken, he will assign us to guard you."

"On what grounds?"

"Your hands, Jewel. And, if I am not mistaken, the gravity of the destruction in the grounds."

"No one's going to believe that once I declare my candidacy."

"No. Not then. But every one of them understands that you are valuable to the House. They also understand that you are not experienced in this type of political game, and that you don't have the stomach for outright slaughter. At least two of the House Council will preserve you if they can do so without loss."

"Elonne and Marrick?"

"Yes."

"I believe," Arrendas added, "that Rymark and Haerrad will attempt to do likewise; they will sacrifice you earlier, however, should the need arise."

She was silent, considering all of the words—spoken and unspoken—trapped and contained by magic in this spacious room. "Torvan?"

He nodded.

"Do you think Gabriel will be happy if Rymark takes the House Seat?"

The Captains of the Chosen exchanged a glance.

Jewel exhaled. "Do you think he means for me to take it, even if Rymark has declared himself the designated heir?"

"What we know," Torvan finally said, "is that Amarais made clear her intent. No more, or less, than that. You must decide for yourself, based on his actions, both in the present and in the future."

She hesitated, as if that wasn't enough. "Do you think, if I do manage against all odds, to succeed Amarais, that he would consider staying as my right-kin?"

Silence. It was broken not by words, but by the opening of the door; Gabriel had finished whatever task he had fabricated in order to give them privacy.

But he exposed some part of his power—or the power of the bookend that served to squelch traveling noise and discourage eavesdroppers; he replied. "No, ATerafin." His voice was grave, his posture formal. But his eyes were ringed with shadow, and his face seemed paler and older than it had.

Remembering everything she'd said about his son, she almost blanched; he walked toward his curtained windows and pulled those curtains wide to let in the clear, blue skies of this cold Henden. "I am not," he said, his back toward them all, his hands gripping the curtain edges, "the Chosen. In my youth—or perhaps in my prime, depending on whom you ask—I admired Amarais. I admired the intensity of her vision. I admired her perfect sense of justice, and her desire to extend that justice, even beyond the boundaries of the House.

"I served her. I served her before she became The Terafin, and I served her after. I accepted the position of right-kin with some reluctance, but I did accept it. Do you know why she offered it to me?"

Jewel shook her head, and then, realizing that he couldn't see the motion, answered. "No."

"Because I was a man with very little ambition. I desired what she desired, for the House. I could run it, could oversee it, because our goals were in lockstep. I have very little pride associated with position."

"You don't need it; you've got Barston."

He turned then, one brow rising. Teller reddened. But Gabriel smiled. "I have Barston, yes. He preserves what *he* feels is the dignity of this office." He let the curtains go. "I am proud of what we achieved. I am proud of what Amarais accomplished. I am bitterly angry that her death was not peaceful. She had earned at least that much.

"But what I felt for her vision, I cannot feel for yours; you are too young, to me. You are unfinished. What Torvan sees, I see, but I am no longer certain that it will be enough." Before Jewel could speak, he shook his head. "I'm aware that what I saw in Amarais in my youth would certainly not seem enough to the man I've become, either; I want safety. I want certainty. Security. I understand that these things are illusion, but even understanding that, I am weary.

"I will hold the regency until matters are decided."

"For her?"

He raised a brow and then met Jewel's gaze and held it until it was uncomfortable for her. "For her, yes. In the end, I wanted what she wanted. I'm still defined by that. I am also," he added, as the door opened on Barston's creased expression, "defined by the limitless disasters that seem intent on destroying our last gesture of respect." Straightening, he turned to the silent captains. "Come."

He left Teller with an obviously agitated Barston, which was too bad; Jewel would have been glad of his company.

The halls were crowded, but the crowds fell silent, parting around Gabriel and his moving party. Discussion would resume, Jewel was sure, once Gabriel's back was far enough away, and much of that discussion would be about Gabriel. House Guards stiffened as the regent approached, even though he seemed to look right through them. Jewel remembered that The Terafin had also had this effect on the House Guard, and wondered if she would ever master it herself.

Wondered if she needed to master it. "Gabriel?"

He didn't consider it necessary that she be invisible. "Please tell me there isn't another emergency that you've failed to mention."

"No, not an emergency exactly."

"Good. What is it?"

"Sigurne is staying over at the manse for the funeral."

"The Sigurne of whom you so casually speak wouldn't happen to be the Guildmaster of the Order of Knowledge?"

Jewel winced. "Yes."

Gabriel pinched the bridge of his nose. Jewel could almost hear his silent prayer for patience. "Very well. I will ask Barston to arrange suitable rooms for her use."

"Oh, she's staying with me. With us."

"Pardon?"

"She's staying in the West Wing."

He was silent for half a hall. "Was this your idea?" he finally asked.

"No."

". . . I see. Very well. *You* will arrange for suitable facilities. I don't need to tell you how important a person Member Mellifas is, do I?"

"No, Gabriel."

"Good." He said it in the exact tone of voice that implied bad. Disastrously bad. As they turned the corner that led to the largest of the galleries and the doors to the grounds at the back of the manse, he spoke again. "She is concerned, then." His tone was different; both softer and at the same time colder, as if he had remembered the importance of his rank and had donned it instantly.

"She is."

"Then it is better for the House to have her present. She is not," he added, relenting, "terribly easy to offend."

"She couldn't be. She works with magi."

He chuckled, acknowledging her point. That chuckle thawed the rigid lines of his face, softening them. Jewel had never known Gabriel well; Teller knew him best, and even Teller was kept at a respectful distance much of the time. But regardless, she'd always liked Gabriel. If The Terafin had earned a peaceful death, Gabriel had earned a peaceful retirement—if that's what he even wanted—and Jewel vowed, silently, that he would get it if it killed her.

But the softness of expression didn't last, for as they approached the doors, they also approached a dozen of the House Guards and three of the Chosen. One of them was Arann. He lifted his hands in very subtle den-sign. Jewel signed back: it's bad.

"Sentrus," Gabriel said, and one of the older House Guards instantly stepped forward and offered the regent a perfect salute. Gabriel weathered it. "Report."

"The Master Gardener is waiting for you by the pavilion."

"What?"

"He insisted, sir. Member Mellifas said that the danger was almost certainly over. In his hearing."

"I see. The rest of the gardeners?"

"He sent them on errands."

"He is alone?"

"No. His two most senior assistants are also with him."

"Have you seen the pavilion?"

"Yes, sir."

"And you concur with Member Mellifas' observation?"

"Yes, sir."

"Good. I will go myself."

This added six armored men to their group, but Jewel had a feeling the Master Gardener's mood made them necessary. She didn't envy Gabriel his position, and was starkly aware that in different circumstances, she'd be the one trying to calm the man down. In fact, that's exactly what she would be working toward in the future.

But the Master Gardener didn't rant, rave, or scream upon sighting the regent. Instead, he fell to his knees, abasing himself in the very rough dirt. This, Jewel thought, was worse, and from Gabriel's expression, he concurred. "Alraed, you did not destroy the grounds, and if you fall apart now, they will *never* be ready. We have the rest of today and the next two days, and we have the funding to expedite any necessary materials."

"In *Henden*?" The Master Gardener all but shrieked. He rose, however, and dusted off his knees.

Gabriel winced. "Even in Henden." He didn't ask the extent of the damage; he surveyed it instead. The Master Gardener's words would have failed to convey the scope. "Have you done a rough inventory?" Gabriel asked, as he began to walk to the ruins of what had once been the center-piece tree. Alraed, done with groveling, walked by his side. Everyone else—guards, Chosen, Jewel and her companions—became either invisible or unnecessary.

Which lasted until they suddenly stopped walking. Torvan and Arrendas drew swords.

Avandar, what is it—what's wrong?

I believe, he replied, in the type of dry usually reserved for drought, *the Winter King is waiting for you.*

Jewel pushed herself to the front of the loose formation, which worked until she reached Torvan's outstretched arm. "ATerafin," he said, with no warmth whatsoever.

"Chosen," she countered, with heat. He turned then, to look over his shoulder. One brow rose, and words hovered behind his mouth; he failed to speak them. He didn't fail to make room for her.

Avandar had—of course—been correct. The Winter King stood his ground at the base of the tree, his head lowered, his tines glittering as if they were ice. Or steel. "Regent."

Gabriel turned to her. "I recognize this beast. I have not seen it since—"

"Yes."

"Is it yours?"

"He, and no. But he serves me in a fashion. Let me speak with him. You're not," she added, glaring at the exposed blades of too many House Guards, "in any danger—but if he's standing there in the open like that, you might be if you continue to walk."

Gabriel nodded and turned to the Master Gardener; what he said was too quiet for Jewel's ears to pick up. Not that it mattered; the Garden was Gabriel's problem for the moment. The Winter King, on the other hand, was hers.

"What, exactly," she said, as she walked to where he stood his ground, "are you doing?" Before he could answer, she added, "In case the House hierarchy is too foreign to you, the man in the fine cut of clothing is the regent. He is, at the moment, the man who commands all of my House. The man beside him is the Master Gardener, and the men in armor are House Guards. Except for those two," she added, waving at Arrendas and Torvan. "They're the Captains of the Chosen."

Her hands fell to her hips in a posture that her Oma would have recognized. "Well?"

If, as your tone implies, these are men of import to you, it is not safe for them to walk here.

"Why not? Sigurne said the danger was past—"

Your Sigurne is a sage, but she is a sage of a lesser time. The immediate danger is past, and I judge you capable of eluding it should you advance. Viandaran is not in danger. But I cannot be as certain of the others.

Jewel pushed her hair out of her eyes.

"A Terafin?" Gabriel came to stand to one side of her; the Winter King allowed it. In a much, much quieter voice, the weary regent added, "we can hear every word you say, Jewel; we cannot, however, hear a response. I feel it best that you keep this in mind."

"Meaning I look insane?"

"Or inebriated, yes."

"Sorry." She meant it. "He can speak—but he speaks to me. I hear his words."

"If you can speak in a like fashion to the stag, it would be best for you."

He is correct, the Winter King told her, his voice grave.

Fine. What is it that you're afraid of? No, let me try that again. What do you think might happen?

Lord Celleriant escaped the dreaming.

Yes?

These mortals might not.

But . . . but he said—

He was safe. He is. But I fear that the mortals will be far more easily entrapped. They do not believe in the old paths, Jewel. They do not lend credence to the Firstborn, if they remember them at all. They lack even the comfort of lore and hearth wisdom to guide them.

Are you saying that our visitors might somehow be entrapped in the dreaming the way Celleriant was?

Not the exact way, no. It is subtle—at the moment, it is subtle. Mortal dreams are not immortal dreams; they lack the substance and the sharper edges; they lack the viscerality and the brilliance. But mortals have never been entirely safe from the Warden of Dream. Dreams sustain him, he added quietly.

She had a very bad feeling about this. *Dreams sustain him.*

Yes.

Even mortal dreams.

Yes.

Turning to Gabriel she said, in the faintest of voices, "Gabriel, how long has the sleeping sickness plagued the city?"

"Perhaps a month."

A month. She closed her eyes and prayed, briefly, to Kalliaris, the goddess she returned to time and again when she faced trouble. Kalliaris, at least, had the grace to remain at a distance.

"Jewel, why do you ask?"

She looked up at the smoldering ruins of the tree; it seemed to her eye to be a hollow, standing trunk. The roots on the ground remained as twisting vines, but they were dry and motionless; their thorns could still sting if one was careless, but at least they weren't moving. "I think what happened with this tree, and with The Terafin before her death, are related to the sleeping sickness."

The regent was silent for a long, long moment. "And the stag?"

"He will allow you to pass if you insist." She said this with more emphasis than she'd intended, most of which was meant for the Winter King. He lowered his tines in agreement, although his eyes narrowed.

"Does he fear that we will be subject to the sleeping sickness if we pass beyond him?"

"I think that's exactly what he fears."

"And if we uproot the tree?"

She gaped at him. "Gabriel—we have two and a half days. Uprooting the tree—"

"It can be done, if we petition both the Kings and the magi; the petition must travel immediately, however."

To the Winter King, she said, *Would that be safe?*

It would be safer, yes. But I fear that the time for safety is passing, Jewel.

Gabriel, given the answer, left quickly, taking Torvan and Arrendas with him. He left the House Guards with the Master Gardener—and with orders that none should pass beyond the boundary set by the Winter King. If they had some issues with taking orders or advice from an animal, they were utterly silent in Gabriel's presence.

They were, Jewel thought, with distinct unease, utterly silent in hers—but it was a weighty silence. It wasn't suspicious—not yet—but it wasn't normal.

No, normal was reserved for the gardeners. The Master Gardener stayed a moment, and because Jewel was feeling pressured, she uncharitably assumed it was for fear of the damage the Winter King might do. Given the state of the grounds, it was a pointless concern; given the mood of the Master Gardener, she didn't feel the need to actually say this. Instead, she headed back to the West Wing, taking Avandar and Angel with her.

She heard a cry at her back and wincing, she turned. The Winter King had vanished. *Next time*, she said grimly, *could you walk* away *from the witnesses before you do that?*

If it proves necessary, I will.

It's necessary.

No, it is not. In fact the opposite is true, in this particular case. You have never commanded men, Jewel; I have. Your regent was correct: they watched you speak to an animal.

You're hardly a—

Yes. I am not. But this is the form I have now, and it is the only form left me. I have merely made clear that your sanity was not in question—unless they wish to question their own. They understand, now, that I am not merely a dumb beast.

They'll be afraid of you.

Yes.

They'll be afraid of me.

Yes. But in the end, that will not be a disadvantage to you; it will merely cause you discomfort.

Sigurne and Matteos Corvel appeared at the doors of the West Wing with little ceremony and a lot of House Guards. The guards were there as both guides and an honor detail, and they took at least the latter seriously. Jewel couldn't imagine armored men roaming the halls of the Order of Knowledge at Sigurne's beck and call, but Sigurne was clearly accustomed to their presence. Matteos carried a large satchel, at odds with his robes. Jewel raised a brow.

"The servants offered to carry our belongings," Sigurne replied, correctly divining Jewel's concern. "But Matteos would not hear of it."

"The regent extends his welcome—"

"He has already done so in person," was the mage's grave reply. "He was on hand before we had passed through the foyer; one would almost suspect he had been waiting for us."

"I actually doubt that—but he probably had a runner in place to notify him if you showed up."

Sigurne smiled. It was a pointed smile, and Jewel made haste to get out of the doorway; she narrowly avoided colliding with Ellerson. Or, to be more accurate, he narrowly—and gracefully—avoided her misstep. "Guildmaster Mellifas," he said, tendering her a stiff and utterly perfect bow, "your rooms are ready. If you would come this way?"

"Of course. Gentlemen, I thank you for your escort. Unless you feel your presence is required within the wing itself, I would be grateful if you would tender both my respect and news of my safe arrival to the regent."

One of the men saluted. Jewel didn't see it, but she heard it; it was a familiar sound, these days. Sigurne then entered the hall and the doors rolled shut behind her. Only then did her demeanor soften. "Jewel, if you aren't too busy, I would be gratified by your company."

Jewel nodded, and as Ellerson led one of her most significant visitors ever to the rooms he had personally prepared, she joined the magi. Matteos was looking less disapproving than he usually did, which wasn't saying much.

"Accept my apologies for our late arrival," Sigurne now said. "We were detained by an urgent request for magical aid—and an accompanying writ of exemption. It appears that my magi are to work in your garden."

"If Kalliaris is going to smile at all this month, they'll have already started."

"That bad, dear?"

"Worse." Jewel ran her hands through her hair. "The Winter King—"

"The Winter King?"

"Oh, sorry—he's the stag I rode up the side of the tree."

Sigurne's hair was silver and white, and a brow that color rose. "Winter King," she whispered to herself. Her robes shifted as her posture did; she pulled several small stones out of somewhere. "I apologize if you've any dislike of magic, but I thought these might be wise."

"Silence stones?"

"They're a little more complex than that, but in essence, yes. I don't see your domicis," she added, making the statement a question.

Jewel stopped herself from shrugging—but only barely. "He's busy at the moment. Since Ellerson's returned, he's decided to leave the running of the daily business of the wing to Ellerson."

"And Ellerson doesn't mind?"

"Truthfully? I think he prefers it. He used to be—he still is—the most fastidious of men, and I think he secretly—"

Ellerson cleared his throat, and Jewel had the grace to redden.

"They're both from the guildhall," she said, in exactly the tone of voice reserved for groveling apologies.

"Indeed, ATerafin," Ellerson added. "Guildmaster, these will be your rooms. Member Corvel's rooms are adjacent. If you prefer, accommodations can be altered so that you are within the same set of rooms, while still preserving some privacy."

"That won't be necessary," Sigurne replied. "However, I do have a favor to ask."

"The stones?"

"Indeed."

Ellerson looked down at the cupped palms of her hands. "If you are willing to leave this task with me, I will place them around the wing. ATerafin?"

Jewel nodded, granting permission.

"Will you see to their activation?"

"I already have."

Ellerson's left brow rose.

"They are within the confines of acceptable legal magic, Ellerson. I give you my personal word that they will not record any conversation held by the den; they are merely here to dampen and possibly to alert those who live within the wing. If your master would feel more comfortable, you may seek Gabriel ATerafin's permission first."

"I am certain that will not be necessary," was Ellerson's smooth reply. He bowed, his hands now full of stones that weren't all that small to begin with. "Guildmaster."

Jewel watched with interest as Sigurne entered her rooms. They were larger than Jewel's, but not as large as some of the rooms used for visiting dignitaries elsewhere in the manse. "Can I help with anything?"

"No. As you can see, the magi are not outfitted in a fashion the patriciate would otherwise expect of men and women of power; we wear our robes. I have robes designed for state funerals, and one extra robe for emergencies; I have no jewelry that is not part of my uniform, and no particular need to use combs and clips in my hair."

Matteos began to unpack his unwieldy bag. As Sigurne had said, she had two robes; one was remarkably fine, even in this waning light.

"Will you have lamps or—"

"Magelight is best. I have, of course, brought my own." The mage smiled, glancing around the room. "This is much finer than many of the rooms I've stayed in as a member of the Order. I assure you that I am content."

"It's not you I'm worried about," Jewel replied under her breath.

"Good."

"Will you take tea?"

"I would love tea. I've heard that the domicis—"

"I'll ask Ellerson." Jewel turned to leave and Sigurne lifted a hand; it was finely veined but entirely steady, remarkably so in a woman of her age. "Is Lord Celleriant in the wing?"

Jewel hesitated. "Yes."

"He is recovering."

"Yes—and I don't think he's happy about it either."

Sigurne smiled almost fondly, as if Jewel's tone had evoked a very pleasant memory. "It makes me nostalgic, Jewel. Very well. I will not ask if he is accepting visitors, but I *will* ask you to make clear that I am, and at his leisure, should he be so inclined to grace an old woman with his presence."

Ellerson was waiting not far from the closed doors when Jewel left Sigurne to find him. It was awkward. Shorn of Angel and Avandar, she met the older domicis in halls that felt more his than hers. And why wouldn't they? He took care of them; she didn't. Her Oma had always felt that your home was the place you cleaned and cooked in. The idea that strangers could be responsible for such a task would have irked the old woman no end.

Jewel had never been a good cook. She could flatter herself by admitting she was a bad one—because that meant she'd tried. Scrounging for food in the holdings made food, period, the most important part of the day; how it was prepared came a very distant second. Somehow, cooking had never become part of her daily routine in the Terafin manse. Neither had cleaning. This man had done both upon their arrival—admittedly with the help of dozens of servants of various levels of seniority—and she had trusted him as much as she'd ever trusted an outsider.

And he'd left her.

He'd left *her*. He'd come back for everyone else. She wanted to be happy for them. She was. But it cut anyway, and she found it hard to be around him for any length of time.

Because he was Ellerson, he knew. "ATerafin."

"The guildmaster would like some tea."

"For two or three?"

"Three would be best, although I doubt Matteos will drink any of it."

"Very well." He bowed.

"Ellerson."

He rose just as easily, his expression neutral, shuttered.

"Who do you serve, now? Who's your contract with? Is it with the House?"

"It is with the den, in aggregate."

"What, they all signed it?"

He nodded gravely.

"And what if one of them dies?"

"Jewel, if, when I serve a master, he loses a limb, and my contract is not defined by length of time, my work is not yet done." He fell silent. She turned from him then, but was drawn back by the sound of his voice. "Let me ask you a question if you will answer it honestly."

Back still toward him, she nodded.

"Would you have survived had I been your domicis? You disappeared months ago, in the Common. Demons were sighted there, and extensive damage was done. Had it been I, and not Avandar, at your side, would you be here at all?"

She was silent.

"And what of your chances now? You will wage war for the House. If I am the man who is by your side, what have I to offer except advice? I cannot wield a sword, and my skill at unarmed combat is lamentable. I have no arcane powers and little arcane knowledge. When you are attacked by a demon—or a small army—how am I to preserve your life?"

She turned then. Her hands were by her sides; her hair was in her eyes. For once, she let it be. Ellerson's expression was not the expression of the domicis, but it wasn't entirely unfamiliar. Even at a remove of over a decade, she remembered what he'd looked like when the lamp lit the underside of his chin in the dark of her nightmare room.

His voice softened at whatever it was he saw in her face. "Jewel. ATerafin. I understood that you would be a member of the House Council. I understood what you had risked and what you had managed, against all odds, to achieve under The Terafin's command. It has never been my goal in life, not even in the guildhall as a callow youth, to serve the powerful."

Jewel was arrested for a moment by the image of Ellerson as a callow youth; she couldn't quite get her thoughts around it.

"I would have served you, regardless. You will be a power. You are one now, although you don't understand what that means well enough to leverage it in pursuit of your goals. But I understood that you were seer-

186 + Michelle West

born, and I understood some small part of what your future would—must—entail. To stay with you—and I believe I said this at the time—would have been a betrayal of my calling. I am not a servant; I am domicis. I knew that what you would need was not what I could provide." He waited, and after a moment, his voice still soft, he said, "Tell me that I was wrong."

She closed her eyes. It was only for a few seconds; she told herself that. "You were wrong," she whispered. "I trusted you, Ellerson. If it weren't for you, I don't think we'd've made it. You taught us how to fit in with the House." She opened her eyes, then. "I mean, fit in as much as we could. We weren't born to this."

"You've grown into it."

"Or it's grown around us."

His nod was grave. He made no move to leave; he knew she hadn't finished. He was Ellerson; somehow he'd always understood much of what she hadn't or couldn't say. He'd left her. She remembered. She remembered vowing never to trust anyone like him again. Fifteen years ago. Sixteen. She couldn't remember the exact date; that wasn't the way she held on to the past.

So much had changed, since then. So damn much. She could remember the shock and the pain of his departure. She could remember the anger that had followed, quick as an unexpected slap.

But she could also remember the domicis who, with his pinched, exact expression and his quiet, annunciated demands, had sat tending the lamp's oil while she slept, afraid of the dark.

"You were wrong," she said again, this time more quietly. "But you were right, as well. No, I wouldn't have survived in the Common had Avandar not been there. I wouldn't have survived in the South, either." She looked up, throat tightening, voice thickening. "Couldn't you have stayed anyway? What you gave me, he *can't*."

After a long pause, Ellerson said, "Jewel, you speak now of your needs, of your experience. Understand that I also have desires and needs; they are born out of years as a domicis. My role is to be the ultimate servitor; it is singular. I do not know how to become the lesser servant, the second fiddle."

The words were almost shocking, coming as they did from Ellerson. Jewel blinked. "You mean I—I couldn't give you what *you* needed?"

"No. Because what *you* need, only Avandar can provide."

"But you came back—"

"Yes. Because what *they* need is twofold. You, first and foremost, for however long it lasts, and me. They need my advice, my sense of order, my sense of the patriciate and the games the patriciate can play; if I never served men of power, believe that I grew to understand them well. I can give your den what they require; I can be that much." He smiled; it was a sad, strange expression. "I am fond of your Finch and your Teller; I am fond of Arann who is happiest in his silence. I am fond of Angel, even if he wanders like your shadow when you are hundreds of miles away, which is quite awkward. I confess that Carver is still a touch on the rebellious side, and I have difficulty learning much about Jester—arguably the most visible of your den in a crowd.

"But I am *also* fond, ATerafin, of you. This is as close as I will ever come to serving as your domicis again—and perhaps I deluded myself, but I felt that if I could watch over and serve your den, I would in the end be doing a service for you that you might value above all others."

Jewel's eyes stung. It was both sudden and unexpected, and she turned her face toward the place where wall met floor beyond the runner's edge.

"My apologies, ATerafin, for the inappropriate timing of this conversation."

"I started it," she said.

"Yes. But I am domicis. We are aware of when—and how—to end inappropriate conversations, and I chose, for entirely selfish reasons, not to do so. I will, however, mollify the reputedly patient guildmaster by preparing a most excellent tea."

Jewel took a few minutes after Ellerson had departed to gather herself in the silent and momentarily empty hall. It was a small hall, a slender one with shorter ceilings than the public halls that led to the wing; it was meant to connect rooms, or at least doors, in a way that suggested home, not the wild opulence of the impressive rich. She didn't give herself more than a few minutes because Sigurne was waiting.

"Enter," the mage said, when she knocked on the door. She let herself in.

"Is everything all right?" Sigurne asked. Jewel had hopes that when she was the age of either Ellerson or Sigurne, she'd be half so perceptive.

"Yes. It took me a little while to find Ellerson." Fifteen years, give or take a couple.

"If you have no objection to chairs, I am fond of sitting."

"Less fond of people who hover?"

"Very much less." She smiled as Jewel took the closest chair. The smile failed to reach her eyes. "What purpose do my magi now serve?"

"They're here?"

"They have arrived, yes."

"The Winter King—and I mention him because I've no doubt your magi will hear rumors—felt that the tree had to be uprooted and destroyed if the funeral rites were to be carried out in relative safety."

"He felt the tree still presented a danger to us?"

"I'm not as clear on that. He felt that what inhabited the tree presented a danger to mortals. I think it's a danger the city is already familiar with." The woman in the seat closest to Jewel's now looked, of a sudden, like the ruler of an Order both arcane and profound.

"Celleriant was trapped in a dream. Or in the dreaming. It was physical, Sigurne; I saw what he saw. I was where he was."

The mage nodded. Jewel would have been more comfortable if she'd remembered to blink.

"The Winter King feels that mortals can be trapped in the dreaming, but not in the same way that Celleriant was. I think—"

"You think the sleeping plague has something to do with your tree."

"With whatever it was that enchanted or inhabited the tree, yes."

Sigurne closed her eyes, which was a relief. When she opened them, she looked distinctly less frightening, but distinctly more unhappy. "I wish that House Terafin were not in the midst of these difficulties. I understand that you are to be embroiled in them—but I feel that it is not in the interests of the Empire at this time."

Jewel had no response to offer, which was fine, because Ellerson, armed with tea, saved her. His timing, as always, was impeccable, and he stayed to serve, which was unusual in this wing. Sigurne seemed not to notice him, which implied that it wouldn't be unusual in most other places. He had, on the other hand, chosen less formal mugs and plates for the service.

"I will speak with the Exalted," Sigurne said, a large mug cupped in two hands. The mugs were warm, and the room was not. Fire helped, but the coming night was a Henden night, and the nights had been cold. "I will ask them about the dreaming."

"Ask them about the Warden of Dreams instead," Jewel suggested.

"Where did you hear that title?"

"The Winter King."

"I see." Sigurne looked past the top of Jewel's head for a long moment before she shook herself and offered a rueful smile. "You make me feel like a girl again." The problem with that version of rueful, in Jewel's opinion, was that it was calculated.

"Is that a good thing?" Jewel asked, because feeling like a girl again—at the wrong age—wasn't a good thing for her.

"No, regrettably, it is not. You have become more perceptive in your absence," the mage added.

"Had to happen sometime. It's not reliable, if that helps at all."

This time, Sigurne's smile was genuine; it was also tired. "I would have you give me good news, if there is any to be had," she finally said.

"Good news isn't my responsibility."

"Is it anyone's, these days? The tea, by the way, is excellent. I notice you haven't touched yours; perhaps you've become jaded."

"I've never been much of a tea drinker. Finch is—but I think that's Jarven's influence."

She stood. "Please fetch Matteos."

"Why?"

"I wish to visit my mages in the garden. It's not what you think," she added. "They are powerful, they understand the legal limits of their power, and they understand the physical limits as well. But they tend to become somewhat fractious where unknown magic is involved, and they often require supervison."

Jewel thought this through. "You mean they won't want to destroy the tree if they know anything about it."

"Sadly, I mean exactly that. If the tree does attempt to kill them, they will of course do what they can to reduce it to ash. Given your domicis' attempts—and his very partial success—I would say that they are in concert only barely a match for what they might face."

"Do you want company?"

"I will accept the company of a member of the House Council, yes. I expect, on the other hand, that Gabriel ATerafin will be doing without sleep for much of the evening."

Jewel stopped by her own rooms to fetch warmer clothing. Warmer in this case also dispensed with the dress. Although all of her dresses had skirts that were wide and loose enough to run in, they made her feel awkward. The one good thing about travel with the Voyani: no one was expected to wear anything as impractical as the Northern dress. Not even the Matriarch.

While she was in her room, she stopped in front of her bedside table. Hesitating, she opened the small drawer that held a few of her gathered treasures. She pulled out the old, battered iron box, and lifted its lid. Wrapped in cloth and nestled in the interior of that box were three leaves. She retrieved a fourth: a leaf of ruby. In the lower light of the room it gleamed not like gem, but like liquid.

She started to put them together and then stopped because her hands were shaking almost uncontrollably. *Avandar.*

Jewel?

Five minutes later—give or take a few—Avandar burst through her door. It was heavy, but he opened it with force. Probably magical, at that. It flew on its hinges, the doorknob clattering against the wood panels. She was seated on the bed, her hands in her lap. "Sorry," she said, looking up.

His frown was quick and severe. "Your hands."

She nodded. "They were shaking."

"They *are* shaking."

"Yes—but not as much. I don't understand why this didn't happen in the South."

"Perhaps the South was not inherently as stressful."

She started to argue, but the words wouldn't leave her mouth. In the South, in theory, it was worse. But in practice? These things were happening in her literal backyard, and they threatened the only people she really cared about. It *was* worse.

"You had a premonition?" he asked. He had taken both of her hands in his and was examining—with care and a little bit of magic—the injured one.

"No." She stopped, looked at the leaf that she'd dropped on the bedspread, and changed her mind. "Yes. But it wasn't strong, Avandar."

"What was it about?"

She glanced at the ruby leaf.

His frown deepened. "I would not keep that, were I you."

"I know. But I think I have to. I think it's important."

"Jewel, you thought the stray dog in the Common three years ago was important."

"We found it a home, didn't we?" She flexed her hands. "Sigurne's waiting for me," she told him, standing. "I'm sorry. I thought I was going to—"

"Understood. It is unwise to keep the magi waiting."

"Why? They do it to each other all the time." Jewel, on impulse, grabbed all four leaves and stuck them in her pockets.

"Exactly. They have therefore reached the limits of their patience. I will accompany you, now that I am here."

"Is Celleriant—"

"He is recuperating. It would be strongly advisable to allow him to do so in peace."

Chapter Eight

MATTEOS CORVEL WAS WAITING. The lower lids of his eyes were ringed with dark circles; if Jewel hadn't known better, she'd've said he was suffering a hangover.

"I'm sorry to bother you," she began.

Matteos shook his head. "I am enough of a judge of character to understand who the actual source of the trouble is. I assume Member Mellifas has asked that you summon me?"

"Yes."

"And I judge from the change in your clothing that we will be expected to go outside, where we might be found until evening makes it truly cold?"

"Yes again."

"Very well. Give me but a moment, and I will join you in Sigurne's rooms."

If the magi were stretched to the very limits of their patience by the simple requirement that they tolerate each other in public, Sigurne's seemed limitless. She was waiting when Jewel returned, Avandar in tow, but she showed no sign of frustration or impatience.

"I must ask your permission," Sigurne said, as she left the room, subtly indicating that Jewel and Avandar were to follow, "to utilize a small amount of magic to deal with the drop in temperature. As I may have mentioned, it's our tendency to travel as little encumbered as possible."

"If it's my permission you need, you've got it," Jewel replied. "But . . . given the laws that govern magic and its use, I'm not sure I'll do."

"You'll do. If you wouldn't mind leading?"

"For form's sake?" Jewel asked. She was certain that Sigurne knew the layout of the manse quite well.

"For form's sake," Sigurne replied. "It is my understanding that the Lord of the Compact has been a frequent visitor, and I would not be at all surprised to encounter him during my stay." From the tone of her voice, she wouldn't be pleased either.

Jewel nodded and led the way to the front doors, where Ellerson was waiting. He handed her a cape that was far too fine. She shook her head.

Avandar, however, nudged her between the shoulder blades. "If, as you expect, you will meet the regent while in the company of the guildmaster, it is better to overdress for the occasion."

"Gabriel knows—"

"As does Sigurne," Avandar said. "But it is not simply a matter of what is known about your personal preferences; it demonstrates that you can, when necessary, put them aside."

"But I *can* when necessary."

"Indeed. What remains to be seen is how much your narrow definition of necessary can be broadened in the weeks to come."

Sigurne was politic; she said nothing. On the other hand, Ellerson said nothing as well—his was just louder. Jewel compressed her lips into a thin line and nodded; Ellerson, not Avandar, slid the cape around her shoulders—but Avandar allowed it.

Avandar, however, pinned it in place with a cape pin Jewel had never seen before. It glowed a faint orange in her vision, which caused her expression to shift.

"It is, indeed, enchanted," Sigurne said, with a slight smile. "Come, Jewel."

As expected, Gabriel ATerafin was at the site of the tree's destruction. He was clothed in a way that befit his rank, although his clothing was suited to the Henden weather. He bowed when he caught sight of Sigurne Mellifas. "Guildmaster Mellifas. Member Corvel. I'm afraid that things have been very busy in the past few days, and my manners have all but deserted me."

"I should have liked to see your manners when they hadn't," Sigurne replied with a smile. "They must have been quite intimidating."

Gabriel chuckled, and ran fingers through his hair. On closer inspection, his eyes didn't look all that much healthier than Matteos'. Jewel wondered what her own looked like, and decided firmly against asking—or looking in a mirror.

"I'm afraid you will have some small wait ahead of you, Member Mellifas—but I assure you they will return. In the meantime, I would like to invite you both to dine. It will have to be the late dinner hour," he added. "If you are not adverse to small dinners, we will dine outside of the hall."

"I am very much unopposed to a more intimate dinner setting."

"Good." He turned toward the tree. "Your magi are efficient."

"They can be. Have they been working continuously?"

Gabriel raised a brow; Sigurne frowned. "If you will allow me, Regent?"

"I will, indeed. ATerafin?" he added, to Jewel.

Jewel nodded and followed in Sigurne's wake. Well, in Matteos' wake. She was not surprised when Torvan ATerafin pulled up the rear. "When did you get here?" she asked, slowing.

"Some fifteen minutes ago."

"Why?"

"I was informed," he replied gravely, "that you would be present."

"Torvan—"

"Accept it, Jewel. Gabriel has designated the Chosen as your guard for the moment. If you prefer, you may refuse that guard outright—but Gabriel will not accede to what I assume would be a polite request without argument."

"I can argue with Gabriel."

"Indeed. Perhaps I wasn't clear. In order to divest yourself of the Chosen, you will have to *win* the argument."

She turned sharply and caught the sliver of a grin that touched his otherwise austere expression. It remained in the lines around both lips and eyes as his tone grew more serious. "Do you expect to find difficulty?"

"I'm . . . not sure."

"Good enough. Please wait here a moment."

* * *

A moment became five, and it produced three more of the Chosen. She recognized only one instantly: Arann. He looked nervous, to her eye—but Arann's nervous was very much like the rest of him; silent, unless you knew what to look for. She signed; he nodded. This was the first night he was to work alongside the Chosen of Terafin. Den-sign didn't divulge simple things like names. She knew the two Chosen who accompanied Arann by sight, but no names immediately came to a mind that felt suddenly and inconveniently empty. One of them was a woman ten years younger than Torvan, the other a broad-shouldered man. He had a beard, although it was very neatly groomed, which was unusual in the House Guard.

"ATerafin," Torvan said, saluting. It reminded her of where she was and who she was supposed to be: a House Council member in service to the regent. One day, she wouldn't need a reminder—or at least that was the hope. She let Torvan and the rest of his Chosen fall into the background as she joined Sigurne Mellifas near the foot of the tree.

The magi had stopped there; Matteos stood by her side, his arms rigid. Her arms were in motion, but it was an unhurried, steady motion—one that implied the slow strength of tree growth, not the quick and vital strength of duelers. Jewel could see her face in profile; Sigurne's chin was raised, her eyes open and unblinking, the lines of her face falling into neither smile nor frown. Her hands were limned in a steady blue light that rose like fine, fine webbing to cover her face.

Jewel had always been able to see magic this way; she couldn't remember what blue meant, and didn't ask. Instead, she waited until the blue light slowly faded and the mage nodded to herself. "If there is magic here that is a threat to us," she told Jewel, without actually looking down from the height of the gutted tree, "it is a magic that I cannot detect. Sadly, in the case of wild or ancient things, there is much that cannot be detected. Matteos?"

"I concur. In both cases. You have Gavin in the lead here; his temper is not yet frayed and he seems to be holding the magi to their task. Will you not retire, Sigurne?"

"I am not yet weary enough to retire," the older woman replied softly. "What do you see when you look at this tree, Matteos?"

"A gutted trunk. It's dark. My eyes are not what they were."

"Matteos, please." She spoke with just a hint of impatience.

Matteos relented. "I see a tree, Sigurne. But I also see the shadow of a tree, as if the two were imposed upon each other. It is not clear to me which of the two is truly the tree; nor is it clear to me which of the two is the stronger. In my opinion, however, the two cannot be separated.

"But you must concur, Guildmaster; the work to uproot the tree proceeds."

"Ah," was the dry reply. "That would be in part because the regent's request for immediate emergency magical aid was granted so swiftly there must be truth to the rumors that Duvari is all but living on the grounds. What he desires in pursuit of the Kings' safety, he will have. It is seldom that the magi work in concert with the *Astari*."

"And I note it is not the *Astari* at risk; it is, of course, the magi."

"As you say, Matteos. But would you have it any other way? Of the men and women assembled beneath the mansion's many roofs, who would be better suited to take such a risk?"

"Duvari," was the prompt reply. "The gods themselves couldn't kill that man."

"I would not be so sure of that. I will, however, concede that the gods themselves could not force him to see reason. Jewel," she added, frowning, "what are you doing?"

Jewel looked down at the leaves in her hands. There were four: silver, gold, diamond, and ruby. Sigurne's sharp question was a perfectly reasonable one; it was just bad luck that Jewel had no answer. She remembered, dimly, shoving the leaves into her pockets in a hurry. What she didn't remember—and it was far more recent—was taking them out. But they were undeniably in her hands, and in the growing darkness of the falling night, they glittered or gleamed.

"Tell your magi," she said softly, "to stop their work."

Sigurne drew one sharp breath. "You will have to explain your reasoning to the regent," she finally said. She nodded to Matteos, and he departed with her unspoken order.

That was a dread for another day. Hopefully, tomorrow. Jewel nodded. "Sigurne, look at the leaves."

"I am," was the soft reply. It was shorn, for the moment, of edges.

"What do you see?"

"I see silver, gold, and diamond. I see ruby."

"Not more than that?"

There was a very slight hesitation, and then the mage said, "I see the ghost of branches, Jewel, attached to each of the leaves."

"Even the ruby one?"

"Even that. Perhaps especially that one."

"Guildmaster!" A man shouted.

Sigurne sighed and turned away. "Yes, Gavin?"

"Why have you signaled a halt to our work? The roots of this tree go deep—we won't have a hope of finishing on time if we're delayed much further."

"It's been a scant few minutes, Gavin."

"Unless you intend to aid us—and second Member Corvel to do likewise—these 'scant few minutes,' as you call them, will be costly."

"I'm not entirely certain there hasn't been a change of plans," the guildmaster replied. "ATerafin?"

Jewel hesitated. The leaves in her hands still looked like precious metal or fine spun glass, but they now felt supple to the touch. They felt warm. Given the deepening chill of the Henden night, the warmth was momentarily welcome.

Do not let it lull you.

Jewel missed the old days, when Avandar was forced, for reasons of propriety, to keep the sharpness inherent in his advice to himself. But she nodded because he was right. "Tell your magi to stand well away from the tree and its roots," she told Sigurne as she failed entirely to take the advice she'd just offered.

The man who had shouted now approached. "Guildmaster—" he began. His voice sharpened and grew quite a bit chillier. "Excuse me," he said to Jewel. "This area is strictly off-limits to all but the magi."

"She is here with me. You probably don't recognize her," Sigurne added, in exactly the tone of voice Avandar might have used had Jewel made a similarly unforgivable political blunder. "But Jewel ATerafin is a member of the Terafin House Council."

"I don't care who she is. Is she magi?"

"Gavin—"

"Then she has no business standing in a danger zone."

Jewel failed to hear him. She'd learned this from Ellerson and was happy to find a use for it.

"She has the permission—and the complete confidence—of the regent. You will stand back, Gavin. Tell the others to do the same."

"What on earth does she intend to do?" he demanded, not noticeably having moved back so much as a step. He was taller than Sigurne—but then again, on most days so was Jewel—but not as tall as Torvan or Arann. What he lacked in height, he made up for in presence—the particular, arrogant presence of the magi.

"Matteos," Sigurne said quietly.

"Oh, no," Matteos replied, with an almost feral grin which looked entirely out of place on his staid face. "I'm afraid I'm in agreement with Member Ossus in this particular case. Jewel ATerafin is special; I won't argue that. But the tree is unique, and the tree has proven to be a danger. Sigurne, you have no idea what she intends. I'm willing to bet she doesn't either."

"Matteos—"

"And whatever she does, she is tampering with a magic that none of the wise understand. I think it highly advisable to continue with the task of removing the tree, since we are short on time."

"If we were not short on time?"

"I would seek the guidance of the Exalted—and, more specifically, their parents. The safer alternative would be to continue with our task here, for which, I might point out, we have received permission in record time."

Sigurne nodded. "It would be the safer alternative given the complete lack of time available. ATerafin?"

Jewel shook her head. She'd meant to nod. The Terafin's funeral was two and a half days away, and the gardeners had already tripled their ranks—which infuriated the Captains of the House Guard because it caused security headaches and Duvari was breathing down their necks—in an attempt to make it ready. Matteos was right, but no meeting with the Exalted could be demanded on such short notice.

"ATerafin," Sigurne said, her voice a delicate blend of age, wisdom, and steel, "I will trust your instincts here. Does what you intend pose a danger to us?"

It doesn't work that way, Jewel wanted to say.

No, Jewel, the Winter King told her. *But it should.*

"I can't promise that," she finally said. "But I think there's a reason I kept these leaves—all of them. And I think this tree is somehow it."

"Very well. Member Ossus." Sigurne's voice was distinctly chillier. "You will have your mages stand down; I will not ask again." When her Oma had used that tone of voice, people bared their throats.

Gavin Ossus wasn't one of those people, but he did stand his men down. "Very well, Guildmaster. With your permission I will remain to observe."

"It is not mine to grant. ATerafin?"

Jewel wanted to tell him to go away. Instead, she said, "I leave that decision in your hands, Guildmaster. Your understanding of the magi is far deeper than my own will ever be."

"Very well, Member Ossus. Stay and observe. Matteos?"

Matteos failed to hear her. His hands loosely twined behind his back, he watched as the magi abandoned their positions around the circumference of what was purportedly the bulk of the tree's roots—it was a much larger area than the trunk that Jewel approached. She noted, as she did, that if the magi left their work, they did not leave their protections; each of the mages was surrounded by pale lights, mostly orange in color, but not all.

Jewel, the Winter King said. He emerged into the darkening evening, his coat a winter silver—a color it had never been in Jewel's memory. Sigurne drew one sharp breath, but she was the only person who made any sound. All others, even the voluble Member Gavin Ossus, were silent in his presence.

You know, you could try subtlety once in a while.

It was not one of my more renowned traits. He approached her as she stood, leaves in hand; the Henden face of the bright moon was high and strong. The pale moon was almost invisible. *Do you understand what you intend?*

No. But even as she said it, she thought she might. *Is it foolish?* she asked, as he knelt on his forelegs, indicating by posture alone that he intended her to mount.

No, ATerafin, although in time you may consider it otherwise. His eyes were sapphire and shining as he watched her move. *I remember you.*

It was a very strange thing to say.

Is it? Do you not remember Viandaran at specific moments? Do you not remember the sight of Lord Celleriant and the mortal bard ascending the skies to bring battle to the heart of the storm in the desert night?

She remembered both very well. *I'm not any of them*, she told him uneasily.

No, nor will you ever be, if you are very fortunate. No more will you be Winter

King, ATerafin. But if you feel that all memorable moments are those that might scar the world, you are young, yet.

She climbed up his back.

I remember the first time I saw you, Jewel.

She said nothing as he rose. *Why is your fur white?*

Is it?

White or silver. In this light it's hard to tell.

She felt his smile like a deep warm place in a landscape that was otherwise ice and snow. *I remember that you stood in the middle of the ancient road, surrounded on all sides by the mystery of the Stone Deepings—a mortal woman, in a place where mortals are forbidden by nature to walk.*

I served the Winter Queen, Jewel ATerafin. I have served her without fail since the Hunt in which she claimed my life that Summer might at last arrive. She is the whole of her world, and where she walks, she is kin to the gods. Yet you stood your ground against her, in ignorance of her long history. You should have died.

I didn't.

No. That is what makes the memory so strong. For a moment, where you stood, I could see the worn cobbles of mundane streets; I could smell baking and ale and sweat. I could hear shouting and laughter and weeping. I remembered them, then, in a way I had not for a very long time, even in nightmare.

And why is that important now? The uneasiness Jewel felt grew deeper as the Winter King turned toward a tree that was mere yards away. He began to walk, each step stately and deliberate, as if she were at the head of a solemn parade or funeral march. She didn't like it. At all.

I did not recognize you, he continued, as if entirely unaware of the effect this conversation was having.

You'd never seen me before, she replied. *Look, let's just—let's just get where we're going.*

You? No. But your kin? Your ancestors?

I doubt you saw any of them, either. They were all here, and they all died—

If it pleases you, remain ignorant a little while longer. But there will come a time, if I am not mistaken, when we will travel the hidden paths together, you and I, and it will be at your behest. It will be because of you that we can travel them at all.

I can't travel those roads again, Jewel replied. *I can't leave the House. Not now. Maybe not ever.*

He said nothing, and for some reason, his silence didn't make her more comfortable. She wanted to turn around. She wanted to slide off the warmth of his back and retreat to Sigurne, who was both mage and infinitely wiser than Jewel. She wasn't certain if the visceral desire was childish or not, because fear was often the foundation for caution, and caution was considered adult.

She remained on the Winter King's back. As he walked, slowly and deliberately choosing his steps, she felt the force of his memories, and they blended with her own, because she remembered what she had held on to when she had faced the Winter Queen: home. Home in the streets of the twenty-fifth holding.

Why there? Half of her life had been spent in House Terafin, and if she succeeded in the months to come, the rest of her life would also be spent here. Why the twenty-fifth? Oh. The street. The road. The texture of the cobbles; nothing glorious or ancient or magical about those stones—or the weeds that grew up in their cracks. Nothing magical about the den she had built there, either. But the den was here, now. Everything they'd built then, they'd continued to build on. This was as much her home as the streets of the twenty-fifth had been. Take these grounds, this garden: she knew it. She could walk it blindfolded. She knew which path would take her to the shrines of the Triumvirate, and which path would take her to the House shrine; she knew which paths would lead to the pavilions at which important visitors were entertained. She knew how to enrage the poor gardeners—it had been an accident—and how to mollify them slightly.

Were there farmers here? No. But she knew the undercooks and most of the servants; she knew the undersecretaries; she knew the merchants, whether they worked on land or at sea. She knew the Chosen, and even cast a glance back at Torvan. It wasn't as far back as she'd expected, because he was keeping pace—at a reasonable distance—with the Winter King.

Tell me, Jewel, why did you take those leaves from the Winter forests?

I don't know. The truth, that they were part of a fairy tale she happened to be in and she wanted some proof that it was real, wouldn't have answered his question.

And the red leaf?

I didn't take this one. It clung to me.

He was silent. *Viandaran is here.*

He was. He offered her a hand and helped her down in silence. But when she was close to him, he said, "ATerafin, understand what it is that you do."

Gods. "Tell me," she replied, voice low. "What am I doing?"

He shook his head, and of all the damn things *bowed* to her.

"Stop it," she told him sharply. "Stop it now." Her arm throbbed, and she knew why: the mark he had placed on her inner wrist was burning. "Avandar, stand up."

He stood. His eyes were dark and distant; they were appraising in a way that was almost entirely unfamiliar. She didn't like it *at all*, and there had been enough that she hadn't liked already this evening. She glanced at the silver Winter King, and he, too, bowed to ground, as if he meant to carry her again.

"Sen Jewel."

"What? What did you just call me?"

Avandar shook his head. "It is an old title, nothing more; an archaic one. I mean no disrespect by it." He joined her, and his eyes were shining. She couldn't even tell if it was because of the effects of magic. Avandar had never seemed young, to her. But he'd always seemed human. Now?

Now, he reminded her of Celleriant.

As if he could hear the word—and given their bond, he probably had—he hesitated. And then he said softly, "With your permission, ATerafin, I would rouse Lord Celleriant."

"But you said—"

"Yes. But I feel that he would consider the lack of rest worth what he might witness. It will be but a moment, and I will not leave your side."

"Avandar—"

He lifted his hands—both hands—in a sudden, sharp reach for the night sky. White light trailed down his palms and arms like liquid, as he spoke words that were entirely inaudible.

The Winter King rose. A breeze moved his fur; it was warm for the cold of the Henden night. He lifted his head, his blue eyes shining in almost the same way that Avandar's were. Jewel had always thought his eyes brown; she was certain they were. Just not tonight.

"ATerafin." Sigurne Mellifas came to stand by her side; it was getting crowded, because so did Torvan and the Chosen. She wanted to send some of them away; she couldn't.

To Sigurne she said, "If you wanted to see Lord Celleriant, watch the skies."

"The skies?"

Jewel nodded. "He's coming, I think. I recognize the feel of the wind."

The oldest of the magi present looked to the sky, her gaze joining Avandar's and the Winter King's. Torvan's gaze was firmly rooted to both ground and Jewel, and she felt comforted by it. He glanced at her, as if sensing her unease.

"Jewel?" The single word was soft.

She shook her head. "It's nothing you can save me from," she whispered.

He glanced at the leaves in her hands. So did she. They were trembling because she was. But she shook her head again. "It's the cold," she murmured.

Arann lifted one hand and signed. She nodded, and he moved away from the Chosen to stand by her side; to stand closer to her than even Avandar dared. He signed again, and this time she signed back, because signing was simpler, and because the words were ones she rarely let herself speak. *I'm scared.*

Where's danger?

She held out the shaking leaves, and he looked at them; he didn't touch. But she thought he could. He could, of all the people here. The thought was comforting. "You were there with me," she told him, as if for a moment everyone else had become backdrop. "You were in the twenty-fifth. You were in the thirty-fifth. You were there."

"You saved Lefty."

"For a little while." They could talk about Lefty, now—but not always without pain. Tonight, the pain was distant.

He touched one of the leaves, the silver one. "It feels like a leaf," he said, with obvious surprise.

"I know. It didn't. I mean, before tonight."

"It felt like silver?"

"Like very fine silver."

"The others?"

"The same." Cobblestones seemed to flicker, for a moment, between his heavy boots—boots that were far finer than any he'd worn when they'd lived in the holding.

"What are you going to do?"

She laughed. "I don't know."

"But you have to do it?"

"Yeah."

His hand fell to the hilt of his sword; he didn't draw it. But he turned his back toward her, and he faced the world outside of their small space. The wind grew stronger, and Jewel finally lifted her face and watched as Lord Celleriant descended from the night sky, dimming stars a moment by his passage. He landed slowly, as if the wind was reluctant to release him. But he landed near the Winter King and Avandar, and he nodded to Avandar.

He glanced at Jewel, and his expression froze for a second in the typical mask of immortal arrogance and distance; the mask cracked as his eyes widened, gray becoming silver. He saw what she carried. He turned to Avandar so sharply the simple motion felt like either an accusation or an attack.

Avandar, however, nodded.

Celleriant straightened. As he did, his hair rippled and fell down his back like a cape—a cape the color of the Winter King's fur. He carried neither sword nor shield, and his clothing was dark and supple; he wasn't armored for battle. To Avandar, he said, "I apologize, Viandaran. I am . . . grateful . . . for the disturbance." To Jewel, however, he said nothing.

She had one chance to walk away. It was now. She knew it as strongly as she had ever known anything: the coming death of her father. The future death of Rath. But her fear felt stupid. She wasn't wielding a sword; she wasn't leading an army or a host. She wasn't commanding the power of the magi. She was standing at the edge of a hollow tree trunk, surrounded by people who—for the most part—meant her no harm; some of them even loved her. She carried leaves out of children's stories in her hands; that was all.

But children's stories came from somewhere. Forests composed of strange trees. Trees of silver, gold, and diamond. Flowers that could cause sleep; flowers that could cause death. In the heart of that forest, a castle surrounded by thorns; a beast in his cave; a magic well.

And yet, wasn't she already walking in that forest, in those stories? To her left stood the Winter King, the stag who had once been man—and King—before he had caught the attention of the Winter Queen. Beside him, Lord Celleriant, one of the immortals who rode in the host of that Queen, part of the Wild Hunt. A little to one side of him, a man who had lived for so long, death was his only dream. Not immortal, no—but not mortal, either.

Add the wizards—the magi—and the knights—the Chosen. How was this any more real than those stories? She was the child who had come to the forest's edge, whether through starvation or flight; she was the one to whom the dark and hidden paths lay open, promising—mostly—death.

She lifted the leaves and she approached that path into the forest. The companions who had followed her this far fell away; only one remained. She turned and smiled; it was a nervous smile, but that was fine. Arann had seen her at her absolute worst, after all. That smile would be nothing. His was steadier, and, as it usually was, silent. But it wasn't a nervous silence. Arann trusted her.

Trusted her, she thought, remembering Lefty. She stumbled; he caught her before she could fall, and he held her arm until she was steady again. The smile she offered the second time did make him wince, because he was Arann, and he knew why. He shook his head. "Do what you have to do," he told her. "I'll be here."

He didn't even ask her what she was going to do. He wouldn't. He figured she'd tell him if it was important—to him. To the den. She didn't feel as if she deserved that—but she also knew she relied on it. Needed it. So she offered a third smile—this one was like den-sign.

She reached out. There was one tree in the darkness, almost in the center of the path she had seen—and could still see, which, given where she actually was, was disturbing. It was a slender tree; younger, she thought, than the rest, because the rest towered into the shadows of night, becoming one with the moonless sky above them.

She touched bark; it was cool and rough. Then she glanced at the leaves she'd carried. Taking a breath, she lifted the silver leaf from the pile in her left hand, and raised its stem toward the trunk. It didn't even surprise her when the trunk grew a branch just to reach that leaf. It was a slender branch, new growth, but even as Jewel watched, it silvered, until it was the color of the leaf itself. It then grew, carrying the leaf with it, until both branch and leaf were completely beyond her reach.

But the branch grew over the dim path; it grew above their upturned faces.

"It's like a story," Arann said quietly. She was surprised that he'd spoken at all, and glanced at his face.

"Here," she told him. She handed him the gold leaf and he hesitated for just a second before he took it. It might have been a butterfly, he held it with such care; his hands were shaking.

"Jay?"

She nodded and he lifted the gold leaf, just as she'd done, toward the slender tree. He held it higher because he was taller and he waited until the tree once again reached out with a branch toward the leaf's stem. That branch became gold as they joined, and even in the darkness of forest night it was a warm, solid gold that spoke of wealth. No, Jewel thought, knowing that this branch and this tree could never be sundered. It spoke of the dreams of wealth, and of the beauty of those dreams.

The reality was of course profoundly different; she'd had both dream and reality. In dreams, you didn't suffer consequences, and your enemies—if you bothered with them at all—were there to offer you victories or vindication.

She waited until the branch stopped its sudden upward growth, and then very carefully held out the leaf of diamond. Its veins shone white in the forest, although the night was dark. Yet light burned in the heart of the diamond branch that the tree now grew, and it flared where the two met: leaf and branch. This growth was the slowest and it seemed the most deliberate, but the branch hung lowest; Jewel could reach up and touch it if she stood on her toes; Arann didn't need that much of a stretch.

"One more," Jewel whispered, as she lifted the leaf of ruby. It was a deep, dark red, and in the dim light, it seemed more liquid than gem, but calling it the leaf of blood was disturbing. She hesitated. As she did, the tree rustled, touched by a breeze that touched nothing else, as if it were attempting to converse.

This tree had once been a normal tree. It had had no voice, no shadows, no leaves other than the ones that budded in spring and fell in a farewell display of color in the autumn. It had been the oldest and the largest of the trees in The Terafin's estates, and it had been respected for its age and its size, inasmuch as trees were ever granted respect.

But this, this last leaf, had come from this tree. She was certain it was the same tree, although it looked younger and slimmer, dwarfed by the old forest in which it had taken root. Celleriant had said it was somehow rooted in a dream world—not a daydream world, that would be too comfortable, too safe.

She turned the leaf over in her palm. Not all dreams were ugly. Not all dreams were bitter. Not all dreams of death led to death—not Jewel's dreams. Her eyes widened. She turned to Arann, who stood in silence, waiting for her to take one action or the other: lift the leaf and return it to the tree, or discard it.

"I dream," she told him softly because he was there and she wanted the kitchen.

Arann nodded, aware of the nature of some of her dreams—and aware, as well, that she woke from them screaming and terrified, and found her way back only in the steady presence of her watchful den-kin.

"I dream," she repeated. "Sometimes I dream of death. I can't control them. The dreams."

He nodded again.

"Can you remember what I tell you now?" she asked, aware that he wasn't Teller, and aware, sharply, that Teller wasn't here.

"Yes."

It was her turn to nod, to draw breath. "I can't control the dreams, but sometimes I can control the deaths that occur in them. They come with me—the dreams—and they drive me in the waking world. It's not perfect," she added, thinking, with sharp pain, of The Terafin, "but sometimes it works."

"The dreams come to me. I don't control them. I don't know where they come from or why. But they're my dreams, Arann. Mine." She lifted her face to the leaves that rustled above them both, as if they were her audience. Their voices were tinkling, metallic, like oddly shaped chimes. "Sometimes I dream of gods."

She lifted the last leaf, the red leaf, and the whole of the tree trunk shivered. Bark grew around it, hardening, darkening; this time when it reached for the leaf, it didn't reach with one branch, but with many—and they were tree branches, and familiar ones at that.

"What do you dream of?" she asked the tree softly.

Trees didn't talk. Not even here. But the branches lifted this single leaf, and instead of raising it to join the others, it drew the leaf in, toward its trunk. A small gap opened in the bark; the leaf vanished as if swallowed. As if, Jewel thought, she had returned its heart.

She waited, breath held; the leaves she had taken from the forest that had surrounded the glass castle in the Stone Deepings did not vanish; nor did their branches become the living branches of a tree of bark. They remained as they had grown, and as she watched, they grew larger, higher, smaller shoots unfurling and adding new leaves that were kin to the ones she had offered.

Silver. Gold. Diamond.

She wasn't surprised when one of each of these new leaves fell toward her upturned face. She caught them, gathering them as they hardened. But the ruby leaf did not return; nor did ruby leaves grow again from branches that had shed them once before. Instead, above, leaves grew.

These leaves, she recognized with a shock: they were the leaves of the trees that girded the Common, and those trees and this one were in no way the same. Large, green, almost the shape of giant's hands, they budded and unfurled, and they rose as the tree gained in height and width, until the roots reached above the dark earth and surrounded their feet.

Arann stared in wonder, a half smile on his face.

One of these leaves also dropped; it was Arann who caught it; Arann who turned it over and over in his hand, the smile deepening. Jewel's answering smile came from a place as hidden as the tree's heart; she reached out, touched the leaf that rested in Arann's hand; it was soft, supple, its edges ivory, its heart green. As a child, she'd gathered the leaves when they'd fallen in the Common; it was forbidden by law to "interfere" with the trees in the Common, but it wasn't illegal to gather what they shed. And, to be fair, it was also almost impossible to interfere with those ancient trees—you could carve your initials in the bark if you were patient and strong, but that would take more than enough time for the magisterians to arrive on patrol, and then you'd suffer—the branches for the most part were too high.

The gathered, fallen leaves had graced her home; they'd graced her Oma's window ledge when her Oma had been sick enough to stay abed for hours at a time; only death had stopped her from entering her kitchen. Jewel had carried them, sometimes in handfuls, as if they were flowers, and her Oma had smiled, smoking her pipe, and twirling the stems reflexively between her fingers before she set them aside.

Those trees were the forest of her childhood, the forest of her youth.

She left the leaf in Arann's hands and walked to the girth of the trunk; there, she spread her arms, as she might have done as a small child in the Common—her father still alive and shadowing her steps—and wrapped them around the tree. They didn't extend far enough, of course.

The tree grew small branches in a place where branches generally didn't grow, and she recognized these as well, but they weren't as comforting a memory: they were like vines or tendrils, and they had thorns for teeth.

One curled around her left wrist, its movement slow and almost gentle; thorns pressed against her skin lightly.

Arann drew his sword. "Jay?"

"No."

"You're sure?"

". . . maybe." She clenched teeth and nodded, her chin scraping bark. The vines tightened suddenly; the thorns broke skin in a rush. She swore in rough Torra, but kept it as quiet as she could. "Don't," she told Arann, although he hadn't moved. "It's—I'm fine. I don't think it's a good idea to try to chop anything off this tree." The pain, in any case, had stopped; it was already on its way to memory, except for the dull pulsing throb.

The vine loosened, withdrew, and Jewel slowly stepped away from the trunk. As she did, she saw that the thorns were now dark with her blood. She watched as her blood brightened, reddened, and spread. The thorns burst open in a rush, as if they were, and had always been, buds, and the leaves that grew from them were red, red leaves.

Hers. Of her.

But their shape—oh, their shape. Edged in ivory, heart of crimson, they were the leaves of autumn in the Common, the leaves that she had laid on her Oma's blanket while she slept.

"Oh, look, look! *There* she is!"

Jewel froze. "Arann, please tell me you didn't hear that."

Arann, however, was now squinting into the darkness that surrounded them. Jewel cringed.

"Where have you been, stuuupid girl?"

She heard the flapping of wings above the newly grown branches, and the cringe deepened.

"Stupid girl?" Arann shook his head.

"What is this? *Who* is this? Where is the *ugly* one?"

"Jay—"

"The leaves weren't the only things I saw in that forest," she muttered. "Maybe if we leave quickly, we can lose them."

"I *heard* that." Jewel, in turn, heard the thump of something heavy landing. To Arann she said, "They're mostly harmless."

"*Harmless? Harmlessssss?*"

Above the branches of the renewed tree, in the light the tree itself shed, there appeared three very large, winged cats. Even in the dim glow, they were instantly familiar: one was white, one was gray, and one was black. The white cat and the black one had their mouths open, and words were spilling out.

"This is just what I need."

Arann gestured in den-sign with the hand that wasn't on the hilt of the sword.

"No. What are you three doing here?"

The white cat hissed in a gurgling way; it was the winged cat version of laughter. "We were *bored*."

"Believe that there's nothing interesting here. At all."

"I don't think she missed us," it said, speaking to the gray cat. The gray cat was the cat Jewel disliked the least, mostly because it spoke less often.

"I couldn't. I couldn't see you to aim."

Another hiss, this from the black cat. He rolled over in midair, and began to rub his left shoulder against the underside of a diamond branch. Even to Jewel, not known for her ability to express appropriate respect, this seemed beyond rude.

The gray cat hissed. It was a very different sound. Jewel stiffened. "Don't you know why we're here, little human?"

"No." She gestured to Arann and started to back away from the tree. He retreated as well—but kept himself between her and the cats. "Did the Winter King send you?"

"Who?" The white cat demanded.

"The Winter King. The man who—"

"Oh, him." In the darkness it was hard to see the cats' eyes—but it didn't matter in this case; Jewel could practically hear them rolling.

She caught Arann's hand and pulled him farther back, wondering when the distance between the tree and, oh, everyone *else* in the garden had grown so large. She spared a glance over her shoulder and didn't much care for what she saw: very dark forest in a very dark night. She stopped even trying to walk backward. "Stay near the tree," she told Arann.

"And the . . . cats?"

"And the cats. We seem to have a minor problem."

Arann, being Arann, said, "You don't know the way back?"

"Not as such."

Fifteen minutes passed. They weren't quiet minutes, either; the white cat and the black cat had decided, for reasons only cats could understand, that they wanted to scratch their backs on the exact same branch, and were busy trying to reduce each other to patches of fur in order to do so. The gray cat didn't appear to have an itchy back. He did seem to have some interest in watching his companions fight, but apparently that kind of fight was only interesting for a handful of minutes. He made his way down to the ground a few feet from where Jewel stood.

Which put him only a few inches away from Arann.

Arann held his sword, but didn't point or raise it. He was tense, though. No reason he shouldn't be. Although Jewel called them cats, there were distinct differences between, say, Teller's cats and these ones, the most significant at the moment not being their wings. No, it was their size. They were as big as smart horses, although they had shorter, thicker legs and a distinct lack of hooves. They also had much larger mouths, in all senses of the word. The gray cat chose this moment to expose his fangs—by yawning.

He then lifted his paws and regarded his unsheathed claws with casual disinterest, flexing them in turn.

Jewel frowned. "Please don't eat him," she said, more curtly than she intended.

"Eat him? Eat him?" The gray cat followed the words with a brief hiss. "I'm not hungry, and it's not fun to kill mortals. It makes almost no difference; they die anyway." He sniffed air and added, "He doesn't seem interesting."

No, Arann wouldn't. It was part of the reason Jewel loved him. "He's not the Winter King, no."

The gray cat hissed again. "Why do you keep *saying* that?"

"Because you should be with him." The Winter King of the great, glass castle had had an enviable effect on the cats; they shut up in his presence.

But . . . he should be dead. Dead or transformed into something that might be of service in the long nights of the Wild Hunt. Ariane had called the Wild Hunt and she had ridden the hidden ways to find—at last—the reigning Winter King.

The cat scratched the ground, lifted his paw, and looked at his claws. "It's dirt," he said.

"Well, yes. We're in a forest."

"Not all forests have *dirt*." He sniffed the air a moment, and then roared. She'd never heard the cats roar before. They clearly didn't do it often, because the screaming hiss and spit in the air above suddenly stopped. Two cats who looked distinctly larger because of the way their fur was bunched and standing on end came to land on either side of the gray one.

The white cat tilted its head and looked at Arann, who happened to be very close. "Are we going to play with him?"

"No," Jewel snapped.

"But we're *bored*."

"Go play with demons instead."

White ears twitched. In fact, so did gray ears and black ones.

"Really?" the white cat finally said, his voice the definition of suspicious. "You let *demons* play in your lands?"

"We don't exactly let them play in our lands, no."

The cat hissed. "That would be more fun," he muttered, sinking down into the earth and resting his chin on his forepaws. "We're bored. Why are you talking about demons?"

"We're pretty sure we have some." As if they were vermin.

Once again, ears lifted. "We could *find* them for you."

"We couldn't," the black cat snarled. He was sulking as well. "Where would she hide demons here? She only has *one* tree." He walked over to the tree's trunk and began to scratch his back across bark.

"But it's an interesting tree, isn't it?" Jewel said. They all stared at her.

"It's too crowded," the black cat replied, sibilance stretching the first short word into the space of the rest. "We don't think it should look like *that*."

She hated to agree, but felt compelled to be honest: they were right. While the silver, gold, and diamond hinted at the children's stories that never died—no matter how old the child listening eventually became—the combination looked wrong.

"I want my *own* tree," the white cat added archly. He stood, having decided that sulking on his belly no longer suited him.

"I'm not a gardener," was her terse reply.

They all broke into the gurgling hiss that Jewel identified as laughter. She wouldn't have minded it as much if it weren't always at her expense.

"Plant them. Plant them, watch them grow." The gray cat moved around Arann so quickly her den-kin had time to spin; he had the very good sense not to attempt to stab the passing cat. He even had to swivel to avoid its wings.

"Plant what?"

The cat hissed. "The leaves, stupid girl." He bumped her hand with his head, and she froze; his head was both soft and warm. Her brows rose, her eyes widening. "You're not—you're not stone anymore."

"No," he said, his voice unexpectedly serious. "We are not stone. We are not ice."

"But—"

"You are neither stone nor ice."

She stared at him.

"You *are* stupid, though. Come, come. The leaves."

"But—"

The cat growled. It was not a friendly sound. "Plant your forest, stupid girl. Plant it *quickly*. They know you now. They know."

"What? Who are you talking about?"

"You have one tree. It is too small."

It wasn't small, now.

"And we each want our *own* tree."

This was the problem with cats. Or at least with talking to cats. She lifted the three leaves that had fallen into her hands. "I was going to keep them."

"Well of *course* you're going to keep them," he hissed, managing to suggest by posture alone that it was with great will and effort that he hadn't appended the words *stupid girl*. He nudged her again, but harder, and this time, his head remained plastered against the underside of her hand. It was so warm. "Hurry, hurry, *hurry*. I hear the ugly man."

Jewel, however, heard something else, and she turned at the sound of breaking branches and heavy feet. She no longer knew which direction the sounds were coming from; she only knew they were getting closer. That, and for some reason, they didn't sound particularly friendly.

The white cat and the black cat began to bristle, but at the same time, began to bounce. The gray cat nudged her so hard she almost fell over. When she looked at him, he looked very put out; it was amazing what could be accomplished with fur, fangs, and the shape of ears. "Hurry, stupid girl, hurry."

"Or you'll miss out on all the fun?"

"Yessss."

Cats. Jewel looked at the leaves. They seemed to be, to her touch, the exact same leaves she had carried with her from the forests that had surrounded a castle made of glass—or ice; it belonged to the Winter King, after all. The Winter King and his only companions: these cats, winged so they might escape gravity; stone so they might escape harm.

They were not stone now. They were not, she thought, cats. It made her wonder about the man the Winter King had once been before he had become Ariane's. A lesson, if ever one was needed, about the nature of immortals and what they did to the mortals who weren't even allowed to die without their intervention.

She leaned into the fur of the gray cat, catching the thought before it unspooled. It was part of what she wanted, wasn't it? To hold what she held; to keep it safe from harm for as long as she lived. To keep her den alive—always alive—no matter who might wish otherwise. Why? Because she loved them. Because they were hers. So, too, was the Winter King claimed, but Jewel was not Ariane. Not the Queen of Winter; not the leader of the Wild Hunt. Had he loved her?

He must have. He must have, even if to Jewel love had seemed irrelevant to Ariane. It didn't touch her; it didn't change her; it didn't show her the way.

She held this thought as well. She had come, terrified, to the Terafin manse in the grip of Avandar's power, on the back of the Winter King. A different King, of course, and yet he, too, lived and died at the whim of the Winter Queen. Jewel shook her head to clear it, and some thoughts made way, but others clung, just as the vines of the tree had.

She loved her den. She loved her House. She loved the ghost of the city she had once grown up in. All of her ghosts, she thought bitterly. The ghosts of her childhood; the ghosts of her parents; the ghost—the voluble ghost—of her Oma. She had never had the power to hold them by her side; she'd had the ability to weep or plead, no more—and weeping or pleading seldom turned hearts. But they'd lived—and died—as men and women; no forest had surrounded them; no Winter Queen had loved them and frozen them, fixing them in place until the last possible moment.

And if you could? She whispered something to Arann as the sound of cracking wood grew louder. Would you have loved them? Or would they have become as animate as any chunk of ice, any frozen thing?

You can't save it all. You can't. You can't hold on to anything forever because people change. *They grow.* So did she, but she didn't fear her own growth. *They're yours because you love them. You're theirs, because you love them. But they are what they are.*

And Jewel? She was what she was, as well. She would let them fight this war; she would keep them by her side for as long as she could. But not longer, even had she the power. She had seen the shadow of eternity in Avandar's dreams; if she looked now, she could see its edges in his eyes. And she never wanted that for her den. Or herself.

But she would do everything she could to protect them. Maybe this was the sole advantage mortals had: everything she could do was not everything, in the end, that the Winter Queen could. She held out the leaf of silver and it shone in the darkness as the cats somewhere at her back began to growl.

Chapter Nine

TREES OF SILVER. Trees with leaves that were forever suspended in moonlight. Trees ancient, profound, rooted in mystery. Jewel had touched them. Had she changed them? No, not more than this: she had taken a leaf, one of thousands. Not more, not less. But she had returned to her home bearing its strangeness and its mystery, as if by so doing she could capture some tiny part of its essence. It had been real.

It was real now.

As real as the cat who padded across ground breaking nothing beneath its huge paws. She touched the space between his ears; his head was still warm. Not soft, not really—his fur was a little too rough for that. "We are," the cat said gravely, "what we are."

She turned in the direction of the only source of light and said, "And they're angry."

"Only a little. We were *very* bored."

"Where did the Winter King go?"

"Oh, away. Away."

"And shouldn't it be Summer?"

"Summer, hmph. We are *Winter* cats."

Jewel stopped. She could see the trunks of the trees that comprised this forest, but never clearly; she could sense their height by the absence of sky. But there was space here, for her leaf; space for her and her cat. She knelt and the cat hissed. "What, this time?"

"You cannot *kneel* here."

"Oh, but you can lie down on your belly and roll around the undergrowth."

"That's *different*."

"How?"

"We're not *asking* for anything."

The men and women who'd frequented Gabriel ATerafin's office over the decades would probably have claimed the same, and with as much truth. "I need to clear some space."

The cat hissed.

Jewel stood. She stood because a new voice had entered the nearby sounds of annoyed cat, and she recognized it. Or part of it. It was cold, certain, and as eternal as the Winter seemed to be.

She said, softly, "Demon."

The cat nodded and hissed. "Kneel if you *must*. It looks untidy, but it won't kill you. Probably."

"It is not the path she must fear."

Jewel stiffened; the leaves were now trembling in her hands.

"If she must kneel—and it is inevitable—she will kneel to *me*."

Turning, hair on the back of her neck rising in a way that reminded her suspiciously of the cats, she stepped onto the road. And it *was* a road, even if it looked like a slender footpath. She felt its shape against the soles of her feet, as if, for a moment, she'd left her shoes behind. As a child, she'd done it often, much to the consternation of her Oma, who'd considered shoelessness a crime against familial pride.

Arann stepped in front of her; she put a hand on his shoulder and gently drew him to her side. Not behind; she wanted to, even if on the face of it it was stupid—but she didn't. The white cat and black cat took to the air, circling the demon who stood on the path yards away from the single tree with its multiple mismatched leaves.

He was not the first demon she'd seen, and she *knew*, meeting his gaze, that he wouldn't be the last unless she died here. But the demons she *had* seen were not this man. He looked human.

No, no that was wrong. He looked immortal, the way Celleriant did. The way the Winter Queen herself did; he was beautiful. It was the beauty of distant mountains; the beauty of the azure sky on a perfect, clear day; it was the beauty of things untouchable by those bound to ground—and life. His lips, in the darkness, were almost red, his eyes so dark they were black. He carried no weapons—but then again, on most days neither did Celleriant.

She had no desire to see those weapons again. "To whom am I expected to kneel?"

"To Lord Ishavriel of the Fist of God, Duke of the Hells."

She turned and glanced over her shoulder.

"Do not look for aid, little mortal. You are lost here, and you have been found."

"No," she replied, voice low. "I'm not lost. Don't you recognize this, Lord Ishavriel? You're on *my* turf, now."

His midnight brows rose over his perfect eyes; his lips tilted briefly at a smile. "These paths were not created for—or by—mortals. You aspire to much. But you are—as so many of your kind—out of your depth here."

The cats circled in utter silence. His expression rippled in a frown. "Leave," he told them, the single word quiet and so deep Jewel wanted to obey it herself.

The white cat hissed in reply.

"I do not know how you came to be here. If you will not—or cannot—leave, that is your choice and your folly; interfere with me here and it will be your destruction." He raised a hand and pointed at the tree of many leaves. Fire left his fingers, but not in a bolt; flames flickered and circled in the air as if they were vines. They reached out, twisting and turning through that air, as if burrowing through something invisible toward the tree's trunk.

Lord Ishavriel's brows rose again, but this time when they fell, they fell across narrowed eyes. "So," he said.

Jewel could never say why she did what she did next: She lifted the hands that contained the three leaves this one tree had returned to her keeping. They glowed like magelights in the darkness.

"This is how your kin came to Terafin," she said, voice a Winter voice. "You *walked*." Heat melted ice and snow; heat of rage. She had learned not to rail against death; it was pointless and it hurt the people around her. Death was faceless and impersonal; it came, in the end, whether it was wanted or no.

But not this death.

Not these creatures.

Was he immortal? Yes. And beautiful. So far above her comprehension that she shouldn't have dared to raise hand against him. But she did; she wanted to raise so much more.

"What are you doing?" the demon Lord demanded, shedding shadow as naturally as the three leaves now shed light. No, not just the three; *all* of the leaves on the tree.

This Lord was her enemy. She felt the truth profoundly; it was so *large* she'd no words big enough to encompass it. He—or his kin—had come through *her* gardens, through *her* grounds; they had passed by her shrines and beneath the eyes of the most watchful and suspicious of men.

Fire burned in the dark air; fire reached for the trunk of the tree. She felt it; saw the lone tree the cats had called hers as if it were natural. She lifted the leaves higher and as she did she felt it: the evening breeze, its chill a balance to the heat of fire. It felt familiar, although it wasn't the wind that carried Celleriant; nor was it the wind that had carried the Senniel master bard, Kallandras.

No. This was a sea breeze. A sea breeze in Henden, heavy with the promise of storm and salt, humid even in the dryness. She could taste it on her lips and her tongue, and it was blessedly familiar; the winds in the desert had had none of her life in them. The wind tugged at the leaves in her hands and she gave them over to its keeping. Hands now empty she made her way toward the tree under the watchful gaze of the man who had called himself a Duke of the Hells.

She placed one palm against the tree, and it was familiar in the same way the breeze had been. It was not the tree in which Celleriant had almost ended his ancient existence; that had been the tree's dream of itself; she understood that now, the insight as sharp as any vision that had ever moved her to action. But the tree was waking. So, too, was Jewel Markess ATerafin.

She reached out for the fire. It was hot—she'd expected that. But hot or no, it didn't actually burn her. Lord Ishavriel's expression etched itself into memory—and it was a memory that would bring her comfort for as long as it remained. The fire stopped moving, but it kept its shape: twisting vines. Where it touched Jewel's fingertips, those vines budded, and the buds burst into crackling red-orange leaves. Leaves this color she'd seen all her life, as the seasons turned. The seasons passed much more quickly now that she was no longer five or six. But they came, regardless, and in the Autumn, the leaves' final burst of color was fanfare. It promised Winter. But it was born from the promise of Spring, was birthed the moment the branches budded. Spring, beginning, youth and growth; Autumn, end, but oh, the beauty of it.

The tree reached out as Jewel did, and it touched those burning, flickering leaves, those echoes of the Autumn of her youth; a branch grew that was the shape and the color of fire.

"It wasn't the leaves," Jewel said softly, to darkness and air.

"No," the gray cat agreed.

The fire left Lord Ishavriel's hands in a rush, leaping toward the tree, where it twined, leaves blooming. The bark beneath it didn't burn; instead, the tree began to absorb the fire and the heat, just as it had absorbed one red leaf.

The white cat dared to hiss, and this time, when fire left the demon Lord's hands, it looked like red lightning. The cat dodged, but the fire had singed its fur.

The wind rose as Jewel watched.

She lifted her voice and she called; the Winter King came down the path at her back. She couldn't see him immediately because she didn't turn, but he was silver now, presence of moonlight, his tines gleaming like leaves—Winter leaves. He reached her side and lowered his head; she touched the tips of his antlers, no more. She'd no intention of mounting. Nor did he kneel to allow it; he waited, his eyes still blue, his gaze upon the demon.

The demon drew his sword in response. It came from no sheath she could see, forming instead, full and whole, in his hand. His hair rose in a wind that seemed to be moving in a different direction from the wind she now felt. She knew that to leave the tree would be to stand in the same wind that moved that hair; it was also death.

Do you see the path, Jewel? the Winter King asked, his voice soft.

She looked at the ground beneath her feet. There had been roots there moments before; she'd almost tripped over at least three of them. They were gone, now. What remained in their wake were familiar cobblestones. They were worn, just as a footpath is, by the passage of so many feet across their surface; they were even cracked in places. She saw the shadows of familiar weeds; the weeds themselves were absent.

"I see it."

Do you understand it?

"Does it matter?" She shook her head, and curls adjusted their fall to land in her eyes. "I know where I am. I'm home. Even here, I'm home."

Lifting her voice, she said, "Go back. Go back to the Hells or wherever it is you call home these days."

In reply, the demon Lord lifted his sword and brought it down, blade first, into the path. The cobblestones shifted—they had to; the ground beneath them shuddered as if it was about to break. Roots lifted themselves from their dirt moorings; leaves fell from the height of distant branches.

The wind took them, gathering them with a flourish that made their descent more a dance than a fall. She watched as they swirled; not even Lord Ishavriel's presence could force her gaze away. Diamond tips brushed her cheeks; gold caught a moment in her hair. But the white-edged leaves of the Common's symbolic forest caressed her forehead like velvet. Like familiar hands.

Lord Ishavriel lifted his sword again, and this time, he brought it down against . . . air. It shuddered to a halt as red lightning spread in a fan around its edge. The Winter King's head rose; his forehooves lifted as he reared. Jewel shook her head, her hand still on the tree.

"You were right," she told the gray cat.

"Of *course* I was right. About what?"

"There aren't enough trees." She smiled. The leaves rose above her head in a hollow column. For a moment they looked like butterflies. They left the folds of the twisting wind, heading in different directions, fluttering as a stray gust blew them back. She watched them the way she had once watched the light shows governed by the magi on the Day of Return. Some spread beyond whatever barrier kept Lord Ishavriel at bay, and he destroyed them, his fire consuming and melting them as they struggled.

But he could not destroy them all; the winds carried them to and fro, where not even he could gather them. Nor did they seek just the air above the demon; they sought the forest behind Jewel's back—and in greater number. Silver wings, golden wings, echoes of moonlight and sunlight, found purchase and haven along the trunks of standing shadows—the trees she could only barely see and had not yet touched.

She said to the cat, "I'm dreaming."

The cat licked its paw and said nothing. But the Winter King said, *No.*

Yes, she replied. *But I've always had dreams. Sometimes they can change little bits of the world, that's all.*

It is not the dreams that have changed them, Jewel. It is you.

She shook her head. *If the world could be changed that easily, it wouldn't be my world.* She thought of the holdings, of the orphans, of the farmers and the tavern owners and the merchants, big and small. Of the living, and of the dead. Her dead. So many people whose lives she would save if she could change them just by dreaming. So many deaths she'd erase. She'd dreamed about making those changes for most of her life.

No?

But the world was the world. Life was life, death was death. There were no guarantees, had never been any—there was struggle, and sometimes, there was triumph. Sometimes there was just bleak loss. Yet out of loss, the den had built its opposite, over the years. Out of sorrow, they'd learned—as if such lessons were needed—to appreciate joy. They remembered pain, yes; it rooted them. It grounded them. But it was the hope and the joy that sustained them.

No. Those people, that world—it's real. It's real and it turns so slowly you might never notice it's moving at all. But I need it. It defines me. It's who I am. The demon's sword struck air again, its descent frustrated by things unseen. She could feel the edge of its blade as if it were a distant pressure. Distant, inexorable. *I'm dreaming, here. Dreaming. It's not a nightmare, not yet. But, it's my damn dream.*

Sometimes, she said again, *I dream of gods.*

She felt the sword fall, and saw that this time it had fallen farther, faster. And why wouldn't it, after all? A demon Lord had no part in her world except as a vulture; these lands were made for all of the creatures like him.

But this particular patch of strange, immortal land overlapped the life she knew. It touched her home. It was as much hers as his.

No. It was more hers than his. It was here that she'd dreamed and cried and slept and ate; here that she'd loved and feared and raged. It was here that she'd given the vow that would define the rest of her life.

"Lord Ishavriel," she said, her hand now gripping the tree's bark, "you are not in your lands anymore. You're in *mine*, and I *don't want you here*. Go home."

As she spoke, the surrounding trees upon which the leaves—her leaves—had settled began to glow; some were silver, some were gold, and some were hard, harsh diamond, warm ice. They grew into their light, gaining the height, the majesty, and the shapes that she knew so well.

His wind flew at their heights; his wind tore at their leaves. Jewel smiled as those leaves were rent from branches. "It's no good," she told him, understanding for just this moment why.

The leaves blew in his storm, but they came to settle on different trunks, different trees, and they took root there, just as the first flying leaves had done. There, in the darkness, transformation began, and it spread. The forest unfolded at her back, to her sides, and directly before her; the path lost shadow and darkness in their growing light. Light, however, did not diminish the demon; it hallowed him. Jewel felt her mouth go dry at the sight of Lord Ishavriel in the gleaming of Winter light. He was beautiful, yes, and cold—but there was something about his expression in the shadows cast by light that implied a sorrow so deep and ancient she couldn't even comprehend it.

She took a step forward and reached out with one hand—it was not the hand that anchored her to the tree.

"Do not be a fool," a familiar voice said. Winter voice. Celleriant had come. He looked up at the height of the tree she now held, and his eyes were a silver that reflected gold somehow. "So," he said softly, when he at last looked back down at the grimy, mortal woman to whom his service had been given.

He did something she could never have predicted: He fell to one knee and he bowed his exposed and perfect face toward that knee. She was speechless, which was admittedly rare. But he wasn't done, not yet. He called the sword she'd hoped never to see again. It came to his hand in almost exactly the same fashion as Lord Ishavriel's had done. But it was blue to Ishavriel's red.

He didn't threaten her. He didn't stand. Instead, he placed the sword at her feet, holding only the hilt to do so. "While you live, ATerafin, I will serve you—and only you." He gestured and his shield came to his arm. "I will be your host; I will be your shield. I, and the things at my command."

"But—but—" She felt the tines of the Winter King lodge gently between her shoulders.

Celleriant met her flustered gaze; his own was implacable, immovable. Immortal. He waited.

What the Hells am I supposed to say? It's not like he asked a question.

"The Winter Queen," she finally managed.

"While you live, ATerafin," was Celleriant's reply. It was cold; he would never be warm; no more would he be open and giving. But there was, in the words, an intensity that defied the distance that cold implied.

Tell him to rise, ATerafin.

Jewel was silent. She understood what he offered. She was afraid of it. Of what it might mean, in the future.

Tell him to rise, and allow him to do what he has sworn to do. Lord Ishavriel will not leave this forest merely because you have claimed it; he will cause no damage to your House and your kin because of your intervention—but you are mortal, and he is not. He is Kialli; *his pride will not allow such a retreat.*

And Celleriant?

Lord Celleriant is a Prince of the Winter Court; the Winter Queen and the Lord of the Hells have been bitter enemies for almost the whole of their long existence together. What Lord Ishavriel cannot do for pride's sake, he can for pragmatism— but not if it is you alone he faces.

He can't hurt me here.

He can, Jewel. Understand that. Your pain is far, far too simple. Can he injure you? No; not here. Not now. But it is not you that he will injure. Not you that he will kill.

But—but what would it mean, to be served by a . . . a Prince of the Winter Court?

Only what you make of it, in the end.

If Ishavriel's pride won't allow him to back down—from me—why would Celleriant serve? Where is his *pride?*

The Arianni and the Allasiani were never the same, although they could be kin. A wuffling breath touched the back of her neck; the Winter King was frustrated. *You will need power, ATerafin. In the coming months and years, you will require it.*

She'd known that. But the definition of power had been money, influence, rank. Not this. Not this forest of radiant metal; not the Winter King; not the Arianni.

Yet her enemy—one of many—was more of this world than the other.

She nodded to Celleriant; he did not rise.

Give me your hand, ATerafin. Do not let go of the tree.

I didn't need to be told that.

His breath again, soft, distinct, and very warm. She held out her free hand and *knew*, the instant before it happened, what he would do: He cut it. It bled. Arann stiffened, and she was suddenly glad that it was Arann, and not Angel, by her side. She grimaced and then lowered that bleeding palm toward Celleriant. His eyes flashed silver light, and gold, and ice, and for a moment it seemed to her—from his eyes alone—that he had swallowed the spirit of this forest, had made it his own.

He lifted his sword from its bed of broken cobblestones, and he cut his own palm; he bled. It looked red in the darkness, and it clearly wasn't frozen. When he placed the bleeding cut above her own she hesitated again; she had to force herself to keep the hand steady.

And he knew it, of course. His smile was thin and cold as any smile that ever touched his lips. But it was fierce, also, and bright. His hand in hers was warm. Warm, living; it might have been a mortal hand, by feel alone.

"You know that this is going to be hard, for you," she told him, the words running ahead of her thoughts; ahead of anything but instinct.

"Will it?"

He released her hand. She wasn't surprised to see that no trace of a wound remained on either of their palms; just the blood smeared by their momentary joining. Rising, he adjusted his shield. In the growing forest, Lord Ishavriel stood, watching in a silence that had lost all frustration. It contained, instead, anticipation.

"Yes," was her soft reply. "Because I'll see the Winter Queen again, and you'll be with me. She'll know."

She couldn't see his expression as he walked toward the waiting demon. But his words, as they drifted back, were clear. "She already knows, ATerafin. She knew the moment you accepted my oath."

The trees sang.

It was a slow trickle of sound, each note attenuated; from a single tree the note might have been the faint protest of breeze through branches. But it was not a single tree that Celleriant heard as he approached Lord Ishavriel; it was a forest. It was not a Winter forest, not a Summer forest— but something profound had touched the trees along this path, and their voices were waking.

He wanted to sing to them. As if he were a youth, and the Winter Wars, the gods and their deaths or their abandonment, had never happened. He wanted to stand beneath their bowers and catch the slow fall of their leaves on his upturned face; he wanted to hear their voices and their long, slow words. He did neither. He carried a sword in the heart of this waking place, and he knew that it did not belong here.

But he was sentinel now; he knew that there were other things that did not belong here, and only the sword might drive them away. Perhaps that was all, in the end, that he was to be allowed, for War was in his blood with its savage, strange joy.

"Lord Ishavriel," he said, inclining his head.

"I see the whelp of the Court has chosen to take his leave of its Queen. Have a care, Celleriant. You have, no doubt, seen the fate of those forsworn."

Celleriant was not kind; he knew well the fate of the Sleepers in their endless dream. "Can you hear the trees?" he asked softly, lifting his sword arm and gesturing toward the whole of the forest in one calculated sweep of motion. He knew the answer, of course. The forest did not speak to the dead.

But the dead could listen. The dead could witness what they could no longer touch or hold. The dead—these dead, the demons of Allasakar—could desire what they could never again touch. They had surrendered all ties to the world and its vast deepings to follow their Lord to his new Dominion; they could not now return to those forests, those hollows, those mountains and caverns.

"I hear the fitful dreams of a child," was Ishavriel's cool response. "No more. I hear," he added, "an ending." He leaped up and forward before the last syllable left his lips, and his sword traced a red arc that glinted off blue as Celleriant deflected, dropping onto his knees a moment. Lord Ishavriel was quick and supple in his movements; he did not remain in any place for long. The winds did not carry him. They could, if he chose to bend his will toward their dominance.

But that would be costly.

Ishavriel carried no shield. For a moment, Celleriant was angered; was he so insignificant an enemy that a shield was not required? The anger slid from him as he watched the *Kialli* Lord, replaced by something colder and infinitely more amused.

"Where have you been playing, Lord Ishavriel, that you've lost your shield?"

Lord Ishavriel's smile was as cold and sharp as Celleriant's.

"In distant lands, little princeling." He gestured, and Celleriant heard the familiar—and entirely unwelcome—voice of the wild fire.

Jewel saw the fire before it started.

Saw it, felt its heat, understood that it was coming. She cried out, wordless, to Arann, and he turned, lifting one hand in den-sign. She answered the same way, with a single urgent gesture: fire.

He looked; no fire existed, no flames, no heat. But she didn't have to tell him that it was coming; he understood that by its absence. "Jay—"

"Come here," she told him, striving for calm. "Come here. Stand in the lee of the tree and touch it."

"But Celleriant—"

"Believe that there is *nothing* you or I can do for Celleriant now."

Even protesting, Arann came to the tree and did as she ordered. She then turned to the Winter King.

You hear it.

Jewel nodded. "Can he stop the fire?"

Not safely, no, as Ishavriel must have guessed. Nor, however, can Ishavriel fully contain it, not here. Not so close to the sleeping earth. Something has angered the Kialli Lord.

I can guess. He has that effect on me, too. Jewel hesitated for a moment, and then she reached up, teetering on toes and balanced on the tree's trunk.

What do you do, ATerafin?

She didn't answer—not with words. Not even with thought, which the Winter King would have picked out of the air anyway. Just beyond her, swords were clashing and lightning singed night air, blue and red, blue and red. Voices were raised, but even Celleriant's was alien, to her. She couldn't understand a word he shouted.

Fire in an old forest was never a good thing.

But fire had come to the tree and the tree had taken it in, absorbing its heat and its essence. She closed her eyes, which didn't help; it made the voices and the sound of fighting louder, harsher. She whispered to vines of fire; whispered to the tree's heart, because she was certain it had one. The darkness behind her lids grew red, and the cool night, warm. She opened her eyes.

Wreathing her arms—both arms, and most of her upper body—the vines grew. They had leaves of kindling flame in a shape she recognized. These, unlike the vines, burned to touch. She was as careful as she could be, because they crackled and hissed without voices.

Slowly, steadily, she withdrew her hand from the tree's trunk. The Winter King reared and she shook her head. "Carry me," she told him instead. "Carry me to them; the fire is coming."

Does it come willingly?

"How the hells should I know? It's *fire*." But the truth was, she did know. The voice of the distant fire was raging fury and crackling heat, and it matched the cadence of Lord Ishavriel's incomprehensible words almost exactly. Its voice defined the voice of the betrayed who destroy, rather than weep. Kin to those voices, it was also full of longing, desire, and recognition turned bitter and ugly.

She shouldn't have cared. Mostly, she didn't—because if that fire was unleashed here, it would spend itself attempting to devour what she had built, and what she had built was new. Its roots hadn't had the time to sink into the earth and grow deep enough to withstand this unwelcome visitor.

Not that trees ever did all that well when facing normal fires; these trees, however, weren't normal. They were dreaming trees and waking trees and they existed in a place where the gods might walk; gods, not mortal girls with a touch of vision and a houseful of people who wanted, in the end, to tell her what to do, how to do it, and when.

What would Haval or Devon say to her now? She lifted her arms, and the vines rose with them, red and fine and thin.

The Winter King knelt and she mounted, taking care—as much care as she could—to keep the leaves above his fur and away from his tines. She ended up losing patches of coat, but the coat smoldered and blackened; it didn't catch fire. Thank Kalliaris.

What would they say to her now? What would Ellerson say?

The Winter King rose.

"Arann, please, if you trust me at all, stay by the tree, no matter what happens."

She didn't hear his reply because the stag sprang forward, tines lowered. With him rose Jewel and the vines and the leaves of flame. She knew that they were part of the tree, that she was still in contact with it, but she felt exposed as they drew close to the fight. Close was yards away from where Celleriant landed, yards away from where he rose, leaping to one side to avoid flame from the demon Lord's hand.

It was not farther away than the voice of the fire; she bid the Winter King stop without even saying a word. But when she tried to dismount, he moved. *I will stay,* he told her.

Go back to Arann.

No. I will remain, ATerafin, or you will not. Lord Celleriant was ordered to serve you. I am not a Prince of the Winter Court. My choices are mortal choices, not Arianni. You will not dismount.

But the fire—

I will ride the fire, he told her.

You can't.

He was silent for a long moment. *Very well. I will* chance *the fire. If you cannot achieve whatever it is you desire, it will not matter; the fire will consume everything. I fear it will consume the fool who called it forth, as well, but that will be little consolation.*

Little's better than none.

What did she intend to do?

What did she know about fire, after all? What did she know about dreams? What did she know about ancient groves of trees that could be woken with a touch and transformed in the waking? The waking . . .

Wait, did you say that the earth is sleeping?

Yes. But not, I fear, for long, and when it wakes, it will be angry. Can you not feel it?

No.

I feel it beneath my hooves.

Why is it sleeping? She didn't ask how.

I do not know. I cannot wake it, Jewel. Of the many gifts my service to the Wild Hunt has given me, that is not one. Even if I could, I would not do it; the anger of the elements is wild and barely contained; it would uproot your forest as easily as the fire would consume it.

Could I?

I . . . do not know. I do not know if it would hear your voice at all; there are mortals who might bespeak it and be heard, if only briefly. His tone made clear to her why he thought it would be brief.

Avandar had called the wild earth in the Sea of Sorrows; he had called the earth in the village of Damar.

Viandaran cannot be considered mortal. Even were he, he was born at the height of the glory of Man.

She took a breath, closed her eyes, and steadied herself. She was on the back of the Winter King, and if he chose to carry her, she'd never fall off.

On the other hand, she'd singed his perfect, silver fur.

She looked at the vines, and then touched them, sliding her fingers between the leaves and singeing skin in the process. They uncoiled from her forearms like leaved snakes might have, and slid toward the ground, leaving a trail of curled, dark fur in their wake. And wool.

They were there when the fire appeared. The Winter King leaped clear of its opening fanfare: an orange-red blaze with a heart of blue. The vines coiled around the bonfire, red to its shaded hues. Its leaves burst into brighter, longer flames when they met, vine and flame, tree and fire.

What are you doing, Jewel?

I'm telling the fire to go back to sleep and dream of forests, was her curt reply. Before he could ask her how, she added, *Watch.*

The vines took root. They took root, however, on what had been path, its beaten dirt blending into worn cobblestones. Stones began to redden as the vines grew; Jewel prayed that whatever it took to wake the earth, this wasn't it. Flames lapped against the vines, and the vines of fire wrapped themselves around the heart of blue, curling and twining until the fires couldn't be seen. The vines melted together then; they formed a trunk that Jewel didn't dare to touch.

Branches, red and sleek, grew out of that trunk, thick around as her arms; they reached for air, as flames might, and they sprouted leaves. Nothing would touch this tree. Not the cool Winter wind, not the rain, not the snow—and she was certain that snow fell here. As the fire summoned by the demon Lord continued to arrive, the tree grew taller, and taller still, until its height touched—and burned—the edges of the canopy the rest of the trees made.

The Winter King was utterly still as he watched.

"Do you hear it?" she asked him.

Yes.

"Will it stay contained?"

Yes, ATerafin. Yes, Terafin. The fire . . . is not yet awakened; the earth is not yet aware.

"That's the best we're going to be able to do," was her soft reply. It was lost to the clash of steel. "Can Celleriant kill him?"

Not yet.

"Will he withdraw?"

The Winter King turned and walked away from their fight. It wasn't much of an answer, but Jewel had the sense that it was the only one she was going to get. That, and the lightning—in blue and red—that flashed across the whole of the sky, not just the patch under which they met, flying at each other—literally—with their ancient swords, in an echo of their ancient war. She could almost see the others as she walked: the dead, *Allasiani* or *Arianni*, in the dim shadows of the forest that existed beyond her trees. She could see the brief gleam of light off metal at chest and the height of forehead; she could see the same gleam off splints on arms or legs. What she couldn't see—what she was suddenly certain she would never see, should she encounter these shadows again—was any hint of their weapons; swords, she thought—and shields.

The path remembers, the Winter King told her. He walked slowly, Jewel ensconced on his back, his hooves touching cobbled stone without breaking or disturbing a single one.

Arann was waiting for her in tense silence that broke the minute their eyes met. "Jay—"

She shook her head. "It's what he wants," she told her den-kin.

"To fight that demon? To risk his life?"

She nodded. "It's what he's lived for for longer than either of us—or both of us combined—have been alive. I could order him back," she added, acknowledging what he didn't say, but what he was nonetheless asking. "But I think he needs this."

"But—why?"

Jewel shrugged. "Because we can't do what he's doing now."

Arann's eyes were dark and wide; his knuckles were white. "Jay—"

"Don't ask, Arann. I don't understand it either. But he'd rather die there than retreat, and I'll let him. We're leaving. He can find his own way back."

He wanted to argue; she saw that clearly. She even understood why, although it surprised her: Celleriant had been allowed into their kitchen, part of their council no matter how far back he stood. Arann did not want to leave one of their own—one of *her* own—behind in the face of such a danger.

But he swallowed the words.

"He's proving himself to me," she said, relenting. "Yes, I know I don't need that proof—but he needs to give it. I think the Lord of the Hells could walk that path in person and Celleriant would still stand on the road, wielding that sword and that shield. He won't care about the collateral damage the fight causes, though."

That much, Arann knew was true—more than true. Celleriant had argued—coldly and passionately at the same time—for permission to run through the manse slaughtering everyone in it in order to end, as he called it, any opposition to her rule. Arann fell in beside the Winter King; Jewel wondered if that was the reason the stag was moving so slowly.

She turned to look over her shoulder; to see the shadows of the two, demon and Arianni, as their movements emphasized their light, their grace, the death that happened all around them almost as an afterthought. They were beautiful. They were beautiful in the exact same way as the tree of fire was: it burned, no matter how careful you were, but for moments at a time, you didn't *mind* the burning.

"Jay?"

Arann's voice brought her back.

"Where are we going?"

"Home."

"Good. How are we going to get there?"

She pointed. Arann's gaze traveled in the direction of her arm, because a man stood in the road—the cobbled road, the road of the holdings. To his side were trees of silver and gold, and leaves touched his hair and his cape. He wore a familiar face, but she expected that. He was Torvan ATerafin.

And he wasn't.

She slid off the back of the Winter King, and this time, he allowed it. "I think there are other ways back," she whispered. "I *know* if I follow this path, I'll reach the manse."

The Winter King nodded. *Who is he?*

"The Spirit of Terafin," she replied.

He wore armor that Torvan would never have worn, but he was of a height with the second Captain of the Chosen. The real Torvan was probably having catfits about now. So, she was certain, was Avandar. She couldn't sense his presence at all; even the brand on her wrist was cool and unremarkable.

But his smile was not a smile that she'd ever seen on Torvan's face. When she was a few yards from where he held the road, he fell to one knee, just as Celleriant had done. Somehow, it was worse. She stopped moving and stared at his bent, helmed head. Lifting only his hands, he removed that helm and set it across one thigh. He carried no sword that she could see, but she was afraid if he had, it would have been a sword very like Celleriant's. Or Ishavriel's.

He smiled as he looked up. "No, Jewel. It would never be that." His voice was grave.

Hers was thick. "You let her die." It wasn't what she'd meant to say.

But it was, clearly, what he'd been expecting. "And so as punishment for my failure, you will not venture to my side; you will not present yourself at my shrine?" He still did not rise.

". . . no. It wasn't as punishment. She's not dead to me until the end of the funeral rites. Maybe not even then."

"You came to me when she was alive, Jewel."

"Yes. Yes, I did. You know why it's different."

His glance strayed to the forest itself, and he smiled. "I know why it is different, yes. ATerafin."

"Are you going to just sit there on the road?"

"Until you give me leave to rise, yes."

She almost left him there. Almost. But Arann was staring—at her, at him. The Terafin Spirit had never appeared before any other member of her den before. "It's not mine to give," she told him, the words more shaky than the brusque she'd intended.

"ATerafin," he said. And then, just as the Winter King had done, "Terafin."

She closed her eyes. When she opened them, she'd shrunk a couple of inches. "Will you force me to carry all of the resposibility? You've always been here."

"I have always been here," he agreed. "Since the advent of the Twin Kings; since before. I have been here. But all things end, Jewel. Amarais was waiting for you, although she did not know it the first day you met. But I? I had hope. These lands are your lands in a way that they have never belonged to any Terafin before you, even myself. And you will defend them, while you breathe, in a way that I cannot. I can guide—but I cannot guide you, in the end."

"But what about those who come after me?"

He said nothing. But he didn't rise, and she hated to see him on one knee.

"Have you always been here?" She glanced at the trees to either side of where he knelt.

"Yes. Here, on the edges of the path, between my lands and the hidden ways immortals fled to when the gods chose to leave the world."

"And the shrine?"

"It is close, as you must know by now. I am not alive, Jewel. I am not entirely dead, but even spirits know weariness. Perhaps especially spirits. I have watched over Terafin for centuries, with some success and some failure; it is time. There is a force in the North that has already begun to twist and remake the pathways."

She closed her eyes. "Allasakar."

He didn't even blink at the use of the god's name. "Even so. Can you feel him, where you stand?"

"I'd rather not try."

"Ignorance avails you nothing."

"Nothing but peace, for moments at a time. I know I can't face a god. I'd rather not attract his attention, since that's the case."

The Terafin Spirit laughed. His voice was rich and deep, and it echoed in the silent forests. Leaves rustled, as if it were a breeze. "While you live, I will serve you in whatever capacity I am allowed. Will you not accept that service?"

"It's not the service," she said. "It's what it means."

"What does it mean to you, Jewel?"

Jewel shook her head.

"Are you afraid of your failures?"

"I'm afraid to fail, yes. I'm afraid—" She closed her eyes. Opened them again, and straightened her shoulders. "It doesn't matter, does it? The war is coming. For the House. For more."

"For far more. You have begun to build not a House but a city, and you cannot see it yet. Where you travel, I have never dared to travel, alive or dead; nor could I. I cannot guide you further. I cannot demand your service, as I have done in the past. What you give, you must give willingly, because so much of it will be done in ignorance."

"And you can't enlighten me."

"No, Terafin." He smiled, and his eyes were the strangest color; she couldn't quite pin it down.

"All right, get up. We need to get back to the others; they're probably worried by now."

He rose then. "Not gracefully done," he told her. "But done, nonetheless. Do you know where this path leads?"

"Yes. The shrine. The heart of the House."

She had never come to the Terafin shrine without passing the shrines of the Triumvirate first, and it felt almost wrong to do it now. But shrines to the Mother, Reymaris, and Cormaris didn't join or touch the road the Winter King now traveled. Only one shrine did, and it stood at the end of that road, as if it were anchoring the pathway.

She could see the altar at the height of its polished, concentric circles; she could see the light of the sconces at the circular height play off the surfaces of smooth stone. She could feel the weight of the House descend, at last, upon her shoulders; if the Winter King hadn't been carrying her, she might have stopped walking for a moment, dwarfed by what she felt.

But he was carrying her. He didn't run or leap, but he didn't pause either. This slow, stately walk gave her whatever time she needed—or rather, granted her the only time she was allowed. He didn't stop at the path's end; he continued beyond it, to the stairs of the shrine itself. These, he mounted; his hooves clicked against the surface of marble, but only lightly, as if he weighed no more than the squirrels that sometimes annoyed the gardeners so much.

She slid off his back at the altar's side. Arann had already reached the height, and he knelt by the altar, bowing his head. Jewel touched its surface; it was cool—but it would be; it was Henden, and dark.

"Are you not going to ask me what I have to offer the House?" she asked the Terafin Spirit. He was there, silent, his face still Torvan's face.

"No. I will never ask it again. This is not an altar for you to make offerings upon, not anymore."

"Then what purpose does it serve?"

"It is a reminder, Terafin, of what others will sacrifice in service to both you and your House."

"And you think I'll need it?" she asked, trying—and failing—to keep the bitterness out of the question.

"You? No. But I am not a seer, nor was I ever one; I cannot tell you, in the end, what you will need and what you will cast away. I can tell you what you must be willing to do—"

She lifted a hand. "Thanks. You've done that already." She took a deep breath and said, "Well, we're home. Shall we go find the others?"

The Winter King nodded, but waited; he intended for her to ride.

"I won't run away," she told him.

But he knelt anyway, the posture the whole of his demand; she gave in because, damn it, she was tired. The Terafin Spirit did not leave the shrine. He stood at its height, beside the altar, as if he intended to remind her of everything that he himself had sacrificed in the name of Terafin. She didn't—couldn't—hate him, but she was aware as she left that he had lost some of his aura of mystery and wisdom tonight, and she wanted it back.

She wanted to believe that someone, somewhere, knew what they were doing; that someone, somewhere, knew what she had to do. Because if they did, it meant there *was* a right way to do things, a correct path to follow, some way of navigating the strange shape of what House Terafin would become. She wanted it, needed it, and knew that it probably didn't exist. Maybe it never had.

But the need for action, the commitment to it, did. She had given her word to Amarais, and she intended to keep it, and as she passed through the most private areas of the Terafin grounds, she felt, for a moment, that she *could*. She clung to that feeling; it was sure to evaporate under the harsh glare of reason if she examined it too closely. There were so many ways in which she could fail, and so many people who intended her to do exactly that.

Some of them weren't even human.

She glanced up as the Winter King paused, and slid off his back at the shrine of Cormaris. He allowed it without comment, and she made her silent prayers for wisdom and the guidance of gods who had chosen to abandon this world so long ago no one really believed they had walked it. She mounted again, and was not surprised when the Winter King also stopped to allow her to offer her respects—or private pleas—at the shrines of Reymaris and the Mother. At the Mother's shrine, she lingered longest, because the Mother knew mercy, of a kind. Mercy, healing, home.

But she wondered, as she rose, if this was the danger the gods presented to mortals: the sense that *someone*, somewhere, knew it all, and knew it well enough that there was no point and no need to struggle to reach a decision; one could leave it, for eternity, in their hands. If the Mother were here, Jewel would have gratefully handed the whole of the war—all of it—into her keeping. What did you become, in the end, if you never had to make those decisions and those mistakes?

Happier, she decided. But the Mother wasn't here. An echo of her existed in her god-born children, one of whom would be here for the Terafin's funeral rites. But if those god-born children had had either the full power or the full wisdom of their parent, would demons exist in Averalaan at all?

Probably.

They'd almost certainly existed alongside gods and other legends. It was a small wonder any of humanity survived at all.

She rose and once again joined the Winter King, but only because he knelt to allow her to mount—and she had no doubt he'd stay that way until she did, even if she left him behind. The night air was cool. The bright moon was high. It wasn't full, but it didn't matter; she could trace the shadows she'd once called eyes from the safety of the stag's white back. White, she thought, and a bit of black that wasn't there by design.

Arann had no difficulty keeping up, and alone of the Chosen, he es-

corted her. He was silent, as he usually was, but that silence hadn't devolved into either awe or fear. The weight on her shoulders sat on his as
well, but it always had. Was it heavier? Yes.

But their shoulders were stronger now. They could bear it. They'd faced
loss before, and they'd survived—Arann, by the skin of his teeth. Had it
scarred them? Yes. But if there was one thing she'd learned in the inter-
vening years, it was this: everyone, *everyone*, was scarred. No one escaped
life unscathed.

But only the unlucky escaped it without knowing what Jewel knew
now: friendship, trust, love. She frowned. "Arann?"

He was staring straight ahead.

The Winter King paused to wait for him, as if she needed an escort.
You do.

Not here, I don't. Not now.

*You do not require it for reasons of safety, no. But you require it for other rea-
sons. I did not meet your Terafin in any significant way; I saw her die. But having
never met her, I can answer the question I now pose to you.*

Jewel bit back a weary sigh. *The question?*

How often did you see her, within the manse that she ruled, unattended?

Only a handful of times, and all of them had been within her private
quarters. She could have numbered them for the Winter King's benefit,
but she got his point, and hers would have been petty or childish in response. "Arann?"

"Jay—the trees."

Frowning, she looked at the trees. They were far fewer in number on
the grounds than they had been on the path, they were a lot thinner and
a lot shorter, and not a single one of them was silver, gold, or diamond;
nor did there happen to be, oh, a burning one.

"Not *those* trees, stuuuupid girl."

Chapter Ten

SHE'D FORGOTTEN THE CATS. Probably because she'd been proven, time and again, to be optimistic or hopeful. Arann's eyes widened, then; she understood why. Returning to the Terafin shrine had been a lot like waking from a dream—or a nightmare. Hearing the cats meant there was no waking.

"We came to *help* you," the white cat said, landing to one side of the Winter King, and accidentally knocking Arann almost off his feet. The cat whirled and hissed at Arann, who'd managed to keep his balance. "*Clumsy.* Watch where you're *going.*"

Please, please, please tell me that they're not going to stay here, she said to the Winter King.

He was silent.

"*I* want that side," the black cat said, landing pretty much on top of the white one. The gray cat, on the other hand, landed to the right of the stag.

"Is it *very* boring here?" he asked, tilting his head to one side.

"If we're lucky, yes."

"Oh," he said, practically rolling his eyes in disdain, "*luck.*"

"What happened to the demon?"

"He burned some fur," the cat replied.

Jewel was silent for a long moment. "What I meant was—"

"Yes, yes, I understand. You have the *wrong* priorities." The cat gave a huff of sound, very much like a long-suffering sigh. He lifted a paw and inspected it. "He left."

"And Lord Celleriant?"

"What, the noisy, ugly Hunter?"

"That's not how he's normally described, but yes, you know the one I mean."

"He's still there. He's *hugging* trees." The cat snickered.

The other two, however, were hissing and spitting, and their fur was quite a bit . . . fluffier. The white cat, much like the Winter King, was looking a little bit blackened and worse for wear; Jewel had no doubt the black cat had received his share of fire-scoring, but on his fur, in this light, it was harder to tell.

"Look, guys—go home. I've got the most important funeral of my life in less than three days and—"

"Is it yours?" the gray cat interrupted.

"No. I'm not particularly going to care about being ready for my *own* funeral; my funeral will be someone else's problem."

"Well," the gray cat replied, "we're hungry."

At this, the white and the black cats stopped in mid-scuffle. It was a scuffle that would make the gardeners rage had they the energy to expend on anything but the funeral grounds.

Jewel had no idea what obviously magical cats ate—and she was pretty sure she didn't want to ask. *Can I get rid of them?* she asked instead.

Yes, I believe you could.

Good. How?

Destroy them.

. . .

"Fine. We're heading back to my home. It is *not* large, we *have guests*, and *I* will be in trouble for every piece of furniture you damage or destroy. There are mortals living in the manse. There are nothing *but* mortals living in the manse."

The gray cat cleared his throat and looked pointedly at the Winter King.

How, exactly, do I destroy them?

How, exactly, he replied, mimicking her, *did you cause the forest to flourish?*

She didn't know. "The mortals are not to be harmed in *any* way. In fact, it would be best if you didn't speak to any of them at all."

"Can we play with them?"

"No. Absolutely not." She urged the Winter King forward, and Arann chose to walk beside the gray cat, rather than between the cat and Jewel. Her den-mate was staring at them, at their wings, and at their size in visible awe—but he still managed to snicker at their interaction. Jewel might have found it funny had she not felt so tired. Or sane.

As the Winter King started to walk, however, the white cat and the black began to eye each other with growing antagonism.

"Enough!" Jewel shouted, thinking with guilt of the raging, weeping Master Gardener. "You," she said, pointing at the white cat, "will walk beside Arann. You," she continued, to a gray cat that looked about to take offense, "will walk in front of the Winter King. You," she told the black cat, "can stay where you are. Do you think you can get along for an hour or two?"

"We're *hungry*."

"You don't get food until we get through the rest of this. Got it? *I* don't get food either."

Where was she going to put them? Where were they going to stay? Could she even offend their dignity by asking if they were box trained? Never mind that, she thought, eyeing the white and the black balefully. "This is your idea of getting along?"

They were trading insults.

"There's no blood," the gray cat said, over one shoulder.

"How exactly did the Winter King put up with the lot of you?"

"He was lonely?" the white cat replied.

The black cat purred. "The Winter Queen doesn't *like* cats. And *we* don't like the Winter Queen."

"So . . . he put up with you out of spite?"

The black cat hissed. But he fell in to her right; the white cat remained by her side and between the Winter King and Arann. She didn't particularly like the way the two were eyeing the backside of the gray.

But she liked it less as they finally cleared the private path that led from the four shrines that quartered the most private part of the Terafin grounds because the cats suddenly stopped their hissing and whining—mostly about boredom—and straightened their shoulders as they walked. They were not small animals, if they could be called animals at all, and while their wings were now folded, they were folded somewhat higher on their backs than they had been. They looked dangerous when they were silent.

And she remembered, then, that they had felled one of the Arianni without taking any injury themselves. They were her escort. Were it not for Arann, she wasn't certain what she would have looked like: she rode the back of a silver stag, she was attended by three giant, winged cats, and she approached the group from the wrong direction, as if by magic.

As if, she thought, grimacing. *Say it: by magic.* But she couldn't.

Avandar was there first, and if the shallow lights of the garden in evening obscured his expression, experience made it clear enough for Jewel. He was *not* happy. By his side, and approximately *as* happy were Torvan and the two Chosen. They did not seem to be surprised to see the newest members of her entourage. Then again, when on duty, surprise was not one of their facial expressions, and Torvan clearly considered this duty.

But the grim, feral padding of the cats was leavened when the white one whispered, *"There's* the ugly one. Can we play with *him?"*

"Not now, and not without his permission."

The ugly one so spoken of raised one dark brow. Avandar looked even less amused. "Where did you find these?" he asked in a tone of voice that implied their presence was somehow a deliberate choice on her part.

"They came on their own. Hopefully they'll leave that way as well."

The black cat hissed. "Leave? *Leave?* Ssstupid girl, don't you know you *need* us?"

The Chosen still failed to evince surprise. They did shift their grips on their swords, though.

"She does not require servants—"

The gray cat felt the need to hiss at this word.

"—who undermine her dignity, and therefore cause those who must also serve to question her power or her authority."

Jewel wondered why the gray cat looked at its paws so often. The inspection, however, was brief; he casually strolled over to the other cats and swatted both of them on the backside, which caused hissing of a different—and much quieter—nature.

"ATerafin, is this entirely wise?"

She glanced at the cats. Since the answer was obvious, she shrugged; she didn't want the cats to complain any more than they already had.

"The magi?" she asked.

"They are waiting. As is the regent, and if you must know, the Exalted of Cormaris and the Mother. It is just possible that the Exalted of Reymaris will have arrived by the time you return to the funeral site."

Her jaw must have weighed a ton, judging by the way it fell open. She struggled to close it. "But—"

"Sigurne felt it necessary to summon them—and in haste. I do not believe their attendants are at all amused."

"But—but why?"

"You will see, if you do not understand yet." He bowed to her. When he rose, he walked to where the Winter King stood, and examined her. "You are . . . singed."

"Yes. There was a bit of fire on the road."

"Which road, ATerafin?"

"You'd recognize it. We walked it most of the way out of the Stone Deepings."

His smile was a twilight smile; it was cold and dark. It suited his face, but at the same time, made it almost a stranger's. "And the fire?"

"Indirectly, the gift of someone who called himself Lord Ishavriel of the hand—or fist—of God. I'm sorry—I don't remember his title." She nudged the Winter King forward, and he began to walk.

When the cats started to fuss about their position, she stopped him and turned on them. "Guys," she said, her voice low and very, very even, "what-did-I-tell-you?"

Their ears flattened. Well, white ears and black ones, at any rate; the gray seemed impervious.

"But we're *bored*."

Jewel swore that if she heard the word "bored" one more time, someone was going to suffer. Someone, she amended, other than her. Teller had always had a fondness for cats that Jewel had never fully understood. She wondered what he'd make of these ones, because they seemed very much like his cats, to her. "I mean it. We're not going anywhere until you can behave." She folded her arms across her chest, and the Winter King turned to look down on them.

There was sulking. There were, however, no other outbursts. Not even when her domicis chose to insert himself between the white cat and the Winter King. "They are no longer stone," he said quietly.

"No. I have no idea why. I have no idea where they came from," she added, trying not to sound defensive. "I wasn't even thinking about them. At all."

"They have left the side of the Winter King; that much makes clear that Ariane found him."

"Yes, but there's no *Summer*," the black cat hissed. "The Hunters were *all* upset about it. So was the Winter Queen. She tried to *kill* us." It hissed again; this one was laughter. "But the castle fell down, and we didn't want to play with them anymore, so we came *here*."

Jewel, astride the Winter King, failed to respond, which was kindest, not that she thought the cats would actually notice. She moved through the garden at night, and as she did, she became aware of the changes in it. Even in the darkness.

"Avandar—" She glanced down at him.

He nodded, the strange smile still curving his lips.

"The Master Gardener is going to string me up!"

"Oh, I doubt that, ATerafin. The changes, after all, are in *his* garden, in his grounds, and they will be celebrated across the Empire. Once," he added, "it is determined that they are not inimical in nature."

She was silent as the Winter King walked in his slow, exact way. "What did you see?" she finally asked.

"I? I saw you touch the tree," he replied. "And I saw you take one step onto the hidden path."

"But—"

"I was not close enough to follow, and you were not kind enough to leave a trail. Had you been, on the other hand, you would have had the company of every mage on the grounds. You may yet have that, if Sigurne Mellifas cannot contain them." He hesitated, and then added, "You are likely to have less welcome company, as well."

She grimaced. "Duvari?"

"As you say."

"And the tree?"

"The tree?"

"The one I touched. The one that almost killed Celleriant."

He didn't answer.

Had Jewel been walking on her own two feet, she would have frozen in shock at the answer to the question she'd asked. As it was, the silence of shock didn't result in lack of movement because the Winter King kept going, oblivious—probably deliberately—to her reaction.

What had been an almost burnt-out husk hours—had it really been hours?—before was now a tree in its full glory, and it was a very familiar tree. Oh, it wasn't silver or gold or diamond, and it certainly didn't burn with leaves of flame, but she knew its shape and form much better.

So did everyone present; who among them hadn't wandered between the trunks of those great, famed trees that girded the Common? The magi were responsible for the festival of lights that occurred there, and the magi often paused at the heights of those trees, heights untouchable by anything save magic and wind.

When the demons had attacked the Common, it wasn't the architectural damage they'd done that had raised the most hue and cry; it was the damage they'd done to some of those trees.

Here, now, in the center of the Terafin grounds, one of those trees was in bloom. In the winter. It was as tall, and as sound, as the trees in the Common—trees that existed nowhere else in the Empire, as far as Jewel knew. But now, one was here.

The magi made room for her as she approached, and why wouldn't they? She heard their whispers—if something that loud could be dignified with the word whisper—as she passed them by, accompanied by Arann, Avandar, and the cats. It was the cats that had grabbed their attention, and she was certain they knew it, but they didn't stop to preen.

She slid off the Winter King's back as they reached the trunk of the tree; by silent assent, she was given leave to do that much. She touched its trunk, felt familiar bark beneath her hands—and more. She could swear the trunk was warm, as if it indeed had a heart of fire encased within it.

"It is not the only one," Avandar said quietly. "If you look, Jewel, you will see that there are several."

But she looked at this one, and understood. No trees of silver or gold or diamond could grow in this soil; no trees of flame and fire could take root here without destroying everything they touched. Hand against bark, she could see them anyway: the Winter Forest, the Winter trees. They also existed, and she could reach out and touch them if she chose.

She didn't. Instead, she bent and retrieved one fallen leaf, and thought of her Oma. She was still holding the leaf when she finally turned to face the crowd that had gathered—at a more respectful distance—from the tree. From her.

The third of the Exalted had, as Avandar predicted, arrived. All of the Exalted stood to one side of the magi, watching her. They watched the cats as well, with some unease; they watched the Winter King. She was grateful that Celleriant had not yet decided to return.

Remembering her first meeting with the Exalted so many years ago, Jewel bowed very deeply. She didn't prostrate herself; she knew it wasn't required. But she held the bow that form did demand until she was told—by the Exalted of the Mother—to rise. It was always problematic when the Mother's Daughters spoke, because their voices had some essential warmth that screamed home in a way that made Jewel want to drop to her knees and crouch by their sides. The Exalted was no exception, but at least tonight that warmth was somewhat stymied by a clear sense of unease.

"Exalted," Jewel said.

The older woman, her golden eyes ringed by lines and lack of sleep, dredged a smile out of somewhere and offered it. Jewel cast a warning look at the cats, who sat at her back in perfect silence. It couldn't last, but if it lasted just long enough, she promised to remember to be grateful.

"ATerafin. We are happy to see that you have returned safely. The guildmaster felt it prudent to summon us—in haste—when you disappeared. Although it is clear you are safe, we do not feel that she was in error." The Exalted then indicated, by dip of chin, that Jewel was to move out of the way, and Jewel had been raised by old women; she moved.

The cats moved with her, eyeing the Exalted in a way that made Jewel's heart skip a beat. She placed one hand on the tops of the heads of the white and the black cats.

"Do you know the history of these trees?" the Mother's Daughter asked as she approached the girth of the trunk. It was significantly wider than it had been scant hours ago, and a hell of a lot more healthy.

Jewel frowned. Did she? She'd heard stories about the trees, of course—anyone who grew up near the Common had. "No, Exalted."

"Ah. There is—was—only one place in the whole of the Empire that these trees are said to grow. They were called Moorelas' trees, in the lays of old."

That, Jewel hadn't heard. "Were they his?"

"I think not. They were also called Summer Trees, and Winter, depending on the teller, and I think the heart of that is closer to the truth. It is not all of the truth." She hesitated, and then glanced at the silent Exalted of the other two churches.

The Exalted of Cormaris nodded, and she raised a white brow. He began to speak.

"Some decades past, ATerafin, you were responsible for drawing our attention—and the attention, indirectly, of our parents—to the crypt in which the Sleepers lie."

Jewel nodded.

"The crypt lies under the shadow of Moorelas, a reminder of death—a reminder of the cost of waking those who must sleep."

She nodded again, but this time more hesitantly.

"That crypt is on the mainland. It is within the bounds of the City proper, within the hundred holdings."

Everyone knew this. She waited.

"It has long been believed, by at least Teos, Lord of Knowledge, that the trees grow in the City because the Sleepers lie here."

"But—"

"But?"

"They're just *trees*."

"Indeed, ATerafin. It is why Teos' beliefs in this matter have been given little credence; they have also been given little play for other reasons. The location of the Sleepers has long been known to the gods alone. In time, it will once again be a matter of myth and children's stories, although perhaps that is the work of decades." He glanced at the tree, but did not approach.

"Now, it appears, there are new trees. We have taken no time to consult with our parents," he added. "Nor will we until we can more coherently report on this night's events. From where did these trees come?"

Jewel glanced at Sigurne.

"I cannot answer," Sigurne said, also drawing the attention of the Exalted. "For my part, I witnessed only the first half of this singular transformation, and I have already told the Exalted what I saw."

"Indeed, indeed, Guildmaster." The Son of Cormaris turned back to Jewel. "Sigurne AMellifas saw you vanish. You walked to the tree, you touched it, and you simply ceased to exist in any way that her magics could detect."

Jewel nodded. "That's not quite what it looked like to me—but I did walk. I walked down a path into a forest." She glanced at her hands; they were full of cat, but otherwise empty. The leaves she had received the second time had taken root as well.

"One of your guards went with you."

"Yes."

"And that guard?"

She gestured at Arann and he stepped forward. He was no longer a boy; even in the presence of the Exalted, he was as neutral as Torvan in expression and bearing.

"Your name?"

"Arann Cartan."

"Of the Terafin House Guard?"

"Yes, Exalted."

"And you saw what your master saw?"

"Yes, Exalted. We walked down a path. I didn't see forest as clearly as she did; I was watching her and the edges of the path. It was dark," he added.

"But it was definitely forest."

Arann nodded. There was no hesitation in the nod. No description either. Whatever was said, Jewel would say, or no one would.

"Sigurne," she said, "I took the leaves into the forest. They took root there." All hesitations were hers here. "There were trees of silver, gold, and diamond on the path by the time they'd finished."

Sigurne glanced at the silent cats.

"The cats came after the trees grew."

"And they are yours?"

Jewel winced. "They're cats," she said, as if that explained everything. "But bigger, and with wings."

The Exalted exchanged a glance, and then gathered by the base of the great tree. And it was a great tree, now; it was taller, wider, its branches higher, than any tree that otherwise graced the gardens.

"ATerafin," the Mother's Daughter said, "Do you understand the nature of the forest in which you walked?"

Jewel was silent. "No," she finally said. "It's not—it's not completely real, to me. It's like a conscious dream; I understood it while I stood on the path. I understood what it meant, how to walk it, how to hold it against all enemies. But now?"

"Can you return?"

Jewel took a deep breath. "Yes. I can."

"Was it night there?"

Jewel nodded.

"Is it night now?"

"Yes. I'm not sure I understand the question," she added, glancing pointedly at the moon. "It's night here."

"Very well. We will be present two and a half days from now; we will ask you that question again at that time." She turned to the guildmaster. "Sigurne."

Sigurne approached, and to Jewel's surprise, the Mother's Daughter held out both of her hands; the mage took them carefully—and it seemed, to Jewel, gratefully.

"You needn't worry that you have roused us for no purpose. We judge the trees in the garden safe, for both the funeral rites, and those who might come to view them. It is not these trees, however, that are now in question, and you have alerted us to a possibility that the wise had not foreseen. Rest easy, if indeed you can; you have expended no political capital, and it is possible we may be in your debt."

"In a matter of this nature, debt cannot be accrued between those who hold the interests of the Empire at heart."

"I fear, in the end, the interests that you speak of will encompass far more," was the Exalted's quiet reply. She withdrew her hands when Sigurne released them, and this time, she approached Jewel.

"You seem a very ordinary girl," she said, after a long moment of silent inspection. It wasn't quite what Jewel had expected, and had anyone else said it, it would have been just this side of rude. The wrong side. "Tell me, ATerafin, why did you step upon that path? I will not ask how. It is not a question I believe you can answer."

"It seemed necessary, at the time. I'm sorry, Exalted; I don't have a better explanation. It was instinctive. I've learned, with time, to trust my instincts."

The Exalted of the Mother nodded kindly. "Your instincts, we have been informed, are very . . . certain. What did you find on the path, ATerafin?"

"The heart of a tree," Jewel replied, knowing how stupid it would sound. "And more. I think—" she shook her head. "I found House Terafin. I found the hundred holdings. I found some part of the city I've known all my life."

"That is not all."

"No, it never is—but they *were* there. They *are* there. I don't know how. But it's not the first time I've walked a path like that."

"And the last time?"

"I met the Winter Queen."

Silence.

The silence couldn't last. Jewel, who rarely valued silence—because it was so synonymous with emptiness—regretted its passing. "It is as we suspected," the Exalted of Cormaris said. He spoke with his usual quiet authority. "She has traversed the hidden paths." He turned to Jewel. "The Exalted of the Mother has said she will not ask you how you could step upon that path, but I must. How, ATerafin?"

"I don't know."

"Do you not? Do you have no suspicion at all that might lead us to an acceptable answer?"

She could have said no, but that would have been lying—and pinned by the lambent golden eyes of the god-born, lies seemed very, very unwise. "Some of my talent expresses itself in dreams," she finally said. "And our encounter with the tree earlier in the afternoon implied—strongly—that dreaming was involved."

"And you are versed in lucid dreams?"

"No. Just ones that come true."

He raised a graying brow at the edge in her reply, and she had the grace—just barely—to duck her head in apology. She was tired. No, she was exhausted. She wanted nothing more than to hobble back to the West Wing, and fall over into the nearest bed. She didn't much care whose the nearest bed was, at this point.

"Something someone said implied that the dreaming here was a . . . space. A physical presence. That I could walk into it, because in some way, I do that already. In my sleep," she added, aware that the words themselves were both true and . . . stupid. "I had to try."

"You've said that you were driven to this extreme by instinct. What, then, did you find on the hidden path?"

Jewel had so hoped to have this part of the conversation in the privacy of Gabriel's very magically protected office—because it meant she could offload the resulting difficulties onto shoulders that were quite accustomed to the patriciate and its politics. She now surrendered that hope. "A demon."

More silence.

Turning to the very rigid Gabriel ATerafin, Jewel said, "Regent, I think I understand how the demons arrived in Terafin." The regent looked as if he hadn't slept in three days; he also looked aged by about a decade. Neither of these were an improvement. He was, in theory, the ruler of the House; in practice—a practice Jewel understood well, even if she sometimes resented the hell out of it—the Exalted had precedence. But there were some things that the ruler of the House, even if temporary, had to be told first, in Jewel's opinion, and this was the only safe way of making that opinion known.

It wasn't, however, Gabriel who answered.

"ATerafin." The Lord of the Compact stepped forward. He even bowed, although it was entirely perfunctory; there was certainly no respect in the look he gave her as he rose. To be fair to Duvari—which wasn't the first item on Jewel's list of social necessities—he also looked as if he hadn't slept and had aged prematurely. On Duvari, however, Jewel had no doubts that both states were temporary.

"Lord of the Compact," she replied, in a tone just as friendly as the one he'd used. He raised a peppered brow, and then nodded; he offered her the edge of a very cool smile. She swore, but not out loud.

"Please feel free to expand upon the information you have just offered the regent."

"I think they walked here from wherever it is they now reside."

"Explain."

"The Exalted spoke of a hidden path. I think this," she said, lifting a palm to touch the living tree, "is on that path. The demons can walk it."

"And you believe they infiltrated the House by walking *through* the tree?" It was clearly not an answer to Duvari's liking. Duvari had a practical mind. A practical, paranoid mind.

"Not through the tree, no. But to it."

"I will not belabor the obvious by asking about the nature of this specific tree; I can see that it is not . . . entirely natural. Will the demon return?"

"Not that way," she replied.

"And you are certain?"

"Yes."

"How?"

She really disliked Duvari. "Because it's *my* tree, in the middle of *my* lands, and I don't want him here. Any other demon that visits will have to come in through the doors."

"These lands have always been Terafin lands," was his quiet reply. It was quiet in exactly the wrong way. "Are you implying that previous rulers of the House ceded entry to the demons?"

Really, really disliked Duvari. "No. You're inferring it." By pulling it out of your—she stifled the thought. Barely. "The previous rulers of Terafin couldn't walk that path; they couldn't touch it. What they couldn't touch, they couldn't make their own."

"And you—"

"Yes. It's mine."

"I . . . see." He glanced pointedly at the heights of the tree above her head. "And if you can accomplish this—which a host of gardeners going back centuries of Averalaan history could not with all of their combined skill and knowledge—what else can you accomplish, ATerafin?"

"I can keep demons from gaining entrance to Terafin using that particular back door," was her grim reply.

Jewel, Avandar said. He was very aware of how little she liked this silent form of communication, and only used it when he deemed it necessary. *Do not antagonize Duvari unless you* plan *to do so.*

Which wasn't something she needed to be told, on most days. Clearly she needed to be told that tonight.

"Lord of the Compact," the Exalted of Cormaris said, "I believe it is late, and the young ATerafin requires some sleep and some time to gather her thoughts. She has already made clear that she acts on instinct."

"Instinct is not—"

"—And for the moment, until we have the chance to confer with our parents—which I assure you we will be doing before the dawn—I do not believe there is further information to be gained. There is, of course, hostility—but while that suits your particular style, it does not suit hers. There is no need to back her into a corner."

"The Kings, the Queens, and the Exalted will be in attendance for the first day of The Terafin's funeral rites," was the clipped and very cold reply.

"We are aware of that. So, too, will all of The Ten, saving only Terafin, for whom a successor has not yet been chosen, all of the guildmasters, and all of the Sacred of the rest of the churches within the city. I understand that they are not your responsibility, but they serve a necessary function within the domain of the Kings that are."

"What Terafin successor will now be willing to countenance the existence of a woman who can literally manipulate reality in their own backyard?"

"That is, as you are well aware, an internal matter; it is not for any of us to decide what the next Terafin can—or cannot—countenance. We judge that the Kings and the Queens will be safe from this particular threat; the Kings themselves would not ask for more."

"And you will give reassurances—"

"Lord of the Compact, I already have; if you fail to find them reassuring, may I suggest you reconsider?"

Duvari fell silent. Jewel recognized the silence; it was one she herself employed when it was absolutely necessary not to offend the person who was busy offending *her*. She enjoyed it a lot more when Duvari was forced to use it.

And that much petty was almost too much. "Lord of the Compact, I understand your concern. If I could answer your questions, I would. But I can barely put two coherent words together. As Member Mellifas is currently a guest in my wing of the manse, any further conversation on our part will delay her much-needed rest."

"Very well. Regent," he said, turning abruptly to face the very silent Gabriel ATerafin, "I request an appointment to speak with you on the morrow. I also request that Jewel ATerafin be in attendance."

Gabriel nodded. "It will not be first thing in the morning; given the difficulties encountered both this afternoon and this eve, some juggling of the schedule will have to be done. Understand that we are aware of the gravity of the situation; we are also aware of the dangers should any harm befall the royal family. The Chosen are already in motion as we speak."

Duvari nodded. "And the *Astari?*"

"The *Astari* are necessary for the protection of the Kings. Any action that they take while in House Terafin, however, must go through the Chosen. No reasonable request will be refused."

"And you are the arbiter that defines what is reasonable?"

"It is House Terafin, Lord of the Compact," the Exalted of Reymaris now said. He had not spoken a word so far this eve—or rather, not a word meant for any ears other than the god-born's.

Jewel, however, was looking at the shade of indigo the sky had become. She turned to her domicis with a pleading expression. "Can you go and see if Haval's waiting?"

Avandar nodded. Turning, he left the grounds—and he could; he wasn't, as a servant, required to interact with the rest of the people gathered near the base of the tree. He was supposed to be invisible, lucky bastard.

Duvari frowned. "Haval? The dressmaker?"

"Yes. I know it seems insignificant to you, and it probably is—but three members of the House Council will have nothing to wear for the first day rites if he doesn't finish his work; he had very short notice, and—"

Duvari lifted a hand. "Guildmaster," he said, to Sigurne. "Regent. I have much to consider and much to arrange, and I will leave you to your . . . own tasks."

The Winter King vanished before Jewel left the grounds, but she didn't really mark it, because when she left, Gabriel left, and they were obviously going to the same place. Sigurne, however, did not; although she had allowed the meeting to be called to an end because she was in theory exhausted, she remained with the magi and the Exalted.

Arann stayed by Jewel's side; Torvan sent the other two Chosen away, but likewise accompanied her. She decided she didn't care for his work face; it was grim and impenetrable, and it did a whole lot of looking past wherever it was she happened to be standing.

Sadly, the cats found it amusing, and she couldn't ditch the damn things. She tried. They mocked her. They bit each other. They attracted the attention of the night shift. The guards would have gaped, but Torvan was present, and it wasn't worth their jobs.

"Jewel," Gabriel said, when they were well away from the grounds, "do you understand the significance of this day's events?"

It wasn't the question she wanted him to open with; it was, however, the one she'd more or less expected. "To be honest, no."

This drew a slender smile from the regent. The smile faded as he walked, hands behind his back in a loose knot. "Be less honest, in future."

She stopped walking. She dearly wanted to get home, where she could eat—if Haval hadn't arrived—and possibly relax for a few minutes. Instead, she turned to Gabriel. "I don't want to live in a House where I can't even be honest with you."

He raised a brow, and the smile flitted back to the corners of his mouth. "I, too, am weary; I was not perhaps being exact in my advice. Be less honest with outsiders."

This, she could accept. "I know the tree was significant. I mean, the dreaming tree. I know what it could have done to most of the significant powers in the Empire just by standing where it stood."

"It is not, oddly enough, of that incident that I now speak."

"Then what?"

"You have now placed a tree that the experts know cannot exist in the soil of Terafin. I will attempt to control word of the source of its arrival—but, Jewel, you must know how effective that will be." He gestured down the hall and began to walk; she fell in beside him. The cats allowed it, but not quietly. He looked down at their heads. "You will keep them?" he finally asked.

They all turned wide-eyed stares on him.

"I don't have much choice, at the moment. Until I understand why in the Hells they're even here, I don't think I have any hope of sending them back."

"Sadly, I concur. You would do best, within the House, to keep them hidden if it is possible. You would, of course, do best to refrain from riding your stag, as well."

She was silent for the length of the gallery. When she reached its corner, she said, "How bad did it look?"

"Bad is not the correct word, ATerafin."

She sighed. "Inappropriate?"

"A better use of language, but it is not the correct choice in this case. There is no appropriate or inappropriate where matters of magic are involved. But magic, for most of us, is in the realm of gods and the mageborn—and it separates those who are touched or tainted by it. You look like Jewel ATerafin, but in the context of these creatures, you also look dangerously other. It is not a look you would do well to cultivate."

"Gabriel—"

"The House Council meets after the funeral—if you are fortunate."

She opened her mouth and closed it again before words escaped.

"The day's events—and the appearance of the Exalted, not to mention the large number of magi—will, of course, be of concern to the House Council. I will do what I can to keep the meeting in its current scheduled time slot, but I cannot guarantee success. Do not, however, be unprepared."

"For an earlier meeting?"

"Of a type. They will be worried, Jewel. It would not surprise me if a series of more personal, and impromptu, meetings occur during the three days of the funeral rites themselves."

She failed to curse; it was close. "Can I ask you a question?"

"Of course."

"How do you feel about me, now?"

His smile was subtle. "You are Jewel ATerafin. Do you understand why the servants have always favored your den in some small part?"

"Carver."

"If you think Carver is the only young man to lurk around the serving girls—"

She lifted a hand. "Never mind. You obviously understand; tell me."

"You came to the House as an urchin; you came with a pack of orphans, all as underfed and poorly dressed as yourself. Yet you saved the life of The Terafin, inarguably the most significant person in the House. You work; they note it. They knew, when she sent you on your earliest missions, the hour of your departure and the hour of your return; they knew how long your days were.

"Had you complained, they would have known that as well; you bore up under the weight of The Terafin's expectations. You were given a wing of the manse out of which to operate—a privilege afforded to very, very few—and they accepted it. Some of the more senior members of the Council were less enamored of The Terafin's decision, but because you had been instrumental in saving her life, they had to swallow the majority of their complaints.

"You knew very little when you arrived here, and you have—by dint of effort and will—become a success in their eyes. They wanted to believe you could achieve success because they—like anyone—want to believe in stories. You are a story, to them.

"But your chief role in that story has always been to be more human than they are; to come from meaner circumstances and to succeed because, in some unquantifiable way, you are worthy of success. You are still, in their eyes, some part of a story."

She understood then. "And even if the things that happen to me now are more storylike and far less real, it's the wrong story."

"That is my concern."

"Do you understand that I don't feel any different?"

"None of us do. I am regent; I do not feel significantly wiser or more competent than I did when I first applied for the privilege of bearing the House Name. What we appear to be to others is never what we look like to ourselves, and you would do best to remember this." He paused as they reached her door. He hadn't finished, but took his time gathering the rest of his words. "You are living in a story of a very different type.

"It may be, Jewel ATerafin, that the trappings of this story will garner you . . . not fear but approval in some quarters. But if that is the case, it makes you far more of a threat to those who wish to succeed Amarais; they cannot be served by someone who outshines them, even if only by accident.

"You will have six days." He turned, and then turned back and offered her a perfect bow. It silenced her because it was so wrong.

She was still silent when she entered the doors of the wing; Ellerson, not Avandar, was waiting. He lifted a silver brow as the cats had a brief struggle to see who would walk through the doors first. "I see Avandar did not exaggerate," he told Jewel quietly. "I have taken the liberty of having refreshments prepared. Teller and Finch are currently occupying Haval, but he is waiting for your arrival."

"Patiently?"

Ellerson did not reply. "ATerafin."

"I have no idea where they're going to stay," she replied. "I know we have a few rooms left—do you think we could open one and see if they destroy too much of it? Before you ask, no, I have no idea if they're house-broken."

The white cat hissed, clearly unamused.

"They're almost never quiet, on the other hand—so maybe the room farthest from any other occupied room?"

"Very well." He glanced at the cats. "Gentlemen, if you will follow me?"

"We're *hungry*," the black cat said.

When Jewel opened the door of the room that was being used for Haval's fitting, silence ensued. It was a silence underscored by widening eyes—Teller's and Finch's—and by narrowing ones. Haval insisted on light for his work, and the room, given the time of day, was astonishingly well lit. It was also unforgiving. The smudges on her coat couldn't be hidden; they were sadly all much more alarmingly dark then they'd looked when Jewel had faced the Exalted.

"Jewel," Haval said curtly. "So kind of you to join us." He glared at the scorch marks on her outer jacket, which she quickly began to remove. "I would appreciate it if you would keep the damage to your *necessary* clothing to a minimum; I have no time, even absent very theoretical sleep, to undertake another commission."

Finch, however, said, "What happened, Jay?"

"We had a bit of a problem with a tree."

"So you torched it?"

"Not exactly." Jewel handed the coat to Finch, who took it and examined it more critically. "It's all superficial. I'm sure it can be cleaned up."

Haval stiffened. If the harsh light was no kindness to Jewel's clothing, it was even less of one to Haval; he looked exhausted. "The rest of the clothing as well. I want to insist that you bathe before you put on what I've finished so far, but I feel the chance that you fall asleep while doing so is high."

"Is Hannerle—"

"She is *quite* awake, thank you."

"—Angry?"

"And quite angry, as you surmise." He stalked over to the table across which lay a dress that was obviously black and white. This he picked up and carried to Jewel. "How did your discussion with Devon ATerafin go?"

In the events that had followed that discussion, Jewel had almost forgotten its content. "It went."

Haval raised a steel brow.

She relented. "It went well enough that he's willing to undertake any negotiations for compensation directly. With you."

". . . I see."

"I think I understand what's causing the plague, though."

He stiffened, which was very, very unusual for Haval; he *must* be tired. Either that, or he wanted to show surprise, which, given it was Haval, was vastly more likely.

"Before you ask," she told him, words momentarily muffled as she pulled a piece of very fine silk over her face, "I should warn you that we have guests."

"Guests?"

She nodded as her hair sprung free. Some of it lodged just in front of her eyes, but she didn't dare push it aside. Instead, she held out her arms as he approached and began to examine his work and its fitting. "You'll recognize at least one of them."

"Jewel, I am in far too much of a hurry to play games. Who are these guests?"

"Sigurne Mellifas and Matteos Corvel."

"I see. You may lower your right arm. No, your *right* arm." He began to pin some folds of cloth. "And they are not currently in residence?"

"No. I think Sigurne's still speaking with the Exalted."

". . . the Exalted."

"Yes. And the regent." She hesitated, and then glanced at Teller. "You still like cats, right?"

". . . Yes. Why?"

"We have some."

"*You* brought cats home?"

"Not exactly. They followed me. I had Ellerson—with any luck—put them in a room as far away from any other room as he could find."

Teller frowned.

"They're not *exactly* cats. They're—" she searched for an appropriate word; most of the ones that came immediately to mind were street Torra.

"They're the size of large ponies, they have wings, and they talk. They talk a lot."

"So, not cats at all?"

"Wait until you meet them."

Haval, however, was done, at least with sleeves. He knelt to fiddle with hem. "Jewel, why exactly do you have winged cats in your personal residence?"

"Because I don't trust them anywhere else?"

He nudged her into a better posture. "Very well. I would like you to return to your supposition about the cause of the plague."

"It's deliberate. Someone derives power from mortal dreaming, and whoever he—or she—is, they needed power. I don't know how it works, but I think he—or she—caused the sleeping sickness as a way of building that power base."

"And will the sleepers now naturally wake?"

"I don't think so. We didn't exactly catch the person involved, and I'm not sure—yet—how to stop him."

Haval stood, and gestured again; she obligingly turned her back to him, aware of the pins in his hand. "How, exactly, did you arrive at your conclusion?"

"The tree. In the grounds. In the back." She sighed and he poked her.

"I will assume that something occurred that involved that tree."

"It did. The tree had been enchanted. No, that's not the right word—it'll have to do for now. It was partially rooted in the dreaming of the people who haven't woken yet, and partially rooted in something entirely different."

"To what end?"

"Given it was the central element of the grounds at which the opening of the funeral rites were to occur?"

"You failed to mention that. Continue."

"The tree attacked Celleriant; Celleriant survived. He wasn't happy."

"Very little could make that man happy, and if it did, it would certainly not please you. I assume he survived?"

"He did. But he understood how he had been attacked, and why the attack almost succeeded, and he explained that much to me. Whoever warped or twisted the tree is almost certainly responsible for the sleeping sickness."

"He said that?"

"No."

"Your intuition?"

"Yes."

"Can you stop him?"

"*Yes.*" She stiffened as the word left her mouth.

"Will the current sleepers survive?"

No ready answer followed.

Fifteen minutes later, Haval allowed Jewel to step down from the stool and change. He also examined the coat Finch still held. "I will be back tomorrow," he told her, as he began to pack up his various implements. "I would appreciate it greatly if you would hold off on any political crises until then."

"What do you want me to do about Devon?"

"I will arrange to speak with Devon ATerafin." He began to insert needles and long pins into one flat, thick fold of pockets, laid out in a row. When he was done, he would roll them into a bundle; it was usually the last thing he did. "Why did you offer to house Sigurne Mellifas?"

"I didn't offer. I agreed to her request."

Haval nodded and continued his work. "Why, then, did she make the request?"

"Haval—I'm not you. I don't know. I think she wanted two things: to be on the grounds on the off chance that her presence was necessary, and to be able to speak with Celleriant, should he condescend to allow it."

"Celleriant?"

"She seemed fascinated by him. No, that's not the right word. But I think she knows something of the history of his people."

He snorted. "Mages."

"Sigurne's not like most of the magi."

"No; she's almost sane. Clearly, however, some of that sanity is superficial. Very well. You mentioned cats?"

"You'll hate them."

"No doubt. I do not like anything you've mentioned this eve. This . . . difficulty . . . with the tree is the reason for Sigurne's presence?"

"Technically? No. I think Duvari is the reason for her presence."

"Ah. Of course; the Kings and the Queens will be present for the opening rites. Let me then return to the tree. How visible was the difficulty you've mentioned?"

She flinched.

"Never mind. How many witnesses were there?"

"The first time? Only a handful."

". . . the first time."

"The second time, the Exalted were present. Duvari was either present or well-informed."

"And your . . . winged cats the size of large ponies?"

"They came the second time."

"With you."

". . . yes."

"Jewel, do you even understand what the word subtlety means?"

She was silent.

Haval would not have been, but as he opened his mouth, there was a knock at the door.

Ellerson opened it at Jewel's quiet word; he was alone. He bowed very formally to both Jewel and Haval. "Forgive the interruption, ATerafin," he said quietly.

"Sigurne's back?"

"Ah. The guildmaster has indeed returned, but it is not the guildmaster who requests a moment of your time."

"Who, then?"

"Council member Haerrad."

"I'm not interested in speaking with Haerrad."

"No, indeed. It has been a very long, and very eventful day. I did attempt to make this clear; the Council member in question is not known for his ability to accept denial."

Jewel frowned. "It doesn't matter whether or not he accepts it. Does it?"

"Perhaps not. I merely felt you would wish to be informed; he is in the waiting room with four of the House Guard and he is unwilling to leave."

She grimaced.

"Avandar, however, is now encouraging his departure."

Her eyes rounded. "I'll go," she told Ellerson.

He nodded.

Chapter Eleven

JEWEL COULD HEAR NOTHING as she approached the closed door at the end of the hall: nothing but the sharp sound of her own breath. Of the House Council members, there was no one—past or present—that she hated the way she hated Haerrad. If Haerrad were revealed as a demon from the Hells, it wouldn't materially change her feelings.

Even the fact that she was almost certain Rymark had arranged The Terafin's death did not unseat him from his most-hated position, although it did give him some company in the inner circle.

Haerrad was the only one who had gone out of his way to injure—not kill—one of her own just to prove a point. Teller had spent weeks recovering from his broken limb; Jewel had never recovered.

She paused a few yards from the closed door and stared at it, hard. If Avandar killed the bastard, things would get ugly. But would they be uglier, in the end, if he didn't? Standing in the hall, waiting, she heard someone cough. It was the type of polite and wordless command that only one man could utter, and she glanced over her shoulder to meet Ellerson's steady gaze.

"He had Teller's arm broken," she told the domicis quietly. "Because he wanted to encourage my support."

"And you are wondering how much more he will do in the near future?"

She nodded grimly.

"Avandar is not a member of the House," was his quiet reply.

It was all he needed to say. If Haerrad died at Avandar's hand, it wasn't, and couldn't be, an internal affair. Not with Duvari—and his Astari— skulking around the House grounds.

"If I go out there, he gets what he wants."

"Yes."

She hated it. Hated it, but opened the door anyway.

Because she hated Haerrad so desperately, she thought he would be the first—and maybe the only—thing she saw in the room; he wasn't. Avandar was. He stood closest to the door that Jewel had opened. She could only see his back and the stiff, straight lines of his shoulders; she could see his arms by his sides, his hands empty and in appearance relaxed. He wore the robes he always wore in service; they were dark, long, and functional; they were also very fine. The years had made slight changes to their fall, to the line of their shoulders, because fashions changed and Avandar understood the importance of fashion as a wordless statement.

That Jewel herself did not was a source of frustration between them; Jewel understood that all her clothing matched, that it was in perfect repair, that it was perfectly clean. She understood when the function for which she was being clothed was important; she understood, for instance, that the funeral dress was *not* about the funeral. But for everyday wear? More than that still seemed an incredible waste.

But Avandar, in his everyday wear, cast a long and sudden shadow; he was cold, as the nights in the desert had been—and just as dangerous. He was also angry.

She walked into the room; the silence didn't change.

"Avandar," she said, when she reached his back.

He nodded. He didn't turn, didn't glance at her. She knew he wouldn't until Haerrad—and she had no doubt it was Haerrad he was staring at— looked away first. A momentary irritation at the games men played came and went. Everyone played games—and everyone thought the games they *didn't* play were stupid.

She stepped around Avandar.

Haerrad was, to her surprise, seated; his four House Guards, however, were not. They hadn't drawn swords—which was good, because it prevented her anger from boiling over, and at this point it had been such a long day, she needed whatever help she could get. But they clustered to either side of Haerrad, obviously waiting for his command.

Haerrad, however, was not a fool. It was one of Jewel's regrets.

"ATerafin," she said, because in spite of the fact she was obviously now in the room, he was still staring at Avandar. When he failed to look at her, she added, "Councillor."

She doubted he would have shifted his gaze at all if a knock at the outer doors hadn't interrupted it.

Ellerson slid past Jewel and headed down the short hall toward the door as if the obviously occupied waiting room were empty.

"ATerafin," Haerrad said, shifting in his chair and surveying the room as if he owned it.

"I have perhaps ten minutes."

He hadn't been smiling to begin with, so his expression didn't noticeably change. "Ten minutes, ATerafin? At this time?"

"It may have escaped your notice, but the first day of the funeral rites is only three days away. I've been absent from the House, and I'm not a vulture; I was therefore not prepared for The Terafin's death."

His eyes narrowed. She was grateful that the door had carried Ellerson away; vulture was not a word she should have dropped so carelessly, and she was glad he wasn't there to witness it. It was, on the other hand, better than the ones it had replaced.

"I've undertaken the hire of a clothier who is—at this very moment—engaged in fittings. He will undoubtedly work well into the night, and possibly the morning, on very little sleep in order to assure that I am suitably attired. Before you point out that he is being compensated, I'd like to point out that it's not a matter of compensation—it's a matter of time. Period."

"And yet, from all reports, you spent several hours in the Terafin grounds—grounds that have been entirely forbidden to any other member of the House Council. Tell me, Jewel, why were you the only exception?"

"I was not. The regent was also present." She folded her arms. This was also something Ellerson disliked.

His eyes narrowed further; this time he rose. His guards made quiet clanking noises as they readjusted their formation. "You have been absent, ATerafin. I grant that much. Perhaps you are unaware of the difficulties that have surrounded the House Council in your absence."

She nodded; it was a stiff motion. It was also what she could manage, because if she opened her mouth, she'd blurt out Alowan's name, and her words might never stop.

"You are aware that Rymark ATerafin has claimed that he—"

"Is the chosen, and therefore legitimate, heir?"

"Yes."

"I am. I'm also aware that such legitimacy counts for little, in the annals of House History. He failed to bring his signed and sealed document to the House Council meeting; if he failed to present it there, I believe he will never present it at all."

She disliked his smile, and he smiled now. "Very well. You were present on the grounds for much of the evening. The Exalted were seen arriving—in haste—as were the magi. What occurred, ATerafin?"

"I can't answer that question."

"Think carefully before you refuse."

"I don't understand what happened, Haerrad. The Exalted, in theory, will now consult their gods in the hope of receiving the answers that you want from me—and if the Exalted don't understand it and they were there, you're asking too much."

"And you are playing games with the few minutes you've said you have. Only tell me what you saw, and I will be content with the confusion of no ready explanation."

"I'm afraid that will not be possible at this time, Councillor."

Jewel froze; Haerrad froze as well. They both recognized the voice. Only Jewel had to turn.

"Lord of the Compact," Haerrad said, his voice quite chilly. "You are here for the protection of Kings, which is certainly a worthy—and trying—endeavor. I do not seek to interfere in your affairs, and indeed, have proved cooperative where the Crowns are concerned, both in Council and in the manse itself.

"You are not, however, here to interfere in a collegial discussion with a fellow Councillor. I find it odd that you are here at all." He glanced at Jewel as he spoke, but his glance contained no suspicion; to Haerrad, Duvari was the greater threat.

"You mistake me, Councillor. I do not seek to interfere in your discussion, but the security required by the Kings takes precedence until after the funeral, and Jewel ATerafin's services are required now."

"And Jewel ATerafin is part of your security precautions how?"

Duvari raised a brow. He looked, to Jewel's surprise, almost bored. It wasn't an affectation he adopted often; she couldn't think of a single other occasion. "You play games as well, Councillor. You are aware of the fact that the undereducated ATerafin has value to the Crowns; you cannot possibly hope to claim the House Seat if you have somehow managed to remain in ignorance of the reasons.

"You are here because you are curious. You are not the only Councillor to have shown an interest in holding such a discussion this eve. You are merely the first. Jewel ATerafin has, however, been seconded to the service of the Crowns for the duration of the funeral rites."

"Meaning?"

"Your audience with Jewel ATerafin is now at a temporary end. After the closing ceremonies, you may resume it in whatever fashion House custom deems acceptable."

"By whose authority?" Haerrad's voice was soft; the words were quiet.

"By the authority of the regent," was Duvari's bland reply. "I am not cognizant of all of the customs of House Terafin," he added, which was almost certainly a bald-faced lie, "but I believe that the regent's word, in this case, will suffice."

It almost didn't. Haerrad stood motionless, considering Duvari. Whatever he had said to Avandar—and, more important, whatever Avandar had said to him—was of less significance. How much less, Jewel could only guess. And hope.

"Very well," he finally said. "I will speak with the regent."

"You will have, I believe, a small wait; if you were the first to come directly to Jewel ATerafin, you will be the last to go directly to the regent. Good evening."

Haerrad left five minutes later. They were distinctly chilly minutes. Only when the door closed on his back did Jewel relax—and even then, not by much, because Duvari was still in the room.

Duvari glanced at Jewel; he didn't speak. She finally did. "You wanted to speak to me?"

"No."

Nonplussed, Jewel nonetheless recovered quickly. "If you came to speak with the guildmaster, she hasn't returned yet."

"I did not; I am well aware of where the guildmaster is currently situated." He didn't move; he occupied the same small space in the waiting room that Haerrad had, without the benefit of either guards or chair. He didn't need them.

"If you would care to inform the Councillor of the identity of the person with whom you wish to speak—" Ellerson began.

"I would not." Duvari loosely clasped his hands behind his back.

"Very well, Master Duvari. May we offer wine, water, or light refreshments?"

Duvari raised a single brow in silence.

"I can assure you," Jewel said, before anyone else could speak, "they won't be poisoned."

The other brow rose. After a pause, both brows settled into their normal position; she could almost hear them snap into place. "That will not be necessary."

"The refreshments or the assurances?"

"Either."

Jewel turned to Avandar. "Leave him here," she said, which was pointless because Duvari had already made clear he was going to remain here anyway.

Avandar had shed some of the don't-come-near animosity, but he was still both stiff and angry. He managed a clipped nod.

She turned toward the door that led to her room, and Duvari cleared his throat. She didn't turn back, but did pause.

"A word of advice, ATerafin, if you are of the mind to accept it."

"It depends on the advice." She realized, as she spoke, that she was angry as well. It was an amorphous anger. Duvari was not a man she had ever liked, but somewhere along the way, she'd lost some of her fear of him. She wondered if it was something she needed to find again, in a hurry.

"You are no doubt aware that you must choose your allies and associates with care."

Jewel nodded.

"Perhaps you are less aware of the fact that you must choose your enemies with just as much care, and vastly more caution."

She turned, then, her hands sliding up to her hips almost before she could stop them. They were trembling. "And are you telling me, Lord of the Compact, that you are, or will be, my enemy?"

"If the events of the night play out in an unfortunate manner, ATerafin, yes."

A hundred words rushed to leave her mouth in heated fury; she slammed her jaws shut on all of them. "How often," she finally said, her voice thin, "do enemies invite themselves into *my* home?"

"Not often, granted. You will find, however, that there are very few Houses whose doors are closed to me. Even yours." He nodded as she managed to fail to reply. "I will not further interrupt your evening's plans, ATerafin."

She turned, opened the door, and almost ran into Haval, who, burdened by bolts of cloth around which he'd painstakingly wrapped his clothing-in-progress, failed to see her.

She managed to steady those bolts, catching them in open palms and pushing against them as Haval rebalanced his weight. He peered between them, looking less friendly than Duvari or Haerrad had.

"Sorry," she told him, cringing.

"Not nearly as sorry as you will be if your hands are anything less than perfectly clean."

Ellerson—not Avandar—moved in to help Haval, adroitly navigating between them. Haval allowed the domicis to touch his precious creations, reserving a severely disappointed look for Jewel.

"Shall I call for a carriage?" the domicis asked.

"Please." To Jewel, he said, "I will return *first thing* in the morning. I will have rather more baggage when I do, and I will require a room in which to work."

"Will Hannerle come?"

"It is a possibility." He took a deep, steadying breath. "She is—" and stopped. Straightening, he offered her a short bow. "My apologies, ATerafin. I believe I now understand the reason for your almost inexcusable clumsiness." He looked through the barely open door.

"We had guests. Haval?"

His smile was thin and strange; it transformed his face, and not in a way she liked. At all. "I believe I will ask you to inform me of *all* of the events that occurred this eve, ATerafin."

"Now?"

"Sadly, no." He glanced at Ellerson. "Guard those against the depredations of your charges as if their lives depended on it."

Ellerson, hands full, nonetheless managed a perfectly crisp bow—a bow that Haval failed to notice. He approached the half-open door and instead of pushing it open, slid between it and the doorframe.

Jewel stood anchored to the hall, Ellerson at her back and a narrow window into the waiting room before her. She could see Haval's back and Duvari's face, and neither gave much away—but Haval didn't give things away; if nuance and expression were items of barter, he was their master merchant.

"Duvari," he said. "It has been a long time."

Duvari was silent.

"You were never one for idle chatter," Haval continued. He turned, politely and pleasantly, to Avandar. "If we might make use of your function room?"

"Of course."

"Duvari seldom drinks. I, on the other hand, am not above it, especially on occasions of import."

"Wine?"

"Yes. A red, I think."

Duvari was still silent. But when Avandar led Haval to the large room with the fireplace, he followed. Jewel glanced at Ellerson, arms still encumbered by Haval's bundles.

"I do not think," he said quietly, "that your presence would be beneficial."

"Would it be forbidden?"

"I cannot say, ATerafin. You must, of course, do as you think wise."

Jewel hesitated. As she did, Avandar left the room and closed the doors behind him. "Ellerson."

Ellerson nodded.

"Give me Haval's clothing. I would be in your debt if you could attend them."

"Of course."

Jewel approached the door and got a face full of Avandar for her trouble. "No."

Her brows rose.

"I am not entirely certain that both men will emerge at the end of their conversation."

She tensed; she couldn't help it. "But I—"

"Let me be more clear. I think there is not a small chance that only one person will emerge from that room after the conversation starts, regardless of how many people occupy it at its beginning."

She stared at him, and then at the closed doors behind his back. "Duvari wouldn't—"

"I said one man, Jewel. I didn't say which." His words made no sense.

No, that wasn't true. They made sense—but it was a sick sense, a wrong one. "Haval—"

"Jewel."

She bowed her head, thinking not of the clothier who had, in his fashion, taught her so much in his time, but of his wife. Of Hannerle.

"Did you not understand what you were asking of him? Did you truly not understand?"

"Avandar—"

"You know nothing of his past. You've said as much. I think it safest, in the end, that you continue to know as little as possible."

"He can't—"

"There is a reason that Duvari waited here. I do not know how Haval was drawn to his attention, but I can guess."

So could she.

"Before you think of strangling Devon ATerafin, consider the action carefully."

"Haval didn't *want* this. He only—"

"Yes. Because you asked. Because you were willing to ask, and willing to make the shoddy attempt at extortion that you did."

"He knew I couldn't do it."

"Of course he did. But he knew that you were willing to try." He glanced at the doors as Ellerson, tray in hand, approached them. Ellerson's expression was as grim as Avandar's; the two men's gazes met, but neither spoke. Avandar opened the door; Ellerson walked through it. Jewel watched his back, afraid now to peer into the room. "I do not know why, in the end, he agreed. But, ATerafin, he did. He is canny in ways that even I was not in my distant youth.

"Had he wished to avoid Duvari, he could have managed it; he has chosen to confront him, instead. You will allow this."

"What if you're right? What if he dies—"

"Either death will be costly. Jewel—you have asked him to advise you. You have asked him, in the end, to do much more. You must now trust him to do as you've asked. Unless you have insight into what might, or might not, occur, you will go back to your room and you will wait."

By mutual—and unspoken—consent, both Haval and Duvari were silent while Ellerson poured wine and water. The domicis also took a handful of minutes to start a fire in the large, central fireplace behind where the two guests were seated. Haval lifted his glass. "I am afraid," he said, in a friendly, conversational tone, "that I am a very busy man this eve. If I seem curt or short, it is due to the inflexibility of my deadline."

Duvari raised a brow, rather than a glass. He didn't touch the water, and had already made clear that wine was not an option. "You are a tailor?" he finally asked.

"I am a *clothier*. It is how I make a living for myself in these diminished times."

"And your . . . living . . . has led you, coincidentally, to Jewel Markess ATerafin?"

"As you can see."

The silence was broken by the slowly growing crackle of fire as it consumed logs; it was broken, as well, by the click the door made when the domicis closed it.

"Why are you here . . ."

"Haval."

"Haval?"

Haval nodded. "It is my professional name."

"Why are you here?"

"I find it slightly annoying that you persist in disbelief; it is not, however, surprising. I am here to make two dresses and one suit—both fine enough to serve their wearers during the Terafin funeral rites. One of the dresses is for Jewel ATerafin."

"And how long have you been clothing her?"

"I have made dresses for her since her adoption into the House, in the four hundredth and tenth year after—"

Duvari lifted a hand. "I am aware of when she joined the House. The other dress?"

Haval shook his head. "If you cannot puzzle that out, even given short notice and the resulting absence of received reports, you are not fit for the job you now occupy."

The silence was cold. Duvari's slow smile did little to alleviate it. "You haven't changed at all, have you?"

"I have demonstrably changed. I have aged, among other things; I am not the man I was in my misspent youth."

"Misspent? Is that how you are now characterizing it?" Duvari rose. Haval watched him.

"It is, indeed." Haval sipped wine. It was a very good vintage.

"Will you insist on playing these verbal games?"

"What do you think, Duvari? If, as you have said, I have not changed, what will I now do?"

Duvari stiffened. He had been tracing a small oval across the carpet between the two chairs, his hands loosely clasped behind his back. They were, nonetheless, visible. He knew that Haval would be watching.

Haval now took a small stone from his interior pockets and placed it, in plain sight, on the small table which also contained the tray that the domicis had left.

"Come, Duvari. Sit. Pacing like a caged beast is not conducive to conversation."

"Very well. It has come to my attention that you have been offered employ by Jewel ATerafin."

"Indeed. I thought I might have a few days' grace in which to dispense with this commission; I see that I was in error."

"You have accepted her offer."

It was not a question. Haval lifted his glass again. "The wine really is very good," he told an unamused Duvari.

"You have remained invisible. You have taken no work that I am aware of; you have, as you intended, all but vanished."

Haval nodded.

"Why now?"

"She made me an offer I could not refuse."

Duvari's left brow rose. If possible, he appeared to be even less amused.

"You doubt it?"

"She is not capable of making an offer that *you* could not refuse. She is only barely capable—in my opinion—of making the attempt; it would not be convincing to any but the youngest of children."

"I see you *have* been keeping an eye on her."

"I keep an eye, as you put it, on all possible House members of significance. In any House."

"And this is why you are angry?"

"I am not—" Duvari exhaled and sat. "I am, as you guess, somewhat annoyed."

"The reason?"

"You know well what it is. You have not come out of retirement for anyone. You have stayed safely hidden on the edges of normal society. You have not, that I am aware, returned to any of your old haunts or habits— and not for lack of encouragement."

"Ah."

"Do you know how difficult your absence was?"

"No. I look at you now, and I see no trace of that difficulty at all. You had the illusion, in my presence, that there was some sort of safety net; that *I* could somehow fix what you yourself could not, should it come to that. It was only ever illusion, Duvari. Had it not been, I would not have retired."

"Oh?"

"I would not have chosen you."

"That was not your choice to make," was the slightly heated reply.

Haval said nothing. He drank instead.

"And now?"

"Now? I make dresses. I make suits. I keep a store with my somewhat annoyed wife."

"Schaudou—"

"Haval."

"Haval, if you insist. What will you do?"

"I will do nothing that will bring us into conflict. Whether or not you choose to believe that is entirely beyond my control. I have no desire to go to war with you; nor do I have any desire to unseat what must never, in the end, be unseated. Jewel is *not*—"

"You did not see the Exalted this eve."

Haval took a sip of wine. "No. I did not. I was rather involved, if you must know—"

"I do not need to be reminded of your *dresses*." He rose again.

"Jewel is not aware of my previous life."

"If she was entirely unaware, she wouldn't have made the offer."

"She's not a fool; she is aware that I *had* a previous life. She is not, however, entirely aware of what it was or what it entailed. I think," he added, draining the glass and reluctantly setting it down, "she would be properly horrified or revolted if she did know. I will thank you not to enlighten her."

"It is not in *my* interest to see you in her employ."

"You would accept me in your own?"

"You were never a man to entirely serve another's interests."

"That is not a yes."

"It is not."

Haval smiled. "If it will ease you at all, I will rescind my acceptance. I am not acting; I am not what I was."

Duvari froze, and then pivoted neatly on one foot. "What game are you playing?"

"None. It is clear to me that one of her advisers traveled directly to you, and if she has some part of your network at her disposal, she will have no need of the scattered remnants of mine."

"She does not, as you well know, have any part of my network at her disposal."

"Ah. And your informant—is he also aware of my past?"

"No. Nor will he be. But if he mysteriously succumbs to illness or poison, I will be forced to move against you."

"Do not," Haval replied. "If I am not what I was, I am not entirely divorced from it; return me to that battlefield, old friend, at your peril. There is, of course, no word that I can give you which will ease your mind in this matter." He rose. "I will see Jewel ATerafin as The Terafin, if she survives. You cannot possibly have objections to this."

"It is a House affair."

"Indeed. But you have taken the measure of the other candidates, and you are aware that one would be a disaster for you and the other—in my opinion—a disaster for far more."

"There are still two remaining."

"Indeed—both of whom are more experienced and less easily led than the young ATerafin."

"Less easily led? You have not spent much time with the girl."

"I have spent enough time. You dislike subtlety, Duvari; you always did. That was your weakness. It was, however, also your strength. I have no such qualms. What she must do, she will do. Not more, and not less."

"And you will be certain that she sees this clearly?"

"If necessary, yes. The Terafin died at the hands of—"

"A demon. Yes."

"You cannot have forgotten the Dark Days—"

"No. That Henden still haunts us all."

"Were it not for her intervention, it might do more than haunt. I have my reasons, Duvari."

"And if the girl proves a threat to the Empire?"

Haval was surprised. He didn't trouble himself to hide it; it was useful. "Are you being serious? I could swear that I was the one who was drinking, not you."

Duvari didn't dignify the question with an answer; he was always serious. A man with less of a sense of humor did not, in Haval's estimation, exist. It was one of the things he had long admired about Duvari, because his lack of humor did not make him predictable—which was otherwise generally the case. He combined his lack with an unswerving devotion to his goals and a pragmatism that such near-fanaticism often failed to allow.

"I have had some contact with the girl over the past decade and a half," Haval said, when it was clear that Duvari would not comment. "There is nothing in her—at all—that implies a threat to the Empire; I would suggest, tactfully, that a full review of known facts, even yours, would indicate the exact opposite."

"And if known facts—such as they are—indicate otherwise?"

Haval rose. "Give me your facts, Duvari. Innuendo has its uses, but none of them apply here. Have I mentioned that I am on a rather unmerciful deadline?"

"You have. You will forgive me if I consider the nature of the deadline itself inconsequential."

"I am not entirely certain that I will. If you consider this a return to old habits, I don't intend it to be a permanent one; any failure here will, of course, impact my business model."

"I had forgotten," Duvari said, glancing at the empty wineglass before he met Haval's gaze, "how hard it was not to strangle you."

"Then your memories are indeed mercifully kind."

"Schaudou—"

"I will not be called that again."

"You will," Duvari said, with the faint hint of a smile. "You will not be Haval if you accept her offer of employ."

Haval allowed that. "Your report."

"It is not, functionally, a report; I will never be in the position of tendering reports to you again."

"Very well. Your *considered* and *rational* opinion."

"My opinion? Some of the events of the evening defy rationality. It is not to my liking."

"No, it wouldn't be. But *people* frequently defy rationality, and our dislike does not figure significantly in this fact one way or the other. What have I told you?"

"There are rules to irrationality which can be used as very strong levers."

"Good. I was afraid, for a moment, that you had forgotten everything. Except, of course, the time. Your opinion, Duvari?"

"I will not prejudice you one way or the other."

"No, of course not." Haval lifted a brow. "Was that your attempt not to offer what I've asked?"

"It was."

"Very well."

"Before you leave for the evening, ask Jewel ATerafin to show you what she brought back from the grounds. I think you will find it enlightening." He unclasped his hands and let them fall, loosely, to his sides. "Schaudou."

But Haval shook his head. He offered Duvari a pained smile that was almost genuine. "Only give me your word that you will support her, and I will vanish into a safe obscurity." Saying it, he knew that no such word would ever be forthcoming.

Duvari did not disappoint him. But he surprised Haval; he bowed. It was not cursory, and it was not insulting; it lasted *just* long enough to be awkward. Haval approached the doors—but he made his approach without ever taking his eyes off Duvari. Respect or no, Duvari was not above using such a gesture as a feint, and an opening, if he felt it necessary.

Haval did not begrudge him this artifice; after all, he had had some hand in shaping it.

He reached the door; Duvari rose. "I am proud of what you have achieved, Duvari, although I have little right to say it. If I do not die in bed at a ripe old age, I can think of no other to whom I would rather lose what remains of my life."

"If it were necessary, I cannot guarantee that it would be my hand that ended your life."

"Ah." Haval opened the door. "If it were not your hand, you could not guarantee my death at all, necessary or no."

Ellerson was waiting to one side of the door—at a distance that implied he had made no attempt to eavesdrop. He had, by his side, standing at a tilt against the wall, Haval's meticulously rolled bolts; by his feet were the baskets in which thread, needles, and other small tools had been carefully packed.

"My apologies," Haval now said to the domicis, "but I must waste even more of my time—and yours. If Jewel is still awake?"

"She is."

*　　*　　*

Jewel leaped for the door when the knock came. Finch and Teller, however, remained in the chairs they'd pulled up. They'd learned to sit, even during the worst of crises; it was a trick Jewel had yet to manage. She yanked the door open and relaxed when she saw Ellerson standing in its frame.

"Is Haval—"

"They are finished," he replied, with just enough of an edge to the words that she knew at least one of the two was in the hall behind him. She hoped it was Haval, and was reminded that luck was entirely Kalliaris' whim; she could smile and frown at the same damn time. Haval was *not* in a good mood.

Finch and Teller now rose and ducked around Haval and Ellerson in a rush to desert the room; Jewel couldn't blame them. She could resent the cowardice, but was aware that in their position, she'd've done the same thing.

Haval gestured to the vacated chairs. "Sit, please," he told her. To Ellerson, he added, "We would like a few moments in private."

Ellerson glanced at Jewel, who nodded.

"That was not an entirely pleasant way to spend a fraction of an evening—especially not *this* one." He sat, the lines of his shoulders slumping.

Jewel watched him in silence.

"I am sure you have questions," Haval said. "I am afraid most of them will have to wait; I consider my own questions of more import."

"He knew you."

Haval said nothing.

"He recognized you. He was waiting for you."

"If you feel that you can get around my questions by positing statements in place of yours, you are sadly mistaken. I will, however, give you some partial credit for the attempt." He ran a hand through what very little remained of his hair. "Yes. I did not intend to speak with Duvari at all; apparently I was overly optimistic. He was, as you may surmise, not entirely *pleased* to see me."

"He's never pleased to see anyone."

"True. Duvari is not a man who likes people, either in theory or practice." Haval raised a brow. "He is, however, a capable man, and there is no better for the position he currently holds. How many attempts do you think have been made against his life?"

It wasn't the question she'd been expecting, although given the rest of the events of the day itself, she was about done with expectations. "I don't know. I wouldn't dare."

"A good answer. I will not be more specific in my reply than 'many.' Duvari, however, is still alive. Were he not capable, Jewel, he would not be able to openly antagonize so many of the patriciate. He draws their fire because he can."

"And his business with you?"

"Oh, that." Haval waved the question away almost artlessly. Haval, however, was never artless. Jewel's eyes narrowed.

Haval noticed it, of course; he noticed everything. "I believe I said I would not answer your questions this eve, and I will now return to that intent and hold fast. You will now tell me everything that occurred since you left my side this afternoon. Leave out nothing."

Jewel, however, folded her arms across her chest and sat stiff-backed against the chair. "You haven't decided whether or not you're going to work for me."

He raised a brow again. It was comforting because it was familiar, even though familiarity from Haval meant little, in the end, and she knew it.

"Did I?"

"Yes. There was a question about compensation."

"Ah, I remember now."

"I wish I had a memory as convenient as yours."

"Yes, you do. I believe it will be necessary to cultivate it in the days and weeks to come." His face lost the look of tired irritation that had graced it from the moment he'd entered the room. Expression bled out of the lines that surrounded his eyes and lips, leaving nothing in its wake. "I have very little time this evening. At my age, sleep is required, and Hannerle—who has been sleeping for far too long—will be waiting in my workroom for my return. She will *not* be happy," he added, allowing himself a brief grimace.

"I do not, therefore, have the time to play games—and, in a fashion, I regret it. This is the first time that you have attempted to sink your teeth into what I would consider a game of note. You could, in fact, win this round with ease; I cannot, however, allow that. Although it is very, *very*, poor form on my part, I will assume that your offer will be neither insulting nor unacceptable. I will negotiate in—what are the words—ah, good faith. I know that you will do the same."

"I won't be the one negotiating," she told him quietly.

"That is more of a problem, but it is not insurmountable; any truly sublime negotiating tactics on my part cannot be used against you. They can, however, be used with no guilt or troubled conscience on my part whatsoever against someone who in theory has experience and knows better. I suggest you get Jarven to intercede on your behalf." At the mention of the name, Haval's mask slipped again; it was brief, but stronger.

She said, "Jarven knew who you were."

"Jarven is an unfortunately canny man; we have *far* too much in common if one scratches beneath the surface. I would also take great delight in attempting to defraud him, because while it would be very, very difficult to succeed, it would be enormously satisfying to try. It would also, however, take time, which is not in *large* supply at the moment."

She rose.

"Jewel—"

"Come with me."

"To where?"

"Oh, just down to one of the guest rooms."

"Very well."

"How do you feel about cats?" she asked Haval before she'd walked halfway down the hall.

He raised a brow. "Is the question germaine?"

"I think so."

"They're cats. I neither dislike them nor like them in any significant way; I won't step on them should they get underfoot, and it's possible I might feed one were it starving. Will that do?"

"It's not a test. *I'm* not the one who's constantly testing."

"No, you are not. Jewel, strong concerns about the events of the day were heavily intimated. I cannot imagine that you have run afoul of Sigurne Mellifas; I *can* imagine that you could run afoul of the Exalted, or at least their various attendants. The priesthood's public face is not known for its excessive good humor or tolerance, with reason."

She took a deep breath, straightened her shoulders, and headed the rest of the way down the hall. Putting her hand on the door, she said, "Let me do the talking?"

He raised a brow again. "Very well. I was not aware that this room was in use."

"I wasn't aware that you were aware which rooms were in use."

He shrugged. "I am observant; some consider it a failing. It is not, however, a characteristic which is easily turned off."

"Or on?"

"Lamentably not." He frowned. "Are you going to stand here for much longer? If so, I will fetch your dress and work on it while I wait."

She opened the door.

The cats were lounging across the bed. They weren't lounging quietly, and the white and the black seemed to have decided that they wanted the same spot. She wondered if they *always* wanted the same spot, regardless of location. They hadn't descended to spitting or clawing, but their insults were growing in volume.

It was, therefore, the gray cat that lifted his head and gazed at the open door.

"*There* you are," he said. He glanced at his paws and then pushed himself, slowly, to his feet, leaping off the bed, but stepping on folded wings—not his own, of course—in the process. "We've been *very* good."

Jewel stepped into the room; Haval, silent, followed her. She closed the door very carefully behind them both, as if a simple door could actually stop the cats from escaping if they were of the mind to do it.

"Who is *this?*"

"This," Jewel told the approaching gray, "is Haval. He is *very* important to me. I need him in one piece."

Haval coughed politely. "And you are?" he said to the cat. As if, Jewel thought, talking winged cats the size of large ponies were an everyday occurrence in his life.

The cat's eyes widened. "You don't know who I am?"

"No. I would, however, like to be introduced."

The cat looked pointedly at Jewel.

"What? You've never told me your names."

This got the black and white cats to stop insulting each other, which made Jewel's shoulders sink; she had a fair idea of who they'd start insulting next.

"What did she *say?*" the black cat hissed.

"She said she doesn't know our *names*," the white cat replied.

"I wasn't asking *you.*"

Turning to Haval, Jewel said, "I'm sorry. This is what they're like."

Haval, however, was watching the cats; her apology made no difference at all to his expression. She was certain he'd heard it; he heard everything.

"I think," Haval told her, without once looking in her direction, "that it would be advisable to name them. Now."

She stared at the side of his face. "They probably already have names."

"I don't think the names they did possess are as consequential to their sense of identity as you might believe. I feel, however, that it would be most prudent."

"Haval," she shot back, with more than a little frustration, "do you *ever* find anything surprising?"

"Frequently. Why do you ask?"

"Have you seen these cats before?"

"Don't be absurd."

"But you—"

"Jewel, it has been a very long day, and the addition of Duvari and your very unusual guests has not done anything to reward the hours of work I have already put in. Nor will either do anything to shorten the hours ahead of me. Their names, please."

"Fine. You're Shadow, you're Night, and you're Snow."

It was the gray cat that now hissed, but the hiss was wordless.

"Very well. Gentlemen, I am Haval. I am pleased to make your acquaintance. I apologize for the brevity of the introduction, but I am severely overworked by your mistress."

"What are you doing?" Shadow asked.

"I am making a dress for her."

Three cats sucked in one breath. Jewel stared at them.

"You make *dresses*?"

"I do. Not one of them, however, would be fine enough for any of you. They are simple creations of cloth, thread, and beads or pearls; they suggest a hint of majesty, but never aspire to more."

Night whispered the word *aspire* to himself with great satisfaction.

"I will have to leave you now, gentlemen."

"But we're *bored*."

"If any of you feel that you are capable of aiding me in my work, I will, of course, accept the offer with gratitude."

"Hannerle won't," Jewel whispered, out of the corner of her mouth.

"Is it a very *important* dress?" Shadow asked Jewel.

"To me?" Jewel had very little experience with the profoundly wild or magical; she accepted the question at face value, and answered it in the same way. "Yes. Possibly the most important one I've ever worn."

"Oh." He turned and batted Snow's left ear. "You *heard* her."

"Why do *I* have to go?"

"Because *you* can help."

"Haval, I really don't think this is a good idea."

"It is possibly not a wise one, no." He lifted a hand to his brow; it was theatrical.

"Do you ever *look* surprised?"

"When I am forced by the expectations of my audience to do so, yes. On occasion, the surprise is even genuine—but I do not express surprise often without effort." He was silent for a very long moment, and then turned to her. "You will make a room available for my use. It will not be cleaned by your servants; it will not be tidied by your domicis—in fact, it will not be *entered* until I am done."

She stared at him.

"I will require a carriage."

"But—"

"And I will also require a room for Hannerle, if she is willing to either work or speak with me after her arrival. She is not fond of the patriciate; she is merely fond of their custom."

"I—I'll speak with Ellerson."

"Good. Snow," he said, bending slightly to bring his face in line with the cat's eyes. "I will accept your offer with gratitude. Understand, however, that the dress is *my* task."

"She could make it herself," the cat grumbled.

"That," Haval replied, "is now my fear."

Jewel turned to stare at the old man, but he wouldn't meet her gaze.

The cats did not stay in their room once Haval had left it, because Jewel didn't choose to stay in their room either. Shadow stuck a paw in the door before she could close that door on their faces, spreading his wings to expand the space between door and frame. When she looked at him pointedly, he said, "We're *bored*."

If she never heard that word again in her life, she'd be grateful. On the other hand, the only way that was certain to happen was if she died within the next few seconds, so maybe she had to reevalute.

"Couldn't you have chosen a *better* name? *Shadow*?"

"What's wrong with Shadow?"

"It's a *kitten* name."

"And Snow and Night are better?"

He snorted, nudging her with his head. It was probably meant to be friendly; it nearly knocked her off her feet.

"Where are we going?" he asked.

"I don't know about the three of you, but I'm going to sleep." She made it three yards and then pivoted. "No, I *do* know about the three of you. You're not to leave the wing; you're not to bother anyone. I don't even know if you *need* sleep. Celleriant doesn't."

"Why are you comparing *us* to *him*?"

"I wonder." She started to head back to her room; the hall was a lot narrower than she remembered it being. The open door didn't help, much.

"Jay?"

Teller, in his dressing gown, stepped into the hall.

"You're still awake?" she asked, surprised.

"I'm debating that right now." He stared at the cats.

She shoved her hair out of her eyes and exhaled. "It's too damn late for the kitchen," she finally said. "I was going to introduce you all when things were less hectic."

"So, next year some time?"

She almost laughed. "This is Shadow, this is Snow, and this is Night. They're—"

"He *knows* what we are," Snow said, shoving his way past Jewel toward Teller.

"I really don't," Teller told the white cat, who shoved his head deftly under Teller's hand. Teller started to scratch behind his ear; Snow purred. It was a very loud, rumbling sound. Teller looked at Jewel and said, "They're cats?"

"See?"

"They're what I think of as cats, yes. But bigger, meaner, and winged. Maybe not meaner. They can do more damage, though."

"Where did you find them?"

"In the backyard. They followed me home." Since this was more or less what he said whenever *he* brought a cat home, she felt it was fair.

"Why are they here?"

She started to answer, stopped, and said, "They can talk; ask them. I'm going to try to get some sleep. The Exalted are likely to be back tomorrow."

He went still. Snow didn't approve. "The Exalted?"

"Yes."

"Why?"

"They weren't entirely happy about the trees in the grounds. You'll see them. The trees, I mean."

"I'll probably see the Exalted as well, if they come through the rightkin's office. You're all right?" he added, with just a hint of anxiety.

"I've got a lot to think about, and I don't want to think about any of it. Have you seen Avandar?"

Teller shook his head.

"Figures. I'm going to bed," she added. "You three—if anything bad happens to Teller, *anything at all*, I will turn you into Winter coats and pillows."

Snow hissed. "We like *him*."

She left the cats with Teller.

She woke screaming.

Bolting upright as she usually did, she hit something that was both hard and soft. Two eyes—two golden eyes—stared at her in the imperfect darkness of moonlight and shadow. There was no magelight in the room, and no lamp. No Avandar either, although she could sense him somewhere on the periphery of the grounds.

"*What* are you doing?" Shadow demanded. It was Shadow; she wasn't certain how she knew.

"Being crushed to death by a cat."

He hissed. "You are taking up *all* of the bed."

"It's *my* bed."

He hissed again, but accompanied it by lying down. Half on top of her. She grunted as she pulled herself out from beneath his weight. Nightmare melted into his voice and the irritation of his presence, fading before she could catch it and hold it tight.

"It's *not* that kind of dream," he told her, stretching out and laying both of his paws across one of the pillows.

He was warm; the room itself was chilly, as it always was at this time of year. She grunted again as she tried to pull blankets free of his weight and only half succeeded; he wasn't cooperating.

"What do you mean?"

He opened one eye; it was faintly luminescent and should have been disturbing. But light, in the dark of night, was never as disturbing for Jewel as its lack.

"What I said." The eye closed.

"How do you know it's not that kind of dream?"

Both eyes opened. "Well, *is* it?"

"I don't know—thanks to you, I don't remember it."

Shadow snorted. "You're *very* noisy," he said. "You won't get *any* sleep that way."

"Shadow—"

"Oh, very well. It's not that kind of dream because it doesn't *feel* like that kind of dream. But you have to be careful of dreams now." He settled his head back down on his paws.

"What do you mean?"

"Your dreams aren't always safe dreams," the cat replied, losing the edge of winsome whine that characterized most of his speech. "What comes from your dreams can hurt you if you do not wake."

"I woke."

"No," he said, shuffling a few inches toward the center of the bed, and brushing her face with his wings as he settled them tightly against his back. "I woke you. It's not the same thing anymore. The ugly one isn't here. He should be."

"I know."

"But he is speaking with someone important. I will stay."

"I don't want you to stay."

"Yes, you do."

"I really don't."

"You *do*."

Jewel had had more productive conversations with walls. "Tell me why," she said, sinking back into her pillow and staring up at the ceiling, eyes wide.

"I will know when to wake you. I will know where your dreams take you. I will bring you back. *If*," he added, "I want to."

She rolled over onto her side. He tilted his head; his eyes looked like small, contained magestones. "Why?" she asked again.

"Do you *always* ask that question? It's *very* boring." His wings rose and spread, one of them hovering across her upper chest and shoulders. "Why do you think the Winter King made us?"

"I don't know." A few hours ago, she'd've said it was because his isolation had driven him insane.

"We watch, little human. We don't *need* sleep. We *eat* bad dreams."

"You—"

"You cannot always watch; nor could he. *We* can watch, while you sleep." Shadow sniffed. "*He* let us play when he was awake."

"I can't afford to have anyone die because of you. They'll blame me."

"Only," Shadow sniffed, "if you *let* them."

"I don't have much choice."

Shadow snorted. "The Winter King was Snow and Ice; we are not sure what you will be yet. But your dreams are no longer safe dreams. The door is open and you have not closed it."

"How do you know?"

"Because," he said, slowly curving the wing around her as if it were a living blanket, "we are still here. Sleep. I will watch."

"But—"

"No more. Sleep." He leaned over and licked her forehead. He didn't even have cat breath.

"Can I?"

"Sleep?"

"Trust you."

"Of *course* you can trust us. You called us. We came. We will be wherever you are until—"

"I die?"

"Mmmm." He lowered his head again, but this time he kept his eyes open. She was aware of his warmth and the soft, strange texture of his fur; she was aware of his wing because nothing about it was human or normal or threatening. She was aware of the darkness, but his presence held it back, kept it at bay.

She thought she could sleep, and the thought surprised her. Her own lids fell slowly because she was, in the end, very tired. "Shadow?"

"Yes?"

"Why did the Winter King turn you to stone?"

"Oh, *that*."

Chapter Twelve

2nd of Henden, 427 A.A.
Terafin Manse, Averalaan Aramarelas

AVANDAR WOKE JEWEL in the morning. In the very, very early morning. "What," he said, in his clipped, short, and very familiar tone of annoyance, "is that creature doing here?"

Jewel pried her eyes open, glanced at the windows, and closed them again. "He came to keep watch over me while I was sleeping," she replied.

"Implying that I did not."

"No, nothing that subtle." She rolled over on her side, facing the window, which was not coincidentally in the opposite direction. "Where were you?"

"Out. I apologize," he added, in a tone that implied annoyance. "If you could tear yourself from your bed?"

"It's too dark to be morning."

"It would be, but you are required to dress appropriately on this particular morning."

Appropriate was always so dire. "Have the Exalted come for me?"

"They are expected within the hour."

She sat up. Or tried. "Shadow," she whispered, pushing his wing.

Shadow retracted the offending appendage. He sat up, stretched, and exposed whole rows of very unpleasant fangs when he yawned.

"Where," Avandar said, in the same pinched voice, "are the other two?"

"With Teller," Jewel replied, hoping it was still true.

"You left them with Teller."

Before she could answer, he lifted a hand. "Your clothes are here. It is not, however, your clothing that will cause difficulty."

No, of course it wasn't. It was her hair. She often longed to be bald at times like this.

"Ellerson has offered to take care of your hair, and if that is acceptable to you, I will agree."

"He has Finch and Teller."

"Finch's hair is not a permanent disaster, and Finch will not be meeting with the Exalted unless they require a character witness."

Jewel wondered, as she shrugged herself out of covers and cat hair, what she'd done in a previous life that was so bad she deserved mornings with Avandar. "Please tell Ellerson I'd be grateful," she said, meaning it.

He bowed.

"Avandar."

His eyes were a shade of dark that suited the desert and the howling winds of unnatural storm. "ATerafin?"

"Are you bleeding?"

"It is not your concern." He left the room before she could argue.

Ellerson never complained about her hair. She did, frequently, as combs and oils were applied with fervor. Shadow sat on her feet, and Ellerson pretended not to notice him. "Haval and his wife arrived some hours ago," he told her as he worked. "As per Teller's instructions, I have made two rooms available for their use. I have informed the Master of the Household staff that one of those rooms is not to be cleaned or entered at all until it is permanently vacated."

"Will that work?"

Ellerson failed to hear the question.

"Did you see Avandar?"

"I did, as you are well aware."

"Was he injured?"

Again, the older domicis failed to hear the question. Jewel grimaced as he fought with her hair. "I don't suppose Celleriant came back?"

"No, ATerafin. Member Mellifas, however, returned, some half hour before Haval did. She and Member Corvel are in their rooms, but they have asked to be wakened when the Exalted arrive. They will be joining you, I believe."

"Is anyone else going to be, as you put it, joining us?"

"It is my hope that your three winged visitors will not."

Shadow lifted his head and glared balefully at Ellerson. He then dropped that head back on his front paws and heaved a loud sigh of boredom.

An hour later, Jewel was more or less ready to meet important guests. She was also served breakfast in the breakfast room. She was often starving at this time in the morning; at the moment, the sight of food was almost unpleasant. Shadow, who sat by her, ate what she wouldn't touch, although admittedly he ate disdainfully.

Sigurne Mellifas and her aide, Matteos Corvel, joined Jewel in the breakfast room; Matteos stared at the cat as if the last faint hope he'd been dreaming had been shattered. Sigurne, however, nodded at Shadow as she took her seat. She was not under the auspices of the domicis—either—and it showed; she wore what she almost always wore, although admittedly the robes had been pressed and cleaned. Matteos was likewise simply dressed, but both of the magi wore the pendant of the Order over their robes, and on heavier than normal chains.

They also looked very underslept.

Shadow began to roll around on the floor, his claws clicking against wooden slats in a particularly annoying way. Jewel would have thought the wings would at least prevent the rolling part, but apparently she would have been wrong.

The three ate as if they were suffering from hangovers; they didn't speak, although Matteos did grunt, once, in part because Shadow had landed on his foot.

Avandar joined them before breakfast had been abandoned; it certainly hadn't been finished. He was dressed in clean robes, which were in all ways superior to the robes the magi wore. Of the four, he easily looked the most awake, although Jewel suspected this was the opposite of true. "ATerafin."

She nodded and rose.

"The regent has sent word; you are to attend the Exalted in The Terafin's audience chamber."

"Alone?"

"I am, of course, given leave to accompany you."

Shadow hissed.

"The guildmaster and her aide are also invited to attend; the regent implied that your attendance," he added, turning to Sigurne, "was not mandatory."

Torvan and Arrendas were waiting outside of the wing's doors when Jewel emerged. Sigurne and Matteos had elected to accompany her; so had Shadow, but he'd allowed himself to be turned away on the right side of the doors. Jewel looked askance at Torvan, who saluted. Loudly. He was wearing armor that might have looked overdone on parade.

"Torvan—"

"ATerafin." His face was completely blank; his voice, however, was loud. Jewel forced her lips up into what she hoped resembled a smile; it was going to be a long morning.

"It could be worse, dear," Sigurne told her, with what sounded like genuine sympathy. "There are only *two* guards."

This was entirely accurate until the small, moving party reached the large, public gallery. In the gallery's wide halls, the House Guards outnumbered them. They were all dressed in their best armor, and they were on perfect, proud display; light from the expanse of windows was beginning to seep in, although it wouldn't be bright enough to illuminate the gallery for a few hours. This hall, and the one on its opposite side and around a corner, led to the two entrances of the audience chambers; admittedly the one farther away was small and informal in comparison.

But the doors that admitted guests into the presence of The Terafin—or, today, the regent—were very, very fine. They were dark and girded on either side by sculptures on pedestals, and because they occupied part of the wall, and not the end of a hallway, they were wider than any of the other doors in the Terafin manse. At their height, engraved in stone, were words in Old Weston. They were, of course, gilded, as if the addition of a layer of gold could make the words of this almost forgotten language more true; it certainly made them more brilliant.

The doors were open.

Jewel, approaching them by Sigurne's side, felt a twinge of sympathy for Gabriel as she entered the very deep room, because he was seated—in full House colors—on the single throne at the room's far end. Two of the House Guard stood behind the throne, and six stood beneath it, fanning out in threes to either side of the wide, flat stairs that approached the throne.

Gabriel, however, was alone; the Exalted had not yet arrived. He gestured, and Jewel approached the throne. She'd seen it used only a handful of times, and its use now made her feel distinctly uncomfortable. For the first time this morning, she was grateful for Ellerson's ministrations, and the stiff and complicated dress Avandar had chosen. She glanced at the magi; if they felt underdressed, it didn't show.

"ATerafin," Gabriel said. The vaulted ceilings of the room boasted very unforgiving acoustics. Jewel approached the throne, and the House Guards let her pass. Sigurne and Matteos, however, now stood back. Avandar did not.

Jewel bowed to Gabriel, who nodded as she rose. On closer inspection, the regent looked like he'd aged ten years in the past ten hours; the lines around both mouth and eyes were deeply etched. It made him look very severe.

"Jewel," he said, speaking softly, "I must offer you some warning. The Lord of the Compact has both demanded—and received—permission to attend this meeting."

"I guessed as much," she replied. He raised a brow, and she added, "He visited the wing late last night. Do you have any idea what the Exalted are going to say?"

"None."

"Any suspicion?"

"No. And before you ask, if insight before the fact is to be gained, *I* am not the person who will offer it. Come," he added. "Stand to the left of my chair. Speak if you are spoken to; if it is Duvari who asks, answer minimally and with care. Your domicis may join you; have him stand near the guards."

Torvan and Arrendas joined the guards at the base of the stairs, standing to the far right and the far left; nestled there, they didn't make Jewel feel quite so out of place as they had in the halls. She glanced down at her hand; there, a heavy, gold ring girded the second smallest finger. Ivory, ebony, and ruby adorned it, coalescing into the geometric representation of a sword. It was meant to be the House Sword, but on the eve of a House War it merely looked martial.

As if he were regarding it in the same way, Gabriel coughed gently. She stiffened, met his eyes, and was rewarded by the slightest of smiles. "There are things you will never learn," he said softly. "You will never dance well. You will never be a swordsman. You will never be an artisan."

She nodded.

"But there are things that you are that no one else will ever be; do not forget it." He lifted his head as the first of the priests preceded the Exalted into the audience chamber.

If everyone else in the room looked as if they required another week of sleep, the Exalted didn't. It was something about their eyes, Jewel thought; they were golden and warm and that light touched the contours of their individual faces, softening the whole and dispelling the shadows cast by something as insignificant as lack of sleep. If hosts were required to dress and comport themselves with the utmost dignity, guests were not. The Exalted arrived in the same robes they had worn scant hours past. Jewel knew this because some dirt still clung to the hems and knees of the Mother's robe. They had repaired to their cathedrals, in theory to speak with their parents, the gods in whose name they ruled their churches.

Jewel felt her throat tighten as she watched the progress of the Exalted. Their eyes appeared to be far brighter than they normally were; she knew, because each and every one of them gazed, as they walked, at her, their expressions troubled. She noted that Duvari was also in the audience chamber, and that he stood with his back to the far wall in the cold silence that passed for a personality.

The priests that attended them carried the ever-present braziers on their long poles, but they stopped halfway between the doors and the throne, and set those braziers—carefully—to one side; they then drew what looked like small stands from somewhere in their voluminous robes and set them up, with care, at three points. The braziers, still wafting smoke, were placed atop them.

This did not seem all that positive a sign to Jewel who, of course, said nothing. She did hazard a glance at Gabriel; he didn't return it. His gaze was on the Exalted as they approached.

Etiquette did not demand that the children of gods abase themselves before any man or woman in the Empire. On occasion, the Mother's Daughter set etiquette aside as a gesture of either gratitude or respect, but today wasn't going to be one of those. She, of the three, was the grimmest, although it took Jewel a moment to realize why she'd reached this conclusion. Some of her Oma's anger—and worse, much worse—fear could be seen in the set of her jaw and the stiff line of her shoulders.

She bowed to Gabriel, who rose. "Exalted," he said, bowing deeply to each of the three.

"Regent," the Mother's Daughter replied. "We have, as promised, asked for the guidance of our parents."

Gabriel nodded, waiting.

"They are concerned with the events of yesterday. While we could answer some of their questions, we could not answer all of them, and they asked for the opportunity to speak with Jewel ATerafin."

The braziers on the ground suddenly made a lot more sense. Following Jewel's gaze, the Exalted of Cormaris now stepped forward. "It is a request," he said quietly, speaking to her and not to the regent. "The gods cannot command you."

Jewel smiled; it was a grim smile. "Not directly, no. But if I were foolish enough to refuse, Exalted, would the gods not then speak to the Twin Kings?"

He was silent.

"The Twin Kings, of course, *can* command. I'm nervous. Gods make me nervous. But I'm not opposed to speaking with them. I would have liked more time to prepare, but I don't imagine the gods actually care all that much what I'm wearing, how my hair is styled, or how I speak."

At this, his lips twitched, and the gold of his eyes warmed. "As you surmise, ATerafin, they do not."

"The Kings *do*. So I'll happily grant the request now."

"There is one more favor," the Exalted said.

"And that?"

"You traveled to and from the garden grounds with . . . unusual companions. My father would like to speak with them, as well. There were three unusual creatures, your mount, and another that we deem immortal."

Jewel winced. She was certain the gods wouldn't find the cats all that charming—and equally certain that telling the Exalted their parents didn't know what they were asking for would be very stupid. She had no idea where Celleriant *was*, and she didn't look forward to riding the Winter King in the middle of a House full of servants who were already stressed beyond their capacity by the prospect of the funeral and its many, many visitants. She finally settled on, "I'll try."

The Exalted of Cormaris raised a brow.

*   *   *

Since she knew where the cats were—and couldn't immediately face the prospect of attempting to herd them—she set out in search of Celleriant. She did not, however, set out alone; the moment she descended the stairs that led to the throne, Torvan and Arrendas detached themselves from the House Guard and followed her. Avandar likewise retreated from the wall behind the throne.

Jewel paused in front of the Mother's Daughter; she bowed. "I'm not entirely certain where some of my companions are to be found."

The Mother's Daughter reached out and caught both of Jewel's hands in hers, forcing her up from the bow. She met Jewel's gaze, held it, and then released her hands.

"I cannot help but think that the gods are unlikely to be impressed by your guardians," Avandar said, when they'd cleared the doors.

"I'm sure they won't, but they asked, and I'm not about to argue with the Exalted. Do you know where Celleriant is?"

"I? No."

"Avandar—"

"Lord Celleriant is not a House Guard, Jewel. Nor is he Chosen. He was ordered to serve, but—"

She shook her head. "He gave me his oath," she said in a soft voice.

Avandar stopped walking.

"Don't look at me like that," she snapped, although she didn't actually look back to see his expression. "I would have told you if you hadn't ducked out." She continued to walk; Avandar didn't. When she was half the gallery's length ahead of him, she turned.

He stood in the slanting light shed by open windows. Dust, like flakes of snow on a dry, cold day, rose and fell in the air around him. "ATerafin," he finally said. She heard the word as if it had been spoken in her ear.

She saw, for just a moment, the face of a different man emerging from the shifting lines of his unfamiliar expression.

"You do not understand," he told her, voice still much closer than he himself. "Lord Celleriant is one of the host."

"I understand."

He shook his head. "How often do you think an Arianni Prince swears fealty to a mortal?"

Torvan and Arrendas now flanked her, and she wished—for just a moment—that they would go away. Them, the guards that were on display up and down the gallery, the visible servants and pages walking briskly to and from other destinations.

She took a deep breath, expelled it, and let her shoulders sink. "Avandar, I don't know." When she met his gaze again, she saw an echo of ancient cities, ancient wars, and ancient deaths. She saw the ghost of a sword in his hand. "Please," she half whispered. "Let me bury her. Let me pay her the respect she deserves. I'll think about all of this after, I promise."

"Jewel—"

"Be what you've been for half my life. Until then. Just until then." She lifted a hand toward him.

His expression slowly shed the ages, but when he walked toward her, it was not as a servant. "I will wait," he told her quietly. "But, Jewel—"

"I know. You want to tell me that it's never happened before. You'd be wrong," she added, before she could stop herself.

He lifted a brow, and this was a familiar expression; she clung to it. "I would like to know more about how I am, as you suggest, incorrect."

"I don't know. I know it's true," she added almost wearily. "But you'd probably have to ask Celleriant, and I'm betting he'd be damned if he answered." She frowned, and turned back down the gallery hall. Torvan and Arrendas followed, as did Avandar.

The grounds were, in theory, off-limits. Theory was tenuous; the Master Gardener still had work to do, and if he had been ordered to wait upon the decision of the Exalted, he was nonetheless working at the edges of what had been a disaster some scant hours past, along with some half dozen men and women who all wore the distinctively dirty colors of the House. House Guards, meant to work and not to present Terafin's best face to visitors of import, were not in the best of moods; arguing with the Master Gardener the day before every noble of note in the Empire was due to descend upon his territory was a task Jewel envied no one.

They did not, however, offer much argument to Arrendas when he spoke with them; Jewel didn't hear what was said, but whatever it was, it allowed her access to the grounds; the House Guards simply looked through her.

"He is here?" Avandar asked.

Jewel frowned, but didn't answer; she walked the newly remade path until it once again gave way to a destruction the distraught gardeners had been forbidden to repair. She moved beyond that with care, aware that a stumble or fall in this dress would be disastrous. But she looked, as she walked, to the tree. To the trees, really. They were so tall and so wide they might have been transplanted from the Common, and they'd shed leaves on the turned dirt and broken stone.

"Celleriant," she called.

She wasn't surprised when he came out from behind the trunk of the central tree. His hands were empty; he carried no sword. He was pale—although, given his complexion, this wasn't as obvious as it could have been. She thought him not fully recovered from his fight—with either the dreaming tree or the demon—but something about his bearing prevented her from asking.

He didn't speak. Didn't bow. But he left the lee of the tree and approached her, his eyes silver-gray in the morning light.

"Celleriant," she said, relief warring with a growing sense of discomfort. "The god-born are here, and they want—they ask—you to speak with the gods."

He raised a pale brow and then shrugged as if gods were of little import. "What is your desire?"

"Politically speaking, that you agree."

"Very well. I agree."

She turned back toward the manse, and he fell into step beside her; Torvan and Arrendas had to widen their paths to make room, and at least one of them didn't like it much. She couldn't blame him. Celleriant looked very much like the reason one had guards to begin with: wild, dangerous, unpredictable. Deadly. But then again, hadn't he always?

She could forget it for moments—or days—at a time. She glanced at him; his hair was long and fine, as unlike hers in color, length, or enviable straightness as hair could possibly get. He'd lived forever; she'd struggled for thirty years. She knew he could kill without blinking; knew, further, that he could face death with anticipation and joy. He wasn't Duster; she knew that. Duster? She'd liked—and hated—foods. Mornings. Cats. She could be embarrassed, could feel guilt, could rage in fury at the oddest moments.

Her ability to kill had never completely defined her.

Jewel stopped walking at the sound of an extra pair of feet—or two pairs. The Winter King had also left the forest.

In the desert, the Winter King and the Arianni Lord had somehow seemed more natural; at the base of the stairs—adorned by House Guards who looked, sadly, a lot less bored as they approached—they clashed with the life she'd worked so hard to build. They weren't part of it. But they would be, and she knew it. What she didn't know was what her life would then become.

To Avandar, she simply said, "Let's go get the cats."

It was a strange procession that made its way through the early morning halls of the Terafin manse, and Jewel was more aware of it on this occasion than she had ever been. She had managed to pry only two of the cats out of the wing; the third, Snow, was closeted in the closed room within which Haval was working, and wouldn't come out. She'd stood on the other side of the door, hesitating, when Night and Shadow offered to go in and get him for her; that made the decision to leave him behind much easier.

Besides which, Shadow seldom fought with either Snow or Night, and if one of the two were left behind, she might be able to sustain the faint hope that the cats would behave. They were certainly behaving now, which she found unsettling. They were silent, and their silence seemed to enlarge them; their wings were folded loosely over their backs, and their fur—black and gray—caught light, gleaming with it, as if they were partly metallic. Their eyes were steady, unblinking, their heads were not held high, but rather, closer to ground, as if they were prepared to hunt.

She hadn't chosen to ride the Winter King, although he had all but insisted; he walked to her right. Celleriant walked to her left; Avandar and the two Chosen took up the rear. The cats, of course, headed the strange procession—and it was strange enough that the House Guard in their full finery couldn't help but stare.

"Shadow. Night. It's on the *right*. The big doors."

Shadow turned one baleful glare on her, but dutifully headed toward the doors she had labeled as big. Night hissed, but it was a relatively quiet hiss, and did the same.

They entered the audience chamber.

Gabriel was seated upon the distant throne, but between the doors and the throne, the Exalted waited. Chairs—fine chairs—had been brought for their use, but they had apparently been declined; the chairs were empty. Duvari was to the right, nearest the doors, his gaze hooded and unfriendly—but this, at least, was normal. And a day where Duvari came as a bit of a relief was far too strange and uncomfortable.

The cats continued to lead, and Jewel walked past the braziers that had been set up in a very flat, loose triangle on the floor; frail threads of smoke rose from their incense. When she approached Sigurne Mellifas, the guild-master nodded. Matteos, however, was watching the cats, Celleriant, and the Winter King as if he couldn't quite decide between awe and worry. On the other hand, it was Matteos; worry was likely to win out.

The cats stopped a few yards from where the Exalted stood. Jewel approached them, but the Winter King and Celleriant likewise held their ground, waiting. This left her with Torvan and Arrendas for comfort, but the Chosen once again took up positions at the end of the House Guards.

Jewel bowed to the Exalted. She held the bow until the Mother's Daughter bade her rise.

"I'm sorry it took so long," Jewel told her. "But my companions were scattered."

The Exalted didn't answer. Instead, she looked past Jewel's shoulder to where the priests were milling. The priests, unlike the House Guards, had clearly not been chosen for their ability to stand at attention. They were staring—some of them openly—at the cats and the Winter King.

"We will begin," the Exalted said, with just enough edge in the simple words that the priests immediately forgot what they were looking at and concentrated on whatever it was they were supposed to be doing. Night snickered.

Jewel turned and glared him into silence, which unfortunately caused Shadow to snicker. She *knew* they could kill, but it was impossible to keep that at the forefront of her thoughts; mostly she wanted to smack them or send them back to their room.

"Are they dangerous?" The Exalted of Reymaris was staring at the two cats; it was the first time this morning that Jewel had heard him speak.

"They can be."

"Will they cause difficulty now?"

"No." Turning to the cats, she said, "Come here."

They did, although Night hissed a little and lagged behind Shadow. She crouched between them. "We're going to the Between."

"What is the Between?"

"The place where men can talk to their gods."

The two cats exchanged a glance. "Why do we have to go somewhere *else*?" Night finally asked.

"Because that's where the gods are."

"Make them come to *us*."

Jewel winced.

The Exalted of Reymaris said, "Oh, they will," as the mists began to roll in.

Something about the way the mists rolled in felt familiar. Jewel rose, but kept her hands on the tops of the gray and black heads with their twitching ears. The walls of the audience chamber faded from sight first. She was surprised when the throne—with Gabriel on it—did likewise. He wasn't here. Neither, she saw, was Duvari, and that would piss him off. The House Guards, like the throne, failed to be encompassed by the fog; the Winter King, Celleriant, and Avandar did not. Nor did the magi.

"Duvari is going to be really, really angry," Jewel said.

"Indeed," the Exalted of Cormaris replied. "But the request did not come from Duvari; nor did it come from the Regent. It came from our parents, and it was tendered, specifically, to you."

"I'd rather you included him. He can't get angry at you—it's me he'll—"

"He will not."

Clearly, the Exalted were used to two things: their position of unassailable power and their position of unassailable trustworthiness. Duvari did not—ever—speak word against the Exalted.

"Child," the Mother's Daughter added, "it is, in its entirety, for your sake that we have chosen to exclude him."

She hesitated and then lifted her chin. "You think something will be said that will make me more of a threat to Duvari than I already am?"

"We cannot say for certain," the Mother's Daughter said. But the Exalted of Reymaris said, "Yes. And it is not to my liking to exclude the Lord of the Compact, although we have had our disagreements in the past."

A glance passed between the Exalted of Cormaris and the Mother's Daughter; the Exalted of Reymaris frowned. "We have reached an agreement," he told them in a cool voice, "and not all agreements require consensus."

The mists rose as they spoke. Night hissed and unfurled his wings; Shadow, however, sat and began to lick imaginary dust off his paw. The cats' eyes were gold and shining, and Jewel thought it odd how very like the eyes of the god-born they were in color, if not shape.

"ATerafin," the Exalted of Reymaris said softly. "Mind your atten-dants."

Frowning, she turned to look at the two she couldn't see, as the cats were relatively well-behaved. Avandar was, of course, himself; starched and cool. But Celleriant had drawn sword, and even as the mists rose, they rose to either side of the blade.

"Celleriant, we're not here to fight," she said, in quiet, evenly spaced syllables.

He said nothing.

"They *like* to fight," Shadow whispered. "It's what they *do*."

She was very glad that Duvari wasn't here. "Celleriant, the sword."

He glanced at her, his eyes narrow. "Do you know what you face here?" he finally asked.

"Gods."

"And now I understand how little meaning that word has to you and your kind. Very well, ATerafin." To her surprise, he sheathed the sword. It did not, however, vanish. He drew slightly closer to her and waited. Mist continued its slow accretion until there was nothing left of the audience chamber except some of the people who'd been standing beneath its vaulted, impressive ceilings.

Jewel glanced up; those ceilings were no longer visible; the sky was as gray as the ground—if it was ground—beneath her feet. No birds flew in the heights; no wind blew; and if the sky knew sun or moon, neither now graced its height.

Night began to hiss; his was the only voice she could hear. His ears straightened, and his fur rose. Shadow, seated, affected nonchalance, but his ears had risen as well.

Avandar gently tapped her shoulder; she startled and then forced her-self to relax. "You have little to fear," he said softly. "There are some things the gods cannot do, not even in this place, unless you ask it of them. And even then," he added bitterly, "it is not always within their means."

They lifted their heads and turned as they heard the screeching caw of an eagle; the gods, at least one, had come.

He came through the mist on the far side of the Exalted, and he towered above his half-kin; Jewel thought him eight or nine feet in height, al-though she couldn't be certain. He wore armor, not the robes in which he was so often depicted. The eagle was perched on his left shoulder, and in his mailed hands he carried not sword, but rod. It was a damn big rod. His eyes weren't gold; they weren't any single color, and that made it hard to meet them; his skin was likewise difficult to pin to one shade. His hair, however, seemed pale, white to Celleriant's platinum, and his face was etched with lines that seemed, at this distance, severe.

His son bowed.

"Bird," Night whispered to Shadow. Jewel swallowed her tongue. She rapped the black cat sharply on the head, and he hissed.

Reymaris came next. Lord of Justice. He, too, wore armor, but he was depicted in a more martial way in the cathedrals of Averalaan. His hair was braided, dark to Cormaris' white; his eyes were the same non-color. He was bearded; he looked, for the moment, like a man in his prime. He also wielded sword and shield.

His son now bowed.

Last to come was the Mother. She wore the robes that the two men lacked, and in the gray of the mists, they were warm with color: burnt orange, brown, harvest gold. A wreath adorned her forehead, and a garland, her neck. She carried a basket from which the hint of harvest could be seen. Her hair was long, and it fell trailing into the mist, but her age? Her age was elusive; she was young and old and in between, her weight shifting and changing, although her robes did not.

The Mother's Daughter did not bow to her, but stood instead and waited.

Jewel felt a twinge of envy when the goddess enveloped her much smaller daughter in a hug.

It was the Mother herself, some eight or nine feet tall, who turned to Jewel. "Jewel Markess," she said. Her voice was not one voice, but a multitude, and it felt like thunder. But in spite of that, it wasn't unfriendly. Just . . . alien.

Jewel nodded; she couldn't speak.

"We meet again."

Jewel frowned, her forehead creasing. She could not remember having met the Mother before—and even if small details of her own life now eluded her, meeting a god was not something anyone could forget.

The Mother smiled. "We did not meet like this," she said. "But I heard your voice and I felt your presence. It was not so very long ago."

Jewel looked, in deepening confusion, to the Mother's Daughter. The Mother's Daughter, however, was silent.

"You prayed to me in an ancient place, one long deserted by your kind—or mine. You prayed; I heard you. You were not alone."

Jewel closed her eyes. "I remember," she said softly. "I remember now." She had been with Duster in the undercity. "You opened the door."

"I did." The Mother's expression grew remote. "Do not give me cause for regret."

This was, in its own way, as confusing as the Mother's greeting. Jewel opened her eyes and shook her head.

But the Mother moved past the Exalted toward the cats, and there she paused. They eyed her from the ground, wings flexing. "How long," she asked Jewel, in the same disturbing voice of the multitude, "have you known the three?"

"Not—not long."

"You summoned them."

"No!"

Night hissed.

"They came on their own."

"How did they know where to find you?"

Jewel had no idea, and made that clear. "I met them—in another place. In the forest of the Winter King."

"It has long been Winter," the god replied. She bent and touched Shadow's head, and he looked up at her without fear. "It has been long, little one. Are you weary?"

"We're bored," he told the Mother in his sulkiest voice.

The Mother rose. To Jewel, she said, "How did you come to be in the forest of that King?"

Jewel glanced at Avandar, who was both rigid and utterly silent.

The Mother now turned to face him. "Viandaran."

He bowed then. It, like his posture, was a stiff, rigid gesture.

"You live, as you desired, so long ago. Were you not told to be cautious?"

"I was."

"And you now understand why."

"I do."

"Why are you here? Why did you take Jewel ATerafin into the Deepings?"

"To save her life."

"It is a perilous way to save a mortal life."

Avandar's smile was shocking because it was offered at all; it was also thin. "Yet she is here, Lady."

"Why did you seek to save her life?"

Avandar said nothing.

"He's my domicis," Jewel replied, in his stead.

"There is no death for you at her side," the Mother told him, as if Jewel hadn't spoken.

Avandar again remained silent.

"Do you think she can give you what you desire?"

"Perhaps not," he replied, relenting. "But there is now one who walks the world who can."

It was the god's turn to fall silent; she did, but turned in that silence toward the Winter King. She spoke to him, and Jewel didn't understand a word she said. But he approached, lifting his head. They conversed briefly, and then the god turned back to Jewel.

"You stood against the Winter Queen upon the open road?" the Mother asked. Her eyes rounded, softening in shape.

Jewel nodded.

"Why, Jewel?"

"Because someone had to—and I could." She hesitated, and then said, "I could see him. I could see the man in the stag."

"And so you now claim the mount of the Queen and a prince of her Court as your servants?"

"No."

"They serve you?"

". . . yes."

The Mother now turned to the two gods who watched—and waited—in grim silence.

Cormaris did not move, but he lifted his head and filled the air with the sound of his voice—his many voices. "Lord Celleriant," he said. "Step forward."

Celleriant, however, stood his ground. "I have not come to be judged by you. I have offered you no oath and no service; I have pledged no allegiance. You are their gods; you are not mine."

This caused the Lord of Wisdom to smile; it was both sharp and resigned. "The passage of time has not changed you at all, has it?"

"Time changes mortals."

"It changes all, Celleriant." He frowned now. "You do not serve the

Winter Queen." It was not a question. Nor did Celleriant seemed surprised by the statement; Jewel certainly was. "Lord Celleriant, if you did not come to be judged, why did you come at all?"

He offered silence, and Cormaris' brow creased.

It was Reymaris who spoke. "Have you given your oath to the mortal?" Celleriant did not answer.

Reymaris moved, where Cormaris had not. He strode across mist, and the ground shook at his passing. The cats moved out of his way, hissing. Jewel, however, did not. She raised her chin as he came to a stop feet away from where she stood. "Yes. He has given his oath to me," she said, because she knew Celleriant wouldn't. "He came because I asked it; I asked because *you* asked it." She met and held his gaze, and as she did, the mist at her feet began to twist into columns that gleamed like polished, new marble. Evenly spaced, they started to her left and right and emerged in two rows beyond his back, encompassing, as well, Cormaris and the Mother.

Reymaris glanced at the columns by her side, frowning.

"Brother," Cormaris called, and the Lord of Justice turned to see how far back the columns went. As he did, the mists hardened and flattened until they were flooring—and something about them looked familiar to Jewel. The stones that had been laid across the ground were large enough that they seemed seamless, and etched into the surface of dark, oddly brown stone, were words.

She drew breath; it cut. Turning rapidly, she looked for—and found—walls.

"Avandar—"

Avandar shook his head.

"Celleriant?"

"I do not know this place, Lady."

She did. She thought she did. She walked past Reymaris, toward the Mother and Cormaris; they watched her, but made way for her as she passed them as well. Avandar followed; Celleriant did not. "ATerafin," he said.

"Why here?" she whispered.

"Where do you think you are?"

"I—" The columns ended. The walls met wall, and in that wall, built it seemed for giants, stood two doors. Familiar doors. She had seen them once, with Duster.

*   *   *

She reached out to touch them and then lowered her hand; there was a bright, bright symbol that crossed both doors, sealing them. The symbol itself was not Old Weston, not Weston, not Torra—not any language she knew. But the gods did.

She turned to those gods, those three, her back to the closed door. She was shaking, and to her surprise, she was angry. She struggled with anger, and won. It was no fault of the gods that Duster was dead.

"You know what lies beyond those doors," the Lord of Wisdom said.

She swallowed. "Why are you showing me this?"

The three gods exchanged a glance.

And Celleriant laughed. His laugh was deep, yet also high and wild. "Lady," he said, as if she were one of the Arianni, and not Jewel Markess ATerafin. "Do you truly not understand what you see?"

This time her struggle to control her anger failed, because the consequences were less profound. "If I *understood*, Celleriant, I wouldn't be *bothering the gods*."

"*They* show *you* nothing. *You* show *them* the past."

She stared at him as if he had lost his mind. "What are you talking about? I'm not *doing* anything!"

"Can you not feel it, Lady?"

"And stop calling me that. Just—stop."

His smile was so cold. "At your command." He walked between the gods, and the gods allowed it; they had eyes for her, at this moment—or for the door at her back. At this distance, she couldn't tell.

"Do you know what lies beyond these doors?" she asked him.

"Yes, ATerafin. I know."

She looked to the gods again; they were watching. "Tell me. Explain what you meant."

"This hall, these doors—they are not visions the gods have granted."

"These aren't visions," was her flat reply.

"Ah, but they are. They are, in this formless land. Visions, ATerafin. Dreams. Nightmares. They are not crafted by the three who have come to meet you here; they are yours."

She shook her head, and reached up to push hair out of her eyes. Thanks to Ellerson's ministrations, there wasn't any. She was afraid.

Avandar placed one hand firmly on her shoulder. "ATerafin," he said, voice cool in warning.

"I'm not—"

"Listen to Celleriant."

"You do not understand the path you now walk, ATerafin," the Arianni Lord continued.

She started to speak. Stopped. The Winter King, forgotten until this moment, crossed the floor in silence; his hooves made no noise. He knelt before her. *Mount, Jewel.*

She did as he asked because for a moment it felt safer than thinking.

"It is as we feared," the Mother said heavily.

"No," the Lord of Wisdom replied. "It is worse." He looked long at the closed doors with their unbroken symbol.

The Winter King walked toward them, Jewel on his back, her hands gripping his tines as if she feared to fall.

"Is it, brother?" Reymaris asked softly. "Viandaran is correct. One at least of our number now walks the mortal plane."

"He has walked it only a handful of years—" the Mother began.

"As has the young ATerafin," the Lord of Justice countered. "And handful or no, he must know that every effort is being made by our kin to halt his progress. If he does not act soon, he might find the war harder than he anticipates."

"Not only your kin," Celleriant said, for he had followed in the wake of the Winter King. "But my Queen. She is hampered by the shape of the hidden ways." He glanced at Jewel, and then added, "but perhaps not for much longer. Regardless, the Winter Queen can stand against Allasakar for some time, and will."

"She is not a god."

"No." It was Celleriant's turn to look at the closed door. "But it was not, in the end, the gods who brought Allasakar low. It was a mortal."

"And it is in the hands of mortals now."

The Mother shook her head. "Jewel is not that mortal."

No, Jewel thought; she couldn't be. Moorelas had been dead so long people didn't believe he'd ever lived—unless they thought the world was ending.

"And Moorel of Aston was gifted with a sword that the gods themselves strove to craft; it was forged in living fire and cooled in living water; it was honed by living stone and given breath by the heart of the wind itself. We could not craft such a weapon again, nor could the master swordsmiths of the Summer Court at its height."

"No," the Lord of Justice said. "She is not that mortal. But she stood in the Deepings and she held the road against the Queen and her host. If she is what we fear, and we allow her to live, she might hold the road against even our brother, for a time."

The Lord of Wisdom frowned. "She is both young and unschooled; she is willful. She will not bend when it is wise to bend. If she can, indeed, build her home at the edge of the ancient, what guarantee have we that what she builds will not be used against our sons?"

But the Mother now turned to Jewel and the look she gave was one of compassion. Or pity, which was infinitely worse. "She will not always bend when it is wise, perhaps; but she has, in the past. She has given much to her House, and perhaps she will give as much to our City in its time. I do not like it," she added, to the Lord of Wisdom, "but she has shown us some of the future here. The day is coming."

"And if we grant her our silence—with my misgivings—what will she then do?"

"What she has already done, perhaps. The kin will find no easy entrance to the Isle from these lands. If what we fear is true, they will find no entrance at all, save the long, mortal road."

Reymaris smiled; it was a narrow, cool smile. "The Lord of the Compact would no doubt agree with you, brother; it is a pity that I was overruled, and his presence forbidden."

But the Lord of Wisdom bowed his head. "So be it. If you will bind me to ancient oaths, I will accept your decision. But I will lay one task upon the shoulders of this mortal." He turned to Jewel and lifted a hand. "You have shown that your hold on the hidden ways is strong; it is strong enough, little seer, that it invades even the neutral lands it borders." He glanced at the columns that all but enclosed them. "Find the path to the Eldest, and undergo her test."

Jewel stared at him.

"I will have your word."

She was silent, but only for a moment. "I can't give you that. I have responsibilities here, and a prior oath I mean to fulfill—or die trying."

"That oath?"

"Was made to The Terafin."

"And if she released you from its confines?"

Jewel's grip on the Winter King's antlers tightened. "She's dead."

"Indeed. But Mandaros' Hall is also known to us, and we traverse it without cost."

"I can't," was her flat reply.

"No. But the children of Mandaros can speak with the dead. They can call her back. If she is summoned—"

"She'll tell you to drop dead." The words fled her mouth before thought could stop them, she was so certain. She had the grace to redden in the extended silence that followed them. "She wouldn't use those exact words."

"Perhaps that is true," the Lord of Wisdom replied. "But The Terafin was a pragmatic woman. If she understood the whole of the threat the Empire faces, she might see the necessity of our request."

Jewel met the god's disturbing eyes as she listened to his words. She heard nothing of Amarais Handernesse ATerafin in them.

And if you had, Jewel? The Winter King asked.

She pricked her fingers on tine's edge, and understood, as she did, that the small cut she'd received was intentional on his part. It stung. So much in life did.

"She didn't make the oath to me," she told the Lord of Wisdom, her voice steady, her hands now in her lap, where crimson welled bright along the side of her left hand. "It was my oath."

His eyes were the eyes of god; he saw much. "You offered it unprompted?"

"I offered it," was the firm reply. "That's all that needs to be known." She swiveled on the back of the stag to look down the row of columns. "What would the test of the so-called Eldest prove? What must I learn, to pass it?"

"It is not that kind of test," the Lord of Wisdom replied. "It is not a ritual which you either pass or fail."

"What, then?"

"It will teach you, seer."

"To do what?"

"To see. To control the fragmentary talent with which you were born, if you have the strength to look into your own heart."

As he spoke, she turned again. It was the Mother's face she sought.

"Yes," the Mother replied, in as hushed a voice as a crowd possesses. "You have seen the seer's crystal, and you know what it is. You knew then.

You are not kin to the gods, ATerafin. We cannot command you." Before Jewel could speak, she lifted a hand. "We understand the Kings' Laws. In spite of all you have said or feared, the Kings, in this, cannot command you either. And if you take the Terafin throne and you sit in the Hall of The Ten, you cannot be moved; you can merely be confined to the full force of the Kings' Laws.

"But you will see war, Jewel ATerafin."

Jewel nodded.

"You misunderstand me. I counsel you to consider, with care, what you have done to these shrouded lands—unknowing, unintentionally. If you cannot, I ask you to consider a different question. From beneath the bower of the tree that has grown above the pavilion at the heart of the Terafin grounds, the Exalted heard the voice of an ancient, ancient enemy. Do you think, where there was one, there will not be more?"

"There's bound to be more," she replied, with just a trace of edge in her voice. "They're demons."

"Yes. They are. And they are the Angelae of the Lord of the Hells. They bide their time and play their games because the Exalted have some measure of power against them—but, ATerafin, the power that our children can bring to bear will not, in the end, be a match for the power that you might wield. You are young, and you are ignorant, but even in your ignorance, you have touched the ancient power of your distant kin, and you have marked out the boundaries of a domain of your own on a path that was once riven and unapproachable by those of mortal blood.

"You are not—yet—a danger. But you will be, and the *Kialli* Lord whose will and command you frustrated will know just how much of a threat you pose. Do you think that the Shining Court will remain idle? They cannot. Even if we do nothing, turning a blind eye to your untrained and untested power, they will not. We watch. We measure. If you are too great a threat . . ."

Jewel slid off the back of the Winter King. Avandar stood to her left; Celleriant stood behind him. To the right, the Winter King stayed his ground. The cats, however, had taken to the air, and were circling. "What will you do?" she asked the gods.

The Exalted stood in their shadows, almost forgotten until the son of Cormaris chose to speak. His voice was thin, but it was not quiet. "They will, as they have always done, advise us, ATerafin. No more and no less. But even given their advice, the decisions are in our hands."

The Lord of Wisdom raised brow; he did not however raise rod against his outspoken son. "In this," he said softly, "we can offer no advice."

This surprised the Exalted of Cormaris; it also surprised the Exalted of Reymaris. The Mother's Daughter, however, merely looked resigned.

"The ATerafin herself has more of an answer for your questions than either of you understand," the Lord of Wisdom continued. "For she has walked in the far South, and she has seen some of what has lain, protected and silent for centuries, beneath the living earth. There, in part, her answers lie. And yours."

Chapter Thirteen

The Exalted were silent.

Jewel was silent as well. But she felt both stunned and slightly sickened as she turned to her domicis. To Avandar, called Viandaran by the gods, as if they recognized him on sight. As if they had spoken to him before, and not in the Halls of Mandaros.

He offered her a slight smile.

"Yes, Viandaran. What you suspect, we also suspect. What, now, will you do?"

"I? I will fulfill my contract with her. While she lives, I will serve."

The Lord of Wisdom frowned. "Your service has been costly, in the past."

Jewel lifted a hand as the landscape beneath her feet began to shift in both color and texture. If she was subconsciously reconstituting images of the distant past, she had no desire whatever to conjure any of Avandar's. In the South, in the desert, she had seen enough. "It will not be costly here. What he did in the past, he will not—*cannot*—do to Averalaan."

"How, if he so desires, will you prevent him, ATerafin? He cannot die."

"He can," she replied.

His eyes widened.

"But not yet, not now. Allasakar is not the only god who can grant him the freedom he desires."

His brows rose. She'd managed to surprise him over the years, but never like this. "ATerafin—"

She lifted her hand again. "I *don't know more*, Avandar. I just *know*."

The three gods spoke among themselves in a thunder of syllables that traveled beyond her comprehension. Judging from Avandar's expression, it was beyond his as well, although he clearly liked it less.

"Very well," the Lord of Wisdom finally said. "Leave us, ATerafin. We have much to discuss with our children."

If she could somehow transform the whole landscape of the Between in which gods and mortals might mingle, it didn't belong to her; she felt the ground shift beneath her feet as the world shattered and re-formed before her eyes, and the throne in the audience chamber snapped into clear view. Girding it were the House Guards; occupying it was Gabriel.

She glanced around; Duvari still leaned against the far wall, and the cats stood by her side, lolling in a way that implied they were very bored. Luckily, they hadn't descended into complaint.

As she blinked, the Exalted began to move toward the three braziers that still emitted their faint trails of smoke. They gestured, and the embers from which the smoke rose were guttered.

"Regent," the Mother's Daughter said, tendering a bow of respect— and exhaustion. "We must repair to the cathedral again. We will return in two days to convene the first day of the funeral rites."

Gabriel raised a brow. "The gods—"

"The gods are troubled, but we give leave to return to your duties; we have much work to do on their behalf before we return to your halls."

Duvari now lifted himself off the wall, his eyes narrowing into unfortunate slits as he strode from the back of the chamber to where the Exalted now gathered. He bowed to them; it was the first time Jewel had ever seen a bow used as both an interruption and a demand for instant attention.

"Lord of the Compact," the Exalted of Reymaris said, as the priests who attended him gathered—and emptied—the brazier. "We do not have the luxury of time. If you wish to speak, accompany us."

Duvari rose. It was not to the Exalted that he now turned. "Member Mellifas," he said, in as severe a tone as he generally reserved for powerful members of the patriciate.

"Lord of the Compact," Sigurne replied. She glanced at Matteos. Matteos, however, failed to notice; he was staring at the ground as if by so doing he could unlock the answer to the Mysteries.

Jewel frowned.

What troubles you now, Jewel?

I thought the magi came with us, but I . . .

She felt the Winter King's smile. It was sharp. *They did. They were witness to the gods and their conversation.*

I don't remember seeing them after the gods arrived.

No. But they were present; they were given no voice and no role. I do not believe it was to the guildmaster's liking, although it is hard to tell.

She wondered how he knew.

He didn't answer; not directly. Instead, he said, *They wished the guildmaster to bear witness; I am not certain why. Did you truly not intend to take control of the landscape?*

You already know the answer to that.

Again she felt his smile, but this time it was less cutting. *I will leave you here, Jewel. I believe the day will be trying, but the worst of it is now over.*

He was wrong.

The return to the West Wing was only a little less demanding of attention than the procession to the audience chambers had been; the Winter King had departed. This left the cats as obvious, out-of-place markers of strange magic. The magi, who accompanied her in silence, raised no eyebrows, however.

Celleriant did not travel to the wing; he veered off at the doors that led to the garden, or more precisely, to the forest. Jewel was content to let him go, because she had no questions she wanted answered at the moment. She was surprised when Avandar excused himself and followed; it made her feel oddly underdressed. The distinct unease of the past several hours had grown sharp enough to scare her, and she wasn't ready to face it yet. *Just give me three days.* Three days. Funeral rites. Last respects. It might be too much to ask, but it was not too much, in the end, to demand. When the first flowers were planted and the last prayers spoken, she would be willing to face the shrouded future.

Sigurne was silent as she walked; Matteos, silent as well. The cats, however, were not; they were restless and very, very bored, a fact they made clear enough that servants paused to see who'd been so ill mannered. Jewel very much doubted they knew what to make of the answer. But that was something she'd have to worry about, as well.

The small party made it to the wing, where Ellerson greeted them at the doors, his expression one of mild concern. "The audience was short," he said quietly, the last syllable trailing slightly upward in tone.

"Was it?"

"Very." It was Sigurne who replied. "It was almost over before it began; Duvari will no doubt be beating a path to your doors in short order. If you've developed an appetite at all, I suggest you eat something; you are likely to miss lunch."

"And you, Member Mellifas?" Ellerson bowed head as he spoke.

"If Jewel's discussion with Duvari does not satisfy Duvari, I am certain that we, too, will be entertaining him. In a manner of speaking, and with my prior apologies, in your domain. I would, I think, like something warm."

"Tea?"

"Indeed. I would not take it amiss if it were, on this single occasion, fortified."

Jewel seldom felt grateful to the gods, but today, she managed. It was, she knew, going to be a long day, and in any event, had Duvari *been* present, he would probably have attached himself at the hip and followed her back to her home. The gods had saved her time, which was in very short supply.

They might have even saved her some of Haval's decidedly short mood.

"ATerafin," Sigurne said, as she turned for the hall. "Will you join us?"

"Yes—but I need to check with Haval first; he'll be in that room all day making clothing that we need to fit properly in two days."

The door was closed. Most of the doors in the hall—including her own— were in this state, but only one of them contained an underslept and therefore cranky dressmaker. Jewel stared at the door for a long minute. Avandar reached over her head and knocked. She wasn't profoundly grateful. A muffled command to enter saved Avandar from being told as much in too many words.

She pushed the door open carefully, aware of what rooms generally looked like when Haval was working in them. He'd only had this one for a handful of hours, which meant she could still see floor—although admittedly not nearly as much of it as she knew existed. At the moment, he was on his knees, rather closer to ground than looked comfortable, fussing with the hem of a dress; he was adding black lace. To her surprise, Finch was still in the room. Teller, however, was not. Jewel lifted her hands and gestured briefly; Finch gestured back, but her movements were muted.

"Oh, do, please, answer her," Haval told Finch. This didn't appear to surprise Finch, although it did make her look momentarily guilty.

"He's in Gabriel's office. When Haval's ready, we're to send for him; Barston is inundated with people he can't afford to offend."

"What, all twelve of them?"

Finch chuckled. "From the sounds of it, yes. At once. On top of each other. I did offer to send them to Lucille, but Teller wasn't certain that would be more merciful."

"I offered to *eat* them," Snow said. He was reclining to one side of Finch's chair, and although he should have been impossible to miss, Jewel had. *Probably wishful thinking.* Finch dropped a hand to the cat's large head and scratched behind his ears.

"Has Snow been at all helpful?" she asked. She asked it of Finch because she was a coward.

It was Haval who answered. He set aside his pins and rose; his knees cracked. "I think," he told Jewel quietly, "you should see that for yourself." He gestured toward a screen that stood in the corner of the room.

"The dress?"

"Behind the screen." She glanced at the cat, who looked very pleased with himself. Then again, when he wasn't fighting with Night, he generally did. "ATerafin?"

She made her way—carefully, to avoid stray pins—across the room, and stopped a yard from where the screen stood, staring at it with a frown.

"ATerafin?" Haval said again, his intonation different.

"Where did you get this screen?"

"Very good. Do you recognize it?"

"No. But I recognize that mountain."

"It was not, before Snow came to assist me, a mountain."

"What was it?" she asked, as if staving off fate.

"Flowers. Not," he added, "terribly *good* flowers, on the other hand. This is better; it is simple but exact."

"It had *bees*," Snow hissed.

"Haval—what did he do to the dress?" Her voice was too loud to be a whisper, but not by much.

Haval did not respond. Instead, he folded arms across his chest—and across the thick apron he wore—and waited, his face a mask.

"How's Hannerle?"

"Sleeping." The word was curt but neutral. "And that was a very sloppy attempt to buy time, ATerafin; I expect better in the future." As she hesitated, he closed his eyes and took a deep breath. Expelling it cost him inches of height. "My apologies, Jewel. If it has been a trying day for me, I imagine that it has not been *entirely* pleasant for you. I am always impatient when I work, and in the end, the impatience will be of little benefit to you.

"You have made at least one significant decision."

"The House?" she asked softly, aware that he was allowing her to stall in a more graceful way, and grateful for it.

"That is one, yes." He glanced at Snow. "Your cats are another, and if they are less considered than your decision regarding the House, they are no less significant. But you fail to see their significance clearly. I fail to see it, at the moment, but I see that it is there. You cannot afford to choose ignorance at this juncture in your career. Ignorance may appear as the more comfortable alternative, but it is not, in the end, the act of someone who will—must—be a power.

"What, exactly, frightens you?"

"I don't know."

"I will allow that. And I will allow you the fear that knowledge brings. I will allow you the ignorance that comes with a surfeit of fact. But I will not allow you to knowingly choose it from this point on. It is a luxury you cannot afford. Fold the screen, ATerafin, and see what a creature without hands has achieved."

"Creature?" Snow said, rising. He shrugged off Finch's hand and ambled across the floor, taking distinctly less care than Jewel had. He was immune to Haval's ire; it was too subtle. Wings spread, he rose, hovering in the air at the height of Haval's shoulders, which shouldn't have been possible given the size of the room and the inadequate height of the ceiling. Shouldn't have didn't cut it. He flew, and to Jewel's eyes, he was glowing; a nimbus of interwoven blue and white surrounded and hallowed his open wings.

His eyes were gold, wide, unblinking. *"Creature?"*

Jewel began to gather the three panels of the trifold screen, slowly collapsing them in nerveless hands. The work steadied her until the moment she saw the dress. This was *not* the dress that she had tried on in pieces as it came together under Haval's rapid needles. It wasn't even close to that dress. It was almost entirely white; there was black that trailed the edges of sleeves that were not, in *any* way, current with Court fashions. They were long, their ends belled in yards of falling fabric. Gold strands of something seemed woven into the fabric itself, catching and bending light. The skirt was far, far too full; it had a train that seemed to contain as much material as the rest of the dress itself.

"This isn't—this isn't the dress we agreed on."

"We did not discuss the dress we purportedly agreed on," Haval replied. It had been one of his common complaints over the years; he expected Jewel to take an interest in current fashion; Jewel expected Haval to be aware of it in her stead. His pride as a craftsman had never allowed him to embarrass her in public, because it was his business that would suffer.

"This isn't—"

"Current fashion, ATerafin? I *am* surpised. No, indeed, it is not. Will you try it on?"

She reached out to touch it, not to take it. Her hands lifted sleeves and dropped them almost instantly. "What is the fabric?"

"You will have to ask Snow," he replied. "It is not a fabric with which I am familiar."

I can't wear this, Jewel thought, staring at the dress. She turned toward the hovering cat.

He slowly alighted. "You don't *like* it?" His brows rose as high as his voice.

"Yes—I like it," she said, too quickly.

"Then *put it on.*" His wings brushed the tip of her chin as he stretched, and then settled them.

"Snow."

"Yes?"

"Look at me."

The cat sniffed.

"I mean it. Look at *me.*"

"Yes?"

"Look at Finch."

He didn't bother. It would have required him to turn around.

"Are we wearing clothing like this?"

"Of *course* not. *I* didn't make *that* clothing." His sniff was the very essence of disdain.

"I can't wear this, Snow."

The great cat froze in place for a minute, and then he turned his head toward Haval. "What did she *say?*"

Haval winced. "What she is trying to say," he told the cat, and in a much softer and friendlier voice than he'd yet used on Jewel, "is that she feels unworthy of such a magnificent dress."

"Oh." Snow looked back to Jewel. He walked to her side and then leaned into her; she stumbled. "You are a *stupid* girl," he told her.

It was ludicrous to have this conversation with a *cat*. She knew it. But her whole life now felt dangerously unstable. If flowers—or gods knew—trees had grown up from the carpets, it wouldn't have surprised her. Things had gone insane the moment The Terafin had died. It was as if Amarais had been the anchor of not only the House, but Jewel's world. She bitterly, bitterly regretted her absence.

"You said it was an *important* dress. You *said* it was the *most* important dress you would wear in your *life*." He hesitated, and then said, "Should it be *armor* instead?"

"No!"

"Should there be more black? I don't *like* black."

"He did, however, listen when I explained why black was necessary."

"No. No, Snow, it doesn't need more black." She laughed. It was not a happy sound. "It needs an entirely different woman. This dress—this is something the Winter Queen could wear."

Snow's hiss was as loud as a growl. "It's *better*."

"Jewel," Haval said quietly. "Come. Sit. Finch, if you will take Snow for a walk?"

Finch rose, but lingered. The crisp command in Haval's request was not enough to drive her from the room. "Jay?"

Jewel lifted a hand, turned it in a swift motion, and then made her way to the chair that Haval was even now arranging for her. He stood behind it. Finch made space for herself—with care—on another chair. Its previous occupant, a bolt of fabric, she removed and set against the wall.

"Be careful with that," Haval said, as the bolt hit the floor. He did not ask Finch to leave again. Finch's compromise was Snow; she called the cat, and he came and plonked his head more or less in her lap. His purr was as loud as his hiss, and Jewel, facing them, watched as Finch scratched behind his ears. But Finch wasn't looking at the cat; she was looking at Jewel.

Jewel, who knew she was as close to white as she ever got. She felt something pulling at her hair, and startled; Haval cleared his throat and she settled back into her chair. He pulled out the pins that Ellerson had so carefully, deliberately, placed into her hair, and as he did, that hair, still heavy with the oils that were meant to keep it in place, loosened.

"The dress is not in poor taste, ATerafin. It is, I admit, unusual; it is also striking. There will not be another like it—"

"Ever." Snow interjected.

"—At the first day rites. It is not daring except in its circumvention of current fashion; it is not revealing. But it is not a child's dress. You," he said, as he began to brush her hair, "are not a child. It is not clear to me that the members of the House Council understand this, because it is not clear to me that you understand it yourself, except when you see those who are. Your Adam. Your youngest visitor."

She stiffened. She had forgotten them. "I'm not a child," she told him, closing her eyes as he continued to brush her hair. Her knees crept up to her chin; the dress she was wearing crinkled loudly as she wrapped her arms around them.

"No, and perhaps I am being too harsh. Amarais Handernesse ATerafin was like a parent to you; she stood between you and the world. While she ruled, you trusted her—and I will tell you now, you trusted her more completely than she ever trusted herself."

"She—"

"She, like any who acquire power while still maintaining a sense of duty and responsibility, bore the weight of fear: fear of the consequences of failure. You allowed this because she demanded it. She cannot demand it now. There is now nothing between you and the future; no safety, no one to stand behind. It is time that you do as she did. Take up the fear, carry it, and protect what you have long sought to protect anyway. No more, no less." He did not set the brush down; he continued. "Wear the dress."

"Is that an order?"

"If it will comfort you this morning, yes. An order I have no right to give you, and an order you have no obligation to obey."

"For first day," she whispered. "For first day, I'll wear it."

"I have work to do here; Snow did not see fit to likewise clothe young Teller or Finch. The work will be done in time if I am allowed to work without interruption." He finally set the brush aside. "Finch," he said, in exactly the same tone of voice he had used earlier. "Take Jewel to her room."

This time, Finch obeyed.

* * *

Shadow was waiting for Jewel.

Unfortunately, he was waiting *on* the bed, and he didn't seem to hear Finch's quiet request that he move. Nor did he feel her less quiet attempt to shove him to one side. After a few minutes of the pointless attempt, Finch folded her arms.

Shadow then rose. He didn't get off the bed, but he did move to one side. "Tell the old woman," he said, "that she is sleeping."

Jewel shook her head. "Sigurne is—"

Shadow leaped off the bed before she could finish, landing behind her. He knocked her over with the powerful swing of a forepaw. He hadn't extended his claws, but it didn't matter; she lost her footing so easily she might have been standing on ice.

"Tell the old woman," Shadow said again.

Finch's arms got tighter, and so did the line of her mouth.

The cat hissed and turned to her. Jewel managed to right herself; she grabbed his tail. She fell over again, still attached to it.

"She needs to sleep," he told Finch, in a much less catlike voice. "And I will watch over her dreams."

"Why don't *you* tell the *guildmaster* that Jewel's sleeping?"

"Will you watch her dreams?"

"I'll wake her if she has a nightmare."

The cat snorted. "You? You will drown in it. You will die."

But Jewel said, "Shadow—I want her to stay."

"But you have *me*."

"Yes. Yes, I do. But—I want her to stay. Just for now. Just while it's quiet. Haval still needs her to be in the wing, and I—"

"I don't want to talk to the old woman," Shadow said, and sat heavily on the floor.

Finch relented, but only slightly. "I'll talk to her. I'll tell her. But I'm coming back, and the door had better not be locked when I get here."

Sigurne Mellifas stared into her cooling tea in the silence left after Finch ATerafin had delivered her message and retreated. Matteos, standing by the fire—which he also tended—said nothing; his gaze caught on flame, as if he were a child fascinated by its caged danger.

Sigurne, however, was not in need of his words. It was chilly in the room; the fire was welcome. The magical wards that protected the magi from simple things like weather were wards Sigurne had always disdained as impractical; at this very moment, that disdain seemed more due to pride than pragmatism. She glanced at Matteos; he moved only to add dry logs to the small blaze. His back, shoulders bent, robes draping, was all that he showed her, but by it, she understood enough.

Sip by sip, the cup in her hands emptied. The alcohol that Ellerson had graced his tea with failed to warm her. She felt old and tired—which, admittedly, she was—but more disturbing, she felt at sea. Demons, she understood. She understood as much as any living mage, with the possible exception of Meralonne. But how much, in the end, was that? They were ancient, deathless creatures—but the ancient was bound in ways she had never fully seen to the mysteries of the gods in their youth. It was now, on the day before the funeral, that she understood how insignificant her knowledge was.

She rose; Matteos, sensitive to her movements, turned.

"You are thinking of Meralonne," he said stiffly.

"I was," she admitted. "But I fear to summon him too often. It is costly, and it is possibly costly in ways he cannot afford."

"That has not stopped you before."

"It has," she said, in mild annoyance. "But while I feel certain that he would have a deeper and broader understanding of the possible threat Jewel ATerafin poses, I am far less certain that he would surrender that information to the magi."

"Or to you?"

"Or to me." She, too, watched the flames. "Do you remember how he trained the warrior-magi?"

Matteos stiffened. "Sigurne—"

"They still have those weapons. The weapons born in part of their power and in part of their force of will. I do not think they will set them aside, having summoned them; I do not think they can."

"And you think Jewel Markess will summon such a weapon?"

Her frown was a teacher's frown—a tired, worried teacher, shorn of all patience. "No, Matteos, that is not what I fear." She turned away from the fire, from its warmth; turned back to her empty cup, and the pot that stood beside it, cooling as well. She poured tea for herself. "You are aware that the loremasters among us have come to prominence since Henden of the year four hundred and ten?"

He nodded.

"You are aware that what was once considered childish story and foolish bardic lay is now accepted as possible truth."

"That gods once walked the earth?"

"The same."

"I am. No reason has been given for their decision to leave, however."

"The gods are not subject to our sense of reason."

"No, indeed." A log cracked at his feet, and he knelt to pull another, untouched, from the pile in the rounded brass bin.

"It is believed—by some, and I confess that at last, I am one—that there were men, mortal men, who could stand in defiance of the gods themselves."

"That I am less willing to grant."

"Allow for the possibility, Matteos."

"As you wish." He set the log carefully on top of those that were already burning and fanned its embers until it, too, was embraced by flame.

"There could not have been many," she continued, after a pause. "And as we have little evidence of what the gods could achieve, we are not certain what level of power might be required to stand long against them. But there have been discussions."

"You believe that Jewel ATerafin possesses the power to stand—against *gods*?"

"I do not know what I believe, Matteos; I do not trust what I know." It was a bald admission from one who was styled the Guildmaster of the Order of Knowledge. "But I believe, now, that we will see the beginning of an answer, some proof of a theory that is so poorly supported by fact it can barely be considered theory at all."

He rose. "Why, Sigurne? Why that girl? Because she is seer-born? Because she has those loud, noisy beasts following her and making nuisances of themselves?"

"Is that all you perceive?"

He grimaced. "I like the girl," he finally said.

"She is hardly a girl anymore."

"I see her seldom, but among the patriciate, she is one of the few I do not dread on sight."

"And you are, therefore, unwilling to see the threat she poses."

"I cannot imagine that she would willingly pose a threat to us." He spoke with more heat than was his wont, and then seemed to realize it; he reddened. "What is it, Sigurne? What did you see?"

"Lord Celleriant," she replied. "I know what he is, Matteos."

Matteos waited.

"He is sworn. To her. Matteos—the names she used. The words she spoke. Did you hear them and remain unmoved?"

"No," he finally replied. "I saw *her*. What will you do, Sigurne?"

"I will attend a funeral. I will attend a funeral, and I will do my best, at this juncture, to see not the girl, but the shadow she casts."

"And if it is dark? If it is the wrong shadow?"

She failed to answer; she drank tea and thought of the ice and the snow and Meralonne APhaniel in her youth.

Jewel woke when Finch called her name. She couldn't immediately *see* Finch, because Shadow lay between them, and his wings were in the way. But she woke in silence, to silence, her breath and heartbeat calmer than they had been all day. "What time is it?"

"It's just off lunch, early lunch," was the quiet reply. The curtains had been drawn, but light leaked through them, gray and yet bright. Jewel rose.

To her surprise, Adam was standing near the door. His hands were behind his back, and his chin low.

"Adam?" She reached for clothing—not the stiff cage of an expensive dress she'd been tied into all morning—and cursed Shadow as she did. Shrugging herself into a dress that didn't require at least two other people's help just to put on "properly," she turned toward him. Shadow stretched and yawned.

"Where is the *ugly* one? Is he gone *again*?"

She cursed the cat under her breath.

"Matriarch," Adam said in Torra.

"Adam, no. Whatever else you want to call me, I'm not that." He nodded, and she gave up. "What's wrong? Why are you here?"

"I am called to Levec's side."

"By who?" she asked, more sharply.

"By Levec."

Her brow felt as if it would be caught in a permanent crease. "Why?"

"He is to meet with the healers from the palace."

She almost smacked the side of her head. "Is Levec here?"

"He sent a message. Teller rerouted it."

Jewel looked up at Finch. "This is about the sleeping sickness?"

"Yes."

"How long ago did he send for you?"

Finch said "He's already over an hour late. He's been going to meet them at least once a week since it started, but—that was before The Terafin's death."

"So this is a *planned* meeting?"

Finch cringed, but nodded.

Kalliaris' frown.

"He didn't want to leave until he'd seen you; you told him to stay in his room."

Well, yes. She had. "I owe you an apology, if something that pathetic will do—Levec's probably knocking down walls by now. With his teeth." That description, at least, made Adam smile. It was a quiet smile, and it reminded Jewel inexplicably of Lander's smile, although the two had nothing else in common besides gender.

"He won't be angry at me," Adam told her, as she opened the door.

"No, of course not. It's just the *rest* of us who'll be forbidden the Houses of Healing for the rest of our natural lives."

Angel and Carver came into the kitchen a full ten minutes after she'd asked Ellerson to get them there. Carver looked wary; Angel—he looked tired. She turned a palm, three fingers folded, in his direction, and he straightened out. Didn't look any less exhausted, though.

"Adam's needed at the Houses of Healing. Can you get him there in one piece with no detours?"

Adam added, "I told her I could travel there quickly on my own."

Carver snorted. "Might as well've told her you could fly. Do you need to take anything with you?"

"No."

"How careful do you want us to be?" It was Angel who asked.

"I'm sending you, aren't I?"

A little of the tired look lifted off his face when he smiled.

Adam was always more comfortable with women than with men; it was something Angel had noticed from the beginning. He'd initially assumed that Adam was comfortable with *Finch* because it was impossible to be uncomfortable around her. But in the time between, he'd come to understand that it wasn't Finch; it was her gender. That and her ability to speak Torra, an ability Angel lacked.

Adam was tall. He was scrawny, the way tall fourteen year olds were. He was also quiet. The quiet didn't bother Angel much, because Angel was capable of the same type of silence. But to Angel, Adam looked like a kid. The fact that he was the age that Angel had been when he'd first set foot in the city, carrying, in a backpack, everything he owned, should have made it easier not to think of him as helpless; it didn't.

"Your Matriarch," Adam said in his strangely accented Weston. "She is angry." The last word rose, making a question of the statement.

Carver said something in Torra, because Carver could speak it. Adam, however, had been the recipient of some of Carver's teasing, and looked hesitant. He answered in Weston. "Matriarchs always worry. Worry is normal."

Angel laughed. He wasn't certain why Adam referred to Jay as a Matriarch, but no one had been able to break him of the habit. "What?" he asked, at Carver's frown. "It's true. She breathes less than she worries."

But Carver shook his head. "Start worrying more," he told Angel, lifting one hand and twisting it, rapidly, in a downward direction.

Angel's hands fell instantly to his sides. They'd almost reached the front doors.

"Next time," Carver said, under his breath, "we take the trade entrance." It was too late, now; they were almost upon the half dozen House Guards near the front doors. The House Guards weren't in a particular formation; they weren't on duty. Or rather, not House duty.

They fanned out, not so subtly discouraging a quick exit. No weapons were drawn, but hands rested on sword hilts as a man emerged from their midst. He wore very fine robes, in the varying shades of blue that passed as House Terafin colors when the clothing was fashionable. His hair, at the moment, was dark auburn, which had been highly regarded in the past; it sometimes showed gray. Not today. Not for the four days to follow.

"Councillor Rymark," Carver said, tendering Rymark ATerafin a very grudging bow.

"ATerafin," Rymark replied coolly. His eyes narrowed as he caught sight of Adam, and Angel stiffened. Stiffened, but kept his breathing regular and even. "I do not believe I recognize your companion. A new addition to your den?"

"Sir," Carver replied.

Rymark ATerafin raised a brow. His expression was severe and unfriendly—no surprise there. His eyes, however, were ringed with dark circles; he was either hungover or exhausted. "I would like a moment of your time," he told them both.

Jay had made perfectly clear how little time they had; they'd already apparently wasted an hour and a half of Levec's patience. Explaining this to Rymark ATerafin was out of the question. Angel glanced at Carver; Carver's gaze was fixed on Rymark.

"I'm afraid we must refuse," Carver replied. "We are on an errand for Councillor Jewel ATerafin."

"And the nature of that errand?"

Carver didn't answer. Rymark looked neither surprised nor pleased; the latter was more of a problem.

"You are not House Guards, and neither of you are servants or pages. You, Carver, are a full member of the House." Angel didn't point out that many of the guards and servants were also full members of the House, but it was tempting. "I am surprised that the Councillor sends named members of the House on insignificant errands."

Carver was an old hand; he didn't bite. He kept a respectful posture—and a respectful distance.

"Very well. You, boy. Come here."

Angel lifted a hand in a brief motion: *danger. Don't move*. Finch had taught Adam some of the basic den-sign, and Angel prayed that basic encompassed his message. Adam failed to obey the Councillor's command. Rymark repeated it in a chillier voice.

Adam remained slightly behind—and between—Carver and Angel.

But when Rymark spoke a third time, he spoke in perfect Torra. Carver didn't curse—with words—but his single gesture more than covered what he could have said. Adam couldn't feign ignorance. They both knew it was important that Adam's power remain hidden; mention of Levec or Dantallon—while it would get them through the unwanted and informal checkpoint—would seriously jeopardize any hope of anonymity.

Rymark repeated his command and Angel lifted an arm as Adam took a step forward.

"Councillor Rymark."

Everyone froze at the sound of the voice. Adam. The House Guard. Even the Councillor, whose expression stiffened into one of extreme dislike.

Carver gestured; Angel nodded. The Lord of the Compact stepped between the House Guards as if they were frivolous decorations. Angel knew Jay disliked Duvari. He privately doubted that anyone who'd met him felt anything but dislike—in the best case. He didn't relax.

"Lord of the Compact," Rymark replied—without turning, without bowing, and without otherwise acknowledging Duvari, a fact that was not lost on Duvari.

"My apologies for interrupting your . . . meeting, Councillor."

"No apologies are necessary." The House Guards moved to the sides to make way for Duvari at Rymark's silent nod. If this was meant as a hint, it failed.

"Good. I would like to ask you a few questions."

"Please do." Rymark still hadn't moved.

"There appear to be some irregularities in our filed reports."

"Surely that is not a House concern?"

"No, indeed, as was made clear to me—by the regent."

Rymark surrendered with very poor grace; he wheeled, his hands curving. Angel admired the way they failed to become fists, because controlled or not, his anger was clear. "*Which* filed reports, Lord of the Compact?"

"Yours."

"I? I have filed no reports with you."

"Indeed. You have, however, made provisions with the House for your entourage at the opening of the funeral rites on the morrow."

"What of it?"

"The regent's report clearly stated that you will have twelve guests, six guards, and two attendants."

"I fail to see the significance."

"Reports indicate that you have, in fact, issued fourteen invitations." Duvari stopped speaking. He glanced at Carver and Angel, in much the same way he'd glanced at the assembled House Guard. "Leave," he told them curtly.

Carver bowed instantly. Angel was slower to bend back, but he did; he almost saluted. Duvari, however, had no sense of humor, and now was not the time to prove it. A quick gesture caused Adam to do the same. Strictly speaking, none of the three bows were necessary; with someone like Duvari—or Rymark, on most days—obsequious gestures never hurt.

*   *   *

"Trade entrance *and* servants' halls on the way back," Carver said, when they were well out of sight of the manse. "Damn lucky Duvari was looking for him. And too damn bad we couldn't stay to hear the rest of the discussion."

Angel shook his head. "That wasn't luck." Adam was watching them both, his lips compressed as if he feared to interrupt them.

"You don't think he just happened to be wandering by either."

"No."

"Watching us?"

"Watching Jay—which means watching us." Angel frowned. "I'd say he was having us watched. Someone must have alerted him; he moved damn fast."

They both glanced at Adam, and then back at each other. Adam, however, shook his head. "I do not think he was watching for me, but I have met him before."

"He knows you?" Carver's visible brow rose into his hairline.

Adam nodded.

"He knows what you can do?"

"He knows I am a healer, yes. Levec doesn't like him."

"No one likes him."

"Why?"

"Because he's the Kings' spymaster and the Kings' assassin."

Angel punched Carver's shoulder, hard. "Don't ever say that again, idiot."

"What? It's what everyone says."

"It's what everyone who *isn't being trailed by* Astari says."

Adam's frown eased into a smile. "Levec doesn't like him, but he trusts him."

"Yeah, well. Not even Duvari could kill Levec. The rest of us aren't so lucky."

The tails were good. Angel gestured, glancing at Carver; Carver gestured back. *No. Three.* Adam watched their brief, wordless interchange in silence.

After the bridge, Angel said; Carver nodded. They lengthened their stride because Adam—unlike Finch—could match it. But they did nothing fancy, nothing difficult, not yet. Angel assumed that their tails were Astari, but he couldn't be certain they were only Astari. He thought about two things as he walked: the first, that Adam was valuable to, and valued by, the Kings, and the second, that Alowan had died. There was no chance at all that the Kings, directly or indirectly, had ordered that death. The killer had been established as demonic. The demon might have gotten into the House—and the healerie—on his own; there was an outside possibility that the demon acted against the entire House, and not on behalf of one of its members.

They'd argued about this in the kitchen for hours, because either was believable. The Terafin's death was far less of a certainty if she happened to have a talent-born healer living in her house; taking out the healer meant a clearer shot at The Terafin.

But no one was certain. No one could be. They did what they could to shore up the argument because they wanted to believe it. Angel grimaced. They wanted. He wasn't as invested in the future of the House, and he had argued against it. To his surprise, so had Jester, his expression so grave it was almost shocking. They'd reached no easy conclusion, but they'd reached no difficult one either.

Carver glanced at Angel and shrugged. In the end, it didn't matter. If the tails were human, they presented a possible danger. If not? They were armed. They were armed with clunky, pretty daggers that made better letter openers than weapons against anything *but* the demonic.

The bridge came into view.

Adam still found the city difficult. It was larger than any city in the South; larger by far than the Tor Leonne. He'd grown accustomed to the smells of the city, but he hadn't yet grown accustomed to the crowds, the tightly packed buildings, the proliferation of carriages, wagons, and sounds. He had difficulty navigating the complicated social structures that governed both the House and the people who came to visit it. He had no difficulty at all hiding his gift, however. It was not considered much of a gift in the South.

He liked Carver. He approved of Angel, but Angel, with his strangely wired hair and his frequent silence, seemed above, or at least beyond, like or dislike. Perhaps it was because he spoke no Torra, but Adam doubted it; Angel had been very strange since Jewel ATerafin had returned.

Jewel herself was difficult. She was Margret's age, or close, but she cringed every time he afforded her the respect she was due. Worse, she denied it. She denied that she was Matriarch, here. She denied that her word was law. He could have accepted that, but while she denied her authority, she didn't deny her power; he saw, clearly that she was blessed with the power that his own sister had failed to show. She could *see*.

His mother, the previous Matriarch of Arkosa, had told him once that sometimes in the strongly gifted their gaze was focused so far away they couldn't see the people around them. *Was that you, Mother?* He shook his head, sliding to one side of a large, angry man. People in the streets were frequently angry.

His mother did not, and could not, answer him. If the winds that scoured the South reached this far North, the dead that rode them were silent. But his mother? She had seen far. She had seen, and accepted, her own death. What did Jewel see?

Carver tapped his shoulder and he let the thought go. *Now*, Carver gestured. *Follow. Watch us.*

Very few men—or women—chose to follow the Voyani the way they now followed Adam, Carver, and Angel. Adam would have said that Carver and Angel were being too cautious, because he saw no one when he looked, or rather, saw so many people it was impossible to tell who among them might be on their trail.

But Carver and Angel seemed to see past the crowds, as if they were a thin, fine curtain, and if the three were invisible to Adam's eye, they were clear to the two older men. So he said nothing. If Jewel was unwilling to be called Matriarch, these were nonetheless her closest family, her most trusted kin, and she had placed Adam's life in their hands. They took the charge seriously.

He therefore didn't attempt to tell them they were going in the wrong direction—although they were—when they moved; he followed. That, he could do.

"Working together?" Carver asked Angel, when they ducked into a small shop at the outskirts of the Common.

"Two, I think. Not the third."

"He'll have to avoid them. *Astari?*"

Angel hesitated, glancing out the doorway. "I'd say the single is *Astari*. I'm not sure about the two."

Carver cursed in Torra, and then glanced at Adam. "Sorry," he muttered.

"I've heard worse," Adam told him. "From my sister."

"I bet. Ready?"

Adam nodded.

"Good. We're running. Keep an eye on me. Don't keep looking over your shoulder."

Adam saw a lot of the Common in the next twenty minutes. Five of those were at a sprint, or as much of a sprint as the crowded streets allowed.

"Got 'em?" Carver asked.

Angel nodded.

"Still three?"

"I think we've lost one."

Carver cursed again. Adam guessed from this that it was the wrong one. He must have looked confused, because Carver said, "The *Astari* knows where we're going. It's not him we have to get rid of. Come on."

It was forty-five minutes before Angel judged it safe to leave the Common. Adam was lost. Angel wasn't. He led them to the House of Healing's front gates, watching the streets in a tense silence. The guards at the gate appeared to be waiting for at least one envoy from House Terafin, because they weren't left in the streets. They were ushered hurriedly into the main hall and told to wait.

Levec entered the hall only a few minutes later, his brows joined above the bridge of his nose, his large hands balled in fists. Those fists relaxed as Adam sprang to his feet.

"I'm sorry, Levec," he said, in the slowest Torra he could manage. Levec's spoken Torra was not very good, but Adam was nervous enough that his Weston would have been worse. "I didn't understand Jewel's orders, and I—"

"Never mind," Levec replied, in brusque, accented Torra. "You two." This was said in Weston.

Angel stepped forward; Carver lounged against the wall, his arms folded across his chest. Angel bowed.

"Yes, yes. Enough. What happened?"

"There was an incident at the manse."

Levec actually paled.

"No—nothing happened to Adam; nothing's happened to Daine."

For some reason, Levec didn't relax. "Adam's services were required?"

Angel shook his head. "The incident had nothing to do with Adam; Adam's off all healing duty anywhere in the manse but our private rooms. But it was large enough and unusual enough that the House Guards were mobilized; things have been chaotic."

"It?"

"You'll have to ask the regent. Or Duvari, if you prefer." The mention of Duvari's name had predictable, common results no matter where it was uttered among the patriciate. Although Levec was not technically one of them, he commanded enough power through his stewardship of the healers that he was considered an honorary member in the eyes of the *Astari*. "Jewel said to tell you she takes full responsibility for the lateness of Adam's arrival. She also asked that you accompany him home if it's at all possible."

"I would prefer to keep him."

Adam hesitated, and Levec marked it instantly. He lowered his voice, which didn't make it all that much quieter, as he turned to Adam. "It's safer for you here." The words were flat, the syllables pressed together like blocks of stone; not a lot of room to move around them.

Angel waited for a moment, but Adam was still hesitant. "Healer Levec."

Levec looked up.

"I won't argue with the general case; it *is* safer for Adam in the Houses of Healing. But for the next four days at least, there probably won't be a safer place in the Empire than House Terafin. Duvari's practically living under its roof."

"Somehow that fails to comfort me," the healer replied, straightening. He was willing to leave the decision in Adam's hands. He wasn't, however, willing to leave the discussion in the halls. "Dantallon's waiting, as are Commander Sivari and the Princess Royale. There are," he continued, as he began to move, "two members of the Order of Knowledge. They've promised they will observe without interfering. They did not, however, promise to observe quietly, and I've a mind to strangle them both."

"Has something changed, Levec?" Adam asked, as he followed.

Levec didn't miss a step; neither did he answer.

Angel and Carver pulled up the rear, which did cause the healer to miss a step. "Gentlemen," he said, in a voice that was more growl than words. "Have you suddenly evinced a meaningful talent in the past few weeks?"

When Carver frowned, Levec added, "If I am to return Adam to House Terafin, I can assure you your services are no longer required."

*   *   *

"You think they followed us?"

Angel shook his head. "I think we'll find the *Astari* tail on our way out." He headed toward the door.

Carver followed, pushing his hair briefly out of his eyes. It was a much more graceful gesture than Jay's, probably because it was a lot less common; Carver's hair always obscured at least one.

Levec's guards were polite; they weren't friendly. They made sure that Carver and Angel exited the halls without taking any unwarranted detours.

Without Adam, however, they were less constrained. Angel gestured as they walked; Carver nodded. The *Astari* tail was, in fact, not far from the Houses of Healing, but he wasn't exactly hanging off their impressive and dangerous fences. Angel gestured again.

"I don't think it's us he was following. You think he's a danger?"

"Not to Adam. Not right now."

The afternoon had started in the streets of the city. If those streets were less crowded directly in front of the Houses of Healing, they were distinctly more packed two blocks away; Angel and Carver could disappear with ease into the crowd that surged around them. But it didn't seem necessary at the moment. They walked toward the footbridge.

"Angel."

Angel nodded.

"Worried?"

"No. The streets are clear."

"I wasn't talking about that."

"What, then?"

"Jay."

"Why worry about Jay? She's got Avandar and Celleriant." He shoved hands into wide pockets; had there been more loose stone in the streets, he might have kicked them. "And Torvan."

"So . . . that would be yes."

"That would be no."

"Fine. Worried about yourself?"

"I'm not a kid anymore. She's not going to leave again until the House is settled one way or the other. If she has the House, we're part of it."

"We are. You're not." Carver could hold a small grudge for a long damn time. So could Angel.

"Fine. She takes the House, *you're* all part of it. Better?"

"Not much. Why are you—"

Angel turned, the footbridge forgotten. "You didn't *see* her, Carver. You didn't see her on the back of that damn stag. I did. I rode up the side—the *side*—of a tree into an unholy mess of branches, behind her back, clinging to antlers the entire way up."

Carver said nothing.

"When the stag stopped, she wanted to get *down*."

"No way." Every member of the den knew how much Jay hated heights. Even in the undercity, when she couldn't see clear to the ground, she'd had trouble moving.

"Yes. And," Angel added, hands curling into fists, "I let her. I let her do it."

Carver exhaled. "You let her do it because you knew she could."

"How in the hells could I know that?"

"She's not dead." He started to move, because they were gathering a small crowd, partly because they were in the middle of the road, and partly because arguments that hadn't gone violent tended to gather interest the way rotting meat gathered flies.

Angel had the choice of ending an unwanted and unexpected conversation, or of following; he was half a block behind when he made the decision to move. Carver was strolling, not striding; it didn't take long to catch up. It did take some effort not to grab him by the shoulder and shove him into the nearest wall.

"I couldn't follow her," he said, making that effort. "I trust her to know what she's doing—even when she can't put it into words. But she was heading into danger, and *I couldn't follow*. Avandar could."

"So he went with her?"

Angel grimaced and shook his head. "Bad example, then. Celleriant could."

"Celleriant was the reason you ran up the tree at all; he was the one in danger."

"How do you know that?"

"Eavesdropping. Jay doesn't make it hard. Did I hear wrong?"

"No."

"So. Avandar wasn't there, and Celleriant was the reason you had to run up the side of what was left of our oldest tree on the back of a big, white stag. You couldn't join her when she dismounted—but money says neither could Avandar. If you're feeling useless, you've got good company, and at least it wasn't your ass she was trying to save. Come on."

This time, when Angel slowed, it wasn't in anger; Carver, knowing, slowed with him. "We weren't even seeing the same thing."

"'We' being you and Jay?"

Angel nodded. "I could only see the drop. The branches. Celleriant was impaled by them, and he wasn't doing much moving. But whatever she saw—"

"She's seer-born."

"She's always been seer-born."

"And she's always seen things we don't—or can't—see. Never bothered you before."

"Carver, she said there was snow. There *was*; it appeared in her hair as she moved. She walked up the side of the damn tree—and once she was free of the stag's back, she didn't have to cling to *anything*. She couldn't *see* the trunk of the tree—she couldn't bloody *see down*."

"And you know that how?"

"Because she told me!"

Carver snorted. "She just happened to tell you that you weren't seeing what she was seeing."

"Yes."

"Because she just knew."

Angel stared. "I—I told her she couldn't get down or she'd fall."

"She didn't think she'd fall."

"No."

"You told her what you saw."

"Yes—she asked. She couldn't see it."

"You told her. Not Celleriant. Not Avandar. Not any of the rest of us."

Angel nodded slowly; his shoulders fell as he did.

"Look, Angel, I don't understand what she is to you—never have. When we were offered the House Name, we knew it was because she'd pulled for us. We took it. You didn't. What we wanted from her—what we needed from her—when she found us, it wasn't what you wanted or needed. But we didn't get that until you turned down the Terafin name."

"What did you want?"

"A roof over our heads. Food in our stomachs. Clothing on our backs. People to watch them." Carver shrugged. "We wanted safety, or as much safety as we could get in the holdings when we had no other family. We wanted what she wanted for us."

"And now?"

The shrug deepened. "Not that much different. Everything's changed—and nothing has. We didn't know what you'd do, when we took the name." He grinned. "Nothing changed, there. But I understand what you mean to her." He stopped walking and turned. "She'll let you go with her," he said, which made almost no sense. "Wherever she's going—if you push, she'll take you."

"I don't want to push her. I don't want to pressure—"

Carver caught his arm. "Do it anyway. Because she won't necessarily take the rest of us if it looks dangerous—and she needs us."

"She doesn't need—"

"She does. She's spent half her life trying to protect what we've built so she only sees danger—to us."

"She's willing to take that risk."

Carver nodded, released Angel's arm, and turned toward the Isle, where the spires of the Triumvirate could clearly be seen, flags flying in the stiff, cold winds at their heights. "Yeah, there's that."

Chapter Fourteen

ADAM ENTERED the largest of the infirmary rooms in the House of Healing. Beds were pressed up against the walls; they were also huddled so close together there wasn't much space between them. Enough for a person with a tray and a small table stand, no more. But more wasn't needed; here, the patients didn't speak, didn't move, didn't attempt to leave. They slept. More problematic, they didn't eat. But water could at least be forced through their lips, and they swallowed.

They ran the gamut of ages, from ancient to younger than Adam himself; the illness struck entirely at random. Only in one household had two of the occupants fallen to the sleeping sickness. Neither the rich nor the poor had been spared.

In this case, however, it was the poor who were lodged within the House of Healing, with one or two notable exceptions.

Before Levec entered the infirmary, he turned. "There is a reason the magi were sent for."

"You didn't—"

Levec frowned. "Mirialyn did."

Of course, Adam thought; she was the highest ranking woman present. "What reason, Levec?"

"Yesterday afternoon, every single man, woman, and child in the infirmary awoke."

"They are awake?"

"They are no longer awake, no. The waking was brief, but they all cried out at once and sat up. Some of them are not strong enough to remain sitting for long."

"How long were they awake?" He spoke Weston, although it was painful.

"For an hour."

Only an hour.

"They woke once again in the evening, with the same cry. This time, they remained awake for longer. Two of those who were wakened are still awake," he added quietly. "Or they were, when I left the infirmary to fetch you." He frowned in his usual single-brow way, and added, "They were also speaking with the magi. I attempted to order the magi out of the infirmary," he added, "but was overruled by Duvari."

"I don't think it will hurt them."

"Oh, and you're now the director of the House?"

"No, Levec."

"Good. Don't forget it."

"What do you want of me today?"

"We'll do what we normally do when we're saddled with the magi."

Adam didn't understand how *Avantari* worked; nor did he understand what power meant in this large and intimidating city. Averalaan was almost like a waking dream to him. For the most part, men didn't even *carry* swords into the streets of the city; if they required protection, they hired guards, and dressed them in the colors of their various Houses. This last, at least, was comforting in its familiarity. But the guards were prohibited from doing the simple things that they could do in the South, most notably in the way they responded to insult or obvious signs of disrespect. They could legally do nothing.

The Voyani weren't serafs; they weren't slaves. Adam was, therefore, used to a measure of freedom, but that freedom had always come from a lack of home and a lack of land. Those who lived on the land were most frequently chained to it, owned by it. That was the truth of the South. But here? There were no serafs. Even the poor in the infirmary were free.

He glanced at them as the doors opened and Levec entered the room. When he entered a room, he was the first person anyone noticed, and if he was in a bad mood—and he was unarguably in a bad one now—he might be the only one noticed.

Levec had already told him that there were two of the mage-born present; Adam did not, and had never, trusted them. Although Levec assured him that the Sword of Knowledge and the Order of Knowledge were in no way the same, Adam couldn't quite bring himself to believe it, in part because Levec had made it perfectly clear that Adam was not to speak when the magi were present. Levec was willing to speak *for* him, and that was the only risk Levec was willing to take. As far as Adam knew, Levec had never even divulged his name.

But it was awkward to remain silent when the Princess Royale asked a question. Levec had had words with her—harsh ones, but he always reserved harsh words for any nonhealer standing beneath his roof, especially among the powerful—and she asked seldom in the presence of the magi, but when she was concentrating or thinking, she could forget.

"Today," Levec told Adam quietly, "we will wake some of the sleepers. The magi," he added, with a grimace, "want to compare interviews between those who woke on their own and those we wake."

Adam nodded, and Levec turned toward the Princess Royale and Commander Sivari. Adam liked the Princess Royale. She was strong, but she spoke in a soft, clear voice. Her eyes were the color of bronze, her hair, the same. She dressed like a Voyani Matriarch, although her clothing was Northern in style; no skirts or saris, no confining dresses, for her. She also wore a sword; it was the lone sword in the room. Commander Sivari did not carry one. Commander Sivari deferred to her without any discomfort at all, as if she were a Matriarch.

She couldn't be.

No, Adam did not understand the North. Mirialyn smiled when she saw him, which was about five minutes after he'd entered the room.

"The mages?" Levec demanded.

"They are still in conversation," the Princess Royale replied. "I know that you don't approve, but the interview has been . . . interesting, Levec."

"Dantallon?"

"He is resting."

Levec snorted and stalked off. Adam glanced at the magi in their familiar dark gowns, and decided to stay put; they were far enough away.

"You were late," Commander Sivari said.

Adam nodded.

"Levec was worried," Mirialyn added. "You are well?"

Adam nodded again, and glanced at Levec's back. Mirialyn smiled. "He will not, I think, mind small talk while he rousts Dantallon. The Queens' healer has been busy since the crisis began, and he is very underslept."

"What have the sleepers been telling the magi?"

"Only of their dreams," Mirialyn replied.

"They remembered their dreams?"

She nodded, her expression becoming more remote, as it often did. "They not only remembered, but they seem to have had the same dream."

"Did the magi talk to all of those who woke?"

"No. I didn't think to summon them in time; the rest were once again sleeping by the time they arrived."

He felt a small pang, a tightness of throat. "Did they eat before they slept?"

She nodded. "It was the first thing Levec demanded of them."

Adam drew a deeper breath. Of course.

"To be fair, they didn't eat much—but they did eat."

He looked more closely at the backs of the magi. Both of the people they were in the process of interrogating were among the older victims of the illness; the children had evidently succumbed to sleep. It was the children who worried him.

"Sigurne Mellifas is staying at our home," he told Mirialyn. He wasn't even certain why, but once the words were between them, there was no way to withdraw them.

"She's staying at the Terafin manse?"

He froze, as if caught in a lie. He had called it home. He had used the Weston word, our.

"Adam?"

He nodded. "Yes," he said, more stiffly than he'd intended. "In the Terafin manse."

Mirialyn frowned. Her frown, unlike the frowns of the Matriarchs Adam personally knew, was not etched in her skin; it took no permanent residence. But it made her look cold and distant. Margret and Yollana had just looked more dangerous.

"Adam," the Princess Royale said, "the sleepers were dreaming of a forest." Watching his face far too closely, she bent and added, "A forest of golden trees and winged lions."

Levec came to the rescue, dragging a bleary-eyed Dantallon in his wake. Dantallon's eyes were green, but seemed darker in the infirmary's light;

his hair was pale and golden, like stories of Northern men. His skin, however, was sallow, not pale.

Tired or no—and he looked exhausted—he made clear, at Levec's request, that the two awakened dreamers seemed to be following the patterns established by Adam's intervention; he didn't expect them to drift back to sleep within the next couple of days.

Levec greeted this news with characteristic grace. "Wonderful. We'll be plagued by the magi for at least another two days."

Dantallon winced, but said nothing. Neither did the Princess. Commander Sivari was watching Adam carefully, and in a way that reminded Adam of the Tyrs of Annagar. He didn't speak.

The magi, however, did speak, at length, when Levec demanded their attention. Adam was shocked to see that one of the magi was female. He knew Sigurne Mellifas was a mage—he should have guessed that other women would also be part of her Order. In the South, it would have been unthinkable—or worse.

But Sigurne *was* a Matriarch; of that he felt almost certain. That she occupied the sole position of power over the Order felt natural to Adam. This woman, half her age, with too-bright eyes and pale skin, did not. She, however, felt no similar lack of ease in Adam's presence; she almost failed to notice him.

The man beside her also failed to notice, but his attention was focused on Levec. "Healer Levec, we have very little time, and we have no desire to waste it. You have already—"

"Insisted that they be given food?"

The man fell silent for a moment; it was clear this took effort. "Dantallon assessed their condition; he did not feel their situation was so dire that they would lack the time to eat before they once again succumbed to their illness."

"Dantallon's responsibility is the Queens' healerie. My responsibility is this one." He glared at Dantallon, who said nothing.

"Do you dispute his diagnosis?"

"What diagnosis can we offer with certainty in this case?" Levec countered. They were speaking quickly enough that Adam had to struggle to keep up.

The man—whose name Adam hadn't caught—jabbed the air with his finger. "We have no certainty, of course—which is *why* it is of utmost import that we be allowed access to information before it is once again beyond us!"

"You will not speak of my patients as if they were artifacts in your possession."

"They are not simple victims of injury or disease—they are practically witnesses."

"This is not a magisterial court. They've committed no crime."

Adam took a step toward Levec, but Dantallon caught his sleeve and gently pulled him back. "They've been brewing for a fight," he said quietly. "They're unlikely to come to blows, and if anyone can afford to anger the Order, it's Levec."

"I don't see how it will help the sleepers."

"No. But can you see any way it will hurt them? Come," he added. "While they sort out their difficulties." He gestured toward the table in the back of the infirmary. It was long and flat, and it served one purpose in this room: it held a map. Adam was fascinated by it. Pins, with different colored wax heads, had been pushed into the map's surface; these indicated the places in which the men and women in the infirmary had lived before they'd been brought here.

Waxless pins indicated possible victims. These theoretical victims existed in the holdings that Dantallon said were wealthier. "There are more?" Adam asked, when he was closer to the table.

Dantallon nodded. "Four that we're certain of; three that we now suspect."

Adam had asked, only once, how they came by these suspicions; Dantallon had made clear that it was not a question that could be answered—or asked—in safety. Dantallon took up a position across the table from Adam.

"If you don't sleep," Adam said, surveying the pins, and noting the new ones that Dantallon had mentioned, "Levec's going to beat you unconscious."

"The very same Levec who threatened to throw me out into the street if I wasted his time dozing in a chair?" Dantallon chuckled. "Your Weston has greatly improved. Who taught you that word?"

"Beat?"

"Unconscious."

"Levec." Adam frowned. "This pin—"

"Yes. It's on the Isle." It was also unadorned by wax. "I will be escorted to the manor this evening, to either confirm the rumor or put it to rest." He ran a hand through his hair. "The Kings are concerned."

"Dantallon—the dreams they've talked about—"

The shouting banked suddenly; the room became instantly too quiet. Dantallon looked up, lips thinning as they compressed. The two guards who habitually adorned the doors outside of the makeshift infirmary were now on the inside, flanking two visitors who had obviously pushed their way past them.

They must be men of import, Adam thought, to trespass so boldly and survive; the guards hadn't even drawn swords.

Dantallon said in soft Weston, "This is just what we need." He straightened out, moving away from the table and toward the two strangers who stood near the doors.

"They're important men?" Adam asked, as he scurried after Dantallon.

"They are not politically important in the same way The Terafin was," Dantallon replied, knowing how little Adam knew of the City's political structures. "But the older man is a very successful merchant, in one of the oldest of the Imperial Houses."

"I've had word," the man was saying to Levec, "that my granddaughter woke. Twice."

Levec's brows were compressed across the ridge of his prominent nose. "She's not awake now," he replied.

The expression that crossed the stranger's face made Adam wince; it was familiar in a way his spoken language was not. Before Dantallon could stop him, Adam said, "But she ate, while she was awake."

The man turned to Adam, ignoring the royal healer who stood just slightly in front of him. "Did she?"

Adam nodded, although he hadn't seen it himself.

"What caused her to wake?"

"We don't know yet. If you ask the magi—"

"Oh, gods take the magi," was the acerbic reply. "If I ask the magi, I'll be standing here for hours and at the end I'll be none the wiser for their response." He removed his very fine, very Northern outer jacket and handed it to the other stranger, who took it without comment and handled it with care.

"Patris," Levec began.

"And gods take you as well," was the acid reply. "I have in my possession a writ which *clearly states* that I will be immediately informed of *any change* in my granddaughter's status. Clearly we define those words differently, and I mean you to understand how *I* define them." He turned to the man who held his coat. "Andrei."

The man bowed.

"Patris Hectore—"

"I will see my granddaughter, Levec." He paused, looked down his nose at Adam, and added, "You may supervise me."

Adam bowed, just as his servant had; the gesture came naturally. This was a man concerned about a child—his granddaughter—and to Adam, such concern was worthy of respect. To Levec as well, because Levec gave a curt nod in Adam's direction—one that wasn't joined by words.

The infirmary was large; the man's granddaughter was slightly separated from most of the adult sleepers; so were the other children who lay abed, breathing deeply and evenly, their lids closed, their hands by their sides.

"She ate?" the older man asked as they walked.

"Yes."

"She ate well?"

He hesitated; the man marked it. "None of the sleepers ate well," he finally said. "They have little appetite."

"Bring me water, boy. And a goblet. Bring me a towel as well."

Adam nodded and bowed.

When he returned, the man was seated beside his granddaughter, his chair wedged in the narrow gap between her bed and the next one. His granddaughter slept by his side, undisturbed by—unaware of—his presence. He was not a small man; his hands were large, and they cupped one of hers, engulfing it.

Adam offered him the goblet; he set the dry towel on the bed within his reach, and put the pail on the floor beside him before he began to withdraw.

"Don't go, boy," the man said. "Stay a moment. Talk me out of my rage."

For a raging man, he spoke quietly, although his voice was strong and certain. When Adam made no reply, he turned. "My cousin thinks me insane. I've many children and many grandchildren, and so far, only two have predeceased me. Sharann is young," he added, his hand still covering hers. "And she is not, that we know, in pain."

"Your cousin thinks you insane? Because you are worried about your grandchild?"

The man smiled. "He's not a doctor, and he's certainly not a healer."

"He has no children of his own?"

"He has three."

Adam shook his head. He was aware that this man must be both powerful and important, and kept any other words of disdain for the man's cousin from leaving his mouth.

"You don't approve?" He frowned. "What is your name, boy? I am Hectore."

"Adam. I am Adam."

"You're not originally from our fair city, are you?"

"No."

"Where is home, for you?"

"In the South. In Annagar."

Hectore's brows rose. "But you managed to make your way to Levec."

"Levec saved my life."

"He's a good man. Remind me that I said that," Hectore added. "I left my grandchild in his care because he is ferocious in defense of those in his care; nothing short of royal edict will move that stubborn—that man, and sometimes, not even royal edict."

"But—"

"She *woke*. She woke, and he did not immediately summon me; he sent me neither word nor notice. She was *awake*, Adam. Do you know what that would have meant to her mother? And instead of family, she wakes to *this*. This is not where she went to sleep; she was probably confused and frightened. And where was I? In my ignorance, I was in the Merchant's Authority, arguing with idiots."

"This is why you wish to strangle Levec."

"Indeed." He now released his granddaughter's hand and slid one arm under her neck, lifting her from the bed. Adam scurried around to the other side to rearrange her pillows as Hectore began to gently dribble water into her mouth. "This must seem strange to you."

"Strange?"

"In the South, men are reputed to care far less for their offspring."

"The Voyani are not like the clansmen," Adam replied, showing this stranger a glimpse of ferocious pride. "We know the value of the children; they are the only future we have."

"So. You are Voyani. I should have guessed. The Voyani are free to travel, although I confess I have met few."

"Have you met any?"

Hectore chuckled. "No."

"We do not come to the North."

"Yet you are here."

Adam fell silent for a long moment. "Yes," he said at last. "I am here. Is there anything else you need?"

"No. I will sue the magi into penury if they come anywhere near my granddaughter, and you may tell them I said so."

Adam frowned, attempting to make sense of the sentence. "You wish me to tell Levec to keep the magi away from her?"

Hectore pursed his lips and then said, in Torra, "I will beggar their precious Order if they so much as touch one hair on her head."

Adam's eyes rounded. "Go on," Hectore said, making shooing motions. "Tell him. He's unlikely to bite you."

Levec was at Dantallon's side, hovering above the map. Adam joined them, sliding between the two healers with the practiced ease of an indulged younger child.

"Is he any calmer?" Levec asked, still glaring at the pins he'd poked through parchment.

"He is not happy that he did not see his granddaughter while she was awake."

"No, he wouldn't be. He hasn't—"

"And he threatened to beggar the Order of Knowledge if the magi go anywhere near her."

Sivari, standing beside the Princess, chuckled. "He just might try. I've seldom seen a man so devoted to his grandchildren."

"You mean you've seldom seen a man with so much wealth or power so devoted?" Mirialyn asked more pointedly.

Sivari nodded. The magi looked vastly less amused, as they were also present.

Adam now looked carefully at the map; he tugged Levec's sleeve and nodded in the direction of the Isle. "The Terafin," he whispered, when Levec bent toward him.

Levec merely shook his head. "Not here, Adam. Go back to Patris Ara-ven and keep him out of trouble. If you can, kick him out of the infirmary—without his granddaughter."

Adam hesitated.

"What?"

"If you are going to wake one of the sleepers—"

"He's already demanded that the magi be kept away from his grand-daughter, and the sleepers woken today will have to endure the magi and their endless questions. They may have to endure more."

When Adam failed to reply, Levec said, "The children all woke, and they were all fed; they ate twice. They are not in danger of starvation for another several days."

"Yes, Levec."

When Adam returned to Hectore, he wasn't terribly surprised to see that Hectore had lifted his granddaughter out of her sickbed, and was cra-dling her in his arms as if she were a much younger child. Glancing at her arms and legs, Adam winced; she, like the rest of the children here, had lost so much weight they looked like victims of famine or drought. Levec always let Adam wake one or two of the children. They were not large, and the lack of food was more telling; if they were awakened, they could be fed enough to guarantee that death wouldn't be due to starva-tion.

"Do many other parents visit?" Hectore asked, making no attempt to once again set his grandchild in her bed.

"I don't know," Adam replied—in Torra. "If any of these children were Arkosan, there would *always* be one of my aunts or uncles in this room. Always." He hesitated, and then added, "I don't know if they would leave an Arkosan child with strangers, though."

"Even if they had no hope of healing the child themselves?"

Thinking of himself, Adam shook his head. "No; if it was a choice be-tween death and strangers, they would risk the strangers. But . . . they would not trust them."

"No." Hectore, speaking Torra as calmly and easily as if it were his own tongue, added, "and it appears with some cause." He glared across to the huddle in the back of the room. "Do you know all of the people present?"

Adam nodded.

"Does the Princess Royale visit often?"

"Yes. She comes with Commander Sivari, and sometimes with Duvari."

Hectore looked like he wanted to spit at the mention of the last name.

Misinterpreting, Adam said, "Duvari never goes near the children. Ever. Levec barely lets him inside the infirmary."

"Yes. And Levec—unlike the rest of us—can get away with it. What do you think of Duvari?"

"I don't. Levec doesn't like him."

"No one likes him."

"But Levec doesn't distrust him."

"I see. Do you live here?"

"In Averalaan?"

"In the House of Healing. In one of them."

Adam shook his head.

"Ah. I'm surprised. Usually Levec keeps his healers very, very close—especially at your age."

Adam froze.

"Ah. You are not to talk about your talent, are you? Especially not with the rich or the powerful. My apologies, Adam. I ask too many questions. Usually it is Levec's hostile face I see when I walk through those doors; it is pleasant to have company that doesn't measure or judge."

"Is he wrong?" Adam asked.

"No, sadly, he is not wrong. And you are a boy among strangers; you have no kin and no family in the city. You would be particularly vulnerable if your ability were openly discussed."

"I have friends here," Adam replied.

"Levec?"

"No. Well, yes, but he is more like an uncle."

"The others?"

"I live with them in House Terafin."

Hectore of Araven left the infirmary half an hour later. Andrei was waiting for him in the hall, in easy view of the guards Hectore had all but humiliated. The guards had, however, recovered their composure enough that they looked right through him when he made his exit.

Andrei handed him his coat, and he donned it in silence; nor did he break that silence until they were alone in the Araven carriage.

"You are certain the boy is always present?"

"He is not, as I stated in my report, always present."

"But he is always present before the sleepers wake?"

Andrei nodded. "He is never far from Levec, and it should be noted for the sake of completeness that Levec is also always present. But the wakings occur only when the two are together."

"Except for yesterday."

"Indeed; that is the exception. I do not believe Levec or his healers were expecting it, judging from the presence of Duvari and the magi."

"Were you aware that the boy is living in the Terafin manse?"

Andrei raised a brow. "You are certain?"

"He said exactly that. He is living with 'friends' in the Terafin manse. I wish to know exactly how long this has been the case, and *exactly* who those friends are."

"At this time, Hectore, that will be exceptionally difficult. The security at the Terafin manse is—"

"How much worse can it be, given the preparations for the funeral, than the Houses of Healing?"

"Much. Duvari only barely keeps informed of the events that occur under Levec's purview. Levec is only concerned with the bodily safety of his healers. He has never lost one while they were within the Houses, so his tendency is to watch outward, not in. After The Terafin's funeral rites are over, it will be less complicated. Can you wait that long?"

Hectore said nothing, but the silence was not permanent. He glanced out at the passing streetscape. "The last healer who lived in the Terafin manse met an unpleasant—and swift—end."

"As did The Terafin herself."

"I am not willing to risk the boy in such a fashion. It appears that my granddaughter's life depends on his, and House Terafin is a totally inappropriate venue for survival."

"At the moment, it is not."

"No; it will become so rapidly, however. Find out who his friends are, Andrei."

Andrei's hesitance was rare, and marked. "Should he have friends with ambitions, Hectore, what will you do?"

"As I have done. You are aware that three of the four Terafin contenders have spoken with me. They have not, of course, demanded my support, but they have asked. If he is indeed housed with one of the three, I will make my own demands in return for some political concessions."

"And if he is not?"

Hectore pinched the bridge of his nose. "I do not understand why Levec chooses to allow him to stay within the manse. Levec is not a fool."

"No, indeed."

"Which makes it imperative that you determine exactly what the situation is; I am unclear on how to proceed, but not unclear on the necessity of that boy's survival."

"Hectore—"

"If he is not known to be a healer, I will not expose him, if that is your fear. I am fully aware of the part Alowan Rowanson played in the last House War." And such a bitter reward, in the end, for those decades of peace and prosperity. But Alowan had at least lived a full life, retaining choice and freedom until the end. What hope did a fourteen-year-old boy—possibly sixteen at the outside—have to negotiate his way into doing the same?

"I want access to him. I wish to be able to interview him when he's not under Levec's watchful eye."

Andrei gave Hectore a very pointed look.

"Yes?"

"Nothing."

"Oh, never fear, Andrei. It's not like I have any intention of adopting the boy, or taking him under my wing; I am concerned about my grandchild. That's all."

"Of course, Hectore."

Levec was not in a good mood by the time the magi were done; Adam suspected he was hungry; Levec seldom ate while working. Adam woke two of the sleepers; a woman in her forties and a man of about the same age. Levec chose them. The magi conducted their interviews—Adam was impressed at just how long each of the magi could talk; he was certain they would still be there had Levec not insisted they leave. They obeyed his bald order with both surprise and annoyance, but at that point, Levec didn't care.

When they were ensconced in the carriage, Levec said, "It was harder, this time."

It wasn't a question; Adam nodded, and then asked one of his own. "Did you sense anything different?"

"Beyond the continuing atrophy of muscle tissue, no. You did?"

Adam nodded again. Levec didn't ask him what; he simply waited while Adam struggled with Weston—and, in this case, Torra—in an attempt to come up with meaningful words. "When I wake them," he finally said, in his halting Weston, "when I have woken them before, it is—" he shook his head. "They aren't quite in their bodies."

Levec frowned; he'd heard this before. "Let me come in with you," he finally said. "I've two hours before I'm to meet with Duvari. I want to hear what your Jewel has to say."

"I am not supposed to discuss this with her," Adam began. He could feel a flush rising in his cheeks, which was made worse when Levec lifted a skeptical brow.

"You're not," he agreed curtly. "Nor, in theory, am I. But I am not about to expose your ability to the magi, and I need a better translator than either you or I. She understands what you can do." It wasn't a question.

When the carriage pulled up the wide drive to the steps of the manse, Terafin footmen were there to greet it. They attempted to offer Levec aid in disembarking, and didn't lose their hands; Adam thought it was close. He accepted the offer of aid, and came to stand beside a glowering Levec.

Levec wasn't glowering at the footmen, however; he was glowering at the man on the top of the steps, just outside of the range of the doors.

"Healer Levec." Duvari bowed.

Levec didn't. "Lord of the Compact. I see preparations for the funeral are keeping you busy."

"Indeed. I've been waiting for you, Healer. Please, walk with me."

Adam was surprised when Duvari began to lead the way to the public galleries, Levec by his side. Servants moved through the wide halls, cleaning and arranging both flowers and candles as they did; guards stood watch as visitors—and inhabitants—passed by. Adam, who had rarely spent much time within the homes of the clansmen, still found halls like these both foreign and astonishing. There were no hangings between rooms; there were doors. There were more windows, more glass, and high, high ceilings, but there were no spaces of elegant silence, no fonts of contemplation, no platforms that faced moon or sun or sheltered behind the artful construction of trees or hedges. He followed behind the two older men as they talked in low voices, apparently oblivious to the constant, moving throngs.

Adam had become accustomed to the perpetual presence of people. It wasn't as if he had enjoyed a great deal of privacy in the caravans. But there the people spoke Torra, and to one degree or another, they were all his kin; one large, moving family, with the responsibilities, rivalries, and affections that implied. The city of Averalaan seemed to him a loose congregation of strangers.

Even this manse, in theory the home of the Terafin line, was in practice the city writ small: strangers, whose duties seldom crossed lines, living side-by-side.

But as he followed Duvari, he realized where the Lord of the Compact was taking them, and he felt himself relax. Each step brought him closer to the doors beyond which Jewel ATerafin and her den lived. They claimed no blood ties, but they understood kinship; he felt welcome there, although he knew Jewel and her friends were often in councils of war. He liked Ellerson, who served, and Finch, who was never harsh, and he worried about Ariel, the child who had come with Jewel from the South. It had fallen to him to care for her, although she was willing to stand beside—or behind—Ellerson when he worked; she didn't speak very much and she hid her hand whenever she noticed its missing fingers.

The doors opened when Duvari knocked. Ellerson stood between them. He acknowledged Adam with a single, silent glance, and then invited the visitors into the wing; Adam stepped through the doors and exhaled.

This was not his wagon; nor could he lie aground and watch the open skies. But here, at least, people spoke his native tongue and here, as well, they followed Jewel, just as the Arkosans followed Margret. They weren't silent and obedient—but none of Adam's cousins had ever been that. They could shout, sulk, or pound tables, but he knew they would follow her no matter where she led, and knew, as well, that they would fight and die for her.

If they knew how.

"Adam," Ellerson said quietly, "Ariel was asking after you."

"Is she—"

"She is well."

"Has there been trouble?"

"There has been some—she is uninjured, but there's been some small argument as a result."

Levec cleared his throat. "We require Adam for a few minutes more. I wish to have Jewel ATerafin's aid in a tricky translational matter."

"Jewel is at the moment occupied, Healer Levec. Might I suggest that Finch would serve your purposes just as well?"

Levec frowned and shook his head.

"Very well. Let me ask Jewel when she can free herself from her duties."

"Thank you."

"Levec—" Adam began.

"Yes, yes. Go. Just be sure to return when I call for you; we're not likely to have more than a few moments of her time, and those moments will probably be grudged."

Adam headed down the hall, leaving a silent Duvari and an annoyed Levec at his back. It pained him to see the healer so worried—because he knew Levec was.

He stopped outside of Ariel's room. Ariel had spent the previous evening with Adam; her Weston was almost nonexistent, and everyone else had been so busy, or noisy, or both.

"Adam," Ellerson called, from the other end of the hall.

Adam looked up, his hand on the door's knob. "Yes?"

"I am not certain how aware you are of the nature of some of Jewel's guests."

Adam froze. "I have seen the Hunter," he said. "And the great stag. Why?"

"They are not her only guests. Ariel, at the moment, is entertaining one of them." He hesitated and then said, "there was some minor difficulty, but she was not hurt, and the situation was addressed—quickly—by Jewel."

Adam opened the door, and froze in its frame. Ariel was seated on the carpet, and curled around her was a very large, very gray, giant cat. It looked up, and as it did, it flexed and raised its wings. While Adam stared at it in shocked silence, it said, "Who are you?"

Ariel rose instantly, but so did the cat. Although it was large and bulky, it leaped in front of the child, standing between her and Adam.

Ellerson cleared his throat. The cat, tail and ears twitching, looked up. "Yessss?"

"Adam is a member of Jewel's den. He lives in the wing. Jewel is very attached to him, and considers him very important. Adam," he added, turning to the stunned Voyani youth, "this is Shadow."

The cat hissed; he clearly wasn't fond of his name.

"This—this is one of the guests who caused the—the difficulty?"

"Ah, no. The two that caused the difficulty have been sent to their room. They broke one of the bed's posts while arguing, which upset Ariel."

Adam couldn't think of a single person—save perhaps Yollana of the Havalla Voyani—who wouldn't find it upsetting. "The other two—are they also winged cats?"

"They are. Snow and Night, named after their colors." Ellerson frowned. "Adam?"

Winged lions. Golden trees.

Ariel rose, ran to Adam's side, and grabbed his hand, dragging him into the room. Because she was there, he went.

"Shadow speaks our language," she told him, her voice very low, her gaze skirting the tip of his nose.

"Ariel, what did Jewel say to the other two after they'd had their fight?"

"I didn't understand it."

"But the cats did?"

She nodded. "They broke it." She pointed to the bedpost. Adam didn't entirely understand the purpose of posts such as these; nor did he understand the reason the beds were so high off the ground. Regardless, it was clear that the carved beam had been snapped in two, although it didn't look as if it had been either bitten or clawed.

"They hit it," Ariel whispered. "While they were fighting. It broke."

"They were *careless*," the gray cat said, slowly padding across the carpet, his claws exposed. His eyes were a disturbing shade of gold, and they were unblinking. He sniffed, snorted, and walked around Adam and Ariel, brushing the underside of Adam's chin—and nose—with his tail. "You're *sure* he's important?" the cat asked Ellerson.

Ellerson stiffly said, "Very sure."

"Oh." He leaned against Adam, and Adam stumbled to the side. To his surprise, Ariel detached herself and smacked the cat on the nose, frowning.

Winged lions. Except they weren't. Adam understood then that although he was hundreds or thousands of miles away from his home, he had found, and was walking, the Voyanne. His suspicions about Jewel hardened to certainty, and that certainty became the silence with which he had always guarded both his mother's and his sister's conversations. Their secrets were the heart of Arkosa. Jewel's would be the heart of Terafin—and no one but a fool exposed a clan's heart.

"Where," he asked Shadow, "did you come from?"

The cat raised a brow and sniffed disdainfully.

Adam reached out to touch him. The cat allowed it, swiveling his head to meet Adam's eyes, light to dark, gold to very mortal brown. The cat wasn't human. Anyone that Adam had tried to heal until now had been; nor did the cat look injured. But Adam touched Shadow as if he were, and warmth spread from his palms into the gray fur, and beyond it, into the body of the winged creature itself.

Shadow roared, and wheeled. His wings rose and snapped; Adam, wingless, flew across the room, colliding with the side of the bed. Ariel shouted. She didn't, however, scream; she was both worried and angry. And it was good to hear her so angry, because she always seemed like the ghost of a child, to Adam; so faint, so attenuated.

Shadow landed on his chest, growling.

Ariel climbed up on Adam as well, her heel landing in the hollow between collarbones, which made breathing difficult. She faced the cat. Adam could only barely find breath to speak her name to tell her to flee.

Ellerson raised his voice and after a few minutes, so did Jewel as she stormed into the room, her face pale, her eyes round.

Shadow turned to her and said, "He is *dangerous*."

"He is *not* dangerous. He's a *healer*, and you will get off him *now* or I'll—"

"Ye-es?" Shadow said, sliding off Adam enough that Adam could sit up—if Ariel hadn't been so precariously balanced on top of him.

Jewel strode across the room to Adam and offered him a hand. He very gently disengaged Ariel, accepted the hand—which was more command than offer—and rose. "What happened?" she asked, in the quiet intensity of worried Torra.

"I—it's my fault," he told her.

"I'll be the judge of that. What happened?"

Adam lifted his hands. They were numb, now. Numb and tingling. "I touched the—I touched Shadow."

"I touch him all the time. I hit him when he's being a pain. He's never tried anything like that."

"You're not a healer. It's not the same." He touched the back of his head and discovered a bump the size of Ariel's fist. "I shouldn't have done it; I wouldn't have, if he'd been—"

"Human?"

Adam nodded. He bowed to her, which hurt. "I won't do it again."

"Shadow."

Shadow snarled.

"Come here. Stop hiding behind Ariel."

He hissed, but the insult to his dignity had the desired effect; he crept across the carpet.

"Did he hurt you?"

". . . No."

"What, exactly, did you think he was trying to do?"

"I don't *know*. It felt *funny*. It felt *wrong*." He hissed again.

"Do you know what a healer is?"

Shadow didn't answer.

"All right, let me make this clear: Adam is our friend."

"You have *too many* friends." His claws raked holes in the carpet.

"If you don't like it, you can always go back."

"To *where*?"

"To wherever it is you came from." Jewel folded her arms. "I'm not joking. If I can't trust you not to kill or injure my friends, you can leave now."

"What if I *don't want* to leave?"

"I'll have Avandar and Celleriant change your mind."

Shadow hissed again. But he sat down heavily, and when he did, Ariel crept back to him and put her arms around his neck.

Jewel then turned to Adam. "Levec wanted to speak with us."

"Levec," Levec said, from the door, "does indeed." The older healer's eyes were narrowed, and his brows were gathered into one thick line. What Adam remembered, Levec also clearly recalled.

"How long," Levec demanded, "has *that* been in residence?"

Jewel had shooed them all out of the room, as she hadn't quite finished whatever she wanted to say to Shadow. Ariel almost followed Adam out, but one glance at Duvari and Levec changed her mind.

"I don't know when he arrived, I'm sorry. It can't have been more than a day ago."

"A day. Yesterday?"

Adam said nothing, aware of Duvari's watchful presence.

It was, therefore, Duvari who answered. "Yesterday. Is there cause for concern, Healer Levec?"

"Where you're involved, there's always cause for concern," was the sharp reply. Duvari raised a brow, but said no more. Adam had a suspicion that Duvari grudgingly approved of Levec's open disdain."I don't suppose you've run across golden trees while you've been spying?"

Duvari stilled in the worst possible way. So, in response, did Levec. He lost color and volume. "Lord of the Compact," he said quietly, "what is going on in the Terafin manse?"

"You are asking the wrong person," Duvari replied. "But if it is any consolation, you are not the only one to ask; the Exalted themselves are concerned."

It wasn't any consolation, of course. Levec turned to Adam. "I want you back in my House," he said curtly, folding large arms across his chest.

The door opened, and Jewel, looking frazzled, slid into the hall before she slammed it shut. "Healer Levec," she said, tendering him a brief bow. "Lord of the Compact. How may I help you?"

Levec opened his mouth, and Duvari lifted a hand, silencing him. "Not here."

Jewel's shoulders fell about two inches, but she squared them and nodded. "Follow me."

She led them to the large room used for formal gatherings, and raised a brow at Duvari as she opened the doors. He returned an almost imperceptible nod as answer to her silent query, and she ushered everyone in. Ellerson appeared, as if by magical summons, before everyone had taken a seat.

"I want Avandar, if you can find him," Jewel told him.

Ellerson nodded and retreated.

"Your domicis is less present of late," Duvari noted.

"Yes. Usually I'd consider his absence a blessing." Jewel glanced at the fireplace, where fire wasn't burning. She headed toward the logs and the small branches used to start one, and knelt there. Adam joined her.

"If your domicis is found," Duvari said behind them, "he will not approve of the way you've undertaken a purely menial task in the presence of guests of note."

Jewel turned; Adam continued to work. "He's the domicis," she replied evenly. "He wouldn't dream of an open display of disapproval in front of said guests of note."

Levec actually chuckled and found himself a chair. "Leave her be, Duvari; the room is chill. Any guest of note would fail to notice. Ah, apologies, any guest of both note and manners."

Jewel found the tinderbox, grimacing. This part, she usually left entirely to Avandar, because he had a more efficient way of starting a fire, and any fire he started tended to keep burning. She gestured to Adam while he worked, taking care to hide the movement of her hands from Duvari; she didn't expect Levec to notice—or care. Adam's answers were both less cautious and slower; although he was more than happy to learn den-sign, he wasn't terribly proficient at it yet.

Stay? Here or there? she asked.

Here. Here, was his labored response.

Certain?

Yes.

Why? She nodded tersely in Levec's direction. Unfortunately, the two motions didn't resolve as the question she'd meant to ask—either that or Adam's minimal knowledge didn't allow him to answer. On the other hand, it was Levec; she was almost certain to know exactly why he'd come the minute they left off building the fire.

Which, she thought, as the door opened, was going to be now.

Avandar stood in the frame; Ellerson was behind him, and from his posture, she assumed Ellerson was carrying a tray. Avandar carried nothing. His brows rose and his lips compressed as he caught sight of Jewel; he left Ellerson in the open door as he walked, briskly, toward the fireplace. "ATerafin."

She rose and brushed her hands against her dress, which didn't appreciably improve his expression. "It was chilly," she told him. "And we have guests."

"At this time, you should not have unscheduled visitors or guests."

"I don't have a Barston of my own to turn them away at the door," she began. "I barely have a functional office here—" She stopped.

Avandar said nothing. The fire sprang instantly to life; tongues of bright orange and pale gold suddenly extended and wrapped themselves around hardwood logs. The small branches and twigs used as starter were consumed in an instant. She hated to admit that she liked anything about magic on most days, but she loved to watch this.

Today, however, it didn't matter. She turned and made her way to Levec; Adam shadowed her.

"Healer Levec," she said, bowing again.

"My apologies for my unannounced arrival, ATerafin," Levec replied.

Ellerson was not entirely pleased by the previous exchange, although it wasn't obvious to anyone who didn't know him. Jewel, who had lived with his absence for well over a decade, was chagrined at how little he had changed. He set his tray down and offered the healer tea. The tea came with brandy, but Levec refused the latter.

"I will come to the point. I am concerned about two things. Let me dispense with the first: I do not feel it is safe for Adam to remain in House Terafin."

"If he isn't summoned to the Houses of Healing, it's entirely safe here," she countered.

"But he *is* summoned to the Houses of Healing; that is not negotiable." Levec glanced at Duvari; Duvari nodded. "I do not want him involved in the current political struggle in *any* way. Can you guarantee that he will not be?"

"I can guarantee that I'll do my best to keep him out of it."

"That is not sufficient."

It wasn't. Jewel knew it. Adam was fourteen years old. But Adam was now separated from the only family he'd ever known, and if he wasn't an orphan—and technically he was—he'd attached himself to Finch in Jewel's absence. Finch, the den, this wing. He felt almost at home here; he did not feel at home with the healers. She said nothing for a long moment, and then, leaving her hands at her sides, she asked, "What was the second concern?"

Levec clearly didn't want to proceed with the second concern until the first one had been addressed to his satisfaction. He drank his tea as if drinking were an act of aggression. Jewel waited, refusing to sit.

It was Adam who broke the deadlock. "Levec wanted you to translate my Torra."

Levec drilled the side of Adam's face with a silent glare, but he did set the tea down. "Very well. Adam wishes to remain here, and I am *attempting* to accept that. You will not offer comment on the success of that attempt."

"I wouldn't dream of it." Jewel then took the seat beside Levec's. Duvari, however, remained standing. So did Avandar, although he always did that. Adam hovered for a few minutes, and then took a chair that was equidistant between Jewel's and Levec's, but across the table.

"Adam?" they both said at once. There was an awkward pause, but it eased when Adam smiled. His smile was almost apologetic, but—it was trusting. He trusted Levec, Jewel thought; he trusted her.

Adam slid into Torra. "Levec asked me what I feel when I heal the sleepers."

"It's different from healing the injured?"

"Or the other sick, yes. I tried to answer, but . . . it's hard. Levec's Torra is good enough that he can speak to the injured—or their relatives—when he meets them. He doesn't think it's good enough—"

Levec lifted a hand. "It's not good enough, and I would thank you not to speak about me as if I'm not present."

Adam reddened. "Sorry, Levec. Yesterday, the sleepers in the Houses of Healing woke. They all woke at the same time."

"Yesterday?" Jewel asked, keeping her voice as steady and uninflected as possible.

"Yes. Twice."

"When?"

"In the afternoon. And later, in the evening. Two of the people who woke in the evening remain awake without my help." He hesitated again, and this time glanced at Duvari. Duvari merely nodded.

"Matriarch," Adam continued, his voice low, his Torra less hesitant. "They spoke about their dreams. The people I've woken don't—they don't seem to have any, or none that they remember. But these ones? They did."

Jewel failed to hear the word Matriarch, but it took effort. "What were their dreams?" She didn't strive for casual because she knew there was no point; she couldn't be casual about this.

"They dreamed," he said, drawing one sharp breath, "of golden trees and winged lions."

Jewel closed her eyes.

Chapter Fifteen

"YOU UNDERSTAND part of my concern," Levec said, when she opened them again.

"Yes. But they're not lions," she added.

Levec's brows rose. He managed to bring them under control before he spoke again. "And the trees?"

"Yes. If you want, we can head out to the grounds now; we'll have to run a gauntlet of House Guards and Duvari's security to get there, though. Or you can wait until the funeral; you'll understand as much as I do, then."

"You'll forgive me if that's not a comfort." He set the tea down without cracking the cup. "How do your . . . guests . . . and your trees affect my patients? My patients are in the holdings on the mainland; you are on the Isle."

"I don't know, Levec. I can guess, but it's not going to be an educated guess."

Adam cleared his throat. "Matriarch?"

They both turned to look at him.

"The translation?"

Jewel reddened slightly. "Sorry, Adam. Please."

"When I heal the injured, I feel the body. For a moment it's as if I can understand it; it's my mother tongue. It's the way I breathe or walk. But when I touch the sleepers, it's different. I *can* touch their bodies; I can do what healers normally do. But there's nothing wrong with their bodies." He hesitated, and then added, "Well, there are always little things wrong with a body—but there's nothing about the body that prevents them from waking.

"They're not *in* their bodies." He glanced at Levec, who was silent, his face momentarily inscrutable.

"How are you certain?" It was Jewel who asked.

"I can see them."

"Pardon?"

"I can see them, standing outside of themselves."

Avandar crossed the carpet, his eyes narrowed. "What do you mean," he asked—in clear and perfect Torra.

Adam glanced at Jewel, who nodded. "When I first woke a sleeper, I didn't see him clearly; not the way I do now. But I could sense him beyond his body. Outside of it. I could call him back."

Levec stiffened, but said nothing.

"Call him?" Avandar's voice was soft, but there was an edge in it. "The way healers call the dying back?"

"I don't know. I've never called the dying. But . . . I've been called, and I don't think it's the same. Wherever they are, they're willing to leave. It's not like—" he swallowed. "They're not near the bridge; they don't want to cross it."

"Where are they, then?"

This was clearly the question Adam had difficulty answering. "I . . . don't know." He took a deeper breath and turned the whole of his attention to Jewel. Not to Levec. "But it's harder, now. I can see them, Matriarch. But it's harder to reach them. I think—I think something else sees them as well, and it holds them."

"Are they dreaming, Adam?" she asked softly.

"They don't remember their dreams when they wake."

"That's not what I asked." She hesitated, struggling with Torra for reasons that had nothing to do with translation. "When you see them, before you call them, are they aware of you?"

He shook his head.

"Can you see where they think they are?"

Creases appeared in his forehead; they'd leave when his frown did. "I haven't tried."

"Try. Try for me."

"ATerafin."

Jewel turned toward Duvari.

"Where do you think they are?"

"In the dreaming," she replied.

"And where, exactly, is that?"

"I don't know." It wasn't the answer Duvari wanted. She bit her lip and looked toward Avandar; her domicis nodded.

"It is not the land of Mandaros," he replied, dragging Duvari's attention—and obvious suspicion—away. "It is therefore not the land the dead or the dying reach. If it were, other healers would be able to rouse the sleepers. They can call the dying back to their bodies because they have the ability to heal the bodies; I suspect Adam can reach them because he can touch more than just the physical.

"They *are* dreaming, in my opinion. They dream small dreams; it is why so many must sleep."

"Must?" Duvari said.

"The dreaming is not part of our world."

"It is not part of the world of the gods."

"It is not, no. But there are ancient roads and paths that exist between mortal fields and forests; they exist beneath mountains and through the causeways of deep stone. They exist in the deserts and in the storms; they exist in the cold of the Northern Wastes."

"If I ask you how you know this?"

Avandar shook his head, a strange smile touching his lips. "You will not ask; you have far, far too much to contend with at the moment to waste your time on a pointless endeavor."

Duvari offered no answering smile. "Continue."

"These ways have long been hidden."

"The hidden path?" Jewel asked.

Avandar nodded.

"Why?"

"Because you know, as I know, that the gods once walked this world. You know that one such god has returned. What you have not completely understood is that when the gods left; their children—those that survived—did not. It is said they could not; they were born of this world.

"The gods agreed to the binding covenant of Bredan. They were then left with a choice: to destroy their children, or to leave them alive. It was a bitter argument. But in the end, a compromise was reached. Do you understand it?"

"The hidden path."

"Yes. It is a place where the gods themselves might once have walked. It is wild in the way the whole of the world was once wild, and it is carved into the ancient earth, the ancient stone. It is called hidden, ATerafin, because very, very few can find it who were not born at the dawn of the world."

Jewel rose, pushing herself up and out of the chair as if by movement she could escape the weight of his words. She knew he spoke the truth; she knew he spoke only as much of it as would make the situation clear to the Lord of the Compact. But she knew, as well, that speaking, he was waiting for her reaction.

"Ariane is the Winter Queen."

"And the Summer Queen, yes."

"She lives on the hidden path."

"Yes. She was kin to gods, and she faced them on the field of battle; she was much feared. There were always ways in which she might find moments of freedom beneath the mortal moon; Scarann. Lattan. There are nights when the hidden paths converge with merely mortal ones." He was still waiting.

"She wasn't the only person I met when you and I walked that path together."

"No. You begin to understand, ATerafin. They came to meet you."

"They came to meet me because I was *on* the path, Avandar."

"Perhaps that is true of Calliastra; she was always willful. I admit that I have never clearly understood Corallonne; she was never my ally. But if they came because they sensed a mortal in their world, the same cannot be said of the Oracle. Do you not recall her?"

"Yes. She appeared as the ghost of my Oma."

"As your dead, yes; not mine. It was not to me that she came, nor to me that she meant to speak, ATerafin. But the three, and Ariane, are all firstborn."

"They're not the only ones."

"No, they are not. And if you have seen the three, it is my suspicion that you have already felt the handiwork of a fourth. Adam, I believe your sleepers are standing on the edge of the hidden path, called and held in the dreaming. What is interesting to me is that you can see them, you can call them back, if even for a short time."

"How is he reaching them?" Jewel demanded, thinking of forests of gold, of winged cats, and of ancient trees; of demons, of assassins, and of The Terafin.

"I do not know," was the grave reply. "I was never prey to the Lords of dream and nightmare."

"There are two?"

"Two?"

"A Lord of dream and a Lord of nightmare."

"There are two who are one."

"You've met him. Or them."

Avandar fell silent. She thought he'd finished; he hadn't. "The dreaming wyrd, ATerafin, the three true dreams which you have experienced more than once in your life: those come at the behest of the Lords."

"No—they—" she fell silent. Celleriant had said something similiar. "The Lords are willing to do the work of others?"

"Demonstrably," was his dry reply. "The tree, ATerafin, and the *Kialli* Lord, are evidence of that. But what the Lords want, I cannot easily say; I am mortal. Nor is that your only concern now."

"No," she whispered. "It's not. If Adam can see the sleepers—"

"Yes. Eventually, if it has not already come to pass, the Lords will see Adam. I do not know if they can touch or harm him where he now stands, but if, in the process of waking the sleepers, he is vulnerable, he is at great risk."

Levec's Torra was not good enough to allow him to follow the entirety of the conversation; it didn't have to be. He watched Jewel's expression shift, saw her lose color, and saw where she looked; it was enough. More than enough. He rose.

Duvari, however, once again came to Jewel's rescue—a fact that would have made her nervous in other circumstances. "It is not what you think," he said in Weston. "They are now concerned that the waking of the sleepers is of great danger to Adam. There should be no sleepers here."

"The—the waking of the sleepers?"

Duvari nodded. "I will speak with the Princess," he said quietly. "And we will determine how best to approach your task."

"What danger is he in?"

"If I understood all of what I heard, and in much simpler terms, he risks falling prey to the sleep itself. If he does, there is no one to wake him, and no one to wake those who sleep now; they will starve to death."

Levec nodded.

"Let us adjourn on the matter of the illness for the three days of The Terafin Funeral. You, at least, will be present for one or two of those days, if you choose to accept the invitation offered."

"Oh, I wouldn't dream of missing it."

The heavy irony of the words appeared to be lost on Duvari, as so much was. "I understand your concern, Healer. But for the next four days, while the *Astari* are in residence in the Terafin manse, no harm will come to Adam. I doubt, given the circumstances surrounding Jewel ATerafin, that he will even be noticed."

But Jewel lifted a hand. "I think I have a solution to the possible danger," she said to Levec.

"And that?"

"The cats. The mouthy, irritating cats."

He blinked.

"I can't guarantee they can protect him, but I can guarantee that they'll know if he's in danger."

"How?"

"I don't know," she replied, turning to him. "But they're part of the hidden path; they're part of wherever it is that the sleepers reside while they dream."

"But they're here."

She nodded. Before she could speak again, there was a loud knock on the doors.

"Enter," she said, because if it was Ellerson, he wouldn't until he heard her voice. It was Ellerson. "ATerafin," he said, bowing. "The regent requests your presence in his office at your earliest convenience."

"Thank you, Ellerson."

The walk to Gabriel's office was hectic and crowded. There were, in Jewel's estimation, half as many ladders in the halls as there were people—and there were a lot of people. The servants who were usually invisible were out in force; Jewel caught a glimpse of the compressed, pinched expression of the Master of the Household Staff and almost cringed. She wasn't, however, required to bow, grovel, or salute; House Councillors weren't, in theory, supposed to acknowledge her at all while she went about her duties.

But Jewel did pause to watch the servants at work, because she had never seen a full House funeral before. The whole of the gallery was slowly changing from the familiar one she knew; tapestries and banners replaced paintings, and some of the standing statues were carefully adorned with black-and-gold shawls. Even the paintings that now hung in the hall were not paintings she immediately recognized, although she recognized some of the names etched in brass on their frames: they were the previous rulers of Terafin.

Avandar walked by her side like a prickly shadow. It was comfortable to have him there, but his absences—and his utter failure to mention their cause—made her nervous. She glanced at him every so often, but stopped when she realized two things: she was checking to see if he was still there, which was bad, and he knew it, which was worse.

When she reached Gabriel's office, it wasn't empty. The doors were pegged open, and there were four House Guards—four Chosen—on either side of them. The room in which one might take a chair if one had arrived early had no chairs to spare—and almost no standing room, either. Jewel stopped just shy of the doorjamb and took a step back, into Avandar.

Jewel.

She took another step away from the room.

ATerafin. What is wrong?

I don't damn it know. It was crowded, but she'd seen far larger crowds in the Terafin manse before—she just hadn't seen one this large compressed into Gabriel's outer office. Maybe The Terafin had had days that contained this many people—but The Terafin had had both Gabriel himself and a dozen of the Chosen standing between her and her visitors. Jewel hesitated at the door, and then turned back down the hall, moving quickly, Avandar in her wake.

"Where are you going?"

"Back to the wing."

"You've chosen to refuse the regent's request?"

"No. I was about to tell you to go find Celleriant, and I've come up with a better idea."

Sigurne Mellifas looked up at the sound of the doorknob. She was seated at the desk in her room, and papers—the lifeblood of the magi—were already stacked inches high to the right and left of her inkstand. A small sigil flaired to life above the height of the lintel; it was gray, but bright enough to read. Frowning, she rose. She had expected yet another delivery from Ellerson. The Order of Knowledge considered its daily business of vastly greater import than anything as simple as a state funeral.

It was not, however, Ellerson; it was Matteos. "Enter."

The door swung open without a creak. Sigurne didn't approve of its silence; there was something unnatural about it. Overly oiled hinges, like paperwork, were instantly relegated to trivial status when she saw Matteos' expression.

"Matteos?"

"Jewel ATerafin has asked that you accompany her to the regent's office."

"The regent wishes to speak with me?" She frowned; that wasn't it. "Where is Jewel?"

"She is in the front hall, waiting with her domicis."

Sigurne exited the room as Matteos held the door; he closed it gently, but firmly, behind her. "I've taken the liberty of preparing a stone—"

"There is no room in this House that is better protected against magic or eavesdroppers than Gabriel ATerafin's inner office, save the personal rooms of The Terafin herself." She headed directly down the hall, walking at a brisker pace than she normally did.

Jewel was, as Matteos had said, waiting with her domicis; she wasn't, however, waiting alone. If Sigurne had been a woman to whom imprecations came easily, she would have run down the considerable list available in this wing; standing at a respectful distance from Jewel was Duvari.

Jewel was pale, which only accentuated the dark rings below her eyes. She immediately tendered a bow as Sigurne walked into the room; it was an impressively correct bow, and she held it for far longer than etiquette demanded. "ATerafin."

"Member Mellifas."

"Matteos implied that the regent wishes to speak with me."

"Matteos," Matteos said, at her back, "did no such thing."

"The regent doesn't," Jewel said quietly. "It's an entirely personal request on my part."

"That I speak with the regent?"

"That you accompany me. I've been summoned to speak with him." Sigurne frowned.

"If you wish to discuss guild fees," Jewel continued, when Sigurne remained silent, "I can do that. It's not a House matter; it would be for direct service to me, for this single occasion."

"In what capacity?"

Jewel swallowed. "As witness, Member Mellifas."

"You are far, far too formal for my comfort, ATerafin. I seldom discuss my own fees because I am *very* seldom available for hire. Member Corvel—"

Jewel shook her head emphatically. "It has to be you."

Something about her tone was so stark and so certain, Sigurne dispensed with the rest of her suggestion. "I am not young," she said quietly. "But perhaps in my case, age has led to wisdom; wisdom is oft costly. Tell me what happened, ATerafin." She was aware of Duvari's presence, and equally aware that she did not have the time to request a writ of exemption from the Kings' office.

It galled her to have to ask Duvari for anything. "Lord of the Compact."

"Guildmaster."

"Your work in the Terafin manse, and on the Terafin grounds, no doubt requires at least one writ of royal exemption."

"It does, as you well know, Member Mellifas, since you are a signatory to all such writs. Why is this of significance?"

Sigurne looked at Jewel, who'd shrunk two inches. The mage could not quite bring herself to speak; to ask a favor of Duvari was the act of the naive or the addled.

Avandar, however, said, "We will wait, Guildmaster, while you execute a writ; I will personally deliver it to *Avantari,* and I will wait until it is countersigned and sealed."

"That is still the work of hours."

The domicis' smile was cold. "No, Member Mellifas, it is not."

Sigurne glanced at Jewel again. She did not like the cast of the younger woman's features. "Very well," she said to the domicis.

Duvari, however, raised a hand.

"Lord of the Compact?"

"Guildmaster. You are aware that any magic covered by my writ is for defensive purposes only."

"Well aware."

"You also understand—"

"That those who are covered by your writ are under your purview while in the manse, yes."

His smile was thin. "And you are willing to be one such servitor?"

"I am not. I am however willing to come to your aid—at your spoken request—should security matters within the House require it. I fail, however, to see how an interview with the regent falls under that category."

"I, however, do not. I formally ask you, as the head of the *Astari*, to accommodate Jewel ATerafin's request."

She stared at him for a long moment. His smile both deepened and cooled as she considered the various angles of approach his game—and it never occurred to her that this was not another of his dangerous games—might take, and how it might damage the Order's power. She could think of only two, and one involved the likelihood that his spoken request was not enough.

Jewel said, "He's telling the truth, Sigurne."

"And you are now also bard-born, with a gift for hearing what lies beneath a man's words?"

"No. Just seer-born, as usual."

"What do you see, then?"

"Nothing. But—I'm uneasy. I don't want to go into that room, not on my own."

"You will have Avandar—"

"I don't know if Avandar can do what—what you can do."

Avandar raised a brow.

"Very well. I accede to your request, Lord of the Compact, with the fervent hope that the writ will not require execution."

Duvari nodded. "Shall we?"

Sigurne almost sighed. She didn't. "You will accompany us?"

"Of course."

That was an unaccounted for third option.

Jewel's hands were dry. Her mouth was dry. The halls remained crowded, but the light that shone in from the wide, long windows seemed gray and harsh on this third passage. She took a deep breath, exhaling slowly as she walked. It didn't help.

When she approached Gabriel's office, the same four Chosen were on guard at the doors, and the room looked, if anything, more packed. She could barely make out Barston's desk, and probably wouldn't have been able to had she not already known where it was. She looked, but didn't see Teller in the crowd, which wasn't surprising; when there was actual work to do, he usually shuffled off, as quickly as politely possible, into his small office.

On a day like today, with a crowd this size—and why in the Hells were all these people here anyway?—the small office would seem like a defensible fortress. She squared her shoulders, looking at the small gap between her side of the door and the office, and then marshaled her polite "excuse-me, pardon-me" phrases and stepped in.

She made it, by dint of those words, and the discreet application of delicate elbows, to the front of Barston's besieged desk. By the time she reached that desk, she understood that half of the people in the room were from the various quarters of the manse itself: people sent from the kitchens, people sent from the grounds, people sent from the stables. They were all here because of last-minute emergencies of one level or another.

The other half, however, were better dressed, and she recognized at least one of them. It did not offer any comfort. Rymark.

"ATerafin," Barston said. Out of deference for his unfortunate adherence to gestures of hierarchy, she lifted the signet ring of the House Council. He didn't technically need to see it; he knew the House Council members—and all of their various aides—on sight. But he did nod, as if her gesture were official.

"This is not the time to speak to the regent," he told her, his voice hovering between stiff and apologetic. "Unless this is *another* emergency."

"Pardon?"

"I said—"

"I heard you. A messenger arrived at the—" Her eyes widened and she suddenly did what for Barston was utterly unthinkable. She levered herself onto his desk, and threw herself over it, landing in a tumbling crash somewhere behind and to the left of his chair. She rolled to her feet, cursing skirts as she spun.

Barston didn't even shout at her, because he could see—clearly—why she'd leaped; there was a long, slender dagger driven into the desk's far edge. Had she still been on the other side of it, the dagger would have passed through her.

Silence eddied slowly from that dagger outward, before crumbling into a storm of sound.

Jewel, however, was already on the move; she dodged as a second knife—this one apparently weighted and shaped for flight—took wing. It impaled the frame of the painting that had briefly been at her back, and that *did* make Barston cry out in panic. He found his voice and shouted for the guards—which, in a room full of people, was not the best option.

A third dagger; this one winged her shoulder, splitting the fabric of the indoor jacket and the stupid sleeves of her dress. She didn't think it had struck skin, and couldn't stop to check; she knew this dance; she'd done it before. She couldn't quite see who was throwing the knives, and that was bad, but she also knew that whoever it was, they were about to run out of opportunity.

She hoped it happened before she ran out of space, because the space was so damn confined. She could hear the Chosen ordering people to leave the room *now*, and she wondered if her putative assassin would be one of them. Given the press of bodies, she was willing to see him escape.

She opened her mouth to say as much, but what came out was something entirely different. "Duvari! Avandar! *Get Gabriel now!*" And then she ducked and rolled.

Duvari didn't even hesitate. The domicis did. Sigurne watched their backs disappear into the office as people in the various uniforms of House Terafin surged out. She stood her ground, and they passed around her in a babbling stream. One of the House Guard—Chosen, she thought, by insignia, raced down the hall; the other three entered Gabriel's office in the wake of Duvari and Avandar.

Sigurne cast a warding spell without lifting a hand or speaking a word. But she also cast a very different type of protection, and that did require speech; it was an old, old spell, and it had been taught to her by the most unreliable of teachers. She had no notes, and very little opportunity to practice—and if she could do one thing to right the world before her death, she would change that very little to exactly none.

But the world was what it was, and Jewel ATerafin had leaped clear across a desk in mid-sentence. Yet she hadn't shouted for help; she had directed two men—one of them in no way hers to command—toward the regent's office instead.

Sigurne stepped into the room. Not all of the men and women waiting upon Gabriel's decision had yet deserted the office, but it was visibly far less crowded. The House Guard had raced toward the regent's office—all save one man, who had drawn his sword and was now heading toward the desk. There, to the right, and toward its drawer side, paced a young man in the uniform of the Terafin gardeners. By the far walls, the men and women in the room had gathered and Sigurne recognized two of them instantly: one was Rymark ATerafin, a member of her Order, and a man she did not trust. The other, to her surprise, was Brialle, another member of the Order of Knowledge; she stood closest to Rymark, and she wore civilian clothing, not the robes of the guild.

I will kill them myself if they interfere with me, she thought, and meant it; she was viscerally disturbed by their presence. Neither seemed inclined to interfere at all at the moment; they were watching the assassin as he paced toward Jewel, knife in hand.

The Chosen reached him. He offered no warning at all; he simply drew the sword back and swung it.

And he was dead before he hit the ground, the stranger in gardener's clothing moved so quickly.

Jewel, you wanted me here, Sigurne thought, as if it were a prayer. She did not cast a spell at the moving man, who had replaced the dagger that was now buried to the hilt in the left eye of the House Guard, not yet; she knew she would have one chance and only one. If she missed, if she used the wrong spell, he would turn the dagger he carried on her just as efficiently as he had upon the House Guard. If the daggers were somehow enchanted, or if her shields did not hold, she would be as dead as the Terafin Chosen, now fallen.

But it was hard, because Jewel couldn't move as quickly as the lone figure that pursued her. He leaped to grab her—and the distance he cleared increased Sigurne's suspicion; Jewel had already moved—barely—out of his path. She survived because she moved just before he did, every time. This, Sigurne thought, was the gift of the seer-born writ small.

How much did Sigurne trust it? How much could she trust it?

She heard the crack of something—lightning, she thought; it was followed by the sound of shattering wood. Shards flew from the direction of the regent's office. Sigurne's hands flew as well. She spoke three sharp, harsh words; the air blurred before her, and the light in the room changed in color and texture.

The assassin wheeled to face her, his eyes widening, his movements significantly slowed.

The air warmed; the light that had seemed so harsh and gray in the context of Jewel's uncertainty turned golden. A warm wind swept through the room; she could feel it, and she could almost hear the sound of leaves rustling high overhead. She reached down, pulled up the hem of her much detested skirt, and withdrew a single dagger from its uncomfortable sheath.

But the assassin was no longer hunting her; he'd turned. He'd turned, slowly, toward the woman who now stood in the doorway, her wrinkled, pale hands lifted. They were golden. *She* was golden, in Jewel's vision.

The assassin spoke; his voice was like thunder in the small room. Jewel smiled. She'd had almost no time to actually look at him while dodging; he just moved too damn fast and she'd had to let instinct take over her body in order to survive him. Now she could clearly see his profile, and she could just as clearly see his eyes. He looked human; she thought he must have been human once, but his eyes were all wrong.

He raised an arm; she saw the dagger in his hand. He even managed to throw it as Jewel approached; it bounced off the air six inches from Sigurne's face. He didn't draw another; instead, he roared and bent to spring.

Sigurne saw him tense and bend into his knees; she knew what was coming, but held her ground, and held him. The power she used was both hers and foreign to her; it was not, and had never been, a comfortable magic to cast. He roared again, and she heard every word the magic did not allow him to say.

He turned, struggling, toward where the two mages—and the rest of the suddenly silent room—stood watching. Then one of the two cast. Fire blossomed around the assassin's heavy gardening boots. *Rymark,* Sigurne thought. Not Brialle.

The fire scorched leather, clothing, and even skin; it did not, however, devour the man. He snarled. "The Shining Court will curse you for your—"

Fire struck again, harsher, and Sigurne shouted Rymark's name in a tone of voice that only the old and powerful could comfortably use. "Cease at once, or the room will burn!"

This caused panicked shouts, because Sigurne was still blocking the door; nor could she easily move from it. But she didn't have to move. Jewel ATerafin now ran at the demon, dagger in hand.

The man—the burning man—turned to her. "Do not interfere with us, little seer, or we will raze your beloved House and your—"

She plunged the dagger into his chest, or tried; her thrust had no strength behind it. But the dagger didn't require that type of strength to wield, and the strength it did require, she had. The man screamed, as blood seeped from the small wound; he roared as light followed it, leaking in spokes that sprayed across the room.

*   *   *

Jewel didn't even wait to watch. She turned toward Gabriel's office, and toward the smoking ruins of what had once been his beautiful, double doors. Barston was standing between the desk and the doors of the office in complete silence; he'd reserved exactly one shout for the damaged frame of the painting, and if he wasn't calm—and he wasn't—he was once again in control.

She ran past him, stopped, and said, "Get everyone out of here. Now." Then she headed toward the gaping, jagged hole in the door; she almost raced through that opening, but stopped inches short, as if something had caught the back of her dress and pulled, hard.

Instinct. Vision.

"Member Mellifas, I think I need your help."

The guildmaster said, "Another moment, ATerafin, and I will join you." It was more than one, and Jewel's hands were balled in fists, but she waited without further comment. Eventually, Sigurne crossed the room and joined her. She looked at the hole in the door.

"I see your difficulty, ATerafin."

"What do you see?" Jewel asked sharply, wishing bitterly that she'd brought Angel with her.

"What you do. There is a hole in the door; it leads into the office. The office, however, appears to be empty from this vantage."

"Empty without any signs of struggle or damage?"

"Indeed."

"I see a bit more than that," Jewel told her, still staring at the jagged hole—which, given the radius of splinters, had to be real. "There's a violet light surrounding the edges of the door."

"The door, not the opening?"

"Yes."

Sigurne said nothing for so long, Jewel actually tore her gaze from the door to look at the guildmaster. Her expression was like carved stone. Once or twice in her young life, Jewel had seen a similar expression on her Oma's face—and that had been a clear sign that Oma was not to be approached. Sigurne, however, was not her ancient grandmother.

"Member Mellifas?"

"Prepare yourself for possible difficulty," Sigurne replied, in a voice that would have frozen water—and shattered it into a million small shards for good measure.

Jewel didn't dare to ask how; to have even half an idea she'd have had to ask what the mage meant by "possible difficulty," and nothing short of—actually, no, nothing, was going to make her do that. This woman—old, maternal, and fragile—was a little like Haval. Age was her cloak and her shield, and she could disarm others simply by donning and exaggerating its effects. She was not, at the moment, concerned with cloaking her power.

The guildmaster was reputed to be a First Circle mage. Jewel, whose knowledge of the inner workings of the Order of Knowledge was dim at best, nonetheless understood that First Circle implied the highest level of power that the mage-born within the Order could achieve. Sigurne Mellifas was the guildmaster, so it followed that Sigurne Mellifas was powerful. It wasn't hard to put these facts together.

Jewel had never done it before, or if she had, she'd buried it so far in memory nothing surfaced now. She stood extremely still and kept her hands by her sides as Sigurne Mellifas stared at the door.

That's all she did; she stared. Jewel frowned as she turned her full attention to the wreckage of the door within its frame. The violet light wasn't dimming—which was what she'd expected; it was brightening. It was also, she realized, changing slowly. Strands of light the color of bright emerald began to wrap themselves around the violet glow—as if either were solid. The strands entwined and thickened as Jewel watched.

But when a third strand entered the mix she frowned; it was gray. Gray. She kept her eyes fastened to the door and kept her frown intent and focused, although she wanted desperately to look at the mage; she knew that Sigurne's object was not the door itself, or not the door in isolation.

She did jump and turn when someone at the far side of the office suddenly cried out in pain and stumbled to the ground clutching the sides of her head. Jewel started toward the stricken woman, but Sigurne reached out and caught her arm. "I believe you will find what you seek now."

"But—"

"Now."

Jewel swallowed and turned back to the door as the sounds of combat rolled into the room.

She almost stopped breathing as she looked for any sign of Gabriel. She could see Duvari, and to her great surprise, the Lord of the Compact was wielding a *sword*. He hadn't been, when he'd entered the office; you couldn't conceal a sword that size. He was fighting one of the House Guards. The Chosen who had entered the office were fighting a different House Guard. Jewel tried to curse; nothing came out. Gabriel's personal office was large enough that two such fights could take place within its walls.

She couldn't see Avandar—and the opening he'd created was large enough that she should have. It was large enough that she could run into the room to check—but not safe enough, in the end. She thought that the men dressed as guards were human; they didn't set her teeth on edge or fill her with that winter chill that spoke of death.

What there was of the fight wouldn't last long. The fight ranged over desks; papers had been scattered, letter trays almost bisected; books had fallen into awkward heaps, facedown on the floor. Duvari had no armor, and the room was tight and small; he could dodge. The Chosen, however, fought two on one—it should have been over quickly.

But it wasn't, and one of the Chosen was injured. Jewel didn't recognize the House Guard; it didn't matter. She couldn't see Gabriel, and she couldn't see Avandar. Turning, she stuck her head out of the large hole bisecting the doors. "Sigurne!"

It was not, however, Sigurne who answered the urgent call, and she should have been surprised at who did: Celleriant. He wore chain that caught light in a cascade of muted, metallic color, and he carried his sword. She cursed. He smiled.

It was not his wild, sharp smile. "Lord," he said.

She wasn't up to the task of reprimanding him for the use of an honorific she disdained. "Help Duvari and the Chosen. Do *not* kill if you can avoid it; we want them alive." She leaped out of the office to make way for Celleriant, and ran behind Barston's desk to Teller's office.

The door was already open, and Teller stood in its frame. "Jay?"

She lifted her hand, gesturing quickly and wildly. His brows rose and he moved past her to where Barston now stood. "ATerafin," the secretary said. "Jewel."

"He's not in his office. Was he?"

"He was."

"Was he *with* anyone?"

"He was." Barston was pale, but the pale was grim; his hands had clenched in fists by his sides.

"Who? Who, Barston?"

Barston gestured at the appointment book; Teller slid around him and flipped it open. He read Barston's meticulous writing and shut the book again.

"Teller?"

Not now. The gesture was sharp, short; it looked like a fidget. "Jay?"

She was thinking. Thinking, in this room, was difficult. She looked for Sigurne and saw the guildmaster; to her surprise, Matteos had somehow materialized while she'd been in the chaos of Gabriel's office. They were both standing over the prone form of the woman who had cried out and fallen, clutching her head. Rymark ATerafin, however, was nowhere to be seen.

Was Gabriel injured? She closed her eyes. Avandar was gone; Avandar had blown a hole through the doors to gain entry, and Avandar had definitely entered them. If he was gone—not dead—he'd left voluntarily. Which meant he'd probably taken Gabriel with him.

There would be two reasons to do that: to take him out of the reach of the assassins—the assassins dressed as cursed House Guards—or to take him into reach of healers. Would he go to Levec? Would he risk that?

No. No, not here. Not now. That left two: Daine and Adam. She wasn't even certain which would be worse. Daine had adopted Alowan's healerie without making a single change; he was as vulnerable there as Alowan himself had been. Adam was in the West Wing, which was as protected— she hoped—as any other place in the manse. But Gabriel didn't know about Adam, and if he was injured in a way that required healing, he would—

Unless Levec hadn't *left* yet.

She lifted the hand at her side just beneath Teller's gaze. Gestured. "Barston," she said, in a more formal voice, "don't worry. I'll find him."

To her surprise, Barston nodded. "Take Teller with you."

"You don't—"

"No. Take him with you—but keep him *safe*."

"Always," she replied.

They raced down the hall toward the medium-sized function room that was used for formal dining. Teller kept an eye out, as if they were once again casing the Common. He didn't speak; neither did Jay. He knew where she was going, and how she intended to get there. The function rooms weren't locked because they were going to be in use in just two days. They were consequently not empty; servants were out in force, cleaning, polishing, and moving bits and pieces of furniture. The damn ladders were also everywhere.

She glanced at Teller. *Tail?*

No.

She nodded and headed into the corner of the room farthest from the door. Because it wasn't empty, she didn't make it all the way there without being stopped; because Kalliaris was smiling, the Master of the Household Staff was somewhere else, making some other part of the servant corps' lives miserable hell. And because she knew Carver, who in turn knew every single servant on staff these days, she recognized the older man who stopped her brisk walk toward the door that was used by servants, and servants only.

"ATerafin," he said, tendering a very proper bow. It wasn't technically required unless they were both in the presence of outsiders, because he also bore the House Name—and in Jewel's private opinion did a much better job of it, at least in terms of dignity.

"Berald," she replied. She didn't bow because hers would be inferior.

He winced, and glanced around. Some of the other servants were close by, but appeared to be engrossed in their assigned tasks. They were; the servants here had no difficulty both working and eavesdropping. They took an inordinate interest in the lives—especially the private lives—of the manse's many occupants. Given the work, Jewel couldn't blame them. "You know you are forbidden the use of the back halls," he said, in a severe voice.

"Yes. I know. But we're in a bit of a pinch here. Someone just tried to assassinate me in the right-kin's office."

His iron-gray brows rose into his hairline, and unlike many men his age, he had lots of hair. True, his hair was tightly pulled back off his face at the moment; it wasn't when he was off duty. "And you've come *here?*"

"Obviously. I need to get back to my wing, I need to do it *now*, and I need to do it in a way that's not easily watched by outsiders. This is the only one I could think of, and I don't have a lot of time to argue—I've just enough to beg. Please, Ber. *Please.*"

"You understand that this job is my life?"

"I do."

He closed his eyes and looked, for a moment, as if he were praying for patience. Or wisdom. Ber favored Cormaris. "Go. You've ten seconds to get out of my sight."

Once they hit the cramped, narrow halls with the much lower ceilings and the total lack of windows in all but the terminal points, they could run. They did. On a normal day, it would have been a hazard; on this one, two day before every single member of the patriciate was to convene to pay their final respects to The Terafin, the servants' halls were empty. Jewel knew the way to her apartments from here. She didn't have the servants' keys, but she didn't need them; she could pick these locks with a hairpin in a pinch. These were the only doors on which she could practice anymore, although admittedly keeping in practice hadn't been high on her list of duties in recent years.

They entered the large function room very quietly; the servants' door, which was also built into the paneling in a way that made it near invisible from the outside, was always kept well oiled. Jewel suspected that the hinges had somehow been enchanted for silence.

The great room wasn't empty. Levec was kneeling on the ground beside one of the long reclining seats; the occupant of that seat was a pale Gabriel ATerafin. Avandar loomed above them both, arms folded.

All three looked toward her as she approached. Gabriel, however, said, "Teller?"

"Barston insisted I accompany Jewel when he realized you weren't . . . in your office."

"I see. How is Barston?"

"He's been worse."

Jewel turned to Teller as her jaw attempted to slide free of her face. "He's been *worse*?"

"Yes. Don't ask. Assassination attempts—as long as they fail—aren't his responsibility; they didn't occur because of anything his staff did, or did not, do."

"The appointment book?"

"I didn't say he looked *well*; I said he's been worse."

Avandar cleared his throat, which ended that discussion. "ATerafin, I see you are still alive."

"I am. The demon isn't."

Gabriel's eyes closed. "Your domicis said you were attacked."

She nodded. "I'm not sure if you were the target or if I was."

"How so?"

She looked, very pointedly, at his bloodied shirt. The fabric was sliced clean through, but the skin—and she could see skin clearly—was whole. "They may have assumed that if I were under attack at the same moment, whatever erratic vision I possess wouldn't give me a clear warning about you. Which sort of implies they know I'm seer-born and also have no clear idea of how the talent actually works."

"You're certain the two are connected?"

"I was sent a message; you wanted to speak with me in your office, and it was urgent."

"I . . . see. Who delivered it?"

"We are working on that now," was Avandar's smooth reply. He was watching Jewel intently, and she wasn't certain why.

"Levec?"

"It was not likely to be instantly fatal," was the healer's quiet reply. "But there may have been secondary infection concerns from the wound, given where it was." He rose. He did not look happy—but he was Levec; happiness wasn't one of his public emotions. According to Adam, it was one of his private ones, but Jewel had her doubts.

Unhappy or no, he was clearly exhausted. Jewel headed toward him; he lifted a large hand to ward her off. It was shaking. She stopped instantly, and examined the dark circles under his eyes. To Avandar, she said, "Get water and something bland for him to eat."

Avandar raised a brow, and she realized he wasn't actually in much better shape at the moment than the healer; he was just much, much better at keeping it to himself. Teller, however, walked quickly out of the room's main doors.

"Duvari?" Avandar asked.

"He'll be fine." But even answering, her gaze slid to Levec. This type of question, Avandar could have asked in silence; he'd deliberately chosen not to, which said something. Once again, *what* it said wasn't immediately clear. "The Chosen were there. The assassins were dressed as House Guards?"

Gabriel nodded uneasily, which answered more than the question she'd asked. They weren't only attired as House Guards; they *were* House Guards.

"Why aren't you using the Chosen?"

His silence was exactly wrong, and when he broke it, he failed to answer. "Your assassin?"

"Mine? Oh. Mine. I think he was a stablehand or maybe a gardener. I know it wouldn't be hard to get a stranger in through the gardening staff." She glanced at Levec. "Is it okay to have this discussion?"

"If he were in my domain, I would forbid it," was the gruff reply. "But he is demonstrably not a patient in the Houses of Healing. You were uninjured?"

His pointed glare at the height of her sleeve made her look down and wince. "Yes. He just cut cloth."

The door to the great room opened. In it were Teller, Ellerson, and a very alert Devon. Ellerson carried a tray. Entering the room he made his way to Levec's side—and the small table to one side of the lounge chair. Setting the tray down, he lifted the heavy, silvered pitcher in its center and poured what Jewel assumed was water into a glass; this he handed to Levec.

"ATerafin," he then said. Both Gabriel and Jewel looked up at him. "Devon ATerafin has arrived to question you about the possible whereabouts of the regent; the Lord of the Compact is . . . concerned."

"Devon," Gabriel said quietly. "Tell the Lord of the Compact I am both safe and—" he glanced at Avandar, "—secure, for the moment. I would be in your debt if you could also inform my secretary of the same."

"I can carry that message," Teller offered.

Both Devon and Gabriel swiveled to look at him; neither accepted. Jewel lifted a hand in brief sign, and Teller winced, but nodded. To Devon, she said, "Duvari is probably still in the office of the right-kin. If he's not, I don't want to know where he is. I need—I need about fifteen minutes. I'll be back."

She made it five feet. Avandar was on her heels at the sixth. "Where," he asked, in the tone of voice she least liked, "do you think you're going?"

"To check on the cats. If you feel like subjecting yourself to gratuitous insults, please feel free to accompany me."

Sigurne Mellifas had never particularly cared for the Lord of the Compact. She was, however, aware that he was a necessity, and on most days could be polite, respectful, and civil in his presence. In fairness to herself—and at this juncture, any fairness was of dubious value—she seldom encountered Duvari carrying a blooded sword. She was aware—as were all who had encountered the Lord of the Compact—that he was in theory a capable man, where capable in this case involved both self-defense and the ability to kill quickly and efficiently. It was seldom, however, that she was called upon to witness the effects of his vaunted and yet unknown training.

She was underimpressed.

Matteos, by her side, was not; he was far too grim, far too angered, to find the detachment necessary. His anger, however, was entirely contained behind the compressed line of his lips and his narrowed gaze. The Chosen had come, in numbers; both of the Captains—Arrendas and Torvan—at their head. They entered an office that was now largely vacated; the regent's unfortunate secretary was still present, and appeared to be attempting to remove a dagger from the frame of a painting. Sigurne almost winced on his behalf as she recognized the painting and the artist. She noted, however, that the long knife embedded in the desk remained where it was standing.

The Captains of the Chosen treated Duvari with all the diffidence due the partially invisible. They ascertained that the dead were indeed Terafin. Barston informed them that the regent had survived the attack, and was now resting in an undisclosed location until further notice, which annoyed Arrendas, and skittered off Torvan. They examined the seared carpet and the remnants of what had once been a demon—of minor power, in Sigurne's opinion, although she felt it politic at the moment not to emphasize this point. They were diplomatic when speaking with the guildmaster, because the matter of magic and writs was not the business of the Chosen; it would be Gabriel's business—and Duvari's.

Duvari, however, grudgingly executed his very broad writ of exemption. It was the only time in Sigurne's long career that she had been grateful for that breadth; she had argued against it biannually for as long as she had held her office, a fact that was not lost on Duvari. Nor, sadly, was the presence of the unconscious Brialle. She was not dressed as a member of the Order, and clearly neither of the Captains of the Chosen recognized her. Were it not for the presence of Duvari, Sigurne might easily have claimed that the woman had fainted in fear at the sudden outburst of both violence and magic. Brialle was a mage of the Second Circle, but she was young and her power had never been adequately tested, in Sigurne's opinion. Given her actions here, it was unlikely that it would be now—not in a way that did not end in someone's death.

Duvari, however, was speaking with Barston about the matter of Rymark ATerafin's use of magic. Duvari could, if bold, go directly to Rymark to demand a writ of exemption—but given that the target of Rymark's magical fire had been the demon, it was unlikely that the writ would be withheld. Sigurne, however, resented it briefly; she disliked the paperwork and the discussion demanded by such a writ, because writs granted after the fact were far more political and far more time-consuming.

"Why, exactly, did you elect to reside in the Terafin manse until the close of the funeral rites?" Matteos asked softly.

"I thought it would simplify things, and, if I am being honest, I desired a small break from paperwork." Sigurne's smile was grim and brittle.

Matteos eyed Brialle. "How long will she be out?"

"I am not entirely certain. She will not wake soon."

He raised a brow.

"I wished to apprehend a criminal; I was not perhaps as cautious as I might be were I in the teaching labs. We will need to contact the Mysterium," she added.

"We will need to get out from under the Lord of the Compact."

Sigurne frowned and Matteos once again fell silent, regarding Brialle. "Go," she finally told Matteos. "Have Eranil summoned; tell him who we have in custody and tell him to be prepared. I will wait upon Duvari."

Matteos clearly wanted to argue, but they had been together for decades; he knew when he could be protective and when he must surrender that role. It chaffed. The magi did not have Chosen, but had they, Matteos would have been their Captain. He nodded and retreated from the room while she watched.

Chapter Sixteen

JEWEL EXITED the great room, leaving Teller in the figurative lion's den. He was more adept at handling the powerful than she was; he was closer to Gabriel, and he had Ellerson's quiet, steady help. She had Avandar, but on balance, she'd left Levec. Devon was a neutral, but given his first words, she was probably being too generous. Avandar, on the other hand, was in a foul mood.

"You cannot honestly believe that the target of that attempt was the right-kin," he said, in scathing, but measured tones.

"ATerafin."

Both Jewel and Avandar turned; Ellerson was standing by the great room's door. "Your cats," he said, "are with Haval."

Haval's work was firmly entrenched across most of the floor, two of the chairs, and the entire window seat. He would probably have commandeered the room's long couch, but Snow and Night were lounging across its length, heads on paws. They looked bored.

Only one of Haval's eyes was visible; the other was obscured by a jeweler's glass. His frayed hair suggested that he had been running his hands through it at far too frequent intervals.

The glass, however, dropped as his expression changed. *"What,"* he said, "have you done to my jacket?"

Pointing out that it was not, in fact, his jacket didn't even occur to her. "First, I didn't do it, and second, it's only the jacket; I'm fine."

Haval's obvious outrage attracted attention. Snow's ears instantly twitched, and Night's head rose. It was Night who got down from the couch, stretching his wings so that one of their tips batted Snow in the face.

"Do *not* step on anything," Haval told Night.

Jewel was shocked when Night hissed—and obeyed. To be fair to the cat, there wasn't much room for paws. "She's cut it," he said, as he approached.

"I told Haval it wasn't me," she replied.

"You let someone *else* cut it?"

Haval had, by this time, fetched the glass that had dropped from his face; he pocketed it, a sign that he intended to forgo work for at least a few minutes. "Please, ATerafin, do answer Night's question."

"I wasn't exactly standing still," Jewel told the cat. "I just couldn't dodge quickly enough."

"And what was the *ugly* one doing?" This was said in a lower, growlier voice.

Avandar, however, failed to answer. It was his general response to the cats if he happened to be in the room with any of them.

"*Avandar*, which is what the rest of us call him, was saving Gabriel ATerafin's life."

Haval's expression shifted again; when Jewel glanced at his face she saw neutrality writ large. It made him look younger, but not in a way she liked.

"If it makes you feel any better," she said to the erstwhile clothier, "he had Duvari's help."

He didn't so much as twitch a muscle. "You are aware, ATerafin, that I have yet to complete either Teller or Finch's attire? I will attempt to work while speaking; you will forgive me if I appear to be inattentive. Please. Tell me what happened."

By the time she'd half-finished, Night was lying across the floor, his head in her lap; this occurred only after she'd cleared some space. His complaints about boredom numbered in the handful, which, for the cats, was good behavior.

"Tell me now what you think occurred."

"Haval, this isn't the time for testing—"

He glared with one eye; the other was still behind glass. "As negotiations for my fee have not yet taken place, and no agreement has therefore been made, you will indulge an old man."

Night snickered. Had he been one of her den, she'd've smacked him across the back of the head. She'd never hit a cat, on the other hand, and even one that was larger than many of the den still counted. "I think," she finally said, "that someone in the House has targeted Gabriel for assassination."

Haval stopped work for ten seconds; she could almost hear him count. "Besides the obvious," he finally said, in a tone that indicated displeasure, "what would lead you to draw that conclusion?"

"The House Council has always known I'm seer-born. I think whoever attempted to kill Gabriel was afraid that I'd give advance warning—somehow—if I weren't occupied myself. My vision has always been pretty reliable when it's my own life in danger."

"ATerafin," he replied, in a glacial voice, "I have had very, *very* little sleep in the past few days, and I am unlikely to alleviate that deficit within the next five. While I realize you might legitimately make the same claim, I would like to point out that *my* ability to reason has not diminished significantly."

"You think the entire point of the attempt was—me?"

He very pointedly said nothing.

Try to remember, she told herself silently, *that you* wanted *his advice.* Closing her eyes, she let herself be lulled into a calmer state of mind by stroking Night's head; he didn't seem to mind, and it helped. "They sent two humans after Gabriel; they sent the demon after me."

"Indeed."

"But—it makes no sense, Haval. The timing makes *no sense.* Gabriel is the only person on the House Council who's made it clear he doesn't *want* anything. He won't remain as right-kin, regardless of who The Terafin is. His regency is the *only* thing the House Council could possibly agree on at this point. There were *no* abstentions on that vote, and it was *fast.*"

"And it would be inconvenient in the extreme to have the regent assassinated two days before the Kings arrive for the funeral. It would be the act of a fool, given the nature of House politics and the very special laws that govern the internal struggles of any House, to attempt such an assassination while the Lord of the Compact is practically also living under this roof."

"I thought you said I was to do my own thinking?"

"I did. I assume that this is what you would have said, given your assessment of the situation, and I believe my version is briefer."

After a long pause, Jewel opened her eyes. Haval's hands were now still; although he still held his needle, he'd removed the glass from his eye, and he was watching her without expression.

"You think that the goal was my death; the cover was the attempt on Gabriel's life."

"Gabriel ATerafin's wound was not fatal?"

"No."

"Would it have been fatal without intervention?"

"Not according to Levec."

"Where is the Member Mellifas?"

"I don't know. She—she dealt with the demon. But—there was an illusion of some sort on Gabriel's door. She—" Jewel frowned. "I think the illusion was being sustained by another mage. I don't know if the mage is a member of the Order of Knowledge or not."

"You are certain that another mage was present?"

"Yes." She opened her mouth and closed it again.

"You look like a *fish*," Night said. There was so much smug in that cat's voice.

"ATerafin?"

Jewel shook her head. "It's Order business, not directly ours; I'm not sure how it will be handled, because the other mage wasn't operating in the manse with a valid writ."

Haval rose. "I am not comfortable with this assessment, but I will allow it for now. I believe," he added, "we have a guest."

She frowned. "Pardon?"

The door slid open. Devon ATerafin stood in its frame. He frowned as he caught sight of the cats; the cats, on the other hand, regarded him with indolent boredom. Jewel attempted to shove Night off her lap, but Devon shook his head. "If I am not interrupting, ATerafin?"

"You are," Haval answered, before Jewel could. "You would be Devon ATerafin."

"And you are . . . Haval."

"I am. We are just now discussing the assassination attempt, if you would care to join us. If you are here to deliver either word or *request* from the Lord of the Compact to Jewel ATerafin, we are not yet finished; as this is not a matter of the security of the Crowns, he will have to wait."

Devon raised a brow.

"It will be good practice for both young Jewel and Duvari," Haval continued. "If she is to continue in her quest to assert some sense of reason in the House, she will have to be able to disregard Duvari when the need arises—and he will have to be able to endure it."

Jewel cleared her throat. "This isn't one of the times I *need* to disregard him."

"No?"

"No. Usually when The Terafin did, he wasn't *in her personal quarters.*"

"Ah. Well, then, this will merely be more challenging. It is certainly not the most challenging of political discomforts you will have to face." He turned his attention to Devon. "ATerafin?"

Devon was smiling. It was a very strange smile; Jewel hadn't seen a similar one on Devon's face before. "If it will not trouble you further, might I clear a space for myself on one of your chairs?"

"It will, as you can obviously see, be difficult—however, given that you show no signs of leaving, I will overlook it. Jewel," he added, "the chair nearest the lounge, if you please."

Jewel shoved Night—with effort—off her lap and went to clear off the chair.

"I fail to see how having Jewel run your errands as if she were the least consequential of apprentices is in keeping with your goal of teaching her appropriate behavior for her station," Devon observed, as he nonetheless took the damn chair and made himself comfortable.

"She could easily have relegated the task to her domicis; that she failed to do so is not my concern. She will suffer no political difficulties from acceding to the request of a harmless, old tailor. I am not the Lord of the Compact; nor am I in any way significant in the eyes of her various political rivals."

Devon seated, Jewel once again took up her spot on the floor; Night was waiting with what passed muster as patience only in the three cats. He flopped his head back into her lap, although he rumbled as he did. "Why, *why*, did you have *all* the fun *without* us?"

"Fun?"

"Well, someone tried to *kill* you. Did *you* eat him?"

"No."

Snow, from the chair, muttered something about waste.

Haval cleared his throat; this had the effect of quieting the cats. Devon was watching Night with the mixture of caution and fascination usually reserved for large fires.

"Gabriel must have been targeted," Jewel finally said. "The doors to his office were magically sealed. Avandar had to force them. By force, I mean break them into a million small pieces, some of which are still in my hair." She hesitated, and then added, "there was also a visitor. Gabriel has House Guards in the office as a matter of course at the moment—just as The Terafin did."

"And that visitor?"

"You'd have to ask either Teller or Barston." She grimaced. "Ask Teller."

"He recognized the name?"

Avandar, however, said, "There was no man in the room."

"Pardon?"

"Gabriel had no visitor."

"That's impossible," was her flat reply. "Gabriel's office is the most magically defended office in the manse; I think he's more cautious than The Terafin was. If you're suggesting the guest was entirely an illusion—" she stopped for a moment. " . . . it's possible."

"It's probable," Avandar replied. "Duvari will no doubt question Gabriel about the spells that function within his office."

"There's got to be something to detect that kind of magic."

"There is. It is not frequently used; it is considered expensive. If there was, as you imply, a mage present, that might account for much; the illusion would have to be continuously maintained and controlled. Regardless, ATerafin, there was no visitor."

"There was a name in the book."

"Indeed; I have no doubt of that." He turned to Haval and nodded. "My apologies."

"They are not necessary. I am willing to allow the possibility that the attempt on Gabriel's life was genuine. I am not, however, willing to allow the possibility that the attempt on Jewel's was merely a small part of that attempt."

"The demon?" Jewel asked, after a long silence.

Haval nodded. He glanced at Devon, who had remained silent throughout. "You have reservations."

"I believe, although I was not privy to the entire conversation, that all of the possibilities have been at least touched on."

Haval folded his arms across his chest and waited.

"Jewel is, however, correct. The timing would appear to favor no one. There is no chance whatsoever that the funeral rites will be postponed."

"If Gabriel had perished?"

"The House Council would be convened almost instantly."

"And a new regent chosen?"

Devon nodded. "A new regent would be chosen by either vote or consensus. Consensus is, of course, to be desired, but if consensus cannot be reached—and I fail to see how, in the short time the funeral rites dictate, it could be—it is likely to be decided by vote of the Council members in question."

"What if one of the contenders then installed their regent of choice?" It was to Jewel that he directed the question.

"It wouldn't do them any good. If one of the contenders made himself—or herself—regent, that's all they'd ever be, unless the governing rules were rewritten. The regent is not The Terafin. If Rymark proposed himself as regent, everyone on the Council would jump for joy, because he'd be saying by that action that he was withdrawing from the race." She hesitated. "If he did that, he'd almost certainly be given the appointment."

"If there were no contenders during the regency?"

"What, if they all died?"

"If that is the only circumstance in which you can see the lack, yes."

"If there were no contenders, the regent would still be regent; he would, in all but name, be The Terafin; he would take the Terafin Seat in *Avantari*, and he would rule the House." She shook her head. "Rymark is far too proud to settle for the title of regent when he wants the House."

"Is it?"

"Pardon?"

"Is it what he wants?"

Jewel blinked.

Haval once again took a seat in front of his beads. "You have said," he continued, picking up his glass and fitting it over his right eye, "that you believe Rymark to be, if not involved with the Terafin's assassination, then at least cognizant of its timing and method."

Jewel said nothing.

"What you have not considered, given your own focus, is Rymark's. You've made the assumption that his focus is the House Seat. I will admit that it is the safe assumption, and it is certainly the assumption from which the other contenders will proceed."

"Rymark was in Gabriel's outer office. He actually attempted to immolate the demon after Sigurne caught it."

"I believe that is significant."

"That he tried to help?"

Haval's whole face creased in an unpleasant frown. He surprised her by answering anyway. "That he raised a hand only after the demon was secured."

Jewel desperately wished that Devon were somewhere else. She was accustomed to Haval's moods; she wasn't accustomed to witnesses whose good opinion she needed in future.

She began to scratch Night's ears again, and Snow got down from the chair and stepped on Night's tail. There was some scuffling, hissing, and recrimination before Snow got what he wanted, which was to take Night's place. While this occurred, Jewel did the thinking that Haval demanded.

"Rymark is a member of the Order of Knowledge. I think he's Second Circle."

"He is," Haval said.

"Finch and Teller are certain that he expected the demon assassin. There are only two ways he could have known."

"The first?"

"In the first case, he could have been approached—somehow—by either demons or those who work alongside demons."

"They would approach him how?"

"He's a member of the Order of Knowledge, which, among other things, appears to breed the idiots. They think they'll rule small parts of the world if they can only learn the art of summoning creatures that are older, smarter, and more powerful than they are.

"It would make sense to contact Rymark through the Order, since we assume that some of its members are at least peripherally involved in schemes to amass knowledge about ancient power. But if he were approached by those mages, or even by the demons, wouldn't they approach him with the offer of the House Seat?"

"It is one possibility, yes. The other?"

She hesitated.

"You have already made a clear statement about the predilections of some of the Order's members—a statement you will, of course, fail to repeat to Sigurne Mellifas in its entirety. You are focused, as I said, on the

House, and given Rymarks' actions to date, it seems reasonable on the surface to assume that he is likewise so focused. Not every mage so approached, not every mage so enraptured, will have any hope of gaining a House Seat—but clearly some of the magi have labored side by side with the demons throughout our long history. If Rymark is not interested in the House Seat, what then?"

"Haval—*I don't know*. He's in contention for the House Seat; he must be interested in it."

"This is not a matter of knowledge; demonstrate some ability to examine the facts—or to *find* the facts—that are within your grasp. You will, as leader, frequently be forced to make choices absent all necessary facts; the ability to identify the things you *don't* know, but could with effort learn, is critical."

Night rolled over on the floor; Snow lifted his head from Jewel's lap. "Eat him?" he asked.

"No. Not yet."

"Why not? He's *annoying* you."

"He's annoying me because he's right. Now hush."

Haval continued to work as he waited. Which was fine. Jewel was silent; Snow's head was warm in her lap. Neither Devon nor Avandar made a sound, although Avandar looked amused. She pushed her hair out of her eyes, and pushed Snow's head off her lap so she could rise and pace, because thought often came with movement, as if her feet were treading on words she couldn't see.

"Allasakar is here, in the world. He's a god; we're not. We're probably considered significant only when we wield power; Rymark does." She drew breath, widening the oval in which she now walked because it was the only safe trajectory; everything else had cats or dress bits on it.

"We can safely assume that Allasakar wants to rule the world. To rule it, he has to conquer it. To conquer it, he has to destroy his natural enemies—or the enemies of his servants. Some of the talent-born—demonstrably—will work with or for him. But the god-born never will; they're too entwined with their parents." She hesitated. "This isn't the first time the demons have tried to assassinate The Terafin." Bitterly, she added, "But this time they succeeded."

"The previous time?"

"The god wasn't here yet. I think they wanted to take the House years ago in order to sow chaos, destabilize the Kings—possibly even kill them." Frowning, she added, "If they controlled House Terafin, they could achieve those goals even now."

"Would those goals serve their purpose?"

"I can't see how it wouldn't."

"And the purpose of the man who claims to be The Terafin's legitimate heir?"

"Every god has his Court," she said, frowning. Her eyes widened. "The demon mentioned the Shining Court."

Haval lifted his head and glanced at the domicis. His face, however, was free of expression.

"If Rymark serves the Shining Court, if he serves Allasakar—and I'm not by any means certain he does—he probably does it because he figures the god will win. Ruling Terafin under the eyes of the Kings doesn't give him as much freedom as ruling under the eyes of a god might, because this god won't care about Justice or Wisdom."

"Indeed. There is always an unfortunate tendency to assume barbarism or savagery on the part of the gods we generally don't name; we assume an absence of *all* beauty, *all* art, all majesty. It is a narrow view, in my opinion. But I have interrupted you, and I apologize. Please continue."

Jewel frowned now. Snow had stepped onto the carpet directly in front of her feet, and he was gazing at her with golden, unblinking eyes. She knelt and buried her face in the fur at the top of his head; his ears twitched. "It's me," she said softly.

"Your reasoning?" Haval asked; he had not disagreed with her.

"The timing." She lifted her face from Snow's fur and turned to Haval, seeing his age and his wisdom as if they were the two edges of a blade. "The cats," she continued, when he failed to react at all. "The trees. The trees that only grow in the Common—but are now growing in my backyard. The hidden path."

"And the regent?"

"I think they meant to kill the regent," she replied, her voice hardening. "In the confusion, my death would mean less than his. But—I don't understand."

"You have demonstrated that you do, in fact, understand much."

"Duvari's here. The manse is crawling with *Astari*." She deliberately failed to look at Devon as she spoke. "Sigurne is here. The god-born. Why wouldn't they wait until after the funeral rites were done? I'd wait."

"Yes, you would. On the face of the facts that you do know, waiting is by far the more intelligent choice; acting now invites the attention of both the Kings and the god-born; it will certainly invite the attention of the Order of Knowledge, although I believe that unavoidable in any case."

She knew that tone of voice. Knew it, took a deep breath, and acknowledged it. "They know more about the hidden path than I do," she said. This time, Haval met and held her gaze. "If they have access to the knowledge of a living, walking god, they know way more."

He didn't even prompt her when she paused.

"If they wait, there's some chance that I'll learn how to do more, and they don't want that."

"No," he agreed. His voice was quiet now, in a way that suggested sympathy. Or pity. "But what you have already done cannot be ignored. It will not be ignored by the god-born, if I am any judge of the disruption you caused; it will certainly not be ignored by the magi." He glanced at Night, and Night rose and padded across the room, stepping carefully over the pins and the shears that were scattered beside bolts of uncut cloth. White cloth, black cloth: the colors of Imperial mourning. The colors, Jewel thought, of Night and Snow, meant to mark the end of an era. "You are afraid, Jewel." It wasn't a question.

She couldn't answer, because she was, and fear wasn't something a girl from the twenty-fifth holding—a woman who wanted to be The Terafin— could admit. Not *this* one, at any rate.

"And that is wise. They attack now. You know that the demons move within the Annagarian pretender's armies in the South. You have seen some hint of the ancient in your brief sojourn with the Imperial armies. Were I the Lord of the Shining Court, my attention would necessarily be with my armies and their battle; I would spare only the scantest of resources on any other difficulty.

"But I fear that they have failed to predict your actions, ATerafin. They have failed, perhaps, to predict your existence, and they must move as they can against you, with far less power than they otherwise might." Haval set his cloth on the table just before Night dropped his head into his lap. "What do you think, Night?"

"I think I'm *bored*."

"Well, yes. Listening to an old man talk is often a very boring but exacting enterprise."

"It *is*," the cat replied as Haval scratched his head.

"What will you do, ATerafin?"

"Pay my respects to the woman who adopted me," Jewel replied firmly.

Haval nodded. He turned to Devon. "The regent will require more . . . careful guards. It has not escaped my notice, ATerafin, that the regent's personal guards are, at the moment, drawn from the Chosen."

Devon said nothing.

Jewel felt part of the world drop out from beneath her feet.

"Jewel will, as well, require the Chosen."

"I have Avandar."

"You have. But you will require guards."

"Us! *Us*! Choose *us*!"

Jewel almost laughed. "Not yet, Snow, Night. Not yet. Unless . . ." She glanced at Devon.

Devon's brows rose. "You cannot be serious."

"Can't I? I can't have the cats as guards. Not in public, not yet. I can have Avandar, because I've always had Avandar. I'll take Arann. I'll take Angel. I'll even take Torvan and Arrendas if I have to. But if I want to gain acceptance, I can't be surrounded by immortal, magical creatures. Not yet." And maybe not ever.

"And you expect the regent to be able to do so?"

"More easily than I can. Inasmuch as the Council members are willing to trust any man, woman, or child, they trust Gabriel. If he dies—if he dies before we can even *convene*—anyone whose concern is the House will suffer."

Devon rose. "Haval," he said, and offered him a very deep, very formal bow. "My apologies for delaying your necessary work. If you have no objections, I will take Jewel with me now, where we might continue our discussion of logistics."

"Please be my guest. If you would, however, return, I believe you and I have much to discuss"

Jewel did not, as it turned out, have much time to speak with Devon, because Torvan, Arrendas, and a dozen of the Chosen appeared at the door of the wing. Ellerson, accustomed to Torvan's presence, bid them enter, which was not an entirely orderly affair.

He then fetched Jewel, who met them, Avandar in tow, at the door. Both of the captains tendered her exact—and perfect—salutes.

"You're just the people I wanted to see," she told them. "Wait here."

*   *   *

"What are you doing?" Avandar asked, when they were mostly out of earshot.

"Making an executive decision," was her crisp reply. She headed to Haval's room, opened the door, and called the cats out. Night and Snow ambled into the hall, looking slightly bouncy. She hesitated a moment, and then decided against fetching Shadow; Shadow was with Adam and Ariel.

Ariel, whom she'd barely had the time to visit in the long, long couple of days since she'd arrived home, was comfortable with Shadow. She'd seen the cats take down one of the Arianni in the Dominion of Annagar; she was well aware of the fact they could be both vicious and deadly when bored—but Jewel wasn't all that attached to the Arianni. Which was beside the point; she knew that the child was safe with Shadow. Ariel was still hiding from her own reflection. It was best for all concerned to leave them together.

She hoped Shadow saw it the same way.

Cats in procession, she headed back into the halls where the Chosen were now waiting.

"Ellerson, has Gabriel been moved?"

"No, ATerafin."

"Good." Turning to Torvan, she said, "The regent is in the great room."

"Alone?"

"Teller and the healer are with him."

Torvan was pale and grim. "The healer?"

"Levec. Probably presenting the House with the bill for his services." She nodded to Ellerson again, and he opened the door. As she walked into the room, she glanced at the lines of his familiar face, and realized with a pang that no matter how deserted she'd felt, no matter how angry she'd been, she was *home* when Ellerson was in the wing.

"If you can find Angel and Carver—"

"They have not yet returned."

Where in the hells were they anyway? If they'd gone drinking, Jewel was going to have both of their heads as kitchen table decorations.

"Torvan, where's Arann?"

"He is in the regent's office."

"Alone?"

"No. He is with Lord Celleriant."

She started to say she wanted him here, but thought better of it; she wanted him there, because that's where Gabriel would be, and she trusted Arann. "Night, do *not* scratch the door. I don't care if you're bored."

Snow hissed laughter, and Jewel glared at him. She could almost feel Avandar's faint smugness.

The Chosen fanned out in the room as Gabriel rose from the lounge chair. His clothing still sported a new, red slash, and he was pale, but he was otherwise whole. She walked straight to Gabriel, Night to her left and Snow to her right.

"Gabriel, you've seen Night and Snow."

Gabriel nodded; he looked dubious, but not surprised. "I have, ATerafin. Admittedly not at this distance."

"They are almost impossible to kill; I've seen it tried by people who can give the demons a run for their money—and enjoy it, too."

Gabriel was not a fool. He was, inasmuch as the right-kin could be, an honest man. "ATerafin, I am whole and uninjured, thanks to the intervention of your domicis and Levec."

"Yes, and I'd like you to remain that way. I want the cats to be your guards."

Torvan coughed, and she turned to face him. "Did you look at the bodies?" she asked, her voice breaking only slightly.

"We did."

"Tell me that they weren't Chosen. Tell me, and I'll believe you."

"ATerafin—"

"Or don't. We can't afford to have Gabriel die; not before the funeral, and not before a new leader is chosen for the House. I trust you. I trust Arrendas. I can name the other Chosen that I would also trust with my life—or with his. But I clearly can't trust all of them."

"ATerafin," Gabriel began again.

"The cats don't need sleep," she continued, as if he hadn't spoken. "They don't need food—"

"We *like* to eat," Night broke in.

"They don't shut up, it's true. But they're capable of dignity and silence when it's necessary."

Torvan coughed again. This time, however, Gabriel offered Jewel a tired smile. "What the Captain of the Chosen is not saying is that the choice is not yours."

She had the grace to fall silent, and to redden. He was, of course, correct; she was tired and running on instinct, which never played well with etiquette in dire situations.

"The assassination attempt was disturbing. It is catastrophic at the moment for the Chosen—something their captains are also not saying. But, ATerafin, there is perhaps a third thing that is not yet stated, and I will ask the Captain of the Chosen to speak his mind plainly."

Torvan then turned to Jewel. "There are protocols with which your cats are almost certainly unfamiliar."

"They don't have to be his *only* guards," she shot back. "I don't care who else you have on his detail. But the cats are fast, and as far as I know, much harder to kill. If something similar happens, Gabriel won't be defenseless."

"He will not be defenseless, as you put it, again," was the grim, cool reply.

Avandar watched Jewel carefully—and in silence. Gabriel was now at her back; she wasn't certain whether or not he'd *have* her back, but at this point, she didn't care.

"Are you mine or not?" she asked, voice flat and hard.

Torvan's brows rose.

"Answer me: Are you mine? The Chosen were not disbanded." Without turning to the former right-kin, she said, "Amarais asked that you preserve the Chosen?"

"Yes."

"For me?"

"Yes."

To Torvan she said, "And you knew and agreed?"

This time he nodded; it was a controlled nod.

"You are not the only Captain of the Chosen." She turned a few inches toward Arrendas. "Captain Arrendas."

He saluted; it was sharp and loud. But his expression was shuttered, as if he now wore a mask or a visor. "ATerafin."

"Did you accede to Amarais Handernesse ATerafin's final request of her Chosen?"

"Yes."

"Then let me repeat my question to both of you. Are you mine, or not?"

*   *   *

Torvan met and held her gaze, and then he smiled. It was a scant smile, harder and harsher in form than most of the smiles she saw on his face. He dropped to one knee and bowed head to her, and Arrendas followed suit in silence.

"Your answer, ATerafin," Gabriel said quietly.

Jewel nodded grimly. "You'll take the cats," she told him, still watching the Captains of the Chosen. "If you're not comfortable with two of them, take Night. I can't," she added. "You know why."

"And you have no care for my reputation."

"I have, as you put it, a great deal of care for it; I just happen to value your life more."

Night snickered.

"Night, Snow—I want him alive. If anyone attempts to harm him, I don't care what you do with them."

Snow was practically preening. "However, in all other regards, you are to listen to both Gabriel and the Chosen. You're to obey them in any other matter."

Both cats' eyes widened in dismayed shock.

Jewel had not yet finished. "How many of the other Chosen chose as their captains did?"

Silence, but it was a different one. "Get up," she told them both. "Looking down at your heads just feels wrong." They rose, making clear that they did it at her command. She thought it might get tedious in the very near future, but held her tongue. "Were they offered the same choice?" She could hear echoes of her Oma's voice: Don't make me ask again.

"We are the Captains of the Chosen," Torvan finally replied.

"Yes, you are. I'm not arguing that. But the Chosen are offered a *choice* when they're asked to serve. They made their vows to *her*. I'm not her. Give them the same choice now. They're not forsworn if they choose not to serve me—I'm not, I'll never be, her." She paused, shook her head, and said, "That's not the way it works, is it?"

Silence.

"Fine. Assemble the Chosen in the back at the House shrine."

Torvan's brows rose. "We have not yet—"

"Yes, I know. It doesn't matter. I'll take Shadow, I'll have Avandar and Celleriant, and most of all, I'll have *myself*. I can buy a few minutes of life if someone tries to kill me, and if the Chosen are assembled, they won't last long—even if they come from the ranks of the Chosen themselves."

"Jewel," Gabriel said quietly, "Perhaps this is not the day. You have said that you will wait to declare yourself—but this action, more than any other, will serve in that stead. If there are, indeed, members of the Chosen who now owe their loyalty to other members of the House Council, your intent will be instantly known."

Jewel almost laughed, but it would have been the wrong laugh. "Yes. Yes, it will. It seems I'm not even to be allowed an appropriate gesture of respect for the woman who—" She broke off, lifting her hand momentarily to her eyes as she turned away. "Assemble the Chosen," she said again.

This time, the only answers were two sharp salutes. "The right-kin?"

"If he's willing, he can stay in the great room with the two cats for the moment; when we're done, his new detail can start. Gabriel?" She turned to him.

Just the hint of a smile touched his lips, although his eyes were shadowed; he looked older. "I will be pleased to remain in your wing under the tender ministrations of your cats and your den's domicis. I would ask that some further word be sent to Barston, but I understand the difficulty."

Teller, silent until this moment, said, "I'll take word if it's necessary. Barston knows you're alive; he would never prize reassurance over an increased risk to your life."

"Send Jester to fetch Celleriant," Jewel told him. "Tell Celleriant to meet us at the House shrine."

"And Arann?" Teller asked.

"Arann will receive word with the rest of the Chosen."

Chapter Seventeen

JEWEL WENT DIRECTLY to the Terafin shrine. She paused at the steps that led down to the garden of contemplation, to stare at the great trees of the Common that now towered over the rest of the grounds in the back of the manse. Morning and afternoon had not erased their presence, although a small army of gardeners had done much to tidy up everything else.

Shadow paced behind her back; Avandar ignored him. He waited, watching the heights of those trees with something very like anticipation. It was silent, but it was strong. "Lord Celleriant is waiting," he told her.

"How did he know to come to me in Gabriel's office?"

"You must ask him that yourself, if you cannot answer the question." His tone made clear that he thought the answer should be obvious; perhaps it was. But she had felt nothing at all, had made no attempt to summon him; she wasn't even certain how she would go about doing any such thing.

She descended the stairs and set foot on the path that wound its way through the shrines of the Triumvirate before reaching the only shrine that truly mattered to her at the moment. Even in the fading light of evening, it was clear that the shrines had been cleaned so well they now gleamed beneath the loose, hand-shaped leaves that had fallen from trees that were at once a day old and ancient. The Mother's shrine had an offering basket that looked simple; it wasn't. Gold and gems and reddish rock had been laid atop the ceremonial stalks of wheat, the harvest of the House under the stewardship of Amarais Handernesse ATerafin.

And so it went: Cormaris' shrine was likewise spotless, almost sparkling, flanked by magestones encased in globes. The eagle, rod in claws, looked almost alive in its stone flight; Jewel suspected that mages had been hired to produce this effect for the three days of the funeral. She paused at Cormaris' shrine; Avandar remained at a distance, on the path. It occurred to her as she knelt that she had never seen him bend knee or head to any of the gods in prayer. But it didn't matter. If he felt himself wise—and clearly, he did—his was not a wisdom she wanted for herself; it was cold, hard, dismissive.

Maybe wisdom was always a matter of context.

She rose, and made her way to the shrine of Reymaris, Lord of Justice. Tonight, she didn't pray, because tonight she knew that there was no way to divide Justice from vengeance in her thoughts. But she remembered as she offered the shrine a brief bow that she had once come here in helpless rage. She'd been just as unable to divide the two—but beyond caring.

She always felt as if she were the same person she'd been on the day she arrived at the manse. The years had passed, and she'd learned how to navigate the complicated political climes of the House and its Council, but those lessons hadn't changed her. Or so she'd thought. *I'm still me.* But what did that mean? How much *me* could she still be, knowing so much more than she had? She was at home in the manse, and at home, at last, on the Isle—a place she had never visited in her youth.

"Jewel."

She nodded without looking back. Instead, she looked up, and up again; she could now see faint starlight through the branches of the towering trees; new trees, all. Yet their leaves weren't silver, gold, or diamond; they were living—dying—leaves. These trees had roots that grew into the Isle's soil, branches that did not sting or cut. Wherever they had come from, they were here now, as real and as improbable as Jewel Markess herself.

She'd been afraid to enter the garden until this moment. The breeze blew hair from her eyes, and a leaf fell, touching her upturned face. For just a moment, she could hear the babble and chatter of the Common at its busiest; could feel the gnarled and callused hand of her Oma in her own.

It was fancy, nothing more; her Oma had never returned as more than a voice and a sharp, biting memory. But the sense of touch was as visceral as those necessary words; it was just rarer. She felt the tug of that hand, smiled ruefully. *Yes, Oma. Yes, I'm ready.*

She walked down the path toward the last shrine.

At the height of the rounded dais, a lone man waited, and even at this distance, his eyes shone.

Jewel left Avandar on the path. It felt natural, and he didn't argue; Morretz himself had seldom accompanied The Terafin to this shrine when she chose to visit the garden of contemplation. She approached the altar atop the concentric, marble circles, and when she reached it, she turned to face the spirit of the man who had once founded the House.

"You know why I'm here."

He smiled. "I do."

"They made their oaths upon this altar."

He nodded. "But they made their oaths to Amarais. She made her oath to me, to my House, and that carried them."

"They are not forsworn," Jewel replied, glancing at the altar. Of the four shrines in this quartered garden, this one had received the least attention.

"The guests will not come here," he replied, as if she'd spoken aloud. "And Amarais herself will never return."

"They'll bring her body here at the end of the final day."

He nodded again. "But she will not be in it, and even I have little use for corpses. She did not remain, as I have remained. Where she is now, only Mandaros knows—and the judgment-born are unlikely to now be called to question her. What will you do, Jewel?"

"I'll address the Chosen."

"And then?"

"I will pay my respects to the woman who made this life possible."

"Ah. It is unlike you."

"Is it?"

"In your youth, you knew that a corpse was just a corpse."

"Yes. And in my age I understand that corpse or no, forms must be observed for the sake of the patriciate. No, for the sake of those that grieve. It's not for the dead that we gather, after all."

"They come, soon."

Soon was two hours later. Jewel stood at the height of the shrine, waiting, her hands clasped behind her back. Above this shrine, the trees also grew. The landscape of the garden had changed. It hadn't changed completely, in large part due to the ministrations of the very overworked Master Gardener and his staff—but it would never be what it was.

Torvan and Arrendas came down the path, walking almost in lockstep. They were armed, armored, as focused as if they prepared for battle within the grounds itself. If they saw her at all, they showed no sign, and because they didn't, she couldn't. The air was chill, but this time, she'd dressed for it; Haval had, years ago, made her a very fine, very dark cape. The clasp was loose because she'd tugged it off her back once too often. Haval had made clear, the last time he'd done his repairs, that he wouldn't do it again in the very near future. It was as close to a dire threat as the dressmaker had been willing to offer.

It warmed her now, as she waited, her hair once again falling across her forehead and into her eyes.

The Chosen came, in the wake of their captains. Like their captains, they were armed, armored; like their captains, they wore their duty faces. She searched for some sign of Arann in this mass of large, moving men, but if he was present, his helm obscured his face. Once, she would have known him by his gait—but a decade and a half in the House Guard had changed it, step by step.

She missed Angel, and it surprised her. But she didn't ask Avandar to find him, in part because she knew the domicis would not leave until she did. He was willing to let her stand—and speak—on her own, but only in his view.

She heard steps on the marble behind her back; light, quick steps. She stiffened, but didn't move, and Lord Celleriant came to stand at her side, his hair caught in a breeze that touched nothing else, not even the leaves above. He was wild now, and like wild creatures, near silent.

"ATerafin," he said, in a voice that didn't carry beyond her ears.

"No," was her soft reply. "Your sword is not necessary here."

The Captains of the Chosen now approached the shrine; they stopped at the foot of its stairs, slamming fists against breastplates like synchronized thunder. They drew swords in the same way, and laid them at their feet before they dropped to knee, bowing their heads.

Did I want this? Did I ever want this?

Did it matter? She bid them rise, in a tone as cool and distant as any she had ever heard Amarais use. They obeyed her quiet command. "Join me."

She turned toward the altar, and saw that the Terafin Spirit remained; she wasn't at all surprised when neither of the captains seemed to notice his presence—although given they were Chosen, there was some small chance that this was deliberate.

"Wait," she told them, watching the grounds before the shrine as they filled, at last, with the Chosen. She counted perhaps fifty men and women.

Seventy, Avandar said.

More than ten.

She felt his brief chuckle. "Captain Torvan, are the Chosen fully assembled?"

"Yes, ATerafin."

"Good." She turned toward the gathered men and women, wishing she recognized more of them, and knowing it didn't matter. They were watching their captains. They were also, she realized, watching her. Waiting. She wanted to ask Torvan what he had said to them, but knew the answer: assemble at the shrine. Nothing more. They had come at his command.

She could not be certain they would remain at hers. Two at least would, and she faced the first of those, seeing the years that had passed as lines in his face and gray in his hair. "I am not The Terafin," she said, clearly enough that her voice carried beyond the shrine which contained them. She couldn't be certain how far, but wanted the words to reach every man and woman who stood waiting in the silence.

She waited for Torvan's response; it was a simple, silent nod.

"I am not The Terafin," she said again, glancing at the other Chosen assembled on the grounds. "Each and every one of you offered The Terafin your oaths of fealty at this shrine when she chose you. You felt those oaths deeply; you risked your lives, time and again, to live up to them, to fulfill your promise.

"Amarais Handernesse ATerafin was born to the patriciate. She was born to the wealthy, educated by the wealthy, and introduced, in her season, to the powerful. She understood the corridors of power, both in Terafin and in *Avantari* as instinctively as she understood how to walk or breathe. But she was fair, and she was just, and in her fashion, she could be merciful; she was wise, and as she understood power, she could hope to wield it *well*.

"But I? I was born to old-stock Voyani refugees in the hundred holdings. I had two names, not five; I was taught to read, but given very little to practice reading with. I was taught to write, but again, with sticks and dirt and the occasional slates and chalk when they could be afforded; in the winters of the holdings, that was never. I was not given fine silks and jewels. I was not given introductions to the men and the women who hold the purse strings of the Empire or the ears of the Kings.

"But I was born with a singular gift. That gift, in the end, brought me to The Terafin's doorstep. This House became my home; The Terafin became my mentor. What I have learned of power, I have learned by her side. When she knew—when *we* knew—that she would die, she did not cry or weep or plead; she did not bend knee to the gods in hopeless pursuit of their intervention. She planned, as she had always done.

"She asked, of me, one thing: that I declare my intent to rule the House she would, by death—and only death—abandon. I was never Chosen; I did not, and could not, serve her in that fashion. But if I did not have the qualities and the qualifications that would make me fit for such a position, I revered her no less, in the end. I gave her my word that I would do as she asked."

They watched her now. He voice had dropped; she knew it. She wasn't accustomed to speaking in front of large crowds, and although she had learned some of that skill from simple observation of Amarais, she had never fully mastered it. But they heard her nonetheless.

Torvan was utterly still as she spoke, but not in his usual way; his attention wasn't turned outward, as it was when he stood guard. He watched her, and only her.

"You have followed the Captains of the Chosen since your creation. You have *never* disgraced the vows you made." She turned full to Torvan. "What did The Terafin ask of you, before her death?" She spoke clearly, cleanly, but forcefully. She meant to have the question answered.

He hesitated, but it was brief, and when he answered, his voice was the louder of the two. "She asked—as her final request—that I hold the Chosen for you."

"And as a gesture of respect, of fealty, you agreed."

He nodded.

She took a breath, glanced once at Celleriant, and then said, "It's not enough."

His eyes widened slightly.

"She's dead, Torvan. If her last command to you was to support me, you are bound to a dead woman—one who will never give another command. Even so, her word will hold sway over mine. And as it's me you're going to serve, it's me who's saying: It's not enough."

She turned, once again, to the Chosen. "You no longer exist to serve

Amarais Handernesse ATerafin. She is dead. You serve the House, but the House is divided. Two of your number have fallen in their attempt to assassinate Gabriel ATerafin, and I *will not* have it, not of the Chosen. The House Guard, yes; they stand to make their fortunes here, if they back the right leader.

"But *not* the Chosen." She took a breath, and said, "The Chosen will disband. They will disband this eve."

Into the silence that followed her proclamation, came one sound: hooves against marble. The Winter King mounted the steps and came to stand to one side of her; it was becoming crowded.

"By what authority," a voice came from below, "do you seek to disband the Chosen?"

"By my own. The Chosen were left intact so that they might guard and support me in my attempt to seek the House rulership. But without The Terafin, they are no longer Chosen. I am not—yet—The Terafin. I don't have the authority to raise House Guards to the level of—of oathguard. I seek it. But I am not Amarais Handernesse ATerafin."

To her side, Lord Celleriant drew not sword, but shield. A whisper traveled through the onlookers; breeze made heavy with syllables. Leaves drifted toward armored men from the heights above as the Winter King lifted his antlered head and gazed into their midst.

The Chosen shifted, their gazes suddenly reaching for the sky as something large flew above their standing unit and skidded to a screeching stop on cold marble. It wasn't terribly majestic, but a winged, gray cat didn't require majesty. Still, Shadow didn't speak; he merely came to sit by her feet—closer to her person than either the Winter King or Celleriant.

"I will seek the House," she continued, reaching out to lay one hand on Shadow's head. "And I will do it with—or without—your support. But if I am to be given your support, it will not be because you feel obligated to honor the wishes of a woman who can no longer lead you. Pay her your respects, as is her due and her right, and then do as I have done: decide your own path and your own future without her.

"If you will serve me, you will serve *me*. I will take your oaths upon the same altar, and I will treat them with the same respect—but I will never be Amarais Handernesse ATerafin; she cannot be replaced."

She turned to Torvan, who waited. "ATerafin," he said gravely.

She smiled and shook her head very slightly. "Are you mine?" she asked him, her voice as soft as his.

He drew his sword and laid it across the altar; it was followed by his helm. He once again dropped to one knee—or he would have. But she'd done enough, endured enough, for one night; she caught his arm—made heavy and cold by metallic joints—and held it. He could have knelt anyway, but it would have been extremely awkward.

He couldn't therefore offer her the one-kneed bow that served as very deep respect. He smiled as she touched the altar with her fingertips, her hands inches from the hilt of his sword. To lift it was to accept him.

"I understood your potential on the first day I saw you at the gates, with your ridiculously mismatched clothing, your den-mates, and your dying. But I was yours the night you came to the shrine to save my life."

"You didn't appreciate it at the time, as I recall."

A glimmer of pain tightened his lips, no more. "We often learn to value what we've been given only years after the fact. I will serve you with my life, ATerafin. What you want for and from the House, I honor as I can by my choice."

She lifted his sword. The altar beneath it was far warmer than it should have been, given the cool air. She had seen The Terafin do this before, but The Terafin had always made the swords seem so weightless; Torvan's was heavy. Her hand shook, although she'd been prepared for its weight. She returned it to him. "Will you be my Captain?" she asked, voice trembling slightly. She lifted his helm and returned it to him; he held it in the crook of his left arm.

He nodded and she turned to Arrendas. Arrendas was watching her with an expression very similar to Torvan's. She felt less certain of herself as the minutes passed. But he, too, drew sword and laid it across the altar; his helm followed. "You never saw her when she was younger," he told Jewel. Mindful of her intervention with Torvan, he didn't sink to one knee. "You can't see the ways in which you're alike."

"And you can?"

"Yes, ATerafin. You're right—you'll never be her. But she," he added, and turned, and met the gaze of the Winter King full-on, "would never have been you, either. I swear that I will serve you and defend you with my life."

"And will you be—"

"Captain? If the Chosen are disbanded, you may have little need of one, never mind two."

"I don't know how many men you need under you before you get to call yourself a captain; apparently you need several thousands before you get to call yourself The Terafin."

His gaze was measured, almost calculating. "How many of the Chosen do you think you'll retain?"

"At least one more," she replied, voice low. "I wasn't even certain you would stay."

"If we're being that honest, ATerafin, I was not entirely certain either. I think it unwise to disband the Chosen, but you have already made that decision."

"Do you think I'm wrong?"

"No. Unwise and wrong are not the same. Understand that your age works against you among the Chosen; you are young."

She nodded.

"But your companions work in your favor, because they feel ancient, and they are willing to serve you." He looked at the assembled Chosen. "You will not retain many," he finally said.

"No. But I can't use them as they are."

"When you rule," he replied, "it is a skill you will need to learn. Most of the men and women who bear the House Name serve the House; not you, not The Terafin, but the House itself. Each such man and woman has opinions and ideas about how the House is best served."

"I know. But I can't watch my back while I'm fighting."

"That, too, is a skill that would benefit you—but we will watch your back, ATerafin."

Shadow snorted. Loudly.

She drew breath and once again spoke to the crowd. "I have said you are not forsworn. Your oaths were given to Amarais Handernesse ATerafin, and received by her; I am not her. What you owed The Terafin, you do not owe me. I will ask it," she continued, as murmurs once again wound their way through the Chosen, "but I will hold no grudge, bear no ill will, to any who do not choose to offer me their service in the way they once offered it to The Terafin. Stay, or go, in honor."

She watched as the Chosen conferred with each other, trying hard not to catch their words. She knew—who better?—that she wasn't Amarais; knew that she couldn't be. She'd given the fate of her den into The Terafin's hands; she'd trusted her almost absolutely. It was a trust that she'd been incapable of extending to herself, a decade and a half past. She didn't honestly feel that she could trust herself that way now. But she did feel that there was no one else that came close, and that was enough.

The Chosen began to slip away, down the path and toward the other shrines—or the manse. They were lost to sight beneath the open sky. It was dark, and if starlight and moonlight shone in the crisp, cool air, it silvered everything, and illuminated only one fact clearly: of the seventy men and women who had gathered at Torvan's command, perhaps two dozen remained upon the short grass and the interlocking stone.

Two dozen, she thought. It was better than she had hoped for.

The first to mount the stairs was Arann; she recognized him because he had removed his helm. He looked pale and tired, which is about how she felt. She smiled, weary; his smile was stronger. He set his helm upon the altar first, and then unsheathed his sword and laid it down as well, and she thought it fitting: armor first, weapon second.

She wanted to tell him that she didn't require his oath, but it wouldn't have been true: she did.

"We're supposed to have three days to decide," he told her.

"I don't have three days. And I don't think three days is going to change anyone's mind—not in my favor, at any rate." But she drew an even breath. "I chose you," she said quietly. "Twenty years ago, I chose you. You followed me. You stayed by my side when we were almost starving. You stayed when we suffered losses, and when we faced death. You stayed when you realized I *couldn't* protect you."

"I knew you would try," he replied, his voice soft where hers was pitched to carry. "I knew you would never stop trying. I couldn't do less, Jay. I won't. Whatever you need me to swear, I'll swear."

But the altar was warm against her palms. "I think this is enough." She lifted his sword and returned it to him, dismayed by its weight. When he'd sheathed it again, she retrieved his helm. "Arann—"

"I've always been one of yours." He saluted, a full Imperial salute. She both hated and loved it, at the moment. But he didn't remain beside Torvan and Arrendas; he saluted them both in turn and then retreated. That was probably for the best, given the size of the shrine and the number of men who waited below, but she wanted to call him back.

She didn't.

Gordon came next, and his smile was broad, loud; he had a voice, when he bothered to pitch it, that could have been bardic, it carried so cleanly.

He didn't have a quiet voice, on the other hand. He set his sword and his helm on the altar, and then he saluted her.

"Will you serve me?" she asked.

"With my life."

"Will you bear the burden of my trust and my faith, even if you feel it misplaced?"

His blue eyes rounded at this departure, and he glanced at his captains. If their expressions gave him any answers, it didn't show in his. But his face grew more thoughtful. "Yes, Jewel. I will keep my faith with you even in the gravest hour of my doubts."

"Thank you." She lifted his sword and returned it to him as Marave approached the shrine behind him. Marave was older than Torvan, but not as old as Alayra had been when she had been assassinated. Her hair was iron gray, now, and it was very, very short. She unsheathed her sword, held it up a moment, and then placed it on the shrine. Her helm followed.

Jewel asked the same questions she had asked of Gordon; Marave's answers were slightly different, because Marave generally had no time for something like doubt. It served no purpose, in Marave's mind, since it wouldn't change her course of action.

After Marave, came Corrin, and after Corrin, Kauran. She took their oaths and their salutes and watched as they retreated into a looser, but obvious, formation. Arrendas left the pavilion and joined them, standing at their head as they faced the shrine.

But when Elton placed his sword upon the shrine, the Terafin Spirit moved. He came to stand across the altar from that sword and the helm that followed; his face was the white of death, his eyes the black of loss, as Elton gave his oath to serve and succor.

The sword's blade cracked and blackened as Jewel's hand hovered above it.

"There was a reason," the Terafin Spirit said, in a remote and cold voice, "that The Terafin took the oaths of her Chosen upon this altar. These are the men and the women who *must* be trusted, and they must be worthy of that trust."

Elton took a step back, narrowly avoiding a tumble down the stairs; his mailed heel wobbled. He had enough balance to retain his footing, but not enough composure to shutter his expression; his face had paled and his eyes had widened. It was those eyes that now sought Jewel's.

"It appears," she said, almost wryly, "that your oath was false." She raised her voice. "I have said that I will hold no grudge against those who will not vow to serve me. I am not so generous with those who have attempted to deceive. So I say to those remaining, those who wish to serve another master, leave now. This is the shrine of the House, and your will and intent will be known."

Elton's eyes were still wide, but this time, he spoke. "This is impossible. It must be magery. Only The Terafin can command the properties of the altar, and only The Terafin—"

"If by magery, you mean magic, then yes, of course it's magic." Jewel almost spoke in Torra, and reined herself in with effort. Her hands were clenched in the type of fists that implied someone was about to be hit, and soon. "If you mean to imply that it's *my* magic, you've been drinking, smoking, or you've always been a *moron*."

Torvan cleared his throat; Jewel ignored him.

Shadow said, "Can I *eat* him?"

"You'll just choke on the bad bits," she snapped, her eyes never leaving Elton's face. "I haven't demanded anything of you. I've asked. I've asked politely," she told him, in as reasonable a voice as she could muster. "As far as I can see, the only liar here is you. If you feel guilty or humiliated, *good*. But don't confuse *my* actions or motivations with yours. I intend to serve the House. I intend to rule it. I intend to rebuild the Chosen. I've made this clear; I can try to use smaller words if it'll help."

"You aren't The Terafin—the altar should do *nothing*."

"Demonstrably whoever told you this was wrong."

Elton's jaw snapped shut. It would have been gratifying if it had been because of anything Jewel had said; she was aware, however, that it had more to do with Celleriant's sudden motion. She caught his shoulder. "No one is to be harmed here. Not in this shrine."

"I have no objections," the Terafin Spirit said.

"*I* have," she snapped back. "And last I checked, the dead don't rule here." Shadow, however, had also risen to his feet; only the Winter King and Torvan—gods bless Torvan—stayed their ground. Turning to Elton, she snarled, "*Leave*."

He did. He was visibly shaken in his retreat.

Grim, Jewel addressed the rest of the men and women who waited to mount the shrine's stairs. "If you have nothing to offer me, leave." She lifted the hilt of his sword; it was cold. The blade, in the shrine's light, was obviously damaged beyond repair. She set it down on the shrine's marble floor and rose.

Three of the Chosen detached themselves from the men who remained and headed, in silence, down the garden's path and away from a meaningless vow. But one—in the darkness, she couldn't clearly see who, turned at the edge of that path. He tendered her not a salute, which would have been meaningless, but rather, a perfect bow.

"Twenty-one," she told Torvan quietly, the fires banked by the unexpected gesture.

"Twenty-one, ATerafin," he replied. He was smiling, although the smile was both slight and sharp.

"Is twenty-one enough?"

"It will be."

She then took up her place by the altar's side, and in the growing darkness of the night, she accepted the oaths of the men and women who remained. When it was done, she was both tired and hungry, but as the men didn't complain, she felt she couldn't. Her stomach mostly agreed as she descended the stairs and joined the not-quite-Chosen on the grass.

Torvan joined her, but Celleriant and the Winter King retreated. Shadow, however, did not—and he made certain he was walking between the Captain of these House Guards and their Lord, or at least he did until she told him to walk on the *other* side, as she had two.

She knew that the men who had left the gathered crowd would report to whomever they meant to serve; her announcement of her candidacy had been made earlier than she'd intended, and not perhaps in the most well-thought out way. But it was done. She led the men to the West Wing; they followed in a sober silence.

Ellerson's silence was less sober when they began to file in through the wing's doors; she sent them into the great room. Only Torvan remained on the same side of the doors she had. Ellerson glanced at Torvan, and then turned to Jewel.

"I have taken the liberty of having a meal—a simple meal—prepared, as you've missed the late dinner hour in the halls. I was not certain as to the number of your guests, but Avandar guessed there might be twenty in total."

There were more. Jewel's stomach complained again, and she ignored it. "I suppose we'd be breaking all the rules of etiquette if we just ate in the great room?"

Ellerson failed to hear her for a minute, after which he nodded. "Not all of the rules, no. But the food will be laid out on the dining table, and if you feel the dining room is too small, some accommodations can be made."

Angel and Carver were waiting for her in the dining room when she entered at the head of the Chosen. No, she thought, grimacing, she couldn't really call them that anymore. Ellerson had set up a sideboard with plates and cutlery, and she pointed the guards in the direction of the food. Arrendas paused long enough to tell her that Gabriel was also in the great room, and would be joining them for food shortly. This was the only thing said that made Ellerson almost visibly cringe, but he made no comment.

"Ellerson said you were looking for us?" Carver asked. Angel was eyeing the food—or the guards; with Angel, it was sometimes hard to tell.

"I was—a few hours ago. Where did you two go?"

"We were down in the holdings, with a side trip to the Port Authority. Are you planning on fighting a small war here tonight?"

"I'm not planning on it, no—but to date, none of my plans have been reliable."

He laughed at that; it was a slightly pained laugh. Then he knelt as Shadow approached and nudged his left knee. The cat raised a brow at Jewel's expression. "What? He's not *doing* anything *useful* anyway."

The guards had noticed that Carver was now scratching behind Shadow's ears, and for a moment, the food on the large serving trays on the table stopped disappearing. Only a moment, though. If they had questions, they wanted to ask them on full stomachs.

The great room was the largest room in the wing; it boasted three fireplaces, several large windows, and walls adorned with tasteful if sparse works of art: paintings, tapestries, one lone sculpture. Ellerson had chosen most of them; the sculpture had come with the wing, and it was, in Ellerson's words, valuable and prohibitively expensive to have repaired if the task of moving it caused damage. Moving it, on the other hand, was the work of several men.

There were, of course, chairs and long tables, but most of these were low and meant for convivial social gatherings. They were therefore mostly impressive for their expense, although they weren't entirely impractical. Jewel plunked herself down on a patch of floor nearest the long table by the roaring fire; it was cold.

Arrendas and Torvan were seated in a similar fashion; the chairs were occupied by various members of the guard, but although half a dozen rose as she passed in an attempt to vacate their own seats, she ignored them. Gabriel, however, was seated.

"I hear," he said, without preamble, "that you've disbanded the Chosen."

She winced.

"I assume you intended to mention it at some point," he added, as Ellerson emerged carrying a tray with a very fine decanter in its center. He carried it straight to the small table at Gabriel's left, and set it down.

"After I'd finished eating, if you want the truth. I didn't think it would take so long to gather the Chosen."

"Not all of the Chosen were in the manse at the time," Torvan pointed out.

"They live here," she replied with a shrug.

"So do Angel and Carver, as I recall."

Carver ducked his head; Angel only looked chagrined.

Gabriel took the cut crystal glass that Ellerson offered him and cleared his throat. "If I am not mistaken, the men and women who are in this room now are all Chosen."

"They were."

"The others?"

"They chose not to serve me."

"Barston is going to have my head over this, you realize. There is no small amount of paperwork to be done, and some deference is owed the Captain of the House Guard."

"I doubt it; he'll wait until the funeral rites are done."

Gabriel chuckled. "He will, indeed. Very well. You have disbanded the Chosen. The men and women here will also be reabsorbed into the House Guard."

"Yes—but assigned to me, as a Councillor."

"If they are assigned to you personally, you are expected to cover some part of their salary."

She swallowed a distinctly underchewed bit of meat and nodded, unsurprised. "You'll take the cats?"

"I will, as you so eloquently put it, allow the cats to serve in a position of honor among my guards. Your own, however . . ."

Torvan nodded. "The men have a few questions."

"They're Chosen for all intents and purposes," Jewel replied, "and I'm used to fielding questions from my own."

"Ah, yes, the infamous kitchen discussions. It is to be hoped that the Chosen are more restrained in their questions."

"And I'm to be equally restrained in my replies?"

He laughed. "Indeed."

Corrin lifted his head. "We want to know about the rest of your guards." He spoke without pause or hesitation.

"You're it."

"You have the three who stood by your side at the height of the shrine."

Ah. "Lord Celleriant is not entirely human."

"He can fight?"

"He can fight like a demon."

"Will you use him in our rotations?"

"I'd prefer not to, if I can avoid it."

"Can I ask why?"

"Yes. He fights as if he *is* a demon, and he tends to have very little respect for life. His own. Anyone else's. He's not particularly kind and he is certainly not gentle. But if we're ever confronted with another demon—or, gods help us, worse—he'll be in the front line. Hells, he might be the entire front line."

This was clearly not to Torvan's liking.

"He'll obey me," Jewel told him. "And he won't interfere in House politics without a direct command; the politics of the House don't interest him."

Torvan and Arrendas exchanged a glance. "The stag?" It was Arrendas who asked.

"He—" she shook her head. "He's harder to explain. Can he fight? Yes. But I don't think he can stand guard in any meaningful way, at least not indoors."

"And the cats can both guard and fight."

She nodded. "I can't speak for their discipline, though."

Shadow hissed.

She thought Torvan or Arrendas would move on and ask about the trees; they didn't. "You will not keep one cat as a guard for yourself?"

"Torvan—I can't."

He raised one brow.

"They're not—they're not exactly normal." Shadow's hiss deepened into a rumbling growl. "Don't growl at me. You're not."

"Normal is *boring*."

"Yes. But most of life is, as you put it, boring. At the moment, we only want the bits of nonboring that appear mostly normal. It doesn't matter if Gabriel's guarded by the cats. He doesn't want to rule."

"And when you take the House Seat, the cats will mysteriously disappear?"

". . . No. But if I have the House Seat, it won't matter."

Again the captains exchanged a glance; it was longer and appeared to be more significant. Torvan then turned to Gabriel and bowed. "Regent."

Gabriel's smile was tired and complicated. "I will leave her detail in your capable hands; I will speak with Jed'ra myself in your absence. This will, of course, have been noted."

Torvan nodded. Turning toward the Chosen, who were all listening intently, he said, "We have five shifts of four; six hours a shift, one in rotation. It's tight, but workable." He began to name names and shifts, paused, and bowed politely to Jewel. "ATerafin."

"I'll just be getting to bed," she replied, because she was very tired and she could nonetheless take a hint. "Will you station the Chosen outside of the wing, or inside it?"

"Two of the Chosen will stand at the doors; two will stand outside of your rooms."

Great. "Our halls aren't exactly—"

"They're wide enough."

Jewel glanced at Angel; Angel nodded. She surrendered and headed toward her room. Avandar trailed after her, as did Shadow; they collided in the door. She turned to Shadow, who was stepping on one of Avandar's feet, and said, in sharp Torra, "Cut it out *right now*. I've had a long day. I'll have a longer day tomorrow, and if I'm very lucky, nothing will try to kill me. I do not need you to play games with Avandar." Pausing only for breath she added, "Or Celleriant, either."

She stalked into the hall, and Shadow said, "But you don't want me to *hurt anyone*."

She wheeled.

"They're *almost* impossible to injure by *accident*."

"Never mind. I'm going to bed. I'm done for the evening, and Ellerson is going to wake me up before the crack of dawn."

Shadow nodded and ambled after her. She wanted to shut the door in his face. Conversely, as she approached her bed, shrugging herself out of her clothing in a way that would have outraged Haval, given that she left it where it had fallen, she wanted to keep him by her side. Avandar was here, and Avandar came with light to ward off nightmares—but Avandar had never been comfortable enough to sit sentinel on her bed, stealing covers and shoving pillows onto the floor.

And, if she were being fair, she would have hated it had he tried. Shadow was a cat. A cat who now bounded past her and leaped up on the bed, taking up more or less all of its center. She made a halfhearted attempt to push him off the other side, but gave up when he deliberately flexed his claws; she could just imagine what Ellerson would have to say on the morning of the first day of funeral rites if Shadow actually shredded the sheets or the mattress.

His eyes were glowing faintly in the dark; they were golden eyes, rounder and wider in shape than human eyes.

"Sleep," he told her, as he settled his head across his forepaws and folded his wings. "Sleep." Lifting his head, whiskers twitching, he spoke across her to Avandar. "It is not a good night."

Avandar, unblinking, nodded. He made his way to the chair that Ellerson had so often occupied on his night watches, and sat heavily. Jewel started to sit up and Shadow placed a paw on her stomach. "Sleep," he said again.

"I think he's injured," she said in a soft voice.

Shadow nodded. "There is blood, but it is dry, and there is not *too* much of it. Sleep, Jewel. Tomorrow it will be harder."

"But why is he—"

"He's been gardening," the cat replied. "Don't snarl at me—it *has* to be done. Celleriant is *with* him."

"Avandar—"

"The cat is correct, ATerafin. It is work that must be done."

"But I could—"

"Yes. It is possible that you could. But not easily, and not—demonstrably—deliberately. Both Lord Celleriant and I know how to traverse some parts of the path without revealing the whole of our presence, as does the Winter King. What we can do, we have done—but I am not certain it is enough."

"What does Celleriant think?"

"In this, I do not entirely trust him." Avandar shook his head as Jewel's expression shifted. Reaching out, he dampened the light. "I would now trust him with your life, and beyond it, the lives of your den, however much it has grown over the years. But the path is not part of his service; it is still wild in places, and what dwells in that wilderness draws beings such as Celleriant."

"Meaning he wants a fight?"

"Meaning, indeed, that he desires a battle that will test everything he can bring to bear. I have managed to make clear that such a battle does not and will not exist by accident; if we prepare and we clear, it will take both intent and will to reach us—to reach," he amended, "you. I dislike the cats, but they serve a purpose."

Shadow hissed as Jewel sank back into the pillows. Staring up at the canopy that served as nighttime ceiling, she said, "But you were injured."

"I was. It was minor."

"And your magic—"

"I *am* a mage, yes. When power is used at too great a rate, there is often some discomfort. I can suffer mage fevers; they cannot kill me. Nothing can," he added, his voice shuttered.

She closed her eyes. She thought there should be comfort in that knowledge: nothing could kill Avandar. Unlike her father, her mother, her Oma. Unlike Rath. But as she drifted toward sleep, she remembered that he had once surrendered the entirety of a city in his keeping to a dark god in order to be granted death; and untold thousands had died at the god's hand, in vain. He lived. He still lived.

She woke to the endless dunes of desert at the height of the day. The sky was azure, the sand gold—a reminder, if it were needed, that gold alone offered no shelter, no sustenance, no safety. It was only in the eyes of men that it could be transformed into any of the three, and the transformation was never perfect.

She was dressed in the vest and leggings of the Voyani, and a waterskin hung at her side. Her hair was secured by a band across her forehead that would catch the worst of the sweat and keep it from her eyes. At her hip was a long knife, and in her boots—her dusty, cracked boots—the hilts of daggers. She could see the caravan in the distance, the large wagons scudding off edges of sand.

She knew she stood in the Sea of Sorrows, and for a moment, she felt as if she had never left it; the endless desert was untouched and untroubled by anything as insignificant as her absence. She began to walk toward the caravan and its gently floating wagons.

But as she approached, she frowned. There was no movement around those wagons; no sign that the Voyani were present at all. There were no children, of course—the Voyani did not bring their children here, where something as simple as desert rain or wind could take them all in a matter of hours. But the wagons *were* here; there were four. No, she thought; there was a fifth as well; it hovered much higher than the rest, and it cast a distinct shadow. Here, shadow was prized, and she found herself heading toward the darkness.

She hesitated before she reached it. Something felt . . . wrong. Yes, this was the desert, and that was wrong enough for a girl born and bred to the harbor city of Averalaan—but it was more than that. There were no people. There was a campfire, nestled in a hollow in the dunes. At this time of day, there shouldn't have been; as the wood for such fires was in such scarce supply, they were rarely lit in the desert—and never at this size.

It grew larger and larger as she approached, mesmerized by the weaving dance of translucent flame in its reds, its oranges, its golds, as caught by their heights as she had been when fire had been contained in a grate in her childhood. But as she reached the lee of the fire, she realized that there was no wood to sustain it. It existed without an anchor, and as it turned toward her, she knew that something as flimsy as wood could never be an anchor for this fire.

You walked my path, the fire said, in a crackle and hiss of a voice.

She started to argue—because arguing with fire made sense at the moment—and stopped herself, remembering: she had emerged from the heart of a fire cast by the four Voyani Matriarchs near the Tor Leonne. It had been a bonfire. She glanced at the wagons that floated not far from the fire, and understood the significance of the four. She was dreaming, and she was aware of it.

"Did you bring me here?" she asked, because she couldn't think of much else to say.

You left me. This was not, from the sudden heat the fire shed, meant to comfort; it didn't.

She backed up the incline as the fire continued to inch toward her, and then turned and ran, the way she almost always ran in dreams: slowly. Horribly, painfully, slowly, each step, each lift of foot and bend of a knee an act of will gone wrong. She reached the closest wagon, and she recognized it as the wagon occupied by the Arkosan Matriarch. But as she approached, she saw the strange magical markings that kept it afloat and scudded to a full stop. They were black and lifeless. Before she could even attempt to climb up to the relative safety of its small platform, the wagon suddenly tilted toward the sand dunes. It fell.

The fire wasn't moving quickly, but it never paused, and as she leaped clear of its low, wide flames, they wrapped themselves around the wagon instead, and the wagon began to burn. She didn't wait to see how quickly the fire consumed it. Feet heavy, breath labored, she turned and made for the next wagon.

It was similar in shape and size to the Arkosan wagon, but it had a lower, wider platform at back on which at least four people might stand, if pressed together. The rails that surrounded that platform were half-height. They were also broken; the remnants of a rope ladder clung to spindles of aged wood. Jewel reached out for it anyway, and as she touched its coarse, dry strands, the wagon creaked, as if groaning beneath the whole of its ancient weight.

It fell. The impact raised clouds of dry dust; they looked, for a moment, like smoke—but only a moment; the real thing came when the fire crawled over its fallen shape, pausing there to feed.

Twice more she ran to the wagons that remained, and twice more she saw the symbols painted on their sides, their doors, as the black and life-less corpses of living magic; twice more, the fire paused in its pursuit just long enough to consume what was left. Lyserra, Corrona, Havalla, Arkosa. The Voyani Matriarchs had clearly abandoned their ancient, moving seats; there was no safety to be found in any of them.

It was a dream, she thought, and began once again to run—almost to crawl, she was bent so low to the ground—toward the last of the wagons she'd seen at a distance. She should've come to this one first, because it was the only one that was visibly, obviously, in the air. But it was *high* in the damn air, and she hadn't sprouted wings in the interim. She shouted, cupping her hands over her mouth, attempting to funnel sound in the dry air, the dry heat; that much she could do, the sound was on the edge of a scream.

The wagon's distant driver must have heard her; it began to move, maneuvering in a way that was deliberate, toward her. She saw the trail-ing, twisting end-knot of a long, thick rope and cursed. She'd never been the world's best rope climber. The thick, ungainly ladders, with their wooden, slat rungs, were her preference. But the fire was an argument she couldn't win.

She jumped for the knotted rope as it swung above her upturned face. Wind blew it out of the grip of her trembling fingers. She cursed again—loudly, deliberately—all the while continuing to strain, arms uplifted; she could feel the fire at her back now, was aware that it was almost upon her.

It hurt. She thought it burned, the pain was so sudden, so pitched—but she smelled no singed flesh, felt no spreading heat. Whenever she'd accidentally courted flame before, the first thing to curl and blacken had always been her hair. She caught the rope on its third pass. The rope wasn't her problem now; it was her weight, her hands, the strength of her shaking arms; she struggled to pull herself up off the ground, hand over hand; she kicked her boots off and thought she heard a brief hiss and pop as they landed.

Chapter Eighteen

"MOVE! MOVE!" SHE SHOUTED toward the floating vessel as she clung. She twisted the end of her rope around her foot, using the large terminating knot as an awkward step. Chancing one downward glance, she saw the fire; it had spread. Each of the wagons was burning in its wake, but the flame hadn't yet managed to reduce them to ash; she was certain that had she been caught in its folds she wouldn't have been as lucky.

Her foot slipped; the rope itself was slippery with dry sand, dry dust. The wagon hadn't budged an inch since she'd started to climb; it was as if she were ballast, anchor, something to hold it in place. The only solution that came to mind didn't involve her survival. Her hands were slippery now; the fire was hotter, wider. It seemed to encompass more and more of the desert sand until all she could see were fields of orange, moving at the whim of different breezes.

Her hands slid. Her foot slipped. She strained against gravity.

"What are you *doing*, stupid girl?"

She'd never been so happy to hear Shadow's voice, and felt almost certain she would never be so happy again. She was certain she would open her eyes—now—and see his, golden and faintly luminescent, in the darkness of her own room. But as she turned in the direction of the voice itself, she discovered she was wrong. She was still clinging helplessly to a stretch of old rope, still attached, very tentatively, to the side of a wagon that wouldn't, without magic and blood, be airborne at all, and still suspended above a fire whose voice nonetheless seemed chill and cold.

Shadow's ash-gray wings were spread, tip to tip, almost motionless as he glided toward her. His ears were pointed up, toward the sun; his hackles had risen, his claws were extended. "Stupid, *stupid* girl!"

"Can you get beneath me and catch me when I let go?"

His familiar hiss was almost a comfort, as he tilted in air. His idea of remaining stationary wasn't helpful, though, and in the end, when Jewel's hands failed to obey her command to take the risk of missing his moving back, he snarled another few rounds of *stupid*, and flew up. She thought he might abandon her, but instead, he came in from above—and grabbed the back of her tunic in what she assumed was his jaws. She started to tell him she didn't trust the strength of the cloth, but didn't have the chance; he didn't tell her to let go of the rope. Instead, he climbed, wings definitely flapping now as he gained height.

What had been an insurmountable distance by length of rope was achieved by dint of annoyed cat. He set her down on the platform that fronted the wagon; she stood with her back flush against the nearest standing surface, and looked down, her hands still bone-white and stuck in a death grip around the rope itself.

He didn't join her, but flew in tight circles in the air above the front half of the wagon.

"Will you *stop* calling me stupid?" she finally said, when her arms had stopped their uncontrollable shudder.

"Maybe when you are *less* stupid. What are you *doing* here?"

"Pardon?"

"Why are you *here*? This is not a good place for you, *stupid girl*."

Her jaw slackened; she slammed it shut in a teeth-rattling way. "This may come as a surprise to you, but it's a *dream*, Shadow. I don't normally get to choose."

Shadow hissed. He landed to one side of her. His wings nearly knocked her off the flying wagon; she almost didn't bother to get out of his way. If she fell, she'd wake up; she'd had that experience dozens of times, at a variety of ages. Age hadn't improved it much. But dream or no, Jewel clung to survival; she always had. She thudded against the cabin as Shadow folded his wings, glaring at his back.

"Stupid."

"You could at least use different words for variety's sake." She frowned as she looked at the minuscule deck beneath the cat's paws—his claws were extended, and they weren't a boon for the short wooden slats. This

was, of course, a dream—and those slats now extended, turning the ungainly, rectangular body of a wagon with largely motionless wheels into
something that might have graced a small ship.

"Jewel," Shadow finally said, his voice lowering into the beginning of
a growl. "Where are we going?"

"Why are you asking me?"

"Because the wagon is *moving*."

"Shadow—it's moving on its own. I'm not steering, you'll notice."

"I *noticed*, yes. That's why I'm *asking*."

Resisting the urge to throttle the cat—largely because she suspected
her hands wouldn't actually fit around his throat—she said, "I'm not the
captain. It's a dream. I have no idea where we're flying; I only know it's
better than being reduced to ash."

"*Is* it?" he hissed.

She looked. The sky had lost its startling clarity in the space of a few
sharp words; it was darkening, and not in a way that implied night. "Tell
me that's not a storm."

He hissed again; water began to fall in large, cold splotches across the
deck. Jewel turned instinctively for the door she knew was there; she
found it, reached for it, and stopped before she touched its tarnished
handle.

Her hand was bleeding.

Shadow's hiss gave way to a far less comfortable rumbling growl, shorn
of words, as her blood fell from her palm to the wooden flooring. She
turned her hand over; it was pale, but uncut. Blood now fell from the back
of her hand, instead. The skies darkened; the rain fell more heavily. Shadow's fur flattened; so did Jewel's hair. She turned toward the door again,
and this time, the blood didn't stop her from grabbing the handle.

It was locked. Thunder suppressed most of the words that followed this
discovery. The door was thick and solid; sun had bleached its timbers,
although the falling rain darkened them now. She rattled the handle, and
then gave up, banging on the door until Shadow almost knocked her over.
She heard another iteration of stupid and girl as she struggled back to her
feet.

"It's locked!"

His eyes became as round as coins. "Then *open* it!"

She remembered why she'd never been particularly fond of cats, even
the small furry variety; if they could talk at all, she was certain they'd

sound just like Shadow. The rain wouldn't have been so bad if the water hadn't been so damn cold. Her hand was still bleeding, but the moving stream of water that now traveled across boards and over the edge of the ungainly, flying wagon thinned its vivid red, washing it clean.

Her hand was still uncut—it was a hell of a lot wetter, though.

Shadow was now making the type of gurgling sound associated with unhappy, wet children. Although she suspected he lived to be annoying, this was the first time she had ever seen him look pathetic. "If you were stone," she told him, between the lulls in the storm's roar, "the water wouldn't bother you."

He hissed. "If it were *Winter*, the water *wouldn't matter*." He roared back at the sky, and even bedraggled as he was, his voice was almost a match for the storm's.

Frowning as his words tickled something she couldn't quite remember, she said, "It *is* winter."

His eyes grew round again, and this time, they shone.

"Shadow—are we *on* the hidden path? Now?" She turned toward the closed door of the wagon, and wondered if she would meet the wagon's Matriarch on the other side of it. There didn't seem to be much way to find out.

But staring, she remembered watching the Arkosan Matriarch painting symbols with her bowl of ink. She raised both of her hands. Margret of the Arkosan Voyani had labored for hours marking the exterior of the wagon with unfamiliar runes; Jewel had inferred only later that without the runes, the wagons themselves wouldn't fly.

There were no runes here, and the wagon was demonstrably in the air. Jewel reached out with the flats of both palms and touched not the handle, but the door itself. She couldn't remember the runes Margret had so carefully painted, and even if she had, the rain would have made repetition of the act impossible. But she remembered that she had given her blood to the ink that Margret had used—and at the moment, the blood that fell from no visible wounds was all the ink she had.

It's a dream, she thought. *It's only a dream.* Finch and Teller had often found it strange that she could be aware of the fact she was dreaming while she was dreaming; they weren't. Nor was she always aware in that fashion; sometimes she was so caught up in reacting to what she felt she'd no time to think. But she knew, tonight; she knew.

Her hands grew warm as she pressed them firmly into the door's wooden surface; her face grew cold. Wind had joined water in its bitter assault; she could hardly feel her cheeks at all. Shadow came to stand beside her—where beside meant practically on top—and leaned into as much of her as he could. He didn't call her stupid, and he didn't ask why she was taking so long. That should have been a sign.

But dreams had their own logic, their own shorthand, their own reality. Blood seeped from her palms, spreading visibly between her splayed fingers like slender, red filaments. These, however, the water didn't wash away; they spread, like the finest of veins in autumn leaves, branching up and out in all directions. She had hoped—had meant—the blood to take the form of runes or sigils, but dreams were unpredictable. Like horses that knew she was nervous, they carried her where they wanted to go, and she stayed on for the ride—if she were lucky.

Today, instead of sigils, they gave her veins. No, she thought, watching as the thunder was joined, at last, by the white flash of lightning that momentarily changed all color, they had given her roots. What had her Oma told her, so long ago? Roots traveled into the ground seeking water. She remembered it clearly because at the time, it had made no sense. Dirt was solid. Water was not. The roots were *in* the dirt. She'd been young enough that she could argue with her Oma and not feel the sting of the older woman's hand; she'd never been young enough to be spared the edge of her tongue.

But Rath had explained it differently, or perhaps, having lost everything that made the world make any sense at all, she'd given up on sense; the tree would die if the roots sought water; they'd drown. These roots were attempting to find their earth. Shadow rubbed his nose against the side of her tunic as they spread across the whole of the door's surface and finally slid beyond it through the seams of its frame. Leaving her left hand on the door, she grasped its handle with her right, and this time, the door opened; she could feel its mechanism click, but couldn't actually hear it over the storm.

Lightning, which had continued its startling white monologue, remained suspended in the sky for a long time, as if it wanted to see what lay beyond the wagon's door. So did Jewel, and she stood suspended for far longer, her hand falling away from the handle to rest on Shadow's head.

"I don't understand," she said. The rain was falling only on one side of the door, but it had become momentarily insignificant. What lay on the other side was nothing small enough—or dark enough, lamps notwithstanding—to grace a wagon. She knew; she'd been in similar wagons before, confined by the cramped and very narrowly spaced walls, the small windows—always latched—the thick air, the lack of sky.

But she'd been in the room that waited on the other side of the open door as well: It was The Terafin's library. Her personal library. Even from this angle, Jewel could see the night sky through the oval glass windows laid into the ceiling at its height.

Shadow, who clearly hated the water, strained toward the threshold—but her hand was an anchor; he didn't cross it. More significantly, he didn't ask her what she was waiting for. The room appeared to be unoccupied, and it looked exactly as Jewel remembered it—books whose titles she couldn't read were stacked in their familiar, slightly unkempt piles, with one or two lying open beneath the glow of magelight. All that was missing was The Terafin herself.

The rain was cold, the cat was loud, the thunder louder still. Jewel stood in the doorway for another long breath, and then she came in, as it were, out of the rain. Only when she had one foot firmly across the threshold did Shadow join her—but he moved faster.

She cringed as he shook himself dry, and opened her mouth to shout at him; water in the quantities they currently carried in either drenched clothing or fur was *not* good for books. No words came; before they could, the door to the library opened. She didn't see it, because she was facing the doors visitors—the few The Terafin chose to invite into her inner sanctum—would have used. But she heard it and turned, dripping water, hair hanging loose and wet in her eyes.

The Terafin entered her library carrying, of all things, a sword. It was a long sword—far too long for either The Terafin's use, or Jewel's. Jewel recognized it almost instantly, although it had been well over a decade since she had seen it last, and longer still since she'd seen it used. It was Rath's sword. Rath had left his wealthy family, his Isle home, and his inheritance; the only thing he had kept for himself—besides the very rare use of his name—was this sword. It had been a gift, Jewel remembered, although she couldn't remember from who.

Jewel had taken it with her on the day she left his final home in the thirty-fifth holding—or perhaps the day after; memory was dim and she'd never been good with numbers of any kind.

Nor did it matter, because she did remember how The Terafin had come by it: it had also been a gift, this time from Jewel, the only other person in the House who could speak Rath's name, and then, only in the perfect privacy of The Terafin's rooms.

This is a dream, Jewel thought, because Amarais walked past her, past Shadow, without comment; she paused at the table upon which her books had been momentarily abandoned. Her color, in the magelight was poor, and her expression caused Jewel to flinch and turn away.

"Who is *she*?" Shadow whispered.

"The Terafin," Jewel replied. She didn't bother to whisper; she *knew* that The Terafin wouldn't hear her speak. Nor did she. The door opened again, and The Terafin straightened shoulders, her face once again settling into a far more familiar expression. Morretz joined her. He held out a great cape, settling its weight around her shoulders. He also pinned it, because she didn't put the sword down.

"Will you do this?" he asked her back. He looked as weary as The Terafin, although Jewel couldn't clearly pinpoint why; she had never completely understood Morretz, although she'd never questioned his devotion to his Lord. The Terafin moved instead of answering, the sword now cradled in her arms, the cloak briefly concealing it. He followed her toward the doors.

Shadow's eyes were luminescent now. So were Jewel's, briefly. She waited until Morretz had cleared the door's frame, and then followed them into the hall. There, by the door, were Torvan and Arrendas, unseeing as they so often were when they were on duty. She resisted the urge to touch them or wave a hand in front of their faces, in part because she saw what their stiff and unmoving faces somehow still revealed as they watched The Terafin walk down the hall, her domicis in her wake.

She wanted to turn, to ask them—no, to demand to know—what day it was, what date, what time. They watched her as if they knew what she knew: that she would die soon; that it couldn't, in spite of their guard, her domicis, and her planning, be prevented.

"She is not like your den," Shadow whispered. "I'm not sure I *like* her."

"No," Jewel replied. "You probably wouldn't have. She's dead now."

The cat hissed. "She doesn't *look* dead."

"It's a dream, Shadow."

A dream that led them, at last, to one of the fountains that graced the terrace that preceded the gardens to which visitors and dignitaries of import were taken during warmer months. It was not, by the way Amarais

drew her cloak more tightly around her shoulders, warm now. Nor was it
day; it was night; the moons were bright, the stars cutting and clear, like
points of the needles she so disliked.

Jewel couldn't feel the cold, although she still squelched water at every
step. Shadow, however, was dry.

The fountain was enchanted in such a way that its water never froze.
The water itself was probably a lot warmer than either the air or The
Terafin. To Jewel's surprise, The Terafin nodded and Morretz began to
gesture; his hands were enveloped by soft, gray light. Were it not so dark,
she might have missed it.

But had she, she wouldn't have missed what followed: The Terafin took
a step up, and the air held her. She took another step, lifted the folds of
her simple skirts to take the third; she now stood above the fountain's low
and very simple basin. Morretz held his hands out, palm up, as if he were
carrying the whole of her weight.

"Thank you," she said. She didn't look back, or down, to see him. Instead, she walked across air, as if a floor of glass had been erected beneath
her feet. Jewel frowned. There was a small statuary at the center of the
fountain, with three deliberately featureless women, hands joined, facing
outward in a very small circle. Their fingers were not distinct, and their
hair was an incline of stone that seemed to drift in one mass down their
equally indistinct shoulders. They were of a height, and at least in this
light, of a color; in the brighter light of day, there were variances in the
stone itself. Jewel had never loved this fountain, but many of the visitors
did.

The Terafin reached the first of these figures; she stood, feet at the
height of their knees. "Morretz?"

He nodded; Jewel saw his grimace; The Terafin did not. She rose, this
time discarding the artifice of steps; only when she had cleared the shoulders of these stone women did she halt. Her cloak and her skirts trailed
over their faces, the representation of their hair, veiling them until she was
clear. When she stood in their center—and it was not a large space—she
called to Morretz again, and this time, she descended.

She still carried the sword, but not for much longer; she set it down,
tip first, as if even now she would change her mind. But that was not The
Terafin that Jewel knew, and no matter how diminished she might be or
become, Amarais Handernesse ATerafin would never be that woman; she
had made her decision.

Her breath was sharp, singular, but she released the sword. It stood, on point, at the very center of the fountain; it didn't fall. When her hands were free and clear, she began to rise again as Morretz gestured. But she commanded him to stop when she was once again at the height of the statues' shoulders, and when she did she knelt, her knees touching air and stone as she lifted her hands—shaking hands—to her neck. In the moonlight, she lifted something over her head—a chain, or something similarly slender and weighted. She draped this, knotting its links, around the hilt of the abandoned sword, and then she lowered her face for a long, long moment.

When she rose, she turned toward Morretz, for she'd knelt with her back to him. Even now, Jewel thought, she guarded all expression of pain or sorrow. But Morretz knew. The Chosen knew. And Jewel, watching, knew as well. It was possible to think of, to acknowledge the fact of, The Terafin's loss, her sorrow—but it was almost always an entirely intellectual exercise. It was impossible to think of her as frightened.

Nor was she as she walked across air toward the man who supported the whole of her weight. She began to descend as she reached him, her fingers shifting the cloak's clasp.

"It is done," she told her domicis.

He said nothing; there was usually nothing one could say to The Terafin when she was like this. She asked for no comfort, accepted no advice, looked for no dream of hope with which she could deny reality. And yet, when she was like this, Jewel *wanted* to give her all these things.

Wanted, Jewel thought, remembering. The Terafin would never be like this again. She was gone, now. The floor of Mandaros' Hall was beneath her feet. Mandaros was god of Judgment, not Justice, and the gods had always said that the dead who waited could choose the moment they approached his throne, bowed head, and surrendered themselves to that judgment.

Duster would take forever, if she ever approached that throne; she might linger on the banks of the river on death's side of the bridge, watching and waiting for her den-kin to join her.

But not The Terafin. For The Terafin, all decisions were action, even the decision to remain inactive. Jewel couldn't imagine that she would sit idle, by those banks, watching for the dead. Maybe, she thought, Rath was waiting there. Maybe The Terafin would finally—finally—be reconciled with the brother she had abandoned.

Or perhaps she had nothing left to wait for; Morretz was also dead. Morretz, whose hands, trembling with the effort of his silent spell, now readjusted the fall of her cloak before he let those hands fall away. He then walked to the fountain, where the sword waited. This time, his spell was more complicated; the colors of the light that left his hands in slender, binding threads varied in brightness and depth of hue.

Jewel watched as the sword grew slowly translucent, becoming a ghost of itself, as insubstantial as the rest of the ghosts that had, and would always, haunt her.

She reached out—for what, she wasn't certain—as the blade vanished, and Morretz's oddly graceful motions of hand and light through air came to a close. His arms dropped; they were trembling. Neither he nor the Lord he served appeared to notice. He bowed to her; she inclined her head, regal as a Queen. A weary, heartbroken Queen, who had at last acknowledged what was lost to her. She had never been young in Jewel's eyes—but she had been young once, and the only physical links to that youth had been broken here. Jewel knew it not because she was seer-born, although that was both her gift and her curse, but because she could see it so clearly in The Terafin's face.

"Amarais," she said, voice breaking between the second and third syllables. The Terafin didn't turn, didn't glance toward her.

"Why are you crying?" Shadow whispered.

She woke, tears trailing down the sides of her face; they were silent; she could do that much. The ceiling above was familiar; it was her bedroom's. She rose. Avandar, contours of his face made sharper by the light that shone in his hands, opened his eyes. He opened his mouth to speak, and shut it as her expression became clear. He offered her no words, made no attempt to comfort. He had never before reminded her of Morretz; the two could hardly have been more different.

But in his patient silence this eve, he did. Even Shadow's habitual whining voice did not break the quiet. She dressed in the partial light, choosing clothing that required no aid to don. Avandar stood and retrieved only her jacket and her cloak. The former, he handed her; the latter, he held up. She turned her back and he slid it over her shoulders, but he didn't touch the clasp.

While she fastened it, he opened her bedroom door.

Torvan and Corrin were standing to either side of its frame. New to the West Wing was the expensive conceit of magelights, which now adorned the walls in even intervals along the hall. Torvan didn't look at her; nor did he speak. But when she turned and walked down the hall toward the exit, he fell in behind her, as natural as shadow, although admittedly more noisy. The other Shadow allowed the captain this much without comment.

They picked up Gordon and Marave when they left the den's rooms. As Torvan, they were silent; their armor made all of the sound they allowed themselves. But where she went, they followed. She didn't want them, but the burden of arguing with Torvan was too costly this eve.

They didn't ask her where she was going. Had they, she might not have gone at all; she might have turned back, crawled under both covers and cat, and attempted to sleep out the night. But they gave her the space she needed, and she came, at last, to the terrace and its famed fountain.

In the darkness, the statues lost the harsh definition of their building materials, and perhaps this was why their sculptor had given them such soft, ill defined lines: they seemed delicate, almost alive, in the evening. The moons were not quite full, but waning, they shed their distant silver light across everything: across the fountain and its constantly moving water; across the gardens and their towering new trees; across the manse, its gates, and the streets beyond which it stood, remote and unapproachable. Although she couldn't see them, she knew the hundred holdings, even the poorest, saw the moonlight in the same way; what the moon saw was different. But people, rich and poor, slept; people, rich and poor, dreamed. People, rich and poor, were being born while the moons watched. They were also undoubtedly dying.

"ATerafin," Avandar said, as she walked across the terrace, rather than toward the steps.

She glanced at him; he was the only man present who spoke, although she was certain the Chosen were equally confused; when she left her rooms at this time of night, it was for the shrine, not the fountain. Shadow glanced at her, and as the Chosen fanned out at her back, he pressed himself into her left side. It was not coincidentally the side that Avandar generally occupied.

"Are you certain this is wise?" he asked.

She failed to hear him; at the moment it took almost no effort. The statues were tall enough and tightly enough entwined that she could get to the small space in their center without climbing up and over their shoulders or arms. Their arms were lower, but much thinner, and if she somehow managed to break or damage them, she wouldn't have to worry about something as inconsequential as a House War; she'd be on the run from the Master Gardener for the rest of her natural life.

"Allow me," Avandar said, from her right. She turned to look at him at the exact moment she began to rise. Given almost no warning, she lost her balance and fell flat out in the middle of the air. He caught her. For Avandar, he was even gentle. The Terafin hadn't lost her balance, and now that Jewel was moving in the same way, she was impressed. Avandar wasn't making air solid beneath her feet, so it wasn't as if she was standing on a platform. No—it was as if he'd gripped both of her ankles in either of his hands, and had hoisted her into the air. What grace or balance she managed to achieve was entirely up to her.

She didn't manage a lot of it, but it didn't matter; her audience was Torvan and the Chosen she'd known since her arrival at the manse. They'd certainly seen her with much less dignity. She paused for just a moment, and glanced at the four, wondering if the night had changed things between them—if they now expected that her dignity did matter. They'd never say anything, of course—but their dignity was never, and had never, been in question.

She would have to live up to the Chosen. Funny, how that hadn't even been a thought when she stood at the House shrine, demanding their oaths upon the altar.

She managed to stay upright as Avandar carried her over the heads of the three stone women. She felt the hint of his curiosity, no more. He didn't know what she sought here, but knew it was of significance to her.

Yes, Jewel, he said. She startled, windmilled, and managed not to fall again. He seldom used that voice, and never when she wasn't in danger or he wasn't annoyed. Shadow, who had the good sense to have wings, pushed himself off the ground; his leap carried him far above her head. To reach her height he had to dive, sweep, and hover.

Avandar set her down as gently as he could. Jewel frowned as she reached out, and her hand passed through air.

"Well?" Shadow asked, from a safe distance above her head.

She shook her head. "It was real," she told him. "I know it." But real or no, her hand still passed through air. Closing her eyes, she cursed her memory; it had felt so real, but she could barely recall what she'd seen.

Morretz had spoken, yes; his voice had been soft enough that she hadn't caught the words. Nor did she expect that the syllables themselves would help her here; they were magic foci, and she was not a mage. But . . . a nimbus of pale light had surrounded his hands: gray, blue, violet.

The gray had been the strongest. Gray was . . . was teleportation, it was motion, lifting at a distance. Blue was water or air, but both of those were beyond Morretz, beyond the merely mortal; what did blue mean? Vision, she thought. Sight. Violet she knew as the casement of illusion. Had there been other colors?

She opened her eyes, let her hands drop to her sides, and looked, once again, at the moonlight.

"It's too early," she said quietly. "The moons aren't at the right height."
Too early?

She nodded. "It's not far off the right time."

She felt Avandar's sudden surprise; it was followed by chagrin. He gave voice to neither. She was not feeling particularly generous, and did. "You didn't think he had this in him?"

"If what you imply is true," Avandar replied, raising voice instead of enforcing privacy, "I admit I did not. He was seldom concerned with this particular type of almost theoretical magery."

"He looked . . . tired, after he'd finished."

"That does not surprise me, ATerafin." He joined her in the small space, leaping as gracefully and powerfully from the stone terrace as Shadow had, but landing instead. There wasn't a lot of room, but Jewel attempted to make space for him, pressing up against the cold stone of one statue's back. He gestured, but it was brief, controlled; in the moonlight, she saw no change at all in his expression. "How long," he finally asked, "must you wait?"

She glanced at the moons. "Not long," she replied.

"What do you hope to find?"

She shrugged; the gesture was her shield.

A quarter of an hour passed. To Jewel, the night sky looked the same; there was a breeze, but no wind, and few clouds to alter or veil the light. But in the narrow space left between her and her domicis, the air began to change.

"Can you see it?" she asked softly.

His silence was his answer: No. After a moment, he asked "What do you see, ATerafin?"

"Light," was her response. "Light. It's pale; gray, blue, a hint of violet."

His frown was now visible. He passed both hands through the empty air, and light eddied around them as if it were smoke; it didn't cling. "I am impressed. I do not think that any save you will find what was placed here. Was it significant?"

"No. The significant things, she left with Arann and me." As she said it, she loathed the words. What had been left *was* significant; it just wasn't political.

"This was not Morretz's idea, then."

"Does it matter?" she asked, irritation sharpening the edge of her voice.

It was Avandar's turn to shrug. "Not, clearly, to either you or the person who placed it here."

She might have said more, but the colors in the air suddenly brightened enough that she had to squint or be momentarily blinded. "I'd move your hands if I were you," she told him.

He did, but with reluctance—as if he wished to test himself against whatever magics Morretz had set in place. If Carver had done the same, it wouldn't have surprised her. She apparently expected more from a man who was, to all intents and purposes, immortal.

He raised a brow, glancing at her; his smile was brief and bitter. "I am a mortal," he said softly. "My inability to die does not change that fact."

"It does, by strict definition."

"And you have now become the arbiter of definition?"

"Of my own, and I hadn't noticed you were speaking to anyone else at the moment."

He chuckled; his hands fell at once to his sides. "Indeed."

"He's dead, Avandar," she added, in a quieter tone of voice.

"So, too, is The Terafin—but you are measured against her, regardless."

"You were never measured against Morretz."

"In my role as domicis, ATerafin, I have never been measured against anyone else in this House."

Her brows rose. "And you cared?"

He chuckled again. "No, ATerafin. No, and yes."

He meant it, which surprised her. "What's the yes part?"

"I am domicis for a reason. If I succeed in learning whatever this position is meant to teach me, I might at last know a measure of peace."

"And if you fail?"

His smile was once again bitter, but it was less brief. Looking up, for a moment, at the moons' faces, he replied. "I will live forever."

The desire for immortality was often what drove the mage-born into the folly of service to the demon Lords and their god; she wondered if knowledge of Avandar's experience could change that desire at all. Given the mage-born and their peculiar focus and arrogance, she doubted it. "And Morretz was a success."

"As domicis? Yes."

"But not as a mage."

"In this age, in this diminished, impoverished age, he would perhaps not be considered a failure. As a mage, however, he had nothing at all to teach me; an infant does not teach a man to run."

"No—but maybe how to crawl, if it comes to that."

"That was my thought."

"I know. Morretz deserves better than that."

He surprised her. "Perhaps."

But she had no more time for surprise, no more time for this conversation—which would continue, she thought, for months or years, unfinished. The light was sharp and harsh, the shape defined: she saw Rath's sword suspended an inch or less above the ground. It shone, as if it were a vessel for Morretz's magic; she reached out with both hands and wrapped them around the hilt.

It wasn't cold. It was hand-warm, as if it had just been released. She lifted it, and it gained weight and substance as she did, the light that surrounded the whole of its blade dimming as she watched. She saw that a necklace had indeed been wrapped around the sword's hilt, and that something hung from it, clinking against the sheath. But she waited for the light to dim. Only when it was done did she turn to Avandar, her arms wrapped around the sword as if it were a slender, heavy child.

"Get us out of here."

He nodded.

She did not examine the sword until she was once again in her rooms; instead she covered it awkwardly with the folds of her cloak as she made her way through the night halls of the Terafin manse. Magelights and oil lamps could be seen no matter where she looked, and everywhere light gathered, so too the servants, a small army of determined men and women. The Master of the Household Staff was in evidence; in the gentle

ambient light, the iron gray of her hair looked as if it had finally surrendered to white. This did not, however, make her appear to be in any way
fragile, and it certainly didn't soften her voice.

Jewel's walk slowed as she watched the Terafin servants at work. No
speck of dust or dirt would dare show itself, when the guests were welcomed into the foyer; no button on uniform would be left unpolished, no
hair would be out of place.

They did this, Jewel thought, for Amarais Handernesse ATerafin. She
was dead, but dead, she commanded this last, singular gesture of respect.
If she was gone, the House she had built remained, and the House would
not expose her reign to ridicule or question. Jewel wanted, for one ridicu-
lous moment, to pick up a cloth and join them as they worked—it was
work that had to be done, and it was simple, if hard.

But the Master of the Household Staff took a very, very dim view of such
interference, and in truth, Jewel would not do nearly as good a job, because
it wasn't hers. She therefore picked up speed again, and reached the relative
safety of her wing. At the outer doors, two of the four guards once again
took up their positions. Ellerson was awake and waiting when she cleared
those doors; he offered her, of all things, warm milk and silence.

She accepted both with gratitude and entered her rooms. Shadow
stepped on her cloak. She kicked him, and he hissed—mostly in amusement. "It's not a very good sword," he said, as she set it on the bed. Avandar gestured and the room was lit, harshly and brightly, by his magic.

"It's what passes for a good sword among the patriciate," Jewel told
him, "and if you use it as a chew toy, I will—"

"Yesss?"

"Think of something horrible to do. Make you eat Carver's cooking."

Shadow hissed again, and bounded onto the bed, where he deposited
himself more or less dead center and began to clean his wings.

Jewel lifted the chain that was wrapped around the sword's pommel; it
had, in the way of slender gold chains everywhere, tangled into small,
linked knots and she had to work to disentangle them. But she did the
work, because she could clearly see what lay at its end: a ring. *A large ring,*
she thought; *a Lord's ring.* It was heavy, solid gold, into which an H had
been deeply, and elegantly, engraved. At the end points of each of the
vertical bars that comprised the letter was a ruby of moderate size. One of
the four was cracked or chipped. She opened the chain's clasp and slid the
ring off it, where it sat with authority in the palm of her hand.

"It's the Handernesse family crest," she finally said, her voice tailing up at the end.

Avandar examined it—without touching it or taking it from her—and nodded. "It is."

"And Rath's sword. The sword his grandfather gave him when he was younger and still a member of the House." She closed her eyes and leaned against the bed's edge, lowering her head. "She left them for me."

"It appears that way, yes. I am uncertain as to why she felt it necessary to go to such extremes to see the items in your hand; were I The Terafin, I would have simply given them into Gabriel's keeping."

Jewel opened her eyes. "I know why."

"Ah."

She lifted the sword from the bed and handed it to Avandar; she slid the chain around her own neck. The ring, however, she slid over her thumb. It was a tight fit—but at least it didn't fall off the way it had when she'd tried it on any of the fingers.

"Let me adjust it, ATerafin," Avandar offered.

"I don't think we have time—oh. You mean magically."

"I do."

She shook her head. "Maybe later."

"You don't intend to wear it for the funeral rites?"

She turned toward the bed, and lifted the scabbard of Rath's sword. After a moment's hesitation, she knelt by her bedside and very carefully placed the sword beneath it. It was what Rath had done with it, after all—for decades.

"Jewel."

She rose, shedding cloak and clothing with care. "I'm wearing it."

"The Terafin did not."

"Not where everyone could see it, no."

"Then may I suggest that you follow her example? She left you the necklace."

"I'll keep it for later," she replied. She set the clothing in a clump on the nearest chair. "Tomorrow, I want to wear it."

His voice softened. "Jewel, she can't see it."

"We don't know what the dead can—or can't—see. Tomorrow, if she's somehow watching, I want her to see the ring."

"Why?"

"Because," she said, grunting as she attempted to push Shadow to the left side of the bed, "She left it. For *me*. I can't wear the sword—I would, if I could think of a way to do it that didn't cause Gabriel headaches—but I *can* wear the ring."

"Jewel—"

"I dreamed of her." She slid beneath the counterpane and the heavy down comforter; Shadow condescended to lift his bulk for as long as it took her to pull both out from under his weight. Her head sank into her pillows; her hair drifted into her eyes.

"A true dream?"

"I dreamed," she continued, staring open eyed at the darkened ceiling above her, "that she took this sword and this ring to that fountain. She and Morretz. Not even the Chosen were there."

"When?"

"I don't know, Avandar. After my departure, but before her death. More than that, I can't say. She meant them for me," she added, her voice finally beginning to crack. "She meant me to find them. I *saw* her."

"Did she speak at all?"

"Yes—but not to me. I wasn't with her, in my dream; I was observing her. I couldn't touch her. I couldn't say any of the things I wanted to say." He was kind enough not to ask her what those were. Her hand closed in a fist around the ring—a fist that would have annoyed Rath endlessly because thumbs-on-the-inside were just asking for broken thumbs in a fight.

"You saw the past," he finally said.

"I saw the past. Before you ask, no, I didn't get to choose what I saw. It was a dream—I'm used to just following those to their end. But I knew what I saw was real. I knew it had happened." She closed her eyes, and then opened them again, turning her head to see Shadow's, unblinking, in the darkness. She reached out to touch his fur, felt it, solid and warm, beneath her hand, and closed her eyes again.

"I was there," Shadow said. She opened her eyes; he was looking at Avandar, his wings folded, his tail twitching.

"Pardon?"

"I was *there* with her. I saw what *she* saw."

Avandar was silent for a long moment. "Jewel—"

"I know. But he's a cat. They go where they want. I couldn't keep him out of my dreams if I tried."

"You need to learn," Shadow told her. "Your dreams will not be safe until you do."

"You could just stay out of them."

He hissed. "If I stay out, *stupid* girl, who will *protect* you from the others? Who will stop you from getting *lost*? Your dreams are real, now. They can kill you."

"Why do you care?"

"It's less boring," he replied. "Now go to sleep."

"Will I dream again?"

He opened one eye. "I will *eat* your dreams. But only for tonight. I don't *like* the way they taste."

"ATerafin," Avandar said softly, "you must speak with the Oracle, soon."

She knew it was true. "Speak to me in four days," she told him. "In four days, I'll be ready to think about anything."

He fell silent.

"Tonight," she told him, surprising them both, "I only want to think about her. She left me Rath's sword. She left me the ring. They weren't for the House—they were for *me*. I'll never be able to talk to her again, and I *want to*, Avandar. I want to ask her all the questions I should have asked and didn't, because I was afraid to take the House. I want to ask her about Gabriel, about the Chosen, about the shrine; I want to ask her about Rymark.

"I want to tell her—" She stopped for a moment, took control of her voice, and spoke again. "I want to tell her that she was my family and I was her den-kin."

"She knew."

But Jewel had seen The Terafin's face on that moonlit eve in which she had given over the last of Rath's items—the last things that bound her, as sister, to the man who had found, and saved, Jewel. There was no one, now, who loved Rath the way Jewel had, and Amarais had hesitated until the last moment, as if in surrendering these private, apolitical items, she was at last surrendering to the inevitability of her own death.

And that was unfair: The Terafin had never surrendered. She had always planned for both failure and success, had always balanced the well-being of her House between the two. She had fought, playing every variant of the game she could see; she couldn't see the demon that had killed her in the end. No one had; had they, there would be no funeral.

She closed her eyes.

"Sleep, Jewel," Avandar said. "I will watch."

"No, don't. Shadow doesn't need sleep; you do. I don't know what you and Celleriant have been doing—and I should, and you'll tell me—but you need sleep at least as much as I do."

"My dreams will not kill me."

"Avandar, I've seen your dreams. If I die in mine, I'd still consider myself better off." She heard his steps, tensed as he approached the bedside. But he stopped there, gazing down at her.

Will you end it? he asked.

She couldn't answer. She knew what he wanted. She even understood why. But she also understood that if he succeeded, he would be gone. She had lived with his arrogance, his irritation, his anger, and his very occasional approval for half her life; she would have sworn, had anyone asked, that she'd be happy to be rid of him. And she would.

But not that way. She was so tired of death and loss.

Chapter Nineteen

4th of Henden, 427 A.A.
Terafin Manse, Averalaan Aramarelas

THE WEST WING was a hive of activity beyond Jewel's closed doors; she could hear moving discussions, shouting—that would be Carver—and the frantic knocking at her door. She ignored it for as long as she could, because she'd slept, and it had been so mercifully dreamless, she didn't want to wake.

When the knocking transformed itself into a snarling roar, however, she rolled bleary-eyed out of bed.

"It's just Snow," Shadow said with a sniff.

Avandar was sleeping in a chair. Guilt therefore made getting out of bed a necessity, and it all but demanded best behavior. She walked quietly past him, slightly alarmed that the noise hadn't jarred him out of sleep.

Shadow had been entirely correct; Snow was bristling in the doorway by the time she had it open. Two of the Chosen were on guard, but it was a different two; they looked distinctly uncomfortable about Snow's presence. Their hands were on the hilts of their swords, but as no one else in the wing—and at the moment, that included Angel and Teller—were reacting much, they hadn't drawn them.

"You two," she said, probably breaking half a dozen etiquette rules, "don't you need to dress?"

They were demonstrably dressed, but they exchanged a brief glance.

"We'll have the chance when the captains relieve us," Gordon told her. "Don't worry."

"Oh, it's not worry," she replied. "Misery loves company, and *I* have to dress for the occasion."

"She does," Teller said gravely. "Haval's waiting."

"Haval didn't even *make* my dress—" she shut up as Snow hissed. "I'll be there after I've—"

"Eaten?"

She nodded.

Ellerson had arranged for breakfast in the breakfast nook; the den were seated in various states of wakefulness around the long, narrow table. Teller, accustomed to the early morning frenzy of Barston post-regency, was wide awake. Finch was wide awake as well; the rest of the den fell into the cracks somewhere between those two and Jewel. Gabriel's office was, of course, closed for the three days of the rites; the Merchant Authority offices had likewise been shut down for the duration. The House was to assemble in three waves. The first wave contained every nonessential person on staff or Council: Jewel, Finch, Teller, Barston, the people who in theory were Important. The second wave would join the ensemble only after the guests had arrived: the guards, the Chosen—or former Chosen. The third and final wave would be the servants, saving only those few who were utterly necessary for the preparations of the offerings after the rites had begun.

All of this had been drilled into Jewel's head by Teller, who, of the den, was most familiar with just how many things had to be arranged. What she'd known before his careful, if weary, reporting was that the Kings, the Queens, and The Ten were, upon death, accorded the full funereal rites and blessings of the Triumvirate, and obviously, gods couldn't be expected to share a day, or anything.

Avandar raised a brow when she ventured this opinion.

"You *are* tired," Carver added.

"The fact of the three-day rite has very little to do with the Triumvirate," the domicis now said, in his clipped voice. "No matter how conveniently the numbers work out in this case, it is not fact."

Jewel grimaced as Carver kicked her—gently—under the table. "Everyone," she said, rising from a half-eaten dish of something with too few potatoes and too much cheese for a morning as early as this one, "Get dressed. We'll meet in the great room. Shadow, would you stay with Ariel and Adam today?"

The cat hissed. "Make *Night* stay."

"Night is with Gabriel. Snow was *supposed* to be with Gabriel as well," she added.

"Dress," Snow said, sounding about as outraged as he did when Shadow stepped on his tail.

"Don't look at *me*," Shadow replied. "You *know* she's not very smart."

"Obviously not," Jewel snapped, "since I apparently agreed to let him make it." She headed toward Haval's room, fortified now by Finch, Teller, breakfast and some decent, if scant, sleep.

"Snow's not as scary as Haval," Finch offered.

"I should hope not; I *chose* Haval."

If Haval ever forgave her, it would—judging by the pallor of his skin, the circles beneath his eyes, and his very unamused expression—be a miracle. A rather large one.

"I'm please to see you could make it," he told them all, gesturing now at the featureless mannequins around which were the clothes several consecutive days' worth of increasingly cranky labor had produced.

"Mine is *better*," Snow told him; he was practically bouncing. Jewel considered—briefly—telling him he looked far more like a puppy than a cat.

"It is, indeed," Haval told him. When Haval spoke to the cat, he spoke gravely and with great respect—which at least showed he was capable of it. To be fair, Jewel didn't doubt that he was; she'd just seen so little of it aimed at her. "Jewel, please—you do *not* have all day, and I'm unable to rest for even an hour if you dawdle here."

"Pardon?"

He pinched the bridge of his nose. "I will, of course, be in attendance. I have less need for obvious finery, and I believe the clothing I transported here will serve my purposes."

"Is Hannerle—"

"No. She finds the presence of the Kings and the Exalted intimidating."

"Who doesn't?" Jewel muttered.

"Hopefully, ATerafin, you." He gestured again, and this time she approached the mannequin that was wearing the garment Snow had somehow created. It was still predominantly white, with edges of black and gold, and it had a train that would sweep floors clean if it were allowed to touch the ground. She grimaced. "Is the long bit at the back necessary? I'm not getting married—"

Snow growled.

"I believe he answered the same way when I asked," Haval said, while he helped Teller into his long coat.

Jewel hesitated again, and this time, Snow began to bat the side of her leg with the top of his head. "Knocking me over won't get me dressed any faster," she told him.

"No, but it won't make you *any* slower."

She unbuttoned the dress from the back and slid it, carefully, off the mannequin; she was afraid to touch it not because it was so very fine, but because she was afraid of damaging it somehow. Not even The Terafin would have dared a dress this ostentatious. She glanced uncertainly at Haval, who was now ignoring her in favor of his own work.

Snow hissed an almost strangled command to *hurry*, and Jewel surrendered to the dress.

To her lasting surprise, it was neither tight nor heavy; nor was it too warm. There was a knock at the door as Jewel examined herself in a slender oval mirror that seemed too slight to reflect the whole of the garment; Avandar entered the room. His attire was very fine, although it was mostly black with white trim and gold buttons; his shoes were also dark, and pointed in the fashion of the Court these past two years. Even his hair had been cut or combed in such a way that it revealed the lines of his face; he seemed very patrician, to her eye.

But he was her domicis, and she was accustomed to him. Or so she thought.

He was silent as she turned; silent as he stared. His face lost the look of arrogant disdain she'd grown to find so comfortable, and she wasn't certain she could even name what replaced it. She stumbled, and Snow hissed in frenzy. Avandar caught her before she could fall—to her knees, as she usually did.

"Avandar."

"ATerafin."

"Give me my hands back."

"Ah, of course. Apologies. Ellerson is waiting."

She nodded, and carefully gathered the train as she headed for the door and the ministrations of the elder domicis. Snow let her leave the room first, but inserted himself between Jewel and Avandar with another hiss.

"If you *step* on it," he growled, "I will *rip out* your throat."

"Snow!"

"I *will*."

Ellerson was waiting for her in her own rooms, which had the advantage of being tidy. Haval's workspace reminded Jewel very much of Rath's; everything strewn over chairs and any surface more than an inch above ground. Here, however, the servants of the House—more precisely the servants assigned to the West Wing—reigned. They did so invisibly, of course, and if Jewel failed to emerge from her rooms, she could generate at least as much mess as Haval. But when she did finally leave, they arrived through their back doors and narrow halls, and they left the same way, having transformed chaos into a tidiness appropriate to the grandeur of the manse.

Ellerson had a chair ready for her, and the mirror had been carefully placed in front of it. His eyes widened when she entered. "As you are no doubt aware," he told her, indicating the chair, "the dress is astonishing."

"Will it hide the fact that I'm not?"

"It just may. I'm afraid that my ability to do the same with your hair is in question."

Jewel grimaced. "That's because Snow didn't make my hair."

Snow snickered. "I could *try*."

"Don't. I think the dress is difficult enough to carry off. If you change anything else, no one will recognize me at all, which kind of defeats the purpose."

"Does it?" Snow sidled over to her chair and deposited his head into her lap. She scratched behind his ears, not worrying about possible damage; if Snow felt it was safe to have his fur all over the oddly soft skirt, who was she to argue?

"One day, ATerafin, it would not harm you to have your ears pierced."

"They can pierce them when I'm dead."

"Will you perhaps allow for jewelry?"

"I don't have any that's worthy of this dress, and before you ask, yes, I noticed you staring at the ring on my thumb, and no, I'm not taking it off." She exhaled, shoulders slumping and hair moving a couple of inches down; it was the hair that Ellerson minded.

Snow's head collided with her chin; he lifted it suddenly and without warning. "I'll find something. You'll wear it." He raced toward the door, and Avandar opened it—which was good; Jewel had the feeling he would have broken it down otherwise. "You couldn't have stopped him?" she asked her domicis.

"Not in a way that would have left much of the room standing, no."

"Can you stop him from coming back?"

"That, I might be able to do—but if I fail, he is unlikely to be amused. I doubt he will bring anything that will harm you."

"Not directly, no," she said, staring down at her lap.

"Not indirectly, in this case. The dress suits the situation, ATerafin."

"Yes—but it doesn't suit *me*."

"If that is the biggest concern of the day," Ellerson told her crisply, "consider yourself very fortunate."

She was suddenly certain she'd remember that later.

Finch and Teller took longer to get ready, because Ellerson had done Jewel's hair first. Jewel's hair was, in the estimation of any servant who'd been forced to help out in Ellerson's long absence, bloody difficult. Mind, they didn't say this to Jewel; they said it to Carver, who saw no harm in repeating it where the Master of the Household Staff was unlikely to be eavesdropping.

Finch had hair that was far less unwieldy; she didn't require Ellerson, but he went anyway, because he knew they were all going to be on edge for the next three days. He even made tea. She had no idea who—if anyone—was fussing over Teller. Teller, on the other hand, appeared to be able to survive without the fuss. The idea had a certain appeal to Jewel.

But then again, so did the reverse: leaving it all in the hands of people more capable. Which, at this very moment, described everyone. She adjusted the ring on her thumb. Avandar suggested that she attempt to fidget less.

And then the door opened. A haggard Haval and a very, very well turned out Finch were waiting in its frame. Haval was still girded by apron and stray bits of thread from the various cloths he'd cut. "If I ever accept a commission like this one again, you have my permission to poison me," he said sourly. "I am simply not young enough anymore."

"Any particular poison?"

"No. At this point, the pain can't possibly be worse. I do request that it be fatal, however." He stopped, pinched the bridge of his nose, and let his hand slide back to his side. "You have, no doubt, seen yourself in a mirror."

"Yes."

"Try to look less frightened when you leave the wing. At the moment, your expression suits a very nervous and underprepared debutante, and at your age, that is no longer appropriate." When she failed to answer, he added, "You are a power, Jewel. You are afraid of what that means, and I accept that; fear of a certain type leads to longevity because it is the foundation of caution. But fear is personal; like love it is meant to be carried close to the heart, and hidden from one's enemies." He reached out and adjusted a strand of escaped hair. In a different tone of voice, he said, "You are ready, ATerafin."

"I don't feel like it."

"No. That is the sad truth of power: when facing the unknown, *you* will never feel ready. But you are." He glanced at the ring on her thumb, but said nothing. "I will see you before the ceremony starts; I must wake and see to my angry wife." He stepped back and then bowed. It was a brief bow, but it was perfect in a way that Jewel never managed in her own gestures of respect.

He smiled, as if reading her thoughts. "Your lack of ability to perform obeisance will be much less of an issue in future."

Absent any reasonable excuse to remain in their apartments, the den filed out the doors. Ellerson joined them. Like Avandar, he wore black; it was edged in gold, and the shirt beneath the jacket was white. The cut of the clothing was, however, very much his usual; he carried a walking stick in his left hand, and he wore a hat.

Angel wore a suit in a similar style, at his own insistence. Carver and Jester had been fitted with suits that were slightly more appropriate to Court than work, and Carver's hair had been pulled back. They knew it was a bad day when they could see both of Carver's eyes; Jester claimed to be shocked that he still had two.

Snow sauntered along at Jay's right. Shadow followed to the door. The gray cat kept all but his claws on the interior of the frame; he was put out, and took no pains to hide it. Ariel didn't come to see them off. Adam, however, did. He froze in the hall, staring at Jewel, his jaw slack; Angel and Carver exchanged a glance and burst out laughing.

"Matriarch," Adam whispered.

Jay cringed. Avandar frowned—at Jay, not at Adam; Adam reddened, and looked at his feet.

Jay snorted and walked back to where Adam was standing. She hugged him while he was saying something in Torra—Angel assumed it was an apology from the tone. His smile was tentative, his face was still red. Angel couldn't remember ever being that young. Jay said something else, in a more somber tone, and the red slowly faded from view as she let Adam go. "Shadow," she said, speaking Weston. "Nothing bad had better happen to either of the two while I'm not here. And keep an eye on Hannerle as well."

"Is there anything *else* you'd like?" he said, hissing heavily on the sibilants.

Looking more like herself than she had all morning, she chuckled. "I'd like for this day to be over. And there's only one way that's going to happen." Turning, she exited the wing again, but this time her shoulders were straighter and she looked taller. It was probably just the shoes.

The Terafin halls had never looked so ostentatious in the galleries meant to impress. They had never looked so metallic in the martial halls and walks, either. Mages had clearly been at work here; the magelights were bright and multihued. The den walked slowly because Jay did. Angel took the opportunity to position himself between Jay and the Captains of the Chosen, and Avandar allowed it with his usual cool grace.

He offered Jay his arm, as Ellerson had taught him; she looked at it for a long moment in surprise—but she did take it, although she muttered something about "these damn shoes" under her breath. Carver made an unfortunate joke—unfortunate because he was well behind Angel and therefore safe from reprisals. Angel wasn't concerned about the mockery. He was worried about Jay. He'd said nothing at all about her dress, but he wasn't immune to its effects: it looked like something not even a painter could get right. It certainly didn't look like clothing.

The white cloth was the color of snow in a bitter Averalaan winter. The black was the color not of night, but darkness—the darkness of the god no one in the city named in Henden; it was deep and absolute and the magelights in their glory did nothing to change it at all. The gold that was threaded throughout was bankers' gold, not harvest; there was nothing remotely friendly or approachable about this dress.

But the hand on the crook of his elbow was warm and solid; it was also callused. The nails had been both smoothed and shaped, and someone had thought to apply powder—but it didn't matter; the hand was sun-dark. Jay stumbled once and cursed her boots; he understood very little Torra, but through long familiarity had picked up all of the inappropriate words. "The ring was hers?" he asked.

"It was."

He didn't ask how she'd come by it, because it didn't matter. Later, maybe.

They walked without speaking through the halls. Jay set the pace. She called it stately. Angel understood why she was in no hurry to reach the gardens, but even walking excruciatingly correctly, they finally did. The doors were open to the early morning chill; the skies were gray and overcast.

Angel winced when Snow stepped on his foot; for winged creatures, the cats were heavy, and all of the den had learned that ignoring them wasn't an option; they craved acknowledgment and ramped up activity in order to achieve it.

Jay stopped a moment, because the cat was trying to speak around something it held—in its mouth. She bent—kneeling in the dress was out of the question unless she was greeting the Kings or the Exalted—and Snow spit something out into her cupped palms. She winced as he began to chatter. He'd brought a necklace—one with a thick-linked silver chain. No, Angel thought, not silver; platinum.

"Put it *on*. Put it *on*."

Avandar stepped in. "May I?" he asked; Jay was still staring at her hands, or at what was in them. Snow snorted and bumped her thigh with his head.

"Where did you get this?" she asked, an edge in her voice.

Snow stopped bouncing and glanced over his left shoulder. "Why do you *care*? It's *perfect* for my dress."

As answers went, it was bad.

"Snow—I mean it. I do care. Where did you get this? Did you make it the same way you made the dress?"

He hissed. "*Stupid* girl."

Avandar lifted the necklace that was pooled in Jay's palms; the chain seemed to go on forever, made thicker and finer and heavier by her growing anxiety. "Avandar, what is it?"

"It is a pendant, ATerafin."

"It looks like it's diamond."

"Ah. I do not think a diamond this large now exists in the Empire, although I have been mistaken in the past."

"If it *does* exist," she said, rising and backing into Angel in an attempt to evade the necklace, "it's going to be owned by one of the men—or women—we're getting ready to greet today. I can't wear it—"

"It is not part of any collection that belongs to the patriciate of this City." He smiled. It was cold and sharp. "Look at it."

She was. She was looking at it with both dread and fascination, because she could see, in the brilliance of light shed by cut faucets, the glimmering strands of luminescence that spoke of magic. She had come, with time, to understand what the colors, on a rudimentary level, might mean—but this pendant was surrounded by all of the colors. All, even the black that only the demons used. She swallowed. "It's not a diamond," she said, voice flat. "Avandar, tell me what it does."

"ATerafin, I do not know."

"Can you see it?"

"See?"

"The magic, Avandar." Her right hand had curled into a fist, and she kept it by her side with effort. Oddly enough, the dress didn't help; it spoke of power first, and dignity second—and at the moment, it was a distant second, and falling behind as the seconds passed.

He nodded slowly. "I can, ATerafin. I can see enough to tell you that it is neither small nor insignificant, and if the magi are watchful, it will be noticed."

"That's all?"

"What would you have me say? That it is ancient? It is. That it is an artifact of a long forgotten people? It is. I will not tell you that it will grant you power, because I cannot say that with any certainty."

"What will it cost, to wear it?"

His smile was slight, but it was warmer. "You are not and will never be a fool, Jewel. There is always a price to pay when dealing with things ancient or unknown; I cannot say what that price will be with any certainty, however."

"And you can't hazard a guess where it came from?"

"I can hazard one. I will not, however."

"The owner—"

"Think of him not as owner but as custodian."

She latched onto the pronoun. "Him?"

"It's *yours*, it's *yours*," Snow hissed.

"While I would desperately like to disagree with the cat on principle if nothing else, I feel in this single instance that he is correct. In the games of the old powers, very little that happens is entirely coincidental, although the shape of the whole cannot always be glimpsed by those who are caught in the threads of its tapestry." The chain dangled loosely from his hands. "I will not force you to wear it," he told her.

"Because you can't."

He raised a brow, but didn't demur.

Angel cleared his throat, and she turned to him for support.

He knew, of course. Her reluctance was so strong it was visible, tangible: she was afraid. Her fear had guided the den through the streets of the twenty-fifth holding, and it had guided them through the halls of the Terafin manse. Both of these were known quantities, now—but they always been knowable, even when the den had been nothing but a small gang of thieves taking the refuge granted them by the woman whose funeral now waited.

But he knew when the fear that shadowed her was fear not of the unknown, but of herself. It wasn't the pendant—or the dress—she doubted here; it was her own ability to carry them well. Angel didn't have the doubt that she could never discard except in rage.

"Angel?"

He glanced at the trees that were so familiar to anyone who'd lived in the lee of the Common and its gates, its guards, its very loud merchants. As if the trees could hear, as if they could speak, a pale ivory creature now stepped out of the shadows that the sun hadn't cast, and made his way up the stairs of the terrace. His tines gleamed in the early morning light, as did his coat; his breath came out in mist as he knelt before her. Angel knew the Winter King could speak to Jay.

It wasn't to the King that she looked; it was to him. He felt both grateful and embarrassed at the gratitude. He wanted to be able to give her what she was silently asking for, but he couldn't. He hated this jacket, with its narrow, useless pockets; he hated the pants, and the boots. The only thing he'd insisted be left alone was his hair—and even that, he'd spent an hour and a half cleaning and binding.

"Jay," he said, and saw her flinch before he'd even said the words. He turned to face not the Winter King, but the grounds behind him. "Things are changing."

"The Terafin is——"

"It's not about The Terafin, anymore. It's about the House, about what you want to make of it—and above all, about how you'll protect it. We don't even understand the whole of the threat. Rymark? Haerrad? We understand those. We understood men like them when we were scrounging for change to stave off starvation." He turned, then, toward the waiting great stag. "We don't understand the trees. We know them," he added, gazing at the creature who clearly intended to bear her. Who had borne Angel up the side of a demonic tree at Jay's behest. "But we don't understand them. You called them," he added, putting into words what she'd avoided saying, even in the kitchen. "And they grew."

"I didn't——"

He waited, but she couldn't bring herself to say the words—not to Angel. "You don't know what the pendant does, but Snow thinks its safe, or he wouldn't have brought it. Right?"

Snow's gaze slid neatly off Angel's face, and also bypassed Jay's. He hissed, his wings flattening.

"Avandar thinks it's safe."

Avandar was not Snow; he said nothing.

"Or rather, Avandar thinks the alternative is less safe."

"The alternative being I don't wear it?" she demanded. "Because I'm not wearing it now, and I've never worn it before—and I'm still here."

"You never moved trees before, either."

"She didn't *move* them," Snow interjected.

"You think I should wear it."

"I think you should try. Because the forest is ancient, and the gods were afraid. Something big is coming. I think it's yours," he added. "I don't know if it'll help; I don't think it'll hinder. What does the Winter King say?"

Jay shook her head.

Avandar held the pendant out—to Angel. Angel took it; the links were surprisingly warm. He held it, waiting, and she finally exhaled a few inches of height and bowed her head. He surprised himself by disliking her hair, it was so tightly wound. Like his hair, hers was an inseparable part of her character; unlike his, she couldn't demand that it remain untouched. She had come from the South and the summer of its perpetual desert; the auburn highlights were bright and red.

The platinum was cold; it looked like sword steel. Unlike silver, it took no tarnish; time wouldn't mellow it. Time clearly hadn't. Angel lifted it; it wasn't particularly heavy. It didn't seem to bear the weight of history that Avandar ascribed to it. He cupped the pendant in his hand for just a moment; it, like the chains that held it, was warm. He thought the light at its core shifted, but he couldn't say how; he didn't try.

Instead, he let its weight once again fall, and he placed the chains around her exposed neck.

She froze for an instant, as if expecting the magic she alone could see to manifest itself in some unpleasant way. Nothing happened. The pendant lay against her chest, almost blending into the fabric of the dress itself.

"It's warm," she said.

Angel nodded.

She glanced at the Winter King; he waited. "He said I should wear it," she told Angel. "And that I should ride."

"Riding won't damage you now," Angel replied. "You're already wearing that dress, and you can get rid of rats and roaches more easily than you can get rid of that cat."

Snow hissed and turned, raising his wings in outrage.

Jay, however, laughed. She then climbed up the back of the Winter King, and he almost leaped to his feet again, as if afraid she'd change her mind. She sat with both legs dangling off one of his sides; the dress didn't allow for anything more practical. But it wasn't required either: the Winter King was willing to carry her.

Avandar walked behind Jay, and Torvan and Arrendas walked in front; a very white, very winged cat walked by her side. Behind them, the rest of the den walked, and Angel reluctantly fell back, making room for Arann; Arann had the sword and the armor of the Chosen.

A fourth guard joined the three. The Winter King stepped down the stairs that led to the heart of the gardens. He stopped for a moment, as Jay took a deep breath. She wore a cape—a white cape—but no jacket. The magi had been at work in the garden, erecting a shield that might keep out the worst of the wind for the service, but the air was still chill. Most of the House Council members were already present, as were their various adjutants.

Rymark ATerafin was there, and of the four, he looked the most regal.

Angel wouldn't have dared in his position, because Duvari was also present, and Duvari's Astari were no doubt scattered among the robed and suited men and women who waited. Some of the magi were also in the gardens, but they weren't here—yet—as guests. The only Terafin servants present were the Master Gardener's groundskeepers; they worked, rather than mingling.

Haerrad wore a suit that implied martial prowess, although he wasn't technically part of the Kings' armies. He had half a dozen House Guards with him at all times, and at least two Council advisers. Where Rymark looked like he was holding Court, Haerrad looked like he was expecting battle.

Between these two, in groups of similar composition, were Elonne ATerafin and Marrick ATerafin. They were, in fact, exchanging cool pleasantries. Angel couldn't see Gabriel among them yet. He could see other members of the House Council on the grounds. The servants moved among them, but offered no food or refreshments; nor would they until after the first day rites had been completed.

People gathered in such numbers, no matter how politic—or perhaps because of how political all such gatherings had now become—made noise. They spoke, they moved, they listened and conversed. Any discussions about House affairs would, of course, be superficial, but they would occur only now; when the guests arrived, no House matters would be discussed at all. But although the guests had not arrived, silence spread through the grounds as Jay at last came into view of the gathering. This unexpected hush leaped from one interrupted sentence to the next, until all but a handful of those gathered here—mostly gardeners—stared, mouths half open.

How could they not?

She rode into their midst like a Queen. No, he thought, not like a Queen; the Queens would walk, attended by members of their Courts—men and women of power and sophistication in their own right. They would have servants, yes, and *Astari*; they would be accorded the respect due their rank. But they would not ride a great, white stag; they wouldn't be attended by a snow-winged cat; nor would they—and he saw this clearly as she approached—be served by a preternaturally beautiful man who claimed not to be mortal. Lord Celleriant waited.

She stiffened as all eyes fell on her; she never liked to be the center of attention unless there was an emergency and she needed people to listen.

Here, however, she had no choice; all her choices had been made in the past few days, and she now had to live with them. Her hands tightened in her lap, and she forced her expression into something that mimed neutrality, lifting her chin and straightening her shoulders as she did.

The Winter King didn't stop at the boundary implied by the gathered men and women. Because he didn't, none of them did: Not the Chosen, not Avandar, not the stupid cat, and not any member of the den. It was easier for them than for her; they knew that no one would be watching them yet. No one would be speaking to them either; they had eyes for Jay. Judging from her expression, Jay wasn't the one who chose her eventual destination either.

The Winter King walked to the place that had once contained the oldest—and tallest—tree on the grounds. A tree stood there now, but it was in no way the same one; it was one of the new trees—trees that had been birthed, ancient, into the Terafin grounds. It was, however, the tallest of the trees that now grew here, and its leaves weren't in bud, but in bloom. Even in the Common, bloom would have to wait for a few weeks; buds would start soon as the worst of winter gave way to Advent, and to spring.

To the trees here, time and its seasons apparently had no meaning. They grew, and as she reached the trunk of the tree, Lord Celleriant came to kneel—in full view of the current assembly—at her feet. It was not a perfunctory gesture, and it stopped just short of the full obeisance offered the Exalted or the Kings. He carried a sword, and the light the blade reflected was the azure of a winter sky.

He wore armor that was entirely at odds with the Chosen; where they wore plate, he wore chain, although the mesh at this distance was fine enough it might have been shimmering, heavy cloth. He wore no helm, no tabard; his boots were supple and fine. He did wear a cape of midnight blue, with a pale edge that appeared to be solid white at a distance, but resolved itself into very fine, very complex embroidery as they approached. His hair was unbound, as it always was, and it fell in a perfect drape down his back, defying movement and breeze.

The Winter King knelt. Jay slid off his back and stood before Lord Celleriant, straightening the fall of her skirts. It was a nervous gesture; the skirts themselves fell smoothly, without obvious wrinkle, and whatever else the Winter King did, he didn't shed. Her hands fell to her sides. She didn't ask Celleriant what in the Hells he was doing; instead, after a long pause, she bid him rise. He unfolded in as graceful a manner as he had knelt, and he joined her Chosen, although it was clear he'd never be part of them.

Neither would Angel, but he felt at home among the Chosen; he felt ill at ease in Celleriant's shadow. It was a shadow he accepted because Jay did; he accepted it the way he'd accepted Duster. Funny, to think of her now, here.

"Are the grounds secured?" she asked Celleriant.

He didn't answer.

She closed her eyes and drew a deeper breath.

"ATerafin," he said, and she opened them. "What do you wear?"

"Do you recognize it?" Her eyes widened, but she narrowed them before surprise was stuck like a signboard across her expression.

"No. But I recognize that it is . . . unusual. In this city, in these lands, it is worthy of remark."

She was silent for another beat. "Just how insecure are the grounds?" She strove for casual, and mostly achieved it. For Jay.

"None of our enemies linger within them now, but they will come."

She glanced at Avandar. Avandar inclined his head. "That is my suspicion as well. I, however, believe that some of them will use the front gates and doors; Lord Celleriant's concerns are other. As, ATerafin, are yours." He stepped back as she turned to face the gathered House Council and all of its tertiary support.

In the morning light of these transformed grounds, in a dress that was too perfect for someone as fragile as she felt, she stood in silence. Angel was almost afraid, but he couldn't decide which way the fear should fall: be afraid for her, or of her. He couldn't stand beside her here, and fell back, indicating that Teller and Finch should join her; they were also members of the House Council, although they had been so for a very short while.

Rymark ATerafin was the first to collect himself. His entourage was still staring, but words had breached the silence, and as they began to spread, movement and sound returned to the carefully arranged clearing. He didn't look pleased—at either their words or Jewel's presence—but she couldn't blame him. She therefore didn't cringe when he began to walk toward her. Two of the members of his entourage followed after a pause, surprised but determined not to show it.

The quality of their surprise was different from Rymark's, although

Jewel couldn't quite pinpoint how. It didn't matter; she was about to get a face full of Rymark, and that was enough of a worry. He stopped less than a yard from Torvan and Arrendas. "Captains," he said, with the barest patina of respect. They ignored him. Technically this was correct behavior, but Rymark had never been all that fond of correct when it didn't suit him.

It didn't suit him now. The Chosen stood between them.

"Jewel," he finally said, as if they didn't exist—which was also correct behavior. "I am pleased to see that you are so well prepared for the funeral rites."

"I held The Terafin in the highest of regard. I owe her my life, and inasmuch as I have it, my freedom from service to the Lord of the Compact. Whatever I could do to show my respect for Amarais Handernesse ATerafin, I have done." She spoke clearly, and without much concern for eavesdroppers; she meant the entire assembly to hear her.

"It is seldom that exotic animals are brought as a gesture of respect."

Snow began to growl. The cats rarely growled, but it wasn't a good sign. Jewel dropped her hand to the top of his head and pressed her palm firmly between his ears. She'd prepared for this. "It is not the first time unusual servants have attended significant members of either the patriciate or the Crowns, and if it is a rare occurrence, I believe it can be forgiven."

"Indeed, indeed," Marrick said, joining them. He was smiling broadly, and the worst thing about that damn smile was that it looked so genuinely friendly. Jewel wanted to dislike him. She certainly *knew* she couldn't trust him. But there was something about him that all but demanded trust. "As long as they aren't killing or eating our guests, I see no reason for complaint. They are," he added, looking directly at Snow, "magnificent."

Snow's growl banked.

"But they are not nearly as notable at the moment as your dress, Jewel. It is very, very fine—I do not recall ever seeing its like in any Court before."

Snow now purred. "You *like* it?" he asked.

Marrick's brows rose. This didn't stop his mouth from moving, on the other hand. "I do, indeed," he said—to the cat. "It is exquisite. I am almost afraid to speak to the woman who's wearing it, and I've known her since she was a child."

"That's not *very* long," Snow said, smug now. "We think she's *very* young."

"Snow," Jewel said.

Snow glanced at her out of the corner of a well-turned eye, and then fell silent. For a minute. "He *likes* it."

Jewel pasted a smile onto her face. When she had first arrived at the House, it was a skill she'd lacked—but at that time, it hadn't mattered. Now, she knew it did.

"I feel I fall far short of your sartorial elegance, Jewel," Marrick continued. "But as it is, all eyes—*all*—will be on you; I should not be surprised if the Kings themselves take note of little else. It certainly takes the pressure off the rest of us." He laughed.

He laughed, and Jewel almost joined him; he had that kind of laughter. She did allow herself a genuine smile. Marrick, even Finch had a hard time disliking. But not as hard a time mistrusting. He bowed to Jewel, and then took her hand and kissed it. His eyes lingered a moment on the ring that she wore on her thumb, but he chose not to comment.

"Come, Rymark, there's no need to look so sour," Marrick added, grinning broadly. "Today, and for the next three days, there will be no woman as grand as the young woman from our House; it is a minor victory for Terafin."

"Perhaps you are right," Rymark conceded, looking very dour. "I should like the name of your dressmaker."

Jewel didn't even hesitate. "Snow, this is Rymark ATerafin, a prominent member of the House Council. Rymark, this is Snow, the dressmaker."

His brows rose in astonishment, and fell almost instantly. She saw suspicion harden into certainty. "If, of course, it's a secret, ATerafin, there is no need for this style of low humor."

Snow hissed.

Marrick glanced at Rymark and then, as was his wont, he moved on. "ATerafin, have you anything to say about the miraculous change in the grounds and the gardens?"

She studied his expression and was rewarded by a glimpse of something far less friendly in the lines of a face that had been etched and defined by laughter. He knew, or had heard. "Very little," she replied, gazing up at the heights of the tree in bloom. She reached out to touch its bark. "But I am very, very fond of these trees; they remind me of my childhood."

"I see. You realize were it not for your dress and your unusual companions, it would be the trees that would be envy of every other House in the Empire?"

"I think the trees will still be that," she replied. "Ah, Elonne."

Elonne ATerafin offered Jewel a graceful nod. More wasn't necessary, and there was nothing perfunctory in the gesture of respect. Jewel returned it. She could not—and did not—feel at ease with Elonne. Elonne had always been cool, correct, graceful; she had never once—in Jewel's hearing—raised voice. Nor did she descend into cursing or obvious signs of anger, even during the most heated of Council meetings. Hers was the voice of deliberation and reason. Of the four, she most reminded Jewel of Amarais. Of course, of the four, she was the only woman, and maybe that explained something.

She had chosen to wear a dress that could be considered the height of current fashion, with its elaborate collar and its high bodice done in white and gold. Like Jewel's dress, it was predominantly white; the sleeves, however, were black, and they trailed across the grass as she walked. The skirts were wider than current fashion dictated; it was the one touch that was old-fashioned. Jewel almost grimaced; she'd clearly spent far too many hours cooped up with Haval and Finch; Haval made no bones about what was, and was not, acceptable fashion for ladies of the patriciate in this season. He was less exacting when it came to Teller, although he did explain the cut of sleeve and collar in both jacket and shirt; he'd also said something about the pants, but that, Jewel honestly couldn't remember. She didn't try very hard.

Elonne was older than Jewel; as old, Jewel thought, as Amarais herself had been when Jewel had first arrived at the front gates. She offered the stonelike Captains of the Chosen a brief dip of chin, both recognizing them and accepting their lack of greeting as if it were the natural order. They failed to acknowledge it, but not in the same way they'd failed to acknowledge Rymark.

"Jewel," Elonne now said. She passed by Torvan, and Torvan didn't move to block her in any way. "The trees are, indeed, very fine. Very impressive. Will they grow in any other House grounds upon the Isle?"

"I honestly don't know. The Master Gardener was shocked that they grew here."

"Ah. I believe he can be forgiven." She glanced at Snow, who was now following her with his eyes. He did not, thank the gods, ask if he could eat her—or any of the other House Councillors; Jewel was grateful, because she wasn't entirely certain she wouldn't allow him to make an attempt at Rymark. "Why these trees, ATerafin?"

Jewel frowned. While it was formal and correct to be called ATerafin, it could also be tiring and confusing, especially in a gathering of this type. Asking Elonne to be less formal, however, had no effect. "I don't know," she replied. "But if any tree could be said to define Averalaan, it's these trees."

"Ah, yes. They do. But Averalaan is not Terafin, and Terafin is not Averalaan. Did you plan this?" she added, her voice as calm and reasonable as if she'd been asking about a merchanting report of some import. She meant for the question to be taken seriously; she was not intimidated by the subject.

"No, Elonne. I would never have planned something so visible and so elaborate without recourse to the Council."

"Yet you had a hand in this."

Jewel nodded.

"May I ask how?"

"Yes, but I fear now is not the time. The Council has been called for the day after the funeral rites are done, and I will report what I know at that time; I've thought of little but the funeral—and The Terafin—since my return to the House."

Elonne bowed her head. When she lifted it, she said, "Of course. My apologies, ATerafin. The Terafin's murder was not what any one of us expected, and it has opened the door to magics that are almost entirely foreign—to me. This tree," she added, gazing up as Jewel had done moments before, "is likewise foreign, and I feel it almost as a danger to the natural order. Do you not?"

"No."

"Ah. Because they are Veralaan's trees?"

"Because what stood here before, in wait, was so much worse."

Elonne once again inclined her head. "Rymark," she said. "Marrick."

Haerrad was the only one who kept his distance. Jewel was grateful for small mercies, because in the foreseeable future, they were the only ones she was likely to receive. It was, on the other hand, a very small mercy because he was watching her as if she were the only person on the green. He loathed Rymark—in the Council sessions, if there was any unpleasantness, it was almost always due to their conflicts—but for the moment Rymark was less significant than she was.

If she wondered why, she was answered—Duvari came to join them.

Duvari, who silenced all conversation by simple presence. If Jewel's dress and her entourage were instantly threatening to the House Councillors who desired to rule the House, they were still less of a danger than the Lord of the Compact. Jewel wondered if Duvari enjoyed their loathing and fear, but not for long; Duvari appeared not to know the meaning of the word "enjoy"—and if he did, he wouldn't condescend to actually engage in any.

"Your dress, ATerafin," he said, with a slight nod, "is remarkable."

Jewel felt her jaw unhinge and caught it before it fell open. She couldn't stop her brows from reaching for her hairline.

"After the funeral rites have been completed," he continued, voice smooth and hard, "we will have to discuss its origin."

Snow hissed.

"Among other things." He nodded to Rymark, Elonne, and Marrick, but did not move away.

They were standing in a loose and silent circle near the tree's base when Gabriel ATerafin at last made his way down the terrace. Night was his immediate escort, although Barston—and a half dozen of the House Guard—were not far away. He didn't immediately join them; instead, Teller broke away from the main group—in which he was all but invisible—and made his way to Gabriel's side. Or to Barston's; it was hard to tell at this distance.

"There has been no further trouble?" Duvari asked. He asked it of the air and the grounds, apparently; he didn't look at anyone as he spoke. He watched Gabriel, Teller, and Barston, his hands loosely clasped behind his back.

No one answered. Jewel glanced at Finch; Finch smiled, but her hand flicked a few words in den-sign.

"My own men will be here, of course," he continued, when no answer was forthcoming. "If the House will play its games of assassination and forbidden magic in the presence of the Kings, it will perish."

Rymark bristled openly. Marrick merely nodded. Elonne, however, failed to hear the words. Jewel should have joined them in their silence, adopting one style or another; she knew it.

"And if it's not the House that's playing these games?" she demanded instead. She kept her voice even, and she kept all Torra out of it, although the latter was harder. Duvari could enrage her on most days simply by breathing.

"Then perhaps the House will fall, for the moment, under the protection of the magi. Writs have been issued," he added, without a ripple of expression. "The current guildmaster of the Order is well known for her pursuit of those who would practice forbidden arts; she is without mercy."

"She is," Jewel replied. "And with cause."

"The House does not require the guardianship of the Order," Rymark interjected. "We are not without magi of our own."

"May I remind you, ATerafin, of the reason for this funeral?" Duvari asked. "The Kings were present," he added. "At the request of the guildmaster. If the demons seek entrance to the city through House Terafin, we are not content to let the matter remain at the discretion of a headless House."

"It will not remain long without ruler," Rymark countered.

"No, indeed. Perhaps the urgency of the situation will encourage the House Council to expedite their vote and their decision." Before Rymark could reply, Duvari left them, walking straight for Gabriel.

"That's as clear a warning as he's ever given," Marrick said, recovering words and humor first. He was to be the only member of the House Council who managed the latter; Jewel couldn't dredge up even the most brittle of smiles. When no one spoke, he added, "It is not costly for us to indulge him in this fashion; it's important that he feels he is discharging his duties, as he will do so regardless."

Haerrad chose this moment to approach. It was safest; it was one of the few in which the House Council was likely to unite in common cause. If Haerrad was known for nothing else, his disdain for the Lord of the Compact was almost legendary. He was not, strictly speaking, rude to Duvari—but he stopped just short of issuing a bald challenge.

Amarais had used this, in the past. If Haerrad could be considered to have a strength, it was this, and any words that fell, bristling, from Haerrad would not be entirely attributed to The Terafin herself, although on occasion she was required to deflect some of the ire they drew. Since it was a role that suited him, he donned it now, and in such a fashion, the House Council united. It was uneasy, but it would be; only for someone as powerful and openly hostile as Duvari would it occur at all.

Duvari joined Gabriel; no doubt the words he uttered there would be similar, although he was marginally more circumspect in his discussions with the regent, in Jewel's experience. The grounds slowly filled as the

House presented its best; Finch left her side when Jarven arrived. Lucille was not yet present.

Jarven, however, strolled in Jewel's direction. He walked slowly, but in a stately manner, and the walking stick he carried lent him an unnecessary elegance; he had extended an arm to Finch, and Finch took it without hesitation. It was clear, from where Jewel stood, that Finch both liked—and trusted—Jarven ATerafin. Jewel, however, had never forgotten Haval's very unusual reaction to the man. It made her cautious.

But he obviously cared for Finch, which was a huge point in his favor.

He stopped ten feet short of where Jewel stood; the Chosen faced not Jarven, but the House Council. He nevertheless failed to breach their invisible radius; instead he bowed. "ATerafin," he said, rising. His expression was calm, untroubled; his eyes were clear. He made no comment about either her dress or the winged part of her honor guard; he made no comment about her pendant or Lord Celleriant. She tendered him a very correct bow.

"Ah, so formal, so formal," he replied. "And without the excuse of outsiders."

"The Lord of the Compact is here."

"Oh, tush. The Lord of the Compact is merely like a little rain at a picnic. Which, given the number of magi on the grounds, won't be a problem for the funeral." He glanced up. "The tops of the trees, however, might get wet."

"Is Lucille not coming?"

"She is, of course, planning to be in attendance—but she's likely to arrive when the guests do; she has work in the office that will not, apparently, wait, and as the office will be closed for three full days, she is attempting to minimize our losses. I really like the look of the grounds," he added. "And when the weather is warmer, they will be an excellent incentive to entertain."

She stared at him. She wasn't the only one.

Jarven, however, responded to her. "Come, ATerafin. You must be well aware by now that the most jaded of men—and women—regularly cross the threshold of the Merchant Authority. They make decisions based on years of experience, but those decisions can be hastened if they are slightly off their guard—or if we, as a House, present something, some new experience, that no other House among The Ten, no other merchant family of significance, can likewise present.

"This garden, and these grounds, have overnight become that: these trees are famed throughout the Empire for one reason and one alone: it is only in Averalaan that they grow—and only in the Common. Men and women have tried, often at great expense, to cultivate cuttings and even seeds—all have withered young. Here, however?" He raised his face again. "Here, House Terafin now has them in full growth, and in full bloom, and one doesn't have to enter the Common to appreciate them." His smile was sharp and anticipatory. Turning to Rymark, he added, "Surely you must agree?"

Rymark very smoothly replied, "Of course," which surprised Jewel.

"It is a promising start," Jarven added. "Come, Finch, if I may presume upon your time?" He bowed to her and when he rose, offered her his arm again.

"We'll need her back before the guests arrive," Jewel told him. "The House Council in full is expected to be gathered to greet the guests."

Chapter Twenty

"IS IT TRUE," Jarven asked, "that Jewel caused the trees to grow?"

Finch grimaced. "Now is not the time to ask that, Jarven."

"It is exactly the time to ask," was his quiet—and serious—reply. "She is bold today. She is dressed in a manner that might befit Queens, should Queens have access to such material and such artistry. Let me assure you, in case you are in any doubt," he added, in a lower voice, "our Monarchs don't. There is no one, no matter how rich or notable, who will compare with the young ATerafin. I admit to being somewhat surprised; I did not think she had it in her." His smile returned, changing the creases in his face; he was at an age where they were always present in one form or another.

"Look at the House Council; they are discomfited. Elonne takes stock; Marrick is being far too jovial. Haerrad approaches her as if she is the foremost of his rivals."

"And Rymark?"

"Rymark concerns me," Jarven replied. "He is ill-pleased, but he does not seem concerned."

"Should he? He's always been arrogant."

"He has; he has never, however, been a fool. To ignore the significance of her presence in that dress, beneath those trees, and at the side of that creature is the act of a fool." He glanced at her, as if waiting.

"You don't think he's being a fool now."

"How perceptive. I should really stop, you know; Lucille will almost certainly be annoyed if I continue."

Finch felt a moment of relief; it was very short-lived. ". . . But she won't be annoyed at me if I do."

His smile was warm, friendly, and just the slightest bit self-satisfied. "She will be annoyed at me if you do, but I am accustomed to that. She'll probably make bad tea for at least a month. Do continue."

"You don't think he's being a fool now, which is why you're concerned; you think he knows something we don't know."

"He most certainly knows things that neither of us knows, yes—but he has made clear that at least one of them involves the neutralization of the young ATerafin, and possibly in a way that would meet with general disapproval."

Finch hesitated. "You know there was an assassination attempt yesterday?"

He smiled brightly at one of the young men who sometimes worked in the Trade Commission office, exchanging a brief and pleasant—if slightly addled—greeting. "I had heard, yes. I'd imagine anyone with half an ear to House business has, although to be fair, the preparations for the funeral rites have occupied almost every echelon of the manse itself, from the regent down to the newest of the servants. I was very disappointed."

Her brows rose, and he rolled his eyes. "Not because of the lack of success, Finch; please, try to be less easily shocked. I was disappointed because it cannot have escaped the notice of any of the contenders that the Lord of the Compact has all but been in residence in the manse in preparation for the presence of the Kings and Queens at the funeral. An assassination that occurs in his lap might still fit the criteria of House Law—but Duvari could nonetheless make life very, very difficult for a House that is so poorly controlled that it cannot prevent itself from such extremes beneath his nose."

Finch said nothing. Jay had made clear that she thought something outside of the House was involved—and something outside of the House wasn't likely to care all that much about whether or not House Terafin came under political fire.

"Ah, Finch, I think our guests are beginning to arrive."

She froze. "The Kings?"

"No. Nor the Exalted; not yet. If it had been either, you would know, have no fear. Unfortunately, I do recognize some of the guests, and I believe I am now expected to make my presence known." He smiled, and offered her an arm. "You will, no doubt, recognize them as well."

*　　*　　*

Gabriel made his way to Jewel's side, taking time to speak a word or two to the members of the House over which he now ruled as reluctant regent. He therefore didn't beat the arrival of the first few guests. Jewel watched them at a distance; they were, for the most part, notable members of the merchant houses on the Isle. With Gabriel came Teller and Barston, although only Barston was likely to remain at Gabriel's side. Jewel offered Gabriel what she hadn't offered any of the Council members: a full bow. She held it as gracefully as she could. Even when Night hissed.

"You are well, ATerafin?" Gabriel asked, when she rose.

"I am well. You are not yet weary of your companion?"

Gabriel's smile froze in place; Jewel wanted to laugh, but managed to keep silent. "It is as you said; he does not appear to require sleep, and if he requires food, our food is apparently beneath him."

She did laugh then.

"It has *plants* in it," Night complained.

"He's good practice," Jewel said quietly. She felt, rather than saw, Avandar's extreme disapproval, and ducked her chin until she could lose the expression. She also failed to say the rest of the words.

"ATerafin," Gabriel said quietly, when she straightened. "That is an unusual ring. May I see it?"

Without visible hesitation, she lifted her normally ringless hand; he caught it—gently—in his own. "Where did you get this?" he finally asked, when he released her.

"It was left for me by The Terafin," she replied, evading the actual question. "It was a personal possession, and of little significance to the House."

"You were not wearing it yesterday."

"Not during the day, no."

"I see. Do you recognize it for what it is?"

"It's the signet of House Handernesse."

"It is. Do you know when she—"

"Yes. I know how it arrived in the manse. I know who wore it last." Frowning, she added, "Why is it significant to you, Regent?"

He shook his head, but his expression was now careworn. "She asked me to watch for it," he finally said. "I don't think she was certain I would ever see it, but she asked." He hesitated again, which was unusual for Gabriel. "But she asked it after receiving a visit from an outsider, a woman I have seen only once in my tenure as her right-kin."

"Evayne." Jewel said. It wasn't a question.

"Indeed." He straightened, his face once again adopting a benign and distant smile. "Your dress is very lovely," he told her.

She managed to say thank you.

The bardic colleges were represented by master bards. Morniel and Attariel had sent two; Brekenhurst and Linden, one each. But Senniel College, alone of the five, was situated upon the Isle; Senniel, therefore, sent all of its master bards, or rather, all of the bards still in residence in the city. Even the bardmaster, of the five, the only one who had been born without the bardic gift for which bards were famed, was in attendance. Solran Marten was tired, and it showed; the War in the South had taken some half dozen of her bards from her halls, and she wasn't certain that it would return them all; war seldom did.

But in the absence necessitated by war, The Terafin had fallen in her own manse, and if rumor was to be believed, in her own Council Hall. Thus, the bards gathered. The regent, Gabriel ATerafin, was a man with whom the bardmaster was familiar; Senniel's bards frequently adorned the Terafin grounds during the height of the season, as they were invited to perform at weddings and festive occasions. They were seldom invited to the more somber funerals—but in the case of a woman of The Terafin's significance, they were necessary.

I am old for this, Solran thought, watching her master bards disperse among the guests. She listened, as she habitually did, for the tone and current of the crowd; although she had no talent-born gift, she knew people as well as any who relied on their wits could. She was therefore drawn, by gossip tinged with both awe and envy, toward one of the younger members of the House Council: Jewel Markess ATerafin.

Lays had been written about this girl, and at the quiet but firm request of The Terafin—now dead—they had been closeted within Senniel itself. It wasn't legally required; the request had been made of Solran's predecessor. But Solran had heard the songs: a seer-born girl, born to poverty in the harsh streets of the poorest holdings, had come to The Terafin with a message of both doom and hope: the Lord of the Hells was traveling toward Averalaan. During the darkest Henden of any living memory—and Solran would never forget that Henden, although she had tried many times—Jewel Markess ATerafin had used her gift to guide The Terafin to the Kings. The Kings had ridden, like Moorelas himself, into the darkness that lay in wait beneath the city, and when they emerged, the shadows were gone.

The lay had only been played for the bards within Senniel; that much, Siobhan could not prevent. The Terafin felt the young woman's life would be in danger were the song widely sung—and Solran did privately agree with this assessment. *Amarais,* she thought, pausing a moment to gather herself. *You will be much missed.*

The moment passed, and Solran once again began to walk. She turned a carefully cultivated corner and the first thing she saw—which stopped her in her tracks—were the trees. Many of the guests, finely attired patricians all, had likewise stopped a moment, in wonder; they discussed those trees, and House Terafin, in the hush of near awe. In some cases, the awe was begrudged, and in one particularly loud one, the speaker determined that these were a tasteless illusion put on by hired mages.

Solran knew they were real.

She walked down the path toward the closest of the trees, and stopped again: Jewel Markess ATerafin was standing beneath it. Solran had had cause to meet the young House Council member, but in truth not often. She had never seen her like this. Jewel ATerafin wore a dress that only song could capture, because it seemed to exist as a feeling, an emotion; it implied gossamer, but at the same time, heavy silk, something luxuriant and full. The sleeves draped in a way that made them part of the dress' fall, blending with the gather of train as if they were liquid, but they rustled. The rustle reminded Solran of the movement of leaves, and she glanced at the branches above the Terafin Council member; they were in full bloom.

Nor was that all—although that would have been enough, in Solran's opinion, to keep the Courts in gossip for at least a half month. Jewel wore a pendant that seemed to harness sunlight's more gentle glow around her neck; on her hand was the ring of the Terafin House Council—and one other, worn on the thumb. There was a story there.

But by her side—by her side was a man who was tall, fair, and cold; he was also beautiful in the way things unattainable are. His eyes were the color of steel in the morning light, and they suited the cast of his face; his hair was pale, and it fell down his shoulders in a way that reminded the bardmaster of Jewel's dress. He drew the eye, but everything about him discouraged speech or even gestures of greeting.

Standing by his side, Jewel should have looked dowdy, short, plain. She did not. It was hard to look away from him—but at the same time, hard to look *at* him. She wondered what his voice would sound like to her bards, and made a note to ask, although she wasn't certain he would speak at all; he had that look of silence about him. She managed to look from this armed stranger to the woman he was clearly guarding; it was easier.

But as she approached, she saw the third strange thing: there was a large cat—a maneless lion—standing by Jewel ATerafin's side; it was white—and winged.

Winged.

She drew one sharp breath and submerged the whole of her complicated reaction, donning an easy, friendly smile. She unslung her harp, and set it against her hip. She did not play, or rather, did not sing, but her fingers couldn't hover above strings for long without coaxing something from them. She was not surprised when she realized what she was playing, but she wasn't embarrassed either. Only the bards here would recognize the song, and once they'd laid eyes on Jewel ATerafin, they wouldn't question it; were it not a funeral, they might bring it out into the open at last.

This woman was no callow child, nor one who required shelter or protection from her gift. She had stepped into the heart of a battlefield no less complex than the fields in the South over which the Kings' armies were, even now, waging their very necessary war against the forces that served the god Solran she didn't care to name. She stood like a young Queen surveying her subjects.

Solran had some experience with Queens, young and older, or she might have been intimidated. But she approached Jewel Markess ATerafin as if she were in truth a Queen, and only realized it when she was almost upon her; she might have changed tact or posture, but Jewel was now gazing at her, her eyes widening in a way that seemed far too young for the dress, the pendant, and the guard.

"What is she *playing?*" the winged cat said, and Solran missed a beat. She'd no doubt hear about it when she returned to Senniel. Or maybe not; a peculiar majesty, unlooked for and almost never experienced, had descended upon the Terafin grounds, and in the end, the everyday mockery of the students for the master might not survive it.

"ATerafin," the bardmaster of the most famous bardic college in the Empire said. She bowed, shifting her lute gracefully as she did.

"Do you like her *dress?*" the cat asked.

Jewel ATerafin dropped a palm to the top of his head, and he hissed but fell silent.

"Is it permitted to answer?" Solran asked, with care.

"It is, although it's probably not advisable if you like either dignity or silence."

"I value both in their proper context—but I have never seen a winged cat before, and I have never heard a talking cat either."

"See?" the cat said, as Jewel withdrew her hand, and with it her silent objection.

"I have never seen a dress like it," Solran told the cat. "It is like—like the dream of a dress, something too pure to be reality."

He nodded and straightened; in his fashion, he was as regal as Jewel ATerafin.

"The Queen of the Winter Court might wear such a dress," Solran continued.

The cat's eyes rounded. "She could *not!*" His wings rose, and his fur rose with them.

"Snow, she meant it as a compliment," Jewel now said. "She's never met the Winter Queen, and if she's lucky, she never will."

"Then why did she *say* that?"

"She's a bard."

"So?"

"The bards know a lot of very old songs, some of them in a language I can't understand. She's speaking because she's probably sung songs about the Winter Queen."

"They're *bad* songs. *Stupid* songs."

The hand returned to the cat's head, as Jewel turned to Solran. "Please accept my apologies. He's not used to this much company and doesn't mean to be insulting."

He demonstrably meant to be insulting, but as he wasn't terribly good at it—and, more significant, wasn't human—Solran had no difficulty forgiving him. "May I ask a question?"

Jewel nodded.

"Have you met the Winter Queen that you can speak so definitively? I have often thought there was far more fancy in the ancient lays than truth."

Jewel's expression shuttered. After a significant pause, she said, "I would love to discuss this with you, Bardmaster, but I fear—"

"Ah, of course. Forgive me. Seeing you, seeing these trees, and seeing your companion—I almost feel I am dreaming, and I'm far less careful about etiquette in my dreams."

"There is nothing to forgive," a man said. Solran recognized the voice: it belonged to the regent.

"Ah, just the man I was looking for. Forgive me, ATerafin," she added, bowing again to Jewel. "I've matters to discuss about the disposition of the bards who will be performing; our practice four days ago involved a slightly . . . different landscape arrangement."

"She will not keep this to herself," Avandar said very, very quietly.

Jewel didn't even look at him; she did nod.

To Snow, he said, "I strongly considered removing your tongue."

Snow hissed. *"Try* it."

But Jewel planted her hand on his head again. "Snow. I don't mind if you speak to the guests, but I will send you back to the wing—with Celleriant as escort—if you call *any* of them stupid again."

"I would prefer silence," Avandar said, his voice louder but chillier.

"I'm sure we all would, but let's concentrate on the possible. I think I see the head of the Guild of Makers."

"If you wish to speak with him—"

"I really don't—"

"Simply stay where you are. He is unlikely to get across the green in any small amount of time." Avandar raised a brow. "Have you some reason to dislike him?"

"None at all; I don't think we've spoken more than a dozen words in total. But I've never managed to offend him, and I'd like to keep it that way." She nodded in Snow's direction. Master Gilafas ADelios was not only a maker; he was an Artisan. He was also the head of the most powerful guild in the Empire, not because he was politically enormously adept, but because the Makers' Guild had so much money they had to spend it on something. Land, buildings, art—anything, really.

They also had first right of refusal on one of the gem mines that the House owned, and they paid top price for those gems they chose to retain.

"Perhaps you are wise, ATerafin. I feel, however, that you might wish to relocate, and quickly. He is most definitely approaching you."

The Guildmaster of the Makers' Guild was, apparently, only a little less desirable and intimidating than the Kings themselves might have been.

Avandar was right—he almost always was—but the man's progress across the green was a series of interruptions, some of which he could not easily avoid. She thought him lucky; none of the rest of The Ten had yet arrived, and had they, he might never have made it through their social gauntlet to reach her.

As it was, he spoke longest with Solran Marten—as the respective leaders of their organizations, they had much in common, and there was genuine respect and a hint of affection in their greeting—but he could afford to ignore or offend anyone else. Not even Duvari got in his way, and Duvari generally made it a point to offend and harass every notable person of any power in any gathering that included him.

Sadly, if Duvari wished to be included, he was. Not even Amarais would have refused him, although her acceptance would have been brittle and distant. He couldn't be excluded from the funeral because the Kings and the Queens would be in attendance. He'd made his presence felt among the Terafin House Council, he'd spoken a few words to Solran Marten, but he'd made no effort to approach Master ADelios at all. Whatever the Artisan had, Jewel wanted it.

She meant to say as much, but couldn't; his expression, when he finally stood only a few yards away, all but forbade speech. He certainly didn't speak to her, although he did turn abruptly to ask a question of one of the women who was following in his shadow. She murmured an answer, but he had already turned away.

"ATerafin," he said, and it occurred to Jewel that what he'd been asking his attendant was her name, "I must ask you from whom you purchased the dress you are currently wearing." It was more or less the question that she'd been asked a half dozen times since the non-House members had arrived, but it was said in a particularly pointed fashion, as if it were the precursor to an argument.

"It was a gift," she replied. "A singular gift. Why do you ask?"

"It is not the work of a mere clothier, no matter how talented; there is an artistry here that is generally found in only one guild. Mine," he added, in case this wasn't obvious. "Yet I see most of the requests for commissions that come to the guild, at least within the city, and I do not recall any such commissions for a dress."

"I don't think many people would go to the Makers' Guild for a dress."

"You would be surprised. You would not, from the sounds of it, be surprised at how often such requests are refused."

"Are there any makers who specialize in—in cloth?"

"There are very, very few. One, at least, does not choose to make her residence within the guildhall, but she is oft fractious and not inclined to work to the deadline most such commissions require. If I am not being impertinent, may I examine the dress?"

He was being entirely impertinent, as he put it, but Jewel's only fear of him was the usual one. He was a person of power she didn't wish to offend. There was something about Master ADelios' interest that was so focused, so extreme, and yet at the same time so entirely impersonal, she might have been a mannequin. "Please do."

"If anyone who is watching feels that they may follow my example in an equally impertinent way, I will deal with them," he replied. His voice was cool and autocratic; he was a man who was used to being obeyed. But this man, or the expression on his suddenly unfamiliar face, was almost a stranger to Jewel; his eyes looked as if they were lit from within. He not only approached her, but knelt with care at her feet. Torvan and Arrendas allowed it without shifting their stance at all.

He reached out, carefully, and lifted Jewel's left sleeve, examining its hem, its weight, the fabric itself. He lifted it, exposed its sheen to as much sunlight as a crowded green let in, and slowly let it fall before he moved—still on his knees—toward the train. This, he touched with at least as much care, paying particular attention to the beaded crystal, the gold embroidery, the onyx stones that anchored the single strip of black.

"The cape," he said, rising, "does not suit."

She almost laughed; for a moment he sounded like Haval.

"But the dress is acceptable?" She reached out and very, very firmly placed a hand on the head of her cat—a cat the guildmaster had failed to notice. Nor had he looked up at the trees, or at Celleriant. He had eyes for nothing, at the moment, but the dress itself.

"The dress is, in my opinion, a Work," he replied. "I do not believe I have ever seen this fabric before—and I have inspected many, many varieties in my time in the guild. The beading does not seem to adhere to the dress by something as workmanlike as thread; nor does the onyx. ATerafin, I ask you again, where did you get this dress?"

Jewel surrendered. "Snow," she said, "This is Master ADelios, one of the *most important* men in the Empire."

The master so indicated frowned, blinked, and shook his head. "That's a rather large cat," he said.

"He is. The dress was a gift, however, from him."

The blinking grew far more pronounced. "You are serious."

She nodded. Snow was watching the guildmaster with far more concentration than his norm; it made Jewel nervous. She kept her hand where it was, and briefly considered the advantage of collars and leashes. The disadvantage—mostly attempting to put one on—outweighed it, possibly by a lot.

"Does that cat have wings?" the Guildmaster asked.

"He does."

"My eyes are not what they used to be, and I was preoccupied. You are saying this cat made this dress?"

"*Yesss*," Snow replied.

The Guildmaster blinked and turned to the silent woman who waited at his elbow, looking like the patron saint of patience in one temple or another. She nodded without speaking.

"You made this, yourself?"

"*Ye-ess*."

He frowned. "May I ask where you came from?" As if talking to a giant, winged cat, while disconcerting, was within the realm of his usual reality. Jewel had always heard rumors that Artisans trod the very fine line between sanity and insanity.

"Pardon?"

"Where did you come from? This dress—it speaks of Winter. Or the end of Winter—at night. It hints at loss, but at dawn; it *speaks*, Snow. Did you do that? Did you make such a thing?"

It was Snow's turn to blink. Jewel, however, glanced at Avandar, and then her attention was caught by Celleriant. If the guildmaster hadn't noticed the Arianni Lord, the Arianni Lord now noticed him. He was silent as he moved to stand closer to Jewel. But it wasn't for her protection; he was watching the maker-born man with as intent a fascination as she'd ever seen him show for the merely mortal. "My Lord," he said to Jewel. "Might I speak with the stranger?"

Jewel hesitated, but nodded as Master Gilafas ADelios finally noticed Lord Celleriant of the Winter Court and the Wild Hunt. The older man's jaw fell open as if it were broken. He turned back to Jewel. "This—this man—he serves you?"

"He does."

"Do you know what he is?"

"She does," Celleriant answered. "But the wonder to me, Guildmaster, is that you do; you see it clearly. You understand what you see." He took a step forward and said, "When have you walked in the Winter realm?"

"I—I—"

"You don't need to answer that question," Jewel said, taking one of his arms—his shaking arms—in both of her hands, as if he were in need of support. She glanced much more pointedly at the young attendant, but the attendant stood meekly by, watching the guildmaster's expression with a mixture of resignation and fear.

ADelios, for his part, seemed to be unaware of either Jewel's hands or her words; he didn't pull away; he didn't acknowledge them at all. His expression was odd; he wasn't afraid of Celleriant, although he had a clear idea of what or who he was. "I saw the Winter Queen," he told the Arianni Lord.

"And you yet live?"

"I know some part of how to walk that road in safety, if such a thing is truly possible," was the more dignified response. "But I lost—I lost someone—there. I lost an—" he shook his head. "Have you come from the Court of the Queen?"

"I have come from the Queen's host, but I will not return to her side unless—or until—Jewel ATerafin is dead."

"How long have you served her?" he asked, pressing his point as if Celleriant presented no danger at all.

"For some mortal weeks," Celleriant replied. He wasn't angry; he was, if Jewel was any judge of the immortal, curious.

"Then you were with the Queen of Winter until that time?"

"I was."

The guildmaster closed his eyes, tilting his head upward, as if seeking sunlight, or the warmth of its promise. Eyes still closed, he said, "Were there mortals among you?"

"There were those who were once mortal."

At that, ADelios opened his eyes. He was pale. "I will not play games with you, but I will make you an offer instead."

Both of Celleriant's brows rose. "An . . . offer?"

"Answer my questions. Answer them truthfully."

"In return?"

"I will make you any object it is within my power to make."

Jewel almost stopped breathing. She glanced, wide-eyed, at her liege.

It had never occurred to her that the autocratic and somewhat unfriendly guildmaster of the richest guild in the Empire might desire any information that Celleriant had; he wasn't a mage, and study of the ancient was in no way his specialty. Nor did his words imply that that was his interest; there was an edge of desperation to them.

"You are maker-born," Celleriant said.

"I am. I am the Guildmaster of the Guild of Makers—an entirely mortal organization, I'm afraid."

"The talent-born are entirely mortal," Celleriant replied. "And of the talents, it is the strangest. Very well. I will entertain your questions, and if I do not feel that they impede my oaths or my duties, I will answer them."

"A mortal girl entered the Winter realm when the roads were passable."

"The roads are very seldom passable to the merely mortal. I will not lie to you, Guildmaster; I have some respect for the makers. If I cannot answer your questions, I will ask for no boon. But if I can, remember what you have promised."

ADelios managed to look offended, but it was a shabby display; Haval would have smacked the back of Jewel's head for such transparent acting. "It was several years ago. She—she had a task set her. She was not merely maker; she was Artisan, and of a power that only legend now contains. She was young. She was not beautiful, not in the—"

"Beauty is not a shared language between our kind," Celleriant said, in a much softer voice. "You cared for her." It was not a question.

The old man—and he seemed old, now—smiled bitterly. "She was in my care, yes. I am not certain why she chose to venture upon the hidden roads; she did not speak often of her gift or her compulsion. But she lived in Fabril's reach, with me."

"Fabril?" Celleriant said. "You almost make me feel young again, Guildmaster."

"Fabril is dead, of course. But he created some part of the building which the guildhall now occupies."

"That would explain much. She came to the road, and she met my kin?"

"She walked to the road with two broken artifacts, and she remade them. I did not ask her how; I'm not sure she could answer in a way that would make any sense to anyone who was not maker-born."

"You fear they killed her."

"I—" he looked away. "I am certain she is still alive."

Celleriant frowned. "Did this mortal girl cause harm?"

"She did."

"To the host of the Queen?"

"Yes."

"How?"

"I believe she cut them down. With a sword."

Jewel was staring at the maker. "How is that even possible?" she finally asked.

But Celleriant said, "I know how, ATerafin. I think I might even understand why."

"Then explain it to me," the guildmaster said. "She was not—I would swear she was not—a violent child; she was not willful except in the way the maker-born are. I remember the carnage—"

"She could not do what she had to do if she did not kill." Celleriant's smile was cold and slender. "We are not close in the ways mortals often are; we do not huddle together for company or our own protection. That is not the way of my kind. But we understand some of the forces behind the greater workings. We have our own craftsmen, our own artists—and art, like love, is in the eye of the beholder.

"Nothing great is worked or made without cost. Nothing. And I believe I know what she wandered the path to make—or remake. No, have no fear; I will not mention her task further. But I will tell you this, although I do not think it will grant you any peace. She could not complete her making without bloodshed. Had she not been upon the Winter road, she might have walked in abandon through your mortal streets, and untold numbers of your kind would have perished before the blade could be quenched.

"I remember the moon and the road of that night. I remember the girl."

"What happened to her?"

"She gave the items so precious to her into the keeping of another mortal, one less foolish, and far less driven, than she. They were the only things she might use to survive if harm was intended, but it was not her own survival that was her concern—and it has ever been that way among the maker-born. You are that mortal?"

ADelios bowed his head.

"Then I will tell you only this: she is not dead. She is alive. I cannot say she is happy, because that has no meaning. But it is Winter, and the seasons have not turned. They would drive a normal mortal mad, but the Artisans have always been mad; they are immune to the fixed season, and they see things in the snow and hear words in the wind; they see, in the shapes of trees and the fall of shadows something to grasp and take and change.

"Will she—will she return to us?"

"Can she resurrect the dead? No. She will never return to you. But in some fashion, she may find peace, and in some fashion, Guildmaster, she may be of great aid to us in the war to follow."

"And if I asked if I might see her again?"

"Then you ask about the hidden ways, the Winter road, and you are aware of the risks involved." Celleriant glanced at Jewel. "The roads will not long remain hidden, Guildmaster. If you seek to find her again, you must ask my Lord for her mercy."

"The Winter Queen—"

"I told you; I serve Jewel ATerafin, until her death. It is she who can grant what you desire—but at a cost that she at least does not fully understand yet."

Jewel, whose hands were still around the older man's arm, said, "It is not yet time, Gilafas ADelios. But the time will come, and you will know it. Come to me then, if you can." Unfortunately for Jewel, those weren't the words she'd intended to say, and she had no idea where they'd come from; she just *knew*, as they ended, that they were the truth.

He accepted them that way, as well; any other man of power and political cunning would have been all over the words in an attempt to pick them apart. She did not understand this man at all. Had he not been such a significant power, it wouldn't have mattered. She let go of his arm as he turned—but he turned toward her and caught both of her hands in his.

"Don't thank me," she told him, before he could speak. "It's not with me that you made your agreement—and I can't imagine that Lord Celleriant will ask for something small or inconsequential in return."

But the guildmaster shook his head. "If you can, indeed, give me the opportunity to see that child again—to apologize to her—I will be forever in your debt." He released her hands and pulled back, dropping into a bow that would have caused Haval to cringe. Clearly, if one had enough money, anything was acceptable.

"I very much like your dress, ATerafin," he finally said, before he allowed himself to be dragged off.

"There is more to this city than I would have thought possible," Celleriant said softly, once the guildmaster was beyond sight.

"There's probably more to any mortal city of any size than you'd think possible," was Jewel's sharp reply. She had watched the guildmaster walk away, and she had watched, with consternation, the way the gathered members of her House now looked at her. She wondered how much they'd seen or what they'd heard, and what they now made of it, because Gilafas ADelios bowed to very, very few, and most of those had crowns of one sort or another on their heads.

"Well done, ATerafin," Avandar said quietly, which only compounded her sense of unease. He glanced at Lord Celleriant. "Fabril's sword and rod?" he asked; his voice barely carried.

Celleriant raised a brow, and rewarded him with the hint of a smile. "You are perceptive, Viandaran. At a later point, you might explain it to our Lord; she does not understand all of what was said."

"She does understand that she's been talked about as if she's not actually here, on the other hand," Jewel said sourly.

Angel, who had been quiet throughout the long morning, laughed. She was surprised by the sound, surprised for a moment to see him standing to one side of the tree, watching, a half smile on his face.

"I was wondering," he said, as she walked toward him, "if the dress had entirely absorbed you."

She raised a brow and he laughed. "I guess not?"

"No. But you look impressively intimidating, if that counts."

"It counts for something," she replied. "But I think it might be expensive in future."

"The future," Angel told her, with a grave nod to the terrace, "has arrived in force."

The Ten had come.

Haval watched Jewel discreetly as the first of The Ten—in order of arrival, and not, in Haval's opinion, significance—made his way down the terraced steps. The Wayelyn was dressed in a somber suit that was appropriate for the occasion, itself a bit of a surprise. The least powerful of The Ten in any practical measure, he was also the most wont to shed, as he called them, the restrictions of the patriciate. On the other hand, his House Council had gathered about him like vengeful schoolmasters; where he looked slightly ill at ease, they looked watchful. The Wayelyn was the first of The Ten to see Jewel ATerafin.

He was also the first to stop dead in his tracks; his sudden lack of motion a deliberate choice, and one that garnered attention. The one thing the man could do at whim was draw such attention; he did it unconsciously, the way his more mature counterparts in the Hall of The Ten drew breath. Haval had never paid particular attention to House Wayelyn; he considered the ambitions of its putative head to be, if not beneath notice, then unworthy of his full intellectual rigor.

The head of the House, in his black and white—colors which did not, admittedly, suit him—immediately made his way toward where Jewel now stood. Various members of the House, and various merchant houses, had made their way toward her on one pretext or another; at least three were trading rivals of some minor note, in his opinion. They had, of course, withdrawn, given the nature of the occasion—but they had not withdrawn so as to be out of line of sight of her.

She was not, lamentably, aware of this; Haval, however, was.

"I trust you are enjoying the view?"

Haval raised a brow at the Lord of the Compact. "I would thank you not to stand there; you are blocking my light."

"Very clever. I imagine that you are not yet queued to join the mourners?"

"I am very, very far down the list, as you are no doubt well aware; I have, however, been cleared for access as a modest clothier with an unimpeachable reputation."

Duvari's expression soured further, although most would not have noticed the change; Duvari was not a man given to any expression that implied friendliness. Or humanity. It was one of the qualities that Haval admired. Haval considered himself too lazy to adopt such a formidable and severe bearing for any length of time; it was far too much work for the very meager amount of information he might obtain. No, Haval's preferred methods were ones he had long practiced. He liked to observe.

If Duvari looked ill-pleased, he did as Haval requested. Haval continued to watch as The Wayelyn offered Jewel an exaggerated performance of a bow. The bow did not please his minders, to be sure, but it was entirely within character. He rose; Jewel had not offered him a hand to kiss, which was unfortunate. He would have to speak to her about that later. "Have you made certain that the magi are watching the arrivals?" he asked, without taking his eyes off the unfolding discussion. He couldn't hear a word at this distance without magical intervention, and while he was not above its use, only Duvari and his operatives would be granted the necessary permissions in this House, on this day.

Snow was conversing with The Wayelyn, and to Haval's amazement, the head of one of The Ten now burst into song. This voice was not a natural voice; it was tinged by the talent that usually drove men and women to the bardic colleges. He therefore had a tenor's natural range, but could stretch his voice to reach lower tones; Haval wasn't certain if this was done with ease or not, but it didn't matter; it was done and made to appear effortless. His song, unlike his conversation, carried the full distance.

Haval couldn't resist a glance at Duvari's expression; it was stone.

Jewel reddened, but as the song continued, whatever embarrassment or hesitation marred that first reaction slowly melted, like snow at the start of spring. What song was he singing now? Haval frowned. It sounded like a children's song, a children's rhyme—about a young girl searching for her young man in an enchanted and dangerous land. It wasn't—quite— doggerel, but in Haval's opinion, came close.

But when he heard:

> *Leaves three, she carried, carried, three leaves*
> *Winter Silver, Summer Gold, Earth's Grief*
> *Leaves three, she carried, carried, three leaves*
> *To find him, to show him the way*

His eyes rounded. Why, he thought, that song, and why to Jewel, now? Haval closed his eyes briefly when the cursed cat leaped off the ground, spreading his wings like contained storm. The Wayelyn, however, did not pause; he sang, now, of the hidden ways, the darkest road, and the nightmare bower that waited. If it were not for the sudden interruption of one of his minders—Haval thought it the wife, Akyna—he might have continued. Most lays of this nature were quite long, and Haval very much doubted they were appropriate for the venue, or at least the context—but he did not doubt that the bard-born voice of the Wayelyn might carry the day.

Had the bardmaster been closer, she might have prevented it, though; she had all of her bards on as tight a leash as one could reasonably expect bards to accept. The Wayelyn, trained under her predecessor, was the exception; he was a bard who no longer owed allegiance to Senniel College, although he was reputed to favor it highly. Akyna then spoke a few words with Jewel; judging by expression alone, many of them were apologies. Jewel, however, was gracious; Haval thought her unoffended once the initial surprise had faded. She did, however, lift head and speak curtly—and clearly—to Snow, who affected not to hear her.

The shout did nothing to enhance her dignity; the fact that she was speaking to a large, flying cat—an obviously magical creature—served to mitigate. Yes, Haval thought, the three days promised to be interesting.

So it went. The eight remaining House Leaders met with Jewel. They spoke, of course, with the regent first—all but Wayelyn, who spoke with the regent last—and spent a few moments in discourse with the significant members of the Terafin House Council; they understood, as well as Duvari did, the nature of the conflict likely to arise within the House at the end of the funeral rites. They did not choose sides, although he was certain at least two of The Ten would attempt to offer money or support to prolong the struggle; a long battle for the House Seat would almost certainly weaken Terafin's position on the Council of The Ten, allowing other Houses to assume a more prominent role. But as they were not yet certain who would occupy that seat, they treated all of the House Council of any note as if they were to become worthy rivals.

Of The Ten, two leaders were absent: Kalakar and Berrilya, swallowed at the Kings' command by the war in the South. Kalakar had, according to rumor, been as much a Terafin ally as one could expect upon a Council of the ambitious and the powerful. In their stead, senior members of their individual House Councils fulfilled their responsibilities, but their absence was a reminder that life—and war—continued unabated beyond the bounds of this singular House, this singular death.

Perhaps Jewel needed the reminder. She was in a strange state of suspension, in Haval's opinion; she moved and acted as if she stood upon ground that, at any moment, might break beneath her feet. She could turn in place, but at most she took a single, uncommitted step outside of her small zone of safety, hiding behind the necessary respect for the woman who had been her mentor.

Or perhaps, just perhaps, he was being unfair. Watching her at a distance, in a dress that had not pleased her in the slightest, she stood as tall as her negligible height allowed, and if she was not perfect in her control, she was—for Jewel Markess ATerafin—as close as she had yet come. Was it enough?

He watched her as she spoke with The Korisama, a man who affected an almost Southern style of dress in prominent, public places. Today was not to be the exception; the colors he wore were white and midnight blue, not black. Only in the Dominion of Annagar did such colors signify mourning or loss. There and in House Korisama itself. Jewel, however, seemed to take no offense at the departure from Imperial tradition; she seemed to understand its meaning.

The Korisama was quiet, and from a distance, respectful. Jewel extended the same courtesy, albeit not for long; the Houses gathered, but so, too, the significant and powerful among the merchants and the guilds. They gravitated toward her as word of her attire and her companions spread.

Haval's attention slid from his young charge toward the House Council members he considered a possible threat. Harraed kept his distance, although he did deign to speak with significant members of the patriciate. Haval recognized two that lingered longest: Servalis and Daetton. They were not of The Ten, of course, but their prominence in the Merchants' Guild was unassailable; they were part of its governing body. So.

His gaze moved on, to Rymark ATerafin, and stopped there. Rymark was not in conversation with anyone of significance—but he *was* in conversation, briefly, with someone Haval failed to recognize. Rymark's arrogance and his disregard for the common class was a hallmark of his personality; if he had words to offer someone insignificant enough that Haval would fail to recognize him, they were offered in disdain or disregard.

But he was clearly engaged with this one man. Haval turned to the Lord of the Compact, still present. It warmed his heart—in a manner of speaking—to see that Duvari had both followed the direction of his own observation and had arrived at the same silent concern.

"Who is he?" Haval asked quietly.

"A very good question," Duvari replied. "I will leave you to your long-distance babysitting; I have inquiries to make in haste."

Chapter Twenty-one

SIGURNE MELLIFAS drew close to Jewel when the girl—and at thirty-two years of age, girl was perhaps unfair—had become almost vacant-eyed. It was, even for Sigurne, hard to look away from her. The man who stood by her side—immortal, Sigurne was certain—helped, but in truth, far less than Sigurne would have expected. The guests had begun some movement toward the chairs, benches, and small platforms erected for their use. When they were seated, the Kings and the Exalted would at last join them. The Kings only milled in this particular way in their own Courts and, truthfully, seldom there.

The Queens, however, had arrived, with their respective Courts. Sigurne was pleased to see Commander Sivari in attendance at the side of the Princess Royale. Only the Crown Princes would fail to make the first day rites; they were to be present to pay their respects upon the quieter and more introspective second day. This was, as far as Sigurne could tell, normal operating procedure for the Crowns, or at least for the man charged with their physical safety.

Princess Mirialyn ACormaris headed toward Sigurne, an odd half smile at play on her lips. She was grave and measured in her approach in almost all things; she clearly favored her grandfather, on her father's side. She wore a Court dress, and not more martial wear, although she was at home in either. Her hair, bronze and long, had been partially captured in pins and braids; pearls and small emeralds had been woven through the strands. They were kept in place by magic, but it was a legal use of magic—if an expensive one.

"Guildmaster," Mirialyn said, bowing.

"Your Majesty," Sigurne replied. "If we are being formal."

Mirialyn smiled; the smile was cautious. "We are being very formal, as always, in grave circumstance. I see you are watching over the young ATerafin House Council member who has caused such a stir in the crowd."

Sigurne raised a brow. She did not, however, deny it; Mirialyn was too observant by half and would only attempt to ascertain the purpose of any lie she cared to make. "I am an old woman," was her austere reply, "and should the need arise, I will be forgiven any interruption or demand on account of that age."

"And not on account of your position as the leader of the magi?"

"No, certainly not on that account. Would you like to speak with her?"

"No; I merely wish to observe. The . . . cat—did it arrive with her?"

"No. Not immediately, but it came shortly thereafter. I believe it appeared during the difficulty in the Terafin grounds."

Mirialyn nodded. "And the Lord of the Wild Hunt?" Her voice was cool, clear.

Sigurne tensed, stiffened, and smiled. "He arrived at her side. It was his sword that dispatched The Terafin's assassin."

"So I was told. You are certain he arrived at her side?"

"As certain as I can be. Jewel ATerafin is many things—some inexplicable and possibly dangerous—but she is almost without guile. I have observed her in her own quarters, among her kin. She has a pack of councillors who are, at the same time, close siblings. At least they squabble as if they were."

"The assassination attempt on Jewel?"

Sigurne cursed privately behind the facade of a tired smile. The Princess was well-informed. But she would be, if she desired it. "You must speak with the Lord of the Compact."

"I have." She glanced past Jewel to her domicis, frowned, and said, "I am not entirely comfortable with the current arrangement."

"Then you must speak with Jewel ATerafin, ACormaris. I believe she will put you at ease."

"It is not Jewel ATerafin that I mistrust. Those without guile are often easily misled," she added.

"It is true. Those without guile are, however, seldom seer-born."

"Has her talent given any possible warning of danger or disaster during this funeral?" Mirialyn asked, watching Jewel at a distance.

"I don't know. It saved her life; I believe it saved the regent's life as well. But you are aware that her talent cannot be directed."

"Ah, no. I am aware that she cannot—yet—direct it; they are not the same thing."

"The guests," Sigurne said quietly, "are being diverted toward the bier's location."

Mirialyn nodded, but her gaze went up to the tree's full branches and rested there in silence.

Teller slid through the crowds to reach Barston—and Gabriel, to whom Barston was almost physically attached, if invisibly.

"Are there difficulties?" The most formidable secretary in all of House Terafin asked, voice stiff and almost inaudible in the milling crowd.

"There are variations to the invitation list that I last received."

Barston frowned. "Impossible."

"So I would have said, given Duvari's presence."

"Who is present?"

"There are two extra guests in the retinue of Lord Sarcen."

Barston's frown deepened. "He is not an insignificant man."

"He is not."

"I almost feel guilty asking you to do this, Teller, but—"

"You want me to find Duvari."

"Or someone who reports to him, yes."

"Now?"

"Absolutely now, while the Kings have not yet arrived."

Teller nodded as Barston turned his attention to Gabriel. The funeral was, to Barston, Barston's office, and therefore anyone of significance who worked with him, a nightmare that would not end for three days. To make matters worse, Lord Sarcen was a member of one of the oldest Houses in the patriciate, and what he lacked in raw money and political power, he made up for in prestige. He had had three daughters, all of whom were advantageously married into families of power and note. He was rumored to have a small and expensive gambling problem; Teller wondered, as he drifted away from the regent's retinue, if Sarcen had actually sold secondary invitations. It wouldn't be beyond what he knew of the man, although admittedly that was very little.

Barston's request, however, was problematic. While Teller recognized Duvari on sight—anyone of any position in any House did—he couldn't easily spot him in the crowd, which probably meant he wasn't *in* it. Crowds had a way of parting whenever Duvari walked into them.

But easy or not, Barston's concern was serious. Teller surveyed the gathering of guests with care before he began to move through it. Even in Haval's somewhat heavy and confining clothing, he hadn't lost the ability to navigate a crowd; it was more difficult when half of the people in the crowd recognized him, however. He considered removing and pocketing his House Council ring; it was new, anyway, and he still wasn't accustomed to its weight—both literal and figurative—on his hand.

"Ah, Teller," a familiar voice said, at his left elbow. He grimaced and turned; the crowd was now thick with moving bodies as people began their surge toward the seats and benches in the distance. Even at a funeral it appeared that attaining the best position was a necessity that allowed for a little loss of dignity.

He turned to see Haval looking at his jacket with a markedly critical expression. "You *did* speak with Ellerson before you left the wing this morning?"

Teller grimaced but ducked his head in a nod. "At least three times."

"Allow me." The erstwhile clothier reached up and straightened Teller's collars, adjusting the gold pins that held them place. They were not terribly expensive and not terribly ostentatious, but suited Teller. On most days. From Haval's expression, this was clearly not one of them. "You are in a hurry?"

"I need to find Duvari."

Haval frowned. "Why on earth would you need to find the Lord of the Compact?"

"Lord Sarcen has two guests in his entourage that weren't on the list. Two extra guests," he added, in case this wasn't clear. He hesitated, because he realized that he was *also* explaining this to a man who made dresses for a living, and he was explaining it as clearly and as quickly as he might have had Jay asked. Not a good sign.

Haval, however, frowned. "I see." He glanced through the moving crowd. "Have they left the grounds?"

"They're with Lord Sarcen," Teller replied, as if that was all the answer required. It was, if you knew anything about Lord Sarcen. Haval's brief and economical nod indicated that he did. It should have surprised Teller; it didn't.

"How long ago did they arrive?"

"I don't know."

"You know the guest list?"

"I don't know it as well as Barston does; I know the original list, but there were about a hundred and fifty amendments by the time it was done, and each and every one of them was an emergency of one kind or another."

"I will find Duvari," Haval replied, his voice losing inflection and irritation and becoming something more distant and inscrutable instead. "You, however, will find Lord Sarcen's guests. Take one or two of the Chosen with you; if you are at all obvious about it, you will attract the attention of one of Duvari's famed *Astari*, and you may need them." He turned on heel—quickly—and vanished through the crowd with an ease that belied both his age and his general demeanor. It was an ease that Teller himself could have managed only in his youth.

"ATerafin," Avandar said quietly.

She was trying—hard—not to shout at Snow; Snow was blithely ignoring her, although she was certain he could hear every damn word she'd spoken. Sadly, she was certain anyone else in the crowd could *also* hear them, and Avandar would make her suffer for eternity if she started cursing in Torra, which she desperately wanted to do.

"ATerafin," the domicis said again, this time with more urgency.

She looked away from the sky and the sight of wings that were both powerful and graceful. "Sorry. Did I miss something I shouldn't have?"

"You did. The first chimes have sounded."

"We're not due to leave until the second."

"They sounded ten minutes ago."

"Oh." She glanced around the flattened grass; most of the guests had departed. One or two remained, and like Jewel, their gazes were pinned to the sky, where the crowning glory of impossible trees met the flight path of impossible cat. Notably, none of the watchers were among The Ten or their entourages. One or two, however, looked like priests from their robes; she recognized the gold and silver of eagle and rod. The Church of Cormaris had arrived. The Exalted, however, had not. Or rather, they hadn't set foot in the grounds yet.

Gathering her skirts, she moved out of the lee of the great tree. Torvan and Arrendas formed up in front of her; Arann watched her back. It was an arrangement that brought her a much needed sense of comfort, if not familiarity. Angel was at her side.

"Did Carver and Jester not arrive?" she asked him, out of the corner of her mouth.

Angel nodded. "They arrived thirty minutes ago, but you were busy."

"And they went where?"

"I don't know. I didn't want to leave your side to babysit."

She couldn't help herself; she snickered. When he offered her his arm, she took it; Celleriant chose to walk on the other side of Arann, leaving Avandar the space to Jewel's left. They made it most of the way down the clearly marked path before Jewel stopped walking. The path was glowing faintly in her vision—the mages had worked here, casting protective spells across the grass, the path, the lamps, and the area itself. Shadows encroached on them now; Jewel glanced up to see that the sky was darkening by shades as clouds rolled in.

"Well," Angel said, "At least the work of the mage-born wasn't wasted; we're going to see storm today." He stopped walking first. "Jay?"

Jewel swallowed. Angel caught the hand that rested against his arm as it tightened suddenly around the fabric of his jacket and his shirt. "Avandar!"

The domicis frowned.

"Where's Teller? Where's Finch?"

"Finch is with the delegation from the Merchant Authority. I am uncertain as to the whereabouts of Teller. ATerafin?"

Jewel's hands were shaking; her eyes were wide, unblinking. For a moment her face was a blank composed of all the familiar pieces: nose, mouth, eyes.

Angel understood instantly what it meant. He looked up at Snow and shouted, and this time, Snow deigned to land. He landed *on* one of Angel's feet, which, given his size and the small space in which he had to maneuver, was no mean feat. But whatever he'd meant to say when he opened his mouth, exposing large fangs, he forgot as he stared at Jewel.

"Oh," he said, his voice dropping. He turned to Avandar. "She is seeing," he told him. The fur on his ears and around his neck began to rise, as did his wings.

She was also trembling. Angel turned to Avandar; the domicis, frowning, had pulled a small rod from the folds of his robes. Jay called it "the bit"; she disliked it, but didn't forbid its use—mostly because when it was being used, she was pretty much incapable of speech. When she dreamed, when her visions came in the dreams that caused a den migration to the late-night kitchen with its multiple lamps and its old-fashioned slates and chalk, she didn't have seizures.

But on those rare occasions when vision—certain vision, not a nameless, instinctive dread—came during the waking day, she could start to tremble and shake so much she couldn't control anything physical at all. *Not today, Kalliaris, not today*, Angel prayed. But he shifted his grip to her shoulders as her mouth began to tremble. She swallowed.

"Angel—Angel *get Duvari*. Get him *now*."

Avandar shook his head. "ATerafin, I will find him. What must I tell him?"

"It's not here—they're not coming *here*, not today, not now."

Avandar didn't ask who she referred to—even odds she wouldn't be certain herself. But in this case, *they* was always bad. He nodded grimly. "Celleriant."

Lord Celleriant nodded, cool now.

Torvan gestured, and Arann joined him. He then said—to both Arann and Angel—"This is a seeing?"

Angel nodded. Arann was slower, but nodded as well. "It's—not good," Arann told the former Captain of the Terafin Chosen. "But—it'll be clearer than most of her 'feelings.'"

Her hands had tightened again; Angel could feel his arm going numb. "Angel—Arann—"

They gathered around her, as if they were in her room or the kitchen, and not in the grand gardens of the most powerful House on the Isle.

"They're going to *Avantari*. They'll kill the Princes. They'll slaughter the Swords, and they'll kill the Princes."

Celleriant was the first to reply. "Are these Princes significant?"

The question robbed every other person present of speech for a moment. It also annoyed Jay, which was not a bad thing. She struggled to take control of her body, to separate herself from vision's grip. Angel understood that this meant she thought she'd seen enough—and was aware that more could be costly on a day when she couldn't afford it.

"They're the heirs to the Twin Thrones," she practically spit. "*Yes*, they're important." She glanced at the sky as if she hated the sight of it, and then at the cut stone beneath her feet. Her knees buckled, but she locked them before Angel could shift to take more of her weight in his hands. "We have time—but not much of it. Not much. Is Sigurne—"

"I am here, Jewel," the guildmaster said, in a tone of voice that Angel had never heard her use. "You are certain of what you've seen?"

Jewel swallowed. Nodded. No one else would have dared to ask.

"How long do we have?"

She shook her head. "Not—not long. Not long enough to ride. But long enough for—"

But Sigurne shook her head. "The magi are under the auspices of the Lord of the Compact; if there is an attack upon *Avantari* in his absence, he will not divert the only mage present who can arrive in safety at the palace in time; the Kings themselves are *here*, and they demand precedence. He will have the magi send word to the Kings' Swords—immediately—and he will confer with the Kings when they arrive. The Kings may countermand his decision, and they may choose to cancel attendance at the funeral, but I fear the argument will not be brief; if there is an attack of significance in *Avantari*, Duvari will see the Kings in safety here."

"Send word," Jewel said sharply.

Sigurne said, "It is already done, ATerafin. The rest, I fear, is in your hands."

I know. I know that. She was trying not to shudder. She could feel the involuntary muscle spasms in her arms and legs, and she knew, she *knew*, that if she pushed it, if she clung to the vision that even now seemed to transform the visible landscape, muddying the colors and the physicality of location until almost everything in it was malformed, she would collapse, fancy dress and guards notwithstanding.

She couldn't afford that, here. It wasn't about the dead anymore. It wasn't about the respect she should show them—and gods knew no one deserved more respect than The Terafin. The living mattered. The living had to matter *more*. She forced herself to see the gardens, to see the grounds; she forced herself to look up at the trees, their branches in full bloom and out of season. As she did, she felt her body slow its frenzied shudder; she closed her eyes, hoping that the lack of visual confusion would help. It at least made her feel less dizzy.

"Avandar. Celleriant," she said, eyes closed, vision blanketed in a red, red darkness, "Go to *Avantari*. Go. Save the Princes."

Celleriant was silent.

Avandar was not—but his voice touched only Jewel. *I do not like it, Jewel. We will leave you undefended.*

The attack's not here—not yet—and I've a record of survival. Duvari is here.

The Exalted are here. The damn cats are here, as are the best of the Chosen. Angel's here, she added. *No one's there.*

They do not empty the palace when—

No one who can face what's coming.

Then send Celleriant.

He won't get there in time if you don't go with him. She opened her eyes and faced him squarely. "You can travel there the way mages do. You brought us *all* from the South to the manse—all of us—and you were still standing. You'll have two. You, Celleriant. You'll still be able to fight." She glanced at Celleriant, who had offered no argument, and she recognized the pale light in eyes that looked, for a moment, silver.

"You're not entirely healed," she told him, knowing in that instant it was true. Knowing, as well, that he didn't care.

"There is not the inconsequential fact that the alarms and defenses across the palace will alert every member of the Palace Guard the moment we arrive," Avandar pointed out, "and the Palace Guard is unlikely to recognize a simple domicis. They are also likely to mistake Lord Celleriant for an enemy."

"They would," a new voice said, and Jewel spun on her feet, nearly unbalancing as her knees gave. Angel caught her. Angel helped as she faced Devon ATerafin; Devon, who was standing beside the previously absent Jester. Jester's face was almost the color of his hair; he'd run, Jewel thought, to Devon and back. And he'd dragged Devon with him.

"How did you know—" she began.

"Teller found me. Teller told me to find Devon."

"And bring him here?"

Jester shook his head. "He didn't say where; I thought you'd know what to do with him."

"And you were right," Devon told Jester, in a deceptively mild voice. "ATerafin." He bowed to Jewel; he bowed low. It wasn't a long obeisance, but it was genuine. She hated it. "I will go with them, if Avandar has the power to take me."

"I have the power to send you both—" the domicis began.

Jewel grabbed his arm and shook her head. "Go."

"I do not like—"

"Go. I can't be there—not yet. It's here I'll be needed, if there's need."

Sigurne was watching Jewel; the guildmaster's expression was still cold and harsh, a Winter face. "She is your Lord," the mage said, and although she should have been speaking to Avandar, it wasn't clear to Jewel that her words were meant for the domicis alone. "She has given her orders."

Avandar's jaw tensed, his face paled, but he offered no further argument; not privately, and not in the open. Instead, he held out his left hand to Devon and his right to the Arianni Lord. "Consider only this: there is no advantage to be gained by the death of the heirs if the rulers themselves do not also perish."

"I have," was her stark reply. "Snow," she told the cat. "Tell Night."

"Shall I call the *other* one?"

She hesitated and then shook her head. "I know he's bored," she said, "and I know he'll be angry—but he's where *I* need him to be, right now."

Snow hissed. It was a remarkably smug sound. "I'll *stay* here," he told her.

"After you warn Night."

"Oh. I *already* have."

Cats. She turned to speak to Avandar, and Avandar exhaled. He spoke a single sentence she didn't understand, but she felt the weight of it as a burden or a geas.

He didn't even gesture. He was standing, grim-faced and silent, and then he was gone—and the men at his left and right were gone with him. Where they had been standing, a harsh, harsh silver light, sculpted and brilliant, remained in their absence.

"He is . . . not without power," Sigurne said. Jewel wondered what she could see, as mage and not as undertrained seer. She didn't ask. She found her feet, and she kept them firmly fixed to the ground, putting as much of her weight on Angel's arm as necessary dignity allowed. "Did we miss the second chime?" she asked Sigurne.

"We did, but we are not yet late, and there will be no argument when—and if—the cause is known."

"You've clearly never sat in on the Terafin House Council," was the wry reply.

Sigurne chuckled. "You may have a point, but I will say that I have endured many more such meetings of the magi."

"I think you win."

"Ah. I was not aware that it was a contest." Sigurne folded slowly back into her age. "I fear the end of this day, Jewel," she said quietly. "And I wish Meralonne were here; I had not thought to miss him in this fashion." She frowned. "I believe I hear Duvari."

Jewel heard nothing, and almost said as much, but she turned in the direction that Sigurne had turned, and saw the Lord of the Compact; he was walking beside, of all people, Haval. Jewel felt her shoulders begin a natural inward cringe, and she even let them. It caused Haval's distant features to crimp in an entirely normal—if slightly disapproving—fashion.

"I will speak with him, ATerafin. Let your Angel and your Arann escort you to the ground, and we will join you."

Snow hissed, and Sigurne raised a brow; as the cat managed to curb its tongue, the mage did the same. "Did you see what, exactly, they would be facing?" Sigurne asked, as casually as she might have asked about the weather.

Jewel hesitated. "Not completely."

"Your men will be unprepared."

She shook her head. "No. If it *has* been faced in the past, they'll know what the danger is. Except for maybe Devon, but he's always been good at improvising."

Sigurne approached Duvari directly, leaving Jewel to the Chosen and her den. Jester joined them, signing briefly to Arann and Angel; only Angel signed back, but it was quick enough Jewel missed all but the affirmative. Snow insisted on inserting himself between Angel and Jewel, rather than walking on the other side, and after a long and annoyed pause, Jewel gestured to Jester and he took Avandar's place. All in all, not a bad trade. She was, and felt, exhausted, and the day had only barely begun; the service chimes had yet to ring for the third time. If they did before she was there, it would be unfortunate, as the third chimes announced the arrival of the god-born: the Kings and the Exalted.

Jewel wanted Finch, wanted Teller; she wanted her room, her bed, and a few days of normal in which to find her bearings again after her sojourn in the Dominion of Annagar, with its ancient secrets, its deadly magics, and its demonic war. Instead, she seemed to have breathed that Southern air, and the ancient and deadly now clung to her, transforming the only home she wanted into something alien and terrifying. She was glad that Avandar was gone; he'd only be annoyed at her whining, even if she spoke none of this aloud.

He would, indeed, ATerafin.

She froze. She had forgotten the Winter King. The Winter King, however, had not forgotten her. "You—when did you disappear?"

She felt the warmth—and the edge—of his smile. *You are never observant enough. You rely on your gift and your instinct; you must learn to see without it, where it is possible, if you wish to command men.*

She started to tell him she didn't, but that was wrong: if she meant to be Terafin, she did.

I have come to carry you, ATerafin. Ride the rest of the way.

"I can't."

You arrived on my back.

"When almost no one was *watching*, damn it. I'm already the object of every curious gossip on the grounds!"

"Then how much worse could it be?" Angel asked. When she swiveled to glare at him, he signed: *you're exhausted.*

And the stupid thing was it was true. Her legs were shaking. She stopped walking and exhaled. "Yes," she said aloud. "Yes, if you'll carry me."

I will carry you, little seer, to the ends of your world, and back if you survive it.

Would you have carried them? Could you have carried Avandar and Celleriant to the palace?

He didn't answer. But he knelt in the grass and waited while Angel gently guided her into the riding position a dress demanded. The Winter King was warm, steady, as he rose; she felt secure on his back, beneath the thicket of his antlers. The wild wind couldn't unseat her, here, and if the earth suddenly broke beneath the Winter King's hooves, it wouldn't cause him a single misstep.

I will stay with you, he told her.

"You can't. It's the—"

I will stay. Celleriant and Viandaran have obeyed your command; they are no longer by your side. In my youth, I was a match for neither, he added. The words were a shock to Jewel, coming from a man who decried all confession of weakness.

It is not weakness to know one's power and one's limitations, he replied. *If there is danger to you here, they will be angry.*

"Celleriant won't."

Ah, no. He will be angry if you are injured—it will be his failure. Viandaran, however, will be angry regardless.

"Mostly at me."

The Winter King's chuckle was dry. *You clearly have little experience with the powerful.*

"No, I have a lot of experience with the powerful," was her somber reply. The bier had come into view. "And I know how power *should* be handled, because I saw what Amarais Handernesse ATerafin chose to do with it. If I'm to follow in her steps, I *can't* be less than she was. And what you want, what they want—that's less, to *me*."

Neither Viandaran nor Celleriant would have perished at the hands of her assassin.

"No. But countless hundreds of others would have perished at *their* hands on a whim, on a bad day. It can't just be about our own survival. It can't—there has to be more than that." She hesitated before she reached out to touch the lowest of his tines. "You were a man, once. You were mortal. A King. You ruled one of the great Cities?"

I did.

"But you looked at the Winter Queen. You looked at the gods. You wanted what they had. I look at them, and I don't. I want what I have. I want," she added bitterly, "what I *had* before the gods and the demons chose to play their games in *my* House. I want my den, I want my friends, I want the people I love—yes, that word, and I don't care if I should hide it. I want them to live, and I want to live among them.

"Viandaran has lived forever, practically—what do you think *he* wants?"

The Winter King didn't answer.

"ATerafin." Duvari didn't shout—exactly. But his voice carried anyway.

The Winter King paused without any need for command, and turned in his tracks, his head and his tines facing the Lord of the Compact as he moved at a pace so brisk it was almost a run. He stopped just in front of the Chosen—Arann, in this case, although he apparently failed to notice Arann's existence.

"I must ask one relevant question, ATerafin."

"Please. Ask."

"Did Lord Sarcen and his retinue approach you at all during the reception?"

She frowned. Lord Sarcen, Lord Sarcen. "No, I don't believe so. Why?"

Haval, beside the leader of the magi, joined Duvari. They exchanged a brief glance and no gestures at all, but somehow Jewel's answer was passed between them. In a sharper tone than she'd intended, she said, "Is there a problem?"

Duvari was not beholden to House Terafin or its leaders in any way, but he answered. "There are two dead guards. They are yours."

Her eyes rounded. "Dead? How?"

"It is unclear. They appeared to be sleeping; they were not. I must ask you to make your way to the bier in haste, ATerafin."

"You fear demons."

"I fear nothing," was his cool reply, "and suspect everything. But it was a significant omission on the part of Lord Sarcen; an uncharacteristic one. It is not his way to avoid what everyone else must see." He joined her, displacing Jester without any apparent effort at all. Jester fell back, walking to one side of Arann. Snow hissed, and Jewel said, "Don't even think it."

Together they made their way to the benches and the chairs that had been placed within the heart of the gardens of contemplation, cornered by four shrines that were largely hidden from view by the trunks of the huge and ancient trees that were nonetheless new. As the Winter King walked between these trees, and between the paths that had, in haste, been reconstructed to take advantage of the unasked for miracle of their existence, Jewel felt a soft, warm breeze touch her forehead and her cheeks. She looked up; saw a bower of leaves, and through them, spokes of sunlight.

Frowning she looked skyward; what she could see was the gray green of encroaching storm, and not a small one, either.

It is as you see it, the Winter King said, the timbre of his inner voice almost hushed. *But these trees remember other skies. If there is peace for you at all, it will be here.*

Or nowhere?

He didn't answer. Instead he continued to walk; his hooves disturbed nothing, no matter where he placed them, and they came out into the assembled—and mostly seated—crowd. There were reserved seats for the House Council members, but not all were occupied; Jewel could see Elonne, Marrick, and Haerrad clearly. She could also see their advisers. They were allowed two guards for the funeral, rather than the customary four, and those guards were to stand to one side of the raised chairs; there were therefore six guards.

No, Jewel though, with a frown; there were eight. Teller and Finch hadn't chosen or arrived with their own guard; Torvan had requested that they allow two of the Chosen—each—to take up positions when they were at last seated. She couldn't see Teller, but she could see that Finch was approaching the platform—and by her side, walked Jarven ATerafin.

Finch was allowed two counselors or advisers; she clearly meant to take a risk and have Jarven seated as one of them.

Jewel was willing to bet that Lucille would chop off both of her legs before she joined them, and sure enough, Lucille could be spotted in the thick of the crowd—and at a distance. Lucille had admired The Terafin greatly—but always at a safe distance. It was a pity; if their styles were different—and they were entirely incompatible—they had something in common. Lucille called it "a spine," but Jewel privately thought it was more than that.

Duvari gestured, and Jewel was aware enough of his presence that a slight gesture was all he required to catch—and hold—her attention. He didn't speak; he merely changed the direction in which he was, apparently, following.

Teller knew Lord Sarcen on sight; Lord Sarcen intended anyone of lesser power or rank or at least lineage in the Empire to know him on sight. He was allowed a small personal banner—all of the Houses who had very specific seating arrangements were—and had actually deigned to use this. Or rather, to have one of his retainers do so; Lord Sarcen was not a man who attended to his own tasks.

The banner was in plain view, unfurled and weighted; it was in the center of the small arrangement of chairs—an arrangement somewhat different from that originally put into place by the regent's office. The chairs themselves—not benches—had been pulled and gathered to one side; they had also been moved forward, displacing some of the other seating that had not yet been claimed.

This would have annoyed Teller—given the hectic days of nothing but emergencies and what would, on the surface of things, appear to be trivial complaints from people who couldn't be treated as inconsiderate boors— but he was already annoyed. Everyone of any import had been invited to attend the ceremony—and as with all such invitations, it had been made clear that the Kings would be present. The presence of the Kings generally implied that the invitation list was strict, not casual, and had that not been clear by implication, it had been made explicitly clear in various follow-up communications.

Nonetheless, there were always men—and women, to be fair—who felt themselves above such petty dictates; those rules, of course, applied to *other* people. Never to the Lord Sarcens of the patriciate of Averalaan. The banner was present, yes, and beneath it, people were seated. Teller recognized Sarcen's third wife—the first two had predeceased him—and two of his daughters. He recognized the sons-in-law, men of wealth but of lesser lineage. He did not, however, see Lord Sarcen; he certainly didn't see any of his guests. He stopped to count the two attendants who had also been allowed entrance; they wore Sarcen's colors, and they attempted to be almost invisible.

But they were accounted for; if there was a breach of security, it would not be there. Not even the servants of attending guests had been beneath Duvari's scrutiny; it had surprised Barston. It didn't surprise Teller; had Teller the need or desire to infiltrate a House, he would do it as a servant, or as a temporary gardener, many of which had been necessary in the manse in the past two days. He wouldn't do it as the guest of a Lord of great self-import—or as a guest of someone with actual import, either.

Jester, however, argued the inverse: that people who were willing to present themselves as important were often overlooked when suspicions were high. If one had to lie at all, the brazen lie was better because brazen lies were so outrageous many people failed to question them. Teller decided that some point in between these two was now called for; he therefore approached the banner.

The servants very politely intercepted him; politely and deferentially, to be certain. They noticed the House Council ring, although they'd done so without being obvious. Teller had long since become accustomed to treating servants as servants; he did so now. "I have a message for Lord Sarcen," he told the older man. "Is he present?" He was clearly not present, but forms had to be observed. Or so Barston said.

The two servants exchanged a glance; the younger, the woman, said, "You may leave the message with Lady Sarcen."

"Ah, no, I'm afraid that would not be possible." He straightened his shoulders, smiled, and said, "The message is from the Lord of the Compact."

The servants were clearly of enough import in the Sarcen internal hierarchy that they blanched; it was the first sign that they were capable of panic. "Please," the man now said, "Lord Sarcen was present but a moment ago, and I am certain he will return."

The woman, however, retreated, heading straight for Lady Sarcen as she did. That Lady, august and severe, lifted her chin as the servant approached. Teller couldn't hear what was said, but Lady Sarcen rose from her chair, and her expression could have cut through walls.

Teller straightened his shoulders. He had seen similar expressions in the office of the right-kin, and similar in the office of the regent, albeit not usually in such public circumstances. Facial expressions were like games to many, many people: a bluff. Not, sadly, to all; the trick was to know which was which. Teller had become adept at it, but he didn't have Barston's certainty of position and territory to fall back on here. This was not the right-kin's office, after all. Any gaffe on Teller's part reflected the whole of House Terafin, on the day for which respects for its most noteworthy member were to be offered.

He kept fear—and grimace—off his face as Lady Sarcen brushed past the servant to whom he'd been speaking.

Jewel heard Lady Sarcen's voice as the small party approached the area clearly demarcated as Lord Sarcen's, and she stiffened. She had dealt with her share of angry merchants in her time—many of them in theory affiliated with the House, and with her responsibilities in particular—in her office; she had not, however, been situated in Teller's position, and the obvious, scathing contempt with which the grim-faced Lady now looked down at her den-kin set Jewel's teeth on an edge so sharp if she bit her tongue, it'd fall off.

Stay, the Winter King said, as she started to slide off his back. *You have forgotten with whom you travel. The Lord of the Compact will speak, regardless; I believe, from observation, that this particular difficulty is best left in his hands. If it becomes a larger problem, you may then make it yours.*

She stared at the back of his head because that's what she could see. He was aware of it, and offered his silent chuckle in response. He never quite stood still, on the other hand, as if aware that she might disobey what was clearly not even a request.

Duvari, however, had no difficulty separating himself from either Jewel or the Winter King. He stepped past them quickly, coming up behind Teller in a way that immediately stemmed the icy flow of Lady Sarcen's unfortunate harangue.

"Lady Sarcen," Jewel heard Duvari say, in a voice at least as unfriendly as hers had been, "*Where* is Lord Sarcen now?"

Teller retreated immediately to Jewel's side.

"Trouble?" he asked her, glancing at her face. His eyes stayed there; the momentary—and trivial—annoyance at Lady Sarcen, her husband, and the patriciate's selfish demands in general slowly drained from his face as Jewel watched. "Jay?" He lifted his hands, sketching the question in rapid den-sign. She knew what he saw; was torn between comfort and irritation.

She answered the same way, her hands dancing briefly above the shimmering fabric that covered her lap.

Where?

They had no den-sign for what she said next. "*Avantari*. Avandar, Celleriant, and Devon have gone." She swallowed, shook herself, and shifted her shoulders, bringing them down her back to change her posture into something more suitable for the dress she wore and the creature she rode. "Come, Teller. We're expected, and we've little time before the third chimes start."

Duvari, however, lifted a hand. He didn't actually look back; he was still in conversation with Lady Sarcen. Jewel grimaced. To Teller she signed, *Go sit. Take Jester. I'll follow when I can.*

Teller hesitated, and she repeated the gestures more emphatically. *You're exhausted.*

Yes. She smiled as she gestured; he winced. But this yes carried an unspoken corollary with it: too tired to have this argument. All of the den understood it; only Angel generally pressed her otherwise. Angel, she thought, and then—for no reason at all—Duster. Duster had been the girl who could never, ever just say yes. Not unless half of the Hells was riding down their backsides and any other syllable meant probable death. Even then, she wouldn't actually say the word—but she'd obey.

Teller grabbed Jester, and then signed a single word: *Angel?*

She hesitated a moment before she signed *Leave him*. Arann was with the Chosen; he would stay until she was allowed to finally join the House Council in their seats. Jewel had no idea where Carver was, but Carver was now Teller's problem; he was in theory to sit with Teller as a member of Teller's retinue for the duration of the first day rites.

She had a suspicion that even today, Carver was sneaking private time with a very harried Merry; the Master of the Household Staff would probably spit him if she caught him. Jewel might not be that far behind, all things considered. Her arms and legs were aching, her throat was dry, and the sky above the gathering had folded clouds into such a dense brew it looked like night; she felt—impatient. Fearful.

Lightning split the sky as she watched, its sustained white flash illuminating the grounds and leaching all color from its inhabitants—flower beds, grass, fabric, faces—thunder followed, drowning out speech, although speech had, for a moment paused. People rose as rain began to fall but resumed their seats once they realized it wouldn't reach them; the barrier erected by the mage-born did its work.

Teller grabbed Jester—almost literally, and in a way that would have made Ellerson wince had he been present. Frowning, Teller scanned the crowd—Ellerson not technically a member of the House, was nonetheless domicis; at some point, he'd be here. Given the way the day had been going to this point, he was probably watching, with that slightly starched frown on his otherwise impeccable face. Teller released Jester's arm, but did some rapid signing, and Jester rolled his eyes, but ducked his head to follow. It was slow; he was glancing back at Jay every half step or so.

"She's with Duvari," Teller said, voice low. "Inasmuch as there's a threat here, it can't be worse than that—but Duvari's selfish; he doesn't share. If he's not going to be the one to bring her down, hard, no one else is going to do it while she's standing under his nose."

That made Jester chuckle, and the sound filtered up through his expression, easing his tension. "Your point," he told Teller, and then added, "And yes, today I'm keeping score. What was with Lady Sarcen anyway?"

"She knows where Lord Sarcen is, and she knows Duvari," Teller replied, although he also felt uneasy. "She's making a clear point to the Lord of the Compact: she's not afraid of him."

"If she has to make that point—"

"It's probably not true?"

Jester nodded.

"Well, she doesn't look like a fool."

"I was thinking more witch."

Teller did laugh at that, and then grimaced, because if Ellerson would frown, Barston would practically explode. "She's a significant Lady of, as they put it, society."

"So was The Terafin."

"No. The Terafin was a power. Terrifying, absolute, and, in her fashion, just." Amusement drained from Teller's face. "And we know what killed her."

"But not why," was Jester's surprisingly serious—for Jester—reply. "No one's really asked why; it's like, if she's powerful, that's reason enough." He glanced once again over his shoulder. "For Duvari, it probably was."

"Duvari didn't kill her."

"No. I'd say he wouldn't have been upset—but given the alternatives are all bad to him, he's probably content to live with the least bad." This time his gaze traveled to the Council seats.

"Do *not* impersonate Harraed here. He'll find out, and we'll all suffer."

Jester said nothing; he didn't, however, deny that he'd intended to do just that. Jester could mock with affection, but not often. His critical faculties for appropriate mockery, however, would only be considered acceptable in the bardic colleges; in a House of any power, it was both suicidal and rude.

Teller took his seat beside Finch. Technically that was Carver's chair, but as Carver wasn't here, no one would raise a fuss. Finch and Teller were both so new to the Council they were expected to take some time to assemble a truly worthy retinue; lack of a counselor or two would be almost expected. Or so Teller hoped. Neither he nor Finch had distinguished themselves to the House by their broad and obvious ambition; nor had they done so by their political acumen, their ability to navigate the jackals that waited within the halls of the Merchant Authority or *Avantari*.

They had been elevated to the House Council by the whim and command of The Terafin and she had left them no option to decline what would otherwise be considered a great honor. She had offered them the House Council rings—figuratively, at the time—and had made clear that they would accept them, or divest themselves entirely of the House Name. Teller wasn't entirely certain she would have done this with Jay away— but he knew, by the threat, how very serious she'd been.

And he even knew why. She had seen her own death—but not its manner—and she had chosen her heir: it was Jay. Jewel Markess ATerafin. Without support on the House Council, the erstwhile youngest member would have no hope of taking the House. Teller glanced at her now, in her dress, the Winter King beneath her, and Snow by her side.

There were things that even the powerful couldn't anticipate, things that couldn't be planned for.

Finch touched his wrist, her hands dancing briefly and elegantly in her lap. Her gestures were slight; they could be attributed to nerves by most witnesses. Not, sadly, by the man who sat on her other side: Jarven ATerafin. He looked mildly interested in his surroundings; he also looked somewhat tired and fragile. Given what Finch said of Jarven, the man was as fragile as Barston on a tear; he was just a lot subtler about it.

Teller signed back; they both glanced at Jewel.

Or at the place where she was no longer standing. Teller frowned; he couldn't help it. Lady Sarcen and Duvari were also absent.

Trouble? Finch asked.

Trouble, Teller replied, after a hesitation. *Angel?*

Not there.

Trouble.

Lady Sarcen was not pleased. She was ill-pleased enough at her treatment that she made a point of complaining to the only House member present, which was, sadly, Jewel. Jewel, however, had enough experience in dealing with the outraged that she could endure with a polite smile and an equally polite apology. Given that the inconvenience was caused in its entirety by Duvari, and given that they were both well aware of it, the demand for an apology was just posturing. Jewel could afford to give in to it, or so she felt—but in truth, she was biting her tongue. Lord Sarcen had been informed—all of the patriciate had—of the very strict security demands laid out by the Lord of the Compact, and had Lord Sarcen not chosen to navigate around those rules, neither woman would now be following in the wake of the Lord of the Compact.

It would have helped if Duvari had been angry. Jewel assumed he was, but he didn't show it; his eyes narrowed, his voice dropped, his syllables came more slowly, and with exquisite clarity. He led them away from Sarcen's seating, and he forbid the two servants who had run interference to follow in any way; to ensure that they didn't leave, he summoned two men clad in the grays of the Kings' Swords—but not in the uniform—to attend them.

This had been the first time Lady Sarcen had balked. But it hadn't lasted; there was something about Duvari at this moment—although to be fair, he was always intimidating—that did not allow for more than the facade of angry words. Actual defiance was beyond her. Beyond them both, Jewel thought.

But when he paused to give a set of instructions to a woman in obvious House Terafin servants' uniform, and those instructions resulted—in minutes—in the appearance of Sigurne Mellifas, Jewel felt something inside of her freeze. She gripped the tines of the Winter King, and held tight, pressing her thumbs into their points as if the pain would brace her, wake her, draw her out of the political drudgery that was also political drama.

Sigurne, at Duvari's side, was not an aged scion of fractious scholars; she was grim and pale, and there was no compassion in her. She turned to Lady Sarcen and offered a very brief, very curt bow. "Lady Sarcen," she said.

"Guildmaster," Lady Sarcen replied, bowing as well, but more fully. The fight had left her face by the time she'd risen; she looked—for the first time—frightened. Looks could be deceiving; she turned to Duvari. "Why have you summoned the guildmaster?" she demanded.

"If you do not know, it should not concern you," was his cool reply. "You will lead me to your Lord."

But she had had enough. She relented, at last, glancing at Sigurne AMellifas. "I will tell you where he is to be found," she said.

"Alas, no, Lady Sarcen. You will lead me to him; if he is not present, you will find him. I cannot afford to lose time to any delaying tactic you might choose to employ."

"I was not invited here as your servant—" she began, although her voice was quieter. She looked to Jewel for help, but Jewel wasn't feeling that generous.

"It is precisely to deal with those who were not invited that you are here and they came at the behest of your Lord." Duvari would not be moved.

Sigurne said, "Lady Sarcen, this is not a game. You will tell the Lord of the Compact where you feel your Lord is to be found; do so, and you may walk between Jewel ATerafin and me. If, however, he is not to be found at the location you name, you will lead—and I cannot guarantee your safety from that position."

Jewel was genuinely surprised; it sounded—to her ears—very much like a threat, and threats were not something she usually heard Sigurne utter. Well, no, that wasn't true; when the magi were beginning their endless bickering, she could often be heard musing about their unfortunate deaths by strangulation—hers—but Jewel didn't count those, since she used them so often herself. There was no affection at all in the words spoken to Lady Sarcen, but Jewel couldn't imagine feeling affection for her.

She also couldn't imagine threatening her, if it came to that.

ATerafin, the Winter King said, *be wary now.*

Of what?

Can you not sense it? The air is wild and the shadows where you now tread do not conform to sunlight.

She frowned, gazing at the moving ground beneath his hooves; he was right. It was subtle, certainly subtle enough to be missed in the presence of Duvari, Sigurne, and Lady Sarcen. It was therefore to Angel that she turned. "The shadows," she whispered, bending to bring herself in reach of his ears.

He passed the message—quickly—to Arann; what Arann heard, Torvan and Arrendas also heard. They were, she noted, finely attired, and as they moved, she heard the sound she'd dreaded—for entirely different reasons—since waking this morning: the third chimes had started.

Chapter Twenty-two

"NOT YET," SIGURNE TOLD HER, divining instantly the reason for her sudden panic. "The god-born will come only after the chimes sound for a third time."

"I'm not worried about their arrival," was the terse reply. "They're here and we have no idea where Sarcen is—or what he's with." She turned to Duvari. "Take us to the Kings," she said.

His gaze was sharp enough to cut, and not lightly. But he glanced at Sigurne before he spoke. "It is too much of a risk," he said, his gaze brushing Lady Sarcen as if she were poison.

"It is," Jewel countered. "But the worst possible threat they can pose is there."

"Is this vision?"

"No. Instinct."

His smile was, like his gaze, quite sharp. "Very well." He turned to Lady Sarcen. "Lead us *quickly*."

For something that had sounded like capitulation, it wasn't impressive. But Lady Sarcen was now a shade of gray that highlighted the powders and colors she'd donned in a very unflattering way. She looked truly afraid, although she was a patrician; she did not deign to give voice to that fear. Jewel wondered, as Lady Sarcen took the lead, what Duvari's instinct must be like, for the Lady moved far more quickly—far more certainly—than Jewel would have in her position.

Even had she been guilty, she would have delayed.

But Lady Sarcen led them, in quick turns, up the terrace. She didn't approach the main house; instead she jogged to the left. Toward, Jewel realized, a familiar fountain.

"I swear to you," Lady Sarcen finally said, struggling for breath, "that the gentlemen in question only had the desire to see the statuary and the fountain; it is famous among those who study the works of the Makers, and they are not significant enough to garner the invitation to view it, although they have petitioned House Terafin and the Order of Knowledge, both."

"They are not here now," Duvari told her. His voice was cool as he approached the statuary.

"Duvari, *hold*," Jewel said; he froze almost in mid-step, pivoting to meet her gaze. "Don't touch the water. Sigurne?"

The guildmaster nodded, lifting her hands. "Be prepared, Lord of the Compact. Lady Sarcen, you may return to your seat. But if you seek not to disgrace yourself, you will do so quickly." As if to underline her words, the third chime sounded for a second time. Lady Sarcen did not need to be told twice; she retreated, gathering shreds of dignity around her as she went. Jewel had no doubt that when she arrived, she would be—or appear—entirely unruffled.

"She is correct, Duvari. There is an enchantment upon this water—"

Duvari turned to Torvan. "Go," he told the Captain of the Chosen. "Tell Arundel he is to take the Kings on the secondary route."

Torvan looked to Jewel; Jewel nodded. Neither gesture was lost upon Duvari, but neither soured his mood; it wouldn't have been possible.

"The nature of the enchantment?" he demanded of the mage.

Sigurne appeared not to hear him, and Jewel thought it no act; the mage was bent in focused concentration, her eyes unblinking, her hands raised but almost immobile. She spoke three words—three words that sounded like thunder encased in syllables. Jewel couldn't have repeated them, even if she wanted to.

The water began to rise.

4th of Henden, 427 A.A.
Avantari, Averalaan Aramarelas

Devon, trained to magic, weapon, poison, and subterfuge, was nonetheless not trained for this. The magi who could comfortably travel from one location to another—instantly, and not at a more leisurely pace—were few indeed, and all of them possessed both power and rank. They could not easily be seconded to Duvari, and Duvari made absolutely certain that they could be seconded with ease to *no one* else. His *Astari* therefore lacked the benefit of experience with this mode of travel. Devon, who had survived the training the Lord of the Compact considered utterly essential, was now grateful for this one mercy.

The Terafin manse, with its fine and very crowded grounds, had been beneath his feet; the young woman to whom he intended to pledge his allegiance in the near future had been standing, grim-faced and determined, to his side. Angel, hair rising like a white spire above his otherwise ordinary face, stood to her right, and at her back, shadowing her, Arann, Torvan, and Arrendas—the men who would form the backbone of her Chosen should she survive her attempt to control House Terafin.

She had given her orders—terse, rough orders—and her domicis, a man Devon had never trusted and would never like, had relented with barely acceptable grace, given his role and station. He had offered hands to Devon and Celleriant, and Devon had instantly clasped what was offered. He understood what was at risk.

He had had no idea what to expect. But the grounds and the people that occupied them melted away below his feet—literally. The earth gave beneath him, the colors of grass and stone turned, in an instant to something only an insane painter might consider representative of either. He had fallen an arm's length—and he could measure the arm; it was Avandar Gallais'. The domicis held the whole of Devon's weight while the sky and the horizon and the manse in the distance blurred into a running stream of almost repulsive color that flowed around him. Around them all.

Avandar did his dignity the grace of maintaining his steely silence. The moving vortex of color began to shift. Had he been any other man, Devon would have closed his eyes; he was not; he watched. Here and there streams and trails of color, trailing smudges as if they were slugs, began to separate, pulling themselves toward the periphery of Devon's vision; as they did, the colors began to spin and move. At their center, three men stood; at their edges, spinning faster and faster, color began to adhere.

It adhered in a totally different shape and tone, and when it was done with its motion and movement, when Devon's eyes had adjusted to the sudden snap of stillness and solidity, he found himself standing in a familiar hall in *Avantari*. It was the hall that led to Patris Larkasir's office—and the offices, therefore, of the Royal Trade Commission.

"Why here?" Devon asked, frowning as he forced his vision and his legs to be steady.

"It is the area of the Palace with which I am most familiar. Were Jewel to be where your Princes now are, I would not be similarly constrained; she is not. We had best hope that Sigurne sent word."

Celleriant drew his sword. He drew it from air, not sheath, and its edge glowed a deep, a compelling, blue. Devon realized it was a blue that belonged in the maelstrom that they had just traversed. "Viandaran?"

"I will not expend the effort to arm myself further," was Avandar's cool reply. "We have already earned the ire of the Kings' Swords, whether it concerns you or not."

"It does not; is it of concern to my Lord?"

"It is. Or it will be. The men here will take no orders from you or me; do not seek to give them. Kill them at your peril," he added softly, as if it were necessary. The pale, long-haired man shrugged; it was all of his reply. If the passage from Terafin to *Avantari* had disturbed him at all, it didn't show; Devon suspected it had barely registered.

He began to jog—quickly—down the hall and away from the familiar environs of his office and its identity. He shrugged himself out of his jacket, which was confining; he also discarded the shirt because of its cuffs and its collar. Avandar Gallais had the singular advantage of the robes of the guildhall; they did not encumber him as he fell into easy stride at Devon's side. Celleriant wore armor; his armor didn't change shape or texture. But it caught light that didn't fall, in a way that no other clothing did.

At their back, Devon felt a cool, gentle breeze. It lifted Celleriant's hair, and strands of platinum streamed across his winter-white cheeks. His eyes were glinting like steel caught in light; he was striking, almost beautiful—but cold. Devon shook himself. Although he prided himself on the ability to notice almost everything in any given environs, this skirted the edge of useless information.

"The wind—" he began.

"It is not—yet—mine," Celleriant replied, gazing ahead through the walls as if he already knew who now invoked it. "How far away are your Princes?"

Too damn far. Devon estimated distance as he began to run. Sigurne must have informed the magi—and the Swords—of the gravity of the situation; they were unhampered, and unquestioned, in their run through the halls, and the only people they glimpsed were the servants who, by duty, were meant to be visible. The Swords had been entirely withdrawn.

Devon knew where they could be found, and he felt a moment's relief.

It was broken almost instantly by the sound of cracking rock; the ground beneath his feet shuddered and stilled.

"She was not wrong," Celleriant said in a soft, soft voice. "There is power here."

The doors that separated the wing in which the Princes held their modest Court were open; they were still attached to their hinges, but they were no longer guarded. From the open door, the halls could be seen, and in those halls, for the first time, the din of fighting was audible: men's voices raised in both command and alarm, steel being drawn—but not wielded, Devon thought—not against similar steel.

He paused briefly—very briefly—by the ornate brass sconce just inside the doors, and he spoke one sharp word. The noise in the hall grew clearer, sharper; the orders were now intelligible. The gold engraving that traced the height of the walls and the trim nearest the floor began to glow, even to Devon's eyes; they were orange, now. He frowned as he watched the colors shift and change.

Avandar said, "What color should it be, ATerafin?"

Devon did not reply, not with words, but he reached into the sash beneath his shirt and he drew two daggers—daggers that were unwieldy, they were so unbalanced. They were ornate and ceremonial—but the ceremonies of the gods had always served many purposes. He offered one to Avandar, who glanced at it and raised a brow; he did not take it.

"I cannot be held responsible for your fate once we enter that hall."

"You cannot be held responsible for it regardless," was the domicis' cool reply. His face was shorn of expression; Devon thought he might even be offended. It eased him.

"You can, as I've said, be held responsible for any deaths you cause here." He spoke to Lord Celleriant. Lord Celleriant did not appear to hear a word. This annoyed, but in its way, it was comforting.

Celleriant gestured sharply; light seemed to come to his hands and glove them, glittering like shards of broken glass beneath a lamp that was held askew. He spoke a single word—a word that Devon could not repeat.

His sword caught the same light, and as he raised his left arm, a shield formed across it. Devon didn't even spare a glance at the wards of warning that now lit the halls. They were there to indicate magic and its possible use in *Avantari*, and only those trained to them might understand the information they conveyed, if they knew how to invoke them at all.

But this magic, he knew, would tell him nothing of use for the conflict to follow, and what information the wards now contained, the magi would dissect without pause until Duvari was satisfied with their answers.

Lord Celleriant entered the halls, and with him, a wind so strong Devon felt its tug as he followed. Avandar followed as well, unarmed and unarmored, his eyes narrowed as he scanned the empty halls. They did not remain empty for long; one turn, and the first of the bodies could be seen.

There were three. One, Devon could not identify at all; the face and the chest had been shredded beyond recognition. From size, he thought it male, and a glance at the shape of the hands confirmed this. It confirmed, as well, one other suspicion: the left hand was callused but clean, the nails short; the right hand was scorched and blistered, the ring finger charred to broken bone. The second corpse was similarly mutilated, its hands smaller but no less callused, the right hand burned in the same way. The third corpse, however, belonged to one of the senior staff servants, one who both lived and worked within *Avantari*. She was—had been—a woman of middling years, and her neck had been cleanly—quickly—broken; there was very little sign of struggle.

He rose. The din of fighting, magically amplified, carried the sounds of orders; he knew the stretched and thin veneer of command that asserted itself when the world had gone momentarily insane. Not fear, but close enough. He didn't insert his voice into that mix; the orders told him what he needed to know.

"The Princes are not—yet—dead," he told his companions.

"Viandaran, there are two."

Avandar nodded. "Do you recognize their voices?"

"I recognize one. You?"

"I will deal with the other."

Celleriant bowed. Devon stared at them for a long moment, but did not speak; Celleriant once again took the lead, and this time, the bodies that lay across the floors of the halls stopped no one, not even Devon. But as he ran, he wondered if Jewel had even a glimmer of understanding of what, exactly, Lord Celleriant was; she had claimed his service, and he had claimed to offer it—but did the earthquake or the tidal wave offer service, and if they did, could it *ever* be contained?

4th of Henden, 427 A.A.
Terafin Manse, Averalaan Aramarelas

There wasn't—there couldn't be—that much damn water in a fount this small. Not if it were natural.

Duvari said a *nothing* that was as cold and silent as a killing frost. Angel drew closer to Jewel, but not for comfort or protection—not his own, at any rate. He was waiting when the rain began to fall.

Rain was wet. In and of itself, this wasn't a significant fact—but the magi had labored for hours to erect a tangible barrier that would protect the guests of these funeral rites from its fall. Yet it fell. Jewel glanced up at the grim, gray-green skies, as lightning pierced their awful color. A cold Henden wind blew in its wake. "Sigurne?" she whispered, watching the wall of water as it continued to lift itself from the basin in which it surrounded the statuary.

The guildmaster did not reply.

She had no need; the rain that had begun its unexpected intrusion now flew at the behest of a wind that appeared to touch little else: the water gathered in beads, and joined what had once merely decorated a fountain.

Jewel had seen the rivers rise from their beds in the distant South; she knew what the water could do. But there were no drummers, no demons—that she could see—nothing that controlled what was now clearly under someone's control. Without those, she had no idea at all how to end it.

4th of Henden, 427 A.A.
Avantari, Averalaan Aramarelas

The Kings' Swords had fallen; Devon thought fully two thirds of their gathered number lay sprawled across the floor. He couldn't be certain how many would remain that way until they were at last carried out and laid to rest, nor did he have time to ascertain this; those bodies formed the treacherous ground across which the battle lay. The Swords had fallen in defense of their future Kings; they should have been accorded more respect than they were. Devon attempted not to step on them as he moved, daggers in either hand, toward the enemies he could now clearly see.

He had expected demons; of the *Astari*, he had the most experience in dealing with the kin. But the two who now occupied the center portion of the halls, surrounded by swords and long spears, were not the demons of his experience; they were tall, yes, and slender, and they were obviously powerful—but they were Winter white, and they were beautiful. Their robes—they wore robes, not armor—were dark, and they flowed like shadows cast by moving flags. The demons were graceful, elegant; they moved so quickly they avoided the simple, inelegant edges of sword and pike. Their hands were red and wet.

Between them and the doors that listed in their frames, a dozen men stood, two deep, and it was behind these doors that the Princes now waited.

Celleriant lifted sword and struck his shield with it three times in rapid succession.

Both of the attackers turned, frowning, at the sound. It did not stop them from killing another man; nor did it make them vulnerable to those who sought any advantage at all that could be gained by their lack of attention.

But one of the two looked—for a moment—astonished. His eyes widened, and his hair—ebon to Celleriant's white—stilled in the air and fell across shoulders and back like a mantle.

"Amaraelle," Celleriant said.

"Celleriant." One of the Kings' Swords attempted to bring his sword up—and under—his guard; he did not even kill the man, but instead swept him away with his left arm. He hadn't once shifted his gaze. "It has been long indeed since you ventured from your Winter Caves to seek a battle worthy of you."

Celleriant began to move forward; Devon would have followed, but Avandar caught—and held—his arm. "If you can, ATerafin, have your Swords clear the area."

"Of what?"

"The dead they can move; themselves if they do not wish to join them. Lord Celleriant's arrival has changed the face of this battle."

"The Princes—"

"Inasmuch as it is possible, they are safe for the moment; they will die if we fall." Avandar smiled for the first time. He gestured, his hands rising and falling in a sharp, sweeping motion that suggested blade's movement without requiring the blade itself. The doors that listed suddenly snapped into place, as if remade, and the two who had obviously been responsible for their damage now glanced at Avandar.

Avandar did not draw a weapon. But the man to whom Celleriant directed the brunt of his attention did: it was a long sword, a great sword, and it was red to Celleriant's blue. A shield joined it.

"Amaraelle, do not speak to me of the Hidden Court when you are here killing mortals in a palace of dead stone and dead wood. I had not realized the Hells needed the equivalent of mortal rat-catchers. If your deeds here are now considered worthy of a Lord of the *Kialli,* the *Kialli* have indeed fallen far—but, please, continue; I will wait while I have the time."

On the face of the creature Lord Celleriant addressed was the slightest twitch of line around mouth and eyes, but the man by his side was not so composed; his eyes—clear, pale, the color of light on water—widened. He threw back his head, exposing the slender line of his neck as he laughed. In so slender a man, the sound was surprising, unexpected; his voice was a low, thunderous rumble, yet laced with sheer delight.

Were he not surrounded by the dead, the dying, the broken, he would have been beautiful. No, Devon thought, as the laughter faded into a sharp, cool smile, he *was* beautiful, framed by the destruction he had so casually wrought. "Lord Amaraelle," he said, "if you care to accept the challenge offered, I will attend to the mice myself; it is rare to be afforded such an opportunity in this dull and diminished world."

Lord Amaraelle did not reply. He watched Celleriant in silence, impervious to the amusement that touched his companion, his sword raised, his shield steady.

"I am afraid," Avandar said, "I must frustrate your meager efforts to find amusement in such lesser work." Devon turned to the domicis, drawn not by what he could see, but by what he had heard: the minute shift in the voice of a man who, domicis or no, defined the arrogance of power almost perfectly. Avandar stepped forward, and as he did, he seemed to shed shadow. Not the shadow that might enshroud the demons or the servants of Allasakar, but the shadow that softened light, diminishing what could be clearly seen.

He drew no weapon—no dagger, no sword; nor did he gesture. The hall wards were sensitive to magic; Avandar appeared, at the moment, to be using none. But he walked toward the two, as uncaring of the fallen as those who had killed them, and as he did, both paused.

The man who had laughed at Celleriant's comment now roared again in delight. "Viandaran! You have still failed to escape the curse of the gods? Truly, I could not have imagined that I would meet you here on this day, in this place; I had heard word that you were in the South, harrying the ancient as you pleased!"

"You oft faced death with delight. Of the *Kialli*, you alone seemed ill-suited to the worship of your Lord."

"My Lord?" was the smiling reply. "Look!" he gestured, stopped, frowned. "You have ruined my doors, Viandaran."

"Yes, although their arrangement was aesthetically pleasing. I, too, serve, and my Lord's orders were quite explicit."

"And those?"

"I feel, at the moment, they do not matter. You are here; I am here. If you will leave Amaraelle to his testing, you will not be beset by the merely mortal."

"Ah, no. I will, it appears, be beset by the desperately mortal. You are ever at a disadvantage, Viandaran; you *want* to die."

"It is true."

The smiling Lord tendered him the briefest of nods, and from air drew a red, red sword. No shield, however, came to his shield arm. Avandar noted it, and Devon saw him raise a brow.

"We are what we are. And it is not in the nature of the *Kialli* to gift to strangers and enemies the things they desire. But I will cause you pain, Warlord."

Avandar shrugged, as if bored. He still did not draw weapon, and Devon had thought at this juncture, he might, for the demon—and the compelling, charismatic man could be nothing else—began his approach, sword in hand.

Avandar smiled. It was slight. "We shall see." He gestured, speaking a single phrase that Devon didn't hear the whole of, for the floor beneath their feet shattered, cracks appearing in black and smoky marble almost as one piece, in a web that reached toward the supporting pillars—and beyond.

4th of Henden, 427 A.A.
Terafin Manse, Averalaan Aramarelas

From the grounds came Matteos Corvel, and with him two of the magi
Jewel recognized, although not by name. He wasn't speaking, but whatever words failed to leave his lips were absorbed by Sigurne regardless.
Duvari watched the column of rising water as it built itself into a wall
that overflowed the basin of the fount and spread across the terrace. Sigurne said three sharp words and Jewel saw light, bright and almost
golden, bisect the same terrace in a single, thin line; the guests were on
one one side of it, the whole of the water on the other.

"It will not hold," she told Duvari, through slightly clenched teeth.

"The rain barrier," Jewel said starkly, turning not to Sigurne but Matteos. "The barrier is more important—Matteos, why did it fall?"

Matteos, grim-faced, almost white-lipped said, "There has been a death
at at least one of the anchor points."

Jewel blanched.

"Two," Sigurne interjected. "Two, at least. This is not where we
thought attack would come, and the magi in charge of channeling power
to the barrier are *not* men meant for war. Almost all of the magi who are
have traveled South with the Kings' armies, and they will not return today."

Not today, Jewel understood, not when needed.

She turned almost wildly and Angel caught her shoulder, releasing her
as she stiffened, but standing by her side. His signing was curt and minimal; hers was frenetic. She sucked in wet air as the rain that had breached
the barrier meant to slough it carefully to one side of the manse or the
other joined the water that waited beyond the protections Sigurne had set.

They would not hold. Jewel *knew* it.

"Send the Kings away," she told Duvari, voice low.

Duvari nodded. "If," he added darkly, "it is possible, ATerafin. I will
find Lord Sarcen—"

"You'll find his corpse, but not today," she snapped back. As the words
left her mouth, she realized they were also true. "What we could do, we
did. I saw Sarcen briefly and he didn't look like a demon, not to me. Go
to the Kings."

"And what will you do?"

"We'll—we'll deal with the water."

*   *   *

There was no doubt at all in her voice; Angel knew all the variations of Jay's voice; he knew her anger when it was buried deep; he knew her fear; he knew her joy, which she hid so completely it seemed to outsiders she had no experience of it at all. She spoke with certainty; she spoke as if every word was the truth.

Duvari heard what Angel heard, and he hesitated for only a moment longer before he turned on heel and ran. It was the only time that Angel had ever seen Duvari move. He might have continued to watch, but the water was undulating in a way that suggested it was about to fall.

"It's just water—" he began, but one look at Jay's face made clear that water could—and had—killed in her presence. She lowered her trembling arms, and the sleeves of the dress itself fell with them, trailing down her sides as if they were a white, white liquid that had captured some essence of the sunlight that storm clouds obscured.

Tines grazed the space between Angel's shoulder blades. He turned. The Winter King's large, dark eyes gazed unblinking into his.

"You cannot *stand* there, *stupid* boy," Snow screeched from above.

"I stand," he declared, "where she stands."

"Then you will die, and she will be very *angry*."

The Winter King did not speak a word; nor did he look away. Angel understood what was being asked—or perhaps offered—but he hesitated anyway. "Find the others, Snow," was his compromise.

"Snow is *stupid*," another voice said. "But *I* can find them.*"*

"You're supposed to be with Gabriel!" Angel shouted at Night. Wind tossed the words where the cat failed to hear them. Still air would probably have done the same. He hesitated and then cupped hands to either side of his mouth. "Find them. Keep them safe. Is Shadow—"

"Shadow stays where she left him. He is *trying* to be obedient."

"Go!"

"Yes, yes, yesssss."

Angel watched their wings cut sky as they wheeled and turned. Not even distance could make them look like birds. He turned to the Winter King and nodded. "Arann!"

Arann sheathed sword. "It won't cut water," he said. The Winter King knelt, and both Angel and Arann mounted his ivory back.

4th of Henden, 427 A.A.
Avantari, Averalaan Aramarelas

Devon had never cared to fight. Fighting was the last resort of the *Astari*; it generally implied a failure of planning, a failure of caution, or a failure of forethought. Watching the Lord, he knew that Celleriant lived for— existed for—battle itself. He was no son of Cartanis; Cartanis was a god of War—but of Just War; the war that must be fought. There was no battle that Celleriant would not fight if he deemed the opponent worthy; no further cause was required.

Avandar was not Celleriant, but in some ways, it was worse; when the floor shattered, Devon knew whose power had broken it. He had seen mages for most of his adult life, often covertly, and while he knew mages hoarded their power, he knew as well that they took pride in it. The magi of the First Circle would easily be capable of this limited and this deliberate an act of destruction—but only one of those magi could travel as Avandar had done—and Avandar had carried three.

It was not the first time Devon wondered who Avandar was, or had been, before his service to Jewel ATerafin; it would not be the last. Duvari did not—and would never—completely trust the domicis, and the scant trust he had grudgingly developed was likely to be greatly diminished if Avandar succeeded on Jewel's behalf.

The stranger laughed. "You have grown addled, Warlord, if you seek to face me without a weapon."

"I do not seek to face you at all. I am not *Arianni*; nor am I *Allasiani*; I have nothing to prove." He gestured, a sharp twist of wrist, and the fractured floor broke as if it were a shell, and something was pushing pieces aside in order that it might emerge. "ATerafin," he said, "order your men to withdraw."

They were not Devon's men, but he didn't argue. He gave the order quickly. The Kings' Swords hesitated; those who could still stand had a duty to the Princes who lay in safety—such as it was—beyond the closed doors. Devon called them again. "Your deaths here will serve no purpose, and it is death you face—not in battle and not in defense of the future Kings, but as afterthought. Come, gather your fallen; retreat to the Halls of the Wise."

"The Princes—"

"They are as safe as they can be; I will remain."

They stood their ground. Devon grimaced. He lifted his hand, gestured, and a sigil appeared in the air, directly in front of his chest. It was the symbol of the Lord of the Compact, the leader of the *Astari*. What common sense could not do, the sigil did; the men moved.

So, too, Celleriant. The broken floor beneath his feet didn't hinder him at all; he leaped to the height of the halls and remained there, his hair flowing on currents of wind that Devon couldn't see. He could feel it and hear it, though. Amaerelle leaped as well; he failed to land. But where his sword struck Celleriant's, lightning flashed, red and blue, and it spoke with the voice of resonant thunder, like a note struck against the shell of the world.

Devon stumbled as the floor beneath his feet tilted. Leaping, he found flat ground, marble with sheared edges. The earth rumbled beneath his feet as he turned. Rising and shedding shards of marble and long splinters of the beams beneath it was a moving mountain.

The earth itself had risen at Avandar's behest.

4th of Henden, 427 A.A.
Terafin Manse, Averalaan Aramarelas

House Guards emerged from the manse and headed toward the terrace, their plated feet striking the stone in a way that implied large numbers.

"Head them off," Arann told the Winter King. When the stag failed to move, he added, "Please."

The Winter King's tines shifted slightly, as if he were nodding; he sprang and landed a few yards from the frontrunners. Arann shouted, "Halt!" and to Angel's surprise, they obeyed.

"The magi and the House Council ask that you remain by the manse; prevent anyone in it from leaving—it is not yet safe. Wait upon the word of the regent or the captain."

No one questioned him. Behind his back, they could see the rearing of the water, and not a single man present felt their swords would do it any harm. They withdrew. "We won't lose anyone here," Arann told Angel quietly. "Unless the water can shatter the walls."

Angel gestured, den-sign, and Arann nodded. He slid off the back of the Winter King. "I'll join them. Will you stay?"

"I'll stay." The Winter King had already turned away; Angel could see Jay's stiff back, and at her side, the gray, plain robes of Sigurne Mellifas. The water now towered above them, its shape changing as he watched.

When it fell, it crashed to the ground; water rose in a spray. But neither Jay nor Sigurne was so much as dampened, although the mage stumbled. Jay caught her arm, righting her; Angel wasn't certain he'd've dared.

She heard the voice of the water. Not in the crash and the thunder of its fall—that much, she'd witnessed before, and at the time, people had fallen to its moving rage. Her grip on Sigurne's arm tightened as she said, "the water—it's angry."

Sigurne said nothing, but the slender line separating the two women from the wall of water that was once again regrouping—as if each drop, each splash of liquid was a single man in an army of tens of thousands—grew brighter and sharper. "I cannot hear the water," Sigurne replied, through clenched teeth. "Nor should you be able to, if my understanding is correct. But if you can, ATerafin, bespeak it. Calm its anger."

Jewel turned to stare at the lined—and tired—visage of the older woman. "I can hear Duvari when he speaks," she murmured, "but nothing I can say—or do—influences him at all."

The water was not Duvari. Not the Lord of the Compact. Not a man. It was bound, Jewel thought; bound, compelled, and angry to be either. She felt the earth rumble at its movements; the ground shook. "We need to get off of the terrace," she told the mage.

"I cannot move and maintain these protections," Sigurne replied.

"The terrace won't last," was Jewel's grim response. "We need to move." She turned to the Winter King as the water struck again.

4th of Henden, 427 A.A.
Avantari, Averalaan Aramarelas

The creature that rose from the remains of the floor was not so much dirt as stone. It was almost the shape of a man, although its fists were fingerless, its head featureless; it wore no armor, wielded no weapon that was not part of itself, but it moved inexorably toward the stranger with the red, red sword. His laughter was wild now, higher in pitch but no less delighted. If demons could be judged by the standards of men, he was insane.

Fists of dirt and stone drove new cracks into the floors as the living earth struck home; the demon was not beneath them, although it was close. His sword struck earth, bit, and lodged in what might have been wrists. It did not sever hands, and the demon's brows rose. "Viandaran, you *have* grown!"

"It is not I who have grown," was the cool reply. "But you who have become diminished. You speak of the gray and empty present, Kincallenne; how much of that now resides in your perception? You are not, you will never again be, part of this world; you are given the flesh you can force from the plane for your brief, brief sojourn."

There was no laughter in response.

"Prove that I am wrong," Avandar continued. "Bespeak the wild earth; tame it, ask for its favor. You were a Lord of the wild earth, in your youth; a Lord of the wild water in your prime." He smiled. It was a perfect, cold expression in a face that had lost color. Devon thought, watching the domicis, that he was pressing his power to its upper limits. The earth struck again, and this time the demon rose.

He rose toward the ceiling, borne aloft by wind that now howled. It was winter wind, the edge of its chill enough to kill the unprepared, and it was far, far louder than it had been.

"What we cannot cajole, Warlord, we *command*."

"There is no other choice left you. Have you now discovered the bitterness of things that must be taken because they will never again be willingly offered?"

"You speak as if we were ever mortal. That curse, that long curse, belongs to you, Warlord, and only you. What care have we for the affections of the wild? What loss are their voices to us? We will remake the plane, Viandaran, and if rumors are true, you alone might witness it—whatever remains of you."

"ATerafin," Avandar said, raising his voice. "You must depart; attend to the Swords, or *Avantari's* magical defenses. The earth and the air have now noticed each other; I cannot concentrate on anything but the earth's voice in this place."

The earth, Devon thought, and the *Kialli*. Lightning flashed beyond the domicis' shoulder, and the sound of unintelligible war cries blended with the sounds of nature's fury; of the two, it was not the former that was suddenly awe-inspiring and terrifying. If the earthen pillar could not be contained, the hall would be destroyed, and with it, the long room in which the Princes now resided, if they had indeed remained there.

They would have Duvari to contend with if they had, and they somehow survived. Not even the Princes were immune to the ice of Duvari's wrath.

*   *   *

The earth rumbled; the wind howled. It was the wind that was safer for the *Kialli*, but Celleriant knew that their mastery of it was forced, enforced; they could not cajole it now. He could, and did, dancing between its thermals, rising and falling at both its whim and his own, plunging past the expert swing and thrust of a Lord's blade as its tip grazed the side of his shield. He sliced at shins and feet; felt some resistance in the arc of the swing. Red light and blue twined in the moving air, like a twisted frame around them.

He heard the wind's voice as his own, and spoke with its breath, challenging the *Kialli*. But he avoided the ground and its moving column of earth, for he knew what Viandaran had done. He could hear the earth and its rumbling anger—was surprised that the anger was directed not toward its ancient enemy, the wild wind, but toward the *Kialli* Lord Viandaran now faced. More than that, he could not discern; even that was a risk. The red blade's edge passed an inch beyond his nose.

The roof shook above them; the support pillars that bracketed the hall cracked.

A thought occurred to Lord Celleriant of the Green Deepings as he asked the wind to shunt aside small falling shards of rock and tile: Jewel ATerafin was not going to be pleased.

4th of Henden, 427 A.A.
Terafin Manse, Averalaan Aramarelas

For years, Sigurne Mellifas had adopted the appearance of the absent-minded fragility assumed to be the natural progression of age; it suited her purposes. But here, now, holding a spell of protection that she knew was far too delicate to provide defense for long, she felt that age as deeply as she ever had; the rain was chill, carried by a Henden wind that knew no mercy. It was as remote as gods, as demons, as far from the human condition as any being that had ever claimed people as cattle or fodder.

"ATerafin," she said, wanting—missing—the fractious and difficult Meralonne APhaniel, "step back, step slowly and evenly. I will cover your retreat." She did not look at the girl; the whole of her gaze was focused on the roiling, rising wall of water. She had lived the majority of her life in

Averalaan; she knew how easily water could kill. The rain fell harder, as if to drive the point home.

"AMellifas. Sigurne."

The girl—ah, no, she was hardly a girl now, except in comparison— had not obeyed the guildmaster, a woman who, in crisis, depended upon obedience. Even from the Lord of the Compact, deny it as he might. "ATerafin," she said again, through clenched teeth, "there is very little time. Retreat. Take your men with you."

"You aren't moving."

"I told you, I cannot move and maintain the shield."

"And I told you the terrace won't last. If you're here—"

"My shields will hold; they will be small enough to contain and preserve a single person."

"You're lying."

At this, Sigurne did glance at Jewel as the water continued its rise. She forced herself to focus again, but she had seen the expression on Jewel's face. "It was not a lie, ATerafin; it was a hope."

Jewel knew no mercy; she was like the howling wind, the driven rain. "It would be hope if you believed it. It's not. If you can't retreat, I won't leave you here to perish. The magi—"

"The magi have their hands full; they are not, now, with me—not even Matteos. The shields that protected—that were meant to protect—the funeral rites from something as unfortunate as weather, have clearly fallen; whether it is by their deaths or their sudden incompetence, I do not know, but I do not suspect the latter. Leave me; go. Finish what you have started here, if you even begin to understand it."

"What have I started, Sigurne?" the question was low, intent; the older woman heard the fear in it and flinched. If she was not by nature a gentle woman, and not by nature a kind one—how could she be, raised to ice and snow?—years of aping either had taken their toll, and the impulse to offer comfort was strong. It surprised Sigurne. It annoyed her, as well.

"*Go,*" she said.

She felt a hand on her arm; it made the whole of her body ache; her skin felt taut, stretched, and so terribly thin, the slightest of touches might tear it. The water hammered at the shields and she felt the force of its blows; water splayed across it, as if thrown.

But Jewel said, "You are a guest in my lands; I have invited you into my home, and I have offered you my hospitality." The words were formal, severe, as if they were issued from the mouth of a much older woman. Sigurne knew, then, which older woman came to mind: she was dead now and waited only the dignity of burial. "Guest or no, Guildmaster, you do not have the right of command here; you are not the Kings, and the Kings are not present. If you cannot retreat while maintaining your defenses, the defenses will have to fold."

"You cannot—"

"I can. Angel."

Her companion was there in an instant. He lifted his hands, fingers flying in the rain in deliberate gestures.

"Yes," Jewel replied. "Help the guildmaster mount the back of the Winter King; he has agreed to carry her to safety. Snow!"

The winged cat now landed, hissing. It was convenient to think of him as a cat; it diminished his glory, diluting the awe that Sigurne might otherwise feel in his presence. And very like a cat, he was swatting at the heavy drops of falling rain, as if by so doing he could kill them or scare them away.

"What are you *doing?*" he asked, and Sigurne now risked a second glance at Jewel ATerafin. The rain that had soaked and flattened the hair of all but Angel ran in rivers through hers; hers had been heated and combed out of its habitual nest. But her dress seemed to take no damage, to allow no water to soak or touch it; it was pale and white, and it glowed, in the darkness of stormy sky, like moonlight.

"What does it look like I'm doing?" she snapped back. "I'm *riding* you."

Wet fur didn't rise in hackles; if it could, Sigurne thought the cat would appear twice his normal size in his bristling outrage. Jewel, however, seemed immune to the threat of his extended claws, the appearance of his long, glinting fangs.

"What? It's not like I haven't ridden you before."

"That was *different*," the cat said, wings widening.

"Don't even think it. How was it different?"

"We had *orders*. We weren't *allowed* to harm you."

"You've got orders now, and you're not allowed to harm me. Be careful or you'll damage the dress. Angel, what are you waiting for?"

"My permission," was Sigurne's reply. It was dry and slightly amused, and given the weather and the threat they now faced, any dryness was welcome. "ATerafin—"

"No one will reach the terrace; if the guards have any brains at all, they won't be anywhere near the back doors."

"Arann's with them," Angel told her.

"Good. Guildmaster, understand: I cannot leave you here. Not like this. If you take insult from it, the regent will no doubt be waiting to offer his most profound and sincere apologies."

"And not you?"

"I won't be sorry." She tightened her knees and the cat sprang up, as if attacking the sky, Jewel ATerafin on his back.

Angel offered Sigurne his hand; her own were splayed forward in the air, as if by physical strength alone she could support what she had, by magic and will, built. "The water won't kill her," he said. "The same can't be said about us, if we stay much longer."

She hesitated; her arms were trembling. If the water did not kill her, other dangers waited; she had used much power today, and this expenditure had been neither planned nor well executed. She glanced at the Winter King, who waited in silence, his wide, dark eyes unblinking. "Can he carry us both?"

"He can, if he's willing; Jay—Jewel, I mean, said he's willing. If you climb him and he doesn't want you to fall, you won't; you might die on his back, but you'll still be there when he stops."

"You speak with certainty."

Angel laughed; there was an edge to it. "I speak," he said, as she surrendered and placed one hand in his, "from experience." He was young; he was strong. He lifted her as if she weighed nothing, depositing her on the back of the stag and clambering up behind her. Before she could say another word, the stag leaped clear of the terrace; he practically leaped free of the earth.

No, she thought, he *did* leap clear of the earth; whatever path his hooves touched was not a path that Sigurne herself could walk without the aid of magic.

In the distance, Jewel could hear the piercing howl of wind; she could hear, as the water broke free of Sigurne's restraints, the rumbling fury of water; she could feel, as the terrace cracked—its steps shattering as if they were made of brittle, thin glass—the implacable anger of the earth. The only blessing given her in the driving rain was the utter absence of fire, and its raging voice.

She had seen mobs in her time; had seen and understood the transformation that came over people she knew—and sometimes liked—when anger and fear spread through them in alternating waves. There was freedom of a kind in the grip of those visceral emotions, but it required a complete surrender of self, of the things that defined self.

She knew that the voices of the wild were not the voices of the human crowd; knew that she was trying to find some similarity to the things she understood because she couldn't grasp the whole of what she could now see unfolding beneath her. But she knew *where* it was occurring, and if she was afraid, she was also angry.

ATerafin.

She heard the clear, low voice of the Winter King above—or beyond—the tumult of the wilderness. *Are they safe?*

Angel and the guildmaster are safe, Jewel. As are your other guests, for the moment. Wet, but safe; the water has not yet reached them.

How?

Listen. Can you not hear his voice?

The only reason I can hear yours over the storm and a bunch of angry elements is—the words, even unspoken, trailed off into a peculiar stillness in the center of what had been a complete, if annoyed, thought.

You begin to understand.

. . . because you're mine.

Yes, Jewel. Given you by the Winter Queen, but given nonetheless. You hear me clearly, and if you put your mind and will to it, you would see me, no matter how hidden I might otherwise be.

Whose voice, then? Whose voice should I hear now?

Ah, no, ATerafin. That is not the way it works. Put no faith or trust—and no power—into the things that have been given you for free; they are worth what you paid. Everything in the wilderness has a cost. Even ignorance, should you choose it; perhaps especially that. Listen, Jewel. Listen and understand what it is that you hear. How did I come to be in your service?

She ground out several choice Torra curses, the syllables lost briefly to the rumble of thunder in the bleak, green-gray shade the sky had become. Lightning followed it a brief beat later: the storm's heart. It was both baleful and beautiful, nature itself answering forces that existed beyond it.

In the Stone Deepings. On the road there. He offered no answer; she knew he wanted more. *I held the road against the Winter Queen.*

Yes, ATerafin. Do you not yet understand how*? It is time; you will know now, or you will not survive to know it. Listen. Learn.*

"He's *very* annoying," Snow shouted, into the wind. "Especially when he's *right*."

Jewel closed her eyes. The rain still fell; the thunder continued to rumble. The steady clarity of the Winter King's voice was absent, withheld; the elements beneath the open sky continued to speak in wild, wild fury. Water rose and fell in fists far too solid to be liquid, although they were; stone broke beneath them; wet, heavy clods of earth spun outward, striking trees, grass, fragile lamps and ornaments.

But the water was not—yet—free to strike and drown as it desired; it moved like a tidal wave writ small, but it moved at the whim of another. Was it the voice of command the Winter King expected her to hear? She could not imagine that any lives were owed to its control.

If something binds the water, she asked the Winter King, *why are the earth and the air awake here?*

They were called. The voice that replied was not the Winter King's, but she recognized it. She'd heard it within weeks of arriving at the Terafin manse, and she'd heard it countless times between then and now, although she had only once seen the likeness of the man who used it: the founder of Terafin, bound to the land in some way that Jewel might never understand.

But she understood the visceral desire to protect what he had built; to guard it, guide it, advise those who must take up the mantle of rulership. She wasn't certain she'd cling to the edges of life in the fashion he had—if he'd even had the choice—but at the moment, she was damn grateful he was here: he spoke to the water. Inasmuch as it could, the water was listening. It did not obey, not exactly, for the Terafin House Spirit—*the* Terafin, the first—did not seek to order or command; nor did he beg.

Terafin!

Yes, Jewel. I am here.

She could hear his voice so clearly he might have been part of her, as much hers, in this wilderness of stone and hierarchy and ceremony, as the Winter King himself.

I am both more and less, he replied. *I wear no reins that can be easily handed between one master and the next, not in life and certainly not in the half-life. You are not my lord, not my lady, not my Queen. If there is service given, Jewel, it comes from you to me, for I am Terafin.*

She shook her head, denying it as storm circled the stage of the sky.

But I am not your lord, not your King; these are not the lands I built, although some semblance of their origin can still be seen clearly if one understands our history. I cannot command you, although perhaps I have been proud enough in the past to try. I am done now with pride, ATerafin. I am done now with stewardship. I am not yours, but what I built—what I hoped to build—might yet be. You are not mine—but you are the heir Amarais chose.

And not you?

It is to her that you grant the greatest of your respect, the most personal of your obeisances. To me, ATerafin, you grant the guilty pride of possession. This is your home; you have built it, made it, changed it; you have touched its shadows and fashioned some part of its light—but you have walked, always, beneath the roof and within the walls of another's construction. Neither of those will last now. The time is coming, has come, and cannot but move forward; you have the option of looking back—but if you cannot turn from the past, the future will take you while you are so blinded.

Jewel, is this your home? You have wandered far, seen much; you have grown. You ride a King of the ancient Cities of Man, and you are served by a Prince of the Hidden Court; even now the immortal bears you above the worst of the water's anger and desire. You wear the raiments of a Queen; visions of the future come to you, whether you will it or not. What you were in the streets of the hundred holdings, you are not now. Is this your home?

"Snow," she shouted, bending head toward his ears, which were almost standing on end. "Land. Take me down."

Snow hissed. "Can't you *jump?*"

She smacked the space between those stiff ears in earnest. "Take. Me. Down."

Chapter Twenty-three

SNOW LANDED IN THE TREES or, rather, came crashing through high branches, their leaves sodden and heavy with rain, but not yet surrendered. Beneath the varied bowers of their crowded heights, no rain fell. Nor did the wind now blow; it was silent, a twilight silence that could not last. Jewel was not surprised to see undergrowth beneath her feet; the carefully manicured grounds, broken by ornaments and artful light, were lost to the forest itself.

She had come here bearing leaves and the leaves themselves had taken root—and they had grown.

Oh, they had grown.

Diamond glittered, thin and hard, in the moon's light; silver and gold seemed almost one shade. She reached out and touched the bark of one of these trees and then let her hand fall away. It was part of this particular forest, but it had come in its entirety from the hidden path. It was, therefore, to one of the ancient trees that girded the Common that she went. It, too, had grown on the night that the three leaves had taken root, but she knew it was grounded in some fashion in the life of Jewel Markess ATerafin. The Terafin grounds had never grown such trees; no land in the Empire could, save the Common itself—or so experts had always said.

In some fashion, it was true.

But if Jewel Markess had never played beneath the tall, grand trees that ringed the Common, these trees would not now exist. If she hadn't watched the magi rise to their heights during festival season, if she hadn't watched the displays of light scatter across night sky like stars captured just for that purpose, she would never have loved them. Those trees endured. One or two had been lost to fire, and one or two had been destroyed by the demons that had inexplicably attacked the Common scant months ago, but at a distance, the height of those trees could still be seen, even from the Isle.

She had seen them up close at the side of her Oma; her Oma was dead. Her Oma, her mother, her father. She had seen them at the side of her den; Duster was dead. Fisher. Lander. Lefty. It had never occurred to her to doubt the trees; they were like the landscape, like the weather, a fact of life.

But it was *her* life. Hers, and the people like her, bound to the hundred holdings by poverty and the ties that living day to day made stronger. It was *her* home, and it was the strength of home that she had called upon to face down the Winter Queen—because the Winter Queen had no part and no place in that life, felt no respect for it at all.

She took a step away from the tree, drew a deep breath, held it while she counted seconds. Snow walked by her side, sodden like the leaves high above them; the dress he had made was dry and unwrinkled, and it glowed very softly in the evening light. And it was evening here, or edging toward it: the light was dusk's light, or perhaps dawn before the sun had fully risen. The earth moved beneath her feet, rumbling with thunder's absent voice. As if she were wearing clothing meant for digging and not for court, she knelt and placed her left palm against the cool earth.

What she heard, she had no words for, not then, and not later; it was like . . . music. Like the music of the storm, or the music of the waves breaking, at greater and greater heights, against the seawall; something she herself could never accompany, no matter how strong her voice. She thought only the bard-born capable of it, and at that, only the truly powerful among their number—but it never occurred to her that any of the bards would make the attempt; there was nothing human in it, no experience to touch and tease into the emotion of melody and harmony.

She rose and began to walk toward the path's end. There was no sun in this forest, rising or setting, but there was light, and it shone on the path ahead, where the Terafin shrine stood sentinel against the wilderness and the hidden ways—joined to it, but not beholden. It was such a small building. She saw that clearly: small, round, almost humble. It had loomed so large in her life, because so much of significance had occurred on its flat, round dais, at the foot of its simple altar. She stopped moving and almost stopped breathing, because as she approached, she saw the source of the light that had led her this far: the altar itself was almost white in its radiance.

She would have feared to touch it, but even thinking that, felt both its warmth and the chill of its winter stone surface in either of her palms. This was Terafin's heart.

Lying across it, arms folded upon his chest, hair unbound, was a man she had both never seen and always seen; she knew him. His eyes were closed, his hands curved in fists; he carried no blade, no dagger, no shield. But absent those things, he was their essence distilled, and he fought in this silent, unmoving state for House Terafin and the people it sheltered. His skin was pale, almost translucent; he looked thin the way the elderly are thin, and fragile. His tabard bore the familiar sword of the House, but its colors were washed out in the spill of light, blue becoming azure, a thing of the sky at sun's height.

Lifting trailing skirts out of habit and not necessity, Jewel ran up the shrine's stairs; she dropped the skirts as she approached the altar that had always been so intimidating. What she saw stopped breath and motion for a long, long moment; time itself seemed to shy away from where she now stood.

He was bleeding. The only dark spot on his body looked all of black against the contrasting light, and it was centered in his upper left chest, just beneath the arms that were crossed in poor mimicry of repose. This close to his face, she saw the lines age, sun, and wind had worn there; she saw the brief rictus of pain transform an expression that defined inscrutable, and she understood that this was not happening *now*. She was seeing the past.

But his eyes opened, long lashes framing them as he grimaced. "Jewel."

She reached out; her hand stopped an inch from his, and hovered there. Snow's claws on marble were the only noise she heard.

"He looks *dead*."

"I am dead," the Terafin Spirit replied. "But even in death, there is an end. Jewel, the House—"

"I know."

"I cannot hold these grounds for long against what has come; I cannot hold them against what will follow. I have tried," he added softly, his voice thin and weak. "But the road is open now; it calls me."

To where? She didn't ask. "You killed yourself on this altar." It wasn't a question.

"No, ATerafin. But I died upon it as the price for the stewardship I have kept these long years."

"You'll forgive me if I don't follow your example."

A wry—pained—smile twisted his lips. He reached out for her hand and paused the same inch away that she had. "Can you hear them?"

She nodded. "I—I don't understand what they're saying."

"No. No more do I; I sense only their abiding anger. I speak to calm it; I do not know what they hear of me when I speak; they hear me, of that I'm certain." He hesitated, and the hesitation made Jewel more uncomfortable than the blackness across his chest. "They might hear you more strongly; you are both alive and *of* the hidden ways in a way that I have never been, save by bargaining and by guile." He reached out again, and this time Jewel moved the half inch to meet him.

His hand was cold. "You have not yet declared your candidacy to the House Council."

"No. But I declared it before the Chosen, and in some ways, that's the larger step."

He coughed, smiled. "You are not one of nature's liars, ATerafin."

"I'm not, no. But I'm not lying; I'm not even trying." She looked up at the lights that rimmed the ceiling, brass holders gleaming. "I can't see the pavilions."

"Nor the rain, no. But when you leave the shrine, you will be in the center of the storm. If you are not cautious, it will devour you; if you are too cautious, it will destroy you. You have not yet declared your intentions to the House Council," he repeated. "But as you surmise, that declaration in this place is decorative.

"Take the House, ATerafin; take it now. You will understand much, much more when you do." His smile was less pained, less stretched; peace touched it. "I have waited, Jewel. I have waited, and now, you are here. I am sorry that I could not protect Amarais."

"You couldn't protect any of them," she heard herself say, aware that she'd been angry at his failure regardless until this moment.

"No. But I did not love them all. Like anyone who is steward and guardian, compromise is necessary. But in her, very little was required. She knew. I told her, as I was able. I gave her that much of a choice."

Jewel snorted. "That was no choice."

"No." His smiled dimmed. "Not for Amarais; for another, it would have been. But she fought her fate until the end; she bought you time, and it was necessary time. Had she died three weeks earlier—"

Jewel lifted her hand. "Don't. Don't say it. I know what you want."

But he shook his head. "It is not what *I* want that is relevant now. What do you want, Jewel?" He smiled again, but this time the pain etched itself into the corners of his lips. It wouldn't leave until he did, and she did not want him to go. "Such a simple question; we ask it of our children time and again. What do you want? Children answer within the context of their knowledge and experience, and their answers are true but ephemeral. Your answer cannot be trivial; it cannot be as simple as 'water' or 'bread' or even 'wealth' or 'power.'"

"Power is an answer that defines the lives—and the deaths—of many," she replied, thinking of Haerrad. Of Rymark.

"It is," was his soft reply. "But it is not an answer you can tender, and not an answer that the land will accept. I ask again, what does Jewel ATerafin want? What will devour the whole of your life, your heart, and your will to bring into being?"

She had already answered the question. She had answered it the day she had come to save Celleriant, walking the edge of the dreaming to where he was impaled, suspended in air, the means by which he might save himself momentarily rendered useless. She had answered it a second time when she had come bearing three leaves—leaves that shouldn't have existed at all, given what she knew of gold, silver, and diamond. Those trees grew, not at her command, but with her permission.

But the trees of the Common were different. They grew for two reasons. The first, the old land, long fallow, upon which she walked, and the second: she loved them. Not the way she loved Finch or Teller; not the way she loved Angel or Arann; not even the more complicated way she loved Carver and Jester, men she was just as likely to throw crockery at as not. No, the trees were the walls and the bowers of her first home, and those walls and bowers stretched unseen all the way to the Isle.

The South had begun lessons she'd never dreamed existed—not for her, not for an orphan. But the learning of those lessons could only be done here, because this was *home*. Home, where Angel now rode the back of the Winter King, Sigurne before him, her hands pale and shaking because she could not quite bring herself to trust her mount; home, where Teller and

Finch now sought to comfort the House Council and its various entourages as the rain began to fall with vengeance; home, where Arann—
Arann!—now took command of the House Guard as if he were a captain,
and not the least senior of the Terafin Chosen. Jester, she could not see
clearly in her mind's eye—but her imagination surprised her, there: Jester
was helping the guests from their increasingly unstable seating; the earth
had shifted, and shifted again, and the carefully planned arrangement of
benches was in disarray.

He held himself aloof on most days, choosing to divert any interest
with a joke or a smile; he stood with them, but he never quite let himself
be caught up in anything but an emergency. So: he knew this was an
emergency.

Carver had left the grounds; he was technically an adjunct to the Council, through Finch, but Council be damned; he raced across the edges of
ruined stone toward doors that were barred by armored guards, and he
managed to get in, racing down the halls and disappearing through the
small paneled doors that only the servants used.

She knew that Daine was in the infirmary; he had taken control, just as
Arann had, although that was less surprising. The House did not—in
theory—know Daine was healer-born; in practice, Jewel very much
doubted it was a secret from many; he had been known to the healers in
the Houses of Healing as a student, and word was bound to travel, greased
by gold or guilt or veiled threat. At Daine's side, drawn and tense,
Alowan's former assistants; two very overworked women. The two who
had died on the day of Alowan's assassination had yet to be replaced, as if
the act of replacement diminished the loss.

Perhaps it did, or would, but Jewel knew after today—if there was
one—that would change. It would have to change. Daine had come to her
in pain and anger, himself a victim of unscrupulous men: men who bore
the name ATerafin. But he had stayed with her, backed by Alowan's support against the ire and fury of Levec. She knew why Alowan wanted him:
he had not expected to survive a second House War.

Anger wouldn't help her here, but it came anyway; that was the problem with helpless fury. A gentler, kinder man couldn't be found in the
streets of this entire damn city, and why had he died? For power. Someone's power—a power that he himself had never desired, although he
could have been both titled and wealthy with just a nod. But in the inter-
vening time, he had trained Daine, and inasmuch as he could have a suc-

cessor, Daine was ready. Nervous, she thought—he was young—but ready.

She could not see Duvari, and was grateful for his absence; she could not see the Kings or the Exalted. But as she turned her gaze toward the manse, she froze because she could see Adam of the Arkosa Voyani. His eyes were dark, round, and unblinking; he was watching her, his hand in Ariel's, hers missing fingers. By her side, bristling but silent, was Shadow. Shadow was also, sadly, staring right at her, in an if-looks-could-kill kind of way.

"Jewel," Adam said, mouth half open.

"You can see me." And hear her, which, given the wail of the storm should have been equally impossible.

He swallowed and nodded. "Shadow can—"

"Of *course* I can see her, *stupid* boy." Shadow stepped on his foot. Adam, however, failed to notice until he applied weight.

"Jewel—what are you—"

"Stay there. Stay with Ariel and Shadow; if I fail, protect them both."

Shadow hissed in astonished fury; it was the first thing that had happened since she'd arrived at the shrine that made her want to laugh.

"What will you do?"

"Tell the world," she replied, "that this is *my* home."

Snow sidled up to her. She knew he was doing the cat equivalent of sticking his tongue out—at Shadow—but at least had the sense to do it behind her back. Or her skirts. He nudged her gently, or what she assumed was meant to be gently, and she nodded, glancing once at the man who lay upon a sacrificial altar. He'd turned his face to look at her; his eyes were glowing softly. He did not move or rise; she wondered if he could now.

No, not now, not yet. Bespeak them, ATerafin, and tell them what they must hear and understand.

She tried to smile back at him, but couldn't quite manage the simple expression. Dropping her hands to her skirts, she bunched them in her fists—which made Snow hiss in shock—before she walked back down the stairs, whose marble, gleaming in the shrine's light, lay unbroken beneath her feet. She hesitated and then dropped her skirts and bent over her feet, where she unlaced the small, uncomfortable shoes that bound them. These she tossed to the side.

Snow said nothing; Ellerson or Haval would have had fits. But Snow hadn't made shoes for her; just the dress, and when the skirts and the train fell properly, who could see her feet?

Barefoot, she stepped away from the shrine and onto the stone path that led to it. When she did, she heard the voices of water, earth, and air so clearly they were physical, tangible. They clamored not for attention, but for dominance, like men on Council attempting to drown out the words of their rivals by raising their voices. Except in the case of the wild, when voices were raised, seawalls fell, stone broke; men drowned, or were crushed.

Men like, very like, Jewel.

Jewel bent to touch the ground, and then stopped, straightening both spine and shoulders and lifting her own voice as she joined the fracas—very much as if it *were* the House Council on a tear. She couldn't understand what the elements were saying, but then again, most of what her enemies on the Council said made no damn sense either, when it came right down to it; the difference was that the Councillors *should.* What sense did one expect from wind or water? What sense from earth?

What sense would they expect, in their turn, from Jewel Markess ATerafin, if they could hear her voice at all?

And they'd hear it. They'd hear every damn word. She *knew* it, as she stood, forcing her arms into a fall by her sides, her hands tense—and straight—as boards. What words were appropriate when dealing with forces that by their very nature rose above the limits of language? What words could she offer that would make them understand?

Jewel Markess ATerafin had never been a diplomat and, with Kalliaris' smile, never would be. The first words that left her lips were:

"How *dare* you?" And they hung in the sky like a long, slow, flash of building lightning.

For a moment, there was silence. The water froze; the earth stilled; even the wind's voice dipped and vanished. Only Jewel's words carried. They should have contained awe, reverence, or some acknowledgment that the forces of nature were in all ways above or beyond her; she might find a roof to shelter beneath, but against this storm, a roof made of sky would be just as useful as a roof of beams and tile. Earth, water, air—she accepted them as necessary, as inevitable, as forces over which she had little control and little say. But they belonged in the wild. They belonged in a storm of magic and gods and things ancient and almost unknowable.

They sure as Hells didn't belong *here*. Here was *hers*. Here was the home she'd built. Was it perfect? Gods, no. And no matter how hard she worked it would never *be* perfect, but then again, neither would she. Everything she loved was here. Everything she valued, everything she trusted, everything she hoped—one day—to be worthy of: all here.

And the voices of the wild would destroy it without even *noticing* the damage they did. If she let them. Anger grew, or perhaps it was merely revealed as the danger of the wild swept the veneer of calm from her grasp. When she spoke again, she spoke two words:

"Be *silent*!"

And the silence which her first words had momentarily invoked extended, like ripples across a pond into which a stone has been thrown. She was that stone.

They turned their attention toward her, as if pulled, and she held her hands out, not in supplication, but in denial. They spoke, but their voices were muted now; rain slowed to a drizzle and the wind that pushed it was little stronger than a breeze. She didn't look to see what had become of the towering wall on the terrace; nor did she look to see what damage had been taken in the slow rise of earth. Her Oma's voice was almost as strong as the voices of the elements: *It can't be undone, can it? Worry about what you'll do now. There'll be plenty of time for tears and recrimination later.*

4th of Henden, 427 A.A.
Avantari, Averalaan Aramarelas

Avandar felt her anger from the remove of *Avantari*, but anger itself was not unusual; Jewel's anger was a constant, to be shunted between events until it was spent. What was unusual was the quality of it, the focus; she had left no room for the conscience that plagued her, waking or sleeping, and no room at all for the doubts that did likewise. She spoke; he was certain of it—but for the first time since he had taken her to his ancient home in the bowels of the Stone Deepings, he could not hear her words.

But he knew the moment the earth did; it froze in its tracks, a misshapen pillar with fists of broken rock. He knew when the wind suddenly stopped its ferocious play for power; Celleriant dropped like a stone, and landed, cracking marble; his opponent lurched and plunged, but managed to retain his command over the element.

"What is this?" Kincallenne whispered, his soft voice audible because almost everything about the broken great hall now seemed to hold its breath.

Avandar turned to his ancient foe. "It is the end of hostilities," was his equally quiet reply. "If you will not be destroyed without recourse, you will take your companion and you will retreat; if you are now tired of the mortal plane, you may remain and return to the Hells."

"And you will send us?" Kincallenne said, brows rising in shock that was only half feigned, lips once again turning up in a smile of manic delight.

"Ah, no. You mistake me, Kincallenne—and you were always perceptive; I must assume you have chosen to do so. It is not I who will destroy you where you stand, not the Swords of the Kings, nor the sons of the gods whom you came to assassinate."

"Then who?"

"Ask the earth, if you dare; it might even answer before remembering its rage at your ancient betrayal. Ask the wind, if you do not."

Kincallenne's frown was sudden, swift; it transformed the whole of his face, edged as it was with curiosity or confusion. He glanced at the Lord with the red, red sword. "Amaerelle, it is not your way, but consider a brief retreat."

Lord Amaerelle did not trouble himself to acknowledge the words.

Celleriant, however, sheathed sword. To Avandar he said, "Viandaran—will we survive?"

The domicis smiled. "If I can guarantee little else, Prince of the Winter Court, I can guarantee that. She is not the Lady you once served, but in her own fashion—her mortal, flawed fashion—what she claims, she holds."

4th of Henden, 427 A.A.
Terafin Manse, Averalaan Aramarelas

She had their attention. It was attention she had never thought *to* want, but it didn't matter; they spoke to her now, and they spoke as politely as forces of natural disaster could. Their voices offered no words, nothing she could easily grasp and hold onto. But what she *could* grasp, she had. She didn't decline to use words, because words were what *her* voice conveyed.

But she spoke in Torra, a concession to her Oma, who had considered Weston a language of merchants and commerce—on her good days.

She also kept it simple and concise; there was no point in talking to elements about petty things like love, loyalty, and trust. "This is *my* home. It is bounded by sea to the east and earth to the west, and it is open to the whole of the sky—but it is *mine*. If you want to walk here, you walk *through* me; if you want to pass through, you *ask* my permission." She gentled her voice and continued. "You have given us gifts, in your time: water sustains us, earth sustains us; we die at birth without air. You are not unwelcome in my home—but you are forbidden to destroy; if you *must* fight among yourselves, you must do it on unclaimed ground.

"This city is mine."

Water spoke; the rain strengthened. She felt its slow and cumbersome movement as it built itself into a wall without containment.

"Yes," she replied, her voice soft. "I know you did not waken here at your own behest. But you will sleep at mine; no one can command you here without my permission, and I *do not* grant it to those who force you now. Be still; be at peace."

She felt resistance, and to her surprise, she realized it was not the water's; it was other. She couldn't see whose, and at the moment, didn't much care. She called on the water, and it came to her in a rush, the wall falling, and the volume of water that had composed it rushing away like a swollen brook in Veral. It pooled at her feet, and she realized that she had walked, unaware of all movement, to stand by its side. But it failed to touch her or the boundary defined by the fall of her skirts. Instead, she reached out to touch it; it slid between her fingers, cool, clear; light absent from the sky seemed to be caught entirely in its folds.

"Go back to the fount," she told it. "Please. It is your home here, and men and women will travel from foreign lands just to gaze upon your movement. Go back and be welcome."

It receded as she spoke, withdrawing. As it did, the broken and ruined terrace was fully revealed; Jewel grimaced, took a deep breath, and let it out in a long exhale. To the earth, she said, "I think I know why you're here. I'm not angry. But help me now; what is broken, I must remake, for I, too, have my duties to my home; they cannot wait. The greatest of my kin, the most worthy, waits upon our farewell; she has waited too long already for the respect that is her due.

"There is no place within my lands where you cannot sleep in peace, but before you sleep, help me."

She gestured again, and watched as the earth moved, touching stone and dirt and flower bed as it rippled carefully outward. Where its first movement had broken the things that lay upon its surface, the second now built and healed; the stones that were cracked re-formed. She had seen this once before, had watched in awe and terror. Now, she simply watched as the earth remade the whole of the grounds.

But it continued beyond the grounds of the Terafin manse.

4th of Henden, 427 A.A.
Avantari, Averalaan Aramarelas

The living, moving column that Avandar had summoned began to dissolve in an instant.

Lord Kincallenne lowered his blade as the broken and cracked marble floors began to seal themselves, becoming flat, smooth—and utterly seamless. A casual observer might think them the same floors as those that had been destroyed when the earth had risen; the *Kialli* were not capable of so casual, or ignorant, an observation. Even had they been, they could not mistake the shuddering reformation of the stone support pillars as they, too, were remade.

No smile touched Kincallenne's lips; what touched it instead was thin and sharp; a brief acknowledgement of pain. "This is not your work, Viandaran, unless you have learned subtlety in my long absence."

"It is not my work," Avandar agreed. "You were ever my superior before the long choice; this, you could have coaxed from the earth without pause."

A shadowed smile replaced the expression of pain, but the wild, exuberant humor was guttered for the moment. "Not without pause," he said, looking down the long hall. "If you survive what must follow, you must explore; I think you will find the architecture somewhat changed in the earth's passage." He nodded. "I will leave you now, but I am certain, Viandaran, that we will meet again, you and I."

"May it be on neutral ground."

"Ah, indeed. I fear that our Lord is not a Lord who accepts such a concept. Amaraelle, it is time."

"I am not yet done."

"Then I will see you in the abyss; can you not feel the power waking beneath your feet?"

"I can, but I am no stranger to the hidden paths."

"You were not, when you lived; what they are to you—or I—now, no one of us can know for certain. If you will test it, test; I at least must depart. Word must travel," he added, his smile growing edged.

Celleriant's sword was drawn again in an instant and he leaped forward, slowed in his passage and his attack by the utter absence of the wind that oft carried him. When he landed, Kincallenne was gone. "Viandaran—"

"Do you think he will not know?" Avandar replied. "Do you think there is any denizen of any note who can walk—and claim—the hidden paths, the sundered ways, who will not know? What he tells his Lord might buy him a moment's mercy."

"They will come prepared."

Avandar nodded. "We cannot tarry; I fear we must leave Devon behind. Our Lord is unaccustomed to the power she now wields, and if she is not careful, it will devour her." He turned and held out a hand to Celleriant, who ignored it.

"Lord Celleriant—"

"It is not necessary to travel that way, not now. It will also be costly, and I fear our Lord intends to continue the ceremonies these events have interrupted; she will require your presence."

Avandar slowly lowered his hand.

"Look, Viandaran," the Arianni Prince continued, his voice softening into hush. "Can you not see it?"

Avandar did not reply, not directly; instead he said, "Lead the way; I will follow if I am able."

4th of Henden, 427 A.A.
Terafin Manse, Averalaan Aramarelas

The earth was slow to move, slow to subside, but Jewel was almost grateful; her feet were now wet, and were it not for the warmth the living earth radiated, they would have been cold. It had seemed a good idea to remove her shoes—why, she couldn't now remember with any clarity—but mud squelched between her toes as she walked. She reached up without thought, pushing wet curls out of her eyes.

Then she frowned, knowing exactly what Ellerson would—or in this case would not—say. To the wild air, she now said, "Give me back my hair pins."

"You should tell it to *put* them back," came Snow's almost meek suggestion.

She glanced at the cat; the water that her dress had failed to absorb had beaded on his wings and had finally penetrated his fur; he looked, to be charitable, bedraggled.

She was curious enough to consider it—but only barely; she felt strangely exhausted by what had, in the end, amounted to simple speech. "If it gets it wrong," she told the cat, "I'm the one who'll suffer."

"If you know *how* to do it *properly*," was Snow's arch rejoinder, "there will be *no* mistakes."

"There's a reason I let Ellerson do my hair for all the important occasions."

"He won't *like* the way it looks *now*."

"It doesn't look worse than yours."

His hiss could probably be heard across the grounds and the back half of the mansion.

"I don't like the pins anyway. They pull my hair so tight it makes my head hurt. But they cost a lot, so I want them back, I just don't want them back *in* my hair. Yet."

The breeze began to finger the hems of her skirt; it was, like the earth, almost warm. It was certainly warm for Henden. She stopped walking and waited; small, slender pins and two enameled golden combs began to dance and spin in the air, weaving in and around each other so smoothly they might have been alive.

She held out an open palm—her left, and they came to rest there one long moment later. Like the breeze and the earth, they were warm.

"You don't have any *pockets*," Snow pointed out, with some satisfaction.

"Pay attention. I do."

"You *don't*."

Jewel shook her head. "I do. Watch."

The cat's wet brows rose; she did have pockets. "I didn't *make* pockets!" His second hiss devolved into what was mostly a growl.

"Don't look at me like that; I didn't make 'em either. But they're here, as needed. Let's find the Winter King and your brother."

"*Brother?*"

"Night."

"Oh, *him.*"

The sky lost the gray-and-green pallor of storm as she walked. Jewel couldn't find her shoes, but didn't look very hard; she couldn't. Although the shape of the path the earth had built—at her request, at her plea—conformed to the path the Master Gardener had designed for this very important occasion, the texture was different; the stone was smooth and it was, to her eye, all of one piece. The flowers that had been all but uprooted and overturned in the slow breaking of the earth resided in beds that were also similar in shape and form, but here, the earth proved it was no deliberate gardener; they were not so uniform in placement as they had been, and many of the stems had been snapped or broken. Yet, free of dirt, there they were.

The shrines had been built so long ago, mages had attended them; they survived the beginnings of the conflict well enough. But the rains had washed them clean. All but the Terafin shrine. There, the altar was now dark with blood; the color was no longer so deep and consistent a red, and the man who had shed it was gone.

The Winter King, Sigurne and Angel still astride him, came upon her as she walked. He lowered his tined head, but did not otherwise bow to ground.

A Terafin.

"Winter King."

He did not admonish her for speaking aloud. *The worst of the danger has passed?* It was a question, not a statement.

"I don't know. The water is free, and it sleeps; the earth and the air are quiet."

Angel slid off the Winter King's back. He was wet, which wasn't remarkable—everyone would be—but he was worried. That much was clear from his expression; he was almost tentative.

"Jay?"

She nodded.

"What did you do?"

"I told them to stop fighting," was her quiet reply.

"Them?"

"The water. The earth and the air. I wish my Oma could have seen me. She'd've been proud. I think. She'd've hated this dress, though."

The Winter King knelt, and Sigurne Mellifas now slid off his back, looking more crumpled but less frail than she had. "ATerafin," she said, in a voice as sharp as any voice her Oma had ever used.

"Yes?" Jewel hesitated as the guildmaster approached. "Sigurne?"

The guildmaster nodded. But she lifted one hand and very gently pressed the back of it across Jewel's forehead. "How do you feel, ATerafin?"

"Strange. I won't have seizures," she added. "But—strange. Like I weigh nothing, or like the world does. Weigh nothing, I mean." She closed her eyes. "I can see the City, Sigurne. With my eyes closed. I can see the Common. I can see the streets of the twenty-fifth holding. I can see people heading into Taverson's—his door needs oiling. People are trying to get out of the rain."

"Open your eyes," Sigurne commanded her. "Open them. Stop looking at the City. Look at *nothing* but your Angel."

"I—"

"*Now.*" To the Winter King, the mage said, "She must be taken indoors." The stag did not move.

"No, I don't know if it will help—but it can't hurt. I must attend the magi and take their reports—if they even survived to make them. I do not know what occurred to presage these events, but I can guess. Angel."

Angel nodded.

"She must go—to the healerie if you judge it safe, and to her wing, if you do not. Do not let her speak of the City or the holdings—do not let her speak of anything *at all* if you value her life."

He looked bewildered. "Sigurne—why? What did she do?"

Sigurne's smile was brief, more of an expression of sorrow or pity than Jewel deserved. "I do not, and cannot, say. But others will, I fear."

"But she saved us—"

"Yes. And it is my belief that every man, woman, and child on the grounds—if only there—heard each word Jewel spoke as clearly as you and I could. I would not be surprised if her voice was heard over half the Isle. Something has changed, and it is neither a small change nor one that will be welcome to those who now rule. Take her, and go. Avoid Duvari if you can; if you cannot, speak for her. He will not allow it easily—it is essential that you do so, regardless." She bowed wearily to both of them. "We are in your debt, I think—but debt does not rest easy on the shoulders of the powerful, and it may be that when we next speak, I will be in no position to give you advice of any kind.

"Therefore, remember: what she has done here, and what she claims to have done, will be heard—but it will be heard by the Exalted, by the Sacred, and by the Kings. It will be examined to the last syllable by the Lord of the Compact; were he not now embroiled in his search for the kin, he would be here now—and I am not certain that it would end well, if it ended at all."

"Look, Viandaran," Celleriant whispered, lifting his face toward the bowers of trees that lined the road. His gray eyes were almost round, and wonder softened the edges of his face. Although he moved with the supple grace that characterized all of his actions, he stepped lightly here, as if afraid too heavy a tread would shatter the landscape.

Avandar glanced skyward in silence. The trees that marked the Common—and that now graced the Terafin grounds—lined a path too narrow to be road to anything but foot traffic. That road, Celleriant had found in the heart of *Avantari's* famous, private gardens; he had done so without pause or hesitation. What he could clearly see, Avandar could only see with effort and long experience, and for the moment, he was content to follow the Arianni's lead. They both knew where this path would bring them; the trees marked it, if nothing else did.

"You are quiet," Celleriant said, after a few moments had passed.

Avandar nodded.

"You understand what you have seen. It begins here."

"It began," Avandar replied, "long ago. But it is possible it will end here."

"And you do not relish an ending?"

"I?" the man once known as the Warlord smiled.

The Winter King carried Jewel. Angel chose not to mount; instead, he walked by her side. For this reason, the Winter King's gait was slow and stately.

"If Duvari appears," Angel said quietly, "take her and go."

The Winter King inclined his head. Angel wondered—briefly—what his voice must sound like; he had never heard it. Jay had, and did. Jay had also heard the voices of the water, the earth, and the air; she heard the voices of ancient forests, and when she called them, they answered. She wore a dress that not even the Queens could wear, and yet somehow it now suited her.

When they reached the height of the terrace, Angel could see the

House Guards in the manse's interior; they stood four abreast, weapons drawn. He hesitated at the doors; the Winter King, however, approached them. He touched them with his tines and they flew open; Angel cringed. On a day like this one had been, he would have chosen a vastly more subtle approach.

But on this particular day, while the House Guards fell into a familiar, defensive stance, Arann appeared. He took one look at Jay, his eyes changing shape before he lifted an arm. "Let them pass." If there was worry or doubt on his face, there was none whatsoever in his voice; the guards obeyed. Arann gestured in brief den-sign. *Where?*

Angel glanced at Jay, and gestured, *home.*

Arann nodded. *Escort?*

No.

But Arann hesitated here, and in the end, shook his head. Turning to one of the older men by the wall, he said, "I'll escort the Councillor to her quarters; take over for me until I return."

The man saluted, a sharp, metallic gesture that was the whole of his reply. It was enough.

"You're expecting trouble?" Angel asked, when they were far enough down the hall that acoustics wouldn't trap and convey the words to any of the guards.

Arann's brows rose. "You can say that after today?" He shook his head. "There are at least four dead. One of the dead is Lord Sarcen; it was not cleanly done. There are two dead House Guards, and one dead member of the Order of Knowledge—but Matteos Corvel implied that there would be more among that number by the time cursory investigation was complete. The terrace *was* destroyed, and apparently, rebuilt *in a day*; Duvari had the House Guards and the Chosen reroute the Kings, and then had their entire progress halted completely. How could anyone sane *not* expect more trouble?"

Snow, almost forgotten until this moment—and that should have told Angel something—snickered.

"Is she all right?" Arann asked.

"Why don't you ask—" Angel glanced at Jay; her eyes were closed. She was listing to the left, but he wasn't concerned; the Winter King held her, and he would not let her fall. "I don't know."

"I heard that," she said. Her eyes, however, remained closed. "And most of Arann's list—which was impressive. The magi—did anyone say how they'd died?"

"No."

"Anyone ask?"

"No, I'm sorry—the House Guards have their hands full at the moment. Duvari won't allow anyone—anyone at all—to leave the grounds; he has every exit and entrance covered by his *Astari*. Gabriel has his hands full; if Duvari weren't known for his blatant disregard of both power and social standing, it would be very, very bad for Terafin."

The rain stopped.

It stopped abruptly, as if a giant umbrella had suddenly been erected; the umbrella was also invisible, by which Finch knew the magi had once again taken the situation in hand. The House Council had had some debate about the expense of the magi and their protection from seasonal rain; she knew that the rain should never have fallen at all. By her side, Jarven was very, very grave.

"That was your Jewel?" he asked, giving voice to the concern of the Councillors who now remained: Teller, Elonne, Marrick, Haerrad. Rymark was not to be seen, which was usually a blessing; Finch somehow doubted it would be that, today.

Since Jarven wasn't technically a member of the House Council, and since he was also known by every *other* member of said Council, she would have been much happier had he retreated into silence; absent that, his usual dissembling would have also been acceptable. But he was sharp-eyed now, his expression so focused this might—might—have been the biggest trade deal the House had ever been offered.

She wanted Lucille, badly.

Lucille, however, was not here. "Yes." Finch took a deep breath, glancing as she did at Teller's hands; they were utterly still. "Yes, it was."

"Impressive," he said, in exactly the wrong tone of voice. She wanted to tell him, then, that Jewel was not—would *never* be—his enemy. She would never be his rival. But she had known Jarven for years; she knew the look on his face. He would not be moved by her words—or even by Lucille's—until he had seen, and judged, for himself.

"She was bold," he said, lips curving in a smile that suited the harsh brightness of his eyes. "She has not, to my knowledge, declared her candidacy for the House Seat."

That sent a ripple through the rest of the Council, a ripple that even the rains hadn't.

"She didn't declare it there," Finch replied, forcing her voice to be as steady as his.

"Finch," he said, looking down—for he'd straightened to his full height almost unconsciously, something he seldom did, "she has done far, far more than that. Did you not hear what she said?"

"I heard it."

He turned to the House Council, eavesdropping, all, with the care of long practice. "Did you not hear what she said?"

There was no definitive answer, although murmurs could be heard, replete with muted syllables that blended into a kind of gray noise.

"Do you not understand to whom—to *what*—she spoke?"

"Jarven—" Finch caught his arm; he allowed this. "This is a House Council affair, and you are not a member of that Council. Please."

At that, he lifted one platinum brow. "Finch—" he paused as a young man careened around a tree, skidding on damp grass. The young man wore the House tabard. He bowed, and if his entrance was unorthodox for a servant of his class, his bow was perfect.

"My apologies," he said. "But the regent has sent for the Council; he requires the authority of their presence."

"Where?" Haerrad demanded.

"In the public gallery. Many of our guests are now there—as are the Kings and the Exalted."

Silence. Jarven, arm still in Finch's grasp, nodded to the young man with all the authority of a Councillor—authority which she had just reminded everyone present he didn't actually possess. Regardless, the young man bowed again; he did not take the nod as a dismissal. "I am to escort you there," he told them gravely. "My apologies for my presumption; the request was made by the Lord of the Compact. Gabriel asks me to tell you all that he is also present in the public galleries."

The Council fell silent, considering the future. But they followed the young man, drawing their guards and their adjutants with them as they went.

Jewel made it to the West Wing. Its doors were open, and almost before the Winter King nudged them wide, Ellerson appeared between them. He glanced at Jewel's hair—it was the first thing he did—and then stepped neatly out of the way to allow the Winter King to enter.

The Winter King, however, did not. He allowed Angel to help Jewel dismount, and turned.

Take what rest you can, ATerafin. If you mean to continue today's task, it will be scant.

She nodded, although by the time the words had penetrated the foggy images and half-remembered words that now passed for her thoughts, he was gone; the halls had failed to contain him. Angel, however, was not. Arann saw them through the door, and turned to leave; she called him back. Her voice cracked.

He looked so much like one of the Chosen she could almost forget he was Arann—and she was tired enough that she hated it. "Torvan?" she asked.

"Torvan and Arrendas have their hands full; the Chosen—those of us who remained by the shrine—are dealing with the House Guard and Duvari. The Magisterium has not yet been summoned."

"Gabriel must be having fits—"

"Gabriel is waiting—for you—in the public gallery. Word was sent that you'd reached the manor." He grimaced, his face folding into a much more familiar expression. "I'm sorry, Jay."

Not half as sorry as I am, she thought. But thinking it, she wasn't certain she could make herself believe it; she let it go. "Go back to the House Guard. I'll clean up here—I'll *let* myself be cleaned up," she amended, "and I'll meet the regent in the gallery. Did he say—"

"No. That was all he said—and it was a small wonder he'd time to get even that much out."

Ellerson followed Jewel to her room, almost tripping over Snow. She fixed the cat with a pointed glare, and he hissed. Ellerson was not a man prone to stumbles in even the most crowded of halls; nor was he a man prone to complaints or accusations. Jewel, on the other hand, was both. Snow's belly dropped a foot or two and hovered a few inches above the floor, as if he were a contrite dog.

The thought made her smile although the smile had edges. It was all she had time for; she was deposited in a chair, Ellerson took the combs and pins from her hands, and started to work. He didn't choose the more elaborate styling he'd spent more than an hour on this morning; he was as aware as she was—perhaps more, given he was Ellerson—of just how little time she had.

But while he worked, the door opened a crack. Adam peered in. She caught his expression in one side of the mirror; his eyes closed and his shoulders sagged.

"I'm fine—" she said, rising.

Ellerson very gently—and completely inexorably—pushed her back into the chair.

He waited.

"Yes," Ellerson told him, although Adam hadn't actually said anything. "Go to the kitchen; get water, bread, or anything else that looks both edible and easily eaten without undue mess."

He returned with water and a tray some very few minutes later, as if he'd already prepared the food and was simply waiting for her return. Instead of water, he'd brought something that looked like hot milk. It was—but it was sweeter; she thought there was honey in it, by taste. It made her smile. It reminded her of her Oma.

"Matriarch," he said in quiet Torra.

She didn't argue. She hadn't the strength for it. Instead, she offered a resigned nod.

"The rains have stopped; the earth no longer moves beneath our feet. But there is something—"

"Something?"

He hesitated. "Something feels—wrong."

"Adam." She glanced at Ellerson, who had apparently failed to hear a single word. "Are you—do you—see?"

He shook his head, and glanced at his hands; they were clasped in the lap his legs made as he knelt on the floor. "No. My mother did, and my cousin; it was not my gift. I am not Matriarch; nor can I be. It's not like that. In the House Levec lives in—"

She lifted a hand, and he fell instantly silent. If only the rest of her own were half as attentive. "Is this something Levec wants you to share with outsiders?"

Adam blinked. He looked truly surprised as if Levec of the bushy eyebrows and the obvious suspicion and ire weren't the subject of fear. "I—I don't know. He's only said I'm never to tell anyone I'm healer-born. But you already know. You know what he knows. You know *more.*"

"I don't know more about healers; I do know I don't want an angry Levec back in my great room any time soon."

He did smile, at that. "I like him."

"I like him, too—at a distance." She grimaced as Ellerson pulled a comb through hair that was no longer straight. "I'm sorry—let's pretend I didn't ask. I interrupt people all the time. What were you trying to tell me?"

"It's *like* the healing. I feel it in the ground—something is wrong; something is injured. It's not—not like touching you, or Ariel. It's—bigger, wider, it doesn't tell me what I need to know in order to heal it. But . . . it's like it's a body."

"You felt it before?"

He nodded.

"Can you feel it without—without whatever it is that healers do?"

He shook his head.

"Can I ask why you even *tried*?"

His face reddened. "I—when the earth started to move, we could feel it; Ariel was afraid. Shadow wasn't helpful there."

"He frightened her?"

"He said we would all die if you didn't do something."

"If *I* didn't?"

Adam nodded. "I wanted to comfort her; I touched the ground."

"Adam, is this something you learned with the Arkosans?"

He shook his head.

"Never mind. I can't take you with me, but I need to hear more—I just need to hear it *after* I speak with Gabriel. Shadow was helpful otherwise?"

Adam nodded. "Shadow promised Ariel she could climb his back and he would fly her to safety if—" he shook his head. "She is on his back, now; she won't leave him. I don't think he minds. Too much."

That made Jewel smile; it was a tired smile.

"I think you should tell Gabriel to wait."

"I'd love to, to be honest. But Gabriel's the regent." She used the Weston word. "It's like Matriarch, only male, and with a lot more formality. As long as I can stand and speak more or less intelligibly, I have to go."

"When my mother had the strongest of her visions, she would sleep for a day. Once, she slept for three; she woke to drink, and she ate very little. I am not a Matriarch; I have received none of my sister's training, and few of the lessons. But *I* was taught to watch for the signs."

"If the world was about to end, would your mother have paid any attention to those signs?"

His head sank. But he shook it.

She rose, and this time Ellerson was satisfied—or as satisfied as he could be, given the obvious state of emergency; he didn't try to push her back into the chair. "I can't either."

"She can't," a familiar voice said, "But *I* can, Adam of Arkosa." Avandar stepped into the room. It wouldn't have been so surprising if he'd actually opened the door first.

The first thing he did was bow. To her. She glanced at Ellerson; Ellerson appeared to be entirely unperturbed by Avandar's appearance. She wondered what—besides poor manners and bad hair—would disturb the elder domicis, and decided she never wanted to find out.

"The Princes—"

"They are safe," Avandar replied.

"You saw them yourself?"

"I left them entirely in Devon ATerafin's care. We were somewhat occupied, as you might suspect." He approached her with the same stiff formality he used in the presence of powerful, political guests. Since none of those were actually present, it made Jewel uncomfortable. "No, Jewel, I did not see them with my own eyes. But there were demons in *Avantari*, and some dozen—or more—dead in their wake. The demons, we distracted."

"Celleriant?"

"He is now outside, on the grounds; he will keep watch while we attend the regent."

"You heard?"

"Yes. Before you ask, I am not aware of the precise difficulties the regent now faces; I am, however, capable of making an educated guess. There were deaths?"

"Not due to the rain—or the earth or air."

"You are certain?"

"Yes."

"Good. Come. If the regent is, as I suspect, besieged on all fronts, he will welcome your appearance."

"I doubt that," she said. Avandar opened the door that he hadn't used to enter her rooms, and waited as she followed. "I doubt that very much."

Chapter Twenty-four

GABRIEL ATERAFIN STOOD in the center of the public gallery; the word public had never felt so appropriate as Jewel approached. The House Guard was on proud display in the halls. Almost all of it, by rough count. Given their numbers, they should have looked like a small army; given the size of the crowd interspersed among them—or behind the uneven lines they could manage to keep—they didn't. Which said something. Given the importance of almost *all* of the invited attendees, Jewel felt the House Guard was, at the moment, severely underpaid.

And given the expression on Gabriel's face—even seen as it was at a distance—this was not a point she was willing to bring up today. Or ever. The matter of the House Guards' pay was best left in their own hands— and judging from their expressions, it was so far down the list of important things to consider, she should have felt embarrassed at the stray thought.

She felt uncomfortable instead, although not due to any action of the guards. The crowd, packed too tightly in the bright magelights of the gallery, adorned in somber shades of white, black, and prominent gold, made way for her. People stepped back, or to the sides—often onto other people—to give her room. She glanced at the skirts of her luminescent dress, itself almost entirely white, with traces of black and gold as befit the funeral of Amarais Handernesse ATerafin; it was easy to believe that people were moving entirely because of the dress.

Snow had adopted the rigid demeanor of the House Guard, which was disconcerting; he was silent, and if he walked with grace, the grace suggested power and danger. Voiceless, he was far more intimidating than he was when he opened his mouth; his silence suggested the death he was hunting could, at any moment, be anyone's if they were unfortunate enough to be close by.

Avandar, in her opinion, walked in the same way, but without the obvious fur, fangs, claws—or wings. His expression in no way suited the domicis robes of mourning he wore. Had she been a visitor, she too would have fallen silent and hastened to move out of his way. But she was not enough of a liar, not today, to attribute that silent, slightly fearful respect, to her attendants. Turning to Angel, she asked, "You heard everything I said?"

He gestured in den-sign. *Yes.*

All of it?

Sorry.

Straightening her shoulders, she offered him a weary smile. "Why? I meant every word of it." That smile hardened and narrowed as she met the stray glances of the Terafin visitors. It was true; she had. But it was also true that she'd worked under the auspices of Amarais for long enough that she knew what was meant was frequently best left unsaid. Her Oma's voice returned, as it often did. *What's done is done. What will you do now? That's all that matters.*

Her smile softened, because if she heard her Oma's voice, she also heard the more steely, patrician tones of The Terafin's as well. *Let the past inform your choices; do not let it foolishly bind them. Regret is a luxury, Jewel. You will find, like many luxuries, it is one for which you do not have the time. If you intend to move forward, it is imperative that you continue to move.* Different words, of course; same meaning.

Amarais, if Mandaros is kind—

She couldn't finish the thought. But it helped, to think of The Terafin; to wonder what Amarais would do in this situation, and to find, in the answer, some strength she could borrow. It wasn't the same, of course— but it would never, ever be the same again.

Haunt me, she thought. *Haunt me, dog my steps, remind me of all the ways in which I might fail if I take the wrong one.* It wasn't the first time she'd prayed for such a haunting, but this prayer was shorter. As Amarais had once said she would be, Jewel was perilously short of time.

She approached Gabriel ATerafin, and noted the changing texture of the guards who stood between them. For one, they were wearing gray, not shades of blue—but far more significant, their livery bore the crossed rod and crown. These men were the Kings' Swords—and where they went, the Kings must certainly follow. Or, she thought, locking her knees to prevent them from bending too suddenly, lead. The Kings and the Exalted were standing only a few yards away from the regent of House Terafin, and between Gabriel and the Kings, of necessity, stood the Lord of the Compact.

She didn't notice, Gabriel thought, that the berth given the Kings was not larger than the space granted Jewel ATerafin. He saw her knees begin to bend, and he saw her lock them in place; she offered the Kings the brief and genuinely respectful half bow of an equal. *Well done, Jewel,* he thought, although he knew that Amarais in her position would have offered a controlled nod to the Twin Kings; she had never liked Duvari, and in his presence, she was wont to be extremely formal and limited in her gestures of obeisance.

The questions—the pointed, almost hostile questions—that Duvari had begun died in that instant; Jewel ATerafin had—and held—his attention. Gabriel knew, as regent, he should intervene—but what regent, what Terafin, had faced events as large and inexplicable as this day's? Perhaps the founder; the founder and Amarais, on a Henden night years ago.

Amarais had faced demons and *Allasakari* and gods; she had come in armor, prepared for war.

No one but the magi and the god-born understood what Jewel had faced; she came accoutred for Court. But what Court, in the end? In what Court did that dress, and that cat, find a home? Gabriel was not a man given to prayer, but had he been, and had he the time, he would have drowned in its intensity, because the answer he wanted was: this one. The Kings' Court.

The Kings, for their part, accepted her half bow without a lift of brow; what they accepted, Duvari must perforce accept. The Lord of the Compact, however, was not inclined to accept anything with grace.

"ATerafin." His voice was cold.

"Lord of the Compact." Gabriel allowed himself a long, slow blink; Jewel's was at least as chilly. She inclined her head and looked through Duvari. "Son of Reymaris. Son of Cormaris."

The Wisdom-born King did arch a brow at her use of the titles; they were technically completely correct; they were perhaps the oldest of the formal titles granted the Kings—but the patriciate used the more royal terms. Jewel left hers unadorned.

"ATerafin," King Cormalyn replied; King Reymalyn said nothing.

She glanced at her immediate surroundings. "Guildmaster Mellifas is not present?"

"She was, but has left to supervise the magi, and to request a more full presence of the Council of the Magi in the manse. She will return shortly; until she does, it has been deemed wise to remain within the gallery, where some rudimentary magical precautions have been left in place."

Jewel's nod remained stiff and formal; what she did not tender the Kings, however, she now offered the triad: she dropped to her knees, bending head toward the floor in a spill of luminescent white. "Exalted. Daughter of the Mother, Son of Reymaris, Son of Cormaris."

"ATerafin," the Daughter of the Mother said. She was flanked by priests in full mourning; she herself wore only the three colors, although the Exalted of Cormaris and the Exalted of Reymaris had chosen to adorn the robes of their full office with black, white, and gold instead. She stepped forward, without a glance to the god-born sons and leaders of the churches of the Lords of Wisdom and Justice.

Gabriel watched; Jewel didn't so much as lift her head until the Daughter of the Mother commanded it. Nor did the Daughter of the Mother bid her rise until she stood a scant yard away. She took an inordinately long time to do so in Gabriel's opinion, as if the silence were a test.

"Rise," she finally said. If indeed she had been testing Jewel, it was not clear, from her expression, whether or not the young House Councillor had passed.

Jewel rose as bidden, shedding the supplicant posture with the ease of long practice. "Exalted."

The Mother's Daughter smiled for the first time; it was a smile as weary in every essential as Gabriel's would have been. "ATerafin. Jewel," she added, her voice softening into a surprising familiarity given the circumstance, "what have you done here?"

It was, word for word, the question Duvari had asked, but in tone and texture it was very, very different.

If Jewel had one unfortunate weakness—a weakness, given the patriciate, that would attract vultures for miles—it was for elderly women. Gabriel was uncertain as to why; he had never asked. There was very little that he had directly asked Jewel Markess; most of his information came by his indirect observation—he watched Teller, listened to Teller. Teller, who now slid between the shoulders of House Council members accustomed to a great deal more space, to reach the side of the young woman he had always considered his leader.

Amarais had known. Gabriel was certain that Barston did not—a deliberate oversight on the part of a man who made sight his vocation.

He noted that Jewel's expression did not change as Teller approached, and he allowed himself a smile, wondering as he did, if Teller would one day occupy the office of right-kin. He would have to find himself his own Barston, however; Barston was due a graceful and well-deserved retirement.

But Jewel did not take time to converse with Teller, and Teller asked no questions or spoke no words that required it, aware that the Exalted's question now demanded the whole of her public attention.

Lifting her chin, Jewel said, "I protected my House." The words were spoken like a soft challenge.

The Mother's Daughter nodded. "You did, ATerafin. For the moment—but I fear your reach extended far beyond that."

Jewel did not hesitate. "Not my reach, Exalted, but my words. Words travel beyond their speaker even in the streets of the hundred holdings, but the speaker is not held responsible for the distance at which they might be heard."

"No; he—or she—is simply held accountable for the content, should the content be considered a genuine threat."

"And were my words considered a threat?"

Gabriel winced; he held his peace, however.

"Not in content, ATerafin. And in my case, not in intent—but there is a reason why the Twin Kings are always direct descendants of the Lords of Wisdom and Justice. Intent exists entirely within the context of a given moment, and it is subject to change with the passage of time and bitter experience. I ask you again, what have you done?"

Jewel squared her shoulders. She lacked the training of the patriciate; her movements said at least as much as her words. She had, over the years, refined the use of the words themselves, but Gabriel accepted that no amount of effort would instill in her the visceral understanding of the language of motion. As he thought it, he saw that her hands had gathered into loose fists; they were shaking slightly.

Teller, however, was completely motionless. He had taken up a position to her right, and at a distance that Gabriel himself might have occupied had she been The Terafin. To her left stood Angel, and between them, the great, white cat.

"I have claimed these lands as my home," Jewel replied.

"They are indeed your home; they are home to many, many citizens of the Empire."

"Then I have not done more. I have not declared myself King—" a whisper went up around her in a spreading circle, a wave of quiet words. "Nor have I declared myself Queen. I have taken no authority upon myself except that claim."

"You have forbidden egress to those who—"

Jewel lifted both of her hands, then. "I told the water, the wind, and the earth that they were to listen to no voice but mine in these lands. I won't apologize for that. There shouldn't be any voice they can even hear, if I understand what the Guildmaster of the Order of Knowledge has said."

"They should not, according to the same guildmaster, hear yours," the Son of Cormaris said, deigning at last to join what could only barely be considered conversation. "Yet it is clear to all present—all, ATerafin—that they did. It is clear, as well, that your voice was heard across the breadth of the Isle when you spoke those words; the priests in our cathedrals and in our service heard them, and what they heard, our Lords hear. In the expert and considered opinion of Sigurne Mellifas, you are not mage-born come very late into your talent; in the expert and considered opinion of the Bardmaster of Senniel College, you have no bardic talent.

"Either the mage-born or the bard-born might—at great risk to themselves—make their voices heard in such a fashion. Yet you have demonstrably done what they could only barely do, and you stand among us."

Snow took two steps forward, his claws gathering carpet in their passage. Jewel reached down—without looking—and placed her left hand firmly across the middle of his head, slightly flattening his ears; the cat hissed, but stopped. No one else in the hall would have dared; she had, and she had done so without fear. *Be cautious, Jewel*, Gabriel thought.

"I stand among you," she replied, "because I am Jewel ATerafin, member of the Terafin House Council. I stand among you because today is the first of the three-day rites that mark the passing of The Terafin, the person I respected most in the world. I'm a citizen of the Empire; I owe allegiance to Terafin, and to the Kings Cormalyn and Reymalyn. I am what I have always been."

"And have you always been able to command, so easily, the elemental forces of nature?"

"I don't know. None of them have ever attempted to tear up my home and destroy the ceremony meant to honor and respect my Lord, before now."

The Exalted exchanged a glance, and the Son of Cormaris fell silent. The Exalted of the Mother now continued to speak. "Do you not understand what you have done?"

It was not the question Gabriel expected; it was not, clearly, the question Jewel expected either. She seemed to lose some of her steel under the steady and watchful gaze of the older woman. "I understand what I did," she said, in a quieter and less measured voice. "But I don't have the words to explain it all. Daughter of the Mother, they were going to destroy my home. Left to run wild, they would have killed everyone on these grounds, and hundreds—thousands—of people outside of them. Someone *else* gave them permission—no, *orders*—to do exactly that.

"Everything I've ever valued, everything I love, is here." She turned her face toward the grounds, as if she could see through the walls that separated them; Gabriel had an uncomfortable feeling that it was not impossible. "There are old, old roads that were carved and built on this Isle long before there were Kings, Exalted, or Jewel ATerafin. They're hidden roads, ancient roads, wild roads. But sometimes—sometimes people who are merely mortal step onto them by accident."

"That was not an accident."

"No, Exalted, not today. I didn't know, before I went South, that the roads existed at all, but in the South—" she shook her head. "In the South, I walked those paths."

"And you came to understand them?"

Jewel shook her head. "I came to understand what *home* means to me, there. I came to understand that on those roads, the force of that certainty *has* power. Even there, even in the South. I could make my stand on those roads because of that. But here? This *is* home."

"And it is not your intent to claim home as your personal kingdom or Empire."

Jewel shook her head. "My House is mine—but I belong to the House just as much. My kin are mine; I'm theirs. Before they died, I lived with my mother, my father, and my Oma. Their home was my home, but the rules were their rules. I don't see this as different."

The Exalted of the Mother's smile was almost pained. "I believe that," was her quiet reply. "But what you see and what others see will of necessity be different." She turned back to the Son of Cormaris and spoke a few low words.

"The Terafin was *my* Lord," she continued, her voice dangerously close to breaking. "If I could give my life in exchange for hers before I took another breath, I'd do it. I can't."

"She would not have allowed it," the Mother's Daughter said, and this time—in front of the gathered witnesses, she lifted a hand to Jewel's cheek and held it a moment, as if to offer comfort.

"No," was Jewel's soft reply. "But I mean for the rites to continue. If we put them off now, we'll never hold them. The rains have stopped. The grounds are safe."

"There are several dead," the Exalted of the Mother said gently.

"Yes. I understand the gravity of those deaths—but there are also people now dead in the streets of the hundred holdings who would be dead regardless. We would have paid our respects to our dead, because we were simply unaware of those deaths, and willing to be so."

"It is not your decision to make." Gabriel closed his eyes as Haerrad's voice—loud, militaristic—echoed in the vaulting of the ceiling.

"No, indeed, Councillor," the regent now said, entering a conversation in which both he and Haerrad were almost entirely superfluous. "It is mine. The Kings may choose to repair to *Avantari*; the Exalted may choose to return to their cathedrals—there is undoubtedly much they must now do. Some of the guests," he continued, lifting his voice, "who have honored Terafin by their presence and their choice to pay respects to the woman who ruled the House for so long, and with so much wisdom, may likewise choose to depart.

"But the members of House Terafin will perform the rites. We owe far more to Amarais Handernesse ATerafin than any to whom she did not offer the protection and honor of the House Name. We deeply regret the interruption and the danger our guests have faced today. As a House, however, we have faced similar in the past, and we are still standing; while we stand, we honor our own." Judging by the expression that briefly crossed Haerrad's face, very few of Gabriel's words had registered; the fact that Gabriel, not Jewel, had spoken them, however, mollified the Councillor, inasmuch as Haerrad would allow himself to be mollified.

"We will attend," King Reymalyn said. He did not speak quietly. His words filled the contours of the arches above the gallery, catching the attention of the delegates and guests who had otherwise not been party, or privy, to the discussion between Jewel and the Exalted of the Mother. "The Queens have also decided that they will remain to pay respects to a woman who exemplified all that was worthy of respect in our Empire."

It was not the decision Duvari wanted; it was clearly the one he expected. He approached King Reymalyn, and the Justice-born King lifted a hand in warning. "There are forces gathered today," he continued, when Duvari heeded the gesture and failed to speak, "that present a danger to our Empire; it is a danger that we will face. We will not ask more of our people than we ask of ourselves." He glanced at Jewel ATerafin as he spoke. "How far, ATerafin, does your . . . determination . . . extend?"

She understood the question, and Gabriel saw her knees begin to bend. He also watched as she locked them, bowing only her head instead. "I am sorry, Son of Justice, but I am unable to answer that question."

"Unable?"

"I can't leave House Terafin, and I can't be certain until I do. I will do so upon your command the minute the last of the rites have been observed."

"Very well. We will wait, ATerafin." He inclined his head and turned to King Cormalyn. To Gabriel's surprise, he hesitated, and then turned once again to face Jewel. "We are in your debt, ATerafin. Only the very wise or the very headstrong attempt to place Empires in their debt."

Her eyes rounded, but her mouth remained shut. Gabriel watched, assessing every gesture, every silence. "That was not my intent," she finally replied. In a much quieter voice, she continued, "I am seer-born; the seer-born, in theory, can look clearly into parts of the future. I therefore consider the actions undertaken in *Avantari* at my command to be my duty to the future rulers of the Empire of Essalieyan."

King Cormalyn's lips twitched in a slight smile. "ATerafin," he said. "You must now attend the regent; he is restive, and there is much to be discussed—and in very little time—before the magi return to us."

The regent was not, of course, the only man to observe, nor the only man to measure Jewel ATerafin's critical performance. In Haval's opinion, Gabriel ATerafin's assessment was, by nature and desire, far too gentle. As a dressmaker, Haval was of course among the least significant of the guests; no one asked his opinion. Or rather, no one should have. He allowed himself a theatrical, if mild, grimace as Jarven ATerafin approached the tall and intricate plant beside which he now stood. The rather better dressed and better known head of the Terafin operations in the Merchant Authority grinned at Haval's sour expression.

"Haval," he said, inclining his head as he adjusted the position of his walking stick. "I hope I find you in good health? You are not notably dry."

"I am an old man," Haval replied, "and not prone to moving quickly merely to avoid rain." He glanced at Jewel ATerafin, who had fallen uncharacteristically silent under the weight of so many stares. "I see you escorted young Finch to the gallery."

"Indeed. An advantage to my position; she has to work with—and for—me."

"I'm surprised Lucille allowed it; Lucille appears to have more sense."

"Lucille was, unhappily, quite busy." Jarven smiled broadly. "And, yes, I'm certain I will hear about it when the offices in the Authority are once again open for business. Finch is astute, and I would say, on the surface, more politically subtle than Jewel."

Haval nodded. "A fair assessment. Jewel is not known for her graceful maneuvers in the political arena. You are concerned, Jarven. If you consider it not entirely unwise, I would be interested in your reasons."

"They are, of course, the obvious reasons. She has certainly made no friend in the Lord of the Compact."

"No head of a House of any import has a friend in Duvari."

Jarven raised a brow. "That was unworthy of you, Haval."

"I felt it was an appropriate level of response for the comment that preceded it."

"Perhaps, perhaps. You are aware that we are now both out of our certain element?"

Haval nodded. "Only one of us, however, is looking forward to the new landscape with any enthusiasm."

"I have very little at risk."

When Haval lifted a brow, Jarven added, "I have lived a long and eventful life, Haval. I have few years left to me, and I admit an absurd level of gratitude that those remaining will not be inconsequential and dull. I do not, I admit, have much of an opportunity to observe her directly; it's almost as if young Finch doesn't trust me."

"That is possibly the highest praise you could give the girl."

Jarven's jovial smile suddenly vanished; no trace of it remained. "What will she do?"

"You will discover that Jewel ATerafin is remarkably straightforward. I consider it both her chief failing and the characteristic that just might preserve her life in the months to come. If she can navigate those with unfailing care, she may survive beyond that. Duvari will, of course, counsel otherwise. I am uncertain what the guildmaster will suggest, and I am equally uncertain what the gods themselves will have to say; if the gods counsel her destruction, it will be . . . tricky."

"Is she even aware it's a possibility?"

Haval, hands behind his back, watched Jewel intently. "In my considered opinion, no. But she will be."

Jarven nodded. "Can you have her do anything about those cats?"

"Sadly, no."

Jewel wanted, desperately, to go back to her room and stay there until the magi sent word. It wasn't the first time she would so badly want something she could no longer have, and the bitter disappointments and grinding fears of an entire lifetime now provided the foundations on which she could—and must—stand. She went—Snow, Angel, and Avandar at her side—to Gabriel.

To Gabriel, in full view of the Exalted, the Kings, and anyone else who was keeping score, she bowed. She held the bow until he cleared his throat, and then rose. What she saw in his face made her regret that. He was tired. He looked, to her eyes, worn—even old. "Jewel."

She nodded.

"The Council will convene the day after the last rites are offered."

She nodded again.

"If the Kings call you on that day, what will you do?"

"I will attend the meeting of the House Council—"

"It is a meeting, in full, of the Council."

She kept the flinch from her expression, or hoped she had. "And then I will travel to *Avantari* and allow the Lord of the Compact to interrogate me for the hours he no doubt intends."

A trace of a smile shifted the lines of Gabriel's face. "And if he demands otherwise?"

"The Laws of Exemption allow my absence at this time."

"Yes. But wisdom and the Laws of Exemption are often in conflict."

"In this case, I cannot afford to be absent from the Council meeting. They'll understand why. Duvari will never be pleased with any choice I make, so he may as well get used to it."

"That really is a very lovely dress."

"A very lovely, suspiciously dry dress?"

He did chuckle then. "Yes, to both. This is not what I envisaged for today. Let us hope that the rest of the funeral will pass without further incident."

Sigurne returned almost a full half hour later. Although she was bent and fragile to the eye, room was instantly made in the crowded gallery for her passage; she reached the side of the Kings in a handful of minutes. Matteos Corvel was at her elbow, looking wet, bedraggled, and determined.

She executed a perfect obeisance to the Kings, the Exalted—and the regent of House Terafin. To Duvari, she granted the nod of an equal. "Your Majesties, the grounds are now deemed safe. We have fortified the shields; the warrior-magi are now in attendance. If there is difficulty in the rest of the City, however, we will be hard-pressed to respond in any timely fashion."

"Understood, Guildmaster," the Lord of the Compact replied. The rest of the City, as Sigurne had so neatly called it, was not his concern. To Gabriel, he said, "The Kings and the Exalted will depart from the gallery; they will follow the route we discussed. The galleries are to be cleared now."

Gabriel nodded. He gestured to the waiting House Council, and they approached, leaving their attendants behind. "I must attend the Kings until the Lord of the Compact is satisfied," he told them; it was not a surprise. "Return to the Council seats; lead the guests by example."

Gabriel seldom gave orders; only Haerrad bridled, discerning the source of those orders correctly. But Haerrad was not a man noted for his grace; the political acumen for which he was—in some circles—admired had little to do with elegant maneuvering and much to do with raw power.

"Where is Councillor Rymark?" he asked, his broad, deep voice traveling the length of the hall. ·

"He is toward the eastern end of the gallery," Gabriel replied curtly. "Before you continue to ask questions that are appropriate for the Council Hall—and only that hall—let me inform you that his disposition was entirely at the request of the Lord of the Compact; he would have been here, otherwise."

Haerrad's brow rose, as did the corners of his lips. The brief contortion could not be dignified with the word smile. "There is much to discuss in the Council Hall when the Council convenes."

"Of that," was Gabriel's dry reply, "I have no doubt whatsoever."

The servants were a moving army across the whole of the green; the Master Gardener's tabard adorned several who now worked at edging the newly turned grass. Murmurs, muted, traveled between these men and women like a living, irregular wave: they had expected a disaster. It was true that the benches were damaged by their fall, but they had not been crushed or destroyed beyond possibility of use; nor had all of the intricate tenting that adorned the pavilions, although the tables had to be—quickly—replaced.

But guiding them, watching them, were the first things that had been retrieved and reinstated: the poles that bore the banners and colors of House Terafin. The coffin itself had not been touched or harmed; it was not wet, it was not scratched, and no trace of dirt adorned it. That also caused whispers to spread, but they were muted and hushed; even the newest of the servants to the Terafin manse knew the story of Jewel Markess ATerafin's humble beginnings, and only a handful had failed to recognize her voice.

It should have terrified them; it didn't. No more had The Terafin herself, when she had ruled these grand, forbidding halls. The only thing that caused them to quake in their boots—or shoes—was the Master of the Household Staff, and as that august and terrifying woman was present, the murmurs never broke a hurried whisper. Nor would they, in any case, when guests—outsiders, all—were present in such large numbers. Many of the servants were ATerafin, and they had received the offer of formal adoption from The Terafin herself. If she had been so far above them they could not ordinarily approach her, she had nonetheless recognized their service, the value of their dedication.

This, then, they could do for her.

The seats were rapidly filled; the desultory greetings and political wrangling that any such occasion demanded had already occurred, and no one was yet in a mood to repeat them. What, after all, could be said? If the strangers and visitors did not recognize the history of Jewel Markess ATerafin—or even the name—they would, in time; they understood for now that they had been in danger, and that that danger had been very, very real. They approached, and resumed, their seats with care; the political zeal for the best seating had quieted, although there were one or two among the patriciate who would cease their jostling for position only at death, if then.

The House Council arrived first; they took their seats in a proud but subdued silence. Last to arrive, and last to sit, was Jewel Markess ATerafin, and the servants—and onlookers—could be forgiven for noticing no one else. It wasn't just her dress—which had weathered an elemental storm without the bother of actually getting wet—or her companion; the servants who worked in the West Wing had spread tales of the sauciness and impertinence of the talking cats as far as such stories could reach, and they were now held in far less fear than they had been. It was her carriage, her bearing, and the way she paused beneath the banner of Terafin and bowed her head.

Her carriage, her bearing, the quality of her silence, reminded all who worked that this was, at its heart, a funeral: that these people—Kings, Exalted, and guildmasters—were here for no other reason.

The House Guard was now out in force, although at the moment, little evidence of their presence could be seen anywhere but along the path that the Kings and the Exalted would walk. That path was silent and deserted, but as the chime sounded, it began to fill, first with the *Astari* and the Kings' Swords, second with the Queens Marieyan the Wise and Siodonay the Fair. Their thrones—and thrones had been commissioned and provided—stood empty as the Queens approached, flanked by their guards. The guards assumed positions to the right and left of those thrones, for the Queens sat side by side.

This was a signal, and the servants now vanished as only servants can, attending to their remaining tasks almost invisibly. The Kings arrived next, and as they entered the clearing, people rose, led by the House Council. They stood in respectful silence until the Kings were likewise seated; the Kings required the presence of more guards and the vigilance of the Astari, but the necessary space had been provided.

Into the clear, cool air, the filigree trace of the smoke burning incense provided could now be seen. The Exalted had arrived. They were preceded by priests of the Triumvirate, in robes that had not yet fully dried; the incense, however, was not so damp it would not burn. The gathered mourners had not resumed their seats when the Kings sat; they waited, tendering the Exalted the respect due the god-born—respect equal in all measures to that due the Kings themselves.

Only when the Exalted had taken their thrones—and the procession was longer and slower than that which attended the Kings—did the guests sit. The House Council remained on their feet, waiting upon the regent's signal, for Gabriel came last to the House Council section. He came without fanfare, without attendants, and without guards; those, he had left with the coffin.

The coffin, however, was now carried—by the Chosen who had served The Terafin with their lives while she lived—into the clearing. A stone bier, faceless and unadorned, had been erected for the occasion, and the Chosen, without so much as a stumble, carried their Lord to that bier and gently laid the coffin upon it. When they stepped back, they stood for a long moment in silence, heads bent. They did not salute her, but brought their hands to chest as if to do so; that pose, they held for one long minute before they retreated.

The bells rang again, and this time, the Son of Cormaris rose. He rose alone. Amarais Handernesse ATerafin had paid respects to each of the gods in the Triumvirate, but it was to Cormaris that she prayed in times of trouble, and to Cormaris that she looked for guidance. The Exalted of Cormaris left his throne—and his attendants, with their braziers, their rods, their scrolls—and walked across the flattened grass until he reached the coffin that had been placed there with such care.

He bowed his head to her, offering her a respect that the Exalted never offered the living by the complicated rules of etiquette that governed the patriciate. Jewel watched. The coffin was closed; it wouldn't be opened, and she wasn't certain how she felt about that. She'd seen the dead before: her mother, her Oma. She had been spared her father's corpse; his employers had dealt with it. There had been no funeral for him, and had there been, it would have been nothing like this one: there would have been no Exalted, no Kings, no rich merchants, no guildmasters. No one of import to the world at large.

Jewel would have been there, and a handful of their neighbors would have joined her.

She swallowed. There had been no funeral for Lefty, for Lander, none for Fisher or Duster; those bodies, she had never seen. Beneath Averalaan, in the sleeping ruins of the undercity, those who had died had been interred without benefit of last rites or burial. She was certain that three of her own were there, somewhere, lost and frozen in time. There was no way to search for them or find them; she'd asked. The entrance to the undercity could be opened only by the Exalted and the Sacred, working in concert, for hours on end.

Even as a member of the House Council of Terafin, she did not have the power to make that request.

But Amarais? She was here. She had built a small Empire within the Kings' Empire. She had touched thousands of lives, tens of thousands. Even thinking it, Jewel bowed her head. Her father had touched so few lives— but one of them had been *hers*. He had been as important as Amarais to Jewel Markess. He wasn't The Terafin, would never be The Terafin; had he lived, he would have worked at the docks until work was beyond him.

It seemed unfair to her that he had given the whole of his life to the people he loved, and it counted for so little. She had loved him. In her way, she had loved Amarais. But the Exalted of Cormaris? He had, undoubtedly, respected her. The Chosen revered her. Morretz had loved her, but Morretz was dead, and the only absence Jewel resented was his. This is where he should be, in a coffin very like his Lord's; this is where he should be buried. He had given his life in her service—and he had died in it as well; Jewel was aware, in a way she wouldn't have been at sixteen years of age, of the difference between the two.

But he was—had been—a domicis. Not ATerafin, not of House Terafin, he had existed only for her. She wondered if he could see the service as it progressed. Would it please him to hear the familiar words of a funeral service spoken by the Exalted of Cormaris? Did it please her?

No.

She felt curiously empty as she watched. She was exhausted, but it was an exhaustion that left her light-headed; as if all her anger and rage had drained away with the departure of the other wild elements. Amarais was dead. The dead didn't care. The whole of this service—every detail, every gold coin—was for the sake of those who remained in her wake. Jewel ATerafin was only one of them. She had looked forward on a very narrow path, seeing that coffin on this day, surrounded by these people; she hadn't looked beyond it. Why?

Because she'd wanted to pay her respects to a woman who was in no way capable of receiving them?

This was the reason her Oma returned to haunt her, or at least things like this; her Oma's voice had been dangerously absent. *The dead are just dead,* she thought. Her shoulders slowly began to unclench. *Only the living give meaning to death.*

Yes, the Winter King said. She lowered her chin, listening to the familiar timbre of his voice. *But look, Jewel; look well. Here, enemies are gathered upon the same ground; they do not lift sword or voice; they have set aside their subtle war. If the dead are just dead—and I will not argue such a fundamental point—the living are alive; this juxtaposition is a reminder. It is necessary, even for you.*

Especially for me, she thought. *It shouldn't be, but it is. Rath, are you waiting for her? Will you finally speak?* Somehow, she doubted it; her smile was brief and hollow. The Exalted of Cormaris continued to speak, and as he did, she heard the low strains of simple music: someone was playing a harp. The details of the funeral—details which she, as a Council member, should have memorized—had been left entirely in Gabriel's hands; the music came as a surprise to her. The bards of renown used their voices as weapons; strange, then, that the music itself could compel so strongly.

But it did. It was soft, somber, strangely gentle. She thought she could listen to it forever. The Exalted of Cormaris did not sing—but the music wound round his words, lifting them, elevating them. There were things that could be sung that couldn't be said, and the flat, rhythmic patterns of a centuries-old sermon—at least—were given a sense of urgency and life by the notes that attended the syllables.

Jewel closed her eyes. In the darkness of lids and attention, she could suddenly see The Terafin, dressed in dark blue, her hair in a net, her face less aged, less harsh. She could see, clearly, the expression she wore; it was the first time they had met, and it had occurred in the safety of Amarais' stronghold. House Terafin was Amarais'. But she had been confident enough that she had opened her home to Jewel and her den at the request of a brother she had not seen for decades—a brother she would never see alive again.

Rath had hated her. Hated her the way that only the loved can be hated.

She opened her eyes to see coffin, Exalted, and banner, and closed them again to see Amarais in the armor of Terafin, the sword of the House strapped to her side beneath the glittering lights of the Terafin foyer. War had come to her House, and she intended to lead, to fight. She had seemed invulnerable at that moment—and less than an hour later, she lay dying, the marble floors broken, the chandelier strewn across what was left. She had survived that attempt on her life only with the intervention of a healer.

And that healer was also dead.

Amarais had been *so strong*, so wise, so certain—and there she was.

Alowan—dead. Morretz—dead. Courtne, Alayra, Alea—dead. Jewel forced her eyes open; it was so dark, suddenly. The three had lived to protect Amarais, each in their fashion. Was her death, then, their failure and a failure of their lives? She had given the whole of her life to Terafin; she had fought and survived one House War to win the right to rule it. She had built a Council that was strong enough to weather the wars that merchant houses fought in the streets, and there had been no war to depose her. She'd built well.

What did it mean now? She was dead; did everything have to crumble with her?

No, Jewel thought. *I gave her my word.* But the truth? She wasn't a strong enough person to live solely by word. Alowan, Alea, even Morretz—they were stronger than she; even Gabriel was, in his way. She needed more, and always had.

But she had built what she loved here. She had built around Amarais, and beside her. What Amarais valued, Jewel valued. Oh, not everything; Amarais loved the arts, and the very few pieces she personally chose to own did not, and would never, speak to Jewel in the same way. But the sword was named *Justice*, and it did. Amarais had given Jewel the House Name, and it had become so much a part of her, it *was* hers, now; it was part of who she was, and even part of who she wanted to be.

When she had first arrived at the front doors, literally penniless, all she had wanted—desperately, viscerally wanted—was a roof over her den's head, a place where they could be safe.

What she wanted now was not so different; what had changed was the knowledge that it had to be built and it had to be defended. She could do both. Breath filled her lungs as she lifted her head, opened her eyes. Yes, she could do this. But she didn't want to have to do it; she wanted—oh, she wanted what children wanted: Amarais back. She wanted the opportunity to tell her all of the things she should have told her before she left for the South; she wanted the chance to ask advice, and to receive her oblique and sometimes harsh comfort.

What she had, instead, was this: the Exalted of Cormaris fell silent, bowing his head for a long, long moment above the coffin. Then he stepped back, lifted his arms, and called sunlight. In the gray and threatening clouds above the magical barrier, it was in very short supply—but it came at his call. A golden, diffuse light surrounded the bier upon which The Terafin had been laid. As the light spread, Jewel felt the warmth of summer breeze—without the stultifying humidity that usually accompanied it.

The Exalted of Cormaris spoke three long words in a language Jewel didn't recognize. He then bowed to The Terafin and said, "Go in peace, daughter." Shrouded in the brief, brief Summer, the Exalted of Cormaris turned to the other two sides of the triad; the Mother's Daughter and the Exalted of Reymaris. They joined him, silent, their robes brushing flattened grass. Their priests remained by their thrones; they stepped into the soft, slow radiance alone.

They then began to speak.

Jewel had heard a variant of this speech very seldom; it was delivered, start to finish, in a language specific to the temples and cathedrals of the gods, and her Oma didn't hold with churches. She had both admired and disdained the men and women who labored under the auspices of the Mother, and when ambivalent, her Oma kept her distance. In her Oma's home, her distance was a distance observed by anyone who wanted to live in relative peace.

The light grew as the Exalted of the Mother and the Exalted of Reymaris joined the Exalted of Cormaris, and Jewel finally remembered where she had last seen it: in the Terafin manse, hours after the attack of the demons, their mage, and their *Allasakari* had all but destroyed the grand foyer. The Exalted had come to examine the bodies of the dead—Chosen, House Guards, and *Allasakari*, all—and they had labored under the warmth of just this light. Jewel stiffened; her hands did become fists. Did they think The Terafin somehow defiled *by* her death?

But she could not hold on to that anger. She had chosen to go South, and her understanding, in any visceral sense, of the events that had led to The Terafin's death was therefore secondhand at best. She had no right to indignation, and it served no purpose. The Exalted of Reymaris and the Exalted of Cormaris fell silent; the Mother's Daughter continued to speak.

The words she chose—in the strange, strange language of churches, hit Jewel, dislodging memory in the way striking events sometimes could. She had heard these phrases before.

Duster had spoken them in the undercity, while the earth rumbled and the distant sound of breaking stone grew closer and closer. At their backs were the biers upon which three preternaturally beautiful men lay at rest, and Jewel's eyes widened as she turned, at last, to catch a glimpse of Celleriant.

He was there, in the distance, at the periphery of the space set aside for visitors. Gray-eyed—steel-eyed—he watched the Exalted, unaware of Jewel's sudden, sharp glance. But his lips turned up in a slender smile—a smile as sharp as his narrowed eyes—at just that moment. He did not otherwise speak or move, and she slowly forced herself to relax; she quickly forced herself to turn her visible attention back to the Exalted, whose prayer was now coming to a close.

And what an odd prayer to grant Amarais Handernesse ATerafin—not a paean to the glory of the powerful, not a meditation on the admiration due the dutiful, but rather, a prayer for the homeless, the orphans, and the lost. Jewel didn't understand the Exalted or the god-born; she was certain that if the House Council knew the full import of those words, they would have taken—silent—offense. She was ambivalent, in a way that reminded her uncomfortably of the sharp-tongued old woman who had raised her, and that lasted until the Mother's Daughter turned—to her—her eyes golden and luminescent with open tears.

They were the tears one might shed for a child, and Jewel found herself transfixed. Amarais did not cry. She did not allow herself to show—and share—that weakness. Jewel, raised on the opposite end of the City in all ways that counted, hated to cry, for the same reason. But the Daughter of the Mother shed tears without fear; it was almost as if she shed them for Jewel, for Amarais—for all of the people here who had loved, lost, and could not reveal how deeply that loss affected them.

It was an act of generosity that almost broke her resolve.

But she knew, if Amarais truly watched from the confines of Mandaros' long hall, that giving in to the overwhelming sorrow and loss would not please her; she held herself as stiff, as still, as she could.

Finch did not; Teller did not; Angel did not. Angel wept openly, although he stood as erect as Jewel herself. His hair, bound in its customary spiral, attracted the odd glance from the patriciate; he was so inured to their reaction he failed to notice it. This woman had offered him her name, and had made clear upon his first refusal that it was his to take at any time he chose.

Like Alowan, he had never taken her up on the offer, but unlike Alowan, he could see a time coming—swiftly—when he might at last do so. Alowan had survived one House War; the rumbling skirmishes that heralded a second had taken his life. But he had prepared Daine to step into the breach his death would leave. He had been a peaceful man in all senses of the word, yet he had found a way to fight a war that he believed in.

The Terafin's war.

The Kings approached the coffin when the Mother's Daughter at last retreated; they did not speak in the strange language of the triad. They spoke in Weston, and they might have been bard-born; their words carried. The praise that the Exalted did not openly offer, the Kings did; they praised The Terafin for her loyalty, her vision, and her mercy. They acknowledged her as first among equals—words which did not rankle the visiting Ten. She was dead, after all; her House was now in the turmoil that death always causes among Councillors of ambition and power. They might benefit from her loss, for they were not themselves in a similar situation—but they would move with care, because they would be, in future.

Angel did not think them vultures, although had anyone chosen to ascribe carrion traits to them, he wouldn't have objected. They were men—and women—of power. This is what the powerful did. Even The Terafin. Perhaps especially The Terafin, a woman who was sensitive to the shifts of power in other Houses, and in particular, the weaknesses that resulted.

She was a Lord worthy of the following she had built; he knew that, and acknowledged it. But he glanced at Jay, just once, while the Kings spoke, because Jay was not The Terafin—and Jay would need to build a following at least as strong if she meant to survive this day's work. He would be there. The whole of the den would be there. Finch, with her roots in the Merchant Authority; Teller with his in the right-kin's office; Carver, the den's eyes and ears among the servants—through whom significant news traveled like fire across a dry, drought-stricken plain. Arann would be part of her Chosen, and what remained of the Chosen, she had.

But she had the cats, as well; Night and Snow were silent sentinels now. They exuded power and danger—mostly because they were silent and still. She had Avandar, who was part of the den, and entirely separate from it; she had Lord Celleriant and the creature she called the Winter King. Any one of these would have been cause for fear and suspicion among the patriciate—but she had the trees, as well. He knew she would never surrender any of these while she lived.

Although the light that surrounded not just the coffin but the dignitaries that now rose around it shone like the heart of midday, Angel thought of night, of endless night. Of war, and its harbingers. Of the deaths that war inevitably caused. Although he acknowledged the loss of The Terafin with the tears Jay herself would not shed, he also thought it might—just might—be better, this way: this war was Jay's war, and she had already begun to arm herself.

Epilogue

6th of Henden, 427 A.A.
Terafin Manse, Averalaan Aramarelas

HANNERLE WANTED TO GO HOME. The finery of the manse—its carpets, its paneled halls, its profusion of both plant life and magelights—did not suit her; nor did the cavernous room in which she had woken to find herself situated. She had spoken, briefly, with Jewel ATerafin, but the small talk had done nothing to calm her nerves; worse, it had produced nothing useful with which she might ward off the worry that all but consumed her.

Haval knew. He had lived with this woman for decades, had watched her slow shift from young, practical woman, to older, practical woman; he had watched her widen, watched her height slowly dwindle the way height will with age. Her hands, callused and strong, lay palms down across the folded counterpane; her face was pale, drawn. Had it only been that, Haval could have deferred a conversation he did not want to have, but Hannerle's lips were compressed in a thin, thin line. She spoke seldom, answered in monosyllables, and took no company; Haval thought she would enjoy the company of either Finch or Teller, but both had been much occupied with the funeral. Nor would its aftermath leave them much time to play visitor.

It was evening, now, although the sun had only barely set; the sounds of merriment—and music—could be heard within the walls. The third day of a funeral was not supposed to be about death; it was a celebration of life, both one's own and the life of the deceased. As such, the wine rooms of the manse had been opened—and possibly emptied; Haval, used to excess, was still moderately surprised at just how much men and women could drink.

But Hannerle, invited, had declined to attend; nor had Haval expected otherwise. She glanced at him when he entered the room, and then let her gaze drop to the hands that tightened, briefly, across the bedding.

"I want to go home," she said quietly.

He was not surprised by her words; he was surprised that she had held them in for so long. The Terafin was not a woman to whom social visits to a clothier were a possibility, and Hannerle therefore had no personal attachment to her funeral. Nonetheless, she had waited until the end of the three-day rites to say what had so clearly been on her mind. Haval moved a chair closer to the bedside, and sat in it in silence, thinking, as he did, that she would sleep tomorrow; without Adam's intervention, she would not wake.

"You know why that would be difficult," he told her quietly.

"I know it would be, but I am willing to return to the Terafin manse—on my own—at the end of three days. I have no desire to sleep my life away, Haval."

"Hannerle, we cannot say with any certainty that you will be wakeful for the whole of the three days, and if you return home and fail to wake—"

"You can have me brought back."

He was silent for a long moment. "Tell me, then, how am I to explain?"

"To who? Jewel already knows, and I can't see that it's anyone else's business."

"Hannerle—"

She now lifted one hand from its place in her lap. "I heard Jewel," she said quietly.

The urge to misunderstand her came and went. "You heard her bespeak the water."

"I heard every word she said, clear as church bells on my wedding day." Having made her quiet statement, she waited, watching him, her lips still thin, her brows gathering above the bridge of her nose. Had it been in folds of anger, he would have found it easier. They were not; she was in pain, and had not yet worked the strange alchemy by which pain became anger. "You mean to help her take the House."

"I do not think at this point she requires much help."

"Haval—answer the question."

It wasn't a question, but he failed to correct her. "I mean to advise her, yes."

"Is that all you mean to do? Advise?" These words were sharper, harsher.

"Hannerle—"

"You promised you were done with your old line of work. With all of it—the lies, the secrecy, the dangerous games. The deaths."

"I have not broken that word. I am here in a different capacity; I am here because Jewel ATerafin considers me knowledgeable, even wise."

"And she is fool enough to trust you." The words were bitter. He had expected at least that much.

Before he could answer, however, the door opened. It had been pushed on its hinges by the white head of Snow, surely the world's most unusual dressmaker. Hannerle's hands became rigid, but she said nothing.

Haval, however, rose. "Snow," he said, in the carefully modulated and respectful tone he used with the cat. "Why are you here? Why are you not beside Jewel?"

The cat hissed and flexed wings. He also flexed claws, causing visible damage to the carpet. "She told me to *leave*," he said. "She wanted *privacy*."

"And you obeyed her?"

"I was *bored*," he replied, gaze sliding sideways and away from Haval's inspection.

"She is now alone?" Haval glanced at the door, which was still ajar.

Snow snorted. "The *ugly* one is watching." He hissed in a way that indicated laughter in the great winged beasts. "She told *him* to leave *first*."

"Ah." Haval resumed his seat. "I am afraid that if you are bored, we will be unentertaining. We mean to simply talk—quietly—for some time."

"Oh, *talk*." His ears twitched. "What about?"

"Sleep."

"Talk, talk, talk. All anyone ever *does* is talk."

Haval glanced pointedly at the door, and Snow, complaining the entire way, took what was only barely a hint. Haval did, however, rise to close the door firmly at the cat's back.

Hannerle was watching the door. "They're beautiful," she unexpectedly said. He heard an echo of a much, much younger girl in her words—and voice—and was genuinely surprised. Hannerle was not a woman given to speaking about the beauty of anything.

"They are fractious, difficult and," he added, glancing at the damaged carpet, "expensive."

"They're not meant to be house cats." She clenched fists briefly, and then swung her legs to the side of the bed, abandoning it. Haval rose to offer her aid, and sat quickly when he received her thunderous glare in response. He hid his smile. This woman was the woman he had married. Her ferocious sense of personal dignity had not yet deserted her; it would do so only upon her death. Her death. He glanced at the floor and when he lifted his gaze again, she was watching his face, her eyes so narrow one could be forgiven for assuming they were closed.

"I like the girl," she said. "I've always liked her. I disapproved—greatly—of her association with Ararath. I have never asked her to what use she put your lessons; I thought I might strangle you if she answered." She set feet gingerly on the carpet. Her own weakness frustrated her, and she was perfectly capable of shunting that frustration to one side or the other, where it might fall on the unwary. "What have you done here?"

"We have never spoken openly about my work—"

"Haval."

"I have made clothing, Hannerle—not the dress that Jewel herself wore, to my great despair. I have spoken at length with Jewel, and in brief with Teller and Finch. I have observed. More than that, I have failed to do."

"And when will you start?"

Haval said nothing for a long moment. "My sources are not always exact when it comes to the interior working of any of the great Houses. I have every reason to be here; I have made use of it."

"And you think you're necessary, somehow? You think she'll fail without you?"

A lie would have comforted her; Haval considered it. But she was Hannerle, and if he frequently omitted truth, he could not bring himself to lie to her. Not yet, although it might have made his life simpler. "She has allies that I did not expect; she has the cats, which I feel a very, very mixed blessing. But she has enemies beyond the scope of my experience, as well as the enemies I feel I understand quite well. I cannot aid her in any way I can see with the former—but given the situation, I feel it essential to aid her with regard to the latter."

"It's only advice?"

He was utterly silent. She understood. She stood, shaking slightly—he wasn't certain if it was due to her weakness or the strength of her anger. But she did not order him out of her room; she did not attempt to leave it herself. Really, it was the best he could hope for.

"And when will it be over, Haval? When she's Terafin? When she's more? When will you stop?"

He said, without guile, "I will stop the moment you can wake on your own."

She was silent, rigid, for a full minute. When she spoke—she started three different sentences before she gained traction with the fourth—she said, "Are you saying that you've made this choice because of *me*? Are you laying that at *my* feet?" He thought she might hit him; there was very little here she could bear to throw, none of it being her own.

"No." He was careful not to touch her, but it was hard. She had always been so prickly in her pain. One had to almost pace around its walls, seeking a way past it. "This is, in its entirety, about me. I was—I *am*—content in our life. I know that I still pay far more attention than you'd like to gossip, but it is a small foible, surely? I enjoy making dresses. I enjoy running our shop."

"But?" she demanded.

"I am not you, Hannerle. I cannot do it without you. The life that we lead—we lead it because I can be content in it *if* you are by my side. If you leave me, it would hold very little."

"I won't—"

"If you die. You cannot be woken by any power in this city except one, and it is only available here. I do not think it coincidental at this juncture." He lifted both hands, as if in plea, although no trace of that action touched his expression. "I will not lie. I find it challenging. But I found the smaller life we built challenging as well, in different ways. I give you my word, Hannerle, the moment you can wake on your own, Jewel ATerafin, be she The Terafin or no, can come to my shop by carriage and take her fittings there.

"I will not say I will not give her advice, if she seeks it; I have given her what advice I can for half her life now. But I will not take part in her Councils."

Hannerle, like Jewel, did not cry. "I want our life to mean more than that, to you."

"You are the heart of life, Hannerle. But I am not a dramatic man; if you are gone, I will continue. I will build what I require in this House. I will begin anew." He paused, and then said, "I *want* our life. I have always wanted it enough to give over anything I had built on my own. I want it enough now to be here, to have you *here*. I know it is not what you want— but can you not accept it, for now? I have sat by your side, I have given you water, I have made the broths that you might swallow, and I have watched you dwindle.

"I will not watch you die if there is anything I can do to prevent it. This is what I can do." It was almost enough. He sighed. "What I can offer Jewel is education; I cannot transform her into someone who might be more naturally suited to halls of power. What you cannot live with, Hannerle, she could not live with. What you would—barely forgive—she would *never* forgive. The entire situation must be handled with care— from the moment we engage, we engage without a full array of weapons at our disposal. I will not lie to you—I may lie to her. It is in my nature. I will not, however, perform services in her name—"

"Haval."

"I will not perform services that I feel necessary without her express permission."

The lines of her shoulders softened slightly, and he now approached her. "I cannot promise more. I cannot take you home. Not for Jewel's sake; that, I'm afraid, I would do. If she cannot deal with such a small risk, she is not fit to rule one of The Ten."

"It's the boy."

He smiled. "You never valued your powers of observation, Hannerle. Never. Yes. I am far too selfish to avoid putting the boy at risk at all; he is the only thing that wakes you, and that act makes him vulnerable. I am not concerned with his welfare, however; if what he does here is discovered, he is at risk—and if he is harmed, kidnapped, killed—you will die. I do not want his health for its own sake; he is merely—"

She slid her hands to their perch on her hips. "That is *quite* enough."

"As you say, dear. Hannerle—"

"I'm not sure I should let you say another word; I'll strangle you myself, and then where would I be?"

"In the Terafin manse—but I'm certain Jewel would forgive you if you told her why."

6th of Henden, 427 A.A.
Terafin Grounds, Averalaan Aramarelas

"Will you not move from this place?"

The moon was high; the evening was cold. The guests and the mourners had left the gardens and the grounds and—absent their singing, their laughter, and their arguments—it was silent. She was not, however, alone. The Terafin's coffin had been placed—as was tradition for the House—upon the altar beneath the curved roof of the Terafin shrine; she would lie there until sun's full height, when she would finally be laid to rest.

Jewel had shed her followers, all save two: Angel, who stood at the foot of the path that led to this fourth shrine in the garden of contemplation, and Avandar, who was somewhere in the shadows. She had not had to tell Angel to wait; he knew. Avandar was angry at the assumed risk she'd taken. She knew that Torvan would know where she was; he probably had the men at his disposal watching the path even now.

"Jewel."

"No." She glanced at the Terafin Spirit. She was angry at his interruption, but grateful for his presence; she had been so certain that she would wake on the second day of the funeral rites to find him gone.

"Not yet," he said, his voice soft. "But soon, ATerafin. I am almost . . . afraid." His smile belied his words. "You have the House Council meeting on the morrow."

"I'll be there."

He fell silent. Kalliaris frowned; it didn't last. "She is dead," he said, his voice gentle. "She is not aware of your presence; she cannot appreciate the respect you grant her in repose."

"I know that."

"Then—"

"No."

"May I ask why?"

Can I stop you? Clearly she couldn't. She even knew he was right. But there was so much she wanted to say. So much she should be able to say. She couldn't. She'd spent an hour and a half, head bowed over the coffin, aching with unshed words—but they were jumbled, messy, inelegant; they were entirely inadequate. She wanted for words, for the *right* words, and they wouldn't come to her. She couldn't even cry because he was here, he was watching, and he'd given his life for the House in a way that even Amarais hadn't.

"You have a visitor," the Terafin Spirit said.

It was almost a relief, although the words set her teeth on edge. She straightened her shoulders, lifted her chin, and turned. There, with as much hauteur as she would ever be able to manage, she froze.

Marrick ATerafin was coming down the narrow, well-tended walk.

The Terafin Spirit instantly fell silent, which was possibly the only blessing Marrick's presence could grant. Jewel set her back toward the coffin, as if she were one of the Chosen, and The Terafin were still alive. Her own, she could tell to go away; this man? No. He was a House Council member, a senior member, and he had already made clear that he intended to take the House Seat in *Avantari*.

Something was wrong; it took Jewel a moment to realize what it was: Marrick came alone. He had no attendants, no House Guards, none of the usual entourage. He did not carry a weapon—or at least not a visible weapon—and his expression was almost unnaturally grave. He was—he had always been—a friendly man. It was hard to dislike him; she knew, she'd tried. Because of Avandar, she continued to try to find fault with his actions, to see his charm as a subterfuge behind which lurked another Haerrad in the making.

But it was only because of Avandar, and in the dark of a clear, cold night, she couldn't even make the attempt. She offered him the polite nod of an equal, and turned away, toward the coffin in which Amarais would greet the dawn.

He joined her. He did not ask permission—but permission was not, strictly speaking, required. But he did not speak either; where she stood, he now dropped to one knee. He bowed his head to the coffin in silence, as if he were alone, and after a moment, Jewel did the same.

"Do you know," he said, although he didn't lift his head, "that I was not a Council member at the commencement of the last House War?"

She hadn't. She knew it was information she *should* know, and was grateful for the lack of any of her advisers at this particular moment.

"I was a young man. A promising, bright young man," he added, with a wry chuckle. "And I was, of course, charming. My mother oft said it was a failing—a bright failing. I am not lazy," he added, "in my own defense. I have always preferred to cajole where another might threaten. But I was not without ambition in my youth." He lifted his head, then, and rose. "I am not without ambition now, as you must know."

She nodded, because this at least she did.

He reached out and laid his right palm against wood that had grown chill with lack of sun in the Henden wind. "She saw something in me, in my feckless youth. She was not yet The Terafin; she was Amarais Handernesse ATerafin, and she was estranged from her family because she had chosen to take the Terafin name. You were aware of that?"

Jewel closed her eyes and swallowed. "Yes. Yes, very familiar. I knew her brother."

"I did not have that privilege, although I knew of him. Handernesse was an old, old lineage; it was not a significant player in the courts of power. Had she stayed with Handernesse, it would have been."

"It would not have been one of The Ten."

"No. But Terafin would not have been first among The Ten were it not for her leadership, either. The finest of swords cannot make a man an expert swordsman; it is the same with the Houses. They have the raw resources, and the reach, but without a man—or woman—who understands the whole of the political landscape, it cannot be expertly wielded, and to advantage. You met her in her prime, Jewel. She was impressive, formidable, and entirely in control of even the slightest of gestures. She was adored by her Chosen, respected by her servants, feted by her merchants."

"When they weren't drunk."

He chuckled. "They could be a tad overfamiliar when drunk; it seldom happened more than once.

"You did not see her in her youth."

"You didn't—"

"I forget myself. When I joined the House, she was young to me—although to you now, she would not have been. She was not a gentle woman in her youth. She was not Haerrad; she was not a monster. But she was a blade, a honed thing, and she burned with righteous anger." His smile was a strange, soft smile. "You could have warmed your hands on her rage on the right days—or the wrong ones. She was always careful with her words—but her words were like a slender dam; what lay behind them could always be felt.

"Perhaps because she was so bold, she found favor in the eyes of The Terafin. It was clear to the House, and to those with ambition, that some bond formed between them; he mentored her, where she would allow it. She was envied, and she was feared, for that reason. But not by me—I was not a member of the House Council; the age of The Terafin signified little in my case."

"And in hers?"

He raised a brow. "I believe that question to be beneath you in your current circumstance."

Jewel had the grace to redden.

"I was ambitious, Jewel, but it was more than that. She offered me a seat on the House Council for my support—what little support I could give her—when she made her bid to take the House Seat." He sounded surprised. Still.

"The House Council is *not* the House," was Jewel's sharp observation.

"No. No, it is not. But it is by general acclaim, by consensus, that The Terafin is finally chosen."

"It's not—"

"Very well. It is by the consensus of those who remain alive *after* the worst of the conflict has occurred. Will that suffice?"

She nodded.

"I accepted her offer." He studied Jewel's expression; in the dark at the end of the three longest days of her life, she couldn't guard it well. "You think I accepted it because I wanted the House Council seat." It wasn't a question. "That is fair, Jewel. I *did* want the seat, and if I were asked at any other time but this one, I would ask, loudly, if there was any *other* reason to accept such an offer."

She waited, now, her hands slowly unclenching by her sides, the night air in her lungs as he turned his gaze to the coffin again. "But this is the shrine at which oaths are made to the House, or of it, and here, I will not lie. It was her, Jewel. When she spoke to me—I wanted *what* she wanted." He smiled. "She was so clear in her principles. She was so determined. She burned, in a way that made fire beautiful.

"You will, of course, declare yourself for the House Seat in the Council Hall on the morrow."

She should have said yes, and knew it; she was silent. There was no question and no doubt in his words. But standing in the lee of the coffin, the woman she respected most in the world enclosed and in all ways unable to return, she could not. She had wanted three days to mourn.

Life doesn't have time for your tears, girl, her Oma's voice said sharply. *You shed them, fine. You're still a child. But you* keep moving *while you cry. If you don't move, the vultures will think you're carrion.*

Yes. Yes, Oma.

"We were not certain," Marrick continued, when she failed to reply. "Until your unexpected arrival at the moment The Terafin was assassinated, your candidacy had been considered a possibility—but you are young, by the standards of the Council Hall, and you have not built an impressive base of power. Or so we believed. When you did arrive—without announcement, and in the middle of the chaos—it became a probability, but the caveat still remained. You are aware that at least four of the senior Council members intended to advance themselves as candidates before the full Council."

Jewel nodded.

"And those?"

"You. Elonne, Haerrad, Rymark. I'd so hoped that Gabriel—" She bit the words off. "Those were the four that I knew about."

"You are correct; if there is a fifth—besides yourself—I am unaware of them." He watched her face beneath the flicker of lamplight; the shrine was not lit by magestones. "On the first day of the funeral rites, my dear, it was clear to at least two of us that you intended to declare. The dress," he added, his smile softening as if the memory were precious, "drew every eye, from the highest to the lowest—and you wore it surprisingly well. I will say that when your cat chooses not to speak, he is fearsome."

Jewel grimaced. "Luckily, that's almost never."

To her surprise, Marrick nodded gravely. "It is lucky, ATerafin. Jewel. He is otherwise too strange and too dangerous. Most of the House has now been exposed to his constant litany about the perils of *boredom*; when they hear him, they roll their eyes and try to go back to their work, in much the same way they would were he a small, cranky child. It favors you."

"He made the dress," she said. She wasn't certain why; Marrick was clearly surprised.

"How? He has no hands—"

"I don't know. I don't really want to know; I never want to wear it again." But she would. She felt it suddenly, sharply, certainly: she would wear that dress again, and the wearing of it might save her life.

He was silent for another moment, and when he spoke, his voice was steady, low, and cool. "The wearing of that dress was a bold move, Jewel.

Fortune oft favors the bold, and no one of us could have carried it off. Nor would we have thought to try. It did not please Haerrad—" He lifted a hand as she opened her mouth, and she shut it. "But Haerrad is not considered one of your natural allies. It confounded even Rymark.

"I have spoken with Elonne; we speak often, as friendly rivals oft will. I have spoken a few words with Haerrad; those are, of necessity, chosen with care—but I have never been Haerrad's natural enemy; in the past week, he has focused the whole of his anger and his attention on Rymark. To be fair, Rymark has returned that regard; they circle each other. It is a pity they are both still standing."

Jewel shook her head; she was smiling. She couldn't help it. "Yes," she finally said. "It is. I don't suppose—" She stopped.

"Don't stop on my account; I am certain my advisers have heard me say far, *far* worse, and in far more descriptive language than you could manage—unless you spoke your native Torra."

She startled, and then relaxed. Of course he knew about the Torra; there was probably very little about her life he—or the other three—didn't know.

"Yes," he said, noticing it. He said nothing else for a long moment; the night was dark, now; the moon was clear where it shone, veiled only by the bowers of the trees—the new trees—on the grounds.

"When the rains started, ATerafin, when the earth began to break beneath our feet, when the waters of the statuary rose like a tidal wave in miniature, we put aside all thought of our own politics and our own ambitions; our ambitions, at that point, were more primitive. We wished to survive. We wished the House to survive. It was a very clarifying moment. I am not a terribly religious man; I do not give much thought to the gods, although I mind with care the dictates of their children. I expect that the gods do the same with regard to me and my desires. I did not, therefore, pray.

"Elonne did. I do not consider prayer a weakness," he added softly, still looking into the slightly moving boughs of the highest of branches. "Amarais was known to pray to Cormaris; she did so publicly. She was not a weak woman. But, Jewel, the strangest thought occurred to me in the moment when it seemed that the whole of the Terafin grounds might collapse beneath those of us who avoided being crushed—or drowned.

"I remembered my youth." He smiled as he said it, and this time he did look at her. "You are aware that a House War is often fought in Terafin when The Terafin dies. The Terafin may assign an heir, but the document of assignation is worth the paper it is written on—and while the paper is no doubt very, very fine, it is not a match for the forces that work against it. If the heir is to be appointed, if consensus is to be reached in Council, it is entirely because the heir has proved himself or herself worthy of the position—and worthiness encompasses survival.

"I have told you I was young when The Terafin took her place on the House Council; she was considered young for it, but not as obscenely young as you were when you were appointed. In the early years of her reign, I do not think she would have dared to appoint you in that fashion. But the House Council understood the part you had played in that wretched Henden so many years ago; we understood that you were a valuable asset—even a crowning Jewel—and that some statement of your value and worth to the House must be sent immediately to the Crowns. We wished to retain you. We did not demur.

"Ah, but I wander. Where was I? Ah, yes. Amarais approached me before I had achieved a Council seat, and she offered to sponsor me, conditional upon my future support. Have you likewise approached any members of this House? No, don't answer; I know you have not. You lacked the ambition that drove Amarais; it was almost incandescent, in her youth. In our youth," he added, "she was ruthless."

Jewel started to speak, and stopped herself with difficulty.

"You think of Haerrad as ruthless."

"Or Rymark."

"But not Amarais. Not Elonne, and not Marrick?"

Aware that he might take the admission as an insult, she fell silent.

"Not Jewel?"

"Not Jewel," she conceded.

"Then you fail to understand what ruthless means in this context."

"I understand what it means."

"Tell me."

"It means there's nothing—at all—a person won't do to achieve their goals. Nothing. There's nothing that causes pause, nothing that deters them."

"It was true of Amarais."

"It *wasn't*."

He held up a hand. "It was, Jewel. Understand that her *goal* was not to take the House Seat; the seat was her means of achieving her goals. She saw a future she felt she could build; inherent in that future were some of the principles you value so highly. She valued them as well; they were, in large part, what she hoped to achieve. Yes, there were some things she would not do—but she would not do them precisely because they were anathema to what she actually wanted.

"Outside of those things, there was nothing she would not surrender. Are you so different?"

Jewel swallowed anger, reaching instead for the words that he'd actually spoken. "Why are you telling me this?"

"Because, Jewel, I heard your voice at the height of the storm. There is not a man, woman, or child upon the grounds—or in the manse—who did not. I heard what you said, and if I did not hear a reply, the effects were writ large in sky and on ground. All those years of planning, of carefully building my own base of power were suddenly made so small and insignificant. Tomorrow, or perhaps next month if I am being honest, reality will reassert itself. But the House Council will not meet in a month; it will meet on the morrow.

"On the morrow, if you will have it, I will offer you my full support."

Jewel was utterly silent. When she could move at all, it wasn't to speak; it was to shove her hair out of her eyes.

Marrick chuckled. "It is not what you expected? You will learn to hide that, in time. I suggest in eight hours' time." His brief chuckle evaporated, his face losing the familiar lines of merriment, his expression so serious Jewel felt momentarily at sea. "I have spoken with Member Mellifas at short length, as she did not have much time for me. It is clear, however, that she feels that what you did should have been impossible. We are alive. I do not think she expected it.

"But, ATerafin, what I heard in your rough, angry speech was what I heard on the day—decades past—that three members of the House Council died at the hands of a man we seldom name; it was the bloody start of a House War that would see dozens dead within the week. On that day, Amarais declared herself. She was always a cautious, careful woman—but not so cautious that she did not know when to gamble; not too proud that she did not know when to concede with grace.

"On that day? She was neither. The House *was* her family. It was her heart's blood. If she came to Terafin thinking it a tool, she was transformed by the experience of guiding it, even as Council member. She had respect for The Terafin of the time, and if they argued—and they did—that respect remained largely undiminished with the passage of time. She knew that there would be conflict when he died; she did not expect it to be so ugly, so swift, and so near complete. She herself survived because of the intervention of a healer." He closed his eyes.

"Alowan." Jewel said. It wasn't a question.

"Indeed. Alowan. He was never ours; he was always hers. She did not rest the week he demanded; she came to the House Council through halls made silent by fear. The sound of the doors opening—and closing—could be heard throughout the manse. I bribed a servant," he added, without a trace of regret, "so that I might hear what she had to say."

"You could have asked."

"Indeed, but that was hardly the point. She was the woman to whom I would owe my future, and she had almost died. I was callow, Jewel; I was not certain with whom to throw in my lot in the event of her passing. She took The Terafin's chair," he added. "There was no regent; the regent was among the three who had died. She did not take her own Council chair; on that day, she took the House Seat, and she waited while the Council Hall filled. She had two guards with her: Alayra was one. You will not have met the other; he perished during the weeks that followed. She had one adjutant—Gabriel, who did survive.

"She was challenged," he added, his voice sliding into a softer register. "For her presumption. She did not even blink; she expected it, and she shunted the objection aside."

"How?"

"She said, if I recall correctly, that there was no one else who was worthy to take the seat, and short of her instant and immediate death, she would not surrender it." He smiled. "She had done one thing in preparation for this singular meeting: she had retrieved the House Sword from its cradle. I don't know how; I asked her only once, and she refused to answer."

Jewel thought she knew, but said nothing.

"She drew the sword, Jewel. She was not an expert swordsman; she couldn't be. But it was clear from her handling of the blade that she had endured some training at the hands of one who was. She said, 'This is the sword of Terafin the Founder. This is the sword that he offered to the first Twin Kings, and the sword he wielded in their war to create the Empire of Essalieyan—an Empire governed by the god-born sons of the Lords of

Justice and Wisdom. The blade's name *is* Justice. The House is not a prize for butchers with the hearts of the most mendacious and unscrupulous of merchants. First among The Ten, it has *always* stood for more, much more, than that.

"'No one who cannot understand what the House *must* mean can take this seat while I live.'" He shook his head. "She had almost died; we all knew it. It galvanized her. It did not force her to reconsider or withdraw; she had faced death; it made her stronger. The butcher sat across the Council table; it was clear to whom she made her challenge. But she made it in defense of the *House*, of what the House must mean." He shook his head. "Heady words, to a younger man. Heady, impulsive, idealistic— even noble words. She spoke with a passionate conviction that the politic never use. And we heard her. I remember the sound of her voice," he added softly. "Tonight, of all nights. Time has—had—tarnished it somewhat; experience had belittled it from a safe distance."

Jewel could imagine Amarais Handernesse ATerafin in that chair, in that hall, the sword in her hands. She could see Alayra—unscarred, determined—by her side. She could imagine Gabriel there as well, steady, silent in his determination. What she could not imagine is what he said next.

"I heard her voice in yours, Jewel. I heard it, from a remove of decades, and I understood what it presaged. I am not seer-born; I have no particular talent that lifts me above other men in any regard. I am on the House Council by dint of my ability to see, and understand, the people around me. And to like, respect, or admire them—as necessary. But what you have, she had; what you have is not in me. She could not have done what you did," he added. "But what she did, in the end, was similar: she risked all, to save what the House meant to her. I would have taken the House if I could. I understand both Haerrad and Rymark; I understand where much of their danger lies. I consider Elonne competent, sharp—and almost appallingly elegant," he added, laughing, "although I will trouble you not to repeat that.

"I am not guaranteed to survive them," he added. "Or, I was not; I felt I was finally being bold, in accepting that risk. But in truth, I also felt Rymark and Haerrad were likely to devour each other, pitting resource against resource, so that they might both be weakened. They are not subtle; neither considers me much of a threat. They assume—with some cause—that I will fall in beside whoever wins the struggle. I will not destroy the House, or risk its destruction, for the title." He waited, and when she failed to comment, he laughed. "I have slipped by a large amount of the unpleasantness by being easily overlooked."

"You're not."

"Oh, indeed. If you mean the organization I've built over the past several years, yes. I am not without influence. The advantage to that influence is its immutability. I am a senior member of the Terafin House Council. Unless I die during this struggle, I will continue to be a senior member of the House Council."

"And your offer of support is contingent on that?"

He raised both brows, and then he laughed. His laugh was low, loud; it pulled at her lips and the corners of her eyes.

"It is contingent, Jewel, on very little. I see the inevitable in the events of this day." His expression shifted; the avuncular warmth drained from his features as he turned, at last, toward the stairs and the path that would lead back to his chambers in the manse. For a moment, he had the lines of a very patrician, very noble man. "I was in the council chambers when The Terafin died. I was on the grounds on the morning of the first day in which she was to be honored. What we face—as a House, and possibly as an Empire—is beyond my ken. If Kalliaris smiles, Jewel, it will not be entirely beyond yours.

"I will leave you with this: I have offered you my support. It is contingent on nothing; what you make of it, if you value it at all, is entirely in your hands. My own advisers will be waiting my return, and I am certain that my movements will have been followed."

"Do you want an—"

"Escort?" He laughed again, his easy, large laugh. "I will consider it very seriously *after* the Council meeting on the morrow, depending on how things play out."

She watched him go. He didn't stop, didn't hesitate, and didn't glance back at her. She stood, shrouded in lamplight, the coffin by her side.

"He could not lead my House," the Terafin Spirit said. "But I do not disdain him. I admire Elonne, but she is too careful, too calculating. She will not attempt to kill you; I do not know what she will otherwise do on the morrow."

"And the other two?"

The Terafin Spirit smiled; it was pained. "I believe you already understand the danger Haerrad and Rymark pose. It is to prevent their rule that you would have declared yourself."

She nodded, swallowed, and said, "It's more than that now."

His smile deepened, although it was a weary, tired smile. "ATerafin, Jewel—it was always more than that. I would keep you with me; I would give you the hours to stand or kneel while you struggle with words—or with your lack of them. But I have the patience, now, of the dead—and the living wait." He closed his eyes.

"Angel waits at the periphery of the path; he is pacing in a tight circle. Your Chosen—and they are yours, and Jewel, their numbers will grow after this day—wait in perfect, rigid silence; Angel is not one of them, nor will he ever be. Your Finch and Teller are even now abandoning their efforts at sleep; they are searching for lights—and robes—in the dark; Finch has just stubbed her toe. They will go to your kitchen, now that it is no longer off-limits at the command of the Master of the Household Staff. Jester is sitting against the wall in his room, and when he hears them, he'll join them. Carver is, I believe, with Merry."

She stared at him.

"Ellerson has a lamp in hand; he is waiting for your den-kin; he expected that sleep would not—in their words—take. He has food, and warm milk. He also has Night and Snow, and there has been some minor damage to the tables in the long hall. Adam is sleeping; Ariel is curled up beside Shadow, and sleeps as well, but fitfully. Daine has woken; he is restless and afraid, and he is being led to the kitchen by those fears."

"But Daine's—Daine's been sleeping in Alowan's rooms, in the healerie—he can't—"

Without pause, as if she hadn't voiced her sudden fear, he continued. "Haval is with Hannerle. She is sleeping—and Jewel, in the morning, she will not wake. But when she does sleep, Haval will join your den in the kitchen. They will wait in silence—for you. Tomorrow, the world changes."

The world had changed three days ago. She swallowed.

"Yes—for you it did. But you are still mortal, and what mortals need, you also need. You will age, and if you are not cautious, ATerafin, you will die."

"Even if I am cautious—"

"Yes. But the deaths are not the same. Go; they are waiting. Perhaps when this is done, and your experiences have changed you, you will find the words that will satisfy you, and you will go to her grave in the crypts, and you will speak them and know peace. That will not happen tonight."

She swallowed. Nodded. Even managed to turn from the shrine. But she turned back. "Where is the Winter King? Where is Celleriant?"

"Ah. The Winter King, Jewel, I cannot see. But I have seldom been able to discern his presence; I see him clearly when he is with you, and only then."

"And Celleriant?"

"He is at rest beneath the bowers of one of the great trees—but he does not stand sentinel; his sword is sheathed."

"He doesn't have a sheath."

"He is the sheath, Jewel. The sword is nascent, now; he carries no weapon, no shield; he wears no armor. The tree's great trunk is at his back; he is seated, his legs against the new earth. His eyes are closed; I believe he is smiling."

She closed her eyes, took a deep breath, and smiled. It was shaky, but heartfelt. Without another word, she turned from the shrine, from its ghost, from the body of her Lord, and she walked down the path, hoping to catch Angel in his circular pacing. She knew the moment that Avandar began to move—but he kept his distance.

She stopped. *Avandar*.

The leaves rustled as he approached. He could approach in utter silence; he was like Celleriant in that. "ATerafin."

"Take me home."

He watched her go. He felt no pang of loss as her domicis joined her and led her away from the Terafin shrine; nor did he feel uneasy or uncertain. He felt pain, yes, but even ghost wounds ached in the cold, and the wind that ran across the hidden path was chill, always chill. Yet now a fire burned near its heart, and it was a fire—at last—that could warm even one such as he.

He had not expected that; it was a singular gift, although he was certain she was unaware of what it might one day signify. In a moment, he would leave the shrine that had been home, throne, and cage for so long. He would climb down the stairs and drift across the path that wound around the shrines of the Triumvirate. Tonight, he would even pause at each of the three, not to pray, and not to make an offering; there was little

598 ✦ Michelle West

of value he could leave in the bowls set aside for the gods; little that men—living men—could gather and offer, in turn, to the Churches.

No, he would offer his gratitude.

Jewel Markess ATerafin.

The Terafin.

Would she stumble? Yes. Again and again, as she sought her footing over ground that was constantly shifting beneath her. But so, too, had he. She would rail, she would cry, she would sit in silence, swallowing all tears and all signs of pain. She would learn.

He smiled. The manse would change, would have to change, under her guidance. But he would not linger long to watch. He felt a pang of regret at that, for he thought her reign would be glorious in a way that no other Terafin's had yet been. It was a loss. He smiled; if he would not be here to see her grow, he would at least be spared her inevitable fall; all things that knew youth, knew age; all things that knew life, knew death.

All mortal things. *Amarais, if you could see her now. If you could only see her now.*

She could not hear him, of course, but had she, she would have heard the voice of a cook named Jonas who had graced his manse with the fire of both his passion for food, and his disdain for "wasteful frippery." It was the only way in which the Terafin Spirit could honor the woman who had given so much, fought so hard, for his House. For a time, she had made it her own.

Jewel will return to the Terafin altar in two days. She will return to you, because she will not allow the coffin to be moved until she does. She will find the words that she failed to find tonight. His smile deepened. *She does not understand why she could find no words at all, but I do.*

She could not offer you the only words you need to hear. But after the House Council meeting, she'll know what they are. She will come to you and she will tell you that she is The Terafin.